WAR RISING

SERVANTS OF MORRIGAN: FOUR HORSEMEN
BOOK THREE

CATERINA NOVELLIERE

Caterina Novelliere & Connections Across Time, LLC
www.caterinanovelliere.com

Publisher's Note: This is a work of fiction. Names, characters, places, and incidents are a product of the author's imagination or a fictional interpretation of a historical personas long dead. Locales and public names are sometimes used for atmospheric purposes. Any resemblance to actual living people or to businesses, companies, events, institutions, or locales is completely coincidental. All historical information in the book should be researched by a reader before it being taken as fact as the author has taken interpretive liberties to modify the century or historical detail to fit the storyline.

Cover Artwork : Consuelo Parra, C.P Book Cover designs -Spain - C.P Book Cover designs
Model: Dragoroth-stock

EBook ISBN:9781732332775
Paperback ISBN:9781732332768

To all my wonderful readers and to those who refuse to allow past mistakes to prevent them from being successful in the present.

ACKNOWLEDGMENTS

I would like to thank Silver Quill & the Williamsburg Writers Groups for helping polish up the manuscript for publication. I know this was a long one and different from *Tale of Rouen*.
Thanks for hanging in there with me.

I'd also like to thank my husband and son for lending me their eyes and putting up with me hiding in the office for long days to get this one written and revisions completed.

Raul - Diego makes a guest appearance in here, too. I won't tell you where. You'll have to read the book. Sorry, not sorry.

PROLOGUE

Córdoba - 806 AD

After spending two months along the border of Andalusia and Aquitaine, Haroun led the Emirate's army home. They returned to Córdoba triumphant in quashing the most recent incursion of the Franks from the East. The curving Guadalquivir River burbled as it passed under the old Roman bridge then cascaded over rocky drops a short distance away; amplifying the burble into a whoosh. With it being spring, the scent of azahar from the blossoming orange trees accompanied by the light fragrance of newly opening jasmine flowers floated on the breeze. Nature extended the first salutation to the weary army that had trekked across Al-Andalus for almost two weeks. Haroun briefly looked heavenward at the azure sky, thanking Allah he and the others lived to see home once more. A smile curved his lips and the heavy weight warfare always hung on his shoulders fell away. In a few hours, he would have a much-needed reprieve from being the commanding general of the army, and God willing, he would finally get a full night's rest in his own bed.

Reaching the outer boundaries of the city, the ranks closed the gaps in their lines. The rhythm of their footfalls becoming steadier and more pronounced as they began crossing the ancient stone structure spanning from one bank to the other. The clip clop of horse hooves and the percussion of boots reverberated off the cream-colored half walls framing the long line of men marching behind the mounted officers, alerting the gatemen on the city walls of their return.

Spotting the Emirate's forces, the gatekeeper sent one of the younger soldiers to notify the Emir that his troops had arrived safely. The teenage boy sprinted through the winding city streets, yelling, "The army returns!"

People poured out of their homes and shops. Crowds gathered at the gate and rapidly filled the city streets to greet long missed husbands, sons, fathers, and brothers. Shouts rang out once Haroun and his two field commanders passed through the massive open gates. The townspeople reached out to touch the famed general and his horse as he passed. Some wanting to be able to say they once met the legendary Black Wolf. Others seeking to change their luck as Allah graced him with favor and fortune. They cheered and murmured about how The Black Wolf, The Great Protector of the Cordovan Emirate, once again brought victory and peace to Andalusia.

Astride a horse the color of midnight, resplendent in black armor and clothing, along with having thick, dark hair, almost the same color as his horse's coat, Haroun very much embodied the moniker the people had given him years ago. A silver and jeweled wolf's head pendant hung from a chain around his neck. Fingertips periodically grazed his arms and legs then his horse's side. To this day, he never understood the community's fanatical fascination with him. There were many other great generals and prominent citizens to revere.

Haroun graciously smiled and proceeded slowly through the streets, ensuring none of the crowd seeking his favor were injured by the warhorse he rode. He periodically stopped to distribute the coin he kept readily available in a small purse on his side to those who looked the most destitute amongst the crowd. Glancing to his left then to his right, Kamar and Fidel, his two field commanders, patiently waited for him to finish distributing the last of the silver dirhams and copper fals.

Once through the throng of people, Haroun and his men entered the high walled courtyard of the palace. His uncle and several of the

Emir's staff awaited them. Haroun dismounted, then hugged his smiling uncle.

"You are blessed, Haroun. Allah smiles upon you like he has no other in the army." Mohammed praised his nephew, pulling back and clasping him by the forearms. "Come! Abdul awaits us inside."

The two walked together through the arched doors to the grand hall.

"You certainly do the Ibn-Ziyad family proud with your service to Córdoba. Some argue you are an even greater general than your father and grandfather."

Haroun grinned. "I would never claim such a thing, Uncle."

"It is true, Haroun. Every word I speak is the truth. While humility is an excellent quality for a man to have, it is fine to accept a compliment every so often."

"Ahhh! The Black Wolf returns to Córdoba victorious once more," Abdul, the Emir, greeted his favorite general. "The gold you bring back refills our coffers and the tax negotiated gives us ample stores for the winter. But most importantly of all, you quelled the fighting on the borders." Abdul lowered his voice as he embraced Haroun. "I also grant the personal request you asked of me. Your father has made the appropriate arrangements. You will see your betrothed this evening. May your union be blessed."

"Thank you, Emir. Your approval of my marriage is the greatest honor that can be bestowed."

Abdul smiled once more. "I want to hear more of your time in France and of the state of my army. Let us adjourn to my library, where we may speak more openly than we can here."

Sunset seemed to take longer than usual to arrive. After the evening call to prayer, Haroun changed into a clean tunic and pants. He wore a blue and silver brocade outer jacket. Its collar and the cuffs of the sleeves were trimmed in gold ribbon. A servant had polished his black boots to a high sheen earlier that afternoon. He presented quite the princely image once his sword was secured on his side.

Haroun inherited his father's height, wavy hair, and broad shoulders. However, his fairer skin and blue eyes gave away his mixed heritage, with his mother being a Saxon, not a Moor.

"You are as handsome as any caliph or king, Haroun," His mother complimented him when he entered the dining hall to await his bride and her family's arrival.

"Thank you, Mother." Haroun kissed her cheek.

After twenty minutes of waiting, his nerves got the better of him. Needing some fresh air, he excused himself and went to the inner courtyard. A fountain in the center gurgled amongst the citrus trees and flowers in the private garden. Looking up at the moon and stars, he thanked Allah for blessing him a second time that day by gifting him the Emir's sanction to marry the woman he loved; a rare arrangement indeed amongst the leading families of Córdoba. Priya had captured his heart the first time he saw her in the palace. After years of courting in secret, she would at last become his wife.

"Haroun!" Priya called out, disrupting his thoughts.

He turned, expecting to see her smiling, formally dressed, and with her family. Instead, she was alone and distressed. Tears streaked her face. She panted as if she had run to his parents' home with a demon chasing her. She flung herself into him. Her long, walnut-colored hair cascaded wildly over his arms when they encircled her.

"What is wrong, jamila?"

"I have condemned us, Haroun!"

"I doubt that. Tell me what distresses you so."

"Abdul knows we are lovers," She blurted out, bringing a hint of a grin to Haroun's face.

"He knows nothing of the sort. What he knows is I seek to make you my wife. I asked his permission to marry you. He gave us his blessing this afternoon." His words shocked her into stunned silence. "We will be husband and wife in a week."

Priya shook her head. "No, he betrays you. Khadijah overheard the guards talking and warned me. I am to be stoned tomorrow. You will not survive the night."

"Abdul would not do such things to us. Khadijah most likely does not understand what she overheard."

"She did not misunderstand, Haroun! The guard are on their way here. My parents have tried to delay them. We must go."

They heard the footsteps and voices of the royal guard coming from the other side of the garden wall.

Haroun listened to their conversation to determine where the unit headed. "Your fears are unwarranted, ya omari. The guards pass to go to the palace. They are not coming for either of us."

Priya calmed after the garden did not fill with soldiers, and their voices drifted away from the Ibn-Ziyad home. Perhaps her friend did not comprehend the discussion she overheard between Abdul and Umar, another Cordovan general.

Priya smiled as it dawned on her Abdul had given his blessing for the two of them to be united. "We are to be married?"

Haroun chuckled, lowering his face to hers. "We are. In a short time, you will be my wife." Haroun kissed Priya, drawing her tighter against him.

Pain radiated from the center of Priya's back. She tore her lips from his, crying out, then collapsed against Haroun's chest.

"No!" Haroun tried to keep her upright. Her blood flowed down his hands and clothing. It spurted from her throat, covering his face, from an assassin driving a second blade into the back of her neck.

"Priya!"

She tried to reach up to him one last time, but her hand fell as life left her. Her eyes rolled up; her body went limp. A painful burn developed below Haroun's shoulder from muscle being pierced by a dagger. Another followed in his side. Grimacing against the sting of the wounds, he struggled to remain standing. Steel dove into his back at least two more times. His own blood intermingled with Priya's on her clothing and in her hair. Growing weaker, his knees buckled. He gently laid Priya on the ground before him. At least he would die with his beloved.

"So much for being a wolf. He's more like a stray half-breed cur," One of the assassins muttered, then drove his knife into the dying man's back a final time. "Umar should be thankful Haroun's whore dies with him. She would never make a fit wife for him or Kamar."

Hearing the man refer to Priya as a whore ignited an uncontrollable rage that coursed through every inch of Haroun's dying body. He would not let her death go unavenged. Her killers would join them in the grave. I will not rest until everyone of them is dead, he swore to himself. His oath drove him back to his feet. He baffled his would-be executioners; turning and drawing his weapon.

Haroun recognized the man who spoke. "Zahar."

"Shaytan" was the only word Zahar could utter.

Haroun plunged his sword into the man's belly, halting any further remarks. The top of his blade emerged from Zahar's back; eerily shimmering silver and red in the moonlight. Running him through was too gentle a death for what Zahar had done. Drawing his arm back slightly, Haroun jerked his wrist sideways, slicing open the man's middle. Yanking the blade free, he cut another gash across Zahar's gut so the man's innards were exposed and then disemboweled him, ensuring the man suffered a slow, excruciating death.

Seeing what befell their captain, Zahar's two compatriots futilely ran for their lives. Haroun easily caught them. In a few short, hate-filled moments, the assassins joined Priya in the grass.

The men's screams brought Haroun's father and mother from inside the house. Haroun's father called for the family guard. His mother ran to Priya. Finding the woman dead, she stared up at her son. She hardly recognized him due to the blood splatter and anguish distorting the features of his normally smiling face. The boy she still saw in her son became a beast she no longer recognized.

Haroun's father understood what his son intended to do when Haroun started toward the rear gates of the courtyard. "Haroun, stay here. We will deal with this as the law dictates."

"The law and Córdoba be damned!" Haroun continued on to the gates.

Father followed son. "Haroun, this is not the way. You will only bring about more bloodshed. Priya would not want that, nor would she want you executed. Allah spared you for a reason."

"There is no God for Priya to be slaughtered. I do not wish to disgrace you, Father, but I will have my vengeance, and no one, not even you, will prevent me from killing Umar this night. Stand aside, or I will run you down." Haroun swung into the saddle of a horse one of the guards left outside the house.

"Please, Haroun. Do not do this. Iblis clouds your judgement with wrath!"

"If the Devil grants me the justice I seek, I will gladly serve him." Haroun spurred the horse forward, narrowly missing his father. Knowing Abdul and Umar were behind the attack, he rode to Umar's. The general would die first, then Abdul would join him in Hell.

Córdoba's revered figure of hope fell from grace, and with him, the promise of peace. A trail of dismembered soldiers lined the way from Umar's home to the palace. Sunrise prevented the now soulless Haroun from killing Abdul. Lucifer called for Haroun to come to his new master. He would have to wait for the next nightfall to continue his quest for blood.

No longer would anyone refer to Haroun as the Great Protector of Córdoba. Instead, the Black Wolf became a monster in cautionary tales to frighten children not to break promises or act with hubris, or else they'd be visited by the Devil of Al-Andalus himself, Haroun Ibn-Ziyad. His horrific tale would be repeated for centuries to come across the Iberian Peninsula, North Africa, and in the lands bordering the Gulf of Arabia. Whispers of Haroun even reached the ears of researchers in modern day from medieval Spain.

CHAPTER

ONE

Córdoba - 812 AD

"Emir, we cannot allow Umar's actions to go unaddressed," Sayyid, one of the leading viziers to the young caliph, urged Malik to take action against the insurrection being carefully staged by Umar.

Sayyid's outburst drew the attention of several servants cleaning Malik's chambers. Malik waved his hand, dismissing them, before sitting down in a large wooden chair. He gestured toward the empty seat across from him, signaling Sayyid to sit. The loud crackling logs in the fireplace only heightened the annoyance the events of the day caused Malik. The two men sat in silence. Lost in thought, Malik stroked his beard.

Coming up with no realistic methods to defang Umar's wickedness, Malik finally spoke. "What would you have me do, Sayyid? Umar is the most powerful commander within our ranks. For me to demand his conspiring cease would be a death sentence for us all. There is not a general alive within my armies that could defeat Umar and his men. If I disgrace him, he will wage war against us or allow the enemy to enter our gates. I cannot let infighting occur within my domain when we are already entrenched battling the Christians from the North and the Franks to the East. Baghdad is eager to see us fall. Harun Al Rashid visits

Charlemagne as we speak. We cannot afford to be fractured if we are to maintain control of Córdoba. We need Umar's favor. If that means allowing him to think he is usurping my authority, then we allow him slight leeway in doing so. He has not removed me from my position yet."

"If you keep allowing this, others will see you as weak, which eventually will lead to your demise, Malik. Your father would never allow Umar to behave in such a manner."

"I am not my father, nor do I have the great army he did. We cannot afford such mercenaries with the state of our treasuries. Tell me who I should seek out to disempower Umar without risking the Emirate, and I will gladly seek him out. But I doubt you know of such a man if I do not. No mercenary or assassin can eliminate Umar between the power he has gathered and the faithful guard surrounding him at all times."

"There was one who could easily decimate Umar. It is a shame Umar used such underhanded tactics to assassinate him."

Malik laughed. "I am beginning to believe the one you reference's abilities are more myth and legend propagated by those who long for the past. In times of strife, people grow nostalgic for golden ages, and the average man becomes a hero beyond imagination."

"Ibn-Ziyad is no legend, nor are his fighting abilities exaggerated. His men followed him without question, Emir. Those still living would even do so today."

"Sayyid, Haroun Ibn-Ziyad died years ago. We cannot resurrect a man long departed to the afterlife." Malik grew tired from the troubles he faced. The dead could not resolve Córdoba's misfortunes.

"Contrary to what everyone is led to believe, the general can be brought back to Córdoba." A woman with strange hair, the color of wine, and onyx-shaded eyes disrupted the private discussion.

Malik straightened in his chair. Where had she come from? No one had opened the door to his chambers. "What nonsense do you speak, woman?"

An equally tall man stepped forward and bowed politely to Malik. "It is not nonsense, Emir. My name is Damien. I believe we can assist one another. For the solution is the same to both our woes."

Neither newcomer looked like any other man or woman Sayyid had encountered before; they couldn't be human. "What are you?"

Damien smiled, flashing iridescent white teeth. "A trader of sorts. The woman is a client of mine. Her name is Isra. Emir, what we are about to propose is a once in a millennium offer."

Rome - Modern Day

Rayne Warwick waited patiently in Campo de' Fiori for Grace to purchase the fruit cup she craved. While Rayne comfortably engaged with the modern world, he preferred the quiet of Italia Antica and a much older Rome. Rome's markets and streets had always contained crowds and noise, but the twenty-first century buzz of raised voices from tourists mixing with locals gathering fresh vegetables and fruit in the small square seemed so much louder. The hustle and bustle of the marketplace paired with the roar of automobiles coming from nearby streets made the noise of the modern city almost deafening.

With the passage of time, the ancient world had given way to the current one. Even an immortal had to learn to adapt to change. Rayne embraced technology and even enjoyed the luxuries modern people took for granted, like public transportation, indoor plumbing, electricity, and climate control. Not to mention his wife, Grace, was born and raised in modernity.

When the Fates described his future spouse as a descendant of the House of the Moon, he had never imagined she would be from a vastly different world than his own. Born in the Middle Ages, he became a man of power through warfare and the good fortune of descending from an aristocratic family. His father, a revered military commander in his own right, was a trusted adviser in the Courts of Spain, Portugal, and France. Many of the lessons Rayne learned during his human years served him well as the Horsemen Commander. The shrewd skill of negotiation, the diplomatic tact of an ambassador, and a touch of charm from his days as a courtier helped him navigate the present-day human realm.

He looked up at the statue of Bruno in the center of the crowded piazza; standing near the same spot he had when witnessing the man's execution in 1600. At the time, he was numb to the smell of the flames, the burning of flesh, and the ending of a human life that did nothing more than threaten the beliefs of a patriarchal institution. Living through centuries of bloodshed could destroy one's sense of empathy if there was nothing to remind them that all life had value. Now, finding the memory horrifying, a shiver ran through him.

Men are often times greater monsters than those they fear from the immortal realm. Though Rayne had little room to judge. He had stood by watching the flames engulf Bruno, listening to the man's screams; unable to intercede, forbidden to help in any way. If he had the wisdom and moral compass he possessed now, Bruno's fate may have been different, or at least found a less painful end.

The tourists in Rome who didn't know what happened in the spot of the colorful market were fortunate. Had they witnessed that tragic day, they would most likely find another spot to buy flowers, wares, and food. Their voices certainly wouldn't be joyfully raised and laughter wouldn't float on the same air the smoke had. The diners sitting on the edges of the square would most certainly lose their appetites.

Grace walked up to her husband and noted the sullen expression on his face. She often paused to study the memorial to Bruno herself. It seemed out of place in the cheery piazza, especially on sunny days like today. "Poor man. Most shopping in the piazza right now have no idea what happened here four hundred years ago."

"Time and name changes have a way of burying the uglier moments of human history." Rayne let the sins of the past go and smiled at his wife. "Let us not darken such a pleasant day with talk of past wrongs."

Grace couldn't help smiling back after he stabbed a strawberry slice with one of the two wooden skewers in the cup she held then offered it to her. She ate the sweet, red fruit. Rayne definitely wasn't in the mood to discuss Bruno. His changing of subjects meant he had personal ties to Bruno's execution. The only time the Horseman refused to share more about an event or the past was when it related to his own. Anything else he'd freely discuss. His eyes, the same color as the sky that afternoon, drifted back to the statue.

Not wanting anything to ruin their first weekend alone in a while,

Grace distracted him from his thoughts once more. "I'm really looking forward to the special exhibition at Castel Sant'Angelo this evening. I bet the fortress is beautiful at night."

"I have no doubt it will be fascinating for you." Rayne skewered a freshly cut slice of pineapple for himself. "In the meantime, what do you have planned for us today, my love? Exploring more museums or torturing me with another couple hours of shopping?"

"Just for that, I should drag you from shop to shop, but I have something eviler in mind. They reopened the Roman wing of the Vatican Museum after adding new pieces to it yesterday."

Still having a mouthful of pineapple, Rayne grunted his displeasure. Finished swallowing the chunk, he openly shared his thoughts on traipsing through the Vatican Museum for the thousandth time. "You would really make me endure another four-hour walk through that building, being herded like cattle with hordes of people to see the one wing, which you have seen many times before for a few new pieces of statuary?"

Grace laughed at the incredulous expression on his face. "You promised me we would have a normal weekend together. This is how humans take in all the many things that Rome has to offer."

"What I had in mind for the weekend was good food, excellent wine, romantic strolls through the Villa Borghese or along the Tiber, making love to my wife whenever I pleased without our children banging on the door because they need something, and sleeping in. Not being woken up at 7 am and playing tourist. If I had known we'd be touring the Vatican and attending some boring lecture at Sant'Angelo, again, I would have insisted we spend the weekend elsewhere."

"How about a compromise? We go to the Vatican Museum next and only see the Roman wing. I am sure you can convince one of the docents to escort us straight there with your charming self. After that, we can go find dinner some place and watch the sunset from Villa Borghese. We attend the special exhibition at Sant'Angelo then head back to the hotel to enjoy a bottle of Brunello together, letting the evening lead where it may. Tomorrow, we can sleep in as late as you like and do whatever you please."

"Whatever *I* like?" One of Rayne's dark brows rose, skeptical of the proposal his wife hoped he'd find a fair one.

Grace played with the hair on the nape of his neck. "Whatever *you* like, my handsome, intriguing, benevolent husband."

Rayne laughed at the way she flirted with him. "We have an accord, my dear wife. There will be no deviation from the agreed upon terms. No matter how much you beg for modification if anything else comes up."

"I am fine with that, but..." Grace lightly hit his chest, ignoring the annoyed huff he uttered after hearing the word but. "...you have to pick where we are eating and make any reservations."

"Already done, leof. I was hoping to surprise you later with dinner and the opera, but you accepted the last-minute invite to the lecture."

"You really are the most amazing husband ever. I am sorry I ruined the evening you planned. We can skip tonight's special exhibit."

"No. We will go to Sant'Angelo. It sounds like this exhibit is a onetime event, only open to those with an invitation. I am curious to see what they discovered with how excited Dr. Rossi was when he called you. But, you can most certainly keep telling me how amazing I am."

"Vanity is a sin, Commander. What happened to the humble side of the man I fell in love with?"

Rayne tucked her hand into the crook of his arm with a grin on his face, beginning the trek back towards the Vatican.

Córdoba - 812

"Malik happily paid your asking price." Damien clinked glasses with Isra in the dining hall of the newly acquired palatial home they secured.

"I am not sure who the bigger fool is, Malik, or the two of you." A raised, deep voice interrupted the celebration. "You do not know what you conjure with this bargain."

"Lucifer!" Damien seemed surprised to see the fallen angel.

The Devil ignored Isra's latest conquest, heading for the overseer who monitored his interests in Spain.

Isra bowed low before her master. "I can manage the man I call forth."

Lucifer roughly grasped her by the jaw. He almost lifted her back to her feet. "Summon Ibn-Ziyad and you instigate your own end. Leave him in the grave." He released the overseer who tried his patience the past few days.

"The agreement is already struck and sealed with blood."

Lucifer's hand slammed against Isra's face, snapping her head backward. A loud thwap echoed off the walls in the room from how hard he hit her.

"Greed and lust shall be your downfall!" Lucifer snarled. "I expect more from the elders in my ranks."

"Master, this arrangement secures our presence in Spain." Isra didn't understand what riled Lucifer.

"No! It jeopardizes our hold here. You are on your own in managing what you have done, Isra. I cannot intervene, nor will I do anything to save you if the man you summon reacts as I expect him to."

Lucifer shook his head, vanishing from the room. He needed to prepare for the events Isra set in motion. He would be further damned, if such a thing is possible, before he lost his foothold in Europe due to some personal vendetta between Isra and the general she planned to provoke.

Rome - Modern Day

For one of the few times in his life, Rayne easily blended into the crowd of dignitaries, celebrities, and academics at Castel Sant'Angelo. Grace admired the striking figure her husband made in modern-day clothing. The custom-fitted black suit he wore highlighted his broad shoulders and tall frame. It was cut to flatter his fit physique. His blue eyes contrasted with his suit jacket and his dark hair. His rugged looks added an air of mystery to him. Thinking about the pair they must make, Grace smiled. His height and dark contrasted her fair coloring, strawberry blonde hair, curvy build, and only standing 5'4. Unlike her husband, she could regularly disappear into a crowd. Though, she never wished for anything different. She'd much rather have the curious mind the Fates blessed her with than look like a supermodel. Besides, it was kind of fun having the stereotypical role of arm candy reversed.

Rayne noted the smirk on her face as she took the glass of wine he offered her. "What are you plotting, leof?"

"Nothing. I'm just entertained by how many folks are curious about you with the whispers I am hearing. They are guessing you're some new American CEO, or maybe even the unknown lead in Sorrentino's latest film that was just cast."

Rayne chuckled. "If only they knew the truth. I don't know which is worse. Managing the press and a hectic schedule of an actor or being mistaken for an American."

"Careful, Warwick. You are married to an American."

"So I am." He sighed as if disappointed then winked at her.

Grace shook her head. The way she smiled before taking a sip of her wine shared that she took his teasing in stride.

"Signora Warwick! It is so lovely to see you again!" A boisterous Italian voice traveled across the room. "And I see your husband is with you this evening."

Dr. Lorenzo Rossi, one of the Vatican Museum curators, cut through a group of people and headed straight for Rayne and Grace.

"Wonderful to finally meet you, Signore Warwick." Lorenzo shook Rayne's hand before greeting Grace more traditionally with a kiss on each cheek. "Do you mind if I borrow your wife for a few minutes? I wanted to show her our latest discovery before the general public sees it."

"Not at all, Dr. Rossi." Rayne smiled at Grace. "I will wait right here for you."

"Are you sure?" Grace knew Rayne didn't like to be left alone at events like this.

"I am sure. Gage texted me a few minutes ago. He and Caitlin are on their way in. They can keep me company while I wait on you."

Rayne watched Dr. Rossi lead Grace off.

Evariste Gage Arsceneaux and his wife Caitlin joined Rayne as Rossi and Grace disappeared around a corner.

"Nice to see you again, Rayne. It's been awhile." Gage extended his hand to Rayne before pulling him in for a quick hug.

"Good to see you, Gage." Rayne turned to acknowledge Gage's wife. "And, Caitlin, you look stunning this evening."

"Not used to seeing you in a suit, Commander. It looks good on you." Caitlin, a redhead with lavender eyes, returned the Horseman's compliment.

The Arsceneauxs and Rayne had known one another for centuries. The three of them served together as military officers for the High Council. Gage and Caitlin were two of the first, outside of the Horsemen, to take Grace under wing when she found herself caught up in immortal affairs.

Gage didn't see Rayne's other half anywhere. "Where is Grace?"

"Rossi is giving her a sneak peek of whatever statue he found that the rest of us get to see after the presentation." Rayne sipped the wine he originally purchased for Grace while he and the Arsceneauxs caught up on what was new in their lives.

A man with brown hair and glasses approached the group. "Rayne Warwick, we are so delighted you and your wife could join us tonight."

Rayne didn't recognize him, but calmly shook his hand.

The man smiled after noting the puzzled look on Rayne's face. "Forgive me. I am Mirko Castelluci, Dr. Rossi's assistant. We met earlier at the Vatican Museum."

"Ahh, yes. Thank you for allowing us to by-pass the normal tour route." The phone in Rayne's jacket vibrated against his chest, startling the Horseman. While he received the occasional text, rarely did anyone ever call him. He only carried the device to blend in with the modern world. Grace's name appeared above her phone number on the screen. Why was she calling him when they could use their abilities to communicate with one another? "Please excuse me, I need to take this."

Gage took Rayne's drink so Rayne could answer the phone.

"Hello... All right... Calm down, Grace." Rayne stepped away from the group. "Where exactly are you?"

"Two rooms over. Go through the small hallway to the left of the room under the Hadrian fresco; follow that hall until the next large room. I am in there." Grace provided him directions, since he couldn't teleport to her with the crowd in the lecture space.

"Everything okay?" Gage whispered, concerned about the call.

Rayne kept the phone to his ear, but covered the mic. "I am not sure. We'll meet you in the lecture room if we aren't back before it begins." Done talking to Gage, he removed his hand from the phone and headed for the door. "I'm on my way, Grace."

Once he reached the hall, he hung up then slid the phone into his jacket pocket. The mass of people in the ancient fortress slowed his pace. He politely pushed through a couple admiring one of the many frescoes on the walls and ceiling.

A guard stopped him from entering the room Grace referenced.

Dr. Rossi overheard Rayne firmly tell the man his wife requested he join her. "It is okay, Antonio. Allow Signore Warwick to pass."

Rayne's eyes skimmed the walls and the objects in the room. He didn't see anything threatening to humanity or the immortal world, but his wife's expression warned of something troublesome lurking nearby.

"What has you so upset?"

She took his arm and led him behind a curtained off section of statuary. "This!" She gestured to the sculpture in the center of the special exhibit space.

The corners of Rayne's lips twitched, giving away his hiding a grin at recognizing the artist's subject. Some ancient Roman sculptor captured Dante Giovanni, the former Horsemen Commander, in alabaster marble.

You find this amusing? There is nothing funny about this! Grace's frustrated voice sounded in his head.

Relax, leof. Whoever crafted this left no concerning evidence of our existence. Most will think it's a random piece of art.

Rayne couldn't quite believe some human accurately recreated one of the Horsemen from memory. The High Council set careful post-assignment protocols in place for any time humans and immortals interacted to ensure their identities disappeared into legend and myth. This was only the third time Rayne ever had to deal with a human-made antiquity surfacing that tied back to a Horseman. The prior objects only hinted at beings aiding humanity instead of replicating one. Thankfully, the artist dressed Dante in Roman triumphal armor and military attire, causing the work to blend in with other Roman historical figures. "Dr. Rossi, any idea who this man is?"

"We believe it is a rendition of Apollo or some other god related to the sun we've never seen before. Research into this particular piece is still ongoing. We haven't discovered another like it."

Rayne glanced at the other artifacts found at the same archeological site. All were typical Roman temple items; the only odd find from the new excavation was a deified Dante. "Isn't Apollo normally featured with a bow or lyre instead of a sword?"

Dr. Rossi never expected Grace's husband to be familiar with ancient art. "Yes, but the decorative cuirass features all the hallmarks of Apollo."

"Professor, I am no expert, but this can't be a Roman depiction of Apollo. First off, he is clothed, which would go against the customs of portraying the gods of the period. Secondly, the sword is a dead give-away that this is an emperor, eques, or someone else who for whatever reason, associated himself with the sun god. Perhaps it is even a more modern creation. Would it not be wiser to pull this from display until you know more?" Rayne casually suggested.

"The carbon dating confirms the artifact's age. It is from the fourth century and is undoubtedly Egyptian marble. But based on your obser-vations, I will remove the placard out of caution until we know more about the subject." Dr. Rossi pulled the small sign offering any informa-tion on the piece from beside it.

"Dr. Rossi, we are ready to begin the lecture whenever you are," Mirko called from the doorway.

"Do you study ancient art, Signore Warwick?" Dr. Rossi wondered about Rayne's assessment of the piece.

Rayne offered Grace his arm. "No, although, I do find it fascinating. History and heritage enthrall me almost as much as they do my wife."

"It is wonderful the two of you have something like the love of Antiquity to share together."

"Our common hobby certainly keeps our conversations interesting and influences our travels a great deal. Out of curiosity, were any other sculptures of deities or men found with this one?"

Rayne's inquiry puzzled Rossi. "No. Do you believe it is part of a larger work?"

"Not at all. But it isn't uncommon to find multiple artistic representations of the gods at an archeological site, especially a Roman one with all the various spirits and creatures they believed in. I also assume with the detail in this piece some wealthy patron commissioned it. Patrons like that usually had multiple pieces decorating their villas or donated several to local temples."

"I believe you are being modest about your knowledge of Roman culture and archeology, Signore Warwick. We must talk more after the lecture."

"I look forward to our conversation, Dr. Rossi. I am definitely interested in learning more about where you found the statue and your work in general."

Rayne and Grace followed Rossi back to the lecture room.

Grace pretended to admire a fresco on her husband's left before whispering, "You are not worried about this?"

"Not at all. On very rare occasion, things like this happen. Relax and enjoy the lecture."

CHAPTER

TWO

Rome - Modern Day

Gage and Caitlin sat next to Rayne and Grace for the presentation. Rayne's hand reassuringly rested on Grace's thigh after slides of Dante's stone replica appeared on the screen.

Now understanding the call Rayne received earlier, Gage shook his head.

The four immortals listened intently to Dr. Rossi's presentation to ensure nothing more than the statue had surfaced. Thankfully, nothing else had. Gage and Rayne whispered to one another as they applauded Dr. Rossi's speech.

The next speaker, a smiling, blonde woman in a brown dress, came to the podium. Dr. Rossi introduced her as Dr. Abigail Blackburn, a medievalist completing a post-Doc with the Vatican archives. Dr. Blackburn shared a detailed history of the medieval church and the Catholic viewpoint on why it was advantageous to support the cause in the East.

No one had mentioned the Crusades presentation to Grace, nor was it listed on the invitation she received. By the expression on Rayne's face, the topic perturbed him. Grace noticed the slight raising of his brows as Dr. Blackburn expanded on a conflict at Acre then a following one in

21

Jerusalem. The gentle squeeze she gave his hand eased whatever troubled him. He grinned, tightened his grip on her hand before bringing it to rest against his heart. She always loved that simple gesture of fidelity.

Stop fretting, Grace. I am finding both lectures rather intriguing.

At the end of the second presentation, Dr. Rossi and Dr. Blackburn welcomed questions from the crowd.

"Dr. Blackburn, do you have any comment on the papal directives published in *The Times* last week?" A reporter a row behind Grace and Rayne shouted out before the mediator could call on any of the raised hands.

The British PhD smiled and came back to the podium. "I assume you are referencing the article on Urban's alleged ties to the Order of Constantinople. There is no evidence to support such an order ever existed, nor do the Vatican archives hold any records of communications with secret assassins tasked with killing Eastern Christians, Muslims, or anyone else the Pope found a threat. Given the political nature of the period, it is certainly possible Urban directed some aspects of warfare, but nothing like the Illumantiesque claims of Dr. Smith."

Various members of the audience chuckled at her response.

"One more question, Dr. Blackburn. Dr. Smith's article mentions a series of letters drafted by Urban and Innocent. These letters frequently reference "the left hand of God" carrying out the Lord's will. Dr. Smith alleges that is code for some sort of assassin. Do you agree with that interpretation?"

"No, I do not. As I just said, there are no records detailing communication with secret assassins as far as I am aware. Furthermore, it is not unusual to see Archangel Gabriel called God's left hand. Many documents from the Middle Ages describe him as such. Gabriel was frequently associated with the destruction of Jerusalem and the herald of the Apocalypse, in addition to being viewed as a messenger by all three faiths inhabiting the Holy Land. No disrespect to my colleague, but I think Hollywood may be influencing his research a bit."

Not wanting to entertain any more outlandish questions, Dr. Rossi ended the Q&A and welcomed everyone to walk to the exhibition hall, then called security over to escort the obnoxious reporter out.

Upon entering the exhibit area, Grace stopped to study one of the mosaics unearthed near the Vatican during recent road repairs.

Rayne left his wife to browse the various artifacts. Grace could spend hours scrutinizing new Roman finds while they only held his attention for a few minutes. He stopped in front of a display of Crusade period documents and objects. A large cross sat at the center of the case along with some of Urban's effects. In stark contrast to the religious symbol, a scimitar and Crusader sword hung from hooks on the right side of the cross. An elaborately hand-illustrated manuscript sat to the left of the cross.

The detailed sketch of a wolf's head drew Rayne's eyes to the center of the page. An intricately drawn image of the archangel Michael made up one side border and Lucifer the other. Across the top of the page, curly golden scrolls joined the angel and Devil, completely framing in the wolf. Under the wolf's head, Latin words spelled out the message: *From the left hand of God, his will be done.*

"Fascinating entry, isn't it?" Dr. Blackburn disrupted Rayne's musings.

"Not something I would expect to find in a Vatican manuscript."

"We didn't find it in the Church archives. It was in Pope Urban's private papers. From what Dr. Rossi explained, you helped fund the project that discovered it. Thank you for your generous support, Mr. Warwick."

Rayne's brows came together, and a look of sheer confusion covered his face. He didn't recall funding any Crusades related projects on behalf of the High Council or anyone else. "I assisted in funding your research?"

"I apologize if I misunderstood. We received a significant contribution from the Warwick Endowment for Historical Research and Preservation."

Now understanding why she thought he was the benefactor for the project, Rayne smiled. "The person you need to thank is my wife. She is the funder and chair of the endowment. Allow me to introduce you to her."

Grace turned after hearing Rayne's voice whisper her name in her head. He motioned for her to come over. Rayne made formal introductions once she joined him and Dr. Blackburn.

Rayne gestured to the propped-up book encased in glass. "Dr. Blackburn is making good use of the endowment award. The manuscript is from Urban's personal papers."

"What an exquisite find!" Grace examined the same sketch Rayne had. Recognizing the wolf, she frowned. She knew it well. The same figure cast in a silver pendant lay in their safe at home. "Odd imagery for a religious text. Is it a Templar manuscript?"

Something about the Warwicks interest in the artifacts bothered Dr. Blackburn. "No, Mrs. Warwick. We are not sure who created the manuscript. It does not have the hallmarks of the Templar Order, nor would it be consistent with their traditions to create such a thing. They swore off worldly goods."

Hazy red beams briefly appeared across the case as Grace changed positions to get a better look. "Perhaps it is a fabricated text to create charges of heresy against the Templars?"

"The book dates to the eleventh century. The Templars did not fall out of favor until the fourteenth. Don't get too close. We wouldn't want you setting off the alarms. I can arrange for a private viewing of it if you like," Dr. Blackburn cautioned, touching Grace's shoulder.

"That would be appreciated. I am curious to learn what else you are currently researching, Dr. Blackburn." Grace smiled, backing away from the manuscript. "Dr. Rossi can provide you with my contact information, so we can find an appointment time that works for both our schedules."

A tall gentleman with light brown hair and green eyes, dressed in a black suit, stood in front of Dante's stone replica. He caught Grace's eye as she spoke. He frowned, as if displeased by its presence. She saw his lips move when his head turned in Dr. Rossi's direction. From the expression on the Italian curator's face, Rossi didn't appreciate his remark. The newcomer shot Rossi a disapproving glare then disappeared through a doorway into the next room.

Rayne nudging her arm with his elbow brought her attention back to the conversation with Dr. Blackburn about the Pope's efforts to retake the Holy Land.

"Any idea what the wolf represents? It doesn't seem to align with the other hand-drawn elements or the passage written." Grace knew by the look Rayne shot her, he thought she shouldn't have made the inquiry.

"I haven't figured that out yet, but have a few theories. The wolf historically has been associated with Rome, so it may represent the Church in some way. Wolves in the Middle Ages were also symbols of death, in particular, wolves were believed to engage in eating men for a variety of reasons, so perhaps the artist illuminating the manuscript meant for the wolf to depict the Left Hand of God better known as Archangel Gabriel since many believed he eliminated enemies of the Church and punished sinners."

Grace doubted Blackburn's theories. First, *The Times* article followed by the surprise Crusades presentation, and now this particular manuscript being on display along with Dante's statue. Someone was trying to get the Council's attention. "Dr. Smith's article mentioned something about the wolf being the emblem of the Order of Constantinople."

Dr. Blackburn laughed. "Don't tell me you believe the drivel he published based on conjecture and centuries-old conspiracy theories? I thought you were a researcher with a specialty in Late Antiquity and the Early Middle Ages, Mrs. Warwick."

"My studies and expertise lie in Antiquity, particularly Roman North Africa, up until the beginning of the Medieval Period. I am also not an expert on the evolution of the Church or all of their policies. But I do find it fascinating that this surfaces shortly after the article did, even if Smith's claims are baseless. It will be interesting to see what you learn about this manuscript as your research into its origins and symbolism continues."

The low hum of conversation around the room disappeared under a growing rumble that reminded Grace of a passing train. The sustained thunder-like noise steadily grew louder, vibrating the walls. As the sound increased, the fortress tremored at a faster and faster pace. The floor rippled. Items fell over in their cases. The statue of Dante rotated, then slipped from its pedestal; shattering like glass into white fragments of varying sizes.

Knocked off balance in her heels, Grace fell into Rayne.

Rayne caught her about the waist. Her hand slid across his shirt and over his jacket to grasp his far shoulder. *I have you, leof.*

Seeing Dr. Blackburn take a step sideways and stumble, he grabbed the professor by the arm to steady her. He kept a firm hold on both women to prevent them from falling. The word 'terremotto' swept through the crowd of people. Once the building stopped moving, he let go of Dr. Blackburn, but not Grace. "Are you both all right?"

Dr. Blackburn looked up at the man who didn't seem bothered in the slightest by what happened. "Yes. Thank you. We haven't had an earthquake like that in some time."

Grace continued to cling to Rayne. "Thank god we weren't hurt and the ceiling didn't come down!"

Rayne found Grace's reaction to the earthquake odd. While it was certainly unnerving, the two of them had been through much worse with having to escape actual building collapses on past assignments.

Security began evacuating everyone.

"For safety reasons, you will need to leave, Mr. and Mrs. Warwick. We'll secure the exhibit, then evacuate the building ourselves."

Now noticing the broken statue, Dr. Blackburn joined Dr. Rossi and Mirko trying to collect the pieces of it scattered across the floor.

Grace glanced back over her shoulder as she and Rayne made their way towards the door with the other attendees.

In the outer courtyard of the fortress, Grace spotted the displeased gentleman who argued with Rossi. She set her hand against Rayne's chest, stopping their forward movement. "Who is that in the dark suit near the cardinal?"

Rayne searched the crowd for whomever caught his wife's eye. The red zucchetto cap of a cardinal dressed in a black simar stood out amongst the crowd of people in the dimly lit area, but it was hard to see the man beside him. After the two men moved closer to the gate, a light shined down on them, giving him a clear view of their faces. He didn't recognize the man. "I am not certain, leof. Why do you ask?"

"He was not pleased with Rossi's exhibit tonight." Grace continued to watch the man and cardinal move through the crowd as she and Rayne made their way to the exit.

"Mayhap, he is one of the museum directors and had not been

advised of what was to be displayed." Rayne pulled Grace back to him after she started in the man's direction. "Whatever angered him is none of our concern."

The cardinal and mystery man walked under the raised castle portcullis.

"I find it odd he appeared just before an earthquake."

Rayne wondered why the stranger perturbed Grace. "You think he caused the quake?"

"I don't know, Rayne. But I get the feeling he is more like us than the other people in the room."

Rayne scanned the crowd once more for the gentleman, but there was no sign of him. "An immortal can't hide from us, Grace. We would have sensed his presence back in the exhibit hall."

The patronizing tone Rayne used annoyed Grace. Her instincts practically shouted there was a connection between the man and the earthquake.

One of the security guards waved at them. "Signore Warwick, your car is waiting."

Rayne gently steered Grace through the crowd towards Gage, Caitlin, and the driver of the private car he hired for the evening. The four climbed into the backseat.

<hr>

"Dr. Rossi, Dr. Blackburn, the drawing in Urban's journal. It is gone!" Mirko flagged his two bosses over to the Crusades exhibit.

"What?" Dr. Rossi doubted his assistant.

They hurried to the display case. The glass remained intact, the alarm actively on, and the journal rested in its stand undisturbed, but the page containing the wolf sketch was missing. The page so cleanly cut one would doubt it ever existed.

"How in the bloody hell did someone steal only one page?" Dr. Blackburn unlocked the case and disabled the alarm. She pulled on latex gloves and carefully turned the ancient sheets of vellum to see if the earthquake flipped the pages. "Mirko's right, Dr. Rossi. The page isn't here."

"We'll see you next week," Grace said goodbye to the Arsceneauxs, stepping out of the car after one of the hotel valets opened the rear door. She waited patiently for Rayne to get out and join her on the sidewalk.

Rayne asked the driver to drop Gage and Caitlin off at their home in Rome, so Gage didn't have to navigate closed roads or crowds to reach his own vehicle still in Vatican City. After the driver agreed, Rayne tipped him, then got out of the car.

With a big smile and a friendly buona sera, the concierge welcomed them back to the hotel and opened the wood and glass front door. The manager on duty nodded to Rayne as they passed the front desk.

Rayne noted how Grace fidgeted in the elevator. "Everything okay?"

"Fine. Tonight's quake and the exhibition rattled me a bit."

Rayne chuckled. "No doubt the earthquake did."

Grace couldn't help laughing. She wondered what caused the mischievous grin on his face when the elevator doors opened. "What are you up to?"

"Nothing. I simply still find the earthquake rattling you humorous. After you, my love." His hand rested on the small of her back while they walked down the corridor. Reaching their room, he slid the card into the electronic lock then held it open for Grace.

The romantic scene that greeted them broadened Grace's smile. Candles sitting on the tables and dresser cast a warm glow over the room, scattered rose petals covered the bed, a bottle of Brunello lay in a wine chiller breathing, and chocolate-covered strawberries rested on the coffee table.

"When did you have time to arrange this?"

Rayne took off her coat and tossed it on the couch. "Days ago. I texted the hotel on the way over and asked them to light the candles."

The earth vented once more; the room briefly trembled and the pictures on the walls rattled. Grace turned, clutching onto Rayne. Her eyes wide with concern.

He reassuringly smiled. "Minor Aftershock. Nothing to worry about, sweeting."

"I still hate the damn things. They're disconcerting."

Between the rumbling earth and the way Rayne held her while lowering his face towards hers, Grace's pulse raced; nerves and anticipation reminded her to live in the moment.

"Even if the hotel crumbled around us, you'd have nothing to fear, leof. I wouldn't let any harm befall you."

Rayne's seeking lips found hers. Grace returned the kiss with as much vigor as he gave it. Her hand traveled up his chest to caress a muscular shoulder. The kiss grew more urgent as Rayne's fingers splayed over her bottom, tamping her hips against him. Grace let out a soft gasp; now feeling the firm bulge that promised a pleasurable rest of the night. Wanting Rayne to fulfill that vow, Grace removed the tie he had already undone in the car and dropped it on the floor. As another kiss began, she grasped the front of his suit jacket. She started to guide it down his arms when something grazed her fingers. The side of her hand brushed against Rayne as she retrieved whatever it was from the inner liner pocket. Rayne groaned in protest when her mouth suddenly departed from his. Wondering what she fished out of his jacket, he opened his eyes.

"Care to explain this, Commander?" Grace held up the illustrated page from Urban's journal. The way he smirked would have annoyed her under any other circumstance, but with how his hands skimmed up her back then descended to her waist, she had a hard time being angry with him.

"Grace Giovanni Warwick, I cannot believe you stole another priceless relic! I thought those days were long behind you." Rayne's lips brushed against the curved white flesh of her ear as he spoke. "There is nothing to explain about that."

"The wolf is identical to your medallion."

"Yes, but the medallion wasn't initially mine. You have nothing to worry about. The manuscript will never tie back to me." Rayne tugged the page from her fingertips, set it on a nearby table, then unzipped her dress. Neither earthquakes nor ancient artifacts would ruin the evening he spent so much time carefully planning. "Now, honor our agreement as promised, my captivating thief."

Grace's eyes closed as he placed light kisses along her shoulder and collarbone. "Technically, it isn't tomorrow yet."

Rayne chuckled against her neck, drawing the two sections of smooth fabric forming a v on her back farther apart. "Now that is where you are wrong, leof. It's after midnight. Additionally, you said you'd let the evening lead where it may."

Discovering the satin lingerie set beneath the gown brought an appreciative grin to his face. He unhooked the bra, slid the straps down her arms. Letting it fall to the floor, he paused his disrobing Grace to admire her full, rounded breasts in the candlelight. His mouth descended between the creamy peaks, then glided along the length of her belly as he slowly dropped to his knees, guiding her gown the rest of the way down her body until it lay in a heap. Rayne unhooked her stockings from the garter belt, whisking his fingers against her skin as he peeled them down to her ankles before he kissed the inside of her bared thighs. He tugged her silky underwear down. She balanced against his shoulders, so he could pull the stockings and panties completely off. Notes of jasmine and orange blossoms wafted up from her skin, heightening his need of her. Those scents and her loving touch would always make him feel home, no matter where they might be. Standing, he swung her up in his arms and carried her the short distance to the king-sized bed.

Grace laid back on the cool sheets, which contrasted with the warmth of the man sliding down her body. His lips once more paid homage to the inside of her thigh. She rapturously sighed from the dark stubble lining his jaw grazing sensitive skin. Her hand rested on his back, in between his shoulder blades. Rayne briefly looked up at her. Her eyes remained shut; unmistakably enjoying the tender caress of his lips and fingers. A startled squeak followed by a moan left her lips as his tongue circled then teased the swollen flesh of her core. He stoked her desire until she quaked and her fingers tangled in his hair.

Adrift in the waves of pleasure coursing over her, Grace let the events of the evening go. After almost eleven years of marriage, she had no reason to doubt Rayne's claim of the medallion never tying back to him.

CHAPTER

THREE

February 1191 - Lateran Palace, Rome

Noticing a hooded figure silently standing in the far corner of the room, the Pope sent everyone out of his office. After the door closed, Clement acknowledged the man. "Thank you for responding to my summons so quickly."

"I always stand ready to serve you as needed, Holy Father." The hooded man bowed his head and knelt down before the Pope.

"I assume you comprehend why your specialized skill set is required for the venture outlined in my letter."

"Yes, Holy Father." The hooded man dressed in the red and black robes of the Order of Constantinople kept his eyes fixed on the floor.

"You must be certain to practice absolute discretion. Ensure no one will ever be able to identify you or draw any connection between your actions and the Church."

"A shadow is all others will see if they have the misfortune of crossing my path."

"Very good. Richard awaits Philip in Sicily. Head south, and join his ranks. You have our blessing to act in whatever manner you deem necessary. We must take back Jerusalem at any cost, even if it requires killing Richard along with Saladin."

"I am prepared to depart as soon as our meeting concludes."

"Remember, the Left Hand reports to a higher authority than any king or man." The Pope extended his hand.

The assassin ignored the gesture which demanded a kiss of the papal ring to demonstrate his subservience to the Church. His fidelity belonged to his brotherhood, not the Pope.

"Always, your holiness."

Not waiting to be dismissed, the Left Hand of God slipped from the palace into the night.

A man dressed in black and gold blocked the assassin's path. "You must not kill the king or Saladin. The humans must resolve this without interference from any of us."

The assassin attacked the newcomer. He quickly subdued the annoying being who pried into his comings and goings the past month. "This is the third time you interfere in things you do not understand, guardian."

Caught in a headlock, the guardian stopped struggling against the arm cutting off his air supply, hoping his lack of resistance would cause the assassin to loosen his hold. "Anger clouds your judgement. You cannot execute your latest orders."

The assassin laughed. "To feel something like anger or grief, one must have a heart or a soul. I no longer have either. I will let you live tonight. The next time we encounter one another, you die."

Silver eyes! The guardian would never forget those silver eyes watching him. "You are greater than this... destined to..." Searing pain traveled from the guardian's temple through the rest of his body. Darkness ruptured forth after a quick flash of light. Unable to hold him, the guardian's knees buckled forward. Rain drop covered, red cobblestones rushed up at him as he lost consciousness.

Curious to learn who so effectively shadowed him, the assassin reached for the guardian's hood. Shouts from nearby guards and the sound of approaching horses prevented him from uncovering the man's face. Needing to escape detection, the assassin concealed himself in the shadows of a nearby alleyway.

One of the riders jumped from his horse and ran to his unconscious peer. "Michael." He checked for a pulse. Finding Michael still lived, he looked in the direction of the alley. *Be prepared, mercenary. The next guardian you meet will not be so easily defeated. You will surrender that day.*

The assassin grinned. *Your order will find itself leaderless if we ever meet again.*

The rider noted the medallion hanging around the assassin's neck. The stolen symbol of an ancient organization once allied with the Council.

Rome - Modern Day

The phone rang, waking Grace. She rolled over, reaching across the empty space where Rayne had slept. Considering the time of morning, he more than likely went to the hotel gym to get a workout in.

"Hello?" She rubbed the sleep from her eyes after answering the phone.

"Mrs. Warwick, I apologize if I woke you. We wanted to be certain we caught you before you headed out for the day. Dr. Blackburn and Dr. Rossi hoped you might be able to spare an hour of your time this morning for the private viewing you accepted last night."

Grace glanced over at the clock. "I am available to meet. What time did Dr. Rossi and Dr. Blackburn have in mind?"

"Would ten o'clock be too late?"

"Ten works for my schedule. Please let them know my husband will be with me, so we don't have trouble coming through the gates."

"Of course, Mrs. Warwick. They will be happy to hear that you can accommodate the meeting request."

Grace hung up the phone and re-closed her eyes, debating going back to sleep for another half hour.

Returning from the gym, Rayne overheard the end of the call.

"That ten a.m. appointment better be a life-or-death matter to interrupt our *personal* weekend in Rome, especially on *my* designated day."

Grace smiled, sitting up now. "An earthquake, a mysterious immortal, and relics associated with you and Dante surfacing all in one night are a more than troubling situation that warrants further examination."

"I told you, none of those things are related or concerning. If they were, the Council would have sent orders for us to investigate them yesterday evening."

"We will have to agree to disagree." Grace held Rayne's gaze as he sat down beside her. His cynical expression relayed he still thought she over-reacted. The man was centuries older than her and more protective of their family than she ever could be. Rarely were his instincts wrong about things, but she couldn't ignore the nagging feeling that the events of the night prior were not mere happenstance. "Anything that presents even the slightest risk to you or the kids worries me, Rayne. If the meeting confirms everything that happened last night was a very strange coincidence, I won't give them a second thought. Please, humor me this morning."

Rayne hated the concern in Grace's eyes. "We better get dressed if we have to be there by ten."

"I love you." Grace brought a chuckle forth from the annoyed man.

"And I you, mia luna. I expect you to keep your word about not giving things a second thought after this meeting. Care to join me in the shower?" Rayne drew Grace to him. "Maybe we'll get lucky and have a few more aftershocks, cancelling your meeting, so I can have my way with you. I rather enjoy how you cling to me anytime the earth rumbles."

Mirko and Dr. Rossi met the Warwicks just outside the Vatican gates.

Dr. Rossi looked tired. "I thought it better we meet you here, so you didn't have trouble with the Swiss Guard. If you'll follow me."

His remark startled Grace. "The Swiss Guard? Are we not going to the museum?"

"Not this morning. We are meeting in the security office due to the earthquake and another matter we wish to discuss with you."

Rayne frowned, but said nothing as they followed Mirko and Rossi to a conference room in the security wing. A gendarmes officer, who had been sitting at the rectangular table in the center of the room, stood up when they entered.

"Grace, Rayne, this is Dirigente Pericoli. Dirigente, Signore and Signora Warwick."

Rayne grew suspicious of Rossi's reasons for wanting a meeting with Grace so quickly. "I assume by Pericoli's presence this other matter you mentioned involves a security or criminal issue."

Pericoli nodded and motioned for everyone to sit down. "Your assumption is unfortunately correct, Signore Warwick. What we are about to share is a delicate matter which requires your absolute discretion. We do not want the media or any member of the general public to learn of it."

Rayne politely inclined his head. With the disclaimer, he nor Grace were under any sort of investigation. "Certamente, Dirigente. Whatever is said in this room will stay in this room."

"A theft of an item on exhibit occurred in Sant'Angelo last night. Did you notice anything or anyone suspicious prior to the earthquake?"

"No, I can't say that I did."

"Signora Warwick?" Pericoli looked over at Grace.

"The only strange thing I noted last night was a gentleman accompanying a cardinal seemed upset with Dr. Rossi. The two looked to be arguing from where I stood," Grace said, surprising Rossi and Pericoli.

Rayne took a deep breath, wishing Grace hadn't brought that up. So much for a short morning meeting.

This was the first anyone mentioned a conflict between the curator and an attendee. Pericoli turned to Rossi. "Do you recall arguing with anyone, Dr. Rossi?"

"Cardinale Orsini's assistant, Michelangelo, was upset that we did not reveal the statue which was broken to the Cardinale before we did the general public. It was discovered on the grounds of one of the palazzos owned by the Orsini family." Dr. Rossi was surprised Grace had noticed the disagreement with her being across the room. "I can point him out on the security footage if you feel the need to investigate the man."

"So far, he is the only lead we have. I appreciate your time, Signore and Signora Warwick. If anything comes of this, we will need a written statement from Signora Warwick and may require her to testify to what she witnessed."

Grace smiled. "I would be happy to provide you with whatever you may need, Dirigente. You have my and my husband's full cooperation. May I ask what was stolen?"

Unsure if he should disclose the item, Pericoli looked over at Dr. Rossi.

Dr. Rossi sighed and waved his hand. "Tell her. She will find out in a few minutes anyhow. We invited her here to view the journal."

"A page from the journal on display was stolen. We were hoping you may have seen someone lingering around the case while you were speaking with Dr. Blackburn. The cameras must have glitched or malfunctioned as the footage doesn't show anyone accessing the case other than Dr. Blackburn after Mirko noticed the page appeared to be missing."

"Perhaps the earthquake damaged them or disrupted their signal?" Rayne suggested, giving the appearance of trying to help.

"Perhaps. The journal is in the office next door if you would like to view it, Signora Warwick."

Pericoli watched Grace carefully turn the journal's pages after she put on gloves.

Grace skimmed each page, looking for any more references to a wolf or the Left Hand of God. Other than the page she and Rayne had, there were no further mentions of the assassin or sketches of the wolf in Rayne's crest. She periodically mumbled fascinating and reverently touched a page here and there. "Such a shame the page is missing. I was anxious to learn more about this Left Hand of God with the controversy around the topic. Not to mention the artwork on the page was absolutely exquisite. I hope you recover it." Grace closed the journal and offered it to Dr. Rossi.

He carefully took it from her then set it in a padded case. "We do as well. If Dr. Blackburn uncovers any additional information about the journal or the Left Hand of God, we will certainly notify you. Grazie again for funding her project along with others."

"It's our pleasure," Rayne said, eager to leave. The faster they left the Vatican grounds, the better. "Sweetheart, we have another commitment to honor. We don't want to be late."

"Since you are short on time, we'll cut through the gardens to avoid the crowds waiting to get into Saint Peters and the Museum." Rossi handed the case containing the journal to Mirko.

Grace and Rayne politely conversed with Rossi about the earthquake and the history of Vatican City as they strolled through the gardens and then into St. Peter's through a staff-only entrance.

Grace stopped to admire Michelangelo's Pieta.

An older gentleman with salt and pepper hair ran up to her. "Mrs. Warwick! We need to talk."

Dr. Rossi shouted for security, then turned to Grace's new companion. "Dr. Smith! I have warned you about entering Vatican grounds." He seized the researcher who started the ludicrous conspiracy theories about the Popes having a secret order of assassins by the upper arm.

The retired professor shrugged free of the curator. "Mrs. Warwick, the order is real! You know it is. You must warn Baelin."

Grace didn't recognize the name the man uttered. "Baelin?"

A security team raced towards them.

"I know what you are, who your prior husband was," Dr. Smith continued, out of breath. "Warn Baelin. Warn the Wolf."

"Warn who of what?" Grace wondered what had the man so frightened.

"They are after the Wolf once more."

Rayne stepped closer. "Who is after the Wolf?"

The professor gaped at Rayne. "Jesus! You aren't a myth!" Dr. Smith grabbed Rayne's arm. "Luc..."

A loud pop followed by the sound of metal sliding against metal filled

Rayne's ears. He quickly pivoted in the direction it came from to see a gunman in the main entrance of the church. The flash from the gun's barrel warned of what flew towards them. Rayne caught the first bullet. The engravings on it and the silver coating surprised him. Demon slayer rounds?

Realizing who the shooter targeted, Grace stepped in front of Dr. Smith.

"Your children—" Smith started to tell Grace something.

The faint sound of a second shot from another weapon with a silencer echoed in the air. Trying to protect Smith, Grace threw herself into him, forcing him backwards. The bullet found him anyway. His body went limp. Something dropped from his hand.

"Dr. Smith!" Grace's shout drew Rayne's eyes to his wife and the man on the floor.

Grace stared at the dead human, stunned by the gaping hole in his forehead. A third round struck her in the side. She looked down to see her shirt changing color and pressed her hand into the wound, trying to slow the flow of blood. The pain between her rib cage and her hip prevented her from standing up.

Rayne hesitated to take action with her injured.

"I'm fine," Grace yelled up at him. "Stop the shooting!"

He yanked the pistol out of the nearest Vatican guard's holster and slid the silver bullet into the chamber. Taking aim at the assailant inside the chapel, his finger tightened around the trigger. The demon fell to the ground after silver lodged in its chest. Spinning towards the door, Rayne hoped the brass ammunition left in the clip would hurt enough to disarm the other demon. As he centered the weapon on the figure in the main entrance, the sound of gunfire again rang out. The being in the doorway fell forward into the church.

"Behind you, Richard!" A newcomer shouted, pointing his weapon directly to Rayne's right.

"Ibelin," Rayne muttered the man's name, surprised to see him.

A third bang reverberated through the large basilica. The bullet killed a priest a few feet from Rayne.

Rayne punched the other demon he sensed directly behind him, knocking the creature out. One of the Swiss Guard handcuffed the unconscious demon then dragged it out of the chapel.

A shimmer of light off something metallic a short distance from Grace caught her eye. Realizing it was most likely whatever Dr. Smith tried to give her, she grabbed it and shoved it in her pocket. Twisting to reach it made the smarting in her side worse.

With the threat eliminated, Rayne focused on Grace.

She winced as he yanked up the side of her shirt to get a better look at her injury. "What did he hit me with? It hurts like hell!"

"A demon slaying round." Rayne untied the pashmina scarf wrapped around the strap of her purse and pressed it into the wound. "It grazed your lower rib."

A Swiss Guard officer knelt beside Grace then carefully pulled her upward so she laid against his lap. "We have her, Richard."

The officer who shot the demon disguised as a priest started to tend to Grace.

"Richard?" Grace wondered who the two men were to address her husband by a name he hadn't used in several centuries.

"Please lie still, Lady Dalglese. I am going to remove the bullet." The man not holding her examined the small hole in her side. He glanced over at a third man arriving with a medical bag. "Federico, I need forceps along with a needle and thread."

Grace thought the man had lost his mind to perform such a procedure in the middle of the church. "We aren't in a sterile environment."

"If this didn't kill you, I doubt bacteria will." The man slipped a strand of black thread through the eye of a needle he held before nodding to his compatriot.

Rayne firmly took Grace's hand in his. The second officer held her shoulders down against his lap.

"Focus on me, leof." Rayne squeezed her hand tighter.

Feeling the sting from the forceps entering her skin then her skin and muscle stretching, Grace couldn't stop the string of profanity slipping out of her mouth.

The officer dropped the bullet into a tray next to him before wiping the blood oozing from the widened wound. "It's out."

"Thank you, Ibelin." Rayne appreciated Ibelin rendering aid to Grace.

Ibelin nodded, cleaned the blood from around the wound, then picked up the needle and thread sitting on top of the medical bag.

Grace cursed again due to the needle repeatedly piercing tender flesh as Ibelin stitched her up. "Rayne Warwick, you'll be the one needing stitches if you even try to tell me today, last night, and you aren't connected."

Rayne chuckled at the threat his wife hissed between clenched teeth. "Hopefully, someone else can offer an explanation for things since your husband is in the dark about the events of the past few days."

"You know how our protocol works. We cannot offer you or your wife any answers." Ibelin tied off the last of Grace's sutures. "We risk enough rendering her aid."

Rayne glanced over at his old acquaintance. "She and I are grateful for your assistance, Ibelin."

Ibelin nodded to Rayne before whispering in Grace's ear. "I will deny ever uttering these words. Your husband has no ties to the events of today."

A feeling of dread alerted Grace to another powerful immortal's presence amongst them. The way Rayne tensed and Ibelin's eyes shot around the basilica warned they too sensed the being.

"Rayne!" Grace gripped Rayne's arm and pointed at the Pieta.

Tears of blood streamed down Mary's cheeks, dripping onto the stone chest of Christ in her arms.

Rayne summoned his sword. "Ibelin, stay with her."

As Rayne rose, all humans vanished from the chapel. Only he, Grace, and Ibelin remained. Time froze, and the immortals found themselves in no-man's-land.

"Easy, Commander." A tall, black-haired, and dark-eyed man cautioned, seeing the weapon in Rayne's hand.

"My wife is injured and a human dead." Rayne tightened his grip on his sword's hilt.

"Your wife's injury is an unfortunate mistake. We weren't aware either of you were present. The human is another matter altogether."

"Care to elaborate on that?"

Grace didn't like the way Rayne's eyes remained locked on the being. The amount of anger and loathing she sensed in her husband dumbfounded her. She had never felt either from him in the manner that she did now.

"Dr. Smith's purpose was corrupted. The one sent to dispatch him inexperienced. You and your wife got caught in the crossfire."

Rayne didn't buy his answer. "Who ordered the execution?"

"Rayne..." The immortal knew denying the Horseman would jeopardize the delicate balance of things.

"Who ordered the damn hit, Lucifer?" Rayne snarled, crossing to the fallen angel.

"You don't want to know," Lucifer choked out as Rayne grasped him by the throat.

"I won't ask you nicely again."

Lucifer laughed before punching Rayne in the face and following up with a kick to Rayne's stomach that forced the Horseman back. "We are on consecrated ground, War. You know the consequences of battling here."

"You drew first blood by killing the human. I am certain the Council will take that into consideration." Rayne slowly pivoted, so the Devil and he remained facing one another.

"No need to involve the Council in this, Commander. Two of my minions are in a turf war. The Vatican is prime territory. I learned of the execution order too late to stop it. I hoped to reach the church prior to the others."

"Which of your regional overseers are fighting one another?"

"Rodrigo." Lucifer hesitated to name the second.

Rayne scowled, already guessing at the other for Lucifer to act as he did. "And?"

"Isra. I warned the two of them not to escalate the dispute any further. That they would eventually catch the attention of the High Council, which would not end well for either of them."

Rayne scoffed, doubting Lucifer did anything to calm the escalation between the two overseers. Lucifer lived for chaos.

"He speaks the truth, Richard. I was dispatched to confront the assassins and to take Dr. Smith into custody." Ibelin hated how his tasking aligned with Lucifer's.

Rayne studied the two immortals. Based on both confirming the cause of the shooting, he could take no additional action on sacred grounds. "Order any agent not with the Papal Guard away from Vatican City then leave here yourselves. Fail to heed my directive, and this will become a Council matter requiring Horsemen intervention."

"As you wish." Ibelin vanished from beside Grace, taking Smith's body with him.

Lucifer smirked. "Like my counterpart, I have no desire to engage you or the Council. I will warn Isra, if she crosses boundaries again, you will be the one she answers to."

Once Lucifer departed, things returned to normal in the basilica. Humans toured the building, and no signs of any shooting existed. Rayne helped Grace to her feet.

"Was that really Lucifer?" Grace had never seen him before today.

"Yes."

"The other man? Ibelin?"

Rayne escorted Grace out of the church. "One of the oldest members of the Papal Guard. We've known one another for centuries. He normally remains hidden in the administrative offices. Demons on Vatican grounds brought him out into public spaces. And before you ask, Dr. Smith, for whatever reason, more than likely tried to warn us about the turf war, Grace."

"How do you know that?"

"Baelin is Ibelin's given name."

"I doubt Vatican City is what the two demons are fighting over. Smith stated they were after you." Grace hated the way Rayne's eyes shifted away from hers and searched the crowd in Saint Peter's Square. "Look at me and tell me Smith was wrong."

Rayne's gaze returned to Grace's. "I can't say with a hundred percent certainty Smith was wrong; however, I can say it is highly unlikely, Rodrigo nor Isra have any desire to engage the Horsemen. Neither would send a hitman after me. They would have come themselves. They are well aware that a stronger demon would be needed to confront one of the Four Horsemen."

"Why would two demons have any interest in you?"

Rayne shrugged. "I have no idea. The last time I saw either both were licking wounds from an engagement with one another. The High

Council sent the Horsemen to remind them humanity was off limits since their previous territorial spat demolished a small town in France. That was two centuries ago. Lucifer normally does a decent job keeping his minions under thumb. If Lucifer states this was a turf war, I am inclined to believe him. Dr. Smith may have misunderstood something he overheard or saw. He was a human tinkering with supernatural sources to draw Ibelin and Lucifer's attention. Neither immortal would concern themselves with a human unless they started crossing into our realm."

"The Council would have dispatched us if a human wandered into our realm."

"We are only engaged when a large breach or material threat arises. Minor issues are handled by others. Whatever Smith did or found wasn't concerning to the Council." Rayne took Grace's hand and led her across the square. "Since we missed breakfast, how about lunch after a brief stop at the hotel? I forgot my watch on the nightstand and would rather not leave it sitting out."

"A man just died, and you're worried about your stomach and your watch?" Grace jerked her hand out of his, halting their walking in the middle of the crowded space. "What about the statue of Mary crying? The Pieta cried blood, Rayne. Her tears landed directly on Christ's heart. Almost as if Mary grieved the loss of her son all over again. That isn't exactly a regular occurrence. The Pieta isn't a living relic."

"Lucifer being in the Vatican caused the statue's tears. Strange things happen in his presence, just as they do when angels and saints appear. Please, leof, do not make more of the morning than what it was." Rayne brushed the hair that the wind blew in her face back behind her ear. "Let's go get my watch, then you can question me to your heart's content about Lucifer and Ibelin over a warm meal."

"Fine." Grace frowned. She would need evidence she didn't have at the moment to prove to Rayne he was wrong about everything not linking to him and the Horsemen. Lucifer said Smith's purpose was corrupted. Ibelin confirmed the same thing. The Vatican and the Devil wanting the same human dead. There was a higher-stakes game at play.

Grace froze in the small foyer of their hotel suite after Rayne opened the door. Their clothing was strewn from one end of the room to the other and in between overturned pieces of furniture. A lamp laid sideways on the floor. Someone had dumped out the bag of souvenirs for the kids. The shattered remains of two bottles of wine carelessly discarded from Rayne's suitcase intermingled with sprawling burgundy liquid reminding Grace of blood against the light marble floor.

"What's wrong, leof?" Rayne wondered why Grace didn't go into the room. Taking a step forward, Rayne took in the same scene she did. "Don't touch anything. Stay right here."

Concerned the miscreants might be waiting for them, Rayne quietly crossed the living room area and pushed open the bedroom door. Thankfully, he found the bedroom deserted. Whoever had been there ripped the sheets from the bed and had forced open the room safe.

Grace couldn't believe someone broke into their hotel room. "What were they looking for?"

"I don't know. Call the front desk while I check to see if anything is missing."

Grace used her cell phone to notify the hotel manager, who said he was calling the police and sending security up.

Rayne didn't know what to think with the contents of the safe being shuffled, but left behind. His watch still rested on the corner of the nightstand. None of their clothing or Grace's jewelry were stolen. "All the valuables and cash are still here, along with our passports. They don't appear to have taken anything."

The manager lightly knocked on the open door, so he didn't startle Grace or Rayne. A police officer and one of the hotel security team followed him into the room.

"Santa Maria!" The manager muttered, carefully walking around the flipped over coffee table.

Grace studied the mess while Rayne talked to the police and hotel manager. Since nothing was missing, the officer assumed they were the victims of a case of mistaken identity. After finishing his investigation of the scene, the officer told Rayne how he could get a copy of the report and that they could clean up their things.

The hotel manager apologized then comped their stay, repeatedly swearing this sort of thing never happened at their hotel.

Rayne thanked the manager. After everyone left, he set his hands on Grace's shoulders, worried about how quiet she was. "Are you okay?"

"Yes. I'm just confused. Why ransack a room and not take anything? To scare us?"

"Possibly, or as the officer said, the thief had the wrong room."

Grace picked up her dress from the night before and carefully folded it then set it in her empty suitcase. She laid Rayne's suit jacket on the couch and brushed some of the lint off it. As she reached for his garment bag, the invitation to the presentation fell from the jacket's pocket. "The journal page!"

She ran to the bedroom, then frantically searched the nightstands for it and behind the bed in case it fell there. "They had to be after the damn journal page. The entry from Urban's journal is the only thing missing."

"The page isn't missing." Rayne gently grasped her arm to get her attention after she continued moving furniture around.

"It most certainly isn't here any longer."

"Before going to the gym this morning, I took it to Sasainn and put it in our safe. I didn't want to take any chances of it being found anywhere that could be associated with us. You are lucky the cameras didn't catch you stealing it, which you needn't have done."

"Like hell I didn't need to take it. Clearly, you've pissed someone off recently. Smith wasn't crazy. He died trying to warn us of something. Why can't you believe someone is doing their best to expose you?"

"You have no proof of that, Grace. I still think this is all an unfortunate series of strange coincidences. Dr. Smith struck a bargain with the Devil that didn't work out in his favor. Ibelin more or less confirmed that. Lucifer wouldn't risk provoking the Council by wrongly killing a human. And for the last time, the journal page is harmless. It has nothing to do with me, nor would it ever tie back to the medallion I own, as the crest wasn't originally mine. Multiple men have worn it."

"You're wrong, Rayne." Grace hated that he wouldn't listen to her.

Rayne wasn't going to keep pointlessly arguing with her. "Finish packing, so we can go home."

FOUR

Sasainn

Grace walked into what used to be Morrigan's private library. Since she died, Raphael Fiore, Morrigan's Liaison to the High Council, and a retired, but reactivated Horseman, used the room as his office now. Some days Grace missed the goddess who originally oversaw the High Council Military Forces. Nothing ever escaped Morrigan's attention. The goddess would have intuitively known the events of the past weekend and inquired about them.

Raphael sat engrossed in reading whatever document he held. In his Horsemen's uniform, Raphael was every bit the Roman Legatus Augusti Pro Praetore he had once been as a human. He managed the affairs of both Isis's troops and the immortal armies of the High Council. While Rayne served as the Commanding Officer of Forces in the combat theater, Raphael was the leading commander in diplomatic circles, similar to a human in the role of Chairman of the Joint Chiefs of Staff. Raphael had mentored Grace and all the Horsemen at one time or another. While Raphael was a trusted friend and advisor, if anything threatened the immortal realm or the Horsemen, it was his duty to take action on it. Whatever she may confide in him about her worries may not stay strictly between them.

Second guessing her decision to seek him out, Grace turned to leave.

"Welcome back, Grace." Raphael never looked up as he spoke, but let her know he was aware she was there. He slowly set the document in his hands on the polished wood desktop, then smiled and gestured for her to sit in the chair on the other side of his desk.

"Thank you." Grace would never get used to seeing the blue-eyed Roman with gray-dusted dark hair sitting where Morrigan used to.

"Enjoy your time in Rome?"

"Up until the last two days of it, I did."

"Caitlin told me of the earthquake. Mother Nature had poor timing. Rayne really wanted to surprise you with a nice trip."

"Our getaway definitely had plenty of surprises."

"Surprises?" Deep lines creased Raphael's forehead. The way she said the word perturbed him. "I had a feeling you weren't simply coming in here to say hello, especially with how you hesitated at the door. Out with whatever question is troubling you."

"Can you tell me what this is?" Grace extended a gold medallion to him.

Raphael sat back in his chair as he examined the object Grace gave him. "This looks like an old codex of some type."

"Isn't a codex a book?"

"It can be, but it can also be a device to store notes or messages in."

"So, it's the Ancients version of a mini-journal or thumb drive? It doesn't look wide enough to hold anything."

Raphael chuckled. "More like an encrypted cell phone. You still have so much to learn about our world, Grace. Magic doesn't require a lot of space. The inscription looks like Aramaic, or maybe Tifinagh."

"It's North African or Middle Eastern in origin then. Can you open it?"

"I can try." The childlike curiosity on Grace's face reflected in Raphael's expression. He hadn't seen one of these codexes in at least two centuries. He extended his arms so Grace could see what he was doing. "First, you need to shift the top half of the medallion until you hear a click or the top sticks in place."

Grace didn't see how the top could be turned. "But it's a solid coin."

"It only looks solid." Raphael gently grasped the top portion and slowly shifted it until he felt the top catch on something. The click from inside it was barely audible. "Usually, there is another small piece that you must pull out to get it to open all the way."

Leaning closer, Grace saw what looked like a hook, not even a millimeter from Raphael's thumb. It was so tiny one would think it was an imperfection in the rounded edge if they didn't know what they held. She pointed it out to Raphael. "There."

Raphael and she exchanged a grin before he brushed his fingertip across the medallion's edge to move the final locking mechanism away from the body of the coin. The medallion split in two, revealing a folded piece of paper on one side. The other side had a brightly painted wolf's head, reminding Grace of a photograph placed in a locket.

Raphael seemed startled as he stared down at the wolf's head. "Where did you get this?"

"Rome."

Seeing Grace reach for the note inside, Raphael handed it to her. She carefully unfolded the cream-colored paper. By its texture, Grace realized how old the document was as it wasn't paper she held, but vellum. Strange sketches covered it. She offered the thin vellum to Raphael. "Any guesses as to what these are?"

"I honestly have no idea." Raphael shifted the page to see if a change in viewpoint or lighting revealed anything he might recognize. It wasn't often he encountered something new. "I've never seen anything like these characters before today. I can ask Isis to examine it if you'd like."

"It's angel script," Lyal said, startling Grace and Raphael.

Grace looked up at Isis's harbinger. "Angel script?"

Blue waves shimmered through the harbinger's straight black locks as the ancient Egyptian nodded. "Raphael doesn't recognize it as it is as old as the Ancients themselves. There are only a handful of beings who can still speak or write it. Each image is a word."

"Can you translate this?" Grace hoped Lyal could.

"La. No. This is a modified dialect, or as you modern-day people would say, the message is encoded. You need to find the key to learn what the author sends to the one they write."

"Thanks, anyway." Grace took the vellum and codex from Raphael.

Raphael studied the once-rogue harbinger. He still didn't completely trust Lyal after her rampage through the ancient world. "Does Isis require something of me or Grace for you to be here?"

"She requests your presence at a Council meeting in an hour along with Rayne's."

"Please convey that he and I will be there." Raphael pondered why the Council requested he and Rayne join their afternoon session. The day's meeting agenda only included administrative matters, not military ones.

Grace stared at the codex. "Raphael, does the name Ibelin ring a bell at all?"

Raphael now shot her the same suspicious expression he had Lyal. "Baelin D'Ibelin? We are acquainted with another."

"I figured you were. How does he know Rayne?"

"We all run in the same circles. Ibelin is an immortal after all."

"So Ibelin works for the Council?"

"Not exactly, but he has aided the Council with several things."

Grace knew Raphael withheld information by his vague answers. "Is there a reason he calls Rayne Richard, instead of Rayne like the rest of us?"

"He was an associate of Rayne's when Rayne went by that name years ago. Old habit for him, I imagine. Any other inquiries, as I need to prepare for the unexpected meeting your husband and I are summoned to?"

"Nope. I'll let Rayne know he's been called to the Council Round. Thank you for your help with the codex." Planning a quick exit from the room, Grace almost jumped to her feet.

"The codex doesn't have anything to do with Ibelin, does it?"

Raphael's inquiry halted Grace as she opened the door. Grace took a deep breath, hoping her smile was innocent enough when she turned around. "Not at all. I got it from a vendor peddling an array of things at St. Peter's. I thought it was a unique pendant until I noticed the engravings on it this morning."

Raphael gave her a skeptical stare, but didn't remark further.

After telling Rayne about the Council meeting, Grace went home. She tried searching through the books in their library for angel script or written languages that might be similar. With as much as Rayne traveled over the centuries, she figured he would have acquired a book of immortal or ancient languages. The man certainly spoke several. Not having any luck, Grace contemplated going to the twenty-first century to do an online search. They were staying in Sasainn for the next few weeks, which limited technology to more useful things like running water and electricity. They couldn't risk a cell phone or laptop getting lost in the surrounding medieval human communities. The local church officials would probably declare the device a tool of the Devil and burn whoever found it at the stake. Not that it would work with no signal or Wi-Fi. Looking at her desk calendar, she wouldn't have a full afternoon free to do a thorough internet search for another day or so. Until then, she needed a secure place for the codex. The last thing she wanted was to lose it before she knew what the message said.

Rayne's safe was most likely the best place to keep it. Only she and Rayne knew how to open the enchanted strong box. She went to the bedroom to put the codex away. As she set it in an empty place on the safe shelf, she disturbed the page from Urban's journal. It slipped to the floor. She leaned down and picked it up.

The front door opened then shut. She recognized Rayne's heavy footsteps on the stairs. After moving a few things around in the safe to better organize its contents, she glanced down at the page in her hand. Hidden in the figures of Lucifer and Michael were smaller images, similar to those in the codex. Grace quickly opened the codex and compared the angel script on the vellum to the miniaturized symbols hidden within the larger images. They matched.

"What in the..." Grace didn't finish her sentence. She shut the safe door with both documents in hand. Completely distracted by her discovery, she walked past Rayne as he entered the room.

"Well, hello to you, too," Rayne said, his tone light and teasing. "Where are you going?"

Grace gave him a quick kiss hello. "I've got to make a call. I will be right back."

After teleporting to modern-day London, she pulled her phone out of her jacket, then scrolled through her contacts until she found Dr. Blackburn's number. Grace cursed when no one picked up by the fourth ring. Surprisingly, the phone didn't roll over to a voicemail box. She let it ring a few more times. She wished they could get cell service in Sasainn, so Dr. Blackburn could call her back if she had to leave a message.

"Hello," Blackburn answered on the seventh ring.

"Dr. Blackburn, it's Grace Warwick. Would it be possible for me to get a second viewing of Urban's journal along with his private papers? Particularly anything with artistic characters, references to a wolf, or the Left Hand of God."

"Of course. Let me know when you would like to meet and I will work on getting the proper clearances."

"Does tomorrow morning or afternoon work for you?" Based on the long pause, Grace's request startled Dr. Blackburn.

"Tomorrow afternoon would work. It would also give me time to rush paperwork through the approval process. Is there a particular reason why you want to come back so quickly?"

Grace didn't see any harm in telling her the truth. "I found a document in my personal collection that I believe may have some sort of tie to the journal and possibly to other items Urban kept. I intend to bring it with me to cross-reference against your sources."

"I am anxious to see what document you have, Mrs. Warwick. Let's plan to meet in my office at one."

"See you then." Grace hung up the phone and teleported back to Sasainn. Now, she had to find someone to take over her duties in the afternoon without arousing Rayne's or Raphael's attention.

Rome - Modern Day

"What are we doing in Rome? Weren't you and Rayne here two

days ago?" An annoyed Ares wondered why Grace insisted on him meeting her at a coffee shop outside St. Peter's Square.

"Because I have a meeting at the Vatican, and I need it off High Council radar."

Ares's head cocked sideways. "What are you getting into now that you don't want them to know about?"

"Nothing too bad. And it's more I don't need Rayne knowing about this until I have the chance to look into a few things. We both know you are the king of executing questionable activities without attracting Council attention." Grace took the last sip of her cappuccino.

"Was that a backhanded compliment, Gracie?"

"Interpret it in whatever way makes you happy."

Ares laughed. "Let me make sure your nosey ex's attention is occupied elsewhere. He's the only one I know of not attending whatever big-to-do the High Council is having today."

"Be quick about it. I need to be in the archival offices at one."

The god disappeared for a few minutes then strolled back into the cafe in his twenty-first century persona: a blond-haired, hazel-eyed, charming, and well-dressed British man who introduced himself as Christian Marshall the Third, emphasis on the Third. He stopped at Grace's table and pulled out the chair across from her. "Is this seat taken?"

Grace laughed at the Greek god who always enjoyed his masquerading more than he should.

"Christian Marshall, *The Third*, at your service, Grace."

She shook her head. "Are we good to go?"

"We are. Surprisingly, Dante is attending whatever symposium those who reign over us are holding, and the Four Horsemen are off on assignment in Persia. With your husband and Raphael wrapped up in that tasking, they won't have any idea you are here."

"Good. Let's go. And if anyone asks who you are, you're the endowment's attorney and risk manager."

Grace paid her bill then the two of them headed towards the Vatican.

"Dr. Blackburn, lovely to see you again. Thank you for agreeing to meet with me." Grace extended her hand to the Research Fellow waiting for her at the main entrance of the Vatican Museum.

"It's my pleasure, Mrs. Warwick. I never expected you to be such a fan of Crusader history with you saying you primarily specialize your projects and studies in Antiquity."

"I am always expanding my historical endeavors. Dr. Abigail Blackburn, this is Christian Marshall, the endowment's attorney and risk manager. He insisted on accompanying me since I was transporting one of the items from our private collection today." Grace introduced Ares.

"Pleasure to meet you, Mr. Marshall." Dr. Blackburn shook Ares's hand.

"Likewise, Dr. Blackburn. Please, call me Christian, Abigail."

Grace rolled her eyes at the way Ares flirted with the woman who actually blushed. "Behave." Grace coughed the word, giving Ares a warning glare.

Dr. Blackburn flashed her badge at the security guard then escorted Grace and Ares into the Vatican archival offices. The conversation stayed fairly benign as the three walked the halls of the enormous structure.

"Almost there." Abigail smiled over at Grace. "I heard about Dr. Smith harassing you in the basilica. It's so tragic that he committed suicide."

Grace stopped walking. "Suicide? I hadn't heard that. Poor man."

"Poor man indeed. I pulled the items you requested from Urban's papers, along with a few others from Clement's which had similar illustrations." Dr. Blackburn unlocked one of the conference room doors. "If you could share more specifics on what you are looking for, I might be able to help you narrow down your search."

"I am looking for any documentation pertaining to the Order of Constantinople."

Dr. Blackburn's expression changed from curious to alarmed. "Oh, Mrs. Warwick! Do not tell me you now believe the conspiracy theories Dr. Smith spewed."

Grace smiled, pulling a pair of latex gloves from her briefcase, and then retrieved the piece of vellum from the codex stored in the bag's center compartment. "No, I do not subscribe to what Dr. Smith theorized. However, I do believe the popes were involved in more affairs than some academics care to admit. I am also not convinced there isn't some grain of truth to those conspiracies. One must sift through all the evidence for a hint of what might have created them. Origin myth fascinates me. Let's start with looking for anything related to 1191 and Saladin."

Recognizing the emblems on the page Grace laid beside the journal, Ares spoke without thinking. "Angel script?"

"What?" Dr. Blackburn wondered why Christian claimed the document was written in an imaginary language.

"Yes," Grace answered them both. "Dr. Blackburn, this is an encoded message I am looking to decipher. The document is believed to be from a medieval order that deployed a made-up alphabet based on symbols so no one outside the order could read it. The knights of the order called it angel script. I believe the order was in touch with Urban and possibly others. This order is the organization which may have caused the false rumors of a supposed Order of Constantinople to spread. I believe they were relaying intelligence to the Pope, not conducting assassinations. Kind of like a medieval spy network. If you look closely, these two images align with the ones hidden in the illustrations. I am just not certain how this particular vellum relates to those pages or what the message could mean."

"This is incredible! I've never seen anything like it. What order do you believe used encoded messages to communicate with the Pope?"

"The Sacred Order of Saint Julian of Jerusalem." Grace hoped the order name sounded believable. "They were a small order, not well-known, so they are easily overlooked."

"I am not familiar with them."

"Raphael was the archangel who represented them in the manuscripts," Ares added to the bogus tale.

"Christian, I could use your help translating the Latin." Grace pushed out the chair beside her.

Dr. Blackburn seemed impressed that the endowment's attorney knew Latin. "You read Latin?"

"Latin, Greek, and a few other dead languages you've probably never heard of, Abigail. We should go to dinner, so we can learn more about our linguistical interests."

Grace snorted, trying not to laugh at the way he said linguistical. "The faster you translate, the faster you can discuss whatever linguistics you'd like with Abigail."

Ares reached for the letter Grace held out to him.

Grace pulled it back. "Gloves, Christian. You are handling documents from the Middle Ages."

Ares loudly snapped the wrist of one of his gloves once they were on, and picked up the letter Grace initially offered him.

The medieval Latin she was reading mentally wore Grace out. She had to slowly translate the official records, then compare them to personal records of the popes, which were written in a mix of Italian and French. As she debated taking a break, Grace spotted the words "Le Loup" in a letter.

"Le Loup?" Grace worried about who the term referenced. Rayne would have a lot of explaining to do if the Pope was documenting conversations with him.

Dr. Blackburn looked up from the letter she read. "Reynald de Chatillon was known as Le Loup."

Grace recognized the name. "The same Reynald who started all the fighting with Saladin?"

"The fighting with Saladin went on a while before Reynald inserted himself into it, but Reynald is the one who broke the truce between Jerusalem and Saladin, which eventually led to the Christian West losing the kingdom. Many people, including myself, believe his lust for wealth overrode his common sense. Had he not provoked Saladin, that part of the world might look very different today."

Grace laughed. "Careful, Dr. Blackburn. That sounds like speculative history to me."

A light brown-haired, brown-eyed gentleman entered the room, disrupting the research session. "Dr. Blackburn, all guests accessing sources this old are supposed to be cleared through the Archival Director and the Head of Papal Security."

"I submitted the proper paperwork through my leadership chain yesterday, and it came back approved this morning." Dr. Blackburn didn't understand how Grace wasn't cleared to access the archives. "I have a copy in my office that I can show you."

"I would very much like to see the paperwork. Mrs. Warwick, her companion, and I can wait here while you retrieve it."

Grace recognized the man from the hit in St. Peter's. Once the room door closed behind Dr. Blackburn, Grace turned to the Vatican security officer. "Baelin D'Ibelin."

"What?" Ares questioned if he correctly heard the man's name.

Grace smiled. "The Executive Director of Papal Security is none other than the Defender of Jerusalem, Ares."

Baelin shot Grace an unimpressed glare.

Grace eyed the immortal concealed in the Swiss Guard ranks. "For you to come out of the woodwork a second time, there is something here you don't want found."

"On the contrary, Defensore. We have nothing to hide from the High Council. Read whatever you like. Although, I am wondering what your husband might say about your return to the Vatican. Did he not tell you to leave this matter alone?"

"I have no idea what matter you are talking about. As to my husband, he allows me leeway to pursue my interests." Grace sat back down at the table and picked up the letter referencing Reynald di Chatillon. "Care to share your experiences with Le Loup?"

Baelin shook his head. "I was warned that you are stubborn. Let us hope you are not as foolhardy as Reynald di Chatillon."

"Unlike Reynald, I respect boundaries."

"You respecting boundaries any better than Reynald is debatable at the moment." Rayne leaned against the far wall with his arms crossed over his chest.

Grace rolled her eyes. "What are you doing here?"

"I was about to ask you the same question."

"I sent for him," Baelin explained Rayne's appearance.

"And I am glad you did. Or I wouldn't have known my wife returned to Rome." Rayne crossed the room and pulled out the chair next to Grace's. He rested his arm on the table after he sat down. He frowned, not liking that Grace potentially entangled herself in either a djinn turf war or a dispute between the Vatican and Lucifer. "Did we not agree to let the whole demon hit thing go?"

"This has nothing to do with demons or Dr. Smith."

"Then why are you rummaging through Urban's records after sneaking off to Rome while I was on assignment? With Ares's disreputable self, no less?" Rayne waited for Grace to try to explain her way out of the Vatican visit.

"I... I have developed an interest in the relationship between Urban, Saladin, and Richard the First. I was hoping to learn more about what the three men thought of each other." Grace broke eye contact with Rayne. Annoyed by the hmmm she heard, she looked back at him to see the hard stare he gave her. The one raised eyebrow and the tension in his jaw screamed he didn't believe her answer. "Fine. I was hoping to find some evidence of the Order of Constantinople and you being the Left Hand of God."

Baelin ran his palm over the lower half of his face, learning what Grace researched. "Merde."

Rayne slowly rapped his fingers on the table. How many times did he have to say that damn wolf would never tie back to him? After a few seconds of silence, he finally spoke. "And what did you find?"

"The Wolf referenced in Urban's letters was Reynald, not you." Grace hated the 'I told you so' look on his face.

"Are you ready to let the past be, or should Baelin and I prepare for more unexpected Vatican visits?"

"Dr. Smith said they are after the wolf!" Grace snapped at Rayne. "Why would he seek me out to say such a thing then panic when he saw you in Saint Peter's if nothing relates to you?"

"Dr. Smith said many outlandish things, Mrs. Warwick. As you yourself identified, Reynald di Chatillon is Le Loup, not Richard," Baelin interjected, hoping she wouldn't look further into things.

Grace locked eyes with Rayne. "The wolf Smith referenced is living."

Rayne knew the determined expression on her face well. She had no intention of backing away from this. "You keep up with modern-day headlines. DAESH recently wrote a letter dedicating one of their terror attacks as an act to avenge Reynald's pillaging of Egypt and Jordan. That is most likely what started the whole wolf rumor and Order of Constantinople nonsense on top of that journal being discovered. Please, Grace, let this go. We are in no danger. If we were, I would have been the one the demon shot in Saint Peter's, not Dr. Smith. You heard Lucifer. He has no quarrel with me."

"Maybe whoever Dr. Smith warned us about isn't Lucifer."

Baelin placed a reassuring hand on Grace's arm. He couldn't fault her for wanting to protect her husband. "If anything hints at Richard being targeted, I will notify you, Mrs. Warwick. There is nowhere I do not have ears. In the meantime, return home. Take it from one who knows, we cannot live in fear or worry about things beyond our control. Nothing from these papers can bring trouble in the present. If they held that power, they would be in the High Council's possession, not ours. And take the troublesome Greek deity with you."

Sixteenth-Century Spain

Grace stopped worrying about the events in Rome after a month passed with nothing additional happening. Maybe Rayne was right about things being an unfortunate coincidence.

"You're quiet today," Rayne said, drawing Grace out of her daydreaming. Normally, she'd talk to him when out riding together, but she hadn't uttered more than a few words the past half hour.

"I am enjoying the sunshine and countryside. It's beautiful here." Sitting behind Rayne on Fahkir, Grace took in the green rolling hills and blue sky. The weather was perfect for horseback riding; not too hot or too cold. A light breeze blew, picking up sections of Fahkir's long, black mane.

"Tarquin, do not get too far ahead of us," Rayne scolded the nine-year-old riding his own horse several yards in front of them. The boy was growing more adventurous and independent with each passing day. A soft laugh from Grace tickled Rayne's ear as her arms tightened around him.

"Aren't you the one always telling me to stop worrying as the

Horsemen watch over Tarquin? That I need to stop acting like an over-protective mother hen."

Rayne grinned and glanced back at her. "I am not concerned about his safety. I merely want to keep him in sight since the gelding is a new acquisition."

Splitting time between their homes in Sasainn and Spain allowed them to better balance their professional obligations and personal lives. Their Spanish home provided a reprieve from the day-to-day training and operations of the High Council Military Forces.

Fahkir began an easy lope after Rayne cued him to do so. The black Andalusian effortlessly made his way up a second hill. Reaching the top, Rayne and Grace saw Tarquin letting his horse drink from a stream in the valley below.

Grace rested her head on Rayne's shoulder. "Tessa missed out by opting to stay at home. I am glad she did. I benefit from being able to ride with her father instead."

"Are you truly enjoying yourself, leof?" Rayne slowed Fahkir to a walk, allowing the horse to leisurely descend the large hill.

"I am. We haven't gone on a relaxing ride through the countryside in a while. I didn't realize how much I missed doing this."

"We will have to make a habit of it then. I am sorry if I am neglecting you."

Grace's laughter brought the gelding Tarquin rode's head up from the gurgling brook. The horse's ears pricked forward, and he looked in her direction.

"You never neglect me, Rayne. Raising a family and periodically saving the world keeps us busy."

"Thankfully, things have been quiet. Now, if only I could get my unruly daughter and wife to behave. Tarquin seems to be the only one not causing havoc in my house this week." Rayne stopped Fahkir to steal a kiss from his wife. With the Hasan gone, he learned to live a less war-centered life. It surprised him how much he enjoyed raising a family with Grace. Now he dreaded whenever a conflict arose.

The hiss of an arrow traveling through the air disrupted the pleasant moment. A silver-tipped wooden shaft slid through the soft cotton of the shirt Rayne wore, burying itself in the muscle of his upper chest.

Grace gasped his name.

Searching for the archer, Rayne whipped Fahkir around. Gritting his teeth and firmly grasping the arrow, he ripped it out of his pectoral muscle. Blood pulsed from the wound, soaking the front of his shirt, and turning it red.

Grace looked in the direction from which the arrow came. With no more projectiles flying and no one in sight, she assumed a huntsman might have accidentally misfired in their direction.

Rayne spotted a group of men in the distance riding towards them with weapons drawn. He cursed, snapping the arrow he held then dropping the pieces. "Retrieve Tarquin and get out of here."

Grace now noticed the men barreling down on them. She pushed herself out of the saddle. Her feet had hardly touched the ground when Tarquin screamed.

A battle cry rang out from the advancing group.

Hoping to buy Grace enough time to reach Tarquin, Rayne rode into their attackers and knocked two from their saddles. His circling the group temporarily halted their charge. One of the men he knocked from their horse slipped past Rayne, charging directly for Tarquin.

Grace sprinted towards her son. May the gods ensure she reached him before the enemy did! While Tarquin was destined to be a Horseman, he was nowhere near ready for combat or capable of fending off an armed attacker.

Fear paralyzed Tarquin in place. He watched his mother and the man rushing at him. Rayne had only recently began teaching him how to defend himself. As the Horsemen's training required, Tarquin fenced and shot archery since he could hold smaller versions of their weapons. Unfortunately, the boy had neither weapon nor knowledge in how to effectively apply what little hand-to-hand his stepfather taught him.

The man stupidly turned to face Grace, placing himself as a barrier between her and her son. She never broke stride as her fist collided with his face, then she dropped to the ground, sweeping his legs out from under him. Before he could react, she was on top of him, yanking his dagger from the sheath on his side. She slammed the long knife down into his upper chest, pinning him to the ground, but not killing him.

With the closest assailant wounded on the ground, Grace glanced over her shoulder to check on Tarquin.

A volley of arrows launched from somewhere on her right. She wouldn't reach Tarquin before the projectiles did. "Ride, Tarquin!"

A soldier in Roman-style golden armor appeared in the saddle behind the boy. The man yanked the reins from Tarquin's hands and pivoted the gelding so quickly the horse stumbled. The rapid maneuvering caused the arrow tips to strike the shield he held along with his metal cuirass and arm coverings instead of Tarquin's exposed skin. By the downward tilt of the man's head, he said something to the boy. Tarquin looked in Grace's direction as the soldier wrapped an arm around him. Her heart nearly stopped seeing her son and the soldier vanish.

"Tarquin!"

The desperation in Grace's cry drew Rayne's eyes in her direction. Tarquin was nowhere in sight. A fist to his jaw brought Rayne mentally back into the conflict. The fury at some foe harming his family fueled each blow he dealt the men engaging them. Even so, Rayne refused to let his anger override his instincts. He would be no good to Grace or Tarquin if a hotheaded mistake caused him serious injury. *We will get him back, Grace.*

The man in gold armor set the frightened boy down on a bed.

Confused by his surroundings, Tarquin glanced around. The walls were gleaming pearl white along with the floor. The dark wood bed under him didn't feel like his bed at home. A woman with silver in her black hair and wearing a strange wine-colored dress stood in the doorway watching him and the soldier.

The soldier nodded to the woman, then gently grasped Tarquin by the shoulder and knelt down so they stared one another in the eye. "You are safe, Tarquin. I need to help your mother and Rayne. Stay right here until I get back. Can you do that for me?"

Tarquin's headed emphatically bobbed up and down. His citrine-colored eyes still wide with amazement.

"Good. I will return as soon as I can."

Ten more riders appeared after Rayne killed the last of the initial wave. Worried about whether or not his daughter was safe, Rayne reached out to Destahn. The Horseman Captain had watch in the barracks that afternoon. As things were quiet in Sasainn, Destahn played a round of cards with Tamir, another Horseman, Sean Watchous, an immortal guide general, and Arturo, Rayne and Raphael's aide.

"Destahn, secure Tessa!"

For Rayne to be shouting orders instead of using telepathy, the Horseman Commander was under duress. The cards in Destahn's hand fell to the table.

I've got Tessa, Rayne. Worry about whomever you are fighting. Destahn confirmed receiving the order before teleporting to Rayne's home, startling Lavinia, Grace and Rayne's cook and housekeeper, who was watching Tessa.

Rayne wanted Grace off the field with not knowing who or what assaulted them. "Go assist Destahn."

"I am not leaving you to face these men alone."

"Do as I ask, Grace. I can easily handle these last ten."

Grace yanked Rayne's dagger from its sheath, since she lacked her own weapons. "My son was just taken. I am not about to risk losing my husband too."

Now was one of the times Rayne hated her stubborn nature. The new batch of riders would be upon them in mere seconds. "Grace, go! Our daughter may be in danger."

The golden-clad soldier reappeared between them. "Your daughter is secure, Commander. Destahn is with her, and Raphael joins them. The only threat your family faces is in front of you."

Before Rayne or Grace could question the man, he charged into their attackers.

The three fought side by side until all ten lay wounded or dead on the ground.

With the assault over, Grace grabbed the soldier. "Where is my son? Where have you taken him?"

"Calm yourself, woman. He is safe in his father's home."

Confused, Grace released him. "His father's home? His father is standing in front of you with no knowledge of his son's whereabouts!"

"*His father* is well aware of where the boy is." The man removed the helmet he wore, revealing his identity. "He sits on one of my guest room beds with my mother tending to him."

"Dante?" Grace's mouth opened then shut while she worked through her frantic thoughts. The dead man the Fates said she was destined for stood before her very much alive. Instinctively, she reached for her first husband. It had been ten years since he died. Ten years since the High Council allowed them one last goodbye on the shores of Greece. For a breathless second, those years left her memory. Grace Giovanni once again wanted to welcome her lost Horseman home.

Dante forced himself to remain outside her reach. He could not touch her without bringing the wrath of the High Council upon them. He foolishly cursed himself by agreeing to their terms. In saving her life, he ended his own existence. Osiris urged him to push back on the requirement to never go near her again. Dante feared if he did, the agreement would fall through after taking so long to be brokered. He would rather spend eternity alone than let Grace and Tarquin perish. However, with the way she stared at him, with her hand extended, he would surrender his hollow farce of eternal life for one kiss, one embrace, before he disintegrated into dust for violating his contract.

The myriad of emotions crossing Grace's face disconcerted Rayne. He wondered if he would lose his wife now that she learned Dante was no different from any other of the deities they served. His heart wrenched as if someone thrusted a knife into it then twisted the blade. Had the years they spent together and the daughter they conceived been for naught?

Grace pulled her hand back, then brought it down hard against Dante's cheek. The loud thwack of the slap echoed through the oddly silent hillside. Her palm and fingers stung from the force of the blow, even though Dante's head hardly moved. The god's eyes briefly closed and his jaw clenched, but he remained silent, not offering any additional reaction to her strike. Tears rolled down her face when their eyes met again.

"You son of a bitch! You could have come back if you wanted to." Unsure if she could keep herself from trying to pummel Dante into the ground, Grace turned away from him. He wasn't worth the anger or tears. No one who truly loves another deceives them as he did her.

Rayne and Dante exchanged concerned glances. Grace's reaction surprised them both.

Needing distraction, Grace went to inspect one of the unconscious riders. Elaborate tattoos marked his skin. An ornate emblem hung on his sword belt. She wiped the remaining tear from her face and tried to focus on solving the motive behind the skirmish. "They are human. Why would they attack us?"

Rayne walked over to her. He stood behind her and settled his hands on her shoulders. "Are you okay, leof?"

Grace didn't turn to face him. She simply placed her left hand on his right one, clasping it tightly. The subtle gesture screamed Rayne had become her rock, the sole holder of her heart. The sapphire in her wedding ring glistened in the stream of sunlight that caught it.

"They appear to be a band of brigands. Perhaps they mistook you for someone else," Dante said before glancing off into the distance. The blue stone and Rayne comforting Grace coldly reminded Dante whose wife she was now. It was one hell of an internal struggle to not pull her from Rayne and tell her she was mistaken in all of her assumptions. That he still loved her and would give anything to trade places with Rayne.

Rayne crouched down to get a closer look at the body. He held the man's pendant in his palm. Recognizing the emblem, Rayne scowled. Afraid of what may be hidden under the man's jacket, he carefully brushed aside one corner of the jacket collar. Seeing the symbol of damned souls inked into the man's skin brought a loud curse from the Horseman. The men served two masters. Why come for him now? "They are Umar's guard."

"Unfinished business from your past, Commander?"

Dante's inquiry made Rayne shudder. "I hope not with having young children to protect."

Movement on the hillside above them shifted Rayne's attention. A man watched the three of them.

Damned observer! Rayne ripped the short sword off the corpse beside him and hurled it in the man's direction. The iron blade churned in the air with a hiss-like whir before it straightened, then slipped through the observer's armor, fixing him to a nearby tree. He took long, intentional strides, walking towards the man to drive home that he considered the observer a lesser being. "Why? Why attack when my wife and child are with me?"

The man smiled, revealing a capsule in his mouth. His teeth fractured the gel coating, releasing the deadly poison it contained before Rayne could yank it out. As he died, he uttered, "Gaudalcete."

The utterance terrified Rayne nearly as much as watching Grace almost die in Alexandria.

Grace noted the fear in her husband's expression. "What is Gaudalcete?"

"A battle, fought long ago." Rayne couldn't bring himself to look at Grace. Instead, he reached for the man's shirt, already knowing what he would find where the man's neck and shoulder intersected. Seeing the demon seal overlaying the damned souls' emblem, Rayne hissed the name Garsea.

Dante understood all too well the significance of Gaudalcete and Garsea. "Tessa and Tarquin can stay with me until this mystery is solved."

Grace shook her head. "No. They can go to the Arsceneauxs, but they are not staying with you."

"Grace, the two will be well cared for. I would never let any harm befall my son or his sister."

"No! God only knows what they will learn in Elysium! I am their mother, and they go where I say for safekeeping."

"And I am Tarquin's father! Did I not remove him from danger while you and Rayne were distracted? Do you honestly believe I would harm either of your children, Grazia?"

Grace couldn't believe he had the gall to argue with her. "My answer is still no. Mothers trump fathers in court proceedings."

"A deity trumps an average immortal." Dante was not about to return Tarquin to Spain with being blind to the reason for the assault.

"Must I remind you I am both the Defensore and a Guardian of the Ancients?"

Dante sarcastically laughed. "Since it comes down to power and authority, god beats everything you can put on the table. What say you, Warwick?"

Rayne studied the soldiers again, then his wife and old friend. "Will your mother assist with tending the children, or are you their lone caregiver?"

"She will help as needed. Rayne, you know my home provides a stronger safe haven for them than they would have in the mortal realm. You also know the laws I break in bringing them there."

Grace's jaw dropped. Rayne actually contemplated the offer. "And you call me the crazy, impulsive one! Would you truly leave our kids with a god that has the history this one has?"

"Leof, hurt clouds your judgment." Rayne took her hands in his, sympathetic to the betrayal raging through his wife after learning it was within her ex-husband's power to return to earth. "Have you forgotten he is a god because he traded himself for his wife and son?"

"Rayne Warwick Dalglese!"

"Enough, Lady Dalglese!" Rayne sternly silenced Grace. He had not seen her this upset in years. Rage created unfounded fear within her. "I would not leave our children with anyone who would do them harm."

"Fine. Tarquin may spend the next two nights in Elysium. We send Tessa to D'Orme. I will ask Arturo to handle the arrangements while we address whatever occurs here."

"You know how close our children are. It is best that they remain together. Tessa will be frightened if we separate the two while we are away."

Grace's frown deepened. Rayne spoke the truth. Tessa shadowed Tarquin everywhere he went, and Tarquin more than happily took his sibling under wing. The two had never been separated since Tessa was born.

Listening to Grace internally debate what to do, Rayne's brow raised. "I have an alternate proposal to ease your angst. You stay with the children, and I will ride to Córdoba to investigate the cause of these men seeking us out."

"I am not letting you ride alone. I will only agree to watch the kids if Dante goes with you."

"Sorry, cara. I cannot assist in this other than offering to shelter your children. I only have leeway to protect my son." Dante earned a glare from her.

"Our son has nothing to fear from humans."

"He most certainly does when they are from another century!" Dante shot back.

"What?" Grace spun to look at Rayne, who refused to make eye contact with her. "Does he speak the truth, Rayne? What century do those men inhabit?"

Rayne took a deep breath. His answer would only irritate her more. "I am not certain. Umar died centuries ago, but these men... these men bear his emblem and wear the uniform of his guard. It is best the children find safe haven in Elysium until we know more."

Grace shook her head in disbelief. "If anything happens to either one of them, Dante..."

"Nothing will happen, Grazia."

"Fine." Grace reluctantly agreed to turn her children over to the man once her spouse.

Rayne hoped a god's home could provide the protection his children needed if Umar and Garsea targeted him. "Destahn, Raphael, bring me my daughter."

Dante's heart shattered seeing the youngest Warwick run from the two Horsemen to Grace. Grace embraced Tessa, thankful to see her unharmed. The little girl's long, gold curls reminded Dante of her mother. When Tessa looked up at him, she had Rayne's blue eyes and dimples. She shyly hid her face in Grace's side.

Grace introduced the two of them, doing her best to keep her voice calm and reassuring.

Hoping to be less intimidating, Dante bent down. Tessa peeked out at him again briefly, then clutched Grace's leg, turning away. He tried to coax her over to him with no luck. Grace's anger only fueled the child's fear of him.

Rayne picked up Tessa after she refused to leave Grace's side. The Horseman smiled as his daughter hugged him and whispered, "Hello, Daddy" before burying her face in his shoulder. Rarely did anything make his outgoing child bashful like Dante suddenly did. "You need to go with Dante, sprite."

Dante watched Rayne gently pry Tessa's small arms from his neck before holding her out to him.

Tessa eyed Dante suspiciously, but settled her hands on his shoulder and sat quietly in the crook of his arm.

Dread filled Rayne as he turned his child over to Dante. "You hold my life in your hands."

"She and Tarquin are my family as well. You know what that means to me, Rayne. I will keep them safe."

Tessa whimpered and reached for her father.

Rayne took Tessa's small hand in his, preventing the tantrum that was about to erupt. "You will be all right, sprite. Dante is one of my oldest friends. He is going to watch you and Tarquin while Mommy and I are away for a few days."

Grace choked up listening to Rayne assure Tessa she was safe. A sob escaped their daughter's lips as Tessa stared up at Rayne.

"Shhh, Tessa. There's no reason to cry." Rayne took a step closer to her, cradled the side of Tessa's face in his hand, then ran his thumb across her little cheek; hoping to soothe the turmoil and fear driving the little girl's need to be back in his arms. He hated the distress Tessa and Grace both exhibited. "I promise you are only going with Dante for a short time, sprite. Tarquin is already in Elysium waiting for you. The two of you will have lush gardens to explore and a large pool to swim in while Mommy and I take care of an important matter. You'll have so much fun playing, you will be surprised by how quickly time passes. Have courage, little one."

Tessa sniffled, then offered her father a weak smile. "I will be brave like you, Daddy."

"Be fearless like your mother often is instead," Rayne whispered before kissing her forehead, and then stepped back.

"There is nothing to fear in Elysium, Tessa. Just to be certain, I will come visit you." Raphael brought a delighted giggle from Tessa. The little girl adored the Roman.

Rayne returned to his original spot beside Grace and wrapped a comforting arm around his wife.

Tessa smiled up at Dante then waved goodbye to her parents. Thinking it best to leave before Tessa could become upset again, Dante departed.

"They are in excellent hands, leof. Dante has help with his mother nearby."

Grace bit back the retort forming on her lips and stared down at the grass to prevent herself from lashing out at Rayne. Someone else caused the chaos of the day. They deserved her animosity, not Rayne. "I know they are most likely safer in Elysium than here. I just fear not seeing them again."

Rayne crooked his finger under Grace's chin and gently lifted her face so their eyes met. "Dante will return Tarquin and Tessa. Otherwise, I never would have allowed him to take them."

Grace nodded and gave him the best smile she could.

Rayne appreciated the attempt. "I am certain we can resolve whatever the issue is in Córdoba quickly. The children will not be in Dante's care long enough for any harm to befall them."

"Córdoba? Should we not ride to Granada? That is where the last caliphate was."

"No. Córdoba is the origin of those men." Rayne looked over at the Horsemen Captain silently taking in everything. "Destahn, meet me at Hayden's in the morning and wear civilian clothing. We need to conduct some reconnaissance into what occurs without alerting many to our presence."

<hr>

Elysium -

Maria met Dante as he materialized in his home with Tessa. "You have guests waiting for you."

Osiris and Poseidon stood outside his study door. Scowls marred their normally stoic faces, warning their visit wasn't friendly in nature. Dante handed Tessa to his mother. "Take her. Their business with me should not last more than a few minutes."

With Dante returning from Spain, Maria guessed the little girl was Rayne and Grace's daughter. "What a pleasure to meet such a charming young lady with pretty golden hair. My name is Maria, carina. What is yours?"

"Tessa." Tessa smiled, instantly taking a liking to the older woman holding her.

Maria returned the smile and settled Tessa on her hip. "Well, Tessa, it is a pleasure to meet you. Would you like something to eat?"

Tessa nodded her head yes.

Tarquin came around the corner and spotted his sister. "Tessa!"

Maria set the little girl down and walked with her hand in hand to the boy waiting at the end of the hall.

Once the three rounded the hallway corner, Dante turned to meet with Osiris and Poseidon. Neither said a word to him as he approached, then politely gestured for them all to go into his study.

"You intervened when your intervention was not needed." Poseidon confronted Dante before he finished closing the door all the way.

"My son was in danger."

Dante's eyes rested on Osiris. The god remained silent. Dante knew his father had to enforce Council directives, but he hoped for once, Osiris might challenge them on his behalf.

Poseidon still couldn't believe Dante flouted a direct order from the Council not to engage in the earlier conflict. "The Horsemen Commander and the Defensore are more than capable of protecting their children from human misunderstandings. You should have stood down as directed, Dante. You are no longer a Horseman. You are a god, a god that has to follow Council decrees."

"If those that attacked them had been human, I never would have violated the directive. Their assailants served a djinn and had a djinn observer riding in their company. They also directly targeted my son, not Commander Warwick or his wife. I was not about to stand aside to please the Council. All of you and your archaic laws be damned!"

"Dante." Osiris's tone cautioned Dante to temper his emotions.

Unlike Poseidon, Osiris expected his son to react this way. Many of the Council lacked the ability to comprehend how deep the love for Tarquin and Grace ran in their new peer. "Defending Tarquin is a forgivable offense. Revealing yourself to Grace, however, violates the contract you freely negotiated with all of us eleven years ago."

"What did you expect me to do, Father? Not return Tarquin and kidnap his sister to ensure they are out of whatever demon instigates all of this's reach? Neither Grace nor Rayne would stand for that. War would track his children right to my door. That is a much worse scenario for the Council and myself than a quick conversation with my former wife."

"Again, you should have remained neutral in the events of the day and allowed the Commander to address them," Poseidon interjected, displeased by Dante's insolent remarks.

"The attack on my son and his stepfather was well-calculated and directed by one in the immortal community. No one, human or immortal, is foolish enough to accidentally attack War and his loved ones. This assault stems from a personal vendetta. Until I know if Rayne is truly the end target or I am, since Tarquin was their mark, I will do whatever I deem necessary to protect my son and myself. Does the law not allow one leeway to defend themselves from harm?" Dante flipped the ancient codes to his favor by shifting the facts to paint him as the potential one being drawn out by an unknown enemy.

Poseidon scoffed. "Your claim of being the target is unfounded."

"Share the evidence you hold that deems me a liar, Poseidon."

When Poseidon remained silent, Dante laughed. "Relay to the Council, until my concerns about my person and my son are belayed, I will take any action I deem necessary to ensure my son remains safe. Furthermore, my oath requires me to protect Tessa Warwick should my assumption be wrong, and it indeed be her father that whatever imprudent creature instigates everything is after. Commander Warwick and the Council appointed me as the girl's primary guardian should anything ever happen to him and Grace."

Osiris bowed his head to hide the grin emerging on his face. Dante remained the reckless, headstrong commander he had always been.

Time as a god under the Council's mentorship couldn't change that part of his son. "You inherited your mother's stubborn nature."

"And my father's steadfast dedication to those he loves when he chooses to display it." Dante once more made the Head of the Council grin.

Osiris knew no matter what he or Poseidon declared, Dante would defy any order to remain neutral in things. "Since there is a remote possibility that one of our own or his heirs are endangered, we will grant a reprieve on any charges stemming from your actions today. We will also allow the two children to remain under your care. However, as much as it pains me to say this, there is to be no more contact with Grace Warwick. Any matters concerning the welfare of the children will be handled through their father or official channels to ensure you do not commit a second infraction of violating the agreement you brokered to ensure the continuation of your legacy."

"Thank you, Father."

Osiris politely nodded. "As there is no need for formal reprimands, let us leave the sun god to his duties."

Poseidon shook his head. Osiris would catch hell for his leniency at the next Council meeting. The Greek sea god vanished from the office.

Osiris gently grasped Dante by the upper arms, proud of his son's actions, even though he could not say so. "I cannot stretch the laws any further as Council Head, Dante. Please do not put me in the position of having to choose between my own son and the responsibilities placed upon me."

"I will do my best to prevent that from occurring." Dante wasn't sure he could keep his word with turmoil shifting fate once more, but he wanted his father to know he understood the risk Osiris took by not punishing his actions. "I am grateful for the quarter granted me today."

"Would you like us to dispatch a harbinger to assist in guarding the children?"

"No. I do not want to shock or frighten them with the presence of a harbinger in my home. They have been through enough today. Not to mention upsetting the children would earn the ire of their mother. She'd come running to their rescue. We do not need to give Grace reason to seek me out, since contact between us is forbidden."

CHAPTER
SIX

Córdoba - Modern Day

Grace and Rayne entered Córdoba as the sun set. Bypassing the residence maintained for High Council officers, they rode to a country home outside the city limits.

While the house wasn't massive, it was decent sized with a large yard judging by the expanse of wall in front of them. The stone wall, tile roof, and the little of the house Grace could see over the wall looked medieval. The curved brown wooden doors of the closed gate reminded her of a castle entrance. She didn't doubt the property served as a fortified structure for a wealthy resident or aristocrat. "This place looks like a historical site, not a home someone lives in."

"The wall and house were built in the Middle Ages, and it's definitely a private home not open to the public. Wait here while I see if the gateman is still awake," Rayne said, dismounting. He knocked on a door in the wall beside the gates.

A few seconds later, a man opened it. He embraced Rayne and loudly greeted him in Spanish. Rayne smiled and briefly spoke with him. The man nodded then opened the gate for them to enter. Another man came into the courtyard and took their horses. Grace watched him lead them off to a stable at the far end of the walled in property.

"Grace, this is Joaquin, the property manager. He runs the estate for the owner when he isn't here."

"It is a pleasure to meet you, Señora Warwick. If you need anything during your stay, please let me know." Joaquin smiled before saying something in Spanish to another gentleman who ran and unlocked the front door of the house. "If I had known you were coming, Rayne, I would have had the house readied for you."

"I apologize for the lack of notice. Unplanned business arose bringing us to Córdoba. Hopefully, our visit will be a short one." Rayne shifted to another language Grace didn't recognize when the man who opened the house for them returned.

Grace listened to Joaquin, Rayne, and the other man converse. She thought it odd they periodically seemed to address Rayne as excellency, emir, and mushir. A strange mix of titles. Knowing at times they all adopted different personas to hide who they were, she didn't inquire about them. Perhaps Rayne had done the same on prior trips to Córdoba. While he didn't seem to like visiting the city, she knew he had to periodically come here to meet with Hayden on behalf of Isis and before her, Morrigan.

After a late dinner, Grace sat across from Rayne in the living room. The Horseman stared absent-mindedly at the fireplace, sipping sherry from a crystal glass in his hand. He heard her muffled huff as she set down the book she held. "Say whatever is on your mind, leof."

"What are we doing here?" Grace wanted to get their investigation started and have her kids home again.

"Culturally, it would not be acceptable to pay a visit to those we need to at this hour."

"Since when do we worry about cultural norms while at war?"

"We are not at war, Grace."

"You don't know that we aren't. You may be just as wrong about that as you were in stating Dr. Smith's warning wasn't to be heeded, or all the events in Rome weren't linked to you. Not even a full month later, someone takes a shot at you, and at our son."

The tensing of his jaw and the slight lifting of a dark brow confirmed her remark struck a nerve, but he remained quiet. His taking another swig of the sherry brought Grace's temper to its boiling point.

"How can you sit there drinking whatever that is after being attacked?" She started walking the length of the room to calm her nerves. "Do you care at all that our children are in danger if they are what this Umar and Garsea want?"

Rayne swallowed the mouthful of liquor. "Our children are perfectly safe. You know they are."

"No, I don't. Osiris will have access to them, not to mention a million other deities, and what does Dante know about raising two young kids."

"Leof." Rayne caught her hand and pulled her onto his lap. "Our children are fine. Dante has been watching over Tarquin since he was conceived."

Annoyed that Rayne patronized her, Grace snorted. "From afar until the past few years."

"No, not just from afar." Rayne brushed her hair from her face. "Long before you were aware Dante was visiting Tarquin, he found ways to see his son. Dante held Tarquin the day he was born after you fell asleep, and has been near the boy as he's grown. He also pays regular attention to Tessa, so there is no animosity between her and her brother."

"The Council forbid Dante to come near us until Tarquin was three."

"When has a Council ruling ever stopped Dante from doing something important to him?" Rayne massaged her back.

"How did you learn he was sneaking into our home to see Tarquin?"

"I suspected it has been happening since the day after Tarquin was born. Dante never freely showed himself for a year. I assumed Osiris sanctioned Dante seeing Tarquin the night he was born for him to appear before Destahn and me. Certainly, Osiris couldn't in good conscience allow his grandson not to meet his father at least once in his lifetime. The next time Dante gave away his presence was on Tarquin's first birthday."

"The giraffe." It dawned on Grace where the little toy had come from that she hadn't seen before that morning.

Rayne smiled. "A present from Dante."

He entwined his fingers with hers, taking them back to that morning, so she could see everything for herself.

Rayne had awakened before sunrise. He heard Tarquin contently jabbering to himself from across the hall. It was hard to believe the boy turned a year old that afternoon. Grace was still sound asleep. He lightly kissed her cheek then climbed out of bed. If he wanted to be home in time for Tarquin's party that evening, he needed to get an early start to the day. Before dressing, he went to check on the toddler.

Sitting in the middle of his crib, Tarquin chewed on a teething ring. The boy's incoming molars must have awakened him. Thankfully, he hadn't noticed Rayne. Rayne took a step back. The floorboard made a loud creak, alerting Tarquin of his presence. Searching for whomever made the sound, Tarquin crawled to the edge of the crib and pulled himself up to a standing position. Hearing the routine morning bouncing begin in perfect rhythm with a chanted dada, dada, dada, Rayne chuckled. The boy knew who was nearby.

"Good morning, Tarquin."

Worried Tarquin would start screaming if he wasn't picked up quick enough, Rayne stepped into the nursery. Little hands were in the air before the Horseman stood alongside the crib. Tarquin's bouncing turned into a happy, unbalanced little dance. The toddler tilted sideways. Rayne caught him before he fell over completely.

"Let's get you changed and dressed. No shrieking when I put you down today. I think you woke everyone within a hundred-mile radius yesterday with that nonsense."

Tarquin laughed and blew raspberries as Rayne laid him on the changing table.

"I can assure you that you are the only one who enjoyed the banshee imitation."

Finished dressing Tarquin, he picked him up and started to leave the room. Tarquin whined and squirmed, reaching towards the crib. Rayne stopped to see what the boy wanted.

"Mama?" He looked up at Rayne, stopping his wriggling.

"She's still sleeping."

Tarquin reached for the crib again. This time more loudly vocalizing his displeasure at leaving behind whatever he wanted.

Rayne almost dropped him with the way Tarquin forcefully leaned forward. The Horseman picked up the teething ring Tarquin had been chewing on earlier and handed it to him. Tarquin angrily squealed and threw the ring. Trying again, Rayne reached for the little stuffed dragon the boy kept at his side. It went sailing through the air, too.

"He's looking for this."

A hand extended from behind Rayne with a small giraffe. Tarquin immediately hugged the toy to him and cooed. Rayne turned, coming face to face with Dante.

"I wanted to wish him a happy birthday. Last time I was here, he asked for a giraffe. He had seen one in a book Grace read to him. You are doing an amazing job raising him and taking care of Grace."

"Thank you, Dante. You are welcome to visit anytime you wish. If Grace asks about the toy, I will tell her I found it in the crib. I will give you some time alone with your son." Rayne handed Tarquin to his father.

Dante took Tarquin in his arms. He wished it was something he could do every day as Rayne and Grace did. "Grazie, il mio amico. I will keep him entertained until you return. I can't promise no screaming. He truly enjoys that ear-piercing shriek. Must be something he inherited from his mother."

Rayne grinned. "His father could bellow orders just as loud. No doubt he gets his lungs from the both of you."

Grace stretched and looked around the bed for Tarquin with Rayne readying for the day. Normally, he would have put the boy beside her.

"Rayne, where is Tarquin?" Grace asked, prior to kissing her husband good morning.

"I left him in his crib. He laid back down with one of his stuffed animals after I changed him. He seemed content. I planned to let you sleep."

"I am going to go check on him."

Rayne sent himself to the nursery to warn Dante, but the god had already left. Tarquin had fallen back to sleep with his new giraffe stuffed under his arm. Hearing Grace in the hall, Rayne returned to the master bedroom to finish dressing.

Grace admired her son sleeping in the early morning light. He reminded her so much of Dante. She briefly wondered about the giraffe clutched in his little fist, but dismissed her thoughts with as many stuffed animals that people had given the boy.

"Everything okay?" Rayne inquired from the doorway, pulling on his shirt and startling Grace.

"Fine. He is sound asleep."

Grace brought them out of the memory and frowned. "Osiris gave Tarquin the sun mark that same morning."

"We've been over this a thousand times, Grace Warwick. The mark is harmless. It merely identifies the boy as Dante's heir."

Rayne wished she would let go of this new hatred of Osiris, which had developed since Dante died. Grace banished the Egyptian deity from their home after discovering the small sun on the back of Tarquin's shoulder. The only time Osiris could enter the Warwick residence was for official business on behalf of the High Council. She further restricted the god to only having contact with Rayne. Surprisingly, Osiris honored her wishes.

"That has yet to be seen." Grace started to leave his lap.

Rayne's arm constricted around her, preventing her from rising. "I love you and our children. I swear to you, no harm will befall Tessa or Tarquin as long as I live. Please cease dwelling on imagined threats. We have a real one to deal with at sunrise." He noted the cynical look she gave him. "I need my wife focused on resolving whatever caused those men to appear today if I am to ensure my family's safety. Do you no longer have faith in me, leof?"

Grace smiled as he hoped she would. "I have full faith and confidence in you. I will do my best to do as you ask."

"Good." Rayne returned her smile, then kissed her.

Grace woke in the middle of the night. Rayne no longer slept beside her. He stood at the large window overlooking the property.

"What troubles you, wolf?" Grace knew well the signs of the predator that lay deep within her husband anytime it was roused.

"I am anxious to learn more about the men who attacked us. They rode a great distance to do so." Rayne continued to watch the activity in the courtyard below. Men loyal to him alone guarded the gates. Grace's arms hugged his chest then she kissed the back of his shoulder.

The howl of a wolf shattered the silent night. She realized why the sound was so loud: the wolf roamed within the walls of the compound. The large black and grey animal crossed the yard. It stared up at her with silver eyes. Could it see her two stories up?

The wolf howled again, making Grace jump.

Rayne smiled. "Demons can't make you flinch, but a lone wild animal frightens you?"

"I know what to expect from a demon. You aren't concerned about the pet whoever owns this place keeps? He is huge."

The animal glanced towards the gate and then lay down before the door of the house.

"Kato is not a pet. He comes and goes as he pleases. And no, I am not concerned. I would never allow a dangerous animal to remain on my property."

"Your property?" Surely she misheard him. He had never mentioned owning land in Córdoba.

"We will discuss this more tomorrow. For now, all you need to know is Kato is harmless. This home is one of the three properties I owned prior to marrying you."

Grace eyed the man she spent the last ten years with. "You swore no more secrets, Rayne."

"And I have kept that promise. I have never denied you any answer you have sought since the day I made it."

"No, you withhold information instead." Grace let go of her

husband and returned to bed. She heard the aggravated sigh from Rayne before he joined her.

He pulled her against him then laid his head on his pillow. "I love you, Grace. Do not go to sleep angry with me."

"I am not angry. Just annoyed. And I love you too. Even with you not trusting me with whatever secrets you have."

"It is not a matter of trust, leof. I am so rarely here. I never thought to mention the house to you. Forgive me for my oversight."

His not disclosing the property in Córdoba worried her, but she gave the man the benefit of the doubt. "You're forgiven. For the moment anyway."

Rayne always kept their family's best interest at heart. Whatever reason he didn't share that he once lived in Córdoba couldn't be anything too terrible. For a brief second, she thought about the four scars on his back that he never spoke about.

A pack of wolves surrounded Rayne. Snarls and growls erupted around him. The beasts stalked closer.

"I am not the man you are hunting."

No matter what he said, the circle of space between him and the animals dissolved bit by bit. He more firmly repeated his words. The wolf directly in front of him leapt simultaneously with the one behind him.

Rayne swung at the first one, deflecting its bite. The teeth of the one attacking from behind tore into his shoulder. He managed to free himself from the wolf then turned, keeping a wary eye on the pack surrounding him.

"I am not who you think I am!" Rayne took an aggressive step toward the wolf that attacked him.

The alpha cowered at the way the Horseman shouted.

"They are no fools. They know exactly who you are, even after all of this time."

Rayne recognized the shadow addressing him. "Isra?"

The laugh he heard chilled the blood in his veins. He shivered in response to it. The only being who could scare the Horsemen Commander walked toward him. Her hand extended and turned upward, reaching for his.

"Welcome home, *my* wayward general."

Rayne started awake. Sunlight illuminated the formerly dark bedroom. Grace slept soundly beside him.

It was a dream, he told himself. It was only a dream.

Rayne wrapped his arms around Grace to better anchor himself in reality. The steady rise and fall of her chest as she slept eased the tempo of his own breathing. He inhaled the light scent of oranges and jasmine her soap always left behind on her skin. The past was dead. Nothing could take away the life he found in the present. He drew Grace tighter against him. The softness of her body alongside his quieted the melee raging within his mind.

The sensation of being gently pulled sideways along with the stubble of a few-days-old beard brushing across her shoulder and neck woke Grace. The way Rayne tightly held her conveyed something bothered her husband. "Are you okay, handsome?"

"I am counting my blessings, leof. The Fates are good to me." Rayne kissed her cheek.

Grace rolled over to face him. "They are good to us both."

Rayne smiled, enjoying how Grace admired him with such pride and love in her eyes. "How would you like to see the Mezquita today?"

"I would like that a great deal. Are you going to give me a personalized tour?"

"If you would like me to. Something tells me it is where we should begin our inquiries about the visitors who interrupted our ride."

Grace walked outside, sidestepping the sleeping wolf who hadn't left the doorstep.

The animal's ears perked up. He lazily watched her from where he lay.

Grace slowly inched forward, extending her hand. Did one

approach a wolf like they did a dog? She almost laughed after the wolf tilted his head as if mocking her actions.

"Kato is it? Rayne assures me you are friendly."

The wolf laid his head on his paws.

She gently rubbed behind his ears, then sat down beside him after he inched closer to her. The wolf licked her face before laying his head in her lap. "You are a big baby. To think I was afraid of you last night."

Rayne stepped through the open doorway. "Only with those he likes. Otherwise, he would tear your arm off."

"Maybe I shouldn't sit so close."

Rayne laughed, closing the door. "You have nothing to fear. Something tells me you are a welcome new member of his pack."

He fed the wolf their breakfast scraps then helped Grace to her feet.

The wolf stepped in front of them, uttering a sound that was a cross between a bark and a growl.

"We will be careful, old friend." Rayne scratched the wolf's head.

"You have quite the rapport with Kato."

"I found him and his brother half dead in Granada. I nursed them back to health. Sulla will show himself before too long. He never wanders far from Kato."

"How long did you live in Spain to acquire an estate like this?"

Rayne looked over at the gates then back at Kato. The wolf turned his head sideways again almost as if waiting to hear Rayne's answer.

"For longer than I care to admit. We need to get going, leof. Destahn is already at the consulate waiting for us."

CHAPTER
SEVEN

Córdoba - Modern Day

Rayne and Grace met Destahn at the High Council consulate. Hayden joined them in the main conference room. "Welcome back to Córdoba, Rayne. For the three of you to arrive together, I assume this isn't a personal visit to the area."

"I am afraid not, Hayden. A group of djinn servants from Córdoba attacked us yesterday." Rayne shared the events of the day prior.

"Djinn servants?" Hayden hadn't expected to hear that. "We do periodically see crimes committed by the local djinn groups, but they haven't attacked anyone recently, as far as I am aware. Any idea who they worked for?"

Rayne shook his head. "Their emblems bore Garsea's seal."

"Garsea is dead. They couldn't be his men." Hayden sat on the edge of the table. Rayne must have misidentified the seal.

Grace wondered if this Garsea had simply gone underground. It wouldn't be the first time a djinn had then resurfaced. "Are you certain Garsea is dead?"

"More than certain," Hayden answered Grace. He noticed the wrinkles in Rayne's forehead and the grim expression on the Horseman's

84

face when he looked over at him. He hoped the Commander might suggest another possible suspect. Instead, Rayne remained silent, his arms folded over his chest, clearly pondering the possibility that Garsea returned from the dead. "Rayne, you can't honestly believe Garsea is back. You killed him."

"I thought I had. But these men definitely bore Garsea's seal. The observer with them did as well. Before the observer died, I asked him why he attacked my family. He told me, Gaudalcete."

Hayden let out a loud breath. "Gaudalcete? The gods help us if Garsea is back."

"It gets worse." Rayne paused, giving Hayden a second to wrap his head around everything. "The uniform the men wore wasn't Garsea's. It was Umar's."

"Umar? As in Umar al-Majid, the ninth-century Cordovan general?" Hayden didn't think Rayne could say anything more shocking than Garsea returning from the dead.

"The same."

"Wait, the men worked for a long dead human general and an executed djinn?" Grace wanted to make sure she followed the conversation.

Rayne looked over at her. "Yes."

As confused as Grace, Destahn crossed his arms in front of him. "That doesn't make any sense. How could humans from the ninth century make their way to the sixteenth, especially if their bosses are deceased?"

"The attack happened in the sixteenth century?" Hayden looked at Rayne for confirmation.

Rayne nodded. "On my land in the Ebro valley. That also suggests Garsea is alive. They wouldn't have been able to time travel otherwise."

"I still find that hard to believe. With the men wearing Umar's uniform, but carrying Garsea's seal, someone is sending a personalized message to you. My money is on Isra being behind everything."

"Isra wouldn't be that stupid," Rayne disagreed with Hayden.

Grace wanted to know more about the entity being discussed. "This is the second time I've heard that name. Who is Isra?"

"She's Lucifer's regional overseer for the Iberian Peninsula. The past few centuries, she and Lucifer have kept a low profile. They normally stick to underground organized crime schemes or black-market sales." Hayden shared what he knew of her. "Rumor has it she is in a turf war with Rodrigo once more, but their fights have remained off the radar with only immortal casualties. As long as they aren't threatening humans, we leave them to their own devices."

"Dirty soul traffickers." Grace knew exactly what Hayden meant by black market sales. "Why would she send someone after Rayne?"

Destahn could see Isra wanting revenge against a Horseman for killing a hired hand. "He did execute Garsea."

Hayden stared at Rayne. "Isra goes through underlings like a snake sheds skin. For her to be brazen enough to put a hit out on a Horseman, War no less, there's something big at play. Any of your assignments put you crossways with a deity or human recently?"

Rayne understood Hayden's line of thought, but the guide was off the mark. "No. In fact, things have been relatively quiet the past few months. The High Council hasn't formally dispatched the Horsemen at all."

"We were caught in the middle of a demon hit at Saint Peter's." Grace wished she would have pushed Rayne harder to investigate Smith's warning.

Rayne scowled at her. "That has nothing to do with yesterday."

"The hell it doesn't. Dr. Smith said they were after the wolf, after you. You blew off the warning." Grace's voice raised as she glared back at him. "This Garsea and Lucifer more than likely hoped to kill Smith to prevent him from telling us whatever scheme they are undertaking. But things went awry with the hit as neither anticipated Smith getting to us first or us being in Rome the same day the hit went down."

"Maybe Grace is right, Rayne." Destahn hated to go against his commander, but Grace had a point. "It's worth looking into. Hayden, who is your local contact embedded in the Church?"

"Father Hernando. If Lucifer or the Vatican are involved, he would know. If he confirms Grace is right, that leaves Isra for us to investigate."

Rayne's frown deepened. The chance of Smith being an associate of Lucifer or Isra's was virtually nonexistent. Neither had use for a man like Smith. Rayne supposed no harm could come from speaking to

Father Hernando. "I planned to visit the Mezquita today anyway. Let's go talk to the priest."

"I'll do some digging to find out what I can on Garsea while you guys are at the church." Hayden's easy day evaporated into one filled with intelligence gathering.

Rayne was quiet most of the ride to the cathedral.

Destahn wondered about his commander's silence. Under normal circumstances, he wouldn't have thought anything of it with Rayne's reserved nature and hyperfocus when working. Today, however, his silence seemed weighted, almost deafening. Yesterday's attack definitely bothered one of the most resolute beings in the immortal realm.

The three walked into the famous converted mosque together. Destahn went to look for the priest Rayne directed him to find.

Grace admired the shifting architecture of each section of the building. Walking from the entrance to the main cathedral through the various additions to the Cathedral-Mosque allowed one to almost time travel through the site's history. She stopped in the Mihrab, a small room on the front of the Mezquita, and stared up at the gold dome decorated with blue, green, and white floral patterns. A blue star formed the center of the ornate mosaicked ceiling. "This place is incredible."

"Yes. It is." Rayne thought the same, staring up at the center star. A heavy feeling of unwelcome nostalgia swept through him. "Are you ready to move on?"

"Sure." Grace cast one last glance at the dome before following Rayne out of the chamber.

Reaching the main cathedral, Rayne and Grace split up. Rayne walked to the center of the chapel as Grace explored the sides of it then made her way through the choir. An odd symbol in one of the carved choir chairs caught her eye. She slipped the codex from her pocket and pulled out the piece of vellum it held. The carving matched one of the images in the codex. What did wood carvings in the Mezquita have to do with Urban's journal?

"Grace." Destahn calling her name drew her out of her musings.

She slid the vellum back into the gold codex before walking towards Destahn and the priest with him.

"Grace, Father Hernando. Father Hernando, this is Rayne Warwick's wife, Grace," Destahn introduced the two of them.

"Nice to meet you. Father, have you ever seen a medallion like this?" Grace held the codex out to the priest.

Destahn shot Grace a puzzled glance before looking at the gold piece the priest held.

"No. I have not. It is beautiful." The priest offered it back to her. "Why do you ask?"

"Curiosity. I am trying to discover the origins of the piece." Grace tucked it into her pocket.

"The markings on it are similar to a language used by the Imazighen who once lived in the area. You may want to speak with some of the community elders. Perhaps they can point you in the right direction."

"Or ask your husband, who reads and speaks several of the Berber dialects." Destahn wondered if Rayne had seen the latest trinket Grace acquired. "Speaking of Rayne, where is he?"

"He's at the front of the chapel waiting for you two." Grace pointed to her right.

Rayne stopped before the high altar, almost transfixed by the ornate decorations and paintings. He looked up at the golden flowers in the main dome that added a burst of color against the cream hues of the ceiling. A frown darkened the expression on his face. He found it difficult to breathe in the sacred space. The enormous walls seemed to collapse inwards on him. Needing fresh air, he pivoted away from the altar.

Seeing Rayne walking towards the nearest exit, Grace grew concerned. "Rayne."

He acted as if he couldn't hear her.

"Something's wrong. Check out the others in the chapel while I see what is going on with Rayne," Grace whispered to Destahn.

The Horseman nodded, then asked the priest for a tour, giving Grace a few minutes to find out what bothered Rayne.

Grace ran to catch up with her husband. "Sweetheart."

Nearing the door, his pace quickened.

Exasperated that Rayne didn't answer her, she resorted to his rank. "Commander!"

"I just need air, Grace. Give me a few minutes." Rayne never looked back at her as he forced open one of the large doors.

Grace followed him outside to the walled in courtyard.

Rayne fell to his knees. One of his arms curled against his stomach. His other hand rested on the grass as if he needed to support himself from a sudden weakness.

Grace slowly approached him. "What is wrong, Rayne?"

"There is blood on my hands. So much blood with coming back here." Rayne stared up at her. Torment contorted his face.

She set a comforting hand on his shoulder. Was he suddenly delusional? "There is blood on all our hands with what we have to do, Rayne. It's the nature of our roles."

"You do not understand, Grace. There were days I slaughtered in the name of vengeance. My enemies could not even find refuge from me in this hallowed space. I lost my way once. My sins haunt me as they never have before with returning here." Rayne confessed a part of him he had not shared with anyone in the immortal officers corps.

The only one who knew the atrocities he committed was Raphael. The first time he and Raphael met was in the Holy Land after the massacre in Jerusalem. When he clasped Raphael's hand, agreeing to ride for Morrigan, the Commander had told him, "The past dies today. You are reborn only Rayne from this moment forth."

How wrong Raphael was! Rayne suspected Dante knew his dark past, but Dante never asked him about it nor judged him based on it.

"I find any of what you said hard to believe. You have never maimed or killed without valid cause." Grace wished she knew how to help the man who assisted her whenever needed. While Rayne was a man of war, he was neither merciless nor vengeful in any quest the Horsemen undertook.

Rayne grasped her arm. "Allow me to make a believer out of you."

Córdoba - 812

A second later, the two of them stood in the heart of Córdoba. Only now, the city looked drastically different. The modern structures disappeared from the skyline along with the cars, vespas, and motorcycles. The paved roads transformed into dirt and stone. Medieval style buildings surrounded them.

Had they jumped centuries? Grace tried to get her bearings, but Rayne's light tug on her arm and him striding forward prevented her from doing so. He led her through the streets to a large home built into one of the hillsides, forced open the door, and waited for her to go in. Looking through the open portal, Grace observed men sitting on one side of the room while a small group of women sat in a partitioned off corner. A mix of Spanish and Arabic was being spoken in whatever this place was. Where had Rayne brought her?

"Ask those inside about me."

"Rayne, why are you—"

"You should know the truth." Rayne shoved her inside. "Now, ask them."

Grace shot him an angry stare.

"Do as asked, woman." Rayne almost growled at her defiance. The door slammed shut behind him.

"I need to speak with anyone here who knows Rayne Dalglese."

The majority of the people in the room ignored her. A few by the door heard her request and eyed her suspiciously, but continued on with whatever they were doing.

"No one has ever lived in the city with that name. I knew a man once called Rayne, but his surname is not Dalglese, nor does he live any longer," One of the older men at a table to her left said.

"What happened to him?" Grace couldn't stop the question from coming out of her mouth.

The man laughed, then took a drink from his cup before sneering at her. "He was executed for offending the Emir."

Rayne stepped forward. "Who claims to have executed him?"

The man knocked his chair over trying to scamper away and then mumbled a name Grace didn't catch. He looked as if he had seen a demon. Grace couldn't believe the way he slinked along the wall until he reached the door then ran out.

"The woman inquires of Haroun Ibn-Ziyad. Can no one tell her anything of him?" Rayne shouted after a table of men cast annoyed glances Grace's way when she asked again about Rayne Dalglese.

The chatter in the room fell silent. Several men's hands went to their swords. All eyes now rested on Grace.

One of the Spaniards stood. "If you value your life, never speak that name here again."

The man's remark startled Grace. Most tales she had heard of Haroun painted him as a hero, but these people acted like he was a monster. "Why does the name Haroun Ibn-Ziyad frighten a mercenary?"

The Spaniard laughed. "The master of this house frightens me more than the man you speak of. He does not allow anyone to even whisper that name."

"Who is the master of this house, and why does he forbid anyone to speak Haroun's name?" Grace approached the man who spoke. He didn't say anything more. Aware the men in the room considered her to be beneath them, she shoved the man down on a nearby table. "Answer me."

The man kept his eyes on Rayne.

Rayne nodded, prompting him to respond to the question.

"You are in the home of Saladin. He does not allow anyone to blasphemy his name, nor that of the traitorous dog you inquire about."

Grace glanced back at Rayne. She had suspected ties between the legend of Haroun Ibn- Ziyad and him, but he had so adamantly denied them. "Who was Haroun that the mere mention of his name makes this room go silent?"

"The worst devil you can imagine." The intensity the man spoke with caused Grace to release him. "Only an insane person courts a djinn. Turn back from whatever fool's errand you are on, woman."

"I don't believe in mythical, imaginary creatures." Grace almost smiled at how convincingly she said those words.

A second man now spoke up. "As you were already told, the one you ask about died several years ago."

"I seek his resting place. I have coin that will make speaking worth your while."

A soldier with gray streaking his dark hair drew near her from across the room. "Keep your coin. You will not find the tomb of the man you seek. It does not exist. We destroyed it to prevent him from returning. Haroun fell from grace, becoming the fiend this man described. The number of bodies he left in pieces, allowing Umar to track and execute him, is more than a woman's delicate sensibilities could handle. Be thankful he is dead. The djinn general would not show a woman pursuing him any mercy if he deemed her a threat. You would find yourself deceased, or worse, if you encountered the one you inquire about."

Grace doubted Rayne's past was as terrible as the man made out. Neither her husband nor Haroun were ever a djinn. "I needn't fear anything from a man you say is no longer living. Instead of scaring me with old wives' tales, tell me, what personal wrong has Haroun committed against you? Or anyone else in this room? I suspect you are spreading vicious untruths about a soldier you fear more than him being any sort of demon."

"Do you think I gave myself these?" The man yanked the front of his tunic open, revealing multiple jagged scars on his chest. "I was fortunate to survive his rampage. My wife and son were not."

What the man shared stunned Grace. "He killed your wife and son? How old was your boy?"

"Seventeen. Haroun cut down my wife when she threw herself between my son and his blade."

Grace couldn't believe Rayne would murder a woman in cold blood. "Is it possible he killed her by accident?"

"I do not believe so. He ran her through with the long scimitar he carried. In one swift movement, my wife and son perished. The monster did not even blink as he moved on to the next man in his path. He left a trail of blood through Córdoba when the Amazigh rebelled against their rightful leaders."

"Rayne was here during the uprisings? Why would England be involved in that skirmish?"

The man sinisterly laughed. "The Saxons and Anglos have no interest in the fight. The man your friend named never rode under a Saxon or Anglo banner. He fought under his own."

"He fought against the Caliphate with the Amazigh?" That confused Grace. The Amazigh fought for freedom from the oppression they felt under Umayyad rule. What was Rayne doing traveling within the region at the time?

"You are either daft or not listening, woman. He betrayed his own people. Abdul offered him wealth and status for handing over the heads of the Berber usurpers. A dog that turns against the hand that feeds him needs to be put down. Umar saved us all from Haroun the night..."

"Anyone who speaks further blasphemies against my son will have their tongue removed so that they cannot spread anymore lies!" A heavily armed man dressed in black shouted from the back of the room. "This is my house! No member of my family shall be disparaged in it. Umar spread lies about the Ibn-Ziyad men to gain power and favor. Never are they to be repeated in my presence! Who started this idle prattle?"

The former soldier shoved Grace forward. "She made the inquiry."

"Careful in how you handle the woman. She travels with one who can ensure you join your family if you put your hands on her again."

The owner of the house's brow raised at the threat uttered from the shadows. "No blood is to be shed in my home. I caution whomever speaks not to make the mistake of crossing me."

Satisfied his warning was heeded after no additional response came from the front of the house, he decided to deal with the woman. The man made his way to Grace.

Grace heard mumbled titles of respect from those he passed. Rayne was the son of an Arab or Berber general? How was that possible when he was an English earl?

The man stopped directly before her. One could not miss the similarities between him and Rayne: their dark hair, their height, their almost identical facial structure and build; beyond a doubt, father and son. The only difference she could see was their eye color and Saladin's slightly darker skin tone. While Rayne's eyes were a vivid ocean blue, this man's were a warm, deep brown.

"Woman, is there a reason you choose to defame my son by starting such vile gossip in my home?"

The stern tone he used reminded Grace of Rayne's whenever he reprimanded Tessa and Tarquin. She took a step closer to him to ensure her eyes weren't playing tricks on her.

His lips twitched into a grin at the way the woman seemed astounded by him. Her bizarre reaction suggested she meant no harm to him or anyone else in the house. He banished the mirth from his face and gave her the most authoritative expression he could muster before speaking in English. "I still await an answer, woman. Do not make me ask again."

Grace snapped out of the daze she found herself in with his changing languages. "On the contrary, I seek to prove your son is not the monster he and these men believe him to be. I simply asked what wrong he committed against that man as far too often misperception and gossip ruins a good man's name."

"How is it you know what my son thinks of himself? The dead do not share their thoughts with the living, especially those who do not believe in the mystical forces around us."

Wanting to throw the man off kilter, Grace switched to Arabic. "I said I do not believe in djinn. I never said our ancestors and the dead do not speak to us."

"A Celtic woman who speaks the chosen language? Whose harem did you escape from?"

"I am my own master. Where I am from, we can learn many languages. Arabic is one of three that I use."

By the way he stared and stroked his beard, the man debated his response. His eyes narrowed after darting to her wrist.

He recognized the distinctive gold cuff that adorned it. Casting a quick glance toward the door, he let out a deep breath then dropped his arm back to his side. "A woman belongs to either her father, brother, or husband if she is not a servant. Since you have no master, you will join my household. Once you have proven yourself trustworthy, I will grant you your freedom back and find a suitable match for you. I have several men in need of wives."

"The woman is married and belongs to another whose wrath you do not want to incur for conscripting her." Rayne emerged from the shadows to stand beside Grace.

A murmur traveled through the room. The man who spoke ill of Rayne paled and crossed himself.

Grace coughed to disguise the laugh that escaped her lips.

Saladin's stern countenance morphed into an amused one. A pleased smile replaced the tight straight line his lips rested in. "Welcome home, Haroun. I suspected the woman was yours with the bracelet she wears and her claiming to want to change whatever opinion you hold of yourself."

Rayne's appearance had not surprised Saladin, but learning Grace was Rayne's wife certainly did. "Her hair should be covered if she is married. Why is she dressed like a man?"

Rayne shrugged. "She may dress as she pleases. Her practices are not ours."

"Your mother will be pleased to see you. I will have your quarters prepared for you."

"No need for that. I will not be staying, Father."

"Nonsense! You cannot journey to Córdoba and not accept my hospitality. Contrary to the greeting the woman received, you are welcome here. You also cannot leave without seeing your mother. She will be devastated to learn her son returned after being gone so long and refused to see her."

"Please give her my well wishes and love."

"General Ibn-Ziyad, Señor Dalglese ..." Grace wasn't sure how exactly to address Rayne's father. "We could use your help."

Rayne took Grace by the arm and turned her towards the door. "We need no assistance."

"Rayne, did the Prophet, peace be upon him, not teach one to honor thy mother and father as Christ did? Did he not teach that a son is to be closest to his mother in companionship, regardless of religious or other division between them? You do not honor your current beliefs or your Islamic roots with our departure." Grace placed Rayne in a position where he could no longer leave without disgracing his parents. He shot her a murderous stare.

Saladin laughed at Grace's maneuvering Rayne to stay. "Well spoken. I rather like you already. Haroun has chosen to use his mother's surname if you know him as Rayne Dalglese. I am Saladin Ibn-Ziyad. Welcome to my home, my new daughter."

"Thank you, Saladin. You bear the name of two important men. Are you related to Tariq Ibn-Ziyad?"

Her inquiry grew the smile on his face. "He is my great-grandfather. Tell me, what is your name?"

"Grace."

"Walk with an old man, Grace. I have many questions for you and my son."

Rayne begrudgingly followed them through the house and outside to the rear courtyard and gardens.

"Who is the other man you believe my name is from for you to say two important men?" Saladin asked, curious to learn who else the woman knew named Saladin.

"An Egyptian official who is an acquittance of ours," Rayne interjected, catching Grace's error before she did. *Leof, the Saladin you are thinking of is from the twelfth century. We are in the ninth.*

Grace offered Rayne an appreciative smile before looking at Saladin again. "Yes, he's a very wise and kind man who helped Rayne and I few times in the past."

"You have been living in Egypt?" Saladin shot Rayne an even more confused look. Why would his son seek refuge in a territory loyal to the Abbasid? Especially with Harun al-Rashid knowing Rayne by sight.

A woman ran into the courtyard, distracting the three of them. She stopped a short distance away. By the softening of Rayne's features, Grace guessed the woman must be his mother.

Saladin smiled warmly at his wife. "Come, and welcome your son home."

She sprinted to them, embraced Rayne, and kissed him on either cheek, then took him by the hand. The two sat down together on a fountain's ledge to catch up with one another.

"How long has it been since Rayne returned home?" Grace still couldn't believe Rayne hadn't told her the truth about who he once was.

Thinking of his son's absence, Saladin frowned. "Too long. After Priya's death and the rumor of his execution, I was certain he would never return."

"Priya?" Grace recalled the name from the strange dream she had in the hospital after being infected by one of Gaelin's parasites. Her subconscious hadn't remembered a folktale as she thought it had. Somehow, she had seen an actual memory from Rayne's past.

"Forgive me if I upset you with mentioning his former betrothed."

"You do not upset me. We both have loved ones in the past. I was once married."

"What happened to your husband?" Saladin wondered if Rayne had stolen the woman. He cast his son a disapproving glance.

Noticing the distaste on his father's face, Rayne stopped speaking with his mother. What had he done to earn his father's condemnation?

Aware of what Saladin suspected, Grace offered the man a reassuring smile. "Rayne did not steal me or harm my prior husband, if that is what you fear. After my husband was mortally wounded in battle, he asked Rayne to marry me. He believed your son was an honorable man, and would make an excellent companion for his widowed wife and unborn child."

Saladin's eyes widened in surprise. "My son is a father?"

"Yes. We have a son and daughter. Zairah reminds me a great deal of her father."

Saladin's earlier smile returned. "Allah be praised! My son returns home and brings with him a wife and grandchildren. You selected a beautiful name for your daughter. It was my mother's name."

"Rayne deserves the credit. He suggested her name. Although, we usually address Zairah by her middle name, Tessa. You never believed your son was executed, did you?"

"When a body was never produced nor a head put on display, I knew Umar lied about the beheading. Umar could never trap Haroun in the manner he boasts he did."

Feeling eyes upon him again, Rayne looked over his mother's

shoulder at Grace and his father. Never would he have believed his wife and father would stand together.

His mother wondered what distracted him. She now saw the lady standing next to Saladin, whom she had not noticed in her haste to see if her son truly returned. "The woman with Saladin..."

Rayne grinned. "My wife."

Shock blanketed his mother's face. "Forgive me, Rayne. Seeing you alive, and learning you have a wife, after all these years."

"There is no need to apologize, Mother. I understand the surprise you and everyone else must be feeling."

"We prayed and hoped for your return or proof that you lived." Lillian looked back at Grace again.

"Shall I introduce you to Grace now, or do you wish to speak for a while longer?"

"It would be rude to leave her waiting with your father. He is most likely interrogating her to ensure she is a good match for you."

Rayne chuckled. "I suspect Grace is the one firing off inquiries. She was rather fascinated by him. The scowl he gave her after she asked about me would send well-armed men running. But not my wife, she merely glared back."

"Then you have chosen your spouse well. Any woman who marries a man with the name Ibn-Ziyad must have great fortitude, considering what that name brings."

He stood and offered his hand to his mother then escorted her over to Grace.

The older woman smiled warmly at Grace. "Welcome to our home, daughter." She kissed Grace on either cheek.

"Did Haroun tell you of his children?" Saladin startled his wife with the question before Grace could return the greeting.

"No. Where are they, Haroun?"

The warm welcome they received overwhelmed Rayne. "We did not bring them to Córdoba."

"You still fear Umar will cause you harm." The older woman's bright spirit dampened some.

"Yes. His men recently paid Grace and I an unfriendly visit."

Grace eyed Rayne. How much did he know about the men that he hadn't shared?

Saladin noted the looks the two exchanged. They seemed to communicate without saying a word.

"Forgive me. I am weary from our ride to Córdoba, but I do not believe I caught your name," Grace addressed his mother.

"Lillian, Lillian Dalglese Ibn-Ziyad. We will leave the men to speak. Come. I will show you to your room. It shall be next to mine." She took Grace by the hand.

Rayne wasn't ready to spend time alone with his father. While he missed the man, his father would have a great many questions he was not prepared to answer. He drew Grace to him to prevent his mother from dragging her away. "No. She sleeps in my quarters. I made a promise that she would never sleep alone. You know I am not one to break my word, especially when I give it to a loved one."

Lillian realized how much her son had changed to disregard tradition. She still saw him as her child, but she also saw a man who had experienced a life many hadn't. His eyes were those of a much older individual.

Saladin sensed there was a great deal of meaning to the oath Rayne made to Grace. He understood, for whatever reason, his son fled from him. "Since our son has sworn to sleep beside his wife, Grace will stay with him as he desires. Haroun, perhaps, you should show her where you two will sleep. You know the way to your old quarters. We will speak more tonight."

Rayne appreciated that Saladin recognized his need to escape. "We shall return by the evening meal."

Grace followed Rayne out of the villa. Neither said a word walking through the gardens surrounding the house. Rayne froze when they came upon a secluded courtyard with a large fountain at its center. She recognized the place from her dream.

Recalling the night that sent his life into a never-ending downward spiral until the day he met Raphael, Rayne's eyes closed. Troubled by the sensation of Priya collapsing against him after the assassins struck, he kept his back to Grace. "I should have stayed away from here."

Grace wished there was something she could do to erase the pain he carried. "It wasn't your fault. You didn't know."

"She warned me! I did not listen." Rayne faced his wife.

The remorse in his eyes made Grace reach for him. Rayne held her so tightly Grace wondered if she would be able to breathe. "You loved her a great deal, didn't you?"

"With all my heart, Grace, almost as much as I love you."

"She forgave you, Rayne. You must learn to forgive yourself. Did you not tell me the same after the battle with Gaelin?" Grace stroked his hair, knowing well the cross the man carried. She bore the weight of it for months after Alexandria. The deep loss, the sense of guilt and helplessness at not being able to save the life of someone you love. God, did she know those emotions all too well.

"I love you, Grace," Rayne muttered, thankful she understood the chaos that the place where they stood surfaced within him.

"I love you. Always." Grace wished he had shared the truth of his human past with her long before now. "We should let Destahn know where we are. I can't imagine the tour Father Hernando is giving him will last much longer."

Learning Destahn had distracted the priest by asking for a tour of the church, Rayne laughed. "Destahn knows the history of that building much more than Father Hernando could ever imagine learning in his lifetime."

Córdoba - Modern Day

Destahn looked relieved to see Grace and Rayne coming towards him.

"Sorry to have kept the two of you waiting. I wasn't feeling well and needed some fresh air. Father Hernando, I presume." Rayne smiled and extended a hand to the priest.

The priest returned the smile and shook Rayne's hand. "It's an honor to meet you, Commander Warwick. Destahn and Hayden think very highly of you. I understand you have some concerns about Isra and a shooting at the Vatican."

"Yes, I do."

"Destahn filled me in on the shooting and the attack. As far as the Vatican is concerned, Ibelin already explained that you were caught up in a turf war between Isra and Rodrigo. There is no evidence to suggest anything to the contrary. Isra remains underground and has not ventured outside the immortal realm. I honestly cannot offer any more information about her. However, I think there is something you should see in my office."

The three immortals walked with the priest to a small office off the side of the main chapel. He unlocked his desk drawer and pulled out several papers.

Grace took them and flipped through the pages. "Dr. Smith's articles. Was he telling the truth, after all?"

"No. But he did steal two relics from Isra. We aren't exactly sure what relics he stole, but she is looking for them. I believe you have one of them in your possession. That could explain yesterday." Father Hernando sat down in his chair.

Rayne thought the priest was confused to suggest they had something of Isra's. "We don't have any relics."

Grace groaned and reached into her pocket. "Actually, we do. Dr. Smith dropped this when he was shot, and I kept it." She handed Rayne the gold codex.

"This isn't Isra's." Rayne scowled, looking down at the medallion he held. "It's Lucifer's."

"Lucifer's?" Grace wondered how Dr. Smith had gotten it.

"Technically, it was Michael's, but he lost it to Lucifer after losing a bet." Rayne opened the codex to find the vellum and painted wolf's head. "You've had this since Rome, and didn't tell me?"

"I didn't think you'd care after blowing off everything else. I went back to Rome to try and translate whatever is written on the vellum, but couldn't crack the encoded angel script the author used."

"Angel script?" Rayne unfolded the note.

Grace watched his eyes skim across each sketched out line. His lips pressed together in a grim line. Whatever the note said perturbed her husband.

"We need to return to my father's." Rayne refolded the vellum, put it back into place, and snapped the codex shut.

"How can you read that when Raphael couldn't?"

"I'll explain later." Rayne grabbed Grace's hand. "Destahn, report to Dante and Raphael it appears Umar and Garsea are working together. Grace and I will learn what we can. Raphael will know where to find me. Father Hernando, thank you for your expertise and time today."

Father Hernando nodded and made the sign of the cross over Rayne. "May God keep you safe on your journey, Richard. Ibelin stands by if you need him."

<hr>

Córdoba - 812

"What in the hell is going on?" Grace demanded, finding herself back in Saladin's courtyard.

"Keep your voice down." Rayne glanced around to ensure they were alone. "You were right about Dr. Smith, Grace. He was trying to warn us about some plot involving Umar and Isra. I am sorry for not taking his words more seriously."

"Apology accepted. Now, I want you to explain how you could read that note."

Rayne shook his head. He'd never hear the end of it once he told her the truth. "The alphabet only mimics angel script. Someone inside the Order of Constantinople was trying to get a message to us. The note advised of trouble here involving Umar acting irrationally. I wish you had shown me the codex sooner."

"Oh, so some medallion dropped by the crazy professor convinces you he is telling the truth, but not your wife being concerned. It seems to me like karma is testing you with listening to the women in your life. And now the fictitious order is real. You still haven't explained how you knew the language the note was written in." Grace glared at her husband.

"I never said the Order of Constantinople didn't exist. I said the wolf sketch and order references would never tie back to me. The order is real. The Vatican claims otherwise for plausible deniability. The members of the order are kept secret. Only those within it know the other members. An order member wrote this note. I can read it because Ibelin taught me the script when he and Lyal trained me before I became a Horseman."

"Ibelin's a papal assassin?"

"I think Ibelin is a liaison with the assassins for the Pope. Only certain order members are papal assassins. Their identities are kept a strict secret. Only the grandmaster and Pope know their names. Most members merely work on the Church security teams."

Grace shook her head. Being mad at Rayne wouldn't solve the conundrum they faced. "How do the order and Garsea tie into Umar?"

"They don't. I am speculating Garsea is the cause for Umar's recent power grab here in Córdoba. The letter only warns that Umar seems to be plotting and my father may be in danger. Djinn like Garsea operate by manipulating human desires for power and wealth. In return for helping mortals gain those items, mortals trade their soul or something the djinn wants in return for their assistance. If Umar has struck a bargain with Garsea, that explains the attack on us. Umar loathes me and my father. We were always a threat to his ability to influence the caliph. If we uncover what occurs here, we thwart any future issues."

"Why didn't you tell me everything about your human years before now?"

"I... I didn't have the words to. Haroun's life, my human life, did not end well. I killed Umar's men in cold blood before my humanity ended. The honorable man I once was died with Priya, only a few feet from where we stand."

Grace took his hand and brought it to her heart. "You redeemed yourself. The High Council saw something good in you to give you a second chance. You have nothing to be ashamed of about your human years. The stories I've heard about Haroun say he was a good man, from an upstanding and kind family."

"I fear the folklorists lie about his goodness as much as his enemies exaggerate his being an evil djinn that turned on the people of Córdoba." Rayne looked away from her.

Grace gently turned his face, so he stared at her again. "If you were half as generous and kind as you are as a Horseman, you led a good life in your human years. The rest is all nonsense Umar made up to discredit you. Now, let's get to work figuring out what is going on and ensure your father is kept safe, Saint Rayne, or Haroun, if you prefer."

Rayne laughed. "You forgive me too easily this time, my benevolent wife."

Throughout the evening meal, Rayne seemed almost a stranger to Grace. His easygoing nature gave way to a more formal, assertive, and guarded presence. He spoke mostly in Kabyle with the other men. Grace took in everything as she ate. The members of Rayne's family and his father's household seemed genuinely friendly. She politely conversed with one of Saladin's soldiers sitting beside her. He reached to stroke one of Grace's gold curls for fortune and good luck.

Rayne's hand snaked out in front of Grace and seized his wrist. All conversation stopped as Rayne came to his feet. "Never touch my wife without my permission to do so."

"Forgive me, Haroun. I meant no offense."

Rayne released his hand.

The man repeated his apology, backing away from the table.

Rayne slowly looked at each person sitting around him. "Any man who values his life will not touch my wife or my children if they accompany me."

Grace knew better than to countermand him. She trusted he had a reason for the out of character territorial display. Once he sat down again, she leaned closer to him. "What was that about? He only wanted some luck."

"I want clear boundaries established. While he was harmless, others may not be. They will test you with a quick touch of the hair then try other things. Stay on your guard with the men here. Not all are friends to the Ibn-Ziyad family even though they sit at this table."

At the end of the meal, Saladin explained to Grace that the men and women did their own socializing for about an hour before retiring for the evening.

Unsure of what she should do, Grace looked at Rayne. "Do you want me to go with the other women or stay with you?"

"Go with my mother. You have nothing to fear from any of the women in the household. They are all family, unlike the men in the room."

Lillian introduced Grace to Saladin's other three wives as the women made their way from the dining hall to their private quarters. Once the group settled into a large open room with colorful mosaics decorating the walls, a servant brought them a tray of apricots, figs, and dates, along with small cups of a medieval herbal tea made from roses and honey. Polite conversation over dessert transitioned to curious inquiries about where Rayne had disappeared to over the past few years followed by more invasive questions about Grace's past and how she became Rayne's wife. Grace politely answered all the ones she could, then redirected the conversation.

Sherifa, one of Saladin's wives, gently grasped Grace's hand. Grace noticed a clay pot sitting beside Sherifa.

"We have a tradition of decorating a bride's hands and feet with henna," Lillian explained as Sherifa dipped a wooden stick into the pot. "I know you already married my son, but may we honor the two of you tonight?"

"If it will not upset Rayne, I see no harm in it."

Sherifa and one of Rayne's sisters decorated Grace's hands.

"Has Saladin always been one of Malik's advisors?" Grace inquired about her father-in-law's role in the Cordovan government as the women painted intricate floral patterns and scrolls on her hands and feet.

"No. Saladin once commanded Córdoba's army and served as head of the royal guard until he was injured in a skirmish on the border of Aquitaine. With his injuries healed, Saladin is as capable a soldier and commander as he has ever been. However, Rayne's ascension in the ranks and his winning the loyalty of many in the army concerned Abdul, Malik's father. Abdul worried if Rayne and Saladin commanded the army together, they would eventually become a threat to his rule. To prevent that, Abdul selected another man named Umar to co-lead the army with Rayne and kept Saladin in an advisory role."

"How does an English woman become acquainted with an Andalusian general?"

Lillian smiled. "Vikings stole me from my village. They intended to sell me in Baghdad. Saladin had been sent to Baghdad as an emissary. Upon inspecting a delivery of tribute and slaves from the West, Saladin found me in the group. My blue eyes and light hair fascinated him. He also claims he enjoyed my wit when we briefly spoke. He told the captain of the guard I was not part of the lot and belonged to him. The captain apologized for wrongly taking a slave from Saladin's personal staff, then ordered my immediate return to him. I was thankful something about me caught his eye. He is a patient and kind man, Grace. He courted me, when by all rights, he did not have to. We spent hours getting to know one another. Over time, I fell in love with the man who married me on a whim."

Lillian offered Grace a blue dress with elaborate gold embroidery to put on. "Blue was always Haroun's favored color. Go change over there. Then we will help you with the headdress and jewelry."

Grace ran her hands down the blue gown, smoothing the front. It truly was beautiful.

"Haroun sends for his wife," One of the servants called from the doorway, not daring to enter the chambers of Saladin's wives.

"Tell him he shall see his wife soon," Lillian answered, draping a matching blue veil over Grace's head.

Rayne heard his mother from the hallway. "Mother, do not make me wait all night."

"Impatience is not an honorable virtue, Haroun." Lillian continued pinning everything in place before setting a jeweled headdress over Grace's curly hair.

Grace could almost envision Rayne scowling and rolling his eyes.

"I will await Grace in the main courtyard," Rayne said, then walked outside to enjoy the pleasant evening.

Satisfied with Grace's appearance, Lillian smiled. "Come. We will unite you and Haroun according to our traditions."

Spotting his mother and Sherifa escorting Grace towards him, Rayne grinned. The elaborate wedding dress and the carefully drawn henna designs showed his family welcomed her as one of their own.

Saladin met the women, politely bowed, and extended a hand to Grace. "As your father is not here, Grace, may I present you to my son?"

"Of course." Grace settled her hand on his.

Rayne straightened as his father approached. If his parents wanted him to honor their traditions, he happily would. He politely inclined his head to his father then Grace.

Saladin extended Grace's hand to him. Rayne took it and gently pulled her forward. He removed the face veil, thereby, officially accepting Grace as his wife.

Saladin smiled then joined his wives waiting only a few feet away.

Rayne chuckled. "Tradition requires me to ask your parents what they seek as a bride's price."

Grace loved the idea of Rayne negotiating a bride price in modern day. Her father would more than likely shoot him. Her parents already suffered a round of shock after she appeared on their doorstep pregnant and married to the best man from her failed wedding. It did not take long for Rayne to win them over, especially after they saw how much he cared for their daughter. Poor Dante had been demonized by the saintly image Rayne presented. "I think they will demand a great deal. I believe I am worth at least two camels, four goats, and one bull. They might even ask you to add Fahkir to the contract."

Rayne guided her through an open doorway on her right then closed the door behind them. "Adding Fahkir makes the contract terms very steep after I pay the gold I am required to provide and present you with the customary wedding gifts a groom gives a bride. You send me to the poorhouse by taking my horse. I cannot provide for my family without Fahkir. I would counter with two camels, four goats, one bull, and Vittore or Diya, since I need neither beast to earn a living.”

“You would give away my horses instead of offering your own for me?”

Rayne held his hands up. “Fine. We keep your two unruly monsters, and I give up my mount.” No longer interested in jesting, he drew her to him. “There isn’t anything I would not give up or do to ensure you are mine for eternity.”

Knowing his family remained in the courtyard pending confirmation that the union was mutually acceptable, Rayne loudly spoke in Kabyle.

Hearing a mix of laughter and voices outside the door, Grace smiled up at him. “I am afraid to ask what you said.”

“I said, I claim the bride presented to me as my wife. She pleases me, and the price she asks to have her is more than fair.”

“Does that mean I am officially the wife of Haroun Ibn-Ziyad, in addition to Rayne Warwick?”

Rayne backed her towards the bed. “Not quite yet. I am about to remedy that. We must consummate our marriage for it to be official.”

“We already consummated our marriage.” Grace enjoyed the way her husband devoured her with his eyes after removing the scarf and jeweled band from her head.

“Not tonight, we haven’t.”

Rayne helped her shed the wedding gown. He let go of all his fears about his past and focused on making love to his wife.

Grace gently bit into his shoulder, muffling a loud moan of pure pleasure.

“Cry out, Grace. It is expected that there be some sort of evidence of what we do.”

She threw her head back and loudly called his name.

CHAPTER

EIGHT

Córdoba - 812

Grace woke to the sounds of birds chirping. Rayne slept with an arm draped around her. Someone had left warm tea and breakfast on a rounded table and opened the shuttered windows, letting fresh air into the room. She carefully lifted Rayne's arm and tried to slide from the bed, but found herself being pulled backward.

"You are not going anywhere."

"The tea and breakfast smell wonderful. My stomach is growling after as many times as my husband woke me last night, emir."

Rayne chuckled at her calling him commander in Arabic. He stretched then walked over to the table.

"Or would it be mushir?"

Rayne grinned again. "I've been called both, but if you are referring to my being the commanding general of the Emirate's army, emir is the better of the two titles. My father is the official military advisor to the ruler of Córdoba, so he would be the mushir."

Grace watched him pour them each a glass of tea and pick up the tray. "Another wedding custom?"

"No, I simply wished to deliver my wife her breakfast."

109

"You will have to teach me some Kabyle." Grace opened her mouth for the slice of fig he held. She loved the smile on his face as he gently settled the fruit on her tongue.

"I would be delighted to." Rayne picked a date from the tray for himself.

Grace sipped some tea after she finished chewing the fig. "I think you have an admirable past, Haroun. Perhaps it is time you share the story of your human years with your wife."

"My wife needs to learn the past does not matter, only the present and the future."

"What am I to tell Tessa of her heritage?"

"That she is descended from a line of great men and women."

"Rayne Warwick Dalglese or Haroun Ibn-Ziyad, whichever you prefer this morning. That is not the answer your wife seeks."

Rayne kissed her. "It will have to do. It is all I am willing to provide her."

Shouting from the hall interrupted their breakfast. The ruckus drew closer to the door. They heard Lillian pleading with someone not to defile her home with violence.

"Took them long enough. I expected them last night." Rayne settled an arm around Grace. "Stay right where you are."

Grace thought he had lost his mind. "I am not dressed, nor are you."

The door slammed against the wall. Three of Umar's officers entered. Lillian and Sherifa begged the men to wait until Saladin returned. Rayne eyed them, but continued to drink his tea.

Grace instinctively reached for the covers only to find them already wrapped around her. Coins from the wedding headdress jingled against her forehead when she moved. What image was Rayne trying to project before these men?

Rayne set his tea down on the table and scowled at the three sent to confirm he lived. "Is there a reason you intrude on my bride and me this early in the morning? I have killed men for lesser offenses."

The tallest of the officers laughed. The other two seemed surprised the djinn from their nightmares sat calmly before them with his wife, just as they might spend the morning with theirs.

"Umar demands you present yourself to be judged for your crimes."

Rayne's arm tightened around Grace after she started to pull away. *Play the naïve, modest wife for me.*

Grace shyly hid herself behind him. "Who are these men, Haroun?"

"No one to be concerned about, habibe." Rayne cast an appreciative glance over his shoulder at her. "Umar would know who the criminal is out of the two of us. Tell Umar, his judgment was previously made and my sentence imposed. Inform him, I do not take kindly to being interrupted when I am eating my morning meal."

The bold one of the three stepped forward with a hand on his sword. "Umar summons you, cur."

Rayne grabbed his dagger from the nightstand.

"Pardon them. They know not who they challenge." Grace pulled Rayne backwards, preventing him from standing. "Blood shed during our wedding will only curse our marriage. You swore to leave your past behind."

Rayne shifted, so he faced her. "As you wish." He stroked her cheek with his thumb. "The woman generously spares the three of you. Umar may summon me himself. Warn him, I may not offer the clemency I do you three today."

Rayne kissed Grace. When the kiss ended, he looked over at the bewildered soldiers. "Why are you all still here? Leave!"

He ran his lips across Grace's shoulder and up her neck before kissing her again. His hand gently grasping the back of her head once her mouth opened, welcoming his seeking tongue. She pressed closer to him as his free hand drew the sheet down her back, exposing her skin as if they were completely alone. He loudly groaned, crushing her upper body against his.

Disgusted by the immoral display, the soldiers departed, slamming the room door shut behind them.

Grace laughed at how they loudly remarked about hedonistic djinn, along with their carnal appetites and poor manners. "You are really using those djinn rumors to your advantage this morning."

"Indeed, I am, leof."

Grace's arms encircled his neck. "You are so sexy when you play the badass, Commander Ibn-Ziyad."

He chuckled, running his fingers down her spine. Her skin quivered in response to his light touch. "General, leof. I was a general. For such an independent woman, it always amazes me how much you enjoy a dominant man in the bedroom."

"We are well matched, my wolf. Part of you needs a woman who enjoys being conquered by her lover." Grace closed her eyes, adoring how his teeth grazed her shoulder before he playfully growled.

Rayne pinned her back on the bed. "Breakfast will wait. I have other things in mind for you."

"Before you start making her howl, give me a second to leave this for you, Warwick. You'll need it this afternoon." Ares threw something on the bed.

Unable to resist, Grace howled, arching up under Rayne.

Ares let out a disgusted sigh. "You two are pathetic if your marriage has gotten dull enough you've resorted to animal noises in the bedroom."

"Go away, Ares," Grace mumbled, pulling Rayne's face down to meet hers again.

<hr>

"I am not complaining at all about spending the morning making love to my husband." Grace paused as she pulled her shirt up her arms.

Rayne glanced over at her after carefully tucking his shirt into his pants. He knew she hesitated to voice whatever bothered her. "Speak your mind, leof."

"Explain to me why we aren't going to confront Umar versus waiting for him to show up on your father's doorstep?"

"It is complicated, Grace. For my family's sake, Umar must appear the aggressor. Challenging him outright would risk bringing the army upon us. I trained many of the men we would be defending against. The last thing I would want to do is injure them when I need their support."

Grace fixed his twisted shirt collar and handed him his belt. "What did Ares bring you?"

Rayne looked down at the carefully wrapped package on the bed. "I am not sure."

He picked it up and untied the strings holding the brown wrapping closed. Seeing what was inside, he dropped it on the bed. There may as well have been hot coals in the package that singed his fingertips with how quickly he yanked his hands back.

"What is it?" Grace pushed aside the paper to reveal the solid black uniform from Alexandria. It wasn't often she saw her husband's face pale. "You are not the monster you think you are."

"You do not know my past sins." Rayne composed himself, not sure why Ares would bring the general's uniform to him.

"I know the man you are now. The man who freely defends humanity, who selflessly gives to others anything they may need. The father who laughs with and teaches his children. The husband who breathed life into his shattered bride. That man is not a demon, Rayne." Grace prayed he heard the truth in her words. He could not have done anything worth an eternity of self-inflicted castigation.

"All of that stems from atoning for my past. My past is why we are here. Obviously, the debt has not been repaid as I hoped."

"Your family stands with you against whatever this past of yours is. The High Council supports you for Ares to appear today. You need to trust that all will be well." She stared at the man christened War by the Fates. It was still near impossible to believe he, of all people, would bear that moniker. "Rayne, why did you really deny the ties to Haroun? I know there's more than not having the words."

Rayne took her face between his hands. "For your safety, as well as the safety of my family who remained in Córdoba after I left."

"Our safety?" Nothing made sense for the past two days. Grace wished he'd trust her with the truth.

A knock on the room door prevented Rayne from elaborating on his claim. He dropped his hands to his side. "Enter."

Saladin stood in the hall with a troubled expression on his face. "Umar awaits you outside the gates."

Rayne grabbed a sword from his old wardrobe.

"I am riding with you." Grace's declaration shocked Saladin.

Aware that Grace would argue with any request for her to stay behind, Rayne nodded. "Meet me outside after you put your boots on."

Saladin followed Rayne to the front door. "You cannot take a woman with you to see Umar!"

"My wife could annihilate your best men."

"What madness is this, Haroun? I would know a warrior if I met one, and your wife is far from Kahina."

Rayne grinned at how his father compared the two women. "They are more alike than you know."

"Umar would slaughter her to remind you of his authority over the land, just as he did Priya."

Ignoring the twinge of guilt his father stirred, Rayne entered the courtyard to find Fahkir already tacked. "Trust my judgment. I would not take a helpless woman into a conflict."

Rayne took Fahkir's reins from the groom. "Ready a horse for my wife."

"Haroun, you place her life at risk as well as ours. Umar has grown even more underhanded since you were last here." Saladin hated the thought of watching his son grieve the loss of a second woman he cared about.

Grace heard the two men quarreling from the doorway. "Is there a problem?"

Saladin turned to find his daughter-in-law dressed in a man's uniform. He noted the gloves on her hands and the sabre hanging from her side.

"My father is worried about you visiting Umar with me."

One of Saladin's men offered Grace his horse. "My mare is fleet of foot. It would be an honor to loan her to you. I will take whatever horse the groom returns with."

"The honor is mine. Thank you." Grace put her foot in the stirrup of the saddle the man vacated for her and swung herself upward. "I appreciate your concern, Saladin. We have confronted much worse than Umar."

Saladin noted the calm expression on her face as she gathered the horse's reins. "This is madness, Haroun. Do not say I did not warn you." Saladin mounted his own horse. "Mohammed should be here shortly. We will leave when he joins us."

Rayne looked away from his father, so Saladin did not see the smirk on his face. He knew Grace wearing men's clothing and behaving as a soldier confused Saladin. Perhaps one day he may be able to tell his father about his and Grace's immortality.

Seeing his uncle arrive with two armed escorts, Rayne gave the order to ride out. Mohammed, Rayne's uncle, fell into his customary position beside Saladin. It was a relatively short ride to the city gates. Rayne halted the group a few feet from Umar and his men.

Grace surveyed the line of cavalry men before them. All dressed in the colors of the Emirate's guard. Daggers and swords hung from their sides. The display of military might would have been intimidating to most that encountered them. She guessed Umar was the man at the center of the line based on the gold medallion hanging from his neck, along with the jeweled rings on his hands.

Umar was only slightly older than a human Rayne would have been. A jagged scar ran from the man's temple, across his throat then disappeared under his collar. Other than the scar, he had an aristocratic appearance and graying dark hair. He was not as fit as Rayne, but had the same knowledgeable eyes, giving away his command experience.

Learning the rumors of Haroun returning to Córdoba proved true, Umar smiled. "The devil lives, after all. I hoped my scouts were wrong. You seal your fate returning to Córdoba after what you have done."

Rayne frowned. Arrogance and ambition made his fellow general an unpredictable foe. He did not trust Umar to honor the neutrality of the land they met upon. Fahkir tugged at the bit, pulling the reins slightly forward in Rayne's hands but did not move from where the Horseman halted him. "You attacked my family after I left you in peace all of these years."

"An unfortunate mistake, Haroun. My orders were to take only you into custody. No harm was to be done to those found with you."

"For some reason, I doubt that." The comment slipped out before Grace could stop it.

Umar's eyes darted to Rayne's right to see who had spoken the insolent remark. He scoffed but said nothing to the woman. She matched the description his men gave of Haroun's wife. Haroun was bold to allow her to ride with him dressed like one of his father's soldiers.

Umar's shifting in the saddle warned Rayne the general's patience wavered. The way Umar studied Grace unnerved him. He never liked when Umar focused on something that intently. "One does not want to provoke a wolf in its den, Umar. I strongly suggest you withdraw the warrant and let the past die. I have no desire to spill more blood, but will do so if necessary."

"If circumstance were different, I would not provoke a new conflict between us. However, it is not in my power to ignore your presence here. Our ruler issued the warrant for you."

Saladin knew otherwise. "Then we shall visit Malik to resolve the matter."

"The Emir exalts you, Saladin. I have no doubt you will gain his ear quickly." Umar hated that the new caliph favored the Ibn-Ziyad family more than the man who commissioned him and Rayne years ago. He signaled his men to leave but remained behind as they departed. He threw something to Rayne.

Rayne caught whatever object sailed towards him.

"You should not have returned, Haroun. You will not leave Córdoba with your wife."

Rayne rankled at the threat but said nothing. Umar wheeled his mount around and followed his soldiers. Only after Umar shrunk in the distance did he look down at what he held. Seeing the emblem in his hand, Rayne shook his head. Umar took orders from Garsea. "I hoped to settle this peacefully. Apparently, that cannot be done."

Saladin placed a hand on Rayne's shoulder. "Malik will hear you out. He is not under Umar's power as Abdul was. We will see him this afternoon. I already have an audience with him."

Rayne nodded, not liking the idea of returning to the palace that held bittersweet memories for him.

Córdoba - 812

Rayne paced the floor of his room, periodically staring at the black uniform Grace had carefully laid across the bed. He reminded Grace of a caged animal. Anyone foolish enough to open the cage door would find themselves mauled or trampled.

"You will miss your opportunity to tell Malik what really happened if you do not change and leave with your father in the next half hour."

Rayne glared at her. "For all I know, his grandfather sent the assassins. Abdul and my father were the only ones who knew where I would be with Priya that evening. We met here to prevent any conflict with Umar. The damn man surveilled my home constantly. No Cordovan ever attacked my father's house before then. No harm should have befallen either of us. Just as I shouldn't be in Córdoba right now. I cannot change the past. I cannot bring Priya back. My presence here endangers my parents. I do not understand why the Fates intermingle my past and present; why they allowed Umar and Garsea to attack me or lure me back here."

Grace ignored the hostility he displayed, knowing it stemmed from fear of his family being injured. She picked up the shirt on the bed and crossed the room to him. Hoping to soothe him, she placed her palm against his cheek. "Calm yourself, wolf. Perhaps this is the Fates way of giving you closure, or a second chance to connect with your family. You've told me a thousand times how much you miss and revere your father. Now is your chance to tell him the same, since you weren't able to before. Things will work out, Rayne. Whatever this is will be resolved without anyone else getting hurt, but you must go with your father. Do not let the past dictate your current actions if absolution is what you truly seek."

Rayne smiled, though the frustration never left his eyes. "You are wise beyond your years, woman."

"My husband and guardian mentored me well." Grace laid the shirt across her arm and grasped the straps of the Horseman's cuirass. "May your wife help you don your uniform, General?"

"She may."

Rayne fidgeted throughout the process of swapping uniforms. He slapped Grace's hands away when she started to fix the twist in his collar. He straightened it himself, still wanting to rip the material from his body. His hands shook as he secured his old scimitar to his side. He picked up a silver chain with a wolf's head dangling from it that was kept in a wooden box inside his old wardrobe. The edge of the moon starting to rise crested behind the ears of the wolf. He settled the large medallion on the center of his chest. When he looked in the mirror, an older version of the mortal general stared back at him. The human face turned into something more sinister in the glass.

Grace appearing beside him erased the monster he saw. Now, there was only a Horseman standing with a woman who believed in him more than he did himself at the moment.

"I can see why Priya was so enamored with you. The red and black is almost as striking on you as the Horsemen's black and gold. Black electrifies those eyes of yours. It is definitely your color, Warwick."

He turned from the mirror to her. Embracing him, Grace offered Rayne another reassuring smile. He kissed her forehead, trying to calm the churn within.

"I wish there was more I could do for you, Rayne. Would you like me to accompany you?"

"As much as I desire to have you at my side, I cannot take a woman with me into Malik's private chambers."

"Please call Destahn or Tamir to go with you."

"This is not their fight."

"We are brothers-in-arms. Any fight you face is also ours," Raphael announced the arrival of the other Horsemen.

Raphael, Destahn, and Tamir dressed in the traditional garb of the Cordovan armies.

Tamir extended his hand to Rayne. "I trust we are properly attired."

Surprised to see his fellow Horsemen, Rayne clasped Tamir's hand. "There is no need for you to be involved in this."

"We want to be involved. Can't let a fellow Umayyad take on a rogue general by himself. I am disappointed you did not previously tell me of our shared heritage," Destahn said, making Rayne grin.

"We have no shared heritage."

Destahn shrugged his shoulders. "I am sure if we looked, we would find some tie. I like Haroun a great deal more than Rayne."

"Disclose my human name outside this century, and you will find yourself addressing me as Commander."

Raphael chuckled at the two of them. "Or he'll be in Tartarus for breaking our laws with exposing the human identity of one of the original Horseman."

Tamir smirked and softly laughed, but did not say anything.

Grace smiled at the banter between the Horsemen. She loved how the four always stood by one another. "I am sure Destahn will eventually end up there for one reason or another, and thank you for coming to Rayne's aid since he is too stubborn to ask for help at times. The four of you can more than manage to persuade a human general to let go of an old grudge. And if Umar won't budge, it sounds as if Malik will."

A knock sounded on the door.

"Enter." Rayne said, knowing the person who knocked was his father.

Saladin studied the men he discovered in the bedroom with Grace and Haroun. They wore the uniform of the Emirate, but he had never seen them in the city prior to today.

"Father, these gentlemen ride with me. Tamir, Destahn, Raphael, my father, Saladin Ibn-Ziyad."

Raphael offered his hand to Saladin. "It is a pleasure to meet the man who fathered one of the greatest commanders in Al-Andalus."

"The honor is mine." Saladin clasped Raphael's hand then looked over at Rayne. "Are you ready to depart, Haroun?"

"Yes, Baba."

Grace accompanied the men outside.

"Honore e gloria," She whispered the first half of the Horsemen's battle cry to Rayne once he was in the saddle.

Raphael winked at her from atop his new horse. "Rayne victorem hodie est."

Grace still found it difficult to believe Raphael talked the High Council into letting him ride with the Horsemen again. Even more surprising, he declined command, stating Dante chose Rayne to lead, then stressed Rayne was the better of the two of them to serve as Horsemen Commander.

Rayne tenderly cupped Grace's chin in his hand. "Swear to me I will find you here when I return. No surprise appearances at the palace and no leaving the safety of these walls for the afternoon."

"I promise I will be here when you return."

Rayne noted how she left out part of what he asked. "And no leaving the safety of these walls with Umar's men about."

"You have my word. I will not depart the premises, endangering myself in any way."

He leaned down to kiss her. "Not exactly what I wanted to hear, but I will settle for it. Until this evening, my love."

Grace went up on tiptoe to meet him halfway. "Return to me soon, Commander." She patted Fahkir's neck then took a step back.

The five men headed to the palace.

"You are a terrible wife to lie to your husband like that," Ares said, standing behind her.

Xander joined them. The silver-eyed demon with long black hair who worked for Hades scowled at Ares.

Grace laughed at the two immortals who always helped her with questionable tasking. "I do not break my word. I promised I would not leave the premises endangering myself."

Ares sighed. "If Rayne learned you kept an eye on things from a distance, he would not be pleased."

"As if you ever worried about crossing the Horsemen."

"Sweetheart, you are married to Rayne Warwick. He isn't just any old Horseman. He's War. Even I have enough common sense not to piss him off."

"Coward." Xander coughed beside the god.

Ares shoved Xander. "Watch your choice of labels, demon, or Hades will learn you are topside without permission again."

Grace rolled her eyes. "Are you two done? We have a meeting to observe."

"If you find yourself grounded once more..." Ares tried a second time to caution Grace to honor her promise to Rayne.

"Going to Olympus is hardly placing any of us in danger. Rayne will never know we watched things. On the off chance my husband learns of today, I will ensure I am the only one who suffers the consequences. I am starting to think Xander's right. Maybe you should be the god of chickens or worrywarts."

Xander grinned, putting an arm around her shoulders. "The longer I know you, Grace, the more I like you."

Olympus -

Theseus eyed the trio that popped into the middle of Zeus's courtyard, disrupting the former king's enjoyment of the peaceful afternoon. "What are you three up to?"

"Can't friends enjoy lunch together?" Grace said so innocently the Greek king snorted.

"Olympus isn't exactly where you three catch up over coffee."

Ares took Grace by the arm and led her away to prevent Theseus from making any further inquiries.

Theseus redirected his gaze to the sun. "Your other half is here. Any idea what she is up to?"

Not liking that Grace entered a realm of the gods, Dante appeared next to Theseus. "No. But her, Xander, and Ares together means it is more than likely nothing good."

Córdoba - 812

Rayne tried to ignore the startled faces and whispering that spread throughout the palace. Gossip traveled faster than they did. Each hall and room he passed through seemed to be filled with people wanting to see the infamous Ibn-Ziyad.

Some people pitied him; others feared him. A minority welcomed him either out of support from prior experiences before the general's darker side emerged or from the romanticization of his legend.

The three soldiers surrounding him were just as much of a curiosity. No one had ever seen their faces in Córdoba before now.

Rayne recognized a few of the people he passed. Entering the receiving room, he nodded to one of his former field commanders standing guard. The man offered a quick smile to acknowledge the nod and mouthed the words 'always my general.' Rayne appreciated that he still had loyal friends within the haras. With the security risk he presented, he would not be left waiting long.

After a minute or two Sayyid, escorted Rayne and Saladin into Malik's private offices. Upon entering the royal chambers, guards seized Rayne. Expecting to be arrested, Rayne did not fight them. The

Horsemen made no move to assist their commander based on Rayne's lack of resistance.

The young caliph looked up at the group that entered his office, disrupting a meeting with his vizier of finance. He did not move from where he sat. Since he was a boy, he heard tales of the general's accolades and the horror stories of the man gone insane. He expected Haroun to look much older. Then again, he expected Haroun to be dead until Damien advised otherwise. "What is your name?"

"Haroun Ibn-Ziyad, Emir."

"The famed general who served my grandfather and father?"

"One and the same, Emir."

The sobering of the twenty-nine-year old's face made Rayne wonder if it was a mistake to think the man would hear him out.

"Your hair is still dark when Umar's has grayed."

Rayne resisted the urge to grin. "One benefit of becoming a djinn is keeping one's youth."

Malik laughed at Rayne's response. "Or you take after your father, who only grayed when he was a few years older than you."

Silence filled the air as Malik debated whether or not to trust the former Protector of the Emirate. "Is it true you murdered Priya?"

Another awkward minute of silence passed while Rayne digested the accusation. Is that what Umar told Abdul? That he slaughtered his betrothed in a fit of rage? The query cut much deeper than Rayne anticipated it could. "No. I loved her. The approval of our betrothal was the greatest reward your father ever bestowed upon me. Someone else assassinated her before failing to take my life. I held her as she drew her final breaths. I could never harm her."

"Did you know Priya and I knew one another, General?" Malik rose and approached Rayne.

"No, Emir."

"She was one of the jewels of my father and grandfather's court."

Rayne hung his head, remembering the first day he noticed her in the palace receiving room. She shyly smiled at him, sitting with her father and mother along the wall. "She was the most beautiful woman in Abdul's court. None other had her honeyed eyes or her soft, long waves of walnut-colored hair. I lost my heart to her the first time our eyes met."

"She once told my father you stole her heart when you looked upon her with eyes the same shade as the ocean."

Rayne raised his head to stare Malik directly in the face.

Malik smiled at how blue the man's eyes were. The wolf adorning his neck lent further credence to the man indeed being the Black Wolf of Córdoba. "She often spoke highly of you. I may be new to ruling, but I am not naïve, Haroun. The only reason my men hold you prisoner is because you allow them to. I do not believe you are the djinn others in my court claim you to be. Release him. The man is no threat."

The guards let Rayne go and stepped back to the walls.

"Close the door. This meeting is not one for all the palace staff and curiosity seekers to observe." Malik took his seat again.

Two guards scrambled to bar the door.

"You believe me?" Rayne hadn't expected Malik to take him at his word.

"Only Umar's men were slaughtered that night. A crazed murderer would not have returned her body so carefully wrapped and gently laid outside her family's door. Her parents repeatedly defended you. They insisted there must be a mistake. Haroun could not have murdered their daughter. Not with as many times as they observed the two of you together. My grandfather never signed your death warrant. He did not believe the news himself. It was my father who feared Umar that finally did. Umar always sought royal favor, and you stood in his way. We have a common enemy, Haroun. Umar pursues my throne since I neither fear nor favor him."

Rayne knew a proposition was forthcoming by the way the man spoke. "What is it you seek from me, Emir?"

Malik laughed. "Wisdom was a virtue always associated with you, Haroun. I appreciate men who are both cunning and frank. I will pardon you and restore your family's standing. In return, you kill Umar and dismantle his army."

Rayne exchanged glances with Raphael. "If you know I am not the heartless beast Umar claims I am, you should know I cannot assassinate the man for you."

Malik eyed him suspiciously. "Why not?"

"I have taken an oath to never harm the innocent nor those that do not threaten me."

"Umar is the last man one could call innocent. He murdered many more than Priya. My father is his most recent victim."

"Treason is a death penalty offense. Place him before a tribunal of elders; eliminate him that way." Rayne hoped to reason with Malik. He could not kill for selfish reasons or the Emirate any longer.

"If it were that easy, it would have already been done. Umar's corruption has had three generations to establish itself. The roots of his deception run deep and the tree grows strong. Any placed on a tribunal that ruled against him would suffer an untimely demise, or their family members would mysteriously disappear. You have nothing to lose and everything to gain, General Ibn-Ziyad. Before whatever this new oath is, you swore an oath to my grandfather then my father and the Emirate of Córdoba. In my eyes, that takes precedence over all else. I raise my hand against Umar, I ignite civil war. You eliminate him and those loyal to him, peace remains in the Emirate."

"I am sorry, Emir. Even with the wrong he committed against me, I can take no action against him." Rayne wished he had killed Umar long ago. The only reason Umar still breathed was the loyal bodyguards who sacrificed themselves while their coward of a leader fled.

"He sent those men to kill you, your wife, and your children, Haroun. He plots as we speak to ransom your wife's life for the opportunity to take yours." By Rayne's recoil from the threat, Malik found the tender spot he needed to force the suddenly passive general's hand.

"Then I will ensure she is well out of his reach."

"Strike him first, and that will not be necessary." Malik rose from his chair and stood before Rayne. "Are you not the same man who left Umar's soldiers diced into pieces with their blood running across the marble floors of his home? Are you not the djinn men and children fear once the sun goes down? Does the wolf in your crest no longer have its teeth to bite?"

Destahn and Tamir stared at Rayne. Today was the first they heard of Rayne's heartless trouncing of his enemies as a mortal.

Not allowing Malik to manipulate his emotions, Rayne remained silent.

"Your wife awaits your return in your father's home, Haroun. Umar watches her closely. Two assassins are stationed outside the gate pending his order to strike. Could you honor this new oath you claim to have taken after finding your wife slain in the one place you mistakenly believe her to be safe?"

Rayne straightened, and his fists started to reflexively clench. He forced his fingers to relax. Only a fool threatened a ruler surrounded by their royal guard. The haras would defend Malik the second Rayne made any threatening move towards him. Carefully tempering his emotions, Rayne stared down at Malik. "I caution you to be wary of provoking me. I am not your enemy. Do not make it otherwise, Malik."

"I would be a fool to make us enemies. My intent is to unite our families against Umar. To prove that to you, I pardon you whether or not Umar dies by your hand. To regain your prior standing and restore your family's honor, you will kill Umar for me."

Rayne wanted to slap the man who smirked at him. The whelp inherited his father's arrogance. He always hated that part of Abdul. Arrogance made Abdul many enemies, eventually costing him his reign from the sounds of it. Malik followed his father's same fatal mistakes based on everything Rayne observed today. "Pardon or no pardon, I will not assassinate Umar on your behalf or mine."

"Do you believe one man alone can foster the kind of corruption Umar has in Córdoba's administration?" Malik piqued the curiosity of several parties in the room.

Raphael stood taller. Saladin glanced over at Rayne along with Destahn and Tamir.

Rayne frowned, wondering what Malik hinted at. "One man or woman can be exceptionally destructive to a community if given the resources and time to deploy them."

"Tell me, General, does your new oath forbid you from striking at one that falls outside the realm of the innocent?"

Rayne exhaled loudly. Malik would not be pleased with any outcome other than Umar dead. "Our discussion is at an impasse, Malik. Córdoba nor yourself command me any longer. I bid you good day."

"Wait!" Malik took Rayne's hand and pressed something into his palm. "Umar does not act alone."

Rayne stared down at the medallion in the flat of his hand. "Garsea."

"Yes." Malik expected Rayne to change his mind upon seeing the seal Isra had given him.

Rayne closed his fingers around the demon seal. Umar and Garsea working together could not only destabilize the Emirate, but wreak havoc across Europe. "Where did you get this?"

"A concerned citizen found it amongst Umar's clothes when washing them. They brought it to me after seeing Umar meeting with what appeared to be a djinn."

Raphael stepped between Malik and Rayne. "Malik, would you be gracious enough to allow Haroun two days' time to think upon your original offer? Over those two days, allow word of his pardon to spread. It will strike fear in your enemy's ranks and draw out the other you suspect works in conjunction with Umar. Dissension will strengthen loyalties to you and weaken Umar, which benefits you, and Haroun, should Haroun accept the task of eliminating Umar and his alleged new master."

Rayne stared at Raphael as if he had lost all sense of reason.

Trust me, Rayne. We may be able to resolve this in a fashion that does not break your oath and makes Malik happy. We need time to explore the options I am thinking may be available to you.

Saladin was not sure what was occurring, but there was something about Raphael he respected. "I would be indebted to you, if you honor Raphael's request, Emir."

Content with how negotiations had gone, Malik nodded. "Of course. Return here on the morning of the third day with your answer, General. I will ensure news of your good fortune is spread far and wide upon this meeting adjourning. I will even give you a hero's welcome home tomorrow afternoon to confirm your pardon and good standing in my ranks."

"You are too kind, Emir." Saladin bowed to Malik.

Olympus -

The tenacity of the young caliph impressed Ares. "Gotta give it to Malik. He's no fool with putting the right temptation before that hubby of yours."

"Rayne knows when he is being manipulated. He won't let Malik damn him for eternity." Grace hated the troubled expression on Rayne's face before he exited the room.

Theseus placed his hand on Grace's shoulder, making her jump. "This does not look like a friendly lunch to me. What are we watching, Defensore?"

"Haven't you ever heard of lunch and a movie? Or do you Greeks not know what a film is?" Grace earned a chiding look from her favorite of the Greek deities.

Ares quickly closed the portal.

Grace held up the plate in her hand. "You are welcome to taste my meal if you doubt we were eating."

"Not a wise idea, Gracie. Ares did make it. It is barely edible," Xander warned Theseus not to take her up on that.

"Shut up, demon! It is fine for those of us who do not enjoy raw meat and rotting flesh." Ares threw some food from his plate at Xander.

"Behave, children!" Theseus prevented any further food flinging. "Care to share what film you were watching?"

"Aladdin." Grace stood. The ride from the palace to Saladin's would only be about a half hour. She needed to get back to Córdoba. "We need to do this more often. I actually miss the two of you a very tiny, minuscule bit."

Ares placed his hand over his heart. "I am touched, Gracie."

"Well, catch you later." Grace started to disappear.

"Not so fast, Grace." Theseus pushed her back down onto the sofa. "I would like to see a bit of the old tale myself. I did not know they made a movie of it. Since you seem to be such a fan, I would value you answering any questions I may have about the film adaptation."

Dante concealed himself standing next to Theseus and reopened the portal, curious to see what the three had secretly monitored.

"Your husband would not be pleased if he knew what you do." Dante flicked Grace in the ear.

"That hurt!" Grace hit Theseus, thinking he inflicted the smarting pain behind her ear.

"You deserve it for spying, instead of allowing Rayne to handle this." Theseus did not clarify who reprimanded her.

"If it were only Malik Rayne needed to manage, I wouldn't be eavesdropping. There is a demon named Garsea behind the scenes."

"Garsea?" Theseus recognized the name. "We all thought he died several years ago after betraying Lucifer and making a power grab to rule Spain. Rayne was the one dispatched to eliminate him. I've never known Rayne to disregard an execution order. Even on the off chance Garsea survived, Rayne still would not want his wife disrespecting his wishes."

Dante shook his head. "I certainly would not want to be Rayne right now. He will have a lot to answer for if he spared Garsea. If Raphael is contemplating what I think he is, Raphael will not find any sort of loophole in the law. We cannot interfere to assist, either."

"You and the High Council members cannot interfere," Theseus corrected, looking over at Xander.

Dante grinned, comprehending what Theseus implied. "If Umar needs to be eliminated, nothing says a demon can't execute a mortal. Doesn't Hades do that for sport?"

"Don't look at me, golden boy. My back still smarts from the beating Hades bestowed for helping you in Alexandria without his consent."

"Golden boy?" Confused, Grace looked behind her to see whom Xander addressed.

"Theseus here has become quite the do-gooder, suck up to the Council," Ares covered Xander's mistake.

"No one said the demon needed to be you, Xander. It was just a passing thought," Theseus redirected the conversation. "Grace, go home before Rayne discovers you are missing. The man doesn't need anything additional to cause him more anxiety."

"You know you are my favorite Greek." Grace kissed his cheek, causing him to roll his eyes.

"I won't inform your husband of your little escapade this afternoon."

Córdoba - 812

"While it is not ideal, it absolves you of any charges." Saladin couldn't understand why Rayne wouldn't honor Malik's request.

Rayne hated that his father entertained the caliph's demand. "And stains my conscious, ruining all I have done to redeem myself."

"Is his death not what you have wanted?"

"Did you not raise me to believe there is no honor in killing a man in such a manner?"

"Haroun, I remember well the lessons I taught you. You face exile or worse again if you displease Malik. Eliminating a man as vile as Umar is a forgivable sin. You can stay in Córdoba if you—"

Entering the house, Rayne reached his breaking point. "I am not returning to Córdoba, Father! Nor am I killing a man in cold blood to please you or anyone else. That is my final word on the matter."

He saw the women of the household sitting together. Grace wasn't among them. "Where is my wife?"

Lillian heard the edge in her son's voice. "She went for a stroll in the gardens. She should return soon."

Her answer set off warning bells within him. "How long has she been gone?"

Grace came through the rear door, offering him a glowing smile. "Only a few minutes. The fresh air and sunshine soothe your wife's frazzled nerves. She fretted for your well-being. I see my worry was for naught. You return with your soldiers in one piece." Ignoring the cynical expression on his face, she kissed Rayne hello. "I am relieved to see you standing safely before me."

Rayne lightly caressed her face with a knuckle, suspicious of the warm greeting. "I will always come home to you."

"Ever steadfast, my saint." Grace openly paid tribute to the man who had become her world. "That is the quality I admire most in you. I am blessed to be your wife. Ana bahebak."

Rayne softly returned the I love you in Arabic, catching Grace's hand after she turned away from him. Out of the corner of his eye, he saw how his mother smiled at the display of affection between him and Grace. Grace's gaze returned to his. The intentional extended eye contact galled Rayne. What had Grace been up to in his absence?

Saladin noted the mistrustful expression on his son's face.

"Something troubling you, husband?" Grace feigned concern for the change in Rayne's demeanor.

Rayne shook his head. "No. I was merely thinking I am the blessed one to have such an honest spouse and two healthy, beautiful children." He ignored the murmuring amongst the women after he spoke.

Grace innocently smiled up at him. "With your permission, Haroun, may I join your mother and the others for a glass of tea?"

"Yes, of course you may, my beloved." Rayne almost laughed at the well-timed request. Now he really wondered what she had done.

All four Horsemen eyed her out of character behavior.

Destahn set his hand on Rayne's shoulder, watching one of Saladin's wives pour a fresh cup of tea then offer it to Grace. "With that display of piety, she has definitely done something worrisome."

Rayne continued to observe Grace interacting with the women of his father's household. Something was glaringly out of place in the normal everyday scene. Where had his wife gone besides the gardens? "Ask Isis where Grace has been today, Raphael."

Raphael drew in a deep breath then did as requested. He hoped the goddess confirmed Grace remained in Córdoba for Grace's sake.

"Isis insists she was here the entire time you were gone." Raphael wasn't sure what to tell Rayne. Something seemed out of place to him as well. "Perhaps everything occurring throws off our instincts, Rayne. You should tell Grace about your meeting with Malik."

"This evening. It is better we discuss it without my parents present."

Raphael and Destahn departed to see if any immortal heard whispers of Garsea returning to Córdoba.

A servant brought a fresh tray of food to the table. Saladin gestured for Rayne and Tamir to join him. He studied his daughter-in-law. The more he learned of her, the more he found she complemented his son. "Grace is a unique woman."

"Thankfully, she is one of a kind." Rayne's remark brought forth a chortle from his father and Tamir.

"Do Tarquin and Tessa have her coloring or yours?"

Thinking of his children, Rayne smiled. "Tessa has her mother's hair and my eyes. Tarquin is the spitting image of his father, from his gold eyes to the dark hair on his head."

"The boy inherits his stepfather's calm and intelligence. Tessa is the wild child of the two," Tamir praised Rayne's raising of a future Horseman.

Rayne glanced over at Grace. "She takes after her mother."

"Or her father in his youth." Saladin recalled his son's own adventurous days. "What made you ask for her hand?"

"I did not ask for her hand. I took her as wife out of necessity."

"Out of necessity?" Saladin didn't conceal his disapproval of what type of scenarios warranted the word 'necessity.' "I raised you to not dishonor a woman of standing. Did I not educate you on methods to avoid scandal when bedding a concubine?"

Rayne grimaced at what his father implied. "We married for honorable reasons, Baba. She and her unborn child needed a protector, and I could provide the security they needed. Her prior husband's arranging for us to be wed upon his death created a troublesome beginning for us. Fortunately, we overcame those challenges."

"Challenges? A bride should not object to the suitor her father, or in this case, her dying husband determines best suits her," Saladin said, reading into Rayne's words. "The man she was married to, you were his friend?"

Rayne recalled the argument he and Dante had the first night he learned of what was to come. "Yes, he was my commander."

"I assume you had to tell her of his passing?" Saladin tried to piece together the parts of Haroun's life he didn't know.

"No, he was killed before her in a battle. I forcibly removed her from the field after she refused to leave his body. That day was one of the worst of my life. I could not stop my commander from being slain, and Grace was injured in the fight. Pure fortune and chance enabled me to save her. Had she died, I would be more lost than I was after losing Priya. I never realized how much I truly loved Grace until she struggled to breathe while I held her."

Shock covered Saladin's face. "You, you had an adulterous affair with a married woman. Is that why her husband arranged the marriage between you two?"

"Baba, do not judge her or me too harshly. I courted Grace prior to her marriage, hoping to win her hand, but it was given to another. And yes, her husband knew Grace and I loved one another when he married her. After an angel told him he would die in an upcoming battle, he had advisors draw up the marriage contract, and as awful as it sounds, condoned our affair."

"Your son is an honorable man, Saladin. What Rayne is not telling you is he argued against the whole affair. He feared for Grace's reputation if such an arrangement became public. But when our commander would not change his mind, he embraced the agreement for Grace's sake. Her life depended on his doing so. Neither fortune nor chance ensured Grace's survival. In all of my years, never have I seen a love so great it could keep a soul from entering the afterlife." Tamir hoped Saladin recognized the strength of character instilled within his son. "Rayne saved more than Grace that morning. He saved the lives of many in those few hours. Modesty is one of Haroun's numerous virtues. I am honored to serve under his command."

Flattered by the compliment, Rayne grinned. "It is those I ride with who ensured victory that day. No commander can win a battle such as that one on his own."

"Your men hold you in high regard, as does your wife, Haroun." Saladin ate another date from his plate. "Did you believe the child Grace carried to be yours?"

"No. I knew who fathered Tarquin. I promised my old commander I would raise the boy and care for Grace if he fell that morning."

Rayne's emotion-laced answers brought forth a sense of pride in Saladin. His son married the woman for noble reasons. He would not inquire further with how his questions bothered the man once a small boy who questioned him about everything daily.

"Your wife blossomed under your care after such great injury. Very few women admire their husbands as she does. Priya's death was tragic, but perhaps Allah had a greater purpose in it. Had you not suffered such a loss, you would not have been able to guide her through hers. I have other matters to attend to this afternoon." Saladin left Rayne and Tamir at the table.

Rayne genuinely smiled for the first time since visiting the palace. He wished he could explain what he was now to the man he revered most.

Grace sat down next to Rayne. "There is nothing preventing you from telling him the truth."

"It is better he not know, leof."

Tamir almost envied the love that slowly grew between Grace and Rayne. Dante and Grace may have been fated, but the knight and thief were made for one another. "So many secrets we all carry. I must return to Sasainn. Raphael will be back with more news by nightfall."

Finally alone with her husband, Grace spoke freely. "You did the right thing telling Malik no. Stop second-guessing yourself."

Rayne pulled back to look her in the eye. "How do you know what occurred?"

"You have been stewing over that discussion since you arrived. Do you honestly think I would not hear your thoughts, especially worrying about you as I do?"

"Forgive me for distressing you." Rayne brushed his lips against her forehead, feeling sheepish. Of course, she would read the churn inside him. She always did when he faced troubling matters.

"Raphael will help you find a solution. You made the right choice."

CHAPTER

TWELVE

Córdoba - 812

A royal messenger wrapped on Saladin's door, interrupting the evening meal. Nervous tension filled the room where the Ibn-Ziyad family gathered. Rayne and Saladin sat straighter in their chairs. Lillian stared at her son, fear overlaying her face. The messenger unrolled the scroll in his hands then loudly proclaimed Haroun received a full pardon for any crimes he was accused of committing.

Grace smiled over at Rayne. "Favor finds you once more."

"I pray you are right."

The messenger continued reading the Emir's decree. "Dancing, music, and horse racing are mandated for the next three nights. All eligible men should compete in the races as tradition requires."

Grace noted the way Rayne smiled at the mention of horse races. He remained beside her, but his eyes followed Saladin and Mohammed to the door. "Go ride with your father."

"Are you certain? With Umar's men about..."

"I will be fine, Rayne. Go capture whatever the prize is. No horse in Córdoba is faster than Fahkir."

Rayne kissed her cheek. "I will send for you when we reach the last race, so you can partake in my triumph."

"Victor's laurels or the bitter sting of defeat, whichever fate grants you tonight, I will be at your side. I am proud to be your wife, Rayne."

Tarquin called for her as Rayne stood.

Rayne grew concerned after Grace's smile vanished. "What is wrong?"

"Nothing. Tarquin wishes us good night. His doing so startled me. I didn't know he could reach out like that."

"Do I need to pay Elysium a visit?" Rayne didn't like the puzzled expression on Grace's face. He could journey to the sacred place if needed.

"No. He's fine." Grace shook her head and smiled. "Go enjoy some time with your father."

"I will see you shortly." Rayne kissed her again, then disappeared into the night to ride in the races as he did in his youth.

Elysium -

Tarquin called for her a second time. Finding herself with her children, Grace looked around their room. It contained two beds; toys and books sat on wooden shelves. A few more toys laid scattered on the floor. Tessa tearfully reached up for her.

"What is wrong, Tessa?"

"I had a bad dream." Tessa sniffled.

Grace hugged her daughter. "It is only a dream. They can't hurt us."

"In my dream, bad people hurt Daddy. Daddy had to live with Zio in Elysium."

"Stop crying, Tessa." Grace rocked the little girl. "Daddy is fine. He is racing Fahkir tonight to celebrate some good news he received."

Tarquin's raised voice wavering beside Grace distracted her. "Please don't be mad, Papa. Tessa wanted Mama. She wouldn't stop crying, so I brought Mama here."

"I am not angry, Tarquin. You did the right thing by your sister. I merely wondered who entered my home without permission," Dante reassured his son all was well from the doorway. He remained there, watching Grace calm Tessa then read both children a bedtime story.

Tessa fell back to sleep with her mother easing her fears. Dante drew back Tessa's covers, so Grace could lay her down. Once Tessa was settled, Grace whispered for Tarquin to get back into his bed.

Dante smiled as Tarquin did as instructed then hugged his mother. Hearing mother and son say 'I love you' and 'pleasant dreams' in Italian swelled his heart with pride. Grace ensured Tarquin knew his father's native tongue and heritage. She and Rayne carefully educated the boy on Venetian, Egyptian, and Italian history, in addition to classical culture.

"May I speak with you, cara?" Dante gestured towards the hallway.

"Of course, Commander Giovanni."

The two walked down the passageway together.

"No one has called me that in a while."

"What do you go by since ascending, Dante? Ra, Apollo 2, or just a generic god of the sun?"

Dante good-humoredly grinned. "Mortals call me sun god on occasion. Everyone else simply addresses me as Dante. How are things in Córdoba?"

"As well as can be expected." Grace knew he stalled with the inquiry. Standing in his living room away from where the kids slept, she openly displayed the hostility she felt towards the newest deity in the Council ranks. "What do you want?"

No matter how many times he rehearsed this conversation in his head, nothing prepared him for it or the animosity in Grace's eyes. "I want to clarify a few misunderstandings."

"Misunderstandings? About what?"

The curtness of her tone stung. He broke eye contact with her. "You and I. I know you told Osiris I abandoned you and Tarquin."

"You did, Dante. You had a choice and chose to leave your family behind with another."

Dante winced at the bitterness in her voice. "Tarquin and you would have perished had I not traded myself. I rewrote fate, so you survived the day and my son came into this world."

"Explain why it is you could visit our son and not your grieving widow? Or how you appeared on the field to protect Tarquin only two days ago, but never shown yourself in full physical form before then?"

"The Council forbid me to go to you. I am banned from any contact with you. Do you know what hell that is? To be forced to stand at a distance and watch a loved one suffer. I would not wish such a thing on anyone, Grace. It killed me over and over again not to be able to comfort you. The Council granted me a reprieve when it comes to Tarquin. I begged and pleaded with them to allow me to visit and protect my son. It took months to get them to agree to that. If Tarquin's life had not been at risk, I would not have been able to assist you and Rayne. I would have never revealed myself to you under any other circumstance."

She scoffed at the passionately spoken words. "If that is the truth, why hasn't the Council sent me from your home?"

"They do not know you are here. Tarquin conceals your presence. I do not know how he does, but there is no trace of you standing before me. If I was not bound to you, I would not have known you were here." Dante stunned her into silence.

Her concern for Rayne, anger, and the lingering love for the god before her sent her mind in a million different directions. "Is Tessa's dream foresight?"

"I do not know." Dante wished he could offer her the answer she desperately needed.

"Is that the truth? Or is this one of those I am not willing to say deity moments?"

"Mia cara, I truly do not know. My wish to speak with you was not to argue or mislead you."

Grace's hand came to her forehead. She let out a frustrated sigh, her hand falling to her side before looking at Dante again. "I can't go through losing another man I love, Dante. Rayne nursed the wounds from the fight with Gaelin until they closed. For weeks, all I wanted was to follow you into the afterlife. He made sure I found my way out of that darkness. Rayne kept every promise he made you and me. Tessa and Tarquin need the stability a good father provides. You told me the same in Greece."

"Grazia." Dante reached for her.

She pushed his hand away, fighting for control over her temper.

The aggressive stride she took towards Dante warned the former Horseman to be careful. The only other person he could recall her staring so menacingly at was Qasim in Damascus.

"I will declare war on the High Council and you if either of you harm another member of my family. I will not give Rayne up without a fight."

"Let us pray you never follow that course, stella. If I learn the dreams are prophecy, I will risk an eternity of torture in Tartarus to warn you." Dante took her hand in his and brought it to his heart. "I swear I will not let the Fates leave you without Rayne or I nearby."

He realized the error he made by touching her too late. The physical contact reignited the old bond between them. Before he could stop himself, he kissed her. Unexpectedly, Grace pulled him closer instead of shoving him away.

They slipped into the past. Back to days when neither knew of the full prophecy. All they knew was their love for one another. The sounds of the Atlantic lapping against the sand in Essaouira filled their ears. A full moon hung on high.

The feel of the Horsemen's crest against her skin made Grace aware that somehow the kiss brought them back to the night of Diego's party. The same night Dante first told her he loved her. Grace tore her mouth from his. The belly dancer's costume she wore brought a fleeting smile to her lips. Letting go of what was, Grace brought them back to Elysium. Neither of them could change the past. "I am not willing to trade what Rayne and I have for you. You made your choice. Contrary to what you thought at the time, with Rayne and Lyal's help, all of us could have walked out of the temple. Instead of trusting in our ability to overcome, you manipulated fate."

"There was no scenario where the three of us left the temple alive, Grace. I did what was best for all of us."

Grace scoffed, wondering how he could rationalize the decision to contractually sign her over to another man. "You took away Rayne's and my freewill by negotiating the outcome without ever including our voice in that decision."

"Rayne loved you then as much as I did. And you loved him.

Without me in the picture, you would have found your way back to one another. I merely accelerated the process." Dante brushed his thumb down her cheek, hating the hurt and frustration on her face.

"I loved you, Dante. I trusted you. You completely betrayed that trust by striking a bargain with the High Council. You put my poor husband through hell by making him a party to something he knew I would loathe. I understand your reasoning for doing so, but the damage is still done."

"If there was a way I could..." Dante wished he could tell her how much he suffered living apart from her. If only she knew how close to her side he had stayed, even though she could not see him. How many times he reached out to brush away the silent tears she shed before she willingly sought Rayne's arms for comfort. He clasped her hand and brought it to his lips. "Know this god is forever a humble servant at your feet, my beloved star. Rayne is a blessed man to have the only woman to hold the sun's heart. Let me return you to him."

Córdoba - 812

Rayne abandoned the celebratory races after the messenger he sent to get Grace advised his wife was nowhere to be found. He frantically searched the house for her. Grace's sudden reappearance in the courtyard told him exactly where she had been.

"Have you chosen a god over a Horseman?"

Shadows danced across his face in the flickering light. Grace's heart was in her throat for the second time in ten minutes. Between the black material of his old general's uniform and his dark hair, the blue eyes locked on her blazed brighter than the nearby torches. He was livid with the way he walked towards her.

"I turned the lion down. I prefer the company of the wolf."

The anger disappeared from his face. She reached for him. His arms enveloped her tightly. Clasping his shoulders, Grace inhaled the comforting musk of leather, clove, and natural scent of her husband. Hints of smoke intermingled with the more familiar smells. She could never trade the peace he gave her or his love for the attention of another. Did he really fear Dante coming between them?

"Irrational old worries anytime he is near you. I can accept that part of you will always belong to Dante, and that he will always love you. But I cannot endure the loss of my wife. I have grown to love you more than I ever thought possible, Grace."

"I love you, Rayne. I hope one day you will learn to trust in that versus fearing some temperamental sun god, not allowed to see your wife, will take her from your arms."

"Grace, I—" Rayne started to say something, but her lips pressing up against his prevented him from continuing. He returned the fervent kiss, mystified by it and the way Grace now trembled. When their lips finally parted, Grace stared up at him with an intensity he hadn't seen in her before. He briefly thought he had gone insane, hearing her whisper the Ancient's binding spell; the Latin words melodiously flowed off her tongue, uniting her soul and his for eternity.

Rayne never expected her to do such a thing. She detested the old spell. Having heard her curse Dante and the Ancients for tricking her into speaking it to Dante, he accepted that she would never utter her portion of it to him. The only reason he spoke the first half binding himself to her was to bring her back to the realm of the living. Her freely granting him such a sacred gift brought tears to his eyes. He buried his face in her neck and hair, not wanting anyone else to see how much his wife's gesture touched his heart.

Grace allowed the immortal to keep his face hidden. She knew his sense of pride. "Forever yours, Rayne. Not even a god can undo that vow once spoken."

He rewarded her dedication with a deep laugh. The joyful smile on her face when he finally pulled back to look at her made his heart soar. She so easily erased the greatest fear that lurked deep within him. "You have asked for your husband's story on so many occasions. For the first time in centuries, he is not afraid to revisit his past."

Grace held his hand tightly while they walked over to the bench in front of the fountain where he had been attacked and Priya killed. He motioned for her to sit. After joining her on the worn wooden seat,

Rayne opened the door to years he had never freely shared with anyone else since becoming a Horseman.

"I was born Haroun Ibn-Ziyad, the only son of Saladin Ibn-Ziyad and his second wife, Lillian Dalglese, in 771. My mother gave birth to me in this house. I spent most of my childhood in Córdoba..."

THIRTEEN

Córdoba - 776

The steady patter of rain against the tile roof shifted to the louder whoosh of a downpour, bringing a five-year-old Rayne running to the front of the house. He climbed onto the oversized chair below one glass pane and anxiously peered outside to observe the darkened world beyond the walls confining him.

Lillian smiled, knowing what brought her son racing from his room. She continued sewing a new shirt for Saladin. Sherifa, Saladin's first wife, wove a delicate cloth on the loom beside her.

Yasmina, Sherifa and Saladin's daughter, chased after her sibling who had escaped from the confines of their play area. The girl was a few years older than Rayne. She shook her head at how the unexpected storm spurred the boy into such an excited state. "I do not understand your obsession with the rain, Haroun."

Rayne saw his father and uncle ride into the yard together. The weather had brought his father home from the boundaries of Al-Andalus. "The rain brings Baba home!"

"Haroun, do not—" Lillian scolded her son.

Rayne tuned out his mother as the sound of male voices grew

louder. He focused on the blurred outlines of his father and uncle. The two men quickly make their way towards the house. Scampering down off the chair, Rayne ran to the front door, not caring that his behavior was not proper for the future patriarch of the Ibn- Ziyad family. He tugged on the metal ring, trying to jerk the heavy door open.

The slab gave way as Saladin carefully pushed it inward. He gently caught Rayne around the waist to prevent him from escaping into the muddy yard. "How many times must I tell you to always be aware of who is at the door before opening it, Haroun?"

"I knew it was you, Baba."

Saladin picked Rayne up and settled him against his side. He chuckled as Rayne asked question after question about the Franks. "You are as energetic and relentless as the storm outside. Perhaps I should have named you Rain instead of Haroun. Allow me to find dry clothing and something warm to drink, and then I will answer all of your questions, my son."

By the dark circles under her husband's eyes, Saladin returned exhausted. Lillian set down her sewing to retrieve Rayne. "He missed you. We all have."

"My beloved, the nights were lonely and cold without you," Saladin whispered. Favoritism amongst the women he married was forbidden, but Lillian was the one woman who held his heart.

She smiled and glanced down at her feet.

Saladin gave her a kiss on her forehead. He cleared his throat, addressing everyone in the room. "I thought of my family this week. We are blessed to live in an untroubled territory."

Saladin kept Rayne in one arm and kissed Sherifa's cheek, greeting her then Yasmina. Once all had been recognized, Saladin headed toward his chambers. He softly called Lillian's name and nodded his head, indicating she should follow him. Lillian walked behind her husband and son.

"Did you watch over your mother and sisters as I asked, Haroun?" Reaching his chambers, Saladin set the boy down to remove his sword and dagger.

"Yes, Baba."

"And if I ask Aziz, he will confirm you completed all of your studies as required?" Saladin raised a brow at Rayne's change in demeanor. The sullen look on the young boy's face meant something occurred with the tutor while he was away.

"He only tested Aziz twice in your absence. I reminded him of the responsibility he has to learn more than the other boys with being your son." Lillian retrieved a dry shirt from a trunk for Saladin.

Saladin pulled Lillian to him and kissed her.

"Our son is watching us," Lillian chastised her husband.

"There is nothing wrong with him learning a husband should desire and love his wives. He will have at least one wife of his own someday." Saladin took the dry clothing she offered him.

The long scimitar and dagger resting on the table fascinated Rayne. Even though his father forbade him from handling the weapons, Rayne found himself drawn to them. Little fingers ran down the leather scabbard that curved, following the long blade it housed. The sapphire and diamond hilt of the dagger shimmered in the flickering lamplight. He quietly pulled the smaller weapon to him. He glanced at his parents. They still spoke after Saladin changed. His fingers wrapped around the dagger's hilt and he slowly drew the blade from its sheath.

"Haroun! That is not one of your toys!" Saladin barked after noticing a flash of light reflecting off the bared silver blade in his peripheral vision.

Rayne dropped the weapon. "I... I... I am.... I am sorry."

"You are too curious at times! While this is smaller than the sword, it is no less deadly. Do not let the gems fool you into thinking it a mere decoration."

Rayne gulped back the tears that welled up at being punished. "Forgive me, Baba."

"You are forgiven. Do not touch any of my weapons again." Saladin placed both armaments in a wardrobe Rayne could not open. Lillian started towards the boy to soothe his embarrassment, but Saladin stopped her. "He must learn the consequences of bearing arms. One shoulders a grave duty once they carry them."

"Ya Baba, have you killed men with the knife?"

Stunned by Rayne's question, Saladin let out a troubled breath. He looked down into blue eyes; eyes a slight shade darker than Lillian's. He did not wish to shatter innocence in one so young, but he could not demand his son speak with honesty if he did not do so himself. "Yes, Haroun. I only ever take a life when there is no other recourse to doing so. There is no honor in arbitrarily killing anyone. Remember that when you come of age to fight for your family and the Emirate."

Lillian dreaded the idea of her son becoming a soldier. "May he become a counselor or vizier."

"Even statesmen must be well-versed in the matters of warfare." Saladin understood his wife's angst. He would prefer his son live in peace over battle, but men did not always have a choice between the two.

Rayne proudly puffed out his chest. "I will become a great general, like my father."

Saladin chuckled, ruffling Rayne's hair. "I see the storm in you once more, Haroun. Let us pray peace reigns when you are a man, and generals are no longer needed. You must learn all you can now, Rayne. Knowledge allows for greater negotiation and leadership than brute strength alone."

"Why do you call me Rayne, Baba?"

"Because you love this wretched weather and possess the same energy the storm does, my boy."

Córdoba - 812

Grace smiled at Rayne. "So that's how you got your nickname?"

"Yes."

"Based on your ambassadorial roles, you took your father's words to heart about knowledge and negotiation."

Rayne grinned. "Not until later in life. Four years passed from that rainy afternoon before my father and I next discussed diplomacy and war. I remember well the day my lessons became about combat instead of the traditional curriculum all boys studied."

Córdoba - 786

An eight-year-old Rayne stared wide-eyed at the horsemen who rode onto his father's property. He had never seen Frankish knights before that morning. The large group of men in armor and flowing white tunics bearing a red cross waited patiently under a flag of truce for Saladin.

Saladin glanced at his young son. "Stay here with your sisters."

For his family's sake, Saladin hoped that the Christian knights would honor the peaceful symbolism of the flag. He had seen them betray the terms of neutrality too many times before.

Mohammed and Sayyid walked across the courtyard with him to the waiting knights. Three men dismounted and stepped forward to meet the Muslim envoy. The duke leading the knights introduced himself with a friendly smile.

Curious to learn what they spoke about, Rayne inched closer to the group. Lillian called him and his two sisters over to her. The two girls obeyed, but he remained where he was.

"Haroun!" Lillian snapped, annoyed that he ignored her.

Lillian's shout interrupted the conversation between Saladin and the duke. They turned to see what caused her to shout.

Spotting the young boy standing a few feet away, defiantly disobeying his mother, the duke chuckled. A mix of curiosity and concern in the boy's expression shared he did not want to leave his father alone with the Christian envoy.

Saladin gave Rayne a scolding glance, then restarted the discussion between him and the duke. Their conversation ended in a friendly fashion.

All the departing knights rode past Rayne, except for the duke. The noble halted his horse before the boy. Saladin and Lillian watched with concern. Saladin's hand rested on the hilt of his weapon as he made his way towards his son.

Unafraid, Rayne stared up at the duke. He was one of the few men he encountered in his young life with eyes almost the same blue as his own.

"Boy, you should mind your mother. Her astuteness, along with your father's statesmanship, will serve you well in the future." The duke placed a medallion around Rayne's neck. "May your courage never falter, Haroun."

Rayne watched the duke ride into the distance before picking up the large crest the man gave him. A silver wolf with sapphire eyes stared up at Rayne. The medallion extended past the edges of his palm and fingers.

"May I keep it, Baba?" Rayne asked his father, who stopped beside him.

"You may." Saladin thought it strange the duke gave such a valuable item to his son.

"Baba, why did those men come to Córdoba?"

Saladin looked from his son to Lillian and his two daughters. "They are an envoy from Aquitaine. They come to meet with Rahman and Abdul. Haroun, go to the armory and retrieve the two sparring swords Mohammed and I use for practice. Wait with them for me in the inner-courtyard."

Lillian watched Rayne disappear into the side building housing tools and arms.

Saladin glanced back at the gate before entering the house.

"Do they bring war to our doorstep?" Lillian anxiously asked her husband.

"No." Saladin's face remained grim. "But it is time Haroun learn the art of soldiery. I fear dark days lie ahead."

Lillian and Sherifa watched father teach son how to hold a sword then basic moves of engagement.

"I lose my sweet boy today," Lillian mumbled.

Saladin disarmed Rayne then gently knocked him to the ground. Rayne lay on his back, stunned. Saladin explained what Rayne did wrong before helping the boy to his feet.

Sherifa hugged Lillian close. "Saladin ensures Haroun's survival. It is a curse all men must bear."

Córdoba - 812

Grace knew boys frequently joined armies prior to the twentieth century; even so, the idea of young kids seeing the horrors of war bothered her. "I can't imagine becoming a soldier so young. Did the Emirate truly allow an eight-year-old into its army?"

"My father shielded me from actual warfare for as long as he could. I spent hours training with my father, then my uncle or my father's soldiers for several years. My father kept most of my training a secret. He feared Abdul conscripting me into the army. Shortly after my fifteenth birthday, Córdoba came under attack. My father commanded the defense of the city."

786 - Córdoba

Rayne followed his father outside. "Baba, I want to go with you."

"No. You must stay here, Haroun. Look after our family. They may need you." Saladin mounted his horse.

"I can fight as well as any of your soldiers."

Pride swelled within Saladin as he stared down at his son. Haroun was caught between the years in which one is neither a child nor a man. "Which is why I leave you in charge of defending our home. Your time for military service will come soon enough."

Watching his father and a group of soldiers ride off into the distance, Rayne cursed. *I should be on the walls of the city with the rest of the men! Instead, I am left behind like a child. I am no longer a boy.* Could his father not see that?

"Secure the gates," Rayne directed the two gatemen before returning to the house.

For the next two days, pillars of smoke extended skyward from burning structures and siege towers. Every so often, the distinctive sound of a stone and clay building shattering from a projectile launched from enemy siege engines echoed in the distance. The loud boom followed by a swirl of white and beige dust always drew Rayne's eyes toward the eastern city walls. If the walls did not hold, the Franks may reach the Ibn-Ziyad home.

Rayne sat on an upstairs window ledge, eating an apple, and reading a book. The morning seemed strange with the birds singing while men clashed over the city only a few miles away.

"Haroun, riders approach!" An out of breath sentry warned the youth Saladin left in charge.

Rayne followed the sentry out of the home's gates to identify if those that neared were friend or foe. Seeing the Frankish banner and red cross, a feeling of dread settled over him. Men carrying those banners and outfitted for war would not pay them an amicable visit. They only had a few minutes before the riders bore down upon them.

"Brace the gate. All women and children must be moved inside."

Rayne called for Lillian as he pulled the weaponry and protective clothing his father had given him from his wardrobe. When he turned, she stood in the doorway, anxiously wringing her hands. "You must go into the tunnels. Take everyone with you. Remain hidden until Father or I retrieve you," Rayne directed, donning the leather vest and chainmail.

Lillian nodded. "Be careful, Haroun."

"All will be well, Mother."

Lillian mustered a smile, then went to gather the women and children under the protection of the Ibn-Ziyad family. She urged them to quietly and quickly descend into the hidden passageway under the main hall. Rayne started to close the false floor to conceal their hiding place. Realizing her niece wasn't among them, Lillian stopped him from locking them in. "Haroun, Nezha is missing."

"I will find her." Rayne secured the door in place.

Enflamed arrows sailed over the walls, announcing the arrival of the enemy. He frantically searched the yard for his missing cousin. The gate would not withstand the battering ram for long. He shouted for the girl a year younger than himself.

She raced from the stable and through the smoke towards him. The gate shattered as she attempted to cross the last fifty yards between them. One of the mounted knights seized her.

Rayne sprinted to them, unsheathing his sword. He sliced through the girth of the soldier's saddle. The saddle slipped sideways, sending the man and Nezha tumbling to the ground.

Before the knight could regain his footing, Rayne knocked him backwards. Rayne mechanically moved through the entire encounter. He swung the heavy blade in his hand, beheading the downed knight. The man's head rolled a few feet away.

Rayne yanked Nezha to her feet. "Find some place to hide!"

Nezha ran off toward the house.

Four more men encircled Rayne, wanting retaliation for his killing their peer. He raised his weapon, prepared to fight them all.

Mohammed rode through the gate just ahead of Saladin after word was sent that the Ibn-Ziyad home fell under siege. He watched in disbelief as his young nephew took down one man after another.

"Haroun, to your back!" Saladin shouted, noticing a soldier taking advantage of Rayne being engaged with another opponent.

The man knocked Rayne to the ground. Saladin spurred his horse forward then leapt from the saddle, landing between the man and his son. His sword catching the knight's blade as it descended towards Rayne. In two swift motions, he finished off the assailant.

Once his home was secure, Saladin felt a slight sense of relief. Things could have gone much worse had Rayne not been left behind. He frowned, observing Rayne searching the courtyard. "The Franks are gone, Haroun."

"I need to find Nezha."

"Is she not inside with the others?" Saladin took in the carnage surrounding their home. More men had been within the home's walls than he initially thought.

Rayne shook his head. "The fight came upon us quickly. She was in the stables and tried to cross to the house."

"Haroun!" A girl screamed.

Rayne and Saladin turned. One last knight held Nezha captive. She struggled against the man using her as a shield.

"Let her go. I will give you safe passage if you do," Saladin bargained for her life.

"As if I would trust a Moor." The man continued toward the gate.

Mohammed and another of Saladin's men blocked the exit, cutting off the man's only path to freedom.

"She dies if you do not clear the gate!" The desperate knight shouted.

Saladin pivoted, keeping an eye on the panicked man. "Do nothing rash, Christian. The girl commits no wrong against you."

Noting the knight had lost his helmet in the fight, Rayne ripped the dagger from his father's side then hurled it at the man holding his cousin hostage. The weapon struck the Franc in the center of the forehead. He collapsed to the ground. Nezha screamed before running to her father.

Saladin stared over at his son. They stood almost the same height now. Rayne's face and shirt bore blood, sweat, and dust, just as his own did.

"Never have I seen such confidence in one's aim as your son displays, Saladin," Abdul remarked, entering the gate. "He is his father's son."

Saladin scowled, but acknowledged the caliph with a nod. "Haroun, go free those within the house."

Rayne thought his father's order strange, but did as instructed.

"Haroun fights as well as any seasoned soldier." Abdul approached Saladin.

Saladin shook his head. "These were not well-trained men, Emir. My son is still young yet. He has much to learn before becoming one of your officers."

"He is fifteen. There are much younger soldiers in our ranks." Abdul knew Saladin would object to what he was going to order.

"I hold out hope of a different path for Haroun."

Abdul laughed. "We all pray for peace. But that can only be achieved through a powerful army to defend our people. Your son held off ten knights with only three other men. He is ready for a commission. If it eases your conscience, I will place him under your command until he proves he is worthy of his own."

"We accept your generous offer, Emir," Rayne cut off his father's forthcoming objection, rejoining the men in the courtyard. "I will report with my father in the morning. We need to ensure our home is secure, and all are accounted for this evening."

"I am pleased to welcome you, Haroun. Good day, Saladin." Abdul departed to ensure other nearby homes did not experience the same attack Saladin's suffered.

"Haroun, you did well today. Now… let us deliver the news of your new position to your mother," Saladin grimly complimented his son, not looking forward to Lillian's reaction once she learned Abdul appointed Haroun a new officer in the royal army.

Saladin waited until after dinner to disclose Rayne's acceptance of a position as a defender of the Emirate.

Rayne stood with his father watching shock then anger cross his mother's face.

"Lillian, I know your feelings on this…." Saladin tried to placate his upset spouse.

"You should have told Abdul no, Saladin." Lillian argued with her husband for the first time Rayne could recall.

"You know I cannot refuse him."

Lillian glared at her husband. "Damn your honor and fealty to a man who places our son in harm's way! He is your only male heir. What shall you do if he dies?"

"Mother, do not be angry with Father. I accepted the commission after he discouraged it. These Frankish men and the men from the North do not ride into Córdoba seeking peace. They murder innocent women and children. It is my duty to take up arms to defend my home," Rayne interjected, not understanding what made his mother irrational. Had he not protected them all that very day and lived?

"You men and your talk of duty, and honor, and war!" Lillian scoffed. "These battles are not your sparring sessions with your father, Haroun. Nor are the men you face merciful. What good do you or your sense of honor do for your family if you are dead?"

Rayne's temper ignited. "What would you have me do, Mother? I am no longer a child needing to hide behind your skirts. I am not naïve and comprehend the risks I will face. I will not idly standby to appease you while foreign invaders, these Christian infidels, slaughter our community, our friends, and our family. If these vile men who pretend to honor their supposed savior's guidance are allowed to continue as they are, all of us will die. I would rather die fighting than cowering here in this house with you frightened women."

Lillian slapped him. "We frightened women raised you, fed you, clothed you, protected you, guided you, and educated you. We will continue to do so even though you are ungrateful for what we do. And these infidel European men you place broad judgment on. You are one of them, Rayne. Or do you forget your mother's ancestry as you do your respect for her? The blood of all three peoples of the book flows in your veins. Your mixed heritage is what caused your father and I to believe you are destined to be something greater than all those before you. Now, I am not certain you are anything more than a self-centered, foolish child who suddenly thinks he is a man. No son of mine would dare speak to his elders as you have, nor ignorantly judge men on shallow attributes."

Needing to be alone, Lillian stormed out of the room.

Rayne didn't know how to react to his mother striking him or the tears streaming down her face.

"Never belittle your mother again, Haroun. Your words wound her deeply. It is upsetting enough for her to cope with the idea of her son riding into battle and realizing the boy she loves is now a man ready to find his own way in the world," Saladin gently admonished his son for his remarks.

"I do not understand her anger over this. All men must serve once of age. Is she ashamed of me?"

"No, son." Saladin shook his head and set a hand on Rayne's shoulder. "Lillian, nor I would ever be ashamed of you. I do not think you will be able to comprehend your mother's concerns or mine until you are a father yourself."

"What wrong did I commit by calling the Christian knights infidels?"

Saladin sighed. If his son was of age to take up arms, he was old enough to learn the truth about his mother. "Your mother is a Christian. She is also of Saxon and Frankish descent."

"I am aware of that." Rayne still did not follow what could be so upsetting about those things.

"Haroun, your mother, your mother was stolen from her village by Viking raiders when she was slightly younger than yourself. Pirates and Persian traders then assisted the raiders with selling her on the slave markets. I met your mother in Baghdad. The Caliph dispatched me at the time to inspect a shipment of slaves and gold offered in tribute to the sultan. I discovered Lillian amongst the slaves that were to go to the sultan's harem. After speaking with her, I could not let her vanish behind the walls of the palace. I lied to the vizier, telling him Lillian belonged to me. That her father betrothed her to me as an act of fealty in Córdoba and the trader stole her from my household. Because of my standing, the vizier believed me. To make up for the perceived embarrassment to the Ibn-Ziyad family, the sultan ordered her release and arranged for us to be wed. I love your mother, Haroun; more than any of my wives. I know it is a sin for me to do so, but I do anyway. If my other wives did not depend on our marriage for their general welfare, and if alliances that bring peace to the region would not crumble, I would divorce them all for Lillian." Saladin paused, allowing Rayne to absorb what he disclosed.

"I will not try to justify my actions when it comes to your mother, as in many respects, they are inexcusable. I believe your mother reminds you this afternoon not to judge others by their faith, ancestry, or any other generic attribute, but instead, judge them on the merit of their deeds. There are varying degrees of good and bad within us all. She and I hope men born of unions like ours will create a better world for future generations. We know you are no longer a child, Rayne. Give her time to calm then apologize to her. Thank her for the good she has done for you and reassure her she will always be important to you. She greatly fears her son turning into a bigoted man obsessed with power and war. That if you fight in the army, you will become the worst of men, like those who stole her or sold her. Prove to her that fear is unfounded, my son. I will do the same when you are not present."

"I am nothing like those men. I only fight to protect my family and home." Rayne still worked through the shock of the day.

"I know you are not. Your moral compass is much stronger than most. But you must learn words hold power, Rayne. They wound as much as the blade. Wars arise out of phrases spoken by men like us when we are angry. I am proud of your actions and courage today. Your mother is too. Just as a wise man understands the power of words, he comprehends the importance of admitting when he is wrong."

"I will apologize to Mother."

<hr>

Córdoba - 812

A shrill cry of alarm prevented Rayne from continuing his story. Saladin shouted orders from the front of the house. Rayne and Grace joined the patriarch of the family in the outer yard. Two men lay dead on either side of the gate. Rayne settled his hand on the nearest one to see what had happened. Grace noticed the way both men's necks were broken.

"Dante," Grace mumbled the god's name. He had to be the assassin.

He was definitely here. Rayne's voice sounded in her head.

"Father, do you know these men?" Rayne worried about the sun god's strike.

"Not well. Your uncle hired them two weeks ago."

"I do not mean to offend you or Mother, but I believe it is best that Grace and I return to my home instead of remaining here another night."

Saladin hated that the assassins Malik warned of were on his property. "Shall I send an escort with you?"

"There is no need to do so. Grace and I are capable of protecting one another."

Grace and Rayne rode in silence back to Rayne's estate. Kato and several other wolves ran alongside them the last half-mile to the house.

"Great. He lives in this day and age too. And he brought friends tonight," Grace muttered under her breath.

The pack settled themselves around the courtyard as the gates closed.

Reaching the house, Grace and Rayne dismounted.

Handing the reins to the groom who ran up to them, Grace looked over at Rayne. "Care to explain how Kato lives as long as he does? Last I checked, wolves don't have that type of lifespan."

"They aren't your average wolf."

Grace shook her head. "What type of wolf are they? Werewolves?"

"We both know there is no such thing as a werewolf." Rayne chuckled, annoying her. "They are a rare, immortal breed."

Kato bared his teeth and growled in Rayne and Grace's direction.

"Kato!" Rayne chided the animal, not believing the wolf threatened them. Seeing the wolf lunge, Rayne drew his weapon and moved Grace out of Kato's path.

Kato attacked a hooded figure neither Grace nor Rayne had noticed.

"Stupid beast never did like me."

The wolf bit into the person's arm. A second silver wolf, almost the same size as Kato, closed in on the intruder.

"Call the damn dogs off before I hurt them."

Rayne whistled. Both obediently sat on either side of him and Grace. "They are excellent judges of character. Care to explain what you are doing here, Xander?"

"Dante sent me. The two men he killed threatened him."

Grace wondered what was going on. "They threatened Dante? Where did they possibly encounter him?"

Xander shrugged. "I don't have all the details, Grace. He only wanted me to warn you. Oh, and he said to give you this from Tessa."

Kato and Sulla growled at the demon as he kissed Grace on the cheek.

"Shut up before I make rugs out of you!"

The remark only made their growling louder.

Rayne praised the wolves after Xander vanished.

Grace shook her head. "Xander is harmless. You shouldn't encourage their dislike of him."

"They hate all uninvited guests. I will not discourage that behavior."

The wolves followed them to the door.

Rayne once again sat in the large chair before the fireplace lost in thought, absentmindedly sipping the sherry in his hand. He had not said a word since they entered the house.

"You never told me the outcome of the races." Grace broke the bothersome silence.

Her voice snapped him out of his contemplations. "I won my three. My father won the others."

"You look tired. We should call it a night."

Sensing he stewed over the events of the day, Grace set her hands on his shoulders. She massaged the tension out of them.

Appreciating how she worked a knot out of the base of his neck, he closed his eyes and dropped his head forward. When it finally gave way, he looked up at her. "Why don't you get ready for bed? I will join you as soon as I finish my drink."

"Don't leave me waiting too long, Commander. I believe you are owed a reward for your victories tonight."

An interested, half grin emerged on his face, surfacing a dimple in his right cheek. "Tribute is usually paid by the defeated, not one who did not partake in the competition."

"A wife honors her husband's might and good fortune. If you will not freely accept her offering, she is more than happy to make you earn it."

"There has been enough conflict today. I would rather accept whatever you wish to offer, leof. I will be up shortly."

Grace let him have the solitude he sought.

Hearing her footsteps move down the wooden hallway floor above then their bedroom door close, Rayne set his glass down.

Elysium -

With the children in bed, Dante was the only one awake in his home. He sat in his study reading Council Records on Isra and other Cordovan djinn, hoping to uncover something that could assist Grace and Rayne. They offered little more information than what he already knew. The quiet solitude of the late hour offered him some much-needed calm for the night. The crackling of flame gradually eroding wood in the fire place eased his restless conscience.

"What were you doing in Córdoba tonight?"

Dante jumped at the unexpected inquiry. Discovering Rayne scowling at him, he frowned. "First, a surprise visit from your spouse, and now you interrupt my evening." He shut the file in his hands and leaned back in his desk chair.

"Answer the question, Dante."

"I went to your father's to apologize to Grace." Dante partially told the truth. Hell, he wasn't sure of why he sought her out. "Upon my arrival, I overheard the two gatemen speaking of assassinating you and her. The messenger you dispatched alerted them to your returning to retrieve Grace. Sensing me there, they attacked me. I defended myself. As soon as I put them on the ground thinking their injuries would eliminate any further bloodshed, they rose up and assaulted me again. The only option I had to ensure they didn't harm you or Grace was to kill them."

"What offense did you cause my wife that required an apology?"

"What affairs did the mortal Haroun conduct for two djinn to attempt to murder him and his wife?" Dante studied Rayne for any hint of insight surrounding the djinn.

"I will take care of the djinn." Rayne left Elysium.

CHAPTER

FOURTEEN

Córdoba - 812

Grace walked with Lillian through the marketplace, buying food and supplies for the next week. She noticed Kato creeping behind the stalls. The wolf kept pace with the women. Grace called him over to her, so he didn't spook people by roaming the market alone. He trotted out from behind the stall then sat in between the fruit merchant and baker's booths. Grace smiled and petted his head telling him to stay.

Seeing Kato beside the fruit vendor's table, Lillian dropped the orange in her hand. "Shoo! Go away!"

"He is harmless, Lillian." Grace doubted her words as she spoke. "Leave him be."

"I have never liked that beast Haroun keeps. A wild animal is never fully tamed, especially a wolf." Lillian retrieved her orange.

The creeping sensation of someone watching them caused Grace's eyes to scan the crowd for anything unusual. Nothing seemed out of place.

A necklace hanging from a rod in the booth in front of her swung in the breeze. She stopped the pendant's rocking, then turned the metal coin, wondering if the Fates tried to send her a message. The outline of someone behind her appeared in the polished surface. With a hand on the dagger she carried, she turned to find herself alone. No one stood to her rear. Instinct warned her to be alert.

Lillian noted how Grace glanced over her shoulder. "What troubles you, Grace?"

"Nothing. I thought I heard a familiar voice. That is all."

Kato remained where he was, calming her some. The wolf would alert her to an enemy.

Lillian thanked the baker for the fresh loaf of bread he handed her. Someone barreled into Lillian, sending the warm bread flying.

Grace yanked the man from her mother-in-law. He shoved Grace into the baker's table. The baskets of bread stacked on the top of it tumbled and rolled all over. She grabbed a broom someone left propped against a nearby wall then turned and whacked him with the wooden handle, briefly knocking him sideways. Now angered that his attempted robbery was thwarted, he ran toward Grace. Using the makeshift weapon, she flipped the thief, so he tumbled backward. Dazed, the man sat on the ground and shook his head.

Kato charged from between the booths, jumped on the man, and pinned him down. The man screamed as the wolf snapped at his face. Two large front paws rested on his chest.

"Kato!" Rayne called the wolf, coming towards Grace and Lillian.

Obeying his master, Kato slowly backed away from the assailant.

Rayne firmly gripped the shirt of the man who assaulted his mother and wife then yanked him to his feet. The man begged the menacing figure holding him hostage to let him go.

"I have never seen a woman fight as you do. Are you unharmed?" Lillian whispered to Grace.

Grace nodded, watching Rayne and the man. Whatever question Rayne posed made the man pale. She knew the inquiry was part threat by the expression on Rayne's face. She didn't need to speak whatever language they used to understand Rayne warned the man about something.

The stranger groveled for his freedom. Rayne released his hold on him. Instead of running, the bandit knelt before Rayne, continuing to plead with the Horseman. His doing so flabbergasted Grace.

Rayne picked up the discarded loaf of bread that landed on the crafter's table and held it out to him. The man snatched it from Rayne's hands. After a quick thank you, he scurried off.

Rayne walked over to Grace. "Damned thief! Are you hurt?"

"I am fine. What exactly was he after?"

"The bread until he noticed your wedding ring."

"He must be starving to risk his life for a loaf of bread."

"Most women he robs do not fight back, nor are their husbands frequently nearby. He told me he was hungry. Umar banished him, making him ineligible for any sort of employment. He honestly meant you and my mother no harm. He only wishes to feed himself and his family."

Being an immortal guardian, Grace rarely had to worry about food or shelter. At times, her status caused her to overlook the day-to-day plight of the humans she and the Horsemen protected. "Do you know where he lives?"

Rayne smiled. "I had a feeling you would ask that."

Grace purchased some dates and oranges from the next stall over, while Rayne requested another loaf of bread from the baker. Realizing what Grace intended to do, Lillian bought the man a freshly butchered piece of lamb. Grace added the wrapped slice of lamb to the basket she carried.

Lillian took the other basket holding the groceries Grace purchased for her and Rayne. "I will ensure your foodstuffs are delivered to your home. Be careful when you visit the man."

Rayne kissed his mother on the cheek. "Thank you, Mother."

Kato jogged beside Grace and Rayne as they walked the winding street to where the thief claimed to live.

Three small children played near a crumbling structure Grace assumed was their house. A woman sent one of the little boys into the building upon seeing Grace and Rayne. The man from the market came outside, the panic on his face conveyed he dreaded the reason Haroun Ibn-Ziyad and his wife came to his home.

"Spare my family, Haroun. Please, emir. They are not guilty of my transgressions."

Rayne raised his hand. "Stop! Neither you nor your family are in any danger."

By the nervous darting of the man's eyes between his visitors and his family, Grace and Rayne knew he feared for his family's well-being.

Grace wasn't certain if the man and his family spoke anything other than Riffian, but she tried to communicate with them in Arabic. "We won't hurt you. We bring you food."

Neither the woman nor the man understood her. Before Rayne could translate, a little girl asked Grace in Arabic what she brought them. Grace pulled one orange out of the basket she carried and held it out. The girl ran up to her, took the fruit from her hand, then peered into the basket on her arm.

Rayne grinned at the girl's willingness to interact with Grace. Leave it to children to freely extend trust and mend broken bridges.

She excitedly shouted to her siblings and parents about what the general and his wife brought them. Grace held out the basket to the woman who cautiously approached.

"It is safe to take what we offer. We know you are hungry," Rayne assured the woman they did not entrap her or her husband.

The woman carefully took the basket from Grace's hand then hurried back into the house.

Confused, the man grabbed Rayne's arm. "I robbed your wife. Why do you repay me with this kindness?"

"Because you committed the offense out of a desire to feed others. I have work that can be done for a wage. What was your profession?"

The man bashfully looked down at his feet, ashamed of harming Haroun's wife. "Before Umar banished me, I was a mason in the palace."

"A mason? I know of a project or two that can benefit from a mason. Come see me in the morning. I will provide materials to repair your home."

"Thank you, emir," The man mumbled, not believing the Devil of Al-Andalus showed such generosity.

Rayne nodded before taking Grace's hand and leading her towards Fahkir.

The man wondered where the horse had come from. He swore Haroun and the woman came to his home on foot.

***

The next morning, the mason arrived shortly after breakfast to see how he could assist Rayne. Grace smiled, standing near a window and watching her husband, the estate manager, and their new employee talking. Rayne returned to the house after he had introduced the mason and estate manager to one another.

"Do you trust him?" Grace inquired as Rayne shut the front door.

"I do. I have seen the man's sins. He only committed them out of desperation. Regular employment will keep him away from any further entanglements with the law or Umar."

"Seen his sins? Can you see such things in people?"

Rayne looked out the window at his new hire before making eye contact with Grace. "All the Horsemen can read people's pasts. There is nothing in his that concerns me."

"That is different from seeing someone's misdeeds."

"There is no difference between the two, my love." Rayne wrapped an arm around her.

Grace returned the glowing smile he gave her. "What are you doing that you need to touch me, Horseman?"

"Counting my blessings."

"Oh? What do you see, Commander?" Grace interlocked her fingers against the back of his neck, enjoying the private moment with him.

"That you were a mean older sister with the pranks you pulled on your brother. Poor Braden, having to be tormented by you."

"He returned the favor many times." Grace laughed, thinking back to those days with her younger brother. "Anything else?"

"No."

"Are you certain there is nothing else? Perhaps, another sin I should atone for?" Grace flirted with her husband. His deep chuckle shared he perfectly understood what was on her mind.

"I will make you complete penance for those thoughts this evening. Unfortunately, I have to meet with Malik's emissary."

Grace kissed him. "Such an honorable man, holding to your commitments instead of succumbing to the lure of blissful temptation."

Rayne laughed. "I try to live rightly, even when my wife tempts me to do otherwise. Raphael awaits me outside."

"Please be careful. Malik doesn't like being told no."

"I can manage Malik."

"I know you can handle the human. It's Garsea operating behind the scenes I worry about. I sense discord today."

"Garsea will meet his end a second time if he delays me returning home to my wife. I fully intend to honor my vow about penance this evening."

A knock at the door ended their discussion.

"Stop worrying, Grace. Raphael and my father will be with me. I will see you this evening." Rayne kissed her one last time before grabbing his gloves and opening the door.

"Good luck!" Grace shouted from the doorway, watching the three men leave for the palace.

CHAPTER
FIFTEEN

Córdoba - 812

Grace strolled alongside a field of wheat hired hands had carefully maintained in Rayne's absence. A small olive grove grew opposite of it. She stopped to admire the surrounding landscape. Rayne owned some of the most fertile land in the area.

A pasture over, the mason and two others repaired a small stone barn. From the roof of the barn, the men could see something large making its way toward the lady of the house. They frantically waved their arms, shouted, and pointed, trying to get her attention.

A loud snarl came from behind Grace. She turned and gasped. A massive, mangy black wolf barreled straight towards her. With the men watching, she couldn't use her powers. She sprinted toward the house, praying she could outrun the wolf.

Elysium -

Dante sat speaking with his mother while keeping a watchful eye on Tessa and Tarquin playing in the rear gardens.

Tarquin stared into the pool he swam in a few minutes earlier. An image of a woman in a field danced across the fluttering surface of clear water before him. The woman looked a lot like his mother. "Mama?"

Dante heard his son's confused whisper. By the panicked look on Tarquin's face and his lack of response, Dante knew something was wrong. "Tarquin?"

Tarquin saw the black beast charging at Grace. "Mama!"

His voice raising brought Dante down the portico steps.

"Run, Mama!" Tarquin screamed.

Dante hugged Tarquin to him. The Horsemen's gift of sight shouldn't be developing in his son at such a young age. Touching Tarquin, Dante could see everything the boy did. The vision didn't originate from Tarquin's destined role in the world. Something or someone else purposely triggered the scene of the wolf chasing Grace. Unable to intervene, Dante requested Ares's help. "Ares, Grace needs you in Córdoba."

The Greek god appeared in the vision, walking in the field with his bow in hand. Grace yelled for Destahn. She hadn't noticed Ares yet. Destahn rode towards Grace. Sulla and Kato followed a few feet behind the Horseman. Crying now, Tarquin clutched Dante.

"She will be all right, Tarquin. Destahn and Ares will help her."

Not wanting Tarquin to see the coming fight, Dante severed the tie between Tarquin and the being who projected the vision. He turned, looking for Maria. "Mama, take him inside. I will deal with whatever black magic this is."

Maria gently guided Tarquin away from the pool. She kept him distracted as they walked to the house.

Dante turned his attention back to events in Spain. The unmistakable frigid grip of dark magic now settled on him. "Using children to relay a message is a dastardly trick only executed by cowards."

Córdoba -

Ares drew back his bow, targeting whatever chased Grace in case Destahn didn't reach her in time.

Sulla flew at the other wolf, trying to take it down.

Grace glanced over her shoulder after hearing a yip. The larger wolf had thrown Sulla to the ground. It closed the distance between them faster than she could run.

Destahn leaned slightly in the saddle and extended his hand towards her. "Grace!"

Grace knew the maneuver Destahn executed. She took another two steps, then sprung upwards, grasping Destahn's hand. The wolf now only a few paces away. Destahn heaved her up into the saddle with him.

Ares's arrow struck the wolf as it bounded into the air. The injured beast landed and slid across the ground before turning to follow Destahn and Grace. She couldn't believe the thing managed to run like it did with an arrow in its side.

"It's still coming."

Again, the wolf quickly closed the gap between them.

Destahn urged his horse to a faster pace. "How is the damn thing moving so fast?"

Worried they might not be able to outrun it, Destahn drew his sword. With Grace in the saddle behind him, engaging whatever this wolf was would be risky.

"Ares, slow it down," Grace called to the god reloading his bow.

As Ares raised his weapon, another's arrow struck the wolf. This time, it collapsed and didn't get back up.

Grace saw the second archer in the distance before he disappeared. *Dante. You risk too much.*

The god didn't respond.

Destahn had seen Dante, too. "He knows how far to push the Council, Grace. I want to know what type of wolf that was. Ares's shot should have killed it."

Destahn rode back to the downed wolf.

"It's stunned, not dead," Ares cautioned after Destahn dismounted.

Grace realized the wolf was no wolf at all, but a demon of some type. "What is it?"

Recognizing what pursued Grace, Destahn shook his head. "Djinn. A very old one. If this bastard gets up again, ride straight to the barn and summon Rayne."

The demon-wolf stared up at the Horseman. Destahn ignored its growl and took another step closer. It snarled one last time before vanishing. He picked up a silver chain and emblem left behind in the grass.

Kato whimpered and nuzzled Sulla.

"Sulla." Grace jumped to the ground and slowly approached the wounded animal that protected her. She stroked the wolf's neck. Blood continued to seep from the bite wound. "Can we save him, Ares?"

Ares knelt down beside the two of them. Kato looked up at the god.

"I think we can. I've never tried this before." Ares handed Grace his bow.

Grace took the weapon, hoping Ares could keep Sulla alive.

Ares whispered to the wolf in Greek while slowly passing his hand over the wound. Sulla let out a low, tormented sound.

Grace reassuringly petted him. "Hang in there, Sulla. Thank you for trying to help me."

Ares picked up the wolf once he closed the wound enough he could safely move Sulla. "Let's get him back to the barn."

Destahn motioned for Grace to mount up. "Just to be safe, you are riding back with me."

Elysium -

Tarquin anxiously looked up at his father after the god returned home.

Dante smiled and set his bow on a nearby table. "Your mother is safe, Tarquin. Ares shot the wolf."

Tarquin threw his arms around Dante's waist. Dante held his son, praying none of the Council noticed what he had done.

Córdoba -

Rayne and Raphael rode through the gates of Rayne's home. Destahn riding towards them with Grace sitting in the saddle behind him surprised Rayne. Ares walked beside Destahn's horse, carrying Sulla. Kato paced nervously between Ares and Destahn.

Rayne dismounted and inspected Sulla's injuries after Ares laid the wolf down. "What happened?"

"A djinn went after Grace. Sulla and Ares slowed him down so I could get to her," Destahn said, looking at his commander.

Rayne rose, not liking how a djinn dared to attack Grace in his fields. An outright attack on his property was the same as a declaration of open warfare from Garsea. "Where is the djinn?"

"Gone. The coward disappeared once we wounded him."

Rayne helped Grace down from Destahn's horse. "Were you hurt at all, leof?"

"I am fine, thanks to these three. We tried to heal Sulla." Grace worried about Sulla.

"He will be okay. Kato!" Rayne called Sulla's littermate. Kato immediately came to him. "Thank you for looking after my wife. Who was the djinn today?"

Kato barked.

"Kamar?" Rayne scowled. "Garsea and Malik should know better."

Grace never knew Rayne could speak to animals. "You actually understand him?"

"Yes. This bodes ill for us. I was a fool to believe Malik would so willingly accept my counteroffer today."

"How do you know Umar didn't send him?"

"Kamar loathes Umar as much as he despises me."

Raphael shifted in the saddle, contemplating how Kamar fit into the overall picture of things. "I am starting to wonder if Malik, Garsea, and Umar are in cahoots together, and their alliance is a threat to someone else for a djinn that hates Umar to go after Grace."

Grace found Raphael's suggestion plausible. She knew Rayne didn't agree by the frown on his face, but he voiced no objection to it. "If they aren't working together, maybe there's another player taking advantage of the chaos? Rayne, I know you believe Garsea is manipulating Umar, but something hasn't felt right about Garsea masterminding all of this."

Her suggestion caused Rayne's brow to arch slightly.

Destahn held out the silver medallion the djinn left behind. "Mayhap, this will provide some insight into Kamar's new boss."

Rayne examined the round silver piece Destahn handed him. "This is not a servant's seal. It is a master's medal."

Ares didn't like the concern on Rayne's face. "Do you recognize the demon it belongs to?"

"Garsea." Rayne approached the uninjured wolf once more. "Kato, are you certain Kamar attacked Grace?"

"Kamar wears the medal to mislead you," said a gray-haired man with pale blue eyes sitting next to Sulla, petting the wolf. "Sulla assisted in Garsea's execution. He feels you should know it would be impossible for Garsea to return after your blade beheaded the djinn."

Rayne politely inclined his head to the ancient shape-shifter. "Ashina."

The half-man, half-wolf smiled over at Rayne. "Sulla also wishes to share his gratitude for how well you care for him and the others. It was his honor to protect your wife. His wounds will heal over the next few days. I will return him to you once he recovers."

"I am the honored one with Sulla and Kato welcoming one not of their kind into their pack. Thank you for tending to him."

Ashina vanished with Sulla.

Grace and Rayne sat in silence as they ate dinner. She noted the glower on Rayne's face and the way any slightly heightened noise from outside drew his eyes toward the door. "Are we not safe here?"

"Nothing uninvited can enter this house, leof. As long as we are indoors, we are perfectly safe."

"Then why do you look so worried?" She wished he would share his thoughts.

Rayne reached across the table for Grace's hand. Her fingers closed around his. "I am worried because whoever is behind everything knows me well. They strike multiple targets at once, causing distraction and dividing my attention between conflicts. Raphael and I thwarted an attack on my mother during the same time Destahn and Ares protected you from Kamar. I cannot be in multiple places at once."

"Protect the humans, Rayne. Djinn cannot kill me."

"They cannot, but the oldest of their kind can inflict severe injury on an immortal. The idea of Kamar harming you..." Rayne closed his eyes, knowing well the torture a powerful djinn could perform on an immortal soul.

"Your wife is a fighter like you. Besides, you do not watch over your loved ones alone. You have Isis's support along with Ares's and Xander's. There are also others who watch over your family."

"Others?" Rayne wondered about her choice of descriptor. "As in Lyal?"

"No, ones forbidden to interfere. A second archer caused the injury severe enough to thwart Kamar's attack."

"God or not, Dante's flaunting of authority will get him imprisoned one of these days. It better not be while he is acting guardian over our children. At least I know they are safe."

"How are you and this djinn, Kamar, connected?"

Rayne sat back in his chair and stared down at the table. The past was intended to be exactly that; yet, he found himself forced to disclose more and more of it to his wife. How much would the present unravel? "I knew Kamar before he became a djinn. He was my second-in-command and is Umar's nephew."

Grace hadn't expected that answer. "Rayne, I will love you regardless of whatever happened in your past. Nothing you've ever disclosed has changed my feelings for you. Do not let fear prevent you from sharing things I need to know to help you resolve this mess."

"Kamar and I received our commissions into the army the same morning. We fought side by side from that point forward. Kamar never possessed the ambition or maliciousness his uncle did. I genuinely liked Kamar. He was a good man then."

"What happened for that to change?"

"Umar executed his brother. The wrath and resentment Kamar internalized turned him into what he is now."

A knock on the door interrupted their discussion. Grace hesitated to answer it after the events of the day.

"If they made it past the sentries and Kato, our visitor is not someone to fear." Rayne eased his wife's nerves.

Grace slowly opened the door. Who stood on the other side surprised her. "Saladin?"

"Forgive me for intruding this late. I have important information for my son."

Grace smiled, pulling the door slab further back. "You are more than welcome at any hour. May I offer you a drink?"

"Tea or water, if you have it, please." Saladin followed Grace to the dining room.

"Father?" Rayne hadn't expected their visitor to be Saladin.

Grace went to the kitchen to make Saladin some tea. By the troubled expression on Rayne's face when she joined them, Saladin did not bring good news.

Saladin briefly paused and took the cup from Grace. "Shukran Jazeelan laky."

"Ahlan wa sahlan," Grace replied, sitting down in the empty chair beside Saladin.

After a sip of tea, he continued with what he was saying. "Jalid eavesdropped on a meeting between Malik, Sayyid, and a woman after Malik dismissed his staff, including the haras on duty, two moons ago. He thought the meeting unimportant until he learned of your return and Malik's request that you eliminate Umar."

Rayne's head ever so slightly tilted sideways, his right brow raised, and the corner of his mouth quirked downward. "You have never been one to concern yourself with palace gossip."

Saladin grinned, seeing himself in his son's cynical gaze. "Normally, I would not. However, Jalid insists this meeting was related to you. Before the guards chased him from the door, he heard the woman tell Malik she knew how you could be brought back to Córdoba. That you were not dead, as most believed. She then directed a fourth man, a Damari, to negotiate the terms of their assistance."

"A Damari?" Grace wasn't sure what a damari was.

"That was the man's name."

The continued skeptical expression on Rayne's face conveyed he trusted nothing Jalid relayed to his father. "Did Jalid happen to hear the woman's name?"

Saladin shook his head. "He does not recall it. When I spoke to Sayyid in confidence about such a meeting, Sayyid denies the discussion occurred."

"If Sayyid discredits Jalid's story, the meeting did not occur." Rayne upset his father.

"Sayyid is loyal to Umar, not Malik. Why confirm a plot to assassinate his benefactor? It was Umar who suggested Sayyid as military advisor to Malik. I believe Jalid's story."

"Allow me the evening to think more about this meeting." Hearing the anger in his voice, Rayne tried to appease his father.

Grace's instincts cautioned the meeting connected to Rayne and the attacks. "Was there anything strange or distinctive about the woman and a Damari that Jalid recalled?"

"Yes. He said a Damari had silver eyes. They reminded him of freshly minted dinars."

"Silver eyes? Sounds like a demon. Maybe you should speak with Jalid, Rayne."

Saladin nodded in agreement. "Your wife is a wise woman, Haroun."

His father clearly missed the demon part of Grace's remark. Rayne contemplated the possibility of a demon or djinn being involved in things. Perhaps a Damari would provide the missing link to Garsea and the attacks on his family. "Does Jalid still live near the market?"

"Yes. Two buildings down from the baker." Saladin smiled, pleased that his son changed his mind about meeting with Malik's servant.

"We will go tomorrow evening after Jalid finishes his duties at the palace. With the hour being late, our guestroom is at your disposal, Father. Grace, we should retire for the evening. It appears tomorrow will be another eventful day."

CHAPTER
SIXTEEN

Elysium

Dante sighed. Tessa cried for Rayne a third time that night. Her sobs and a periodic 'Daddy' traveled down the hall from the children's room. Nothing seemed to prevent this nightmare she kept having of Rayne being hurt or killed. When he questioned the Fates about it, they assured him prophecy was not a gift she inherited. She simply missed her father. He fully dressed after climbing out of bed. There was only one thing that would ease the little girl's fears.

Tessa stared up at him, sniffling, when he opened the door to the children's room. Dante sat on her bed and wiped the tears from under her eyes. "Tessa, mia carina, stop crying. Your father is safe."

"But, but the mean lady." Tears streamed down Tessa's face again.

"There is no mean lady. She is a figment of your imagination. It is okay to admit you are scared of being away from home. I was frightened the first time I spent a night away from my home as a child." Dante smiled down at her. "I have a surprise for you, but you need to be very quiet where we are going. Can you do that for me?"

Rubbing her eyes, she nodded her head.

Dante glanced over at Tarquin, amazed the boy slept through all the ruckus. Once Tessa composed herself a bit more, Dante picked her up. She laid her head on his shoulder and clutched his neck with an arm.

"Remember, cara, we need to be very quiet."

"Like sneaky, little mouses."

Dante chuckled. "Yes. Like mice."

Córdoba - 812

Feeling a sudden weight on his chest, Rayne started awake.

"We have to be quiet, Daddy. We can't wake Mommy," Tessa whispered, calming the alarm within her father.

"Tessa? What are you doing here, sprite?"

She missed you. To the point it is giving her nightmares. I wanted her to see for herself that you were safe. Dante stood two feet from him.

"Nightmares? About what?"

Tessa placed a hand over Rayne's mouth. "Shhh... you will wake Mommy."

We will speak in the library then. Rayne scooped Tessa up in one arm and walked to the hallway.

Dante followed them. The library was only two rooms down from the master bedroom.

Rayne motioned to chairs where they could sit. He settled Tessa on his lap. "Now, sprite, tell me about these bad dreams you are having."

Before Tessa even opened her mouth, the tears flowed again. Rayne smiled and wiped them away with his thumbs. "Calm down. There is no reason to cry." He tickled her when she started to whimper and her lower lip jutted out. "No more crying, sweeting. I cannot help if you do not tell me what is wrong. Can you tell me about the dream without crying?"

She nodded, staring up at him. "A bad lady hurt you. You died. We couldn't see you anymore. You lived with Zio."

"Zio?" Rayne wondered who Zio was.

Tessa pointed over at Dante. "Zio. Tarquin's papa."

Dante shrugged when Rayne looked over at him. "She started addressing me as uncle a few days ago."

"Oh, Tessa, that is a scary dream." Rayne hugged her tightly. "I can promise I will not leave you, Tarquin, and Mommy. There are no bad ladies in Spain. Try dreaming about us doing something happy together if that dream starts again."

"Like riding ponies or tea parties?"

Rayne ignored the laugh Dante choked back. "Those are perfect things to dream of instead."

"When are we going home, Daddy?" Tessa snuggled closer to her father. She missed being with him.

"Soon, Tess. As soon as I take care of one more thing here." Rayne laid his head on top of hers, praying he told her the truth. That Fate wouldn't surprise them with an unexpected twist, lengthening his stay in Córdoba.

"Your daughter is beautiful," Saladin said from the hall. Unable to sleep himself, he had gone for a walk around the enclosed courtyard.

There was no other way for Rayne to explain Tessa's presence than to reveal his immortality. His father would never believe Dante randomly rode into town with his daughter in the middle of the night.

Saladin entered the room and knelt down to better view the girl resting her head on her father's shoulder. "As-Salaam -Alaikum, Zairah. It is a pleasure to meet you."

Small blue eyes filled with curiosity studied him.

"You look like Daddy."

The little girl's words curved Saladin's lips upward into an amused smile. "That is because your father is my son, little one. I see Rayne and your grandmother in you. When he was your age, Rayne had nightmares as well. He used to wake up his mother and me often." Saladin removed the hand of Fatima he wore and tied it around Tessa's neck. "We gave him this to ward off the djinn causing them. Keep it. There will be no more bad dreams with Fatima watching over you."

Not wanting to interrupt or send Dante fleeing with Tessa, Grace observed everything through the cracked door. Saladin's simple gesture endeared him to Tessa and Grace. Through the sliver, she could see Tessa yawn.

"Getting sleepy, sprite?" Rayne grinned as Tessa shifted against him then hugged him once more. He rubbed her back, lulling her to sleep.

All three men remained silent, allowing the child to drift into dreamland. Tessa's hold on Rayne's neck gradually loosened, her breathing eased to a slow, steady pattern.

"I had a feeling all she needed was a few minutes with you," Dante whispered, taking in the serene scene. "You quiet the storm in her as you do in her mother."

Rayne softly laughed and carefully handed Tessa to Dante. "This one is much easier to calm than her mother. Tell her I love her when she wakes."

"I will. Hopefully, your family will be reunited in another day or two. Until then, the children are safe with me." Dante nodded to Saladin then vanished.

"Baba..." Rayne wasn't sure where to begin, how to explain what he had become. Would his father even understand?

Saladin held up his hand, silencing his son. "I have known since you were Tessa's age that you were destined for something great. I assumed all this time it was to be a powerful general. As long as you walk with Allah and live rightly, I do not care what you are now."

Grace opened the door after father embraced son. "Rayne is a powerful and great general, Saladin. He is a champion for the innocent and the weak. One of four special guardians selected to keep evil at bay. His primary charge is protecting humanity from anyone who would do it harm. That is why he cannot strike at Umar for personal gain."

CHAPTER

SEVENTEEN

Elysium

Dante sat on his bed, unlaced his boots, then removed his shirt, hoping to sleep for a few hours before the kids woke again. Keeping the two children as long as he did both wore on him and exhilarated him. The abilities and intelligence of his son awed him. When Tarquin officially joined the Horsemen, the boy would exceed Dante's own fame in the immortal world, or so the Fates claimed. Tessa brightened his day with her imagination and tender heart. She befriended everyone and delicately handled everything she encountered. Dante could see her becoming a healer, but her future was not yet written.

"Does he die, Dante?"

Dante's eyes immediately shot to where the inquiry came from. "Grace? You should not be here."

"I need to know. The nightmares of death repeating makes them foresight, not freak chance."

"I have assurances they are nightmares only. You need to leave." Dante turned on the bed so his back was to her. He hoped none of the Council learned she was in Elysium.

Grace grabbed his arm. "Assurances from whom?"

"Osiris and the Fates."

Fury ignited within Grace. "You are lying, Dante Giovanni. You know more than you are sharing."

"Grazia, go back to Spain."

"I will leave after you tell me what you know."

Dante resisted the urge to yell at her. "If the Council learns..."

"They already know I am here. Osiris was my first stop tonight. Lyal is the one who sensed there is more than he would share. I came to you hoping you would be honest with me since the other Council members chose not to be." Recognizing the combination of anger and fear on his face after Dante stood and faced her, Grace's stomach churned.

"Grace, they will rescind my rights to Tarquin. I cannot protect the children if they do. Leave, before an enforcer is sent to remove you."

"Protect them from what? You said I have nothing to fear. That Tessa's dreams are merely nightmares." Grace hated how he remained silent. "I swear on my life, Dante, I will do everything in my power to ensure you always have access to our son. They banned you from seeing me. I was not forbidden to see you. I came here freely. You never sought me out. The Council will hang themselves on their own technical over-sight if they try to punish you for tonight. Now, answer my question, cavaliere."

Dante brushed the disobedient curl that regularly covered her left eye from her face. "Everything and everyone I have consulted says he lives. Tesoro, please stop obsessing over this and go back to Córdoba."

"You only call me 'tesoro' when you are hiding something."

Once more, silence was his only response. Dante turned away from her, staring into the fireplace. "Return to your husband, Grace."

She could see the tick in Dante's jaw. *Rayne will not be another sacri-ficed Horseman! I am not leaving until I know the truth.* The stiffening of Dante's back confirmed he heard her. *We loved one another once. Does that mean nothing now?* She played with the hair on the nape of his neck before placing her lips against the bronzed skin of his shoulder. She heard him sharply inhale.

Il mio cavaliere. Grace slid her arm around him and laid an open palm over his heart, mimicking the many times he had settled her hand over it and promised to love her in this lifetime and the next. *Parla con me, mio marito.*

Shoving her hand from his chest, Dante spun around. Gold eyes narrowed in anger. "Do not test me, Grazia. I am not the man I once was."

"God or not, you are still my Horseman, Dante Giovanni. You are still the man who saved my brother and me from Qasim. The man who dressed as a priest and sent his captain into enemy ranks to protect a woman you hardly knew. My gladiator who defied the Council and seized any opportunity presented to him. The same man who refused to give up on a woman blinded by a foe. I promised myself I would never be blind again. I see every part of you, cavaliere. Even with as much as I disagree with what you did, I see the nobleness of it. I see the sadness and pain within you. Do you truly wish for another to carry the same burden when you can prevent it?"

"There is nothing endangering your current spouse's soul." Dante looked away again.

Grace turned his face back to hers. "Bugiardo! Tell me the price to save him. What bargain do I need to make?"

"Grace, there is nothing to bargain over."

"Stop lying to me."

Since reasoning and appealing to his heart wouldn't get Dante to reveal the truth, Grace resorted to the only other thing in her arsenal. She drew the dagger she carried and settled the blade alongside Dante's neck. "Rayne will not needlessly die for whatever stupid cause the Council and Fates have now."

Dante immediately seized her hand holding the knife. "To threaten a god as you have is a death sentence."

"I'll gladly give my life for his. The Council, the Fates, nor you may ever harm Rayne. Now, tell me what you have not."

Having enough, Dante yanked her wrist sideways, spinning her body around. He applied enough pressure to the tendons and muscle of her arm that she dropped the knife. His foot caught her ankle, sending her falling backwards into his bed. He pinned her underneath him. "Basta, you insane woman! Please tell me you were not so foolish in your discussions with my father."

"You and your father be damned! I am not surrendering Rayne without a fight. You are either with me or against me in this, Dante," Grace hissed up at him, trying to get free.

"I have always stood with you, Grazia. That will never change."

Anger shifted to want as he looked down at her. Her hair splayed out around her, her face flushed, her chest rising and falling from her rapid breathing, her robe partially open, revealing the swell of her breasts under her nightgown. The feel of her body underneath his destroyed his self-control. Forbidden or not, they had already violated the terms of his agreement with the Council. What was one more offense? He pressed his lips to hers. Grace's arms wrapped around him. She eagerly returned the kiss. His hand slid under her robe and followed the curve of her hip before slipping between her bottom and the velvet of his comforter.

Her legs encircled his. "I know the one thing you want most, Dante. You can have it."

"Grazia," Dante breathed her name before kissing her again, his fingers squeezing her flesh. It would be so easy to take her.

"Just tell me how many nights are needed to save him."

Dante groaned, struggling to regain control over his traitorous body. "Such an arrangement would condemn us both."

"The Council restrictions be damned. If it will keep Rayne alive, I will do whatever you require; just promise me he survives."

"For both our sakes, I will pretend you never put such an offer on the table." Dante forced himself to pull away.

"Then what deity do I need to barter with? I won't let the Council or anyone else murder him. They took you from me. They will not take Rayne." Tears ran down Grace's face.

"Oh, mia stella." Dante drew her into his embrace once more. "Fear is leading you in the wrong direction."

Grace buried her face in his shoulder. "I can't lose him, Dante. I can't go through having my heart ripped out again."

"I swear that isn't what lies ahead. You will never have to endure that again." Dante rocked her. "I won't allow the Council to subject you to such suffering twice, cara."

"You won't act to stop whatever is to come."

"Grazia, Rayne is one of the most powerful beings in the immortal community. All creatures that encounter him sense he is not to be trifled with. Even Lucifer possesses a healthy respect for your husband."

Dante forced himself to let go of her. With a shaking hand, he poured himself a glass of amaretto from the decanter sitting on the table in his room.

"Yet, Umar challenges him." Grace watched Dante down the amber liquid before setting the empty glass down. "There is more at play here. Your drinking gives that away."

"Malik and Umar are vying for power. Rayne is caught up in a political confrontation between the two. Nothing more. Your husband's future is secure."

Dante removed the crystal stopper to pour himself a second round. The liquor numbed the throbbing ache for Grace. Maybe if he drank the entire bottle, he could forget the exquisite sensation of her body underneath his, along with the tears she wept over his death and the potential loss of another she loved.

Grace wanted to believe Dante told her the truth. "How do you know his future is secure?"

"I see your fate whenever I touch you, cara. War will have a son of his own. The boy won't be conceived any time soon, but he will join us. If Rayne's life was in danger, I could not see the child."

"What if that is only one possible path, Dante? Not all things are predestined."

Dante ignored the urge to pour a third drink. Instead, he faced the woman watching every movement he made. Her eyes pleading with him to tell her the truth. "When it comes to you and Rayne, almost everything is predestined. Rayne is, and always was, your future. He knew it all along but chose to remain silent. Unconsciously, I knew it too. I selfishly wanted to keep you as long as I could. After Rayne resisted fate, I was placed in your path under a false prophecy to ensure the next generation of Horsemen would be born."

"What?" Grace didn't know how to respond to what Dante shared.

Dante approached her now that he regained control of his emotions. "Rayne has loved you since the encounter on the Watchtower."

Fleeting images of Rayne and her on a castle tower overlooking an aqua sea appeared before Grace. "That was a dream."

"No. It is real. As are the other fleeting memories you have of him before you actually encountered one another in Rome. They are forbidden meetings created by you two needing one another. The Fates blurred them after altering your stories."

Grace doubted she and Rayne ever had any such interaction. "The Council banned the Fates from doing such things long before Rayne and I ever encountered one another."

"The prohibition was not issued until after the Fates' second time meddling with immortal affairs. Only a warning was given when they altered Gage and Caitlin's memories as the two of them requested the Fates do so. After learning the Fates altered your and Rayne's paths without telling anyone else, the High Council restricted their abilities as much as could be done."

"You are wrong, Dante. I never dreamed of the Watchtower and Rayne until Damascus, which was long after Rome. The first time that vision clearly appeared was the same night Rayne interrogated me about Raphael and the serpent."

Dante shook his head, completely understanding why she mistrusted him. "You two knew one another when Rayne appeared in Osvaldo's carriage. He recognized you immediately. Finding himself face to face with you shook him to the core. He saw the visions you had of him at Osvaldo's. I've never seen him so dazed. He berated me for a good hour that evening, alleging I failed to adequately warn him about who the woman I planned to apprehend was, and then again, when I brought you to Essaouira. At the time, I couldn't understand why he was so angry. I thought his reaction originated from irrationality or maybe jealously, but as the discussion went on, I realized Rayne legiti-mately found himself terrified by something, by the mere presence of a mortal woman. I should have guessed then you two were destined to be romantically linked. The only time Rayne acts irrationally is when something he has tried to bury surfaces. He didn't disclose to me that he knew you would become his wife until after the whole parasite fiasco."

"How could Rayne have known any of that? Rayne does not see the future as you and I do. The visions I had when we kissed cautioned me about his immortality, nothing more."

"Rayne rarely sees another's future, but his was revealed to him when he took on the mantle of War. He disregarded the visions of you along with those of Tessa, thinking his role as Horseman nullified them. Not to mention how long it took for you to appear in his and my lives."

"I never felt the immediate bond with him that I did when I first touched you."

"That is because I was to love you first. But Rayne knew the truth, and while the bond wasn't the same, did you not find yourself drawn to him as more time passed? Did you not see both of us protecting and loving you in Rome?"

"Falling for either of you was not anything I foresaw the first time I kissed Rayne. I only saw him riding after you and me."

Dante settled his hands on the sides of her face, surfacing the old vision. "Look closer at yourself and him. Allow things to play out completely this time."

With Dante's help, the hazy vision became vividly clear. She noticed the sapphire wedding ring on her finger matching the one on Rayne's hand carrying the drawn sword. Dante appeared more ghostly riding ahead of Rayne. Originally, the vision had stopped at this moment, but now it continued.

Rayne glanced back over his shoulder as if watching for something following them. The sound of baying hounds grew more distant. "We are in the clear, Grace. Destahn, do you have the prince?"

"The future king is safely on his way back to his father. Disaster averted." Destahn's voice calmed Grace's pounding heart. "You drawing the tracking party away worked perfectly for us to retrieve him."

Rayne nodded to Dante. Dante vanished as Rayne sheathed his sword.

Grace smiled up at Rayne after he rode up alongside her. "How did you get us through the witch's barrier?"

"A little help from an old friend. Why Filaura thought kidnapping a human prince was a wise idea is beyond me. That stunt almost ignited warfare between humanity and ourselves."

"But as always, you prevented such a travesty from happening."

Grace's hand settling on Rayne's thigh prompted Rayne to lean towards her.

"I will be damned if another war breaks out endangering our family, especially with the pending arrival of my daughter." Rayne grinned at the startled expression on Grace's face then kissed her.

"Your daughter?" Grace pretended to not know what he was talking about.

Rayne chuckled. "You should have told me of the child yesterday, leof."

"We didn't exactly have a quiet moment when I could have told you, nor were you in the mood to hear your wife was with child." Grace enjoyed the way he kissed her a second time.

"No more unnecessary risks now that this assignment is complete. I also expect you to demand a moment of my time to tell me you are pregnant if you ever become with child again. Even if I am in the middle of fighting off hordes of demons in the apocalypse."

Dante pulled his hands from her face, returning them to the present.

Grace didn't know what to say. The day happened just as Dante shared. Could Rayne have seen the whole thing when she only saw the first few seconds of their ride to distract Filaura's guard? "Can you share whatever Rayne may have foreseen in Rome if he could truly see his and my future?"

"He saw everything. The matching wedding rings, making love to you in the baths after being wounded, and the birth of his daughter. If only you knew how badly you rattled him. I am shocked he managed to conceal how disturbed he was until he and I met to discuss strategy after dinner. He challenged Isis's directive for the Horsemen to protect you in Morocco. He tried everything he could to forget those visions."

"I don't understand, Dante. You yourself advised the agreement between the Council and you rewrote fate. How could Rayne have foreseen any of those things if they weren't written yet?"

"I ended the Triad and ensured you lived with what I brokered. Your intuition that there was a chance we all survived Alexandria wasn't wrong, Grace. There was a very slim possibility we all walked out of the temple victorious. We might have even found a way to live amicably as the Triad. But the probability of a happy ending was lower than I was willing to risk. Rayne and you were born into your roles, Grace. Nothing that has happened to either of you is mere happenstance."

"If what you say is true, Tessa would not dream of her father being killed. She is my daughter, a descendant of the moon. I do not doubt prophecy is one of her gifts."

Dante's gaze dropped to the floor. Grace seized his right hand. "Please, Dante! Alexandria cannot repeat. I will not survive it again."

Dante laid his forehead against hers. His thumb captured one of the glistening droplets on her face. It reflected the flames in the fireplace beside them. God or not, he could never stand to watch her cry. He'd face the Council's wrath if only to stop her tears.

"Death does not beckon your husband. Another does. Rayne must not kill Umar. Should he be provoked into killing the man, he becomes lost once more. He will be tested soon. Stay close to his side, Grace. That is how you save him. You must not let him fail if you value him enough that you would trade yourself to a god to ensure his safety."

"Rayne will not strike down Umar. I will do everything I can to keep them away from one another. Thank you, Dante." Grace hugged him; grateful his loyalty was still stronger to her than the Council.

Dante stroked her hair, memorizing the details of her face for the millionth time, and treasuring the silken texture of gold curls against his fingers. The gratitude in her eyes warmed him. She once again saw him as a hero, not a villain. "You will be the death of me, yet, cara. Be thankful my willpower is stronger than most. Another would have taken you and done nothing to protect the man you are trying to save. You know better than to negotiate with a deity or the Fates."

"You are not any old deity. You are my cavaliere." Grace brought a smile to his face.

"Go home, Grazia." Dante willed her back to Rayne.

Córdoba -

Rayne woke a second time to pressure on his chest. His eyes opened to find his wife staring down at him. "Grace? What..."

Her lips on his cut off the question. "Nothing is wrong. I just need my husband."

Rayne enjoyed how she kissed him again. The way she tugged the sheets covering him out of the way further roused him. The gentle nipping of her teeth along his neck and shoulder sent his pulse racing. She took the hard length of him inside her, joining their bodies. His arousal heightened hearing the soft cries that gradually grew louder with each movement of her hips. It had been a while since she had awakened him in the middle of the night to make love. He certainly had no complaints, loving the way his wife pleasured them both, but he wondered what brought on such urgency within her. His name falling from her lips and the shuddering of her body against his banished any concerns about her behavior. He rolled her underneath him, thinking only of the delight their lovemaking gifted them both.

CHAPTER

EIGHTEEN

Córdoba - 812

Rayne appreciated how Grace so easily embraced his past and family. Their time in Córdoba reignited an all too familiar reckless passion in his marriage. Grace and he always had a loving relationship, and the two never neglected each other. But something revived those early emotions between the two of them; reminding him of their secret meetings in the woods of Sasainn and the private moments in Rome where they hid away from the world. Rayne experienced the same emotional high and infatuation he had the weeks following the promotion ceremony when Grace formally became his wife.

Overhearing his thoughts, Grace smiled. "I thank the Fates every day for giving you an unending supply of patience. A weaker man would have abandoned course."

"I nearly did several times."

This was the first she heard of him doubting their relationship. "What caused you to keep moving forward?"

"Slightly wounded pride, fear of the wrath of a newly made god for breaking my word to him, and a dwindling sense of hope that the woman I shared so many tender moments with in secret would again

191

one day look at me as she did the afternoon I retrieved her from the woods in Sasainn."

"No doubt I look at you much differently now. Back then, I could not fathom how much you could mean to me, nor how much joy you bring me." Grace's expression grew somber. "There is nothing I would not do for you, Rayne. I love you, in this lifetime and the next."

The emotion in her tone unsettled Rayne. "What troubles you, leof?"

"Nothing." Grace started to rise from where she sat.

Rayne gripped her forearm, stopping her. "Do not shut me out, Grace. With my past laid bare, I need to know my wife stands with me."

"Nothing is wrong. I was remembering how hard things were those first few days in Greece, and how you never faltered. You loved me in my most hateful moments. Those dark days seem a lifetime ago. Let's go for a ride or a walk. It is a beautiful morning."

The two strolled alongside the fields, getting lost in the warm sunshine. Grace held his hand or gently hugged his arm the entire time if it wasn't around her. They broke the rules of decorum for the century, but Grace needed the innocent contact with Rayne today. He seemed to sense that, as he didn't gently chide her about period correct behavior. Anytime she looked up at him, he smiled down at her.

Once they returned to the courtyard, the gurgling of a small fountain drowned out any whispers of worry in Grace's mind. She studied the wolf's head pendant Rayne now regularly wore. "I saw this somewhere before we married."

"I periodically carry it attached to the horseman's blade. You also saw it the night you told me about Anubis being in Rome."

Grace remembered the time he referenced. "No. I saw it long before complaining about the Council."

"Perhaps in the visions the day we met." Rayne vividly recalled the first visions she ever triggered within him. She sent his world reeling, seeing him as Haroun. No other had ever associated him with the general after Lyal's death.

"Maybe."

Rayne removed the large medallion and settled it around her neck. "My lady moon, think of your husband whenever you look upon this."

"You will need the crest when you visit Malik."

"He knows who I am without it. Wear it in good health."

The two returned to the house. Grace sat in a chair by the open room doors. She hummed softly to herself, sewing a button Rayne had lost back onto one of his uniform shirts. He caught her casting an admiring glance his way as he changed into more traditional clothing for his meeting with Malik. At times like this, it was hard for him to believe they were from such different backgrounds. He returned the glowing smile she offered him.

"Rayne?"

"Yes, leof?"

She held out her hand to him. "There is something we must discuss."

"Oh? And what is this matter?" Rayne took her hand and knelt down on one knee to be eye level with her.

The wood slab of the room door colliding with the clay wall halted whatever words Grace started to utter.

Saladin marched towards them with angst etched across his face. "You said you could not kill Umar!"

The accusation flustered Rayne. He dropped Grace's hand. "I cannot. My oath prevents it."

"Umar was found dead this morning. His throat slit while he slept."

"What have you done, Grace?" Dante raged from the opposite side of the room.

All three men stared at her. She set aside her sewing and slowly rose.

The condemnation in Dante's expression made Rayne shudder. He prayed Grace wasn't guilty of what he suspected. "What has happened, leof?"

The question confused Grace. "I am not sure."

Dante snatched Grace by the arms. "Do not lie, cara. The Council Guard is almost at the door. They come for you."

The hints of panic intertwined with anger in Dante's voice worried Rayne. What did the god know that he did not?

Now understanding what Dante thought she had done, Grace's eyes locked with Dante's. "I did not kill Umar."

"Grazia, per favore, cara. Is that the truth?"

"Who is the man to appear like he does?" Saladin questioned his son.

"A god." Rayne didn't have time to offer his father long explanations.

Saladin knew only one thing drove a man to act as Dante did. "The god loves her?"

Rayne nodded yes, regaining a level head before Dante did. He separated the furious sun god and his wife. "Leof, he is right. We do not have much time. Swear to me you did not slay Umar."

Raphael materialized with representatives from the other pantheons to arrest Grace. Seeing the restraints in his hands, Grace clung to Rayne.

Rayne cursed, feeling her fear as if it were his own. He drew her closer. There was little sanctuary he could offer with the High Council issuing the arrest warrant.

"Rayne, I swear, I promise on my life, on our kids, on anything you need me to. I did not take the man off the earth."

Rayne glanced over at Raphael. "May I go with her?"

"I see no harm in that. You must surrender your sword if you wish to accompany her. We cannot risk you doing something as stupid as she is accused of."

Rayne's hold on Grace tightened. "It is in the chest near the bed. I will turn over the Commander's ruby until this is resolved."

"That is not necessary. You are not facing indictment. Dante, recover Rayne's weapon for me." Raphael redirected the sun god's attention to eliminate any risk of him trying to free Grace.

"It will be all right, leof," Rayne said the words for himself as much as he did for her.

Raphael closed a heavy, black shackle around Grace's wrist. The sheer terror in her eyes as she stared up at Rayne worried both commanders.

CHAPTER

NINETEEN

The Council Round

Rayne and Grace stood in the center of the round meeting room of the High Council. The size of the room disconcerted Grace. She never stood before the Council prior to today. Only Raphael and Rayne briefed the body of deities. She slowly turned, finding herself surrounded by high walls, at the top of which stone partitions separated distinct seating areas. The structure reminded her of the Coliseum in Rome. Deities from every walk of life filed into the various sections.

"I feel like I am about to be fed to the lions." She swallowed and tried to calm her nerves. The Council would try her before issuing any sort of sentence. The ruling organization was bound to the law of the Ancients, like she was. Nevertheless, the pristine white and gold surroundings petrified Grace.

Rayne did his best to muster a reassuring smile, but struggled to do so. For the Council to charge her, they had some sort of damning evidence. "It is intimidating to stand here for the first time or two."

"Rayne, I would never violate my oath by arbitrarily killing a human."

"Say nothing more until we know the actual charges." Rayne loathed silencing her, but worried she may accidentally harm herself by uttering anything that could be misconstrued if one of the Council overheard it.

Poseidon took the overseer's chair once the room quieted. "Grace Gillingham Giovanni Dalglese Warwick, we charge you with taking a human life without sanction. The penalty for such a crime is your soul being sent to Tartarus for eternal imprisonment. What say you to such a charge of reckless delinquency?"

Having never been in a court such as this one, Grace wasn't sure what to say. "Not guilty?"

"Please note the Defensore claims innocence. Before this trial begins, I must ask the following individuals to recuse themselves from the panel: Osiris, Isis, Ares, Zeus, Theseus, and Anubis as all have had interaction with the accused or her husband which may bias them in deciding the Defensore's fate. The newest of our ranks is asked to do nothing more than give testimony since he declined a position on the Council."

Dante materialized beside Grace and Rayne. "I will honor the Council's wishes."

"How in the hell do I end up in these messes?" Grace muttered, after all parties who knew her well were removed from the judicial panel.

Dante raised a disapproving brow. "I often wonder the same, cara. Be thankful the two people who care about you most are a god and a Horseman or you would be dead by nightfall."

Grace worried whoever targeted her might harm Tessa or Tarquin next. "Who is watching our children?"

"My mother, with Gage and Sean. Give me some credit, Grazia."

Grace surveyed those left to judge her. There was only one potentially harmful person present. "Poseidon, do I have the right to request that one of the judges be dismissed?"

The Greek god sought administrative guidance from Osiris.

Osiris smiled reassuringly at Grace. "If the Defensore can prove just cause for the dismissal, the named judge may be removed."

"Then I demand Hera recuse herself as well."

Hera gasped as if offended. "What ill will would I bear against you, Defensore?"

"Mothers are vindictive when someone wrongs their child. My ex-husband slept with one of your son's wives. All three of us standing before the Council have beaten Sanjur in battle on more than one occasion. As my soul is on the line, I would like to know those who judge me are impartial."

Poseidon motioned for Hera to leave. The goddess obeyed the temporary Council Head's direction.

"Commander Fiore, we are ready to begin," Poseidon directed Raphael to take his customary place, guarding the exit.

Raphael stepped back from his fellow officers to ensure no one entered or left the round until the hearing concluded.

Grace didn't like that a guard was posted at the door. Why was Poseidon worried she might attempt to escape? She had no reason to run. She had done nothing wrong.

Osiris knew he shouldn't say anything to Grace, but wanted to ease her fears. "Commander Fiore serves to protect you from those who accuse you more than the Council being concerned about you becoming a flight risk."

Osiris's trying to calm Grace confirmed for Dante his father did not believe she committed the offense leveled at her. That gave him some hope of the charges being dismissed. Perhaps the trial was a formality to meet the requirement to investigate such a severe crime.

Hades stepped forward. "We all know an officer gone rogue is not an offense to be taken lightly. I was greatly distressed when word reached me that an arrest warrant had to be issued for the Morte Defensore. I am certain everyone will be as disturbed as I was when I present the evidence against Grace Warwick."

Grace shook her head. "You have got to be kidding me. Hades is the lead prosecutor for the High Council?"

"Did you wish to say something to the Council, Defensore?" Hades smirked, looking over at Grace.

"No. I will reserve my comments until after I learn what I have supposedly done."

Grace, Rayne, and Dante listened intently to the charges.

Hades narrated the case like the annoying announcer in movie trailers. "In the early hours of morning, someone entered Umar's bedroom and slit his throat. There were no signs of forced entry suggesting this was not a random attack. Umar's killer was either immortal or someone with the skill to sneak past his guard and pick his door locks. We all know the Defensore's prior occupation."

"That is conjecture, not fact. Do you have any actual evidence I was at Umar's residence?" Grace interrupted Hades's performance.

"Patience, my dear Defensore. I have not finished presenting my case." Hades cleared his throat. "As I was saying, it is almost as if the killer was a trained assassin, or more accurately, a master thief. No one witnessed anyone entering or leaving Umar's quarters once he went to bed. Umar's manservant discovered his body shortly after dawn."

"Grace is not the assailant. She was with me the entire night," Rayne defended his wife against the ridiculous accusation.

"Was she, Commander?" Hades grinned, eyeing Grace.

Grace paled.

"I have eyewitness testimony that places her in Dante Giovanni's bedroom only a half hour before Umar's demise."

Rayne stared at Grace and Dante in such a manner Grace wondered if her husband would condemn her before the jury could.

"Is this true?"

Grace hoped he would allow her to explain why she had gone to Dante. "Rayne, it isn't how Hades makes it sound."

"The question requires a simple yes or no answer, Grace. Did you leave our bed in the middle of the night to seek out Dante?"

"Yes," Grace meekly whispered, aware of the chaos the truth would unleash.

Rayne fought back the wave of betrayal he felt to prevent himself from hurting Grace's case.

A murmur washed across the room.

Hating how Hades relished manipulating the court for dramatic effect, Dante placed a hand on Rayne's arm, then stepped in front of Rayne and Grace to address the Council directly. "She only came to comfort her daughter, who suffers from night terrors. We briefly spoke for a few minutes in my bedroom so that we did not disturb the children once Tessa fell back to sleep. Nothing more occurred. To imply anything else did, damages the character of this court, the accused, her husband, and myself."

"Care to share the nature of the conversation, Dante?" Hades stirred the already roiling pot.

Dante's eyes narrowed at the secondary inquiry.

Rayne braced for whatever Dante's answer may be. Between Grace paling and Dante's reaction to the question, something more than talking happened.

Raphael groaned and brought his hand to his face, then ran his palm down towards his chin. Dante's expression declared he was guilty of some sort of improper behavior. Hades definitely struck a nerve. *Please Fates, do not let Armageddon begin here today.*

Hearing Raphael's remark, Dante glared over at him. After taking a second to compose himself, Dante turned to the Council and Hades. "I am happy to disclose more about our discourse. The Defensore was concerned the nightmares Tessa is having of Commander Warwick dying are prophetic visions. I advised her, as far as any of us knew, they were merely manifestations of Tessa's fears with being separated from her parents. That was the extent of the discussion. I sent her back to Rayne after belaying her worries. Are there any further questions about her time with me, Hades? I will gladly answer any additional inquiries the Council or yourself may have. Though I warn you to choose your words wisely."

"I do not see a need for further questions, Dante. In addition to establishing the Defensore was not in her bed sleeping, as her husband naively assumes, the human authorities found this at the scene." Hades raised Grace's dagger above his head. The blade was still caked with Umar's blood.

A second round of whispering circled through the room.

Getting over the shock of seeing her weapon, Grace found her voice again. "While the knife is mine, I did not slay Umar. Someone must have stolen it to commit the act."

An immortal man in black stepped forward, sending more murmuring through the room. "Then you did not exercise proper care over an immortal weapon, Defensore. Mayhap, a mistake was made in selecting you for such an esteemed position."

Rayne knew the well-dressed being better than he cared to admit. The immortal had stayed away from the Council Round for centuries prior to today. "Lucifer. What draws you back to the Council after renouncing your place here?"

Lucifer laughed. "Sin is my specialty, Commander Warwick. When one of this magnitude is committed, I am compelled to come forward. Lust, temptation, and wrath are three of the deadliest. Each contributed to what brings us all here today." Lucifer made it a point to stare at each offender in the same order of the sins he named: Dante, Grace, and Rayne. "The question Hades fails to ask is how far can a guardian fall? Was the temptation to protect her husband so great the Defensore could not resist it?"

Grace held the Devil's gaze. "I did not murder Umar. No matter how tempting it may have been."

Lucifer grinned. "So you say, Defensore."

Rayne's eyes shifted color to a stormy gray, warning all in the room his patience waned. He did not appreciate Lucifer's presence, nor the accusation made against his spouse. Rayne slowly turned, giving the leading council members a disapproving stare. "Each one of us here knows the Defensore's character. If Grace states she did not kill Umar, she is not the assailant. Regardless of what weapon was found. Further investigation needs to be conducted into this matter before the Council may accuse my wife of anything. Even humans do not bring their own to trial without due diligence as was done here today."

Poseidon did the only thing he could for Grace. "You are correct, Commander. The warrant for her was issued prematurely. I stay any additional inquiries until we know more. At the same time, we cannot risk a rogue or corrupted immortal roaming freely. Until more information becomes available, the Defensore shall be confined. Raphael, escort the prisoner to Purgatory."

"Interesting that Poseidon shows mercy to your wife, Rayne. The past tends to repeat itself until we learn from it. Have you learned the lessons you were meant to?" Lucifer poked at Rayne.

"My past has nothing to do with my wife."

"Rayne, I cannot delay the Council's order." Raphael prevented any further antagonism from Lucifer.

Rayne nodded, then followed Raphael as he escorted Grace through the crowd of immortal onlookers and out of the Council Round. Dante trailed behind the three; following them outside and down a white stone staircase. Destahn waited at the bottom of the steps.

Once they reached Destahn, Rayne could no longer hold back his temper. "I gave you my surname, a home, protection, everything one man can give a woman. Most of all, I gave you my trust and heart, Grace. This is how you repay me? You sneak off to Dante while I sleep?!"

"I didn't—" Grace was well aware Rayne thought the worst due to his ex-wife Anne's affair and the start of their own relationship. "Yes, I went to see Dante in the middle of the night. I know how it must appear, but it isn't what you are thinking."

"We both know damn well Tessa did not need her mother last night. Dante lied. There is only one reason I know of that would cause him to do so."

"I did not lie. I simply did not provide any more information than was needed to answer the question. This whole affair is strange." Dante drew all of their attention. "Your wife came to enlist my help in protecting you, Rayne. Nothing more."

Raphael noticed the first members of the Council emerging from the building. Lucifer stood with them, observing the turmoil within the Horsemen's ranks. Not wanting the bickering between the three to garner any more attention, Raphael gently guided Grace forward by the elbow. "We need to keep moving."

Rayne glanced over at Dante as they walked behind Grace and Raphael. "Protecting me? From what?"

"Yourself." Dante wished he could provide more insight.

"Myself? Care to expand upon that, Dante?"

"I cannot."

Rayne shook his head and let out an annoyed laugh. "Funny how you break the law when it is to your benefit to do so, but refuse to do the same for others."

"I have broken more laws than you will ever know of to protect you, Grace, and the children. I would not be surprised if I am charged with some sort of crime for disclosing what little I did to Grace in the interest of keeping you out of harm's way. Even I have my limits, Rayne!"

"Since when does anything limit your ambition, Dante? If you had limits, you would not place a woman you claim to love and protect in the Council's crosshairs. You compromised her reputation with a questionable situation instead of immediately returning her to her husband, and discussing whatever you disclosed with both her and me."

"Stop fighting! Whoever is behind this wants you two at odds with one another." Grace tried to stop the escalating argument as they entered Purgatory prison.

Destahn hated that Rayne and Dante argued. "She's right, Rayne. Who would benefit from a rift between you and Dante?"

"Dante is the only one who benefits from what is done." Rayne doubted anyone else would drive a wedge between Grace and him, especially with the agreement Dante signed years ago. "I have a murderer to track down, then I will deal with my wife privately."

"Rayne!" Grace tried to call him back after he vanished.

Raphael opened her cell door and set a comforting hand on her shoulder. "He will return once he calms."

By the troubled look on Destahn's face, the Horsemen Captain struggled with joining Rayne in his search or guarding her.

"Watch over him, Destahn." Grace decided for him.

"Keep yourself safe, Grace. Trust no one outside of the Horsemen and this one." Destahn clapped Dante on the back, then vanished to assist Rayne.

Grace sighed before sitting down on the bed in her cell.

Raphael swung the door shut and locked it. The grating iron lock sent a chill through Grace. Raphael noted the intensity with which Dante watched Grace. The god found Grace's imprisonment as distressing as Rayne did. "Whatever you are thinking, Dante, I strongly caution you to remember the pact you made with the Council."

Dante stepped around Raphael. "If you stayed with Rayne the rest of the night, how did the dagger end up at Umar's?"

Grace came to the door. "It must have been stolen from Rayne's wardrobe."

"I want to believe you, Grace." Dante doubted her. The timing of Umar's death so close to their discussion was too much of a coincidence.

Grace extended her hand through the bars. "See for yourself, cavaliere."

"Dante," Raphael halfheartedly reminded the god of his supposed neutrality.

Dante glared over at Raphael, silencing him, then took Grace's hand. He saw the end of their conversation, her making love to Rayne then drifting to sleep in his arms, and her not waking until sunrise. She stayed with Rayne until her arrest, exactly as he had advised her to do. He wished what he saw was enough to clear her of the charges, but it wasn't. Rayne needed to find the killer with the dagger being discovered at Umar's. "Who else would have access to Rayne's weapons cabinet?"

"I do not know. I assume Saladin and Rayne. They are the only ones besides myself with keys to it."

"Do nothing that will make matters worse." Dante let go of her hand and walked towards the prison entrance.

"As if I could from a cell." Grace sat down again.

Raphael smiled. "I will ask the warden to bring you water and some lunch. This will all get sorted out, Grace."

Grace lay back on the bed after Raphael departed. She thought through everything that had happened.

A few hours later, four guards and Dante returned to the barred door.

Grace heard the rattling of keys and came upright. "What is going on?"

Dante's face remained solemn. "The Council agreed to release you into my custody. You will stay with your children in my home until this matter is resolved. You are forbidden to leave Elysium. I sent word to Rayne of your new location."

"Thank you." Grace appreciated what he had done, knowing the test it would be on him.

"You are welcome."

The sharp tone he used and the clipped diction of the English phrase instead of his normal response of di nulla or prego hinted that the negotiations for her release had been heated.

CHAPTER

TWENTY

Córdoba - 812

R ayne and Destahn rode to Umar's property. Both walked the extensive grounds, searching for clues of who the man's killer might be. Nothing was disturbed outside the home. As Hades said, there were no signs of forced entry.

Rayne bribed the estate manager to give them access to Umar's private chambers and bedroom.

Destahn noted the frustrated look on Rayne's faced after they found nothing suspicious inside. "Either a professional did this or one of his household did."

"We have to be overlooking something." Rayne's eyes scanned the door again. The lock was in perfect condition, not a scratch anywhere.

"There's only one thing we haven't tried yet. The murder did happen at night." Destahn hinted at their ability to tap the past and act as invisible voyeurs with the trauma that occurred in the room.

"I was hoping to avoid having to do this." Rayne held his hand out, pausing time. He settled his other hand on the bloody sheet left on Umar's bed, willing the events of the night prior to replay.

The two Horsemen found themselves standing in the darkened

room, halfway between Umar's bed and the door. A black-garbed figure sprinted past Rayne and Destahn into the hallway, its face and hair concealed by a long black scarf underneath a cloak hood. Black leather gloves covered the assailant's hands. Based on the height and slimmer build, the murderer very well could have been a woman.

Rayne walked over to the bed and stared down at a deceased Umar. By the way he lay, the man remained asleep until the assault began. His body was only slightly off center, so Umar's end came quickly, but not without pain. Rayne noticed Grace's dagger carelessly discarded on the floor a few feet from the bed. He pulled the neck of Umar's bloody nightshirt down to get a better look at the wound running across his neck.

Lucifer peered over Rayne's shoulder. "Jagged edges. The blade more scraping and tearing versus a clean cut. Someone inexperienced inflicted the fatal blow. If the Defensore was Umar's executioner, the wound would be straight and smooth. The murderer obviously didn't have a steady hand. Appears your wife isn't the assailant. We both know those you train know how to kill properly."

Rayne turned to face the Devil. "Two appearances in one day, Lucifer? I am starting to wonder what connection you have to the events of last night."

Lucifer laughed. "If I were behind this, Umar would have died much more painfully. The injuries would have been more professional in nature. With all his wrongdoings, I have my top demons fighting over who gets to torture our surprise guest of honor, who showed up on my doorstep before he should have. Such a headache to deal with as the Lord of Hell. That being said, it really makes me wonder who would want your wife to take the fall for this?"

Destahn folded his arms over his chest and eyed Lucifer. "Grace has no enemies."

"We all have enemies, Captain. Most just don't have the courage to confront us or go to these extremes." Lucifer grinned, looking at Rayne once more. "But I don't think the individual behind this is after Grace. They wanted her out of the way. Now, who did you make angry that would be clever enough to devise such a scheme, Rayne? Besides myself."

"The only two beings stupid enough to threaten my wife are you and Garsea."

Lucifer tsked. "We've already determined I am not the one instigating this."

Destahn's annoyance with Lucifer interrupting their scene investigation grew. "No, *we* haven't, and I am growing more suspicious of you the more you talk, Lucifer."

"Let him keep speaking, Destahn. Have you not heard the phrase give a scheming man enough rope and he will eventually hang himself?"

"If I wanted a fight with the Horsemen, I would have taken Grace hostage, not framed her for murder. Isn't that right, Rayne?"

The scowl on Rayne's faced deepened. "I should have killed you the first time you made such a vile mistake. I regret I didn't every day, Lucifer. Who revived Garsea?"

"Garsea is no more. No human or immortal comes back from the dead when they perish under your blade."

"Kamar attacked Grace not too long ago. This fell off his neck." Rayne tossed Lucifer the silver medallion Kamar left behind.

Lucifer shook his head, examining the medal. "Isra and Malik certainly have you fooled, don't they?"

"Isra wouldn't dare cross me. She knows what I would do to her if she came anywhere near a member of my family."

"She doesn't have to come near you, or anyone else, for that matter. Not when she has Malik, Narcisco, and Kamar to do her bidding."

Rayne doubted Isra would ever challenge him like this. "Isra isn't that bold."

"She's grown bold over the past century or two. You saw what happened at the Vatican. She wants control over the entirety of the Iberian Peninsula as well as Italy and France. Isra can't get that without a powerful minion to do her bidding. She needs a skilled military leader and assassin to lead her legions. Think about it, Rayne. Why an attack on you by Umar's men? Why leave signs of Garsea returning from the dead? Who else would know how to expertly draw you back to Córdoba? Isra *is* the master strategist, placing the pieces she needs in the right places on the board. If you can't see that, mortal and immortal alike are in grave danger. And let's not forget, you're the one who got away. The darkest desire of every djinn is to possess what they can't have." Lucifer disappeared after finishing his monologue.

"The one who got away?" Destahn tried to hide his smirk as he posed the question.

Rayne wished Lucifer would have kept that remark to himself. "It isn't what you are thinking."

Destahn held his hands up and chuckled. "No judgment here, Rayne. We've all had lovers we later regret becoming involved with."

"Isra and I were never lovers," Rayne snapped, unfreezing time. "And if you ever imply such a thing again, you'll find your mouth sewn shut to prevent you from repeating such nonsense."

"I guess that's better than having my tongue cut out." Destahn followed Rayne out of Umar's room and down the hall. "You're rather touchy about Isra. That makes me think you're lying about not being romantically involved with the djinn."

The glare Rayne shot Destahn warned him not to push the issue any further. Destahn decided it best to change subjects. "Where to next, Commander?"

"My father's, to see if his key to my weapons chest is still in his possession. Then we'll pay a visit to Malik."

CHAPTER

TWENTY-ONE

Elysium

Tessa and Tarquin sprinted to Grace after she and Dante entered Dante's home. The scene of a mother embracing her children eased his doubts about deciding to negotiate for Grace's freedom. She belonged in Elysium with Tessa and Tarquin. He could also protect her from any further harm better than the prison guards could.

Tarquin practiced his Italian with Grace. In spending just a few days with Dante, Tarquin's fluency matched Grace's. The boy would speak the language more proficiently than she did if he remained under Dante's tutelage.

Tessa poured her mother and brother a cup of imaginary tea.

"You need to drink your tea. It is getting cold," She scolded Grace and Tarquin after the two kept talking while holding the little cups and saucers she gave them.

Tarquin rolled his eyes.

Grace picked up her cup and pretended to sip out of it. "It's very good tea, Tessa. Thank you for making it."

Dante heard Grace whisper for Tarquin to humor his sister. Tarquin slugged his down like a shot, earning a disapproving stare from his sibling.

"That isn't how you drink tea, you mannerless barbarian!" Tessa shouted, swinging for her brother.

Grace gently grasped Tessa's wrist. "Do not hit your brother, Tessa. Tell him you're sorry."

"But, Mommy, he didn't sip his tea."

"Tessa." Grace's voice cautioned not to argue with her further.

"Fine. I am sorry, Tarquin."

"Whatever. It didn't hurt anyhow, and I can drink my stupid imaginary tea anyway I want."

Tessa picked up Grace's cup and threw it at Tarquin, nailing him in the forehead. Grace immediately grabbed a hold of Tarquin, who now swung at his sister.

"You are such a spoiled brat, Tessa. You are lucky Mama is here."

Tessa stuck her tongue out at Tarquin. "I am not a brat. You're a mean brother and a Neanderthal!"

Dante chuckled, giving away he had been watching from across the room. Tessa was certainly her mother's daughter to call Tarquin a Neanderthal. She had been fairly well behaved until today. This was the first display of rebelliousness he had seen from her. He was beginning to doubt Rayne's stories of the four-year-old's temper.

"Zio should hit you with a lightning bolt for being mean."

Grace kept the two squabbling siblings apart. "Both of you, stop it!"

"Zio is my father. He would hit you with one before me."

"No, he wouldn't. Zio would get in trouble with Daddy for hitting me."

Tarquin snorted. "As if Daddy could scare Papa. A Horseman cannot beat a god. Daddy would run away from Papa terrified if he ever had to fight him. He is only the Horsemen Commander due to Papa dying."

"Tarquin Enzo Giovanni!" Grace scolded her son.

For the first time, Tarquin dared to really test his mother. "All I said is true, Mama. A god is stronger than all the Horsemen and you. I wish Papa never fought Gaelin! Rayne would be the Captain and not the

Commander. He would not be my stepfather! We would all be Giovannis, and I wouldn't have a stupid, annoying sister!"

"Enough!" Dante's voice resounded over theirs, drawing their eyes to him. He gave both children a hard stare as he approached. "Tarquin, a Horseman once killed a god. Never underestimate their importance or the power of one riding in their ranks. I do not want to hear any more disparaging remarks about Rayne, nor should you ever refer to him by his first name. The man loves you and raises you as his own flesh and blood. You will show him respect, even when anger makes you forget that. Now, apologize to your mother and sister."

"Yes, Papa." Tarquin hung his head. "I am sorry, Mama. I did not mean what I said."

"It is okay, Tarquin. I know you were angry." Grace kissed her son's forehead, accepting the hug and apology he offered.

Dante arched a brow after the boy did not freely say something similar to Tessa. "Tarquin, make amends with your sister."

The boy mumbled a half-hearted apology.

"And you, young lady," Dante knelt down, so he looked Tessa in the eye, "as your mother said, you do not throw things at your brother." He set a hand on each of the children's shoulders. "You are family. The two of you should always do your best to get along. When you have differences, talk through them. Now, hug one another, and no more fighting. Or I will zap both of you with lightning bolts for misbehaving."

Grace did her best to conceal the smile creeping onto her face with how quickly the two apologized and hugged one another. They raced to their room once the hug ended to play a game.

"What is this about you and lightning bolts? Have you one of Zeus's powers now?" Grace took the hand Dante offered to help her up.

"I have no idea why they suddenly think I have that ability. That is the first major argument they have had since coming here."

Grace smiled. "They are smart. More than likely, they are sensing the tension in the house and reacting to it, or they are getting more comfortable around you."

"Mayhap a bit of both. Tessa certainly takes after her mother. Rayne and Tarquin will have their hands full keeping the type of boy she will attract at bay."

"She won't need either of them. I will ensure she can hold her own. I do pity any man who breaks her heart considering who her father and apparently zio are."

Dante laughed. "I could not answer her questions to her satisfaction about how I am Tarquin's father since you are married to Rayne. She appointed me her uncle after the discussion. Tessa doubts me any time I tell her you and I were married."

Tessa and Dante having that sort of conversation intrigued Grace. Tessa never asked her or Rayne about Dante. She just accepted Dante was Tarquin's Papa. "Did she say why?"

"I am only a god, while Rayne is the most handsome and brave Horseman ever. And something about girls like knights better than toga-wearing gods. She wanted to know where my toga was since I claimed to be a god, which led to a question about why does Osiris wear a dress." Dante had never adopted the white toga as standard dress. He preferred to wear his own clothes or the Horsemen's black and gold uniform.

"Please tell me you explained that people from different time periods wear different styles of clothing."

"I agreed that knights in black and gold are much more handsome than toga-wearing gods. I also suggested she ask Osiris about his dress if she ever meets him."

Grace burst out laughing. "Your father will have a stroke if Tessa refers to his robes as a dress."

"I am more interested in seeing Ares's or Theseus's reaction to her opinions about toga-wearing gods. Osiris will smile and calmly correct her. He wouldn't want to risk angering you again."

"Mommy! Tarquin and I want to show you Zio's fountain," Tessa called from down the hall.

"Go enjoy a walk in the gardens, cara. The fresh air will do you good."

***

Once the kids were in bed, Grace changed into the nightgown and robe she found lying on the guest bed. Rayne hadn't come to Elysium as she hoped he would. Unable to sleep, she made herself a cup of tea then wandered to the living room. After settling into a comfortable spot on the couch, she studied the stitching in the cuff of the silk robe she wore. Dante always made sure she had anything she needed when life turned upside-down. Rayne and he were both generous with their time and wealth. If only people knew the truth about the two immortals mislabeled War and Death.

"Your welfare always came before mine." Dante invaded her musings, surprised to find her curled up on the couch, watching the swaying flames in the center of the hearth. He thought she had gone to bed an hour ago. "Stop worrying. Rayne will come back to you."

"I wouldn't be too sure about that. I haven't seen him look so hurt or betrayed before this afternoon."

Dante smiled, then sat down on the opposite end of the couch. "Rayne loves you as much as I do. No matter how furious you made me, you could never drive me away. We both know you tried your damnedest to do so."

Grace chuckled, thinking back on the tumultuous relationship she and Dante had shared. "I wish I knew where Rayne was. I can't see him when I try to. Why would he block me like that?"

"Rayne isn't blocking you. The Council stripped away most of your abilities. That is why you can't see or communicate with him."

"The Council has to know I would never randomly kill a human."

"They know, but due to the nature of the accusation, a thorough investigation must be conducted. Unfortunately, they must limit your ability to do harm until it concludes."

"Wonderful. My husband is convinced I betrayed him, and the Council doesn't trust me any longer."

"No one has lost faith in you, Grazia. There are protocols which must be followed in this type of situation. Rayne went back to Spain to find whoever killed Umar. If he truly believed you betrayed him, he would not be trying to prove your innocence. He will come straight here when he can do no more searching today."

Other than the crackle of the logs, a tense silence fell upon the room. It intertwined with Grace's frustration; almost smothering her. She closed her eyes, forcing the negative energy away. She recalled happier times. There were many nights when she had sat curled up with Rayne before a roaring hearth. She and Dante also used to end the day together with quiet time before the fireplace. Neither immortal offered her comfort tonight. Rayne was angry, off somewhere, and Dante sat a few feet away, not allowed to have more contact than necessary with her. Fate threw the three of them into bedlam again. Why had Umar reached out from the past after leaving Rayne in peace for so long? Who killed Rayne's old rival that would have access to her weapon? She stared at the god offering her and her children shelter. There were plenty of prior occasions where Dante eliminated threats to her. Had he done the same now? Finding the courage to ask the inquiry circling in her head, Grace broke the silence. "Did you kill Umar?"

"No, I did not. If I wished to reclaim my wife, there are other ways I would go about it."

Rayne stood in the room doorway, uncertain if he liked finding Grace and Dante together at this late hour. "Her husband will keep a wary eye on his wife's new protector, hearing he has contemplated claiming her again."

Relieved to see him, Grace jumped over the back of the couch and ran to him.

Rayne embraced her. "Forgive me, leof. I was irrational in the Council chambers. The chaos of the day inflamed my temper. I know where your heart rests."

"I should be the one asking forgiveness." Grace smiled before he kissed her hello.

"Mama!" Tarquin called for Grace, interrupting their reunion.

"Go see what he needs." Rayne kissed her forehead before dropping his arms from her side. He noted the way she hesitated to leave. "All is well between us, Grace. I will be waiting for you right here."

Once Grace disappeared down the corridor, Rayne looked over at Dante. "I never freely came between you and Grace. I am asking you for the same courtesy."

Dante arched a mocking brow. "Courtesy? Like the courtesy you showed me in Rome? I know all about the evenings and afternoons I was away, Rayne. If I am not mistaken, she wore a wedding ring and Giovanni was her last name then."

"The only reason that occurred was because you signed my name to a contract as your successor in all things. The Council deemed her mine alone at that time, and the Fates manipulated us until we could not stay away from one another. Your blessing of everything was freely given. It was I who objected to the agreement. I begged you to remove the clause requiring me to marry Grace; to leave us the right to freely decide what may occur after your death, but you refused my request. Is your memory faulty, god, or is mine?"

"This is not easy for me, Rayne, nor were things eleven years ago. I apologize for questioning your integrity. You have my word. I will not touch her in any carnal fashion. If my word is not good enough, one of the terms of her release is I cannot be closer than arm's length to her person. If I violate that... put simply, you'll need to find someone else to watch the children."

Rayne sarcastically laughed. "What else did you negotiate for the Council to release her into your custody?"

Dante understood how Rayne could suspect ulterior motives being at play. "Nothing which concerns you or her. My intent in bringing Grace here was only to protect her, Rayne. Someone went to great lengths to frame her. I would never try to take her from you. I know reclaiming her is impossible. Should you forsake her and the Council ban be lifted, I will seize that window of opportunity and never let her go. Otherwise, I respect that she is your wife. If it is her loyalty that causes you to voice such concerns, you are well aware of how to learn the truth from her lips." Dante motioned to the open window and full moon hanging on high.

"One minor misunderstanding is not cause enough for me to abandon my wife. Grace has never given me a reason to question her fidelity. Now that a cool head prevails, I trust my wife to honor her vow."

Grace returned to find Dante and Rayne staring each other down. Their relaxed stances were deceptive, with the stern expressions on their faces. "What has you two at odds with one another?"

"We are merely clarifying our position on a delicate issue, cara. Nothing comes between us." Dante smiled at her, then looked over at Rayne. "Is my statement incorrect, Commander?"

"No. I am glad we understand one another, amico." Rayne ignored the skeptical look Grace gave him.

"Well, I am certain you two have much to discuss. You are welcome to come and go as you please, Rayne. I bid you both good night."

Grace and Rayne watched Dante stroll down the hallway toward his office.

"Rayne."

"Stop," Rayne halted the second apology she began to utter. "Where is our room? I am tired and want to enjoy what little is left of the evening with my wife."

"Is that really all you want?"

"Yes."

"This way then." Grace showed Rayne to the guest bedroom.

Rayne bathed and readied for bed. He drew the drapes open, contemplating the events of the day. Moonlight flooded into the room. When Grace joined him, he tenderly kissed her.

She sighed after he gently spun her so her back was against his chest and she faced the window. "It comes to this, does it?"

His hands lightly caressed her skin and he murmured, "I love you" against her hair.

"Stop trying to be noble and ask me whatever question you are holding back." Grace wanted to heal the rift opening between them.

"Grace, it isn't..." Rayne couldn't finish the sentence. No matter what he said, it would merely be a shallow excuse.

"There is no need to deny it, Rayne. Part of you needs the reassurance that I answer honestly. Otherwise, you and I wouldn't be standing in the light of the moon right now." Grace turned and stared up at her husband. "Speak your mind, Rayne Warwick."

"What did Lyal share to send you running to Dante last night?"

"The gods concealed something once again. You are in more peril than I initially believed. Osiris refused to answer my inquires. After Osiris's refusal, I went to Dante, suspecting he knew whatever was being concealed. We argued for a short time, then he warned me you must not kill Umar. I returned to Spain hoping to keep you and Umar apart."

Rayne wished she had confided in him. If she had, she wouldn't be under house arrest. She still emotionally bore the scars of Dante's deception. They ran deeper than Rayne thought they did. One day, she would fully grasp he would never intentionally hurt her like that. "Next time Lyal warns you of something, come to me. Just the other day, I promised you I would not ever again ignore any warnings you give me."

"If I don't know what threatens you, I can't offer you adequate warning." Grace brought a grin to Rayne's lips.

"My wife telling me to be on my guard would be more than enough for me to be cautious in my dealings."

"After telling you Rome and Dr. Smith were connected, you downplayed everything. I didn't want you to do that again."

"I had cause to doubt Rome and Dr. Smith tied back to me, Grace." Rayne took her hands in his. "Lyal cautioning us about something is an entirely different circumstance."

"Rayne, someone, something, was setting you up to kill Umar. They were positioning things to leave you little flexibility in deciding whether or not to slay your old rival. Whoever finished the man off foiled whatever being we are up against's plans."

"I wouldn't have killed Umar."

"You think you wouldn't, but I am not so sure. Dante said you'd be severely tested. It sounds as if this Garsea might be able to make you go against your conscience. Did you find any sign of him today?"

Rayne shook his head. "No. Lucifer claims another djinn instigated recent events, contrary to what evidence appears to indicate."

"You don't believe him."

"I do not know what to believe. It is late, Grace. We can worry about Garsea and Lucifer in the morning. For now, I want to enjoy the company of my wife and get some sleep." Rayne brought her against him and settled his arms about her waist.

They stood in silence, staring out the window once more.

After a few minutes, Grace looked up at Rayne. While he held her, he may as well have been somewhere else with the way he stared into the night. The distant look in Rayne's eyes made Grace wonder what her husband thought about.

Reading her thoughts, Rayne smiled. "How much I love my wife and family." He brushed his mouth across hers. "How relieved I am that Dante got you out of Purgatory." He kissed her again. "How thankful I am that I can share moments like these with you while you are under a Council investigation. This is so much better than worrying about you locked away alone in a cell. Let's go to bed."

Once they settled into bed, Rayne wrapped his arms around Grace. She quickly fell asleep with her head on his chest. Unlike her, his troubled conscience kept him awake.

He admired his wife, thinking about their constantly evolving and complex relationship. Seeing her in Othello's carriage for the first time shocked him. The mysterious woman from the British Isles actually sat before him. Time froze when she boldly kissed him in a vain attempt to manipulate him. The second the vision played of Haroun on horseback, he knew the woman's fate and his were entangled.

Learning prophecy promised her to another nearly destroyed him. The two times he lost her to Dante, the Fates ripped his heart out. How could they so easily take her away from him after declaring them to be soulmates? The morning he learned Dante signed her life into his care, genuine panic and fear set in. Did he love her enough to face the storm Dante's death would bring? Would she forgive him for not warning her of the agreement? Was their love strong enough to survive that awful test? What if she grew to hate him? Worse yet, what if he couldn't protect her from his past? Would she and his new stepson lose their lives? Time abated those terrors until the past few weeks.

Rayne forced old nightmares from his mind. No new harm would befall his family. He kissed the top of Grace's head and ran his hand through her hair. "We will find Umar's murderer and clear your name."

Unable to think coherently anymore, he allowed his eyelids to surrender to the heaviness overcoming them.

A few hours later, a sinister presence brought Rayne back to consciousness. He stared at the window where the energy came from. His eyes shimmered silver. An involuntary, visceral snarl arose in his chest. Wicked laughter drifted across the distance. Rayne slipped from the bed. He slowly walked the length of the window, searching for the djinn baiting him from outside. Demons and djinn could not enter Dante's home.

The djinn sneered at Rayne from the other side of the glass, no longer hiding himself.

"Kamar." Rayne recognized his former field commander.

"I never believed the day would come when a god would offer a being like yourself shelter in Elysium. Then again, none of us knew you survived the second battle of Gaudalcete until we tangled with the Horsemen in Gibraltar. More than I was surprised to see you riding in their ranks. How does a monster like yourself gain favor with a Council member, Haroun?"

"Abandon whatever fool's errand you are on and go back to Córdoba, Kamar."

Kamar snickered, intentionally looking past Rayne into the darkened room. "The woman you share a bed with is an intoxicating mix of fragile mortality and magic. She must be quite pleasurable to fuck for you to be so quick to send me on my way."

Rayne stepped through the glass, so he and Kamar stood an inch apart. "Careful how you speak of my wife."

"Your wife, you say?" Kamar nervously swallowed and took a step back. "What creature is she to marry you? She is not one of us."

"Why are you here, Kamar?"

"Malik wished to remind you of old debts you still have to repay."

"I have no debts. Remind Malik of my warning not to make an enemy of me."

"If you wish to keep the woman safe, remember whom you pledged your loyalty to before Morrigan. If you do not, a stronger reminder may be sent."

"Our prior friendship ensures you return in one piece to the caliph tonight. If you fail to heed my warning, I will forget we served together."

Kamar inched towards Rayne, curious to learn if Rayne would make good on the threat.

Rayne flipped Kamar onto the ground. The Horseman's blade grazed Kamar's shoulder, cautioning he would indeed kill to protect his wife.

Noticing bright silver eyes staring down at him, Kamar grinned.

"You wear a new uniform, but are still the same beast, Haroun. I will deliver your message."

Rayne gave the djinn room to regain his feet.

Kamar slowly backed away. "We never escape our bondage, Haroun. We are damned men, you and I."

"I found my salvation. Perhaps one day you will do the same."

The djinn let out a loud laugh. "I am curious, Rayne. What was her reaction once you shared what you are? What all you had done?"

Rayne broke eye contact with Kamar, knowing well the tactic he employed. Lucien played that card too many times. Only fear of a more confident being prompted a djinn to such manipulation.

Kamar waved a finger in Rayne's face, further annoying the Horseman. "Salvation doesn't exist for you and me. Once your sins are laid bare, you will become one of those wolves you foster. The mighty Haroun, nothing more than a mongrel: feared, hated, and condemned to the traitors pack. She won't love you upon learning the truth. They never do. Kato and Sulla should have taught you that lesson well."

Kamar vanished.

Knowing the theatrics ended for the night, Rayne returned inside. Grace still slept soundly. He wondered why Kamar's presence hadn't disturbed her. Just as he pulled the covers over himself, Grace softly laughed, mumbling the word 'commander' with a smile on her face.

Rayne propped himself up on an elbow. "Do you dream of me or Dante, leof?"

Rayne's inquiry woke her. She started to stretch then changed her mind. She hugged him instead. "You, my wolf."

Her answer brought a grin to his face. He kissed her forehead before drifting off to sleep.

Córdoba - 812

Kamar went down on one knee before Isra. "I can confirm Haroun's children are still in Elysium. The sun god, Dante Giovanni, offers them sanctuary."

"And Haroun's wife?" Isra hadn't heard the Council's judgement against her yet.

"Arrested, but released into Giovanni's custody."

Her release flummoxed Isra. It wasn't often the Council would show leniency to an immortal accused of going rogue. "You are certain she is in Elysium and not Purgatory?"

"I saw her myself, mistress. She was sleeping beside Haroun in the sun god's house when I arrived to confirm the children were still there."

The sun god harboring Haroun's wife and children complicated matters. She would have to change course or lure them out of Elysium.

CHAPTER

TWENTY-TWO

Elysium

Dark shifted to light as orange and red intermingled on the horizon. Rayne quietly got out of bed, trying not to wake Grace. After putting on his uniform and body armor, he picked up his boots and sword, then carried them into the hallway. The door latch clicking into place reverberated loudly; the early morning silence deceptively amplifying it as Rayne pulled the door shut. Reaching the living room, he glanced at the large window and glass doors.

Dawn further unfurled. Long streaks of black and navy blue futilely fought to retain their hold on the sky. Vibrant hues of pinks, oranges, purples, and reds gradually weakened night's hold on the heavens. As spectacular as the display of color was, the red undertones warned of a pending melee. Rayne frowned, tugging on his boots. Things were chaotic enough. He didn't need anything hindering his investigation. The faster he could clear Grace's name, the better.

The distinctive aroma of Italian roasted coffee teased his nose. He turned his head to see Dante standing beside the couch with two cups of coffee in his hands. "You are the only being who ever manages to sneak up on me."

Dante chuckled. "Then it is a good thing we are friends."

Rayne grinned, taking the cup Dante extended to him. "Grazie per il caffè."

"Prego." Dante noticed how Rayne stared out the window as he sipped his coffee. "The red sky and Kamar's visit are not related."

Not surprised Dante knew about the djinn's late-night visit, Rayne softly snorted. "Day is your domain, Dante. What warning does the sky bring if it is not related to Kamar?"

"The Fates do not share everything with the gods, just as they do not with the Horsemen."

"Do you honestly expect me to believe a sun god has no insight into omens that appear at daybreak or sunset?"

"Believe whatever you wish. I cannot convince you otherwise." Dante disliked Rayne's new distrust of him. "We are still friends, Rayne. I am not involved in whatever is going on."

Rayne resisted the urge to respond. He forced himself to take another gulp of coffee, then loudly set the cup down on the coffee table. "Keep Grace and the children safe."

He grabbed his sword and started for the front door.

"Rayne." Grace's voice halted him. She walked toward him in her nightgown; her robe fanning out around her, the sides of it rippling in a manner that reminded him of a flowing silken river. The breeze her quick stride created pressed the thin material of her nightgown against her torso, outlining the curves of her breasts and hips. The deep v neckline revealed just enough flesh that if he didn't have a murderer to track down, he'd sweep Grace into his arms and head for the bedroom.

Dante slowly lowering his coffee cup made Rayne aware of the god admiring Grace. Rayne caught the way Dante's eyes quickly traveled up and down her body. An unconscious, appreciative grin appeared on Dante's face.

Anger prompted Rayne to pull Grace against him. His mouth descended upon hers, delivering a bruising, fervent kiss; his hand possessively grasped her hip. The territorial display reminded Dante of whose wife she was.

"Well, good morning to you, too." Grace smiled up at her husband, surprised by the passionate greeting. "That more than makes up for not waking me and letting me know you were leaving for the day."

"After all the excitement yesterday and how late we went to bed, I didn't want to disturb you." Rayne kept his eyes on Dante as he lowered his lips to Grace's ear. "May I suggest closing your robe, my love? We are guests in Dante's home. No telling who may randomly appear."

Dante's brow shot upward at the way Rayne emphasized the words "my love."

"Sorry." Grace hastily tied the belt of her robe. "I was worried you'd leave before I reached you."

Raphael, suddenly standing in the living room, drew all three immortals' attention. Rayne grinned, resettling his arm around Grace. Raphael's timing proved his point.

"What brings you by so early in the day?" Dante addressed his new guest.

"The Council is in an emergency closed session. Isis advises that the three of you are to remain here and should expect a summons in an hour or two."

The early morning gathering worried Grace. "What are they meeting about?"

"I do not know. I'll return later when they are ready to speak with you." Raphael vanished as quickly as he appeared.

Grace let out a worried groan. "What now?"

"I am certain whatever it is, we will find a way to resolve it. In the meantime, may I offer you a coffee, cara? Or perhaps a cappuccino?" Dante downplayed Raphael's message, hoping to ease Grace's angst.

"I haven't had one of your special cappuccinos in years. I would love one."

Rayne gave Grace's shoulder a gentle squeeze. "I brought several changes of clothes for you. You'll find them in the bag on the chair closest to the dresser."

"Shouldn't I wear my uniform if we are going before the Council?"

Rayne shook his head. "I am sorry, leof. With the Council temporarily stripping you of your rank, you can't."

"Go change, Grazia. It will take me a few minutes to prepare your cappuccino. I will also throw together something for breakfast since none of us are going anywhere for a few hours." Dante offered Grace a reassuring smile then walked to the kitchen.

Rayne sat back down on the couch, thinking about Kamar's warning. He knew the red dawn promised trouble, contrary to what Dante claimed.

A few minutes later, Dante returned with a tray of pastries, fruit, Grace's cappuccino, and a small pot of coffee. He settled it on the coffee table before sitting in a large chair across from Rayne.

"The Council meeting is more than likely Lucifer's doing than Malik's." Dante held up the coffeepot, offering to refill Rayne's empty cup.

Rayne put his hand over the top of his cup, no longer interested in coffee or food. "I am good. Thank you."

Dante refilled his own cup. "Did you find anything yesterday?"

"Nothing that can clear Grace's name. Destahn and I saw the murder. Whoever the assailant was disguised themselves well. They left no trace of who they were. I was able to track their footsteps until they reached town. Any sign of them disappeared after that."

"So the killer has an immortal assisting them." Dante leaned back in his chair, not liking the idea of that.

"It appears so. I suspect Kamar or Narcisco to be the one who aided the killer with Kamar's appearance last night. Kamar always enjoyed gloating when he thought he got away with something clever."

"Kamar? Where did you two run into one another?" Grace interjected, rejoining them and picking up her cappuccino from the tray.

"Córdoba." Rayne hated lying, but he didn't want Grace to worry any more than she already did.

Distracted by the sweet taste of amaretto crossing her tongue, Grace missed the reproaching glare Dante shot Rayne. She smiled, enjoying the pleasant surprise ingredient Dante added to her coffee. She never knew what to expect when he made them for her. Sometimes they would be plain. Other times there would be hints of chocolate or cinnamon, but the shot of amaretto was a welcome addition for a stressful morning. When she smiled over at Dante after swallowing her first sip of coffee, Dante winked at her. The soft laugh she let out caused Rayne to give her a suspicious look. Grace ignored Rayne, picking up a strawberry from the plate of fruit then eating it. "This is divine, Dante."

"I am glad it meets with your approval, cara. Tell us more about the assailant you saw, Rayne."

"There isn't much to share. They were dressed in black and concealed their face. They could be a human or a djinn. Complicating matters, their build could also be that of a woman or a man. If Umar's wounds had been clean cut, I would immediately suspect a djinn or a professional assassin. In contrast to their efforts to disguise their identity, they didn't take the time to perfect their skill with a blade."

Dante shook his head. He had hoped Rayne would have found more to develop a defense for Grace.

Grace recalled something that might help with the investigation. "Hades said he had eyewitness testimony I was here the night before last. Did you or Osiris tell him I was here?"

"No, cara. My father offered no testimony, nor did Hades question him about the evening. I learned of the murder charges when my father warned me a warrant had been issued for you. Knowing I only had a few minutes to reach you before Raphael did, I went straight to you. Hades and I did not have any sort of discussion until the Council charged you."

Rayne wondered if there even was a witness. "Then who is this witness Hades spoke of?"

"I am not certain. My mother and the children were asleep. Grace and I were the only ones awake in my home. Kamar was not here. I would have known if he was." Dante suddenly scowled as he realized who the witness might be.

The way Dante's expression darkened from reflective to furious told Rayne the nature of the potential witness. "Nothing like the wrath of a jilted lover. Who's been warming your bed, Dante?"

Raphael reappeared in the room, halting their discussion. "The Council requests all of your presence immediately."

Grace wasn't sure how they could comply. If the three of them left, no one would be in Dante's home to watch Tessa and Tarquin. "We can't leave the kids unprotected."

"I will remain here with them." Raphael eased Grace's worries.

As she took Rayne's hand, she noticed Lyal standing in the darkened hallway. What was she doing there? Before Grace could stop Rayne, he teleported them to the Council Round.

The High Council Round -

Hades, Osiris, Isis, and Poseidon gathered together in quiet deliberation while other members of the Council conversed amongst themselves.

Since they had not been acknowledged yet, Grace whispered to Rayne and Dante. "Why is Lyal in Elysium?"

Dante thought he misheard Grace. "What?"

"I saw her in the hall, Dante."

"Lyal is not in Elysium. The only women to visit my home besides yourself are my mother and sister."

"You lie, cavaliere. I just saw her." Grace hated how Dante kept so many secrets. What had happened to the two of them that they became what they were? Had their relationship fallen that much prior to his death?

Grace's unspoken questions disturbed Dante more deeply than a harbinger hiding in his home. "Lyal couldn't be in Elysium without me knowing she was there."

"Exactly my point, Dante. She hates you and your father. The only way she would be there is if someone dispatched her. What is going on that you requested a harbinger to guard your home?"

"I didn't make any such request," Dante said loud enough that Hades and Osiris looked over at them. He lowered his voice once more. "I am more than capable of defending my home without her assistance. I think the stress of recent events is wearing on you."

"I know who I saw." Grace stepped closer to Dante.

Rayne slid himself between the two to prevent the disagreement from escalating. "If Grace believes she saw Lyal, perhaps we need to investigate the matter, Dante."

"I know when someone enters the confines of my home, Rayne. Lyal is not there."

"The hell she isn't!" Grace snapped at her ex.

"Keep your voices down," Rayne chastised, noticing various Council members now observing them. "We can figure this out later."

Dante's temper pricked, he couldn't let the matter go. "I understand you are angry, Grace. The only way a harbinger could lurk in my home..."

"Commander Warwick," Osiris addressing Rayne cut off Dante's statement.

Dante's eyes narrowed. The realization of who must have sent Lyal to Elysium and hidden her presence set in. "Father, before we begin, may I have a word with you?"

Curious as to why Dante made such a request, Osiris materialized beside them.

Rayne's arm encircled Grace's waist, pulling her back against his chest. "This is neither the place nor the time to fight with Osiris."

Grace hated the warning whispered in her ear. Muscle would become steel if she made any threatening advance towards Osiris.

"Grace believes Lyal was in my home this morning." Dante closely watched for his father's reaction.

Osiris's features remained stoic. "Lyal cannot enter your home without you knowing. All gods are aware of those around them."

"Tarquin mentioned seeing a woman with black eyes yesterday."

"What?" Grace impulsively took a step toward Dante and Osiris. Rayne's arm constricted across her torso. "And you didn't investigate Tarquin's claim before now?"

"Calma, tranquilla, Grazia." Dante waved his hand, asking Grace to calm down. "I searched the house and found no one after Tarquin told me about the woman in the rear garden." He returned his attention to Osiris. "Are you certain you are not aware of anyone dispatching the harbinger to my home?"

"This is most concerning, Dante. The Council issued no directive for Lyal to surveil your home or the children." Osiris now seemed puzzled by Tarquin and Grace alleging to have seen Lyal.

Grace hated the way Osiris thoughtfully stroked his chin and beard. "He's lying."

Osiris cast Grace a dismissive glance. "I do not lie. The Council did not dispatch Lyal."

"The Council may not have, but someone did. And I'd bet that someone was you."

"Grazia, silenzio, per favore." Dante took a deep breath, as frustrated as Grace was by Osiris's denial. "Father, if you dispatched Lyal, admit that you did, and tell me why she is there. What do you fear will happen?"

"Dante, I did not send her to your home."

"You deceitful, lying bastard! I can sense you know more than you are sharing, Osiris," Grace snapped at her father-in-law.

"Grace, do not do this here." Rayne tried to remind Grace of their surroundings.

"It's no secret that I can't stand Osiris."

"Najmati…" Osiris hoped to soothe Grace's temper.

"You do not get to najmati me, Osiris. I am not your star anymore. Not after everything you took. If anything happens to my kids, I will find a way to kill you."

Rayne couldn't believe she threatened a council member in the Council Round. "Have you lost all sense of reason, woman?"

"Well, isn't this a touching family reunion? The only thing missing are the kids," Hades interrupted the growing disagreement, now walking towards them.

Rayne firmly clamped a hand over Grace's mouth to prevent any retort headed Hades's way. "Say nothing more, leof."

Hades snickered at the Horseman's quick silencing of his wife. "Let her speak, Commander. She only hangs herself."

"What is the purpose of the summons this morning, Hades?" Dante eyed the god of the Greek underworld, mistrustful of his motives.

"There's been a new development in the case against your wife. My apologies. I keep forgetting you gave her to Rayne. Having Grace under your roof must be a frustrating arrangement for both you and Commander Warwick."

Dante did not allow Hades to provoke him. "Are you going to share this new development?"

"One of Umar's servants saw a woman running from Umar's house.

She disposed of this just outside the estate's gates." Hades held out a black cloak. "Would you kindly try the cloak on, Defensore Warwick?"

Grace stared down at the garment. "It isn't mine."

"Humor me, Defensore." Hades more forcefully thrust it toward her. His hand pressed the cloak into her chest.

Rayne shoved the god back. "While you have the dispensation to make requests, you have no right to touch my wife."

"It's all right, Rayne. The cloak won't prove anything." Grace swung it behind her so she could settle it on her shoulders. Cold traveled up her neck as the black material made contact with her skin. She heard a muffled female voice talking to someone, and a blurred outline of a woman with blonde hair and silver eyes appeared.

Osiris saw the startled expression on Grace's face. "What did you see?"

"A female immortal. She has pale blonde hair and silver eyes. I can't place her face."

Hades smirked. "You are certain you don't know her?"

"I've never seen her before." Grace could still see the woman's face as she pulled the cloak off. "Who is she?"

"A djinn, who claims you sought her out to make a private arrangement to kill Umar. One which would prevent the Council from seeing your actions," Hades said, revealing the reason for the impromptu meeting.

Panicked by the additional false allegation, Grace shook her head. "I would never do such a thing."

"You just threatened a council member. You clearly have no problem straying from our laws and traditions."

"She has reason to be angry with me, Hades." Osiris surprisingly came to Grace's defense. "I am the one who approved the pact Dante made."

"Are you saying you do not believe the Defensore is capable of such an act?" Hades seemed entertained by Osiris's statements.

"I do not believe it is in her character to do such things. While all beings are capable of atrocious undertakings, Grace Warwick would not enter into a negotiation of that nature. As demonstrated earlier, she prefers to be open with her actions and words.

That is one of the many reasons we selected her to become the Defensore."

Hades scoffed. "She's a former Hasan thief."

Dante wondered why Hades was so convinced that Grace murdered Umar. "All of us know Qasim and Fariq lied to her and presented themselves as her rescuers. A human in shock, after learning she was kidnapped and time traveled several centuries, would be susceptible to that sort of deception."

"She drugged you and stole a relic from your bedroom, Dante."

"To save her brother's life. If she was on trial for theft, your case would be on more solid ground, Hades."

"You confirm she committed two crimes to protect her brother. What makes you certain she wouldn't kill to save the man she loves?"

"It isn't in her nature." Dante raised his voice. Hades's vindictive pursuit of Grace wore on him.

"Do you have any actual evidence of my wife bargaining with this so-called djinn?" Rayne doubted Hades did. This was another show for the Council.

"Indirectly." Hades shrugged, not elaborating.

Rayne laughed. "Hearsay proves nothing in a case like this."

"You might think differently, Commander, after you learn more about Grace and Dante's discussion the other evening."

Dante didn't like the smug look on Hades's face. "I already disclosed the nature of my discourse with the Defensore."

"In light of the djinn's claim, there might be one detail you left out that the Council needs to know about."

Dante glared at Hades. "And what detail is that?"

"Maybe it is better we hear about this matter from Grace herself. After all, she is the one on trial." Hades knew Dante would wordsmith any answer offered. "Defensore, did you not offer yourself up in exchange for Commander Warwick's life?"

"I fail to see what this has to do with Umar's death."

"Please answer the question, Defensore. Did you offer yourself to Dante in exchange for Commander Warwick's life?"

"Being willing to trade my soul for someone else to live does not make me a murderer."

"You still haven't answered my question, Grace. Please inform the Council of your negotiations with Dante."

"Yes, I offered myself to Dante if it meant I could ensure Rayne would survive whatever test lie before him. I would freely give my life for my husband and children if needed."

Hades laughed. "To be clear, you didn't nobly offer your life up for your husband. Allow me to quote what my witness overhead, "I know what you want most. You can have it, Dante, Just tell me how many nights are needed to save him.""

"Trying to humiliate an accused is not acceptable conduct of the Council Prosecutor!" Dante interjected. His eyes shot up into the Council ranks, landing on Volupta. The way she held her chin higher and glared back at him confirmed she was the witness. He'd strangle the petty goddess for endangering Grace's life.

Poseidon noticed Volupta's reaction to Dante's remark. So Hades's pursuit of the Defensore was not solely in the interest of seeing justice done. Grace was caught in the crossfire of a vendetta between the goddess and Dante. "Strike Hades's comment from the record. Hades, I am cautioning you as Dante has that anything said in these proceedings must support the case against the Defensore."

Hades smiled. "I assure you, the quote has relevance. I am demonstrating that when desperate, the Defensore is willing to barter whatever services are necessary to accomplish what she believes is the right thing. Defensore, please reconfirm your last statement for the Council. I want to ensure whatever is recorded is accurate."

"I said I would give my life for my husband and children."

"Clearly, you'd do more than give your life. What lengths would you go to if Commander Warwick or your children were endangered?"

Grace hated how Hades phrased his question. She had no other choice than to honestly answer the inquiry. "I would do whatever was necessary to protect my husband and children, including give up my body or my entire being for them. Does my answer now satisfy the prosecution?"

"Not quite yet. You said you would do whatever is necessary to protect Commander Warwick. Would you also conspire to commit murder to protect your husband, Defensore?"

"No. There is a vast difference between surrendering my existence and robbing another of theirs."

"Please elaborate on your answer, Defensore," Aphrodite directed. She could see Grace was innocent and was moved by how much the woman loved her husband. She also sensed lingering feelings for Dante within Grace. No wonder Volupta had so readily come forward.

"Goddess, my life, body, and soul are mine to give. They are all I truly have to trade. They are all I would ever trade since taking my oath to the Council. As the Council knows, Qasim and Rasil tortured and almost killed me. My sense of hope and self-worth were ripped from me by the actions of three heartless immortals. It took years to repair the harm done. A decade later, Commander Warwick, my husband, was left with no other choice than to take my humanity from me after I sustained a mortal injury in the last battle with Gaelin. While his reasons for saving me were noble, I still had no voice in whether I died or became immortal. All of you know the bargain Dante struck with the Council, which took my freewill away once again. No one has the right to rob anyone of their freewill. No one understands that more than someone who lost their freedom to choose on multiple occasions. I also simply value life and the gift of humanity. I never asked or sought to become immortal. Murdering Umar, in his sleep, for selfish reasons would go directly against my own beliefs and values, not just the oath I took to the Council. I could not take a soul without sanction, even that of a human who has done the despicable things Umar has. As much as I love my husband, I could never justify trading a life other than my own to save him. I would find another way."

Aphrodite smiled. "Defensore, I have another request of you. Please share with me why you would barter with Dante, and not another deity. After all, you shared Dante contributed to your loss of choice."

Grace glanced over at Rayne and Dante. The trademark annoyed clenched jaw and twitch in Dante's cheek returned. Dante was clearly furious Aphrodite made the inquiry. In contrast, Rayne nodded, encouraging her to answer. He recognized how Aphrodite gave Grace the opportunity to dismantle the picture Hades attempted to paint of her going rogue out of desperation.

"Yes, Dante did. It is no secret I harbor some resentment for his doing so. At the same time, Dante has always protected his brethren and me. Even when doing things I vehemently disagree with." Grace paused and stared at Dante. His eyes stayed locked with hers as she continued her answer. "The truth of the matter is, Dante is the only deity I would trust to follow through on his end of the agreement. He rarely breaks promises once he gives them. On the rare occasion he does, it is because he knows his doing so will serve the greater good. As we've all seen, he'd sacrifice his own needs for others anytime it is required of him. Besides Rayne, Dante is the only immortal I would ever freely negotiate with. The rest of you aren't so honorable."

Some laughter and murmurs swept through the Council members observing the trial.

Waiting for them to quiet, Grace looked back at Rayne. Surprisingly, he smiled at her.

Perfect answers to Aphrodite's inquiries, leof.

Once silence settled over the hall again, Rayne stepped forward. "As you've all now heard, my wife would not barter with a djinn or a god, other than Dante. In order to give my wife a fair defense, with the Council's approval of course, I would like to question the djinn who allegedly met with my wife, and have them stand before the Council, so we may all hear the nature of the supposed agreement struck. Hades, may I have the name of the djinn who claims to have entered into a contract with my wife?"

"I offered the djinn anonymity in exchange for their testimony."

"None of the Council approved such an arrangement," Poseidon spoke up, displeased Hades acted outside his authority. "The judges panel finds this evidence to be circumstantial at best as Commander Warwick earlier deemed it. We also find the Defensore's explanation of why she would never barter with a djinn credible. We release the Defensore back into Dante Giovanni's custody until the investigation concludes. I strongly urge you to execute your duties with haste, Hades. Commander Warwick and the Defensore need to return to their normal duties. This proceeding is adjourned for the day."

Still incensed about things, Dante walked over to his father. The Council members scattered, talking with one another or left the building.

Rayne discretely rested his hand on the small of Grace's back as they stood together watching the commotion around the room. "Hades tries the Council's patience. I have a feeling they will dismiss the charges soon."

"You aren't angry with me?" Grace expected him to be furious after his reaction to everything the day prior.

"No. I suspected the exact nature of your conversation with Dante when I learned of it yesterday. It's the only thing that explained Dante's behavior with both of you readily denying anything more than talking took place. So when the truth came out today, I was prepared to hear it. While I understand why you did what you did, please never do such a foolish thing ever again. As I promised last night, I won't disregard your concerns in the future."

"Believe me. I've learned my lesson well on this one."

Rayne smiled. If he wasn't in uniform and standing in Council chambers, he would have embraced and kissed her to reassure her everything was okay.

Grace leaned into him. His hand moved to her side and he gave her a quick one-armed hug. "I love you, Commander. And I'll make this one up to you."

"No need, leof. I wasn't exactly on my best behavior yesterday. We'll consider things even."

Finished speaking with Osiris, Dante returned to Grace and Rayne. "How many blonde-haired, female djinn are in Córdoba?"

"A half dozen or so, but none have silver eyes." Rayne wondered why Dante asked.

Volupta coming down from the seats to the floor to mingle with other Council members redirected Dante's attention. The statuesque, mahogany-haired goddess glared at Dante.

Grace hadn't seen the woman giving Dante a death stare before. "Who is that?"

Rayne frowned. So Volupta was Hades's eyewitness. "Volupta. Daughter of Psyche and Cupid. She isn't a Council member, and rarely ventures into the mortal realm."

"She's beautiful."

"Only on the outside," Dante said loud enough Volupta heard him.

"Otherwise, she is a petty, vindictive stranza with a black heart."

Grace rarely heard Dante speak so derogatorily of a woman. "I'll steer clear of her then."

"Wise decision, cara. Rayne, you said none of the blonde female djinn in Córdoba have silver eyes. Why is that?"

"A silver-eyed djinn would be an enforcer or a descendent of a demon. There are no demon and djinn offspring in Córdoba, and there was only one silver-eyed enforcer that I am aware of, but he's long dead."

"Are you certain he's dead?" Grace asked as the three of them walked towards the doors of the Council chambers to go back to Elysium.

"I am. I killed him."

TWENTY-THREE

Elysium

"Rayne, do you think Hades lied about the djinn?" Dante inquired as they walked through the rear gardens towards his home.

"I honestly don't know. Whether or not he did, something is off about this djinn's claims. Djinn aren't powerful enough to hide something from the Council. I can't see one even contemplating an agreement requiring such a thing. And, as I said earlier, only a djinn enforcer or demon would have silver eyes; neither of which would act as a soul broker. Hades alleges Grace traded her soul in exchange for mine and killing Umar served as the payment for the exchange. An agreement of that nature would require either a soul broker or an enforcer. Unless the bargain was made with an overseer. None of the soul brokers or enforcers in Córdoba are silver-eyed, nor is Isra."

"What color eyes would they have?" Grace asked, not knowing much about djinn.

"Dark eyes." Rayne halted as the words left his lips.

It dawned on Grace why her husband suddenly froze. "Like Lyal's?"

"Get to the house." Rayne's eyes scanned the gardens and backyard for djinn.

Patrolling one side of the yard while Rayne walked the other, Dante reached out to Raphael. *Raphael, where are Tessa and Tarquin?*

Hearing the concern in Dante's voice, Raphael checked the weapon on his side. *With me in the kitchen. Why do you ask?*

Lock the doors, and keep them inside. We have uninvited company. Grace should meet up with you any second now.

"Mommy!" Tessa loudly greeted Grace from the table.

Grace is here. I am moving to the back door. Raphael glanced over at Grace then put his undrunk cup of coffee on the table.

"We're going to play a game, sprite," Grace whispered, hugging her daughter. "One of the rules are we have to be very, very quiet."

"Zio taught me the mices game!" Tessa pretended she locked her lips shut.

"Good girl, Tessa. Now, I want you and Tarquin to hide between the couch and the coffee table in the living room, so no one can see you through the windows. Tarquin, go with your sister."

Tarquin knew something was wrong. "What is happening, Mama?"

"Nothing for you to worry about. Please do as I ask. Keep away from the windows, and no matter what happens, stay on the floor with Tessa."

"Yes, Mama." Tarquin took Tessa's hand. The two hurried to the living room. Grace tried to give them a reassuring smile after they crouched down between the two pieces of furniture.

Raphael touched Grace on the arm when he passed her. *Whoever is out there won't get to the children.* He continued on to the door. Reaching it, he rested his back against the wall, doing his best to keep out of sight while still being able to view the rear yard and gardens.

The front is clear. Dante's voice sounded in Grace's head. *Coming around the east side to help Rayne finish sweeping the rear elevation.*

Dante met Rayne in the center of the yard. "Find anything?"

"Nothing. Whoever was here is gone now. Or like Grace claims, Lyal is lurking nearby, and she is who Tarquin saw."

"Either way. It is probably best we stay on guard." Dante didn't like the idea of djinn being around.

Rayne gave Grace and Raphael the all clear.

Grace and Tessa joined Raphael at the back door. Excited to see Rayne, Tessa bolted outside. She ran straight for him. "Daddy!"

Rayne picked her up when she reached him. "I've missed you, sprite."

"I miss you, Daddy. Are we all going to live with Zio now?"

Rayne laughed as his daughter gave him her best bear hug. "No, we are not living with Zio. We are just visiting him."

"But I like Zio and Nonna Maria."

"Zio and Nonna may visit us anytime they like."

"But Nonna can't leave Elysium, and Zio can only come to our house as a ghost cause Mommy isn't supposed to see him."

Rayne pretended to ponder Tessa's words. "Hmmm...I suppose we could live here. But, if we do, what will happen to poor Lavinia? And who will feed Fahkir, Diya, and Vittore?"

"Oh?" Tessa's eyes grew wide at the thought of Lavinia, the cook she adored, being alone and no one taking care of their horses. "Lavinia would be sad."

"Yes, she would."

"And the horses would be starving."

"Most likely." Rayne's smile grew as Tessa reasoned out the need to go home.

"We should go home, Daddy."

"We will. Once your visit with Zio is over. He needs you and Tarquin to stay and play for a few more days." Rayne gave Tessa one more hug. He set her down as Grace joined them.

Tarquin stared at Rayne from the steps.

Rayne noticed the angry glare on the boy's face. "Is everything all right, Tarquin?"

Tarquin rolled his eyes then went back inside.

Grace had never seen Tarquin treat Rayne in such a manner. "What was that about?"

"I am not sure." Rayne wondered about the defiant behavior himself.

Dante must have seen Tarquin as he now walked up the steps towards the house.

A shrill scream from Tessa caused all four of the adults to turn around. Tessa futilely swatted at a man dressed in medieval Spanish garb who grasped her arm.

Rayne recognized the massive djinn holding Tessa captive. "Let her go, Narciso."

"What a lovely little girl you have, Haroun."

Rayne drew his sword, moving toward the djinn. "Release my daughter."

Grace started forward, but Dante blocked her path. "Allow us to deal with this. Without your abilities, you could get hurt."

Rayne lurched sideways as if something tackled him from his right. For a brief moment, Rayne found his shoulders pinned back against the ground. He grabbed his attacker's face and forced their head backwards; giving him enough clearance to get his full arm between him and them.

Watching Rayne fling the invisible assailant from him, Dante pulled his weapon.

Rayne climbed to his feet, staring at whatever was in the yard. "I can see you, Isra."

"Isra?" Grace wondered who exactly Rayne fought and why they attacked him in Elysium, of all places.

Lyal materialized out of nowhere beside Narciso. Before the djinn could react, Lyal snapped his wrist and slammed the elbow of her other arm back into his face. The large djinn had to let go of Tessa to recover his balance. In a split second, Lyal grabbed Tessa and teleported over to Grace.

"Your daughter, Defensore."

Grace took Tessa, relieved she was safe. "Thank you."

Dante engaged Narciso. The djinn got in one swing before Dante's sword plunged into his chest, sending Narciso back to Hell.

"You're alone, Isra. It was foolish to only bring Narciso with you." Rayne cautiously closed in on the being no one else could see.

"We had a bargain, Ibn-Ziyad."

A column of dark smoke swirled and danced a short distance from Rayne. Raphael and Dante formed an armed barrier between Grace and the solidifying being in the yard. Dante muttered under his breath, worrying Grace. The column dissipated, revealing a tall woman with sangria-hued hair, dark eyes, and honey-colored skin dressed in a deep, dark red.

"Eternal servitude was the price for what you desired, Haroun."

The tip of Rayne's blade stayed trained on Isra as the overseer moved to his right. "Umar did not perish as promised that night."

"So it took me a little time to see to the general's end. Now that my end of the agreement is fulfilled, I expect you to fulfill yours."

Rayne laughed. "I don't think so, Isra."

"Then I demand adjudication from the Council prosecutor."

The request snapped Grace out of the mental shock she was in. "You have no right to demand any such thing."

Hades appeared in the yard. "On the contrary, Grace, any immortal may demand adjudication if a party fails to honor an indenture of servitude freely given to another. May I review the indenture?"

Isra handed Hades a document. The god unrolled the scroll, then his eyes skimmed over it.

Grace shot Rayne a panicked look after Hades let out an 'ahem, interesting' as he continued reading.

Raphael recognized the contract Hades held. "Isra released Rayne from any further service in Jerusalem."

"A deal is a deal. The Commander's consent was freely given." Hades shrugged, siding with Isra after examining the contract. "The silver lining to all this is it appears you are off the hook for Umar's murder, Defensore. I will file the appropriate documents to set a release hearing." Hades re-rolled the scroll and offered it back to Isra.

Grace handed Tessa to Lyal. "She cannot have my husband."

"I'm sorry, Grace. My hands are tied in this matter. Rayne freely made the agreement."

"Hades, are you really turning the Horsemen Commander over to a djinn? What exactly do you think a regional overseer will use War for?" Grace couldn't believe any of this was happening.

Isra snickered, relishing the chaos she caused. "I will gladly take your daughter's soul instead. She is developing some intriguing gifts that benefit me more than your sword, Haroun."

Rayne's eyes turned storm-colored at Isra's audacity to request Tessa fulfill a bargain he made. "My daughter's soul is not up for trade."

Isra gestured towards Grace. "Then perhaps the woman?"

"You will take no one from this yard, Isra."

The overseer's eyes briefly fell on Grace, then drifted towards Lyal and Tessa. She noticed Tarquin watching from the doorway. A cruel smile twisted her lips before she focused on Rayne again. "I never expected you to be a family man, Haroun. Not with how you enjoyed killing and pillaging. I was rather surprised when Kamar reported that you had a wife and daughter hidden away. You wouldn't want them to learn what you really are, would you? Spare them the horror of seeing your true nature, bid them farewell."

Rayne's eyes shifted to a darker shade of gray. "Why would I bid them farewell? I am not going anywhere."

"Did you not hear Hades?" Isra smirked, more than happy to fight with the Horseman.

Raphael took a step towards Isra. "We all know the contract is a forgery. You test all of us far too much with this nonsense."

Hades doubted Raphael would violate the law, even for another Horseman. "Raphael, your job is to enforce Council decrees, not to defend criminals."

"Nothing will be enforced today." Dante glared at Hades. "I invoke full Council review of the contract due to *cremin falsi ab falsus procurator.*"

Dante's deployment of the old law intrigued Hades. "Based on what justification, Giovanni?"

"You aren't as clever as you think you are, Hades. Rayne is my successor in all things personal and professional. There is no higher decree than that of the Council. Even if the indenture were legal, it is null and void. Rayne has sworn an oath to the Council and myself. An immortal promise supersedes any bargains a human may strike with a djinn."

"In light of this new evidence, the Commander remains a freeman." Hades nodded to Dante then disappeared.

With everyone distracted by Hades's exit, Isra lunged at Rayne, sending him to the ground once more.

Rayne wrestled with his old mistress. Isra had grown stronger than she used to be.

"Leave my father alone!" Tarquin sprinted from the house, shooting past Grace and Dante.

The boy's declaration confused Isra. She looked up at the running boy, who was clearly Dante's son. "Your fath—"

Tarquin jumped on top of Isra and slammed a knife he held into Isra's side, silencing the overseer mid-word. "Get off my dad!"

"Never come back here!" Tarquin screamed, holding up the blood covered blade then forced it down into her back

"Tarquin, go to your mother," Rayne yelled up at the boy. He couldn't vanquish Isra as long as Tarquin was on her back.

Lost in his rage, Tarquin brought the knife he held up again. "You can't have either of my fathers, demon."

Fearing Isra would harm the boy, Rayne grabbed Tarquin by the ankle, yanked him off Isra, then shoved him away. Finally having a clear target, Rayne drove his own blade up through Isra's chest, vanquishing her.

All eyes rested on the nine-year-old who appeared to be more of a wild animal than an immortal. He had moved so quickly no one could intervene in his irrational attack on Isra.

Amber met gold as Dante slowly approached his son. He knew the fear that prompted the boy to take action well. "Give me the knife, Tarquin."

Tarquin obediently handed over the weapon, then hugged Dante.

Seeing Dante had the knife and Tarquin was safe, Rayne let his head fall back onto the grass. He closed his eyes, taking a deep breath to slow the pulse pounding in his ears. Thank the gods no one besides Isra was seriously injured.

Dante dropped the knife beside him and held his son. He never wished for Tarquin to suffer this sort of conflict so young. Rage and fear were the only emotions Dante felt for years after witnessing the murder of his mother and sister. He hated that his own son dwelled in the midst of those dark sentiments now. *May the Fates spare Tarquin the anguish I endured.* "Rayne, your mother, and I will never leave you, Tarquin. We will always be with you. You are very brave, mio figlio. There is one rule of war you must learn and master. Never arbitrarily strike an enemy in anger as you did today. That will lead you to injury."

"Is that how you died, Papa?"

Dante frowned. Now was not the time for such a discussion. "No. The answer you seek is much more complicated, Tarquin. It is one you are not wise enough to hear yet."

"So you did abandon us! You don't love me or Mama as you say you do."

Tarquin's words wounded Dante. The hurt they caused etched itself across the chiseled features of the god's face. "That is not true, Tarquin. I love you and your mother more than life itself. I wish I could explain everything to you, but you are too young to understand the choice I made."

Tarquin shrugged free and ran into the house.

"Tarquin!" Grace started to go after the boy.

Rayne climbed the rest of the way to his feet. "Wait! Allow me to speak with him. I understand how he feels better than you do."

"You understand..." Grace couldn't bring herself to finish her sentence noticing the color of Rayne's eyes. They were no longer executioner gray as they normally would be moments after an intense conflict, instead, they were a vibrant silver. The same luminescent color of Xander's eyes!

There was no more hiding his past. Grace and everyone else could clearly see the eyes of the enforcer he once was. "Grace, I can explain."

Grace shook her head, still not believing Rayne stared at her with silver eyes. "Tend to Tarquin. I need a minute."

"As you wish."

Grace watched Rayne disappear into the house. A few seconds later she heard Rayne say Tarquin's name, then Tarquin shouted, "I hate him." She glanced over at Dante. He remained kneeling on the grass, his head hung, grappling with his own emotions.

Osiris appeared behind Dante and placed a hand on his shoulder. "Your burden is lifted and your debt paid. The Council releases you."

Dante sarcastically laughed at what his father thought was a welcomed gift. "The Council releases me? The burden will never be gone! The price paid follows me through eternity, along with my son. Is that not evident to you with the events of the day?"

"More than you can bear, but not more than you can overcome, Dante." Osiris motioned for Lyal to follow then vanished.

Tessa asked Grace to put her down. The second her feet hit the ground, she ran to the sun god. Tessa hugged Dante. "Don't be sad, Zio. Tarquin loves you. He's just being mean."

Moved by her tender, little heart, Dante returned the hug.

"Smile, Zio. Smiles make us happy."

The best Dante could do was a half grin. "Grazie mille for trying to give me hope, little one."

Knowing Dante needed Grace, Raphael gently took Tessa by the arm. "Come on, ragazza. Let us go inside."

Grace crossed the short distance to the god on his knees. She ran her fingers through his dark hair. Dante refused to look up at her.

"My wife and son despise me."

Tears stung Grace's eyes. "We don't hate you, Dante. We simply do not understand."

Dante buried his face in her belly, grieving again for the loss of his family. "I never meant to hurt either of you. I only sought to protect the two of you, to give you a good life, no matter the cost to myself."

Grace realized letting her and Tarquin go tolled him more than she ever imagined. "Mio misero bello cavaliere."

"Si. Sempre tua solo, cara." Dante reaffirmed his heart was hers alone.

Grace slowly came to her knees. Today, she wiped the tears from his face. "Grazie, Dante. One day, our son will understand and thank you, too."

The softly spoken words seared through him. Twice now, she offered her gratitude to him after years of distance and anger. For the first time since becoming a god, Dante embraced Grace without fear or reservation, welcoming the comfort she offered. "Go back to hating me, Grazia."

Grace laughed. "You once reminded me you could live with the way I felt anytime I said I hated you."

Dante recalled the night in Damascus when he told her exactly that. "Oh, mia Grazia, how I wish I never made that wretched agreement."

"I would be dead, and you would be the one cursing me."

"No, mia stella, I would have demanded my father send me into the afterlife with you and Tarquin." Resisting the urge to kiss her, Dante took her face in his hands. He drew her to him and rested the side of his head against hers; finding solace in the feel of the soft strands of her hair against his face and the light scent of jasmine and oranges from the soap she used.

Rayne returned with Tarquin. The boy left his side to embrace Dante and Grace. He observed the three Giovanni's comforting one another. For the first time in centuries, the feeling of being an unwelcome outsider settled over him. Raphael and Tessa stood behind Rayne.

Grace looked over at Rayne quietly observing everything. "What bargain did you make as a mortal?"

"It is better you two discuss this privately," Raphael halted the conversation.

Grace shook her head. "How is it Raphael and Dante know and your wife doesn't?"

"Do not be overly angry with Rayne, cara. He has told no one other than Raphael about the agreement with the demon. I only know due to being his former commander." Dante kept his arm around Tarquin.

"A demon?" Grace fought to control her temper. "A fucking demon, Rayne!"

"Mommy! That is a bad word!" Tessa scolded from the doorway, wagging a finger at her mother.

"Your father is about to learn a few more twenty-first-century bad words in more than one language," Grace grumbled before grabbing Rayne by the arm. "You killed the silver-eyed enforcer of Córdoba, my ass. You lied to me this very morning, Rayne Warwick! You better have a damn good explanation for everything."

TWENTY-FOUR

Elysium

Grace paced the guest room, trying to comprehend all Rayne told her. He had actually sold his soul, so he could kill Umar.

"How does a mortal even find a djinn to make that sort of bargain?"

"Isra found me. In my state of despair, all I could think of was avenging Priya. I wanted Umar to suffer. Lucifer and Isra enflamed my anger and desperation. Remember how you felt after watching Dante die? Unlike you, there was no one to guide me."

"Eternal servitude as a demon, Rayne? In my darkest hours as a human dealing with the Hasan, I never would have agreed to that."

"You are a stronger person than I was. Not all of us had the same conviction you possessed as a mortal. If I had any idea of what I would become... what I would do, how many years I would have to kill for that witch, I would never have allowed Isra to convert me."

Grace stared at Rayne with such horror on her face it terrified him. "You told me you were immortal before you met Raphael."

Suddenly feeling ill, she grasped the bedpost. Rayne reached to help steady her on her feet. She slapped his hand away. "Get away from me."

Honoring her request, Rayne took several steps back. "I am not a fiend, Grace. Please don't look at me as if I was one."

"The hell you're not, Rayne! I saw your eyes in the yard. You weren't just a mercenary for Lucifer and his flunkies. You were a djinn or demon yourself! The man at your father's spoke the truth."

Rayne hung his head, ashamed of what hate had once turned him into. "Yes."

"How convenient you left that out of your tale the past few days."

"Grace, I was foolish and angry. I did not understand what the blood oath would commit me to."

"How many innocent lives did you take for you to turn?"

Rayne closed his eyes, struggling to find the words to answer her.

Disgusted, Grace glared coldly at her husband. "You weren't looking for redemption when you left Spain. You were fleeing from yourself!"

"Grace... Leof... Do not condemn me. You do not understand. It was not..."

"Wasn't like what, Rayne?" Grace stalked towards him. Her emotions a whirlwind of anger, confusion, and condemnation. "You didn't even discriminate, did you? How many women and children died or were tortured by the men you commanded? Or worse yet, died by your hand?"

"I am not certain."

"You are not certain? You are a monster!" No longer wanting to be around him, Grace spun on her heels.

"I am not that beast anymore!" Rayne shouted and grasped his wife by the arms to keep her from leaving the room.

Desperation resounded in his tone. Anguish traveled from his being into hers. Grace closed her eyes, drowning underneath the surge of her husband's pain and grief.

"I have done penance for centuries, Grace. Tried to earn forgiveness for my sins; to right every wrong I ever committed. I prayed the Fates had finally granted it the night you added my last name to yours. Then again, the morning I learned we would bring a child of our own into the world. Can you no longer see any good in the man you once called a saint?"

Aqua eyes studied the face of the soldier she always knew was far from the saint she called him. Very few men of war had clean hands. Despite all the effort made to protect the innocent, that was not always possible. "I see the wolf clearly. I still see the man I say 'I love you' to each night. The father, who teaches and guides his daughter and son. The Commander who accepted the rank forced upon him. Now, I also see the enforcer that sleeps within you. The djinn is still there. Isra sees him, too. I wonder if he has passed part of himself on to our daughter."

Rayne didn't know what to say. Her eyes said what her lips didn't. She could only see the darkness now. "My misdeeds cannot be passed onto my children or you."

"But we must deal with the consequences of them."

"I alone will bear the cost of my mistakes. I won't let Isra or anyone else harm my family."

Grace couldn't stop the angry laugh from escaping. "You won't let anyone else harm your family? Two djinn just traumatized our children, Rayne! I am in Elysium under false pretenses, most likely due to something Malik or Isra plotted. Tarquin stabbed Isra, terrified she'd take you! Your family is more than paying for your mistakes. How in the hell did you not come to the conclusion that vengeance served you poorly once Umar escaped? One does not become an all-powerful djinn after one assault."

"I had no choice, Grace."

Grace hated how her body trembled from the rage and hurt she barely controlled. "No, you had a choice. You chose self over others. You are no better than Dante."

The comparison to Dante stung. Grace's being eternally angry with him sucked all hope from Rayne's being. Isra's play to force him back into her clutches dealt damage much worse than those early days when he served her and Lucifer. A death knell sounded deep within; Isra finally managed to break him after all these centuries.

Grace saw the defeat in Rayne's expression. He had never looked so tired after any other conflict they faced.

Rayne lost the will to fight with her any longer. "It was never that simple once I was in Isra's clutches. I prayed for death every moment I spent under her control."

"Ten years ago, you promised no more secrets; no more lies, Rayne.

You broke that promise, not just once, but at least twice today alone. How am I to trust anything you say from this point forward?"

Grace knew he could not offer any answer after a tense, silent moment passed. "I don't even know who you are anymore."

Needing space to cope with everything, she fled the room.

Rayne let her go. Solutions to ease her concerns were well beyond his grasp.

Dante stepped out of Grace's way when she passed him in the hall. He looked through the open guestroom door. Rayne's out of character, slumped over posture worried him. "Never would have I believed War could be defeated. Surrender isn't in your nature. Do not give up hope, Rayne. You and Grace will come through this."

Rayne shook his head. "I am not so certain this time. She believes I deceived her far worse than you did."

<hr>

Isis waited for Grace in Dante's gardens. Lyal stood beside the goddess.

Grace wasn't surprised to see Isis blocking the pathway. "News travels fast, doesn't it?"

"You are understandably angry after what was revealed today. But you must not let the anger blind you. Rayne needs you more than ever."

"I have previously warned you and Osiris that neither you two nor the High Council are welcome to stick your noses into my love life. What is it going to take for you to comprehend what butt out means?"

Lyal snickered beside Isis. "They do not care about your wishes or anyone else's, najmati. Your anger with your husband weakens the immortal guard requiring their interference."

"Rayne may be shaken, but he will not forsake his sacred duty to the High Council. If anything, he'll be more dedicated than ever without his wife and children to distract him." Grace doubted things were that serious. Rayne always remained steadfast in anything he did, regardless of what happened in his personal life. She had seen that first hand after Dante rashly spoke the binding spell. Rayne carried on after the loss of her then. He would carry on now, no matter how things played out.

"Grace, you and the children are his greatest motivation to ensure the balance is kept. How do you not understand the destruction your rejection brings?"

"Speaking of my children," Grace looked over at Lyal. "Thank you for guarding them today."

Lyal politely nodded. "It is my responsibility to ensure no harm befalls the descendants of the House of the Moon."

Grace shook her head, wondering if Qasim would have gotten his claws into her if Lyal wasn't trapped in Tartarus back then.

Isis did not like the direction Grace's thoughts strayed. "There is a purpose behind everything those destined to serve as Horsemen or the Defensore endure."

"What purpose does turning one destined to be a Horseman into a demon serve, Isis?"

"Grace, that wasn't Rayne's fault. In many ways, it was the Council's failure. You must forgive him."

"I don't need to do anything. Where is my immortal father-in-law?"

As if on cue, Osiris joined them. "I am pleased we are on speaking terms once again, najmati."

"Only for the next few minutes, Osiris." Grace gave the god an icy stare. Her gaze shifted between Isis and Osiris. "You bound me to a demon and a god? How much more cliché can the High Council get?"

"A former demon, who only knew darkness a short time." Osiris annoyed her further.

"Long enough to make Genghis Khan look like an amateur with the tales I hear of evil Haroun. Lyal?"

"Yes, najmati?" Lyal bowed respectfully to Grace.

"Warn me if Osiris withholds anything or lies to me in this conversation."

"As you wish, najmati."

Isis frowned. "Grace, you do not need to mistrust Osiris so. He has never acted with malice towards you."

"That depends on one's perspective, doesn't it, goddess?" Grace ignored the irritated expression on Isis's face and focused on Osiris. "Did Isra kill Umar?"

"Indirectly."

Grace glanced over at Lyal. The guardian gave no sign of concern with the answer. "Indirectly? Who assassinated Umar for her?"

"One who rises and another who lost their son."

Grace turned to Lyal, looking for confirmation.

"His response is honest."

"Good. Observe him closely with this next request. If there is even a hint of dishonesty or withholding of information I should know, I give you liberty to do as you wish with him."

Lyal grinned at the opportunity presented and reached for her blade. Osiris's eyes narrowed, reminding Grace a great deal of Dante. The god did not say a word, but Grace knew she pricked his temper.

"Was Rayne's contract discharged as Raphael claims?"

"The contract is no more. Isra released him after Raphael bested her. Raphael burned the contract, giving Rayne his freedom. Rayne assumed the rank of Horseman from that moment forward."

"So, what Isra produced is definitely a forgery?"

"I believe it is."

Grace stared back at the house. "How many Council members are needed to ratify a declaration of action?"

"That depends on what you seek to ratify. A war declaration would require majority approval and my seal."

"What about approval for an isolated action?"

Isis exchanged worried glances with Osiris, but answered Grace's question. "You would need four senior members' signatures, including the Council head."

"That's it?" Grace figured with the way the High Council operated she would need more.

"Yes. Why do you inquire?"

"Curiosity. Lyal, maintain your post protecting my children. The rest of you can leave me to figure out how to deal with this mess."

Osiris raised his finger. "May I suggest—"

"No, you may not. Your prior suggestions have injured me and my loved ones to the extent I no longer value your opinion."

Grace wanted all the craziness to stop. She walked away from the three deities to the opposite end of the gardens, trying to think coherently. After clarity evaded her, she shouted up at the sky. "No more demons, no more prophecy, no more ghosts, no more death!"

"We all hear you, Grace. No need to shout at all of creation," Theseus answered her unspoken plea for guidance. Ares accompanied him.

"The Council sends you two." Grace almost laughed at their new delegates, noting Osiris and Isis left the yard.

Ares smirked. "Would you rather Osiris? We can ask him to return if you'd like."

"I suppose anyone is better than Mr. Green, conniving, lame-ass father-in-law, ruler of the afterlife."

Ares's jaw dropped in mock surprise. "Rather childish of you, Gracie. Do you call him that to his face?"

"Some days. You won't take it personally if I give Theseus's counsel more weight, will you?"

Ares grinned and placed an arm around her shoulders. "Didn't expect anything different. You never listen to me anyhow. What can we help you with, Defensore?"

Grace's face sobered. "What do I do?"

"Open a bottle of Dante's best vino and have a threesome with your two husbands. In the morning, the three of you will be all lovey dovey then kick some demon ass just like in the old days." Ares ignored the scowl she gave him.

Grace looked over at Theseus. "Please tell me you can offer better direction."

"I am afraid I cannot offer an answer which will make you any happier than Ares's did. Heal the god and the Horseman. You will find your way from there."

"Did you just repeat what Ares said in a nicer way? I have no doubt a threesome between a god, a demon, and the Defensore is illegal, not to mention immoral."

Theseus shrugged. "There is no law preventing you from enjoying the company of both men. Last I knew, you were married to both."

Grace huffed at Theseus's remark. "Considering one died and has been MIA for ten years, I am only married to one."

"Dante never really died. The Council merely forbid him to see you. The sun god respects the wolf's claim, but still very much considers you his wife. As far as I am aware, he has not been with another since ascending, much to the disappointment of a goddess and a muse. Didn't Isis remind you this whole monogamy thing is a human invention?" Ares teased, well aware Grace wouldn't like the suggestion.

"We prefer not to have our husbands trying to kill one another and to know who our children's father is."

"Then pick the one you like most, Guardian, and leave the other to lick their wounds." Ares vanished.

Theseus took Grace's hand. "You have options. Regardless of what you decide, Dante and Rayne need to know they are welcome in your life. The Horseman internalizes his fears much more than the god. Remember that."

"Thank you." Grace knew he was not supposed to direct her. As always, he gave her a gentle nudge anyway.

"I don't envy you. It will work out whatever path you choose."

"Theseus, can Rayne ever go back down that road?"

He thought about the scenario she suggested. "I do not know. I would like to think he never would. However, Lucifer is an exceptional manipulator. He tricks all creatures, not just mortals. He offers them dreams that are nothing more than smoke and mirrors. There is a reason humans view him as the Devil. Isra learned well from her master and effectively deploys his tactics. Men of war who love deeply like Rayne frequently fall victim to the darker sides of themselves. Rayne always held power he never knew of with being fated to be a Horseman. Lucifer recognized that. He and Isra waited for the opportune moment to recruit him. It is a shame the Council did not bring him into our ranks sooner. The Fates seemed as surprised by Priya's assassination as Rayne was. I half wonder if Lucifer intentionally drove Umar to order her death, and if he discovered Rayne's destiny before the rest of us did.

"It took a great deal for Lucifer and Isra to turn Rayne. That is something you should ask him about before you make any judgement of his character. As much as I hope Rayne would remember who he is and the guilt he once carried, loss and vengeance are a deadly combination. War drew his sword against the Council one time before."

"What? Why?" Grace didn't think she could be surprised by anything else after learning her husband was once a demon working for Lucifer himself.

"He feared you would die in Alexandria after you returned to the temple to try to revive Dante. Rayne was willing to take on the High Council to ensure you lived. I have no doubt the urge to protect you is even stronger now. I cannot imagine what he would do if your life or your children's were ever placed in great peril, nor do I know what will occur if you decide to leave him." Theseus left Grace to determine the path she would walk.

Grace looked back at the house, then towards the far end of the yard. Dante, Raphael, Tarquin, and Tessa ambled together. The four seemed to be recovering from the excitement of the day. Dante stared in her direction, but did not come towards her. She exhaled the breath she had been holding. Dante could not intercede between her and Rayne with the temporary release agreement he negotiated. Though the concern in his expression warned he was tempted to once more violate the Council's terms.

I will be fine, cavaliere. If you want to help, keep Tarquin and Tessa safe.

Dante looked away, but brought his hand to his ear, pretending to scratch behind it, signaling he heard her. She smiled when he cast her a quick glance over his shoulder.

Tessa picked something up from the grass and showed it to him and Raphael. With Raphael's attention elsewhere, Dante quickly gave Grace the hand signal for commander and go. *Rayne needs you, Grace. His wrong does not stem from the nature of mine. He has never set out to deceive you. Please, show some compassion. Go to him.*

Grace closed her eyes and saw Rayne wrestling with his fears in the guest bedroom. He needed to quickly confront Isra after her boldness today; however, he worried his leaving without reconciling with her would worsen things. She could feel his anxiety. It heightened her own.

What he had done was horrifying, but he had become something greater. He freed himself from a fate she couldn't imagine and probably saved her from going down a similar path. She remembered the panic in his voice when he made her promise she would live her life and be thankful she was spared. Rayne loved her unconditionally in her worst moments.

CHAPTER

TWENTY-FIVE

Elysium

Why couldn't the Fates have allowed his past to surface in a less destructive way? Or left things well enough alone? Rayne mused, looking down at the marble floor beneath his boots.

He sensed he wasn't alone any longer. Noticing Grace in the doorway, he quickly stood. Fear, guilt, and distress muddled his mind and paralyzed his lips. He couldn't even utter her name with the furious expression still on her face.

Slowly crossing the room to him, Grace stared up into ocean blue eyes. Isra's enforcer was reborn and transformed into her saint. "You should have told me."

Unsure of what to say, he nodded. "I know."

Grace's arms encircled his shoulders. Relief cascaded over him. She still wanted him after learning the truth. He nearly crushed her he held her so tightly, thankful she chose not to let this destroy them.

"Slay the bitch for threatening our son and daughter. If you see Lucifer, feel free to eliminate him too," Grace whispered in Rayne's ear. Neither the High Council nor a demon would take happiness from her again.

"That is one execution order I will happily fulfill."

Tamir and Destahn ran into the room. "Bedlam is breaking loose in Córdoba. One of Umar's former divisions is raiding your father's property."

Grace smiled up at Rayne. Humanity needed the Horsemen once more. "Go help your father and stop the factions from fighting."

Rayne worried there was more they needed to discuss. "The others can secure the property without me."

Grace lifted the hood settled against his back and raised it into place on his head. "There is nothing more to say, my wolf. Your heart and marriage are safe. Córdoba needs you."

She picked up his sword from the bed and offered it to him. Rayne clasped the hilt of his weapon; his eyes still resting on Grace. He pulled her to him with the sword, bringing the gold and steel handle with her hand to his heart.

Grace nodded, acknowledging his re-pledging his fidelity to her. Seeing him lean towards her, she went up on tiptoe. Her lips met his for a goodbye kiss. Needing assurance that she truly forgave him, Rayne prolonged the kiss.

Destahn loudly coughed from where he stood.

Rayne glanced over at him. "I am aware that you two are there."

"The cough was to remind you of the attack on your father's property. She can wait for your attention. It can't," Destahn prompted Rayne to leave.

Rayne gave Grace another quick kiss. "I will be back by nightfall."

"Be careful," Grace called after the three men as they faded from sight.

Worried about the conflict in Spain, Grace went to find Dante. She heard multiple voices coming from the front of the house. Several deities stood with him in the foyer, discussing Isra. Raphael missing from the group let her know the Roman rode to Spain with the other three Horsemen.

Seeing Grace coming towards them, Dante stepped away from the Council members. He met her in the hallway.

Grace appreciated him coming over, so she didn't have to interrupt the impromptu meeting. "Am I free to leave?"

Dante shook his head. "No, not yet. The charges must be formally dropped."

"Then you must go to Córdoba."

"I cannot partake in that fight, Grace. It is Rayne's to manage."

"Rayne is shaken by all that occurred today. He would benefit from having you on the field."

"Rayne is more than capable of handling matters in Spain."

"Dante, you can shadow him without being involved in the conflict. Shadowing does not violate the Council's stupid rules."

"Cara, the Horsemen watch over one another. He will be fine."

Grace grabbed Dante's hand. "Isra is there. I sense Lucifer is too. You fell facing a partial god. Raphael fell fighting a man that was half demon. Rayne is still reeling. Do not leave him to fight Isra and Lucifer on his own."

Dante glanced over at Tarquin playing with Tessa in his study, where he had sent them to keep them away from the Council discussion.

"If you will not do it for me, do it for our son. You promised Tarquin both his fathers would always be with him." By the way his brow arched, she knew Dante would risk the ire of the Council.

"Do not fight with my father while acting as my delegate. Be certain to conceal any thought of where I am."

"Thank you."

Dante nodded then excused himself from the Council discussion. "I apologize. An urgent matter has arisen that I must attend to. I will rejoin all of you as soon as I can. In the meantime, the Defensore shall represent me in my absence."

Osiris gave Dante a perplexed look, but motioned for Grace to join the group of deities.

Hades waved his hand in Grace's direction. "Should she be involved in this discussion while under investigation?"

"Based on what Isra shared today, we know the Defensore is innocent. If my son deems her worthy to serve as delegate, then I, too, believe her worthy to render opinion on this matter." Osiris almost dared Hades to challenge Grace's presence again.

Hades scowled, but said nothing further.

Zeus winked at her. "I find Grace's participation crucial to our decision making. After all, she knows the Horsemen Commander better than any of us, and can provide a military perspective we lack with the Horsemen and Dante unable to be present."

The subject of the discussion honestly surprised Grace. Isra's attack on Rayne had the Council's full attention. Before Dante left, he had been arguing Isra's actions necessitated the Horsemen be formally dispatched. The overseer's scheming risked exposure of the immortal realm to humanity. Lucifer's appearance in the Council Round confirmed Isra's ploy may be more far-reaching than a power grab in Córdoba.

"Do you agree with Dante's position on Isra's actions, Defensore?" Poseidon drew Grace out of her thoughts.

"I do not have the foresight any of you do. But based on what I have observed so far, I am inclined to think Dante is right. Rarely were his instincts wrong about an enemy when he was the Horsemen Commander. If he believes formal involvement is needed, the Council should grant it."

Córdoba - 812

After quelling things at his father's, Rayne and Destahn returned to Umar's. Neither went inside, but walked the edges of the property, searching again for any signs of a djinn being on site. Kamar's narcissistic personality would have left a calling card of some type. After an hour's search, nothing surfaced.

"Anything?" Rayne hoped Destahn had better luck than he did.

Destahn shook his head. "Nothing. Maybe Kamar wasn't the killer."

Rayne noted the closest other home was a hundred yards away. It was that of Umar's estate manager, a deeply religious man terrified if anyone even whispering the word djinn or shaytan around him. Something moving in the citrus orchard caught Rayne's eye. A black-cloaked figure watched him and Destahn. Rayne teleported to them. Destahn followed his commander. Spotting Destahn, the figure ran from the Horsemen. Rayne caught up to them in just a few quick strides and grasped their arm.

A female voice came from under the hood. "I meant you no harm. They asked me to watch the property for men matching your description."

Rayne kept a tight hold of her. "If you meant no harm, then why did you run?"

"Would you not run if the Horsemen pursued you, Haroun? Do you honestly think no one here recognizes you?"

Destahn yanked backed the woman's hood to reveal a blonde-haired, dark-eyed djinn. "Looks like we found our killer."

"I didn't kill anyone!" The djinn denied the accusation, earning a skeptical expression from Destahn and Rayne. "I swear on my oath to my mistress, I did not murder anyone in Umar's household."

"Then who did?" Rayne asked.

The djinn laughed. "Last I recall, you murdered Umar's guard then went after the general, Primus."

Annoyed by her laughter, Rayne gave her a rough shake. "I meant the recent attack on Umar. Now, who killed Umar a few nights ago?"

"I do not know, but it wasn't me. I also don't think the assassin was a djinn. My mistress asked me to watch the property for you or any other Council officer that might appear."

"Did anyone else appear besides us?" Rayne let her go. She wouldn't run now that her face was revealed.

"Besides yourselves? Hades and Xander. They said they investigated Umar's death because an immortal was involved. No one in the djinn community killed Umar, though a great many of us would have liked to. He harmed as many djinn as he did humans."

Destahn doubted a djinn didn't commit the murder. "If the djinn have no love for Umar, why wouldn't they kill him?"

"Our mistress forbade us from doing so. She needed to maintain her leverage over her former primus should she ever need him again." The djinn sank down to her knees, bowing before Rayne. "As she said you would, you returned when Umar drew his last breath, Primus Ibn-Ziyad."

Unimpressed, Rayne glared down at her. "Get up, and address me as Commander Warwick if you value your head."

"Yes, Commander Warwick." She rose as instructed.

"If djinn weren't involved, did you notice any suspicious humans around the night of Umar's murder?"

"I wasn't here that night, Commander. But I can make some inquiries for you."

"Please do. Bring us any information of value, and I will reward you well for it," Rayne appealed to the djinn's greedy nature.

"Yes, Ha... Commander Warwick."

"One other thing before you let her go." Dante revealed his presence in Spain. "Confirm your mistress's name."

Unsure what to think of Dante, the djinn sneered at him. She had never encountered a god before.

Rayne had no patience left for djinn rascality. "Answer him."

"Isra, Primus," She said, then ran off into the countryside.

Destahn grinned, looking over at Rayne. "A djinn is bad enough, but a primus, Rayne? Considering how scary you can be as a Horseman, I don't even want to imagine what you were like as an enforcer."

"Then don't provoke me by bringing up my past, Destahn."

Dante chuckled. "Multiply the most destruction you've seen him wreak on the battlefield by at least ten, and you'll have an idea of what he was like as an enforcer."

"Then maybe I shouldn't say I understand what Lucifer meant by the one who got away much better now." Destahn loudly laughed at the annoyed glare Rayne shot him.

Rayne raised a brow, muttered something under his breath, then looked over at Dante. "You are welcome to return to Elysium if you intend to instigate insubordinate remarks instead of helping unravel whatever Isra is up to."

Elysium -

Just before sunset, Dante walked through the front door of his home. Grace, Tarquin, and Tessa sitting in the living room together brought a smile to his face. Maria called for Tessa to come help set the table for dinner.

Grace saw him in the hallway when Tessa ran off toward the kitchen. Rayne not being with him worried her. "Where is Rayne?"

"He and the others are tying up loose ends in Córdoba. He will return shortly." Dante walked over to her and kissed her cheek.

The way Grace hugged him conveyed that the confrontation in Spain troubled her more than she let on.

"Stop your fretting, mia stella. Rayne is well. He also didn't need my assistance." Dante pulled back slightly to look down at her; his arms hung about her waist. "Now that the truth is out, Isra holds no sway over Rayne. Your forgiving him destroyed the most powerful weapon she could wield."

"I pray you are right, Dante."

"I am most certainly right, cara. Isra made a grave mistake by coming here. She drew the Council's attention today."

"Mama, did you kill the man like Hera and Hades say?" Tarquin interrupted their discussion.

The unexpected inquiry flummoxed Grace. It took a second for her surprise to fade, so she could answer him. "No, Tarquin. Someone else did."

Dante frowned, looking over at his son. "Where did you hear such a thing?"

Tarquin's lower lip quivered.

Dante gave Tarquin's shoulder a gentle squeeze. "There is nothing to be afraid of, Tarquin. I am not angry about the question, nor is your mother."

"You can help Mama prove she didn't kill Umar, can't you?"

Dante reassuringly smiled at his son. "Isra's actions today proved your mother's innocence. The Council is dismissing all charges against her. Did you overhear the Council meeting yesterday?"

Tarquin lowered his gaze and fidgeted with his hands. "I am sorry,

Papa. I only came inside as I wanted a glass of water. I swear I wasn't eavesdropping."

"I am the one who is sorry, Tarquin. We should have met elsewhere."

TWENTY-SIX

Elysium

Feeling the bed shift multiple times, Grace woke to Rayne mumbling in his sleep. His body shuddered and jerked. Whatever he dreamed about must have been something horrific. She set her hand over his heart, invading his sleep to see if she could ease whatever troubled him.

Hell - 806

The putrid smell of centuries old mold combined with ash and sulfur in the stale air, taking her breath away as she entered a dark chamber. The trapped smoke from the fireplace created a thick, suffocating haze, which made her cough. She looked through the smog and saw Rayne.

Rayne squinted against the worsening sensation of burning and watering in his eyes. Garsea and Isra believed the heat and ash in the air added to the misery they inflicted on those being tortured. They weren't wrong. He would give anything to be able to rinse and rub his eyes, if even for a few seconds of relief. The chains trapping him between two stone pilings kept his arms forced outward. There was no way for his hands to reach his face.

A loud crack, then a hissing whistle warned that braided leather traveled towards him. The sharp bite of the whip brought forth only the slightest grunt from Rayne as the strap once more tore through the exposed skin on his back.

"You disobeyed me on the battlefield, Haroun." Garsea, Isra's militia commander, sent the long length of black leather sailing at Isra's newest recruit again.

The only signs of pain displayed by the former human consisted of clenched fists and a loud hiss of inhaled breath, even though his body lurched.

Rayne's vision briefly blurred after several large drops of sweat traveled down his forehead then fell into his eyes. Even so, he managed to glare over at Isra. He wrapped his fingers around the chains holding him in place, bracing for another round of torment. "I will not kill those I have no quarrel with. Do your worst. I will not deviate from my morals."

Isra laughed. "You lost your claim to any principles when you sought vengeance against Umar."

"You asked for my soul, not my sword. I owe you nothing more than my existence, which matters not without Priya."

"The nature of your servitude is determined by your mistress, not by your desires. I have no use for a slave or another soul to torment. I need skilled soldiers after you slaughtered my troops in Guadalacete. As a former general, you shall more than adequately take their place."

"I will not fight for you or any other demon, Isra."

The defiant eye contact he maintained twisted Isra's lips into a cruel smile. She struck him across the face. "You will do as your mistress and field commander instruct, Haroun."

The she-demon sat down in a large chair a few feet away and poured herself a glass of wine the same color as the blood coating Rayne's back. She sipped from the chalice, entertained by the man's disobedience. He will learn. They all eventually did, even the proudest who bargained with her for something.

The once mortal man stubbornly kept his gaze fixed on her; enduring lash after lash without screaming. An occasional grunt or groan escaped his lips and his eyes would briefly close, but he refused to display any other signs of suffering.

"There will be no muscle or flesh left on his back if I continue." Garsea lowered the whip. He hated to admit it, but he was impressed by how long Haroun remained on his feet. Many more senior demons and djinn would have collapsed into unconsciousness by this point. A newly created djinn withstanding a torture session like this one was unheard of.

Isra set her glass on the table, then inspected the gaping wounds on Rayne's back. She noted how blood and sweat-covered muscles trembled. Now that she stood beside him, she heard the rapid pace of his breathing. "If you are hoping for death, Haroun, it will not come."

Rayne's voice tremored more than his body did. "I will not serve you."

"Resist all you like. You indentured yourself freely, which means you will learn to obey."

Fighting the weakness and pain coursing through him, Rayne stared at the floor.

"I own you."

"You own nothing, Isra!" Rayne looked back up at the overseer. "I will not murder for you. I will not lead your armies. I will never be one of your minions!"

"Isra, the color of his eyes!" Garsea never before observed a militia member with silver eyes. The only others to have silvered eyes were immortally-born demons. "We must tell Lucifer of this."

Isra noted the swirling of silver and blue before her. "Whatever your fate, you belong to the darkness now, Haroun. I will break you. Lock him in his cell, and then we will tell Lucifer of our recruit's unique appearance."

Rayne stayed upright long enough to stumble to the cage they kept him in. Once Garsea and Isra disappeared from sight, he collapsed to the floor. He thanked whatever deity may exist for distracting his captors before his strength dissipated.

Another demon in the cell across from Rayne wondered about his fellow prisoner. "No one, djinn or human, can withstand the whip as you did. What are you?"

Rayne briefly raised his head to see what manner of creature spoke to him. "Nothing. I was once a man, but now, I am nothing." He allowed himself to drift into the darkness clouding his vision.

Elysium -

The tender touch of Grace's fingertips on his cheek pulled Rayne out of the nightmare. His eyes flew open, searching for whoever touched him. Their mercury shade worried Grace. His fingers encircled her wrist; painfully gripping it as if she hurt him. Panicked, he yanked her hand from his face.

"Rayne, it's me. You're in Elysium, not Hell, or wherever that was."

Now recognizing Grace, he let go of her hand. Her fingers lightly stroked his shoulder, soothing his restless soul. Silver faded to blue. His pulse slowed to a normal rate. His mouth felt cottony; his lips parched and stuck together. He swallowed, staring up at Grace in the darkness before wetting his lips with his tongue so he could speak. "How much did you see?"

"Everything."

Rayne looked away from her. The way he broke eye contact shared his shame.

"I am sorry, Rayne. I misjudged you earlier."

"Your judgment wasn't completely wrong, leof. Isra eventually turned me into exactly what you accused me of being. Thankfully, the Council and Fates believed I could be better and righted my course."

Watching the sunrise, a new sense of calm settled over Grace. A spectacular dawn always gifted hope to every living being waking to the majesty of a color-filled morning sky.

Rayne joined Grace in watching night become day. She hadn't spoken a word since waking. The extended silence worried him. For the first time in a decade, he felt a terrifying distance from his wife. While she said she forgave him and apologized for misjudging him, her reserved demeanor screamed she may not have. "Is all well with us?"

Grace searched what she once considered the most honest eyes she ever encountered for hints of any more hidden secrets. "I am still hurt and angry that you chose not to tell me the truth about your past, along with the reasons why you avoided Córdoba. But, more importantly, I love you, and will be damned before I allow a demon, djinn, or whatever Isra is to take my husband from me. We will work through this."

"I hold no other secrets, Grace. You now know everything about your wolf." Rayne hoped she believed him.

"We shall see."

A light knock on the door ended their conversation.

Grace wished whoever was at their door had waited a few minutes longer. "Come in."

"Poseidon sends for you both." Raphael noted the way Rayne's jaw clenched and Grace sighed. "They are formally dismissing charges, Grace. Neither of you has anything to fear."

Dante came down the hall towards Raphael. "They should have done that yesterday while they were here."

Raphael grinned at his former mentee. "You know formal charges require public meetings. They've also requested your presence, but did not share why it was needed."

Dante grunted; Raphael knew the reason, he simply didn't want to share it. "Liar. Relay that I will be there shortly."

The High Council Round -

Rayne and Raphael stood on either side of Grace in the Council Round. Poseidon nodded to the three of them. Osiris stood behind him with a smile on his face.

"As I see Dante is late as usual, we will begin with addressing the charges against the Defensore," Poseidon addressed the chamber. "Grace Giovanni Dalglese Warwick, in light of Isra's confession before Hades and Dante yesterday, all charges against you are being withdrawn.

We reinstate you to your former position, and your freedom is fully restored. The High Council extends our deepest apologies for the confusion resulting in your arrest."

"You owe her husband and me an apology for the chaos you wrongly caused in our households, not to mention the trauma your actions put our children through." Dante shot an annoyed glare at the Council Court members as he walked into the Council Round.

"Nice of you to finally join us, Giovanni," Poseidon acknowledged the tardy god's arrival. "Allow me to also apologize for any harm this may have caused your child..."

"I think the apology would be more sincere if Hades extended it on behalf of the Council," Dante cut off the acting Council Head and stared directly at Hades.

Hades rolled his eyes. "The Council Head issues formal apologies for the rare mistake the Council may make, not the prosecutor!"

"As charges have been dropped, I will resume my place as Council Head," Osiris interjected, trading places with Poseidon. Once Osiris settled himself in the Council Head's chair, he looked over at Hades. "I am also inclined to agree with my son's suggestion as the Council Prosecutor insisted action be taken against the Defensore and brought the matter to formally charge her to a vote while others of us felt more evidence needed to be gathered."

Hades shot Osiris a scathing glare before looking back at the four immortals in the Council realm.

Dante met Hades's gaze and arched a brow, daring the god to disobey Osiris.

Hades forced a smile before speaking again. "Commander Warwick, Defensore Warwick, on behalf of the Council, allow me to extend our most sincere apologies for any distress our investigation caused your children and yourselves. Dante, as your colleague, the Council nor myself ever intended for our actions to foster ill will between deities, but certainly you of all beings understand that any hint of an immortal violating their oath or going rogue must be swiftly addressed to prevent the loss of life as demonstrated several centuries ago when Lyal succumbed to bloodlust, and the Council debated what to do."

Dante bit back his thoughts about the Council's execution order for

Lyal. "Now knowing more about that awful day, I question what drove Lyal to bloodlust. Regardless, I accept your and the Council's apology."

Worried Dante's remarks may anger several members of the Council, Rayne stepped forward. "My wife and I appreciate and accept the Council's apology. We also want to express our deepest gratitude for the Council quickly dismissing the charges after additional evidence came to light. The Defensore and I do realize the seriousness of such an accusation against a High Council Officer, and we understand why certain members of the Council felt it necessary to limit any potential harm that could result should one of our own go rogue."

Isis smiled at Rayne. "As always, a very courteous and diplomatically phrased response, Commander Warwick. I move we close discussion on this matter and move on to other things."

"Agreed," Zeus said, aware that Hades wanted to smite Dante where he stood. "I believe the release of the sun god from his contractual duties is next on the list of items to be discussed."

Osiris nodded. "Dante Giovanni, Guardian of the Ancients for the House of the Sun, the High Council affirms that you have fulfilled all terms of the contract you struck eleven years ago to ensure the continuation of your bloodline and to protect the Defensore. All restrictions and servitude that agreement bound you to are discharged. Additionally, with the dismissal of charges against the Defensore, the release agreement is also terminated. We would like to once again extend to you a seat on the High Council. Your dedication to this Council, the human and immortal communities, along with your family, in addition to your valor as one of the Horsemen, more than supports your worthiness to become a Council member." He hoped Dante would accept the position this time.

"I am honored the Council once more deems me worthy to sit amongst them. I humbly request a few days to consider such a prestigious offer before rendering a response." Dante politely bowed to his father.

Isis set her hand on Osiris's arm after seeing the disappointment on her husband's face. "Take all the time you need, Dante. We know this has been a trying time on you, just as it has been on the Warwicks."

Osiris frowned, but pressed on with his duties. "We need to

continue our deliberations of what action to take against Isra and whether or not the situation in Spain warrants Council intercession."

Once the Council, Dante, and the Horsemen were engaged in discussion, Grace quietly approached Khonsu, the deity overseeing the House of the Moon.

"How may I be of assistance, Defensore?" He whispered, so they didn't disrupt the Council meeting.

"Are there documents anywhere detailing Lucifer's relationship with the Council or any dealings Isra made with Rayne?"

Khonsu shook his head. "The Council does not keep written archives. Why are you inquiring about such matters?"

"I wish to help my husband and the Council. Understanding the past would assist me in doing so."

Khonsu pondered her request. His eyes widened as a solution to the lack of written records came to mind. "Come. I believe there is a way to learn the information you seek."

Rayne noticed Khonsu leaving his chair and guiding Grace towards the chamber doors. He set his hand on Dante's shoulder to slip behind the god listening to Zeus's report on djinn activity. Dante watched Rayne stop Khonsu and Grace.

"Where are you going? You cannot leave a Council meeting without being formally dismissed." Rayne kept his voice low as he spoke.

"I am taking the Defensore to the Repository, Commander," Khonsu answered the inquiry.

Rayne thought it odd that Khonsu wanted to show Grace something in the Repository. "The Repository? Why?"

"I believe learning the information the Repository holds aids your cause against Isra."

Now Grace was confused. "I thought you just said the Council didn't maintain an archive."

"We do not, at least not the kind of archive you are accustomed to, Defensore. Commander, your wife will be safe with me. She also isn't leaving Council grounds; therefore, she does not require formal dismissal. We shall return shortly."

Rayne inclined his head to Khonsu, respectfully honoring the god's desire to show Grace whatever he felt she needed to see. *If you need me...*

I will immediately call for you, Grace assured Rayne she wouldn't get herself in any sort of trouble.

Rayne retook his place beside Dante. The god gave him a puzzled look then briefly glanced back at Grace and Khonsu. Grace assumed Rayne told Dante where she and Khonsu were going.

"Come, guardian." Khonsu motioned towards the door.

Grace followed Khonsu through the doors, and down a side hall she hadn't noticed before. "If you don't keep written records, what am I going to find in the Repository?"

"You shall see." Khonsu reassuringly smiled, leading her down another turn in the hallway.

Two golden doors appeared before them. Khonsu opened them and led her inside a large room with a shimmering energy pool of some type in the center. White waves bounced off the golden walls encircling them.

"To understand all that occurs with your husband and Lucifer, you must view what your husband will not speak of and learn of the Horsemen's origins."

"View what Rayne won't speak of and the Horsemen's origins?" Grace hated how the deities always spoke in such a strange fashion.

"Into the past you must go as an observer."

"I cannot channel the past as others can." Grace still didn't understand how this so-called Repository stored information.

"You do not need to channel it. As the Guardian of the House of the Moon and the Defensore, you may travel to the past as the Council members can."

"Why do I need the Repository to time travel? I can do that on my own."

"Not when the Council hides the past and our dealings from history. One must know where to look to discover the hidden past. And unlike the time travel you do, you may only observe events stored in the Repository. These moments are not changeable as others might be. May time reveal all the secrets you seek, daughter of the moon." Khonsu shoved Grace forward so she fell into the pool before them.

CHAPTER

TWENTY-SEVEN

The High Council Round - 806

Lucifer stared at his fellow Council members seated around the large table. "With the unrest escalating between humans and immortals, we need to designate a special guard to ensure things do not worsen. The role of this guard will to be to serve as balance keepers for our two communities."

Zeus saw no need to create such a guard. "We already have harbingers who serve that purpose."

Lucifer connivingly smiled. "While the harbingers are efficient at their tasking, they may only kill with our sanction or deliver Council ordered punishments. Their limited numbers fail to prevent the skirmishes arising in the mortal realm and ours. The new guard I am proposing should be granted the ability to use their own judgment in dispatching instigators of discontent. Empowering them to do so mitigates growing warfare."

"Or worsens it." Morrigan distrusted gifting that sort of power to any creature. "We have seen the destruction that corruption amongst the highest deities causes."

273

Lucifer rested his hands on the smooth surface of the table. "Precisely why this group of Council selected soldiers should be gifted independent judgment authority and the ability to terminate any member of the immortal community, including those of us on the Council, should we ever find ourselves tempted to destroy creation or one another."

Worried about Lucifer's proposition, Osiris and Morrigan exchanged troubled glances.

Osiris could not kill the proposal without allowing Lucifer the benefit of formal consideration. "We shall consult the Fates on this idea of yours and open further deliberations our next session."

"Thank you for being willing to consider my recommendation, Osiris. I look forward to our next session." Lucifer politely bowed to the High Council Head before leaving the Council chambers.

Morrigan eyed her peer. "Please tell me you merely extended a courtesy review and are not contemplating establishing a special guard."

"You know what protocol requires." Osiris stood, not wanting to further comment.

Isis set her hand on his. "Lucifer seeks to captain this guard. We agree to this, and he will select his own minions or the others in our ranks loyal to him more than to the greater good. He is the least trustworthy of us. We cannot endow him with such power."

"Nor may we ignore his proposal. A blanket dismissal of this guard and an accusation of nepotism against Lucifer would fracture some of the Council allegiances. We cannot risk such a thing. Additionally, I want to ensure Lucifer has not already selected the members of this special unit without Council sanction. Trust the Fates to provide the proper guidance on this matter." Osiris understood his wife's and Morrigan's concerns well.

"I will ask Hades to discretely dispatch Xander to ensure Lucifer has not taken the liberty you fear," Zeus supported Osiris's handling of the situation.

Osiris nodded, granting formal approval of Xander's information gathering through unofficial channels.

806 - The High Council Round - Six months later

Lucifer grinned, delighting in why the High Council suddenly reconvened. Now was the time to whittle away at Osiris and Morrigan's power. The two held dominion over the Council for far too long. Lucifer happily entered the Council Round, eager to learn the outcome of the Inner Council vote.

"We discussed your request for a balance keeper guard. In light of the massacre in Gaudalcete and the warring of rogue immortal against human in Persia, we agree that your proposal for the formation of a new guard has merit." Osiris hated that the words left his lips.

Morrigan shook her head in disgust. It was a troubling day when the Council conceded anything to Lucifer.

"It saddens me that some of our kind violate our code of no harm to humanity. But desperate times do warrant desperate measures." Lucifer concealed his pleasure with the Council's decision behind a solemn expression. "I offer my services to the Council in assembling and leading our new balance keepers."

"While your offer is appreciated, we already selected those best to fulfill the role," Isis said, almost enjoying the disbelief on Lucifer's face. "As recommended by the Fates, there will be four of these elite guard. We have agreed to call them Horsemen. Furthermore, the Inner Council decided it best they report to one of us due to our extensive knowledge of warfare without a volatile history of unnecessarily provoking battles within the realms."

Lucifer's expression devolved into a livid scowl. "I have served as a harbinger and a Council member; brokering many an important accord that ended conflicts. I cannot think of another on this Council who possesses a deeper understanding of what motivates beings to do reckless things. I believe that more than demonstrates how the Horsemen would best serve Council interests under my purview."

Snickers at Lucifer claiming such a thing sounded around Council chambers. Muttered commentary traveled throughout those gathered for the meeting.

Osiris holding up his hand silenced the laughter and whispers. Once the room quieted, he continued the meeting. "As three of the four

Horsemen currently report to an Inner Council member, we decided that deity shall maintain direct reporting authority over them. The entire High Council will hold indirect command for broader reaching issues. This shared authority ensures the Horsemen are only deployed when needed and limits any risk of exploitation for one deity's personal gain. Allow me to introduce our Horsemen."

Lucifer turned to see three armed men enter the Council Round.

"Raphael shall serve as their field commander and Liaison to the High Council. Gabriel, at the moment, is the second-in-command. The being serving as second-in-command shall bear the rank of Horsemen Captain. With Michael fulfilling dual roles of Council Guardian and Horseman, he shall be the third rounding out their ranks."

Lucifer's face tinged a light shade of red as he fought to restrain his temper. "Morrigan's guard. The Inner Council awards a goddess of war command of a force that could kill us all? Is that truly wise, Osiris?"

Morrigan couldn't help smiling at Lucifer's reaction. "My domain extends well beyond war, Lucifer. I oversee victory, sovereignty, and am tied to the Fates. My ability to incite warfare is limited to protecting those under my care. Do not confuse me with my Greek or Roman counterparts. If my ranks take arms, it is because there is a need to do so."

"Where is the fourth Horseman?" Zeus inquired, only seeing three.

All eyes turned to Lucifer, causing him to wonder if he was to be the fourth.

"The one destined to be the fourth vanished from our sight three weeks ago," One of the Fates solemnly informed the Council. "He must be found."

Córdoba - 806 - The Dungeons of Isra's Estate

Lucifer watched Rayne pace the length of his cell. He noted the way the former human's blue eyes shifted from their human hue to the silver of a full-fledged demon. Isra hadn't lied when she sent the message that her new minion displayed surprising abilities. The energy pouring off the caged man suggested the human evolved into something well beyond a low-level djinn. A strange gray light surrounded him instead of his aura dissolving into darkness as it should have.

"How long ago did he barter his soul?"

"Almost a month now." Isra noted the predatory stare Rayne leveled at them.

"Only a month? That is not long enough for one to become like us. When did his eyes begin to alternate between blue and silver?"

"In Guadalacete, after he slaughtered the division of djinn he marched with. Garsea himself had to battle Haroun on the field to prevent our turncoat minion from decimating our ranks."

"Haroun is his name?"

"Yes, Master. He was General Haroun Ibn-Ziyad."

Lucifer's brow lifted. "The Protector of the Cordovan Emirate?"

"One and the same."

"My how the righteous do fall." Lucifer drew closer to the cage, now recognizing the former general's face. "What turned the famed virtuous man into one of your djinn?"

"A vengeance oath. One of his fellow generals murdered his betrothed and assassinated him. His rage at her death was so great it reached me. I halted his passing and promised him a chance to kill Umar in exchange for servitude. He initially agreed. Now, he refuses to serve."

"Umar survived. That voids our agreement," Rayne snarled at the two beings watching him.

Isra rolled her eyes. "Your thoughts on your failed vengeance killing do not matter to either Lucifer or myself. The blood on the parchment is enforceable, whether things turned out to your satisfaction or not."

Rayne laughed, taking a step towards Isra. "Let me out of this cage, and we will see if you have the power to enforce our broken agreement."

Isra raised her hand to reprimand him.

Rayne grasped her wrist, stopping the fire bolt she conjured from materializing.

Lucifer smirked at his boldness. "Release her, General."

Finding her hand free, Isra flung the energy burst at Rayne.

Rayne teleported out of the bolt's path and caught the orb. The flame sat in the center of his palm, changing from red to a blue-tinged white.

All three watched the fire dance in Rayne's hand until Rayne closed his fist, extinguishing it.

"He teleports and controls dark flame?" Lucifer hated to admit he was more than impressed with Isra's new acquisition.

"He not only controls it. He can conjure it. The reason he killed so many on the field was due to a speed I haven't seen another possess. We had to enchant the cell bars to keep him within them." Isra baffled her boss.

Lucifer wondered if an immortal woman hid within Saladin's household. "Saladin is your father. Which of his wives is your mother?"

Rayne ignored the question.

"Lillian." Isra quashed the possibility of Rayne being a half-breed. "Lillian is a mortal of Saxon heritage. She was born in Britain to Celtic parents. Haroun was human when I turned him. His powers only recently developed."

"Celtic? Is she pagan?"

"No. Christian." Isra wondered what her master pondered as Lucifer stared thoughtfully at Rayne. Hoping to be helpful then rewarded for her efforts, Isra shared the local myth about Haroun Ibn-Ziyad. "Many Cordovans believed Haroun to be a being of hope with his mixed heritage and his victories, not to mention his charitable nature. There is a tale of him earning the respect of the Duke of Aquitaine as a young child. Aquitaine gave him the medallion of the Order of Constantinople in recognition of his courage. Some townsfolk believe the duke gifted Haroun the Fates' favor."

"The Duke of Aquitaine is one of Morrigan's guides." Lucifer smiled, realizing who Isra corrupted. "They say as a human you wore a crest with a wolf emblazoned on it. Is it true that your men called you the Black Wolf of Córdoba?"

"What does any rank or name used to address me matter?" Rayne halted his pacing just long enough to make eye contact with Lucifer. The grin on the Devil's face expanded. Rayne went back to striding alongside twisted black iron bars, thinking of how he would make Lucifer and Isra suffer if he ever regained his freedom.

The sinister laugh that emanated from Lucifer sent a ripple of hatred and wrath through Rayne.

"You do not even know what you are, what abilities you truly have."

Rayne's hand snaked through the bars, capturing Lucifer by the shirt. Lucifer's body slammed against the twisted iron pillars preventing Rayne from mauling Lucifer and Isra. "The only difference between your other minions and me is I don't fear you. If these bars weren't here, you and the deceitful bitch that works for you would no longer exist."

"And why is it you have no fear of me? Others wouldn't dare utter a threat like the one you just did. You are not some random minion, Haroun."

"If you are so wise, you tell me what I am, Lucifer."

The Devil teleported out of Rayne's grip.

Rayne loathed how Lucifer laughed even more.

Lucifer extended his arms outward, elated by this freak stroke of luck. "I hold the Council's lost balance keeper! This is a surprising turn of events. For you to be christened a wolf, you belong to the House of the Moon. What Council member do you serve, Haroun?"

"Council member? I know nothing of this nonsense you and Isra consistently utter."

"Has a deity or one of their messengers not visited you?"

Rayne snorted. "I did not believe in deities other than Allah or djinn until encountering you and Isra. What reason would one have to visit me?"

"You are not alone in wanting the answer to that question." Lucifer believed Rayne held no insight about his destiny or the power granted to him. "Keep him caged until I return. We need to know exactly what our new general is capable of doing."

Isra found the order strange. "Where are you going?"

"To the Council Round. The House of the Moon seems to be short their wolf."

"Their wolf?" Isra glanced at Rayne before returning her gaze to her master.

Lucifer grinned. "This may play out very nicely in our favor."

The High Council Round - 806

"What is the meaning of this interruption?" Isis demanded as Lucifer boldly strode into the Inner Council chambers.

The newly designated Horsemen turned to see who invaded the sanctity of a sealed meeting.

"I am afraid I have troubling news for the Council that cannot wait to be delivered." Lucifer threw Rayne's medallion onto the table in front of the four highest ranking Council members. "My troops found a man's body bearing this crest in Spain. I suspect the corpse is that of our missing Horseman."

Morrigan cautiously picked up the medallion. While the goddess remained stoic, the concern on Isis's face revealed the identity of the fourth Horseman.

"One of our ranks strays beyond our laws to kill an immortal guardian." Lucifer hoped to draw out more information. "I will dispatch Garsea and any other resources necessary to hunt down whomever defies our decrees. In the meantime, I offer to serve as a Horseman until a replacement can be found."

"Bring Aquitaine here," Morrigan whispered to the priestess beside her.

Raphael straightened as Morrigan's eyes found him.

Zeus doubted Lucifer randomly stumbled across the individual destined to complete the Horsemen. "Where exactly did your men find the body?"

"A half hour ride from Córdoba. The man's features bore a striking resemblance to Haroun Ibn-Ziyad. The general has been missing for almost a month. That would match the timeframe the Fates said the fourth Horseman disappeared from their sight."

Osiris's whispering with Isis halted.

Aquitaine entered the room then bowed to Morrigan. "You sent for me?"

The goddess offered him the crest in her hands. Aquitaine's expression sobered.

"Was this once yours?" Morrigan prayed the duke said no.

"Yes. Please tell me the one I gave it to is safely in Council custody."

Lucifer placed an empathetic hand on the Aquitaine's arm. "Sadly, the man who wore the seal is no more. We discovered his body outside of Córdoba."

Aquitaine shook his head. "What a disturbing development."

"Again, I offer to stand in the man's stead as needed." Lucifer tested the Council.

Osiris glared at Lucifer. "You cannot serve as a substitute until a replacement is found."

"Why ever not? My powers are greater than the other three combined."

Raphael chuckled and approached the Council table. "While you are powerful, Lucifer, you will never be a balance keeper. You lack mortal blood."

Raphael's words puzzled the Devil.

Morrigan disclosed the failsafe the Council designed to ensure Lucifer could never become one of the balance keepers he argued so passionately for. "We, and the Fates, felt it best a Horseman be a mix of both realms. Otherwise, there is a risk of favoring one realm over the other. It also ensures a Horseman empathizes with the tribulation of man. Immortals often do not understand things that afflict the human condition."

"You stupidly made four of the most powerful beings fallible!" Lucifer almost shouted at the deities and their entourages.

Michael now rose. "Watch your tone in here."

Lucifer laughed disbelievingly. "I have seen some ludicrous things carried out by the Council over the centuries, but requiring a Horseman to have mortal blood is by far the most foolhardy. Humans fall to temptation more easily than any immortal."

Osiris glared at Lucifer. "The Fates do not share your opinion of man."

"I hope the Fates quickly find you a new fourth Horseman, since they believe a human can be trustworthy enough to wield such responsibility." Lucifer vanished from the room.

"When Lucifer set his hand upon me, I saw Haroun, alive, in a dungeon." Aquitaine shared the vision Lucifer triggered with the rest of the Council.

Raphael frowned. "Lucifer has Haroun?"

"I am not certain of that, but I know who I saw."

Osiris needed more than a random vision to indict a fellow Council member. "We cannot arrest Lucifer without evidence. If we charge him without finding Haroun, we split the Council."

Morrigan hoped Aquitaine could offer more information. "Did you recognize anything in the vision that might share where Haroun is?"

"No. It is someplace I have never been." Aquitaine frustrated the goddess.

"Raphael, go to Córdoba and learn what you can about Haroun. Lyal, you have informants within Lucifer's ranks. Perhaps they may know of a human recently taken captive in Córdoba and being held somewhere." Osiris dispatched the Horsemen and Isis's field commander on their first joint assignment.

Córdoba - 806

Lucifer appeared out of nowhere, startling Isra. "You need to find a way to better control him. He cannot spend eternity in that cage."

Isra looked over at Rayne calmly sitting in the rear corner of his cell. "I was contemplating killing him. He is proving to be a worthless investment."

Lucifer grinned. "One destined to be a Council Harbinger is hardly a worthless investment. You merely haven't found the right tactic to manage him."

Isra's eyes widened in surprise. "A harbinger? That explains the silver eyes and his abilities."

Lucifer approached the cage. "I have an offer for you."

Rayne ignored the immortal and tossed a rock across the floor.

Annoyed, Lucifer entered the confines of the cell. "There will be no more ignoring orders or your masters, Haroun."

Wary of Lucifer, Rayne came to his feet, but remained silent. He prepared to defend himself should the Devil make any threatening advances toward him.

"I can tell by the way you are staring at me that you want to utter some flippant remark. Speak it, Haroun."

Rayne locked eyes with Lucifer, refusing to make even the slightest sound.

Lucifer smiled at how the former human flaunted his and Isra's authority. "Defiance, rage, loathing. They all lead you straight to me, Haroun. You will indeed be one of the strongest and most powerful of those who serve me."

Rayne snorted at what Lucifer said, but still wouldn't speak. He wouldn't serve Lucifer any more than he would Isra. Neither would have him as a mere minion or a general at the head of their legions. There was nothing more Lucifer or Isra could do to force him into doing their bidding. He survived the torture sessions and the whip. They had taken his freedom. It had been days since he last was outside the cage Isra built to contain him. Every tactic they deployed failed to break his resistance. He'd gladly die or spend eternity in the confines of his new prison.

"A man always has a weakness to exploit or something he wants more than anything else." Lucifer let Rayne know he could read his thoughts.

"I want nothing, and there is not enough of my conscience left for you to exploit."

Lucifer loudly laughed. "Oh, I doubt that. It's amazing what you humans will do with the right motivation. What event brought you to him, Isra? A rage of vengeance against a rival? Umar, wasn't it? What if I give you a second chance to kill this Umar?"

"I will not slaughter entire populations for you or Isra, even for a second chance to finish Umar."

"I do not want you to kill entire populations. I want you to eliminate three problematic immortals. Isra will dictate your other tasking since contractually you are her servant."

"My sword is not yours to wield against any creature I have no quarrel with." Rayne turned his back on Lucifer.

"Do not give your back to our master," Isra hissed, entering the cell, raising the whip she held to strike him.

Rayne caught the whip as it sailed towards him. He would not tolerate being beaten any longer. Twisting the leather strap around his bleeding hand, Rayne yanked the butt of the weapon from Isra's grip.

Lucifer laughed when Rayne retaliated by striking Isra across the face with the end of her own whip. The large knotted butt bruised and cut into her cheek, drawing blood. Lucifer held his hand up in front of Isra, preventing the she-demon from attacking Rayne. "It appears you have some fight left in you, after all."

"I have quarrel with Isra." Rayne threw the whip to the far side of the cell. "As to the three immortals you want dead, kill them yourself."

Rayne returned to the spot along the wall that he routinely leaned against and sat down, refusing to acknowledge Lucifer any longer.

Lucifer shook his head then departed, only to return a few minutes later with a woman struggling in his arms.

"Haroun!" The woman cried out seeing Rayne.

Rayne rose, doubting his eyes. She had to be a mirage Lucifer conjured. "Priya?"

"It appears I've found the proper leverage." Lucifer laughed at the rage on Rayne's face.

"Haroun, help me." Priya reached for Rayne.

Lucifer jerked her back to ensure she was well out of Rayne's reach. "Do we have your sword now, Haroun?"

"No." Rayne struggled with his conflicting emotions. His mind screamed the woman couldn't be Priya, but his heart shouted back it was her. "Priya is dead, Lucifer. Umar's assassins murdered her. I saw her die."

"Oh, she's dead, Haroun, but her soul isn't. It's amazing what one can find wandering in the afterlife. Tragic deaths prevent a soul from immediately crossing over." Lucifer brought Priya to the cell door, so Rayne could better see his betrothed. "You will destroy Malaca as Isra desires, then you will take care of the three men I need eliminated."

"If I refuse?" Rayne already knew the answer with Lucifer holding Priya.

"She pays the price." Lucifer set Priya ablaze.

"Priya!" Rayne tried to reach her through the bars. He wasn't sure what he could do to stop her suffering, but he'd damn well try something to put the flames out. She was just outside his reach. The flames that consumed her singed his fingertips. Her tormented screams tore at his conscience. He tried summoning the magic he recently learned he possessed to suffocate the fire or force Lucifer back, but the elusive power refused to come. All he could do was watch Priya die again.

Lucifer let her charred body drop to the floor.

Rayne collapsed to his knees. He reached out to touch her scorched hand. It crumbled into gray ash under the weight of his fingers.

"I can torture her soul for days, Haroun." Lucifer re-summoned Priya.

"She is innocent in all this, Lucifer!"

"Your obedience buys her peace."

"Torture me instead!"

Lucifer smirked. "I am torturing you, Haroun. Whether or not she burns again is up to you. Do I have your sword and obedience, General Ibn-Ziyad?"

Rayne closed his eyes. He couldn't watch Priya repeatedly burn, but he couldn't do as Lucifer asked either.

"Must she endure another round so quickly?"

Priya screamed after Lucifer conjured hell fire again.

Rayne's eyes flew open. The fear in her scream! Why weren't the gods interceding now that he knew they existed? He understood their abandoning him with being a man of war and what all he had done, but to abandon a woman who lived as the rules of their faith required? Priya had done nothing to warrant this.

"Haroun, Haroun, please." Priya wept as Lucifer grasped her by the hair and waved the flame around her.

"Stop!" Rayne shouted, watching the flame in Lucifer's palm mere millimeters from Priya. "Do not harm her. I, I will do whatever you wish. Allow her to cross over into the next life."

"She will not find salvation until you fulfill your oath."

"I will honor my promise to you and Isra, Lucifer. Release her." Rayne may not have been able to give Priya the life she deserved as a human, but he could ensure her afterlife gifted her whatever existence she desired.

"Once Malaca is no more, she will go free." Lucifer vanished with Priya.

Rayne shook his head, slamming his fists into the floor. The dungeon rattled from how hard he struck the stone.

"Like it or not, you're one of us now." Garsea almost felt a hint of pity for the broken general who resisted Lucifer and Isra longer than any other being had previously.

CHAPTER

TWENTY-EIGHT

Malaca - 806

Rayne rode in the middle of the large horde preparing to sweep into Malaca. He stared at the city walls a short distance before him. They would be breeched in a matter of seconds by the demon and djinn army. An army he would help unleash on the citizens of the unfortunate town. Stone would crumble to dust. What sections didn't fall, hordes of demon and djinn would scamper over like a mass of ticks thirsting to bury their heads in the flesh of a stray dog. May the supposed gods help the poor residents who sought shelter inside the city. A wave of nausea washed over him. He forcefully swallowed the bile down that rose in his throat. Never had he dreaded a battle as he did this one.

Isra and the other djinn surrounding him thrived on the townspeople's fear. A sinister, cat like smile covered Isra's face while she looked at those same walls, already savoring her victory as she rode beside Rayne. "You will crave this after today, Haroun. Once you spill blood as a djinn, bloodlust will drive you to consume evermore death. Each soul taken will build your strength. You'll welcome the frenzy of human suffering with the euphoria it always brings."

Rayne prayed she was wrong. That something would free him from Isra's clutches. "I will never desire blood as you do."

Isra laughed. "Just as you'd never wield your sword for Lucifer and me? I will relish the moment you once more learn how wrong you are about your fate. Mark my words, Haroun, there will come a day when you anxiously await my directives to take another town or to kill one who defies me or Lucifer."

Garsea rode up to them with a grin on his face, ready to conquer and claim new territory. "I give you the honor of leading the advance, Haroun."

Rayne stared at them, mortified, but forced his face to remain emotionless. He tried to focus his thoughts on the pending fight, if one could call it that. He did his best to rationalize what he was about to do. *You set Priya free with this one act. You can do this one time, then kill whatever these Horsemen are that Lucifer needs out of the way.*

"General!" Isra's tone warned her patience with him waned.

Rayne dispatched the order to advance. The walls fell quickly along with the human army. Thinking the siege over, he handed Isra the keys to the citadel and the town's flag. "Malaca is yours, Isra."

Narciso pointed to the humans they herded together. "What of the women and children, mistress?"

"Kill them," Isra calmly directed.

Appalled, Rayne spoke out against the order. "Do not do this, Isra. They are no threat to us."

"Are you failing to honor your oath, Haroun?" Isra conjured Priya to remind Rayne of the consequences of disobedience.

"There is no honor in genocide, Isra. At the very least, free the children."

"We do not fight for honor, Haroun, nor do we need any future rebellion instigators left alive." Isra sent Priya back into the afterlife. "I will be kind this engagement and only order you to ensure my wishes are carried out. Next time, you will be the executioner."

Rayne took a step towards Isra, his hand on the hilt of his blade.

Garsea blocked his path. "Do not be foolish, Haroun."

While Rayne refused to back away from Garsea, he moved his hand off his sword hilt. "One of these days, I will be your executioner, Garsea."

Garsea laughed. "The more your hatred festers, the faster you turn. You will be freely serving Isra soon."

The djinn walked away chuckling to himself, leaving Rayne to finish their siege on the city.

Narciso awaited the instruction to attack. "Your orders, General?"

May god forgive me. Rayne closed his eyes as he surrendered himself to the darkness he could no longer fend off.

Utter the words, a feminine voice whispered.

The phrase repeated, almost like a strange echo from behind him, then again on his right. Rayne glanced towards the city gates to see a cloaked figure standing in the darker billows of smoke.

Trust the Fates. Give the command, Haroun.

Rayne wondered if he hallucinated, but what was left of his conscience compelled him to believe whomever spoke. *I place the outcome in God's hands.*

His voice sounded foreign to him as he gave a command he never thought himself capable of issuing. "Kill them all. Burn what remains of the city."

Rayne remounted his horse as the djinn and demon horde moved towards the humans corralled near the city gates. He tried to block out the screams of those about to be slaughtered when the djinn dragged the first several people forward for execution.

A man in black and gold emerged from the nearby flames, decapitating one of the djinn restraining a woman. A second later, five other djinn lay dismembered on the ground. The humans huddled together, terrified by the djinn, demons, and whatever beings moved through the smoke striking down their captors.

"Get the humans out of here!" Raphael shouted to the High Council soldiers that accompanied the three Horsemen.

Through the flames, Rayne saw three similarly dressed men leading a defensive strike, while another small band of soldiers wearing silver and green escorted those still alive to safety. They looked human, but moved similarly to djinn. What manner of creature were they?

Furious the Council interfered in his plans, Lucifer materialized beside Rayne. "You may fulfill both your promises in one day, Haroun. Those mounted officers in black and gold are the three I need eliminated. Priya is forever free if you eradicate the Council's Horsemen."

Rayne turned his horse and charged for the man who appeared to be the leader of the troops.

With his eyes locked on the evacuation teams, Raphael didn't notice Rayne until Rayne's blade collided with the armor covering his back, knocking him out of the saddle. If the blade had hit slightly higher, he would be headless.

Standing up, Raphael cursed. He drew his weapon. How did a mere djinn have the power to unhorse him? He waited patiently for the djinn rider to pass him once more. Teleporting to the opposite side of the horse, Raphael ripped Rayne from the saddle.

Finding himself rolling in the dirt, Rayne somersaulted back onto his feet. He quickly raised his scimitar, blocking the black steel blade traveling towards him.

Impressively, the scimitar circled Raphael's broader blade and scraped across Raphael's shoulder, forcing the Horseman to step sideways.

Gabriel rode up to Michael. Both watched the unknown djinn leading Isra's forces engage Raphael. They hadn't encountered one who could match their commander's skill with a sword prior to today. The way the man fought reminded them more of Lucifer or one of Hades's demon guard.

Gabriel glanced over at Michael. "I've never seen a djinn that could catch Raphael by surprise."

"Me neither. If I didn't know better, I would say he was a harbinger, but that's impossible. A corrupted djinn can't become one."

Rayne's blade found a weak spot in Raphael's armor. He forced the tip through the metal, piercing Raphael's side.

Raphael grunted from the quick burst of pain traveling his side. His dagger-wielding fist collided with Rayne's face, bashing him sideways. Rayne's head tilting back from the blow exposed his throat. Raphael dropped his hand, so the edge of his knife made its way to Rayne's jugular. The jagged blade bit into Rayne's flesh, but did not inflict the damage Raphael hoped it would.

Ignoring the smarting in his neck and watching his opponent, Rayne carefully retreated. The injury he dealt the soldier would normally kill a man. "How are you not dead?"

Raphael laughed. "I was wondering the same about you. Most djinn and demon burst into ash when their jugular is opened."

The two engaged one another again.

Realizing Raphael couldn't take down this particular djinn, Gabriel and Michael rode forward to assist their commander.

***

Aquitaine shouted the all clear after one of his men advised any living human was safely out of the burning city. He turned to see the three Horsemen fighting a lone djinn. It sent Michael and Gabriel to the ground before turning to Raphael.

Recognizing the being, Aquitaine ran towards the Horsemen. "Stop, Haroun! Drop your sword and surrender to Raphael. We will grant you quarter."

Raphael noted how the djinn glanced in Aquitaine's direction. No wonder he wouldn't go down. He was destined to be one of them. Raphael lowered his blade slightly; hoping to reason with the being before him. "Is your name truly Haroun Ibn-Ziyad?"

"Haroun Ibn-Ziyad died with the people of Malaca today." Rayne drove his dagger towards Raphael's chest.

Raphael grasped Rayne's wrist with both hands to prevent the weapon from penetrating the armor he wore. "Surrender, Haroun. You can't fight us all."

Aquitaine could sense Haroun wouldn't capitulate willingly. The man wasn't much different from the boy he was years ago. They needed to weaken him to take him into custody. Aquitaine hurled his knife at Rayne, striking him in the throat.

Losing blood and stunned by how accurate the duke's aim was, Rayne collapsed to his knees. No man could hit such a small target from that far away.

"Take him alive! Morrigan can salvage his soul," Aquitaine shouted above the fray.

Gabriel gripped Rayne's shoulder.

Raphael extended a hand to him. "You lost your way, wolf. But you are still one of us. Allow us to set you back on the right course."

Rayne instinctively grasped Raphael's hand. His grip loosened as weakness overcame him.

"What?" He mumbled, not understanding why the soldier would say such a thing.

Raphael pulled the blade from Rayne's neck. Michael tore the tunic of a dead soldier lying near them and pressed the cloth against Rayne's wound, trying to stop the bleeding.

"Why are you helping me? Allow me to die."

"We cannot do that, Haroun." Michael looked over at Raphael. "He may be too far gone with the blood he's lost."

Something collided with both Horsemen, forcing them down onto the ground several feet away from Rayne. Both twisted to look back at where Rayne laid. They glimpsed black feathered wings. The wings and the injured djinn they tried to save disappeared into the ground.

"Lucifer!" Raphael bellowed, knowing exactly who took Haroun.

Granada - 806

Darkness engulfed Rayne. He plummeted ever downward as if someone pushed him from a cliff. The speed at which he descended churned his stomach. Unexpectedly, his free fall came to a jarring halt. What stopped it? Rayne forced his eyes open. Had he finally died?

"You failed me today!" Lucifer fumed down at him.

Rayne screamed as something singed his skin. His face burned after Lucifer struck him.

"And now they know you are alive."

"Who knows?" Rayne tried to make sense of Lucifer's words as he struggled to sit up.

Lucifer handed Isra Rayne's indenture papers. "He is yours to do with as you please. He is not capable of killing the Horsemen as I thought he could. The only thing he is good for is being an enforcer. If he disobeys you, remind him Priya is easily available for another torture session."

"Thank you, master." Isra relished the thought of controlling such a powerful being. An enforcer was a rare gift from Lucifer.

Lucifer watched Rayne prop himself up on one arm. "Get him out of Spain. Morrigan will send the Horsemen for him. If they find him, everything we planned will be for naught."

"We can send him to Lucien in France until Morrigan abandons her search," Isra suggested hiding Rayne with a djinn that wouldn't dare challenge her ownership of him.

Lucifer nodded in agreement.

The Spanish prison doors shattered a floor above them

"Lucifer! Where is he?" Raphael shouted. Lucifer was there somewhere. Lyal had tracked him to this location. "I know you are here!"

"I will deal with the High Council. Move him. Now!" Lucifer hissed before teleporting upstairs.

"Where is who, Raphael?" Lucifer casually looked up from the chair he sat in and closed a book between his hands as if he had been reading.

"You know damn well who I am asking for." Raphael hated how Lucifer played the games that he did.

"I am afraid I don't."

"I saw you in Malaca, Lucifer. The Council knows you have the missing Horseman."

Lucifer acted confused. "Malaca? Why whatever happened in Malaca?"

Lyal sensed Rayne. "He is beneath us, Commander."

Lucifer poured himself a glass of wine with an amused smile on his face. "Who is beneath us? The two of you act as if I kidnapped the harbinger the Fates lost. As if I would do such a thing. I welcome you and Lyal to search the entirety of this place for a man we all know died three weeks ago. When you do not find him, I expect an apology and restitution for the door you shattered."

Raphael nodded toward the stairway. "Retrieve him. I will handle Lucifer."

Lyal dissolved into the stone layers beneath her. She found Garsea and Narciso lifting an injured being from a cot in the center of a cell, who matched Aquitaine's description of Haroun.

Ripping her knife from its sheath on her arm, Lyal launched it into Narciso as she ran towards the three. The enchanted blade immobilized the djinn against the wall.

"Give him to me."

Lyal's shimmering black eyes held Rayne's attention. Her hair matched the dark shading of her eyes. Like the three men in Malaca, she moved like a djinn, but her attacking Narciso suggested she was something else.

Garsea lowered Rayne to sit on the cot again, then pulled his weapon. "Come and take him, harbinger."

Rayne watched amazed as the woman laughed then engaged one of the most powerful in Isra's ranks. The female creature easily evaded Garsea's blade. She sent the five other demons that entered the room back into the hall before sealing the door shut with magic Rayne only read about in stories.

Two more men in uniforms of black and gold, along with one wearing clothing of green and silver, materialized out of thin air then moved towards him. They swatted away the demons attacking them as one would gnats buzzing around them on a humid summer evening.

The man in green and silver's eyes locked with Rayne's. "Haroun."

Rayne knew that voice, he knew those eyes. They were almost the same shade of blue his had once been. Where had he and the man met before?

An explosion rocked the fortress. Stone fragments tumbled down upon them all.

Isra walked through the falling rubble. "Garsea, take him to Lucien."

Rayne watched Isra unsheathe her blade for the first time since being in her custody. She sliced open one of the black uniformed men's faces then sent the sword through the side of the man in green and silver. The one Garsea called harbinger ordered the others to fall back then knocked Isra's weapon from the she-demon's hand. Black eyes rested on him as Garsea seized a hold of his arm.

The High Council Round - 806

"Did you find him?" Morrigan anxiously asked as Lyal and the Horsemen entered Council Chambers. Osiris, Isis, and Zeus sat with her.

"We did, but were not able to secure him. Aquitaine was injured along with Gabriel. Both are being treated in Sasainn," Lyal advised the Council heads.

"Where was he, Raphael?" Isis asked the new Horsemen Commander, originally expecting them to return without finding any trace of the man.

"Isra held him in Granada. I would wager at Lucifer's order. We could find no trail leading us to where they relocated him. All we can do is wait for him to resurface." Raphael hated how Garsea slipped away with the newly made djinn, who could quickly become a concern for the Horsemen.

Zeus scowled. "Did you find any evidence linking Lucifer to his conversion?"

"None other than the two being located under the same roof. Lucifer denies any knowledge of Haroun being kept in the dungeon. Examination of the cage they kept him in shows an enchantment placed upon the bars by Isra alone."

Osiris pondered a way to gain the evidence they needed to remove Lucifer from the Council. "Mayhap, we can persuade Isra to disclose how Haroun came to be in Granada."

"We would have to find her first. She disappeared with Haroun and Garsea." Lyal further frustrated the Council members.

Córdoba - 812

"Rayne!" Grace shouted, finding herself brought back into 812 by whatever powered the Repository. The pool sent her to Rayne's home in Córdoba instead of the Council Round.

Hearing her scream his name, Rayne ran into the room. "Grace? What are you doing here? I thought you were with Khonsu." The way she clung to him crying unnerved him.

When she looked up at him, tears streaked her face. "All that you endured... how are you not still a djinn?"

Damn Khonsu for sharing stories that weren't his to tell! Holding her tighter, Rayne was afraid to ask what exactly she had seen. "I had centuries of assistance to restore my faith in the greater good, leof. The Council also gave me the gift of hope for better things to come."

CHAPTER

TWENTY-NINE

Elysium

"How are you holding up?" Dante asked Rayne, offering him a drink.

Rayne took the glass and enjoyed the smooth liquor as it traveled across his palate. "As well as can be expected. Though I am worried about Grace. Whatever Khonsu showed her in the Repository troubles her."

"Have you not asked her what she saw?"

"I have. She only responds with the Horsemen's origins and the Council's search for me."

"I can see how both topics might be disturbing for her. She hasn't shared any more details?"

"No. Whenever I ask her to tell me more, there is a strange emotional distance between us, yet she literally clings to me for comfort. It's almost as if the Council forbade her to share the contents of the Repository. I don't understand why they would. I know every little detail of those moments. Hell, I lived half of them. The ones I didn't, I learned when I took the Horsemen's Oath."

"The past the Repository holds can be overwhelming for those of us who have lived in the immortal realm for centuries. I imagine as new as Grace is to our ways, she is doing her best to understand whatever was shared."

"That does not ease my fears, Dante. I worry about what part of my past is going to surface next and how Grace will react to it. Do you have any idea what is like to have every possible misstep or event of your past revealed to your spouse? How much strain that places on your marriage? Not to mention this is all happening as we must confront Isra and Lucifer to prevent whatever plot they are deploying from taking root in the mortal world."

"Perhaps, perhaps, you should take Grace and the children away from Elysium and Córdoba for a few days to reconnect. The other Horsemen and I can manage Isra and Lucifer to ensure Armageddon doesn't begin, at least not until you return."

Rayne contemplated the suggestion. "You don't mind monitoring Isra while I am gone?"

"Now that I am free to do as I wish within immortal laws, investigating what trouble an overseer is causing isn't a problem at all. We have the Council's full sanction to do whatever is necessary to foil Isra's and Lucifer's plans. Go home with your family for the next couple of days."

***

Sixteenth - Century Spain

Rayne took Grace and the kids to their primary residence in sixteenth-century Spain. Two days of quiet at home calmed the children's nerves and Grace smiled more often. Their third morning home, the Arsceneauxs stopped by for a visit, along with Dante and Raphael.

They all stood outside, enjoying the sunny weather. Tessa and Tarquin chased one another around the yard. Grace periodically checked on them as she spoke with Caitlin. Tessa wandered to the banks of a pond they periodically swam in on warm days.

Rayne looked over his shoulder after Tarquin and Tessa stopped talking. Silence almost guaranteed the kids were doing something they shouldn't be. Thankfully, their discussion ceased because the two had split up versus causing mischief. Tarquin skipped a rock on the pond while Tessa stood a few feet away, fascinated by something in the water. She called Tarquin over to look at a fish she discovered. Some days Rayne wished the world still held all the wonder and innocence it had when he was young. Listening to Tarquin agree that the fish was neat, he smiled. The two stepped closer to the water and ran a foot or so following the little minnow darting in and out of reeds along the bank.

"When do you plan to return to Córdoba?" Raphael asked, drawing Rayne back into their discussion.

Grace felt eyes on her. She looked towards the men and saw Dante staring at her. Gage joined the Horsemen, redirecting Dante's gaze. Spotting the general, Tarquin called hello to Gage, who waved the boy over. Eager to join their discussion, Tarquin happily ran to the adults. The boy looked up to Gage as much as he did the Horsemen. He was growing up too quickly. She went back to watching her daughter. Tessa stepped to the very edge of the grassy bank.

"Tessa, do not go any closer than that," Grace cautioned, worried Tessa would happily wade into the pond to chase the fish.

The little minnow darted into a patch of grass. Tessa leaned slightly to see where it had gone. A shadow came towards the shore.

"Daddy!" Tessa softly called for her father.

Rayne stepped away from the group. "Yes, sprite?"

Something grabbed her ankle then dragged her into the water.

Rayne sprinted towards where his daughter had stood. "Tessa!"

Her arms flailed, splashing water everywhere as her body briefly bobbed back up above the water. "Daddy!"

Rayne dove into the center of the pond.

Lyal stopped Grace from following him into the water.

After what seemed an eternity, Rayne's head broke the glasslike surface. A sputtering and crying Tessa held onto his neck as he swam towards the shore. Grace stepped into knee deep water to meet them. Rayne waded over to her.

"Go with Mommy, Tessa."

Grace took Tessa from Rayne. The shivering preschooler cried into her shoulder and wailed about a monster in their pond. Grace kissed Tessa's forehead, thankful Rayne reacted as quickly as he did. "You're safe now, Tessa. You're okay."

Whatever was in the pond yanked Rayne backward into the deeper center.

"Rayne!" Grace instinctively moved toward the pond again.

Dante pulled her back.

Rayne managed to free himself from the green and brown vine-like extensions encircling his legs. Thicker tentacles wrapped around his waist. A second set inched up his back towards his neck. "Get the children in the house!"

He filled his lungs with air before the creature submerged him in the depths of the normally safe pool.

Seeing the panic on Grace's face, Dante took her by the arm. "Do as Rayne asks. I will assist him."

Tarquin remained near the porch, wide-eyed and watching everything.

"Go inside, Tarquin!" Dante shouted at his son.

Tarquin ran through the front door then peered out the window.

Dante's gentle tug on Grace's arm caused Grace to hurry towards the house. Hearing a loud splash, she stopped and turned.

Rayne escaped from whatever tried to kill him. Prey turned to captor as Rayne now held the monster hostage. It struggled against the Horseman's grip on the back of its head.

Grace pressed Tessa's face into her shoulder. "Close your eyes, Tessa."

Rayne heaved the creature onto the grass. "First, you attack my son. Then you threaten my wife. Now, you go after my daughter."

"Haroun. Emir. Primus." The being tried to crawl away from the immortal stalking him. "We were brothers once."

"Silence!" Rayne watched the djinn changing shape before him. "I let you live the other night. I will not make the same mistake today, Kamar." He jerked Kamar upward.

Dante stood beside Grace and blocked Tessa's view of her father.

"For endangering my son." Rayne sliced off the man's left arm. "For harming my daughter." Rayne severed the right one.

Kamar howled in pain a second time.

The brutality Rayne displayed transfixed Grace in place. She had seen the executioner in him before, but never like this; pure wrath made up Rayne's being.

"You must take Tessa inside. She should not see this part of her father," Dante whispered to Grace.

Lyal gently pried Tessa from Grace's arms. "I will see to the child. Tend to Grace. Rayne's rage overwhelms her. She fully bound herself to Rayne only a few days ago." Lyal teleported herself and Tessa inside.

Worried about her husband, Grace walked around Dante.

Rayne reached into the beast's chest and ripped out its heart. "For chasing my wife."

"He did that barehanded," Grace mumbled, not believing Rayne would ever behave as he did now.

Rayne dropped the still beating heart on the ground.

Astonishingly, Kamar remained alive. "Isra will bring war to your doorstep for this, Haroun."

"I am War, Kamar. You will atone for desecrating the sanctuaries of my family." Rayne severed Kamar's head then drove his sword through the djinn's heart. When the heart stopped contracting, Kamar's body imploded into a fine black ash.

"Tariq!" Rayne summoned his old vizier that still served Isra. The djinn immediately appeared with head bowed to his former master.

"Yes, Haroun?"

"Take this to Isra with the message my wife and children remain off limits." Rayne thrust Kamar's head into Tariq's hands. "Since she fails to honor the prior warning, War comes to destroy her. No mercy will be granted to her or any who serve her."

Tariq bowed then disappeared with Kamar's head.

Dante and Grace watched Rayne approach them. Molten silver concealed blue. Whenever the enforcer took over, Rayne's physical presence seemed larger than normal.

Dante thought Rayne took things too far. "You begin an immortal war without sanction."

"Do not stand in my way, Dante. We both know this must be done." Rayne's shoulder hit Dante's as Rayne continued on to Grace, forcing the god to take a step back.

Rayne stopped before his wife, hating how concern filled her eyes. "I swear to you, Isra will never come near our children again. I will hunt her down and dispatch her."

Grace looked up at Rayne. The dark part of her husband did not disappear now that all danger was past. The being that intrigued and frightened Lucifer remained before her. "Isra does not scare me. Losing my husband to his prior self is what terrifies me."

"Your husband retains his conscience. Do not let the silver or other physical changes fool you. They will fade as the executioner and enforcer quiet once again." Rayne gestured towards the house as his opposite arm slipped down Grace's back.

She noticed how he positioned his body as a barrier between her and Dante before he escorted her inside. Grace glanced back at Dante. The god frowned. He vanished instead of following them.

Grace cleaned up Tessa then changed her into dry clothes. Tessa tightly clasped Grace's hand, unwilling to leave her mother's side. She stayed close to Rayne or Grace, gripping either their hand or leg for the rest of the afternoon. The little girl calmed some after Rayne held her for a while, but it wasn't longer than a few minutes after climbing off Rayne's lap that Grace found her fingers caught in the firm grip of Tessa's small hand.

"Tessa, I need to start dinner. You may stay in the kitchen with me, but I need my hand to cook. Please let go."

"But the monster might take me if I let go!" Tessa's lip trembled.

Grace hugged her daughter. She heard the irritated breath Rayne let out. "Tessa, no monsters will ever take you from this house. We are safe in here. They'd also have to fight Daddy if they made it past the barrier spell."

Tarquin offered Tessa his hand, hoping to help ease his sister's fears. "Daddy would defeat them before they made it through the front door, just like he did the pond monster, Tess."

"Thank you, Tarquin." Grace smiled at the two children.

Tarquin led Tessa to the table and pulled out a book to read to her.

Rayne watched Tessa and Tarquin reading the book together. "My children no longer feel safe in our own home. Damn Isra and Kamar for taking that from them today."

Grace reached for him. While he wrapped an arm around her, his gaze remained focused on the children. The angry set of his jaw and the unshed tears in his eyes warned of how deeply the strike at their home disturbed him. "Rayne, in time, they'll feel safe here again. Do not give Isra a victory."

"She has no right to take a child's sense of security. It is one thing to come after me, but another entirely to terrorize two young children." Needing to calm his temper, he left the kitchen.

Rayne did not join Grace and the kids for dinner. After eating, Grace went to check on him. She found him staring at himself in their bedroom mirror.

"My wolf. I truly worry about you."

Rayne turned from the mirror and offered Grace a reassuring smile. "There is nothing to be concerned about, leof."

"What were you thinking? And do not tell me nothing with as intent as the expression on your face was."

"I was recalling when I escaped Isra the first time." He took Grace's hand, sharing the memory.

***

France - 810

"What is happening to me?" Rayne rasped, looking up at the black-eyed woman kneeling beside him.

"You are dying." She placed a hand on his chest, checking his heartbeat.

"I am a djinn, an enforcer. I cannot die." Rayne struggled to breathe. His body tingled, growing numb.

"Immortals can die. We are merely harder to kill than humans."

"What?" This was the first Rayne heard of anything other than his master being able to finish him off.

"One of your own poisoned you. The wound from the battle hides what they have done."

The woman tilted his face up to check his symptoms. Wide silver eyes almost missing their dark pupils and the strange shade of gray over taking his lips confirmed what caused his weakened state.

"Kamar." Rayne knew exactly which of his peers would do such a thing. Kamar and he had toasted to their pending success the night prior. The lower-ranking djinn must have tainted the wine with a slow acting toxin. Finding it ironic that he would die from something he never anticipated, Rayne laughed. Kamar's vindictiveness for Rayne's inability to stop Umar from executing his brother was the thing that granted him freedom from Isra. "Salvation finds me at last."

"There is no salvation awaiting you. Damnation and an eternity of torture are your path for the offenses you committed." The woman-like creature placed her hand flat on his chest. "I can save you from that, Haroun."

"At what price? I am done serving anyone besides myself." Rayne flung her hand from him. The movement temporarily cut off his air supply. To his dismay, his eyes opened again to see the Egyptian still watching him. "Let me die, woman. I know you delay my passing."

"You can right your wrongs, General. Your soul and conscience can be regained."

Rayne willed her away. He prayed if there was a god left in heaven that he would die rather than be forced to obey the bloodthirsty whims of Isra. He could no longer live with what he had become over the past few years. As Isra predicted in Malaca, he slowly came to crave causing suffering and death. While bloodlust didn't drive him into a frenzy as it did the others, he could feel its pull anytime he was sent to execute or threaten an enemy of Isra's. After witnessing his young cousin's death at the hands of Lucifer and Lucien, he grew numb inside to everything. They had taken what sliver of humanity he had left. Now, he only fleetingly felt a tingling of emotion from the sickening pleasure of torturing someone or seeing the fear in a being's eyes before he ended their life. Not even carnal pleasures could make him feel alive any longer. Whenever he took a woman to his bed, it was to relieve the primal ache of lust that consumed dark beings, along with needing to quell the animalistic urge to make certain women he encountered submit to the enforcer they frequently found so fascinating.

How had he fallen so far without even being cognizant of it? If he sold his soul, why in the past week had the battles and murders started haunting him? Why did he feel so much regret and guilt? An enforcer should be remorseless.

"General, your fate is greater than that of a demon. Evil knocked you off course. The High Council sends me to give you the opportunity to find your way home."

"The High Council? The same council who allows fiends such as Isra and Lucifer to run amuck? The Council who abandoned me to be tortured in Granada? If they gave a damn about right or wrong, monsters like myself would not exist."

"Even monsters have a purpose. Do you want to learn yours?"

"Why do I feel as if this matter is already decided?'

The woman actually smiled down at him. "Some things are out of our hands. Destiny dictates events more than even I care to admit."

Rayne now recognized her. "You are the harbinger Lucifer spoke of... the one from Granada. It appears you will have to report failing at bringing me before the Council a second time."

"If you know I am the harbinger from Granada, then you also know absolution from the High Council is a rare gift one should not carelessly discard. I caution you to choose your next words wisely, General."

Rayne would have laughed if he wasn't convulsed by so much pain; the poison wreaked further havoc traveling throughout his body. His abdominal muscles involuntarily contracted. The sensation of a thousand scorpion stings crept up his arms to his shoulders. He wanted to roll to his side and vomit. The harbinger's hand bearing down against his chest kept him from doing so. He could swear she smirked, taking pleasure in his suffering.

"Your heart is failing. The pain will heighten as it slows."

Rayne winced and cursed from the stinging sensation descending to his groin and thighs.

"Worse awaits you in Tartarus."

The stinging intensified; almost as if his nerves scalded muscle and flesh before penetrating his bones, boiling the marrow. Rayne didn't even want to contemplate what could be worse than he experienced now.

"What are their terms, harbinger?"

"You will learn them soon enough. For now, your word that you will do as the Council messengers direct spares you from Hell."

Rayne loathed the thought of indenturing himself once more. Still, something compelled him to accept the offer. "You have it."

Energy surged through him, burning every inch of his body. He blacked out from the pain.

Rayne briefly woke to find himself in some sort of odd chamber. The harbinger who allegedly brought him the opportunity to regain some sense of humanity spoke with another bejeweled woman dressed in white. Two soldiers in black and gold armor stood with them.

One of the men glanced over at Rayne. "The poison doesn't kill that quickly."

The harbinger grinned. "Accelerating and exaggerating its affects helped the general accept the Council's offer."

"We need the man's trust, Lyal. Tormenting him does not gain his confidence," The other soldier snapped at the harbinger. "Let us pray he never learns what you did today."

"You worry too much, Raphael. He will heal and the Council will have their coveted balance keeper."

"I agree with Commander Fiore. There will be no more harm done to Haroun. Prepare him for his role as needed, nothing beyond that." The bejeweled woman reprimanded the harbinger.

The harbinger respectfully inclined her head. "As you wish, Isis."

"Isis?" Rayne quietly repeated the goddess's name, wondering if he really saw her or if he was dreaming.

All four of the immortals now looked at him.

Rayne slipped back into darkness as Isis came towards him.

CHAPTER

THIRTY

Malta - 810

When he finally regained consciousness, he found himself alone, lying on a bed in a stone walled room with one small window. A far cry from the elaborate chamber he dreamed seeing Isis and her men-at-arms in.

"Where am I?" He muttered to himself, not expecting anyone to answer.

"Malta," A man in monk's robes advised from the open doorway, startling Rayne. "Lyal, the Andalusian is awake."

The harbinger came from somewhere in the hall and made her way to his bedside.

Rayne's mind became clearer as he sat up. "What am I doing in Malta?"

"Isra cannot sense you here. Tomorrow, you will begin your training."

"My training?" What training could he possibly need?

Lyal seemed annoyed with him. "You must learn our ways and how to fight our kind."

"I know how to fight." Rayne wondered if he merely traded masters.

"Against humans. You must learn to identify and fight immortals, gods, their descendants, sorceresses, and all kinds of creature you never knew existed. You will learn how to identify friend and foe."

Rayne scoffed. He should have never agreed to the Council's terms. "Next, you will tell me fairies and elves actually exist."

"They are as real as you and I, wolf."

"I am no wolf." Rayne looked around for his clothes. Where were they? His boots sat at the foot of the bed, but his garments were nowhere in sight.

Lyal handed him the medallion lying on a table by the bed. "This is your emblem, is it not?"

"A Christian knight gave it to me years ago." Rayne tossed the crest onto the bed beside him.

"That man was no more a knight than you are a saint, Haroun. He was a Council messenger sent by the Fates. The medallion tells those of us who walk amongst you your destiny. Like it or not, you are a wolf; a very specific wolf at that. One day, you will protect the moon."

Rayne laid back on the bed. "You suffer from insanity, harbinger."

Lyal laughed. "Then so do you to trust me."

"Trust you?" Rayne snorted, watching the odd being sitting next to him. "I do not trust you. I agreed to this to earn my freedom. Nothing more."

"And you shall have it. Once you are ready for it." Lyal smirked at the way the man eyed her.

"What exactly are you?"

"My name is Lyal. I am Guardian of the Ancients for the House of the Moon."

"If the moon already has a guardian, then I am not needed."

"I serve as the Commander for the House she will be born into. Only the wolf can ensure the moon is lifted into the sky and safeguard her."

Her strange statements confirmed the harbinger was more delusional than Rayne initially thought her to be. "Born into? The moon already exists."

"The moon has not yet become immortal, wolf, nor is the moon the orb you view at night. She is a woman. One with a destiny, almost as great as yours."

Rayne shook his head and stared up at the ceiling. What had he gotten himself into with this supposed Council and their harbinger?

The bed shifted as Lyal stood then walked away. Upon reaching the doorway, she turned and hurled a dagger at him.

Coming upright, Rayne caught it in mid-flight. "Do not test me, harbinger. I have no qualms with killing a woman."

The smile on Lyal's face grew as she stared at the former enforcer. He recovered from the transition process much faster than she or Isis anticipated. She sensed a raw inner strength in him which mirrored that of the other three Horsemen.

"Good. As you know, evil comes in all genders and forms. You must not hesitate in extinguishing it. Consider the new blade on your knife a gift. It was forged to kill Isra should she ever try to reclaim you. Rest, Haroun. Your training will require you to be at your best."

Rayne studied the silver blade, now free of nicks that he held in his hand. The sapphire hilt of the weapon was the same, but the razor-sharp end was entirely new. "I assume you are to be my teacher."

"Your guide for this part of your journey. Ibelin and Morrigan's guide general, Sean Watchous, shall be your first instructors. You will meet them tomorrow morning."

"What type of creature is a guide?"

"You will learn that soon enough." Lyal shut the room door, leaving him to mull over everything.

For almost a year, Rayne trained in Malta. The days of bouting and exercising were brutal. His sessions started before the sun rose and lasted until well after dark. He frequently crawled into his small, uncomfortable bed, aching and exhausted. Even as a human training under his father then in the Cordovan army, he could not recall being this sore or fatigued. He cursed the sun every time it started to rise his first few months there. His body never seemed to get enough rest. His mind screamed for more sleep, but he pressed on anyway.

At first, he doubted the things he witnessed. Lyal took the most pleasure in throwing new tricks and mirages at him. After being trounced for two weeks, he learned not to be deceived by his eyes. His three teachers taught him how to use weapons and magic not even the djinn community knew. He mostly trained one-on-one with Sean, Lyal, or Ibelin. On rare occasion, he had other new immortals join him or he faced off against all three of his instructors. Slowly, he learned to better control and command the immortal battlefield. Once he embraced the new tools given to him, he could easily determine what entities surrounded him. He moved effortlessly through the shadows without detection. Every three months, deities randomly appeared to see his progress.

The first time he noticed a hooded man in black standing at a distance with Lyal watching his sparring sessions, the man's presence distracted him from an engagement with Ibelin. The knight got in a bruising blow then took Rayne down, dislocating Rayne's shoulder. Rayne regained the upper hand in the fight as Lyal called for them to halt. Ibelin and he looked in her direction. The observer with her shook his head no. By the irritated glare Lyal shot the two of them, Rayne correctly assumed the assessment of his performance wasn't satisfactory. Disgruntled, tired, and in pain, Rayne returned to the monastery. He went straight to the infirmary and removed his tunic so the order's healer could examine his shoulder.

"Do not lose faith already, Haroun. It takes time to learn our ways." The medic smiled, tying a sling for Rayne's arm in place. Rayne only grunted in response to his words. "Rest the arm for a day to give the shoulder time to heal."

"Injuries rarely bothered me as a djinn." Rayne stared down at the sling. He doubted Ibelin or Lyal would grant him leniency or the rare reprieve of a day off.

"Your body will adapt to your new status as your stomach has to a normal diet. The body needs a few weeks longer to get there. You are already healing faster than you used to. Soon, you will heal overnight as you did as a djinn, only this time it will be white magic, not black sustaining you."

Astoundingly, Lyal and Ibelin allowed him one day of rest before his preparation to be a Council soldier once more intensified. They routinely pushed him to the brink. There was more than one night where he returned to the monastery bruised and bleeding. During the third week of the new regimen, Rayne managed to surprise Ibelin and Lyal as he figured out the new tactics they deployed. Rayne routinely began overtaking and outmaneuvering them. No member of the order could best him any longer. Ibelin found himself continually defeated in his bouts with Rayne.

"Time for you to step out, Ibelin. He can anticipate any strategy you execute. Lyal and I will take it from here." Sean clasped Ibelin's hand, grateful for all Ibelin had done and Ibelin's willingness to continue helping to hide Rayne from Isra and Lucifer until Rayne could stand on his own against the two.

The second time Rayne noticed Lyal and the man in black, a woman with gold hair in green and gold robes who he sensed was a deity accompanied them. Today, he could hear their conversation in his head.

"Your evaluation of his progress?" Lyal asked the man after Rayne defeated a group of ten guide soldiers.

"Better, but still not good enough. I will check back in another ninety days."

Exasperated, Rayne flung the sword in his hand. He just took down ten immortal soldiers and defeated eight other humans.

"What more can you and the Council possibly expect of me?" He shouted, staring directly at the man in black.

Stunned Rayne could hear their discussion, Sean, Lyal, the man in black, and the golden-haired woman turned toward him.

"Your best, and then some, Haroun. You have yet to show me that," The man in black yelled back. "Push him harder, Sean. Enlist the assistance of whoever is needed to help him get there."

"Perhaps it is your help we need," Sean whispered, so Rayne couldn't hear him.

The man in black looked back at Rayne. The reformed djinn brushed the sweat dripping from his forehead away. "You know I can't train him. Someone else must see him through the trials." He and the blonde deity vanished.

Rayne shook his head and picked up the sword he had thrown as

Sean came towards him. "I don't understand what they want. I took down every immortal I fought. No man in the order can get near me on the field. Djinn nor demons can stand against me any longer. What other creature is there left for me to fight?"

"Rayne, you rely too much on your physical strength and your swordsmanship still. That is holding you back. You need to trust your instincts more and tap the power within." Sean gave him an empathetic pat on the back.

"I don't like the lack of control when using magic or these new abilities. They remind me of my time as one of Isra's djinn."

Sean smiled. "Those days are behind you. Trust me when I tell you, you are something much greater than what you were. You'll better control your abilities the more you use them. Do not be afraid of them. With the enemies you will face, you need every advantage gifted to you. Warfare, as you will fight in, can break even the strongest of us. Life literally hangs in the balance whenever men like you and me are called to arms. We must react quickly and calmly in those moments. Our abilities allow us to do so. Meet me at dawn for a run, then we will work on giving the Council exactly what they want to see their next visit."

"Who was the woman that appeared today? I sense she is a deity, but do not recognize her."

"Morrigan, the Celtic Goddess of War. She directs the High Council Forces. If you pass the Council trials, you will see her on a more frequent basis."

"And the man in black?" Rayne noticed the grin on Sean's face.

"One of her personal guard. I am not at liberty to say any more about him."

Three months later, Rayne walked alone on the hillside encircling one of the island's lagoons. The clear turquoise water tempted him to indulge in a swim, but he needed to be back at the monastery in half an hour. A warm wind rustled his hair along with several small bushes tipped with bright yellow flowers growing in the rocky landscape. The serenity of the afternoon vanished when he heard something other than the wind to his backside. He ducked, so the oncoming blade missed his head by mere centimeters.

Spinning, he pulled his own weapon, but used magic to force his attacker back. Rayne couldn't identify who or what his attacker was. The man was his height, but broader in build, dressed head to toe in black, and his face was concealed beneath a hood. He relentlessly came at Rayne again and again. Rayne met each blow and deflected each attack, but had difficulty landing any sort of retaliatory hit with how the man evaded his blade. Whatever this being was, it would not be satisfied with anything other than his death or surrender.

Forced into using every bit of magic Sean and Lyal had taught him along with his combat experience, Rayne finally relied on his instincts to guide him through the confrontation. By letting go of his need to control everything, he could almost see the being's next moves before he made them. Battle shifted into a mix of magic, hand-to-hand, and swordplay. Rayne slowly gained the upper hand over his opponent.

"Enough!" Rayne slammed his blade into the ground. The earth tremored and the ground split open. His opponent clung to one of the rocky edges, dangling over the new chasm. A ring of black and blue flame surrounded them.

"Now, you are ready," a voice sounded behind Rayne.

Rayne twisted sideways to see Morrigan, her guard, Lyal, and Sean standing a short distance away. "This was another test?"

To Rayne's surprise, the being who attacked him laughed and extended his free hand towards him. "It was, Haroun. Now help me out of this hole you dug."

Rayne grasped the man's hand and pulled him onto solid ground.

"Well done, brother. I've never seen anyone conjure dark flame and hell fire as you can."

"Gabriel," The man in black spoke his opponent's name in a reprimanding tone.

Gabriel chuckled. "We look forward to you joining us." He clapped Rayne on the back before walking over to Morrigan and the others.

Rayne nodded, but said nothing.

Morrigan raised her hand, closing the gorge and putting out the fire. Her eyes rested on Rayne, but her face remained emotionless as she spoke. "Now that he earns the Commander's approval, I shall go to the Council to determine the next step in his fate."

The goddess and man in black, as usual, vanished from sight. They never stayed longer than a few minutes. The man he fought spoke briefly with Lyal then disappeared as well.

"Excellent work today, Rayne," Sean called to his pupil now staring off into the distance.

Irritated by everything, Rayne looked over at Sean and Lyal. "Next step in my fate? I am not certain I want to serve a Council that treats those who serve them as pawns to be toyed with whenever the whim strikes."

Understanding Rayne's frustration, Sean grinned. "You are far from a pawn, Rayne. While today pleases Morrigan and her liaison, you have yet to win the Council's favor."

Lyal deviously smiled, proud of him and empathizing with his current thoughts about the High Council. "The wolf embraces himself entirely. Now, we wait for the Council to render guidance."

"Your Council is unpleasable to put a man through the hell they have me for almost a year and still not find me worthy," Rayne said, then headed to the monastery. He didn't need Ibelin berating him for being late. It was disturbing enough to learn he passed the combat trials, but had to await his fate for an even longer time.

Two months passed with no word from the Council. While Rayne waited, he remained in Malta training with Ibelin and Lyal. He also helped with various tasks around the monastery. Tired of waiting on the Council, he underwent the initiate rights for the Order of Constantinople.

Wondering if the Council had changed their minds about him, Rayne watched a ship sailing in the harbor from the shoreline. Lyal stood beside him. They had walked to the port together. She suddenly settled her hand on the back of his neck and gently pulled his face towards hers.

Rayne jerked back. "I am not foolish enough to become one of your lovers. I know well what happened to the last two."

Lyal laughed. "The Fates chose the moon's mate well."

Rayne would never understand Lyal's antics. The harbinger had a warped sense of self. Even so, she earned his respect. She was one of the most remarkable military commanders he trained with and fought beside. Nothing frightened or deterred her. "You have no shame to pursue a man destined for another woman."

"She isn't in your life yet. There's no harm in enjoying yourself until the two of you meet. You've earned your freedom, Rayne. We will find you again when the time is right." Lyal sauntered off towards an immortal man in black and gold standing at the far end of the beach.

Rayne recognized the man from what he thought was a dream about Isis. The man's eyes briefly met his before the man smiled as if amused by something, then shifted to look at Lyal.

"Where am I to go?" Rayne wondered what he was supposed to do until the time was right.

"Anywhere you wish," Lyal called back over her shoulder before she vanished with the other harbinger.

Rayne looked back at the sea. So, the Fates abandon him once more.

"They do not abandon you. You will never walk alone going forward, Richard." Ibelin joined him.

The name puzzled Rayne. "Richard?"

"Your new identity. You are Sir Richard Dalglese, a knight and senior member of the Sacred Order of Constantinople. Use your mother's heritage to create your story. I am to book you passage on any ship you choose. Do not return to Spain; only trouble awaits you there. Gather your strength, redeem some of your sins, and then you may return home. Doing so will ensure Isra fears you enough to stay away."

Córdoba - 812

"I stayed away from Córdoba for centuries. Isra knows exactly who and what I am now. Not even War is enough to keep her at bay any longer. My children are terrified of being alone in their own home. They should never fear a thing within these walls."

"They don't, Rayne. They fear what is outside them, and in time, their fear will subside. Your ability to protect them is something they revere. You heard Tarquin yourself today. Daddy will defeat any monster that tries to come in." Grace soothingly ran her fingers through Rayne's hair before kissing him. Hoping to keep his mind off Isra, Grace asked, "Where did you go from Malta?"

"Normandy. I became one of William's mercenaries then ended up in England, as you already know, when he invaded Britain."

"So the Council let a few hundred years pass before making you a Horseman with you not going to the Holy Land until 1191?" Their waiting that long mystified Grace.

"I hadn't proved myself worthy until then."

"Did you have other wives during that time with you not marring Anne until 1180? It must have been strange to William and others that you were an unmarried man at your age."

"No," Rayne said, a bit startled Grace asked him that. He had disclosed the serious relationships he had prior to marrying her. "I spent the majority of those years alone, serving the order, the Pope, and whoever was on the throne. You and Anne are the only women I have ever married. I should have never married Anne. The warning signs were all there: she pursued me, Lucien periodically showed up on Britain's shores when he had no business being there after she came into my life, and the odd interactions I witnessed between him and Anne. But I ignored them, chalking everything up to strange coincidence."

"What was the final straw for you if you knew what was going on behind your back?"

"I didn't know, Grace. I was gone so frequently, and Anne seemed so genuine in her intentions towards me. Maybe I convinced myself that she loved me. While I suspected something might be occurring, never did I think Lucien was the other man until the day I caught them together."

England - 1191

"Anne!" Rayne called for his wife, entering his home for the first time in several weeks. He returned from Italy a month earlier than expected due to calm seas and favorable winds expediting the voyage home. He smiled down at the bracelet he held. Anne adored sapphires.

His maid hurried past him and out the door as if frightened by something.

Rayne smiled at his steward after finding him in the dining hall. "James, have you seen Lady Warwick?"

"I believe Margaret advised that Lady Anne felt ill and retired to your quarters to rest."

"Ill?" Concerned, Rayne headed for his bedroom. Hearing a man's laughter, his steps slowed ascending the stairs. Coming down the hall, he realized where the laugh originated from. Anne's muffled giggle sounded from within the bedroom after a deep voice muttered something he couldn't make out. He silently opened the bedroom door.

The bracelet fell from his fingers. His wife wasn't alone in his bed; the same bed he made love to her in and that she spent so many nights sleeping beside him. Anne's long, dark hair hung around her nude body. She laughed again, sitting astride her lover, unabashedly grinding against him. The two of them smiling and panting; clearly having intercourse. He recognized the man's side profile as her companion raised himself up to kiss her. *Lucien?! She beds Lucien!*

Lucien grinned before stealing a second kiss. "There are rumors of Richard summoning Rayne to join him in Sicily. May your husband earn another increase in rank, but die soon thereafter."

"I almost feel sorry for the poor fool believing I truly love him." Anne added to the hurt surging through him.

"Rayne is far from poor. Why do you think I insisted you ensnare him, my love? We needed his coin and his influence. I told you it wouldn't take much to turn him into a besotted lover. The man even stupidly married you. Now, we need to find a way to make him mysteriously disappear, so I can comfort then marry the devastated, windowed Countess of Warwick."

"I do enjoy the benefits that come with his wealth, and he is an attentive lover."

"Better than I?" Lucien's tone held a hint of jealously.

Anne laughed again. "Nowhere near as good as you." She wrapped her arms around Lucien as he rolled her underneath him.

Not willing to engage another djinn after promising Ibelin he would do his best to stay out of Lucifer's sight, Rayne picked up the gold bangle he dropped. There were better ways than an altercation to get even with Lucien and Anne, starting with ending their access to his purse. He rode directly to the cathedral to meet with the bishop.

Seeing the earl's large frame in his office doorway, the bishop started. "Lord Warwick?"

"I want a divorce from Anne. Draw up the papers, so they may be delivered accordingly."

"My lord, these things take time. Mayhap your marriage is salvageable?"

Rayne slammed his hands down on the bishop's desk. "She beds Lucien Plamondon as we speak. I saw them in my bed myself. Draw up the divorce decree."

The bishop swallowed nervously. The scandal from the earl suddenly divorcing his wife would rock the small hamlet the noble oversaw. The people loved Anne as much as they loved Rayne.

Rayne laid the wolf medallion and cross he carried on the polished dark wood before the bishop. "Do not tell me no twice. My marriage is finished."

The head of the local church recognized the emblems of the secret order of assassins loyal to only the Pope himself. No order other than the Templars served the Pope so zealously in carrying out the harsher parts of protecting Christendom. "Give me an hour, Richard. Your marriage will be absolved, and you will be free to find another bride should you so choose."

Unable to utter any sort of response, Rayne nodded to the man, then went to the sheriff. "Drag my harlot wife and her lover through the streets, so all can see their lady's true nature, but spare her life. I want her to live with the same humiliation she caused me. You will find them both in my bed."

Rayne watched as the sheriff and his men dragged Anne and Lucien from his house then paraded them naked through town. He kept to the shadows behind the crowd of confused and startled onlookers. Anne cried and made excuses for herself as they led her toward the prison. Lucien escaped the guards, abandoning Anne. Once the prison door slammed shut behind her, Rayne rode to the harbor to secure passage to Sicily. He sent a messenger to James with written instruction to give Anne one dress only and a pair of shoes along with a basket of food. Everything else of hers was to be removed from his house and burned. When Anne was released from prison, no shelter, aid, or support of any kind was to be extended from his household. If he caught any of his servants disobeying his order or assisting Anne in anyway, they would be punished harshly upon his return. He also wanted his bed burned and a new one commissioned to replace it.

Standing on the shores of Malta, Rayne read the letters James and the bishop sent him confirming Anne's removal from his estate, that his instructions were fully carried out, and advising the Pope approved his annulment. The parchment they were written on crumpled as his fingers closed around them.

Never will I naïvely love a woman so deeply again.

The notes burst into flame before vanishing in Rayne's hand.

Rayne pulled the sapphire cuff his mother gave him so long ago from his jacket pocket. *I am sorry, Mother. The only way I will trust another woman enough to marry her is if she wears this band, and it is given to her by one of the ancient guardians our ancestors once believed in.*

He hurled the heirloom into the expanse of aqua before him. The waves took the last material reminder of his human years far out to sea.

Poseidon retrieved the bracelet. "We failed him again."

"No." Osiris shook his head. "He journeys to Morrigan's Horsemen. He nears his last day as a member of the Order of Constantinople."

THIRTY-ONE

Córdoba - 812

Since the strike at their principal residence, the enforcer stayed ever present in Rayne. Nightmares continuously haunted his sleep. Dark circles surfaced under his eyes after several nights of little rest. The calm demeanor he normally displayed vanished, replaced by a cynical skepticism. He snapped at Grace on more than one occasion. He barked orders at the Horsemen, and argued with Dante.

Rayne rode back to the Cordovan house. Dante was due to report in to him shortly. He walked inside to find Sulla and Kato sleeping on either side of a chair where Grace sat reading. They rarely came into the house. "Did you lure them in here with food?"

"No, they followed me in after I took a walk."

"Hmm." Rayne patted Sulla on the head, then kissed Grace hello. "What has you two watching over my wife so closely?"

Sulla yawned and laid his head back down.

Grace smiled. "Based on that yawn, most likely their owner's angst. Any luck locating Isra?"

"None. The damage she caused is setting in. Malik's advisors are at one another. My father and I had to separate two of them."

"I searched the southern part of the city, and there is no sign of her." Dante loudly announced, striding into the living room. Noticing Grace wore the wedding ring he gave her on her right hand, he froze in place. "Forgive my manners, Lady Ibn-Ziyad. I did not see you there."

"Such courtly behavior for a god. Normally, you all just barge in here whenever you please. I don't recall you ever addressing me as Lady Ibn-Ziyad."

Dante grinned. "The maid is in the hall. It would be strange for me to address you in any other fashion. Haroun, if she were my wife, I would make sure she knew never to refer to a man as a god."

Rayne good-naturedly smiled. "Perhaps if you attired yourself in a humbler color, you would not invoke that image in her head."

Grace laughed at the two of them. She watched Rayne disappear down the hallway to retrieve something from the library.

Dante knelt beside Grace to see what she was reading. "*A Thousand and One Nights*? You never tire of that book, do you?"

"No, I am rather fond of it. What trouble are you causing to smile so much?"

Dante shook his head. "None, mia stella. I am merely overjoyed to see the moon honors the sun by adorning herself with a jewel he gave her." He took her right hand in his and held it against his heart.

Rayne returned to catch Dante brushing his lips across Grace's knuckles. Dante settled her hand against his chest, over his heart as he leaned in closer to her. Flattered by Dante's attention, Grace smiled and her head tilted downward.

"So much for remembering whose wife she is." Rayne disrupted the affectionate moment then spun on his heal. His feet heavily struck the wood floor, creating a rapid, loud rapping against the polished planks; warning all occupants of the house about his displeasure.

Sulla and Kato raised their heads from their paws. Their ears perked towards the door.

The angry rhythm faltered after the thwack of iron meeting plaster resounded from the entryway. The shattering of clay and lath then chunks of them tumbling to the floor as the door handle punctured the wall broadcast War's departure.

Sulla growled at the door slab bouncing forward.

Grace ran after Rayne. She caught him by the arm at the edge of the porch. "Rayne, wait!"

He brushed her hand aside, continuing to descend the front steps. "Give me some room to breathe, woman. I will be back later."

Dante followed Grace onto the front porch. Rayne wheeled Fahkir around then galloped out the gate.

"I am losing my husband," Grace said, shocked Rayne reacted to things as he did.

Lyal stepped out of the shadows. "You are not losing him."

"Have you not noticed his eyes, Lyal? They stay silver. He has not slept well in days, and now this."

Dante sensed something drifted further awry. He forced the feeling away. Grace didn't need more to worry about. "Rayne will defeat whatever memory causes his restlessness."

Grace didn't understand what Dante referenced. "Memory?"

"Isra can no longer rile him by being near his loved ones. While she wants Rayne, she won't risk her own existence. She is deploying another tactic. Rayne is strong. He will figure it out before she can ensnare him."

"What part of his past is she wielding?"

Dante shook his head. "I have no idea. I can speak with Somnus if you would like me to."

"Please do. I'm reaching my breaking point with all of this. I've never seen any being wield this sort of power over Rayne. The fear and anger he harbors devastates me at times. I don't know how he manages it."

"You feel those emotions so strongly because of the newness of the soul bond. In time, you'll learn to navigate them better."

"I don't understand. This didn't happen with you when we spoke the binding spell."

"You weren't immortal when we bound ourselves to one another. Even a human endowed with magic does not experience things the same way an immortal does. Not to mention, I am not normally angry."

"Rayne didn't use to be either."

"Rayne buries his emotions more than I do. Perhaps he feels them more deeply."

Dante's choice of words made Grace smile. "There have been many a day I described you as shallow."

"And heartless, or my personal favorite, an egotistical Neanderthal." Dante enjoyed the way she now laughed. "Let me go see if Somnus can offer any helpful insights into what troubles your husband."

"Maybe you should check on Rayne instead."

"With what just occurred, Destahn or Raphael are better suited to do that. We do not need to incite his temper more." Dante kissed her cheek. "Take care of yourself, Grazia. I sense discord around you more than Rayne this morning."

***

After two hours passed, Grace paced the living room. Multiple questions circled in her head. What was taking Dante so long? Should she go after Rayne? What were Rayne and Destahn doing? Only Narciso was seen recently in Córdoba. Where had Isra gone?

The wolves and Lyal watched her cross the living room for the thousandth time.

"You worry unnecessarily. Isra's choice of weapon this round is a weak one."

Surprised by Lyal's statement, Grace halted midstride. "You know what causes Rayne's nightmares."

"Rayne does not want you to interfere in this."

"I don't give a damn what my husband wants. He is not thinking clearly after a week of virtually no sleep."

"Najmati...."

The old nickname annoyed Grace. "You are as bad as Osiris when it comes to keeping harmful secrets then trying to all najmati me."

"I am nothing like Osiris." Lyal loathed the comparison to the deity she hated most.

Grace grinned, discovering the one button she could push to rile Lyal. "Then don't behave as Osiris does."

"Be thankful I serve as your guardian. Otherwise, I would take great pleasure in ensuring you never uttered such a vile comparison again."

"As you remind me you are a guardian of the moon's house, I order you to tell me what is happening to my husband."

"He is haunted by the past."

"Show me what memory disrupts his sleep."

"It is forbidden to alter what has already occurred."

"I am not altering it. I only seek to understand how better to assist in the present."

Lyal laughed. "No need to lie to me. I must warn you, if I send you back as you ask, you risk drawing the Council's ire."

"My oath is to protect humanity and preserve the sacredness of the Ancients, not to make the High Council happy."

"You swore to uphold their laws."

"Fuck the Council and their laws. War is becoming corrupted. I need to stop that for humanity and myself. Now, tell me what I must do to preserve the future."

Lyal handed Grace the Defensore's sabre. "Then it is decided, we go to war against Isra. Without Rayne's or the Council's blessing."

Grace's clothing morphed into the Defensore's uniform and armor. She was done standing aside and letting Rayne fight this battle alone. "I'll ask them for forgiveness later."

"I wouldn't lower myself to that. You are doing what should have been done after the strike on your family."

Grace smiled; she loved her rogue guardian. "What incident do I need to correct?"

"Stop him from striking down the children. He never intended to harm them."

Lyal shoved Grace backwards, sending her into the past.

Hastings, England - 1066

Grace dropped into the middle of a medieval battlefield. Knights and soldiers filled the green rolling hills around her. The lush countryside would be beautiful if a war did not rage, despoiling the soil.

Not seeing Rayne, she grabbed a nearby soldier tending a wound. "Where is Rayne Warwick?"

The soldier gave her a puzzled look.

"Haroun?" She tried again. This time receiving a disgusted expression and a nasty response in Norman French. By the dialect he used, she guessed this battle was one Rayne fought while serving William the Conqueror. "Où est Richard Dalglese?"

The soldier pointed across the field. A knight stood out from the rest in the middle of the fray. His armor slowed his movements, but the fighting technique was distinctly Rayne's.

Grace made her way towards him. She watched him cut down two men before being attacked by three more. *Lyal, what do you mean by stop him from slaying the children? There are no children on the field.*

They are there. Find them.

Once I find them, how do I stop things from playing out? I do not hold the power to change fate. As far as Grace knew, only Dante or the Council could rewrite the past on the rare occasion such a thing was allowed. Changing one minor detail could set both realms on a trajectory towards chaos.

Your instincts will guide you in this. Do not fear for the larger outcome. You only shift War's path a minuscule amount.

Define minuscule, Lyal. The Council wouldn't outlaw these acts if there wasn't a ripple effect.

We shall find out the consequences after you return to the present.

Grace cursed, but continued to search for any sign of civilians. The plundered town was abandoned. The field on the town's outskirts only held combatants. All that remained were armed men fighting one another. Where were these damn kids?

Out of the corner of her eye, she saw something move. She realized two little ones sought shelter in a hallowed out fallen tree trunk hidden by the tall grass. Both seemed terrified. The eldest reached for the sword of a fallen knight near him. The boy's raising of the weapon would attract Rayne's attention.

A man jumped from behind the tree engaging Rayne and buying Grace the precious seconds she needed. She sprinted forward and tackled the small boy struggling to pick up the weapon.

A sudden flash and reflection of sunlight on Rayne's own blade warned Rayne of danger to his backside. Once he dispatched his current attacker, he spun with his sword cutting through the air.

The heavy blade collided with Grace's side and then swept up her back as she fell forward onto the grass. She clutched the boy to her chest to keep him safe. Chillingly, cold steel scraped her neck but missed the back of her head. The loud curse she heard confirmed Rayne jerked his sword upward to prevent any further injury to whomever he struck.

Doubting his eyes, Rayne ripped the helmet from his head. A woman in men's clothing glanced over her shoulder at him from the tall weeds. Where had she come from? How could she survive a blow that would have killed armored men twice her size? Why was she not bleeding?

"Spare us, Dalglese."

She knows my name? Dazed, Rayne shook his head. What language was she speaking? It was not one Lyal had taught him or that the Council recognized.

Grace realized by Rayne's puzzled expression he did not yet understand modern-day English. She lifted her upper torso and waved her hand toward the ground.

Now he saw the small boy curled up in the grass. The woman threw herself before his blade to protect a child.

"Is he dead?" Rayne asked in French; horrified he might have killed an innocent soul, breaking his promise to the Council and the Order.

"No, he lives." Grace used the only French she knew. It was more modern, but Rayne understood.

Shouting drew their eyes back to the fighting further up field.

"Take your child and flee, woman. It is not safe here." Rayne yanked the terrified boy to his feet. "Hide in the tree line over there. Hurry! Run now!"

The little boy looked up at Grace.

"Do as he asks."

"But my sister, my lady." The little boy looked around for his sibling.

"I will find your sister. Go while it is safe for you to do so," Grace reassured the boy.

Rayne and Grace watched the boy run across the field to ensure he made it safely.

Taking advantage of the distraction, a rival yeoman crept up behind Rayne. Grace saw the man before Rayne did. Rayne wouldn't have time to defend himself. *So much for not significantly altering the past.* She swept one of Rayne's legs out from under him.

Falling toward her, Rayne cursed. His eyes widened, noticing the woman drew a sword from her side. The black and gold weapon blended in with her clothing. He expected to find himself impaled on the tip. Unpredictably, her arm slipped upward under his, her blade missed him completely. His palms met the damp, cold soil. He stopped his fall enough that he did not crush the woman. He had never seen eyes the color of hers. They were an odd mix of aqua, green, and blue, reminding him of the Mediterranean.

Blood splattered down on them. Grace angled her blade so it would only wound the man. The man she stabbed screamed, freed himself from her blade, then staggered away to tend his injury.

"Be more careful, Rayne. You have too great a destiny to die in some English farmer's field."

"Que, mademoiselle?" Rayne wished the woman spoke in French so he could understand her. Her saving him made no sense. He was an invader, taking her homeland and endangering her children.

A little girl suddenly bolting from under the fallen tree bewildered Rayne even more. She sprinted across the field to where her brother waited. The two children embraced one another, then crouched down, trying to hide behind a bush while staring out at Grace.

Grace smiled up at Rayne when he looked back down at her. She sent herself to the two terrified children.

Shocked the woman vanished, Rayne quickly rolled sideways and spotted her in the tree line with the boy and girl. An immortal with children? What were they doing on the field? The village and it were supposed to be cleared of noncombatants before the clash began.

Grace picked up the small girl and took the boy by the hand. She cast Rayne a quick glance over her shoulder then walked into the mist-filled woods.

After returning the children to their mother in a nearby village, Grace looked heavenward. "Anything else, Lyal?"

Jersey - 1191

Finding herself now standing on the rooftop of a castle tower, Grace let out an annoyed groan. Altering two days in the past almost guaranteed a stint in Purgatory. Rayne better not have many more buried secrets. Lyal could only block the Council's ability to track her for a short time.

Needing to get her bearings, Grace looked around to see a distinct russet and rose granite block used in the castle and walls resting on top of jagged brown rock and cream-colored sand. Muted turquoise waters reflected the stormy sky. She recognized the castle and her surroundings.

"Mont Orgueil? Why am I here?"

A lone watchman across the tower from her stared down at the sea. He climbed onto one of the open crenels between the stone merlons of the battlement ringing the top of the tower wall.

"Never mind. I see him."

Rayne harbored more loss and self-loathing than she could ever imagine he did. Was he truly contemplating jumping from the tower? Worried he might think her a djinn if she used Arabic, Grace hoped Rayne could understand modern French well enough.

"The fall won't kill you. After a few days in bed, you will be as good as new, drawing suspicion about what you are."

Rayne eyed the cloaked figure strolling towards him. "Most die upon impact."

"Most people aren't immortal." Grace earned a scowl from Rayne. She casually looked over the ledge at the synthesis of burnt umber and gray coloring the rocky cliff he selected for his descent. "The road you walk is not an easy one, Haroun. You will find purpose again."

"You know nothing of my story."

"Do you still mistakenly think you are alone? Did Ibelin not tell you otherwise? The darkness will pass. You will have the redemption you seek."

Grace had never seen Rayne doubt himself to the point of utter despair. She was surprised to learn his past held such an episode. He survived his time with Isra and his training with the order. By human standards, he lived a successful medieval life. He won the favor of a king who granted him title and land. Would losing Anne to Lucien truly drive him to harm himself?

Rayne's face turned seaward again. He watched the surf roll onto the rocks below with it being high tide.

Grace tried to shift his thoughts away from suicide. "I never would have believed infatuation and loneliness would so thoroughly conquer a djinn."

Rayne looked down at the woman. The female immortal could see his innermost battles. Why did she care about his fate?

After a few tense seconds of silence, Grace gave up trying to reason with him. "You never listen once you think you know the best way to handle things. Since you must learn the hard way." She walked back towards the stairs leading to the keep.

Wisps of fog rolling in around them added to the mystery of whoever visited Rayne. He stepped down onto the stone roof and followed the woman. He seized her by the arm. "I recognize your eyes. You save me on the field; yet, encourage me to take my life in a cowardly fashion." He ripped the hood of her cloak back, revealing her face. "Who are you?"

"I can't answer that." Grace reached for her hood to pull it back up.

His hand settled on top of hers. "I already know your face. If you walked in a crowd, I could readily identify you. If the Council required you to conceal yourself, you should have worn your cloak in Hastings."

Grace smiled, pleasantly surprised that she had his full attention. Maybe he would listen to her after all. "How would you identify me amongst the mob with only meeting once before?"

"No one else has your sea-colored eyes. They should never be concealed, especially from me."

"I am flattered, Rayne. Is there a particular reason to never hide them?"

"Those seeking trust with nothing to hide stare me in the face."

By the intensity of his gaze, Grace knew he was trying to determine what she was. "Even looking you in the eye, I am required to limit what I share."

"Will the Council allow you to disclose why you appear to me?"

"The Council does not sanction my visit. I am here of my own accord."

"Of your own accord? What would cause a Council messenger to be disobedient to those she serves?"

"Sometimes the greater good requires one to violate the law. I am willing to face whatever punishment this visit warrants to ensure you continue on to Jerusalem."

"What benefit do you gain from me doing so?"

"None." Grace maintained eye contact as they spoke. She needed him to believe her. "You will do amazing things, Rayne. Soon, you will learn how much the world needs you."

"The world needs me? You aren't being honest." Rayne arched a distrustful brow. "I would wager your presence here has more to do with you needing something from me versus anything I can do for humanity. Why exactly are you so interested in my welfare? Did Isra send you?"

Grace laughed. "I work for one much greater than Isra or Lucifer."

"How do you know what I am?"

"Continue on your crusade, wolf. An immortal named Raphael will make you an offer in the not-so-distant future. It will be one you mustn't turn down."

Rayne didn't like how she ignored his prior inquiry. She knew the task the Pope sent him to dispatch. "Your name, lady. Do not deny me an answer."

"Let me go, Rayne. I linger too long."

Rayne's grip tightened on her arm. "I will release you once you share your name."

"Lady Dalglese, Countess of Warwick. The final wife of Richard Dalglese."

Rayne stepped closer to her, searching her eyes for any signs of deceit. The ink on his divorce decree wasn't dry, and this woman claimed to be his next wife. Normally, he could sense a lie, but in this instance, all he sensed was honesty. Was it possible she spoke the truth?

"Swear to me, my so-called countess, this future you speak of is worth living for."

She took his free hand in hers then brought it to her heart. "Stay the course; no matter how rough the waters become, Rayne. Your faith won't go unrewarded."

The sapphire ring carefully styled to match the design of the one on his right hand caught his eye. Did his future spouse truly stand before him? He gently grasped the back of her head, trying to read who she was. Her past was an amalgam of jumbled images; none of which made sense. *Show me what lies ahead since you cannot speak the words aloud without the Council hearing.* Rayne kissed the woman in an attempt to lower her defenses.

Aware it was an unwise thing to do, Grace returned the kiss, drawing him closer. A stifled groan sounded in his throat.

He recognized the power within her. Her soul was immortal, but in contrast to a djinn, it was filled with light. A strange, comforting warmth flowed into him. Visions of him marrying her and him being promoted in some military ceremony circled his head. Rayne stroked her cheek, desperate to believe his life would once again have meaning. That the woman wasn't some cruel trick deployed by Isra or Lucien to lure him out of hiding. "Please, give me some sort of assurance what I saw is real."

Grace unclasped the pendant she wore and settled it around his neck. "I can't give you any further proof. The Council would punish me harshly if I did. You must choose whether or not to believe."

I love you. She pressed her lips against his. *Believe, Rayne. Your children and I need you.* By the bewildered expression on his face, he heard the words that never left her lips.

My children? I have no children.

Trusting that he would eventually continue on his way, Grace smiled then returned to ninth-century Córdoba.

Rayne lifted the pendant from his chest. A silver wolf's face with sapphire eyes and a diamond moon rested in his palm. His fist tightened around the medallion that once belonged to him. How had the woman obtained it?

Córdoba - 812

Destahn and Rayne rode along the outskirts of Córdoba searching for signs of Narciso. Damien had disclosed to Xander that the djinn general inhabited the valley just beyond the city's boundaries.

Confused by the sudden blurred images he experienced, Rayne shook his head. Grace, Mont Orgueil, and Hastings? What triggered the rapid flashes of the past? He halted Fahkir and scanned the surrounding hillside. Everything seemed as it should be, but something definitely changed. The restless side of him calmed for the first time in a week.

Destahn didn't like the dazed look on Rayne's face. "What's wrong?"

"I don't know. I felt lightheaded. Whatever it was seems to have passed."

"Rayne, I don't like this. You look like hell, had another fight with Grace, and now this spell. Mayhap we should seek a healer. After you are evaluated, we can resume our pursuit of Narciso."

"There is nothing wrong with my health, Captain. I am merely tired. Now, let us focus on the task at hand." Rayne gently tapped Fahkir's side with his heels to get the horse moving again.

Destahn shook his head, following Rayne. "You are a stubborn medieval ass at times as your wife claims, Commander."

CHAPTER

THIRTY-TWO

Córdoba - 812

Lyal followed Grace into the master bedroom. "Perhaps you should await Rayne's return."

"Did you not just help me defy the Council?"

"Fighting for your husband's well-being is one thing. Confronting Isra alone is another."

"I never thought I'd see the day you were afraid of a djinn."

Lyal slammed her hand down on the dresser, rattling everything on top of it. "Isra is centuries old. That makes her powerful. There is a reason Lucifer uses her to keep his rabble in Spain and Portugal under control."

Ignoring Lyal, Grace stared at her reflection in the mirror. The sun reflecting off the sabre on her side caused a shimmer in the silver glass. Living in peace the past few years, she had become complacent; wrongly assuming evil was done with her and her loved ones. Grace yanked on her gloves. "Am I not the Morte Defensore and a Guardian of the Ancients? Isra does not frighten me."

"She enslaved your husband. It was her magic that confined him to the cage. You saw what he endured while under her control."

333

Grace tightened the straps holding a concealed knife to her arm then shifted the dagger on her hip so it was easier to pull if needed. "She trapped a desperate soul you and the High Council failed to protect."

Lyal stepped in front of her. "Then do not repeat our error. Leave her to the Horsemen."

"I am not repeating it. I am aiding my husband as you all should have. Did you not state we are going to war with Isra?" Grace maneuvered around Lyal and walked to the doorway. When Lyal remained where she was, Grace turned and looked back at the harbinger. "Are you coming or not?"

"No. If you choose to face Isra, you do it alone, najmati. Not even I am foolish enough to anger Rayne by doing such an idiotic thing."

"I know how to manage my husband's temper."

"Rayne will want blood for this."

"So it's Rayne you fear? Seeing he's the one being who scares you enough that you won't defy him when you will the Council gives me all the incentive I need to do this. I also won't forget 'we' really means me." Grace yanked up her hood. She had an idea of how to find Isra without Lyal's help.

"War will demand his pound of flesh from your backside."

"He can have it. At least, he will know his wife freely fights with him, unlike the Council and the harbinger who trained him centuries ago."

***

Grace entered the tavern Hayden once described as the Cordovan devil's den. Thugs, thieves, demons, and djinn filled the dismal place. The smell of smoke and stale beer greeted her as she strolled to an empty table. A bar maid passed. Grace stopped her and ordered a drink. The bar maid nodded in acknowledgement. Grace sat down. Now, all she needed to do was wait.

"This table is reserved. I think you need to find another" A good-looking man with blond hair and bright yellow eyes grinned down at her.

"Oh, I think I am seated at the right table. I was waiting on a piece of shit soul broker and, lo and behold, he appears."

Now seeing the gold insignia on whoever sat at the table's collar, the soul broker took a step back. He had no desire to tangle with one of the High Council's officers.

Grace grabbed him to prevent him from teleporting. "I am not sure what you've done, Damien, but whatever it is, I am not here to punish you for it. I need your help."

"Waheeda?" Damien recognized the officer's voice and relaxed. "For a second, I thought you were someone else."

Grace kept a tight hold of his arm. "Maybe a Council harbinger cashing in the warrant for you?"

"That is a misunderstanding between Hades and me." The demon tried to squirm out of her grasp.

She shoved the demon down into the chair beside her. "Answer my questions, and I won't alert the Council to your hiding place. I might even put in a good word for you. You are more of a pain in the ass than a killer, anyway."

"What do you need to know?" Damien wondered why the thief rumored to have turned hero would do him a favor.

"You ever heard of an overseer named Isra?"

Damien laughed. "Know her well. Get yourself back into trouble again, Waheeda? I heard you had gone straight."

Grace wanted to slap the smirk off his face, but resisted the urge to do so. "Where can I find her?"

"I am not sure. Last I heard, she was chasing down an escaped servant named Haroun. Try the Underworld." Damien picked up Grace's drink and took a long gulp from it.

Grace yanked the tankard out of his hand then sat down across from him. "The Underworld is a big place, Damien. You've got to do better than that or I will summon Xander, so Hades can take the coin you stole out of your hide."

"How did you..." Damien stammered, shocked she knew exactly what he had done.

"I've learned some new tricks since Thebes. Would you like to find out a few more of them?" Grace slammed her dagger into the table, just missing the demon's hand, trying to intimidate him. "Xander, I sum..."

"She's hiding in a house three properties down from the palace. Malik gave it to her. It has arched doors made of black iron and decorated with golden faces and flowers. The only one like it on the street."

"Malik? The Emir?" Grace wanted to ensure she had the right Malik.

"One and the same. He struck a bargain with her to get rid of Umar and some other general after the general refused to kill Umar. Whoever Haroun is, Isra salivated once Malik agreed she could have him." Damien swiped Grace's tankard again.

"And how do you know of the Emir's and Isra's deal?"

A large smile spread across his face. "I brokered it. Turned a nice profit off it, too."

"How much was Haroun's soul worth?" Grace wanted to kill Damien with his bragging about instigating the latest storm in her life.

"My weight in gold. The poor fool should have killed Umar with what is headed his way. He made me a very rich demon." Damien laughed then took another swig of her drink.

Xander ripped Damien out of his seat. "That should be just enough to pay the interest on what you stole from Hades."

Damien turned paler than normal, staring over at Grace from the floor. "But you didn't finish..."

Grace chuckled, knowing justice would be served. "Looks like the deal wasn't such a good one after all. Next time you sell someone's soul you don't own, know who their friends are."

Xander dragged Damien into a corner, so he could disappear into the Underworld without many noticing.

Grace walked out of the bar and removed the officers laurels from her collar. She wasn't working for the High Council today.

Sunset was a few hours away. Time was on her side. Isra was at her weakest during the day. Grace followed the winding side streets to the home Damien described. Two djinn guards sitting near the front door confirmed for once Damien told the truth.

Using an invisibility spell, she slipped past the two without detection. The house was dark. Heavy curtains covered all the windows. Intuition guided her down two long, dark corridors to an open room lit by a blazing fire surrounded by a black marble mantel.

Isra sat in a black throne-like chair facing the fireplace, patiently waiting for the sun to set. Sensing something in the room disrupting her solitude, her head turned slightly. Odd, not a presence she ever encountered before. "It is not often an immortal seeks me out. My powers cannot extend to our realm. My jurisdiction is merely that of humanity."

Grace took a cautious step forward. "Since you know who I am, you should also know I do not come to trade my soul."

The chair swiveled round unexpectedly. Isra stared at Grace. Annoyance painted across her bronzed face. "I know what you are. I do not know your purpose here."

"You made a bargain recently for an immortal's soul. Neither the one who brokered it, nor offered it, have a claim to it."

Isra set the silver chalice she held down on the table beside her. "Tell me, who might this immortal be?"

"The Horsemen Commander, Rayne Warwick."

Isra laughed. "Haroun? Haroun is an escaped enforcer who belongs to me. I can assure you, I have a valid claim to his soul."

"Raphael Fiore won Haroun's freedom. You have no claim over him."

Isra slowly came toward Grace. Her stride fluid and deceptive. Dark eyes judiciously sized up the unannounced visitor. "What is your interest in Haroun?"

"He swore an eternal oath to the one I serve. I am here to see that he carries it out. Surrender any false claim you mistakenly think you have on him, Isra." Grace calmly watched Isra circle her.

"Your name, guardian?"

"Waheeda." Grace used the old name Qasim gave her.

Surprised by the being's supposed name, Isra froze in place.

"Waheeda? That is the name of a Hasan master thief, which I have not heard in almost twenty years. Did she not die in a clash with Qasim?"

"If I am dead, how can I stand before you?"

"Qasim never had dominion in Spain."

"I no longer work for Qasim."

Isra flew at her. Having seen the way Isra attacked Rayne, Grace expected the strike. She moved out of the way then sent the overseer to the floor. Isra recovered and swung at her. Grace blocked the blow, twisted her upper body, then used her elbow and upper arm to knock Isra off balance. She drove a dagger into Isra's shoulder as the overseer stumbled, pinning her down against a large wooden table.

Grace pulled her other two daggers and kept the djinn's neck in the center of v'ed steel. "I could kill you in a breath, Isra."

Isra stared at the sapphire in the hilt of blade piercing her shoulder. "Haroun's weapon. Where did you find it?"

"The dagger and Haroun belong to me. Give me the new contract for him."

"I will give you Kamar in his place."

"Do you think me a fool? Kamar is dead. Hand over Haroun's contract, now!" Grace threateningly ran a blade down the side of Isra's neck.

A rolled parchment document appeared on the table beside them.

"I don't need his soul. The enforcer within him will return him to his rightful place in my legions," Isra hissed up at Grace.

Grace forced open the scroll to ensure it was indeed for Rayne. Malik's seal on the bottom confirmed it was.

"Whoever your master is, guardian, they will suffer for this insult, and so will you."

"We shall see." Grace ripped Rayne's dagger out of Isra's shoulder.

Isra shrieked as the dagger backed out of her flesh, alerting the guards to the attack on her.

Grace quickly slammed the blade through Isra's heart, vanquishing the overseer. So much for slipping out of the house unnoticed. Between the demon and djinn, they'd see her regardless of what spell she may use. She tucked the document into her cloak, then sprinted towards the main entrance.

Two hulking demons stepped into the hall, blocking the front doors. Predictably, one leapt at her. Once he was airborne, Grace dashed under him and stabbed him in the chest. While she missed his heart, it slowed him enough; allowing her to bring her other hand around and slice his jugular.

Out of breath, she turned to face the second. "Well, come on. Let's get it over with."

He laughed, drawing a sword, mistakenly thinking he had the upper hand. Grace ducked under the blade as he swung it towards her neck and grabbed his wrist. Her dagger severed the tendon running from the muscle in his bicep to his upper forearm, making his weapon hand useless. Growling, the demon knocked her away from him with his other arm.

"You've lost your damn mind, woman!" Xander struck the second guard, sending him backward and clearing the doorway. "Get out of here before your husband learns where you have been."

Grace yanked open the heavy iron and oak slab. "I owe you one!"

"You owe me more than one for this!" Xander punched the demon in the face as it started to rise again.

Grace laughed, running into the daylight towards Diya.

She rode straight to Rayne's home. Galloping towards the closed gate, she shouted at the gatemen to open it. The guards scrambled to get the gates open, so the lady of the house didn't crash into them.

Rayne heard the commotion from the stable. He looked out the door to see Grace leaping off Diya's back. Diya was winded and covered with sweat. A cloaked Grace sprinted inside the house. The way she stripped her uniform of all insignia disturbed him. She had never done such a thing before. Her odd behavior reminded him of Lyal when the harbinger went rogue. Concerned, Rayne teleported to the house.

Grace set the rolled indenture on fire. Once the flame flourished, she tossed it into the fireplace. She picked up a small glass bottle of liquor, removed the lid, and sniffed the contents. The pungent smell confirmed it more than likely had a high enough proof to be flammable. She threw whatever the liquid was into the fire then stoked the logs. The flames shot upward, engulfing the parchment.

The loud crackling in the fireplace caught Rayne's attention as he entered the room. "What are you burning?"

"Nothing important." Grace set the bottle on the table.

Rayne spun her to face him. "What was that?"

"A forged contract."

"A contract? For what?" Rayne knew he wouldn't like the answer with the way she stared up at him from under the black hood.

"You."

"Me?"

Grace held up his ancestral dagger, disconcerting him more. "Malik bartered you as the payment for Umar's demise. Once you killed Umar, Malik would have given you to Isra."

Rayne yanked his weapon out of her hand. He would strangle Grace if she struck some sort of deal with Isra. Hell, he'd beat her within an inch of her life if he learned she foolishly went anywhere near Isra. "Did you bargain with Isra for the contract?"

"With all she has done to try to regain control over you, do you really think she would give you up at any price?" Grace noted the way Rayne's body tensed and the hard set of his jaw. "No bargains were made. I obtained it via hostile means through a third party."

Relieved to hear no negotiations occurred, Rayne embraced her. "Hostile means? We aren't going to end up before the High Council again, are we, leof?"

Grace held him tighter. "No. I broke no oaths. I only disguised myself to hide who I was."

"Thank the gods for small miracles." Rayne looked down at her. "Should I be preparing for unexpected company with the way you rode in?"

Grace let out a short laugh. "The one I took it from has no clue who I am, and I gave the one who did identify me to Xander."

Learning of Xander's involvement, Rayne frowned. "Hayden told me he had seen Xander wandering in Córdoba earlier today and drinking in the Devil's Den. I should have gone into town after that disclosure. I assume that is where you met whoever this third party you robbed was. Larceny is also conduct unbecoming for a High Council Officer."

Grace shrugged. "Once a thief..."

"You ceased being a thief long ago. Thank you for ensuring my freedom." Rayne shook his head, still a bit surprised to learn Malik indeed bargained with Isra. Jalid had been telling the truth. "I never thought Malik could be worse than Abdul."

"Malik didn't come up with the idea on his own."

"What do you mean by that?"

"Damien brokered the deal between Malik and Isra."

"Damien?" Rayne didn't know the name

"A low life soul broker. Not that he can be trusted, but he was summoned to the palace to negotiate the deal between Isra and Malik for you. He's who Jalid is calling a Damari."

Rayne's scowl deepened. "How much was I worth?"

"Damien's weight in gold, which is quite a bit. He isn't a small being."

"Well, at least I am worth a fortune to someone. What else did you learn, Grace? I know you are hiding things from me."

"Isra wasn't only getting you out of the deal. Malik gave her a house in town as a down payment for her help. A large one with golden decorations on the gate, a block from the palace."

"I know the home. It once belonged to one of the Visigoth merchants who was allowed to remain here until he crossed Rahman. Rahman beheaded him for allowing Christian usurpers to enter the walls of the city. To ensure an example was made of the family and no one else would support any future usurpation attempts, everything the man owned became part of the Emirate's treasuries. Rahman turned it into a fortress to house his armory and his leading general was granted temporary residence there with its proximity to the palace."

Rayne picked up the pitcher on the table and poured Grace a glass of water while she removed her cloak, pulled off her gloves, and unbuttoned her collar. The warm day made the black uniform unusually hot to wear.

Grace voiced one of the things that had been troubling her the past few days. "How did you manage to escape without your contract being discharged? That suggests you regained some sense of right and wrong. Otherwise, you wouldn't have rebelled against Isra."

Rayne took a deep breath, uncertain he wanted to relive those times. He offered Grace the glass of water. "I never really lost my ability to differentiate between right and wrong. I grew numb to the guilt and regret of committing wrongful acts."

Grace took the glass, not sure what to think of his answer. "Maintaining any sense of right and wrong makes me wonder if something in you resisted converting fully to an enforcer. I've assumed all this time Isra was a djinn and not a demon for you to become one. Is she?"

"Isra is an ifrit, a dark being in the djinn community. Closer to a demon than a djinn. As ancient as she is, she could most certainly turn a soulless human into either a djinn or a demon. Especially one destined to be a Horseman."

"While I knew djinn could be good or bad, I had no idea there were different types depending on your beliefs." Grace realized how much she still didn't know about the immortal realm.

Rayne almost smiled at the remark. "We all learn more about the immortal world over time, even I am still leaning. Considering you were raised in the modern, westernized world with a healthy sense of skepticism toward otherworldly beings, you've learned more than most and embraced our ways. I also struggled a great deal early on to comprehend the variety of beings in the realms and changed religious beliefs multiple times until I arrived at my own personal sense of faith."

"Speaking of faith, what exactly happened in the Holy Land before you met Raphael?"

"Do you really want to know?" Rayne worried she may not like what she learned.

Having just taken a deep gulp of water, it took her a second for Grace to answer. "Yes."

"To redeem my sins, I indentured myself to the Church, more specifically the Order of Constantinople. I was the Left Hand of God for a brief time, as you suspected. Ibelin was the one initially asked to kill Richard and Saladin. He objected to the Pope's request, finding it immoral. When he refused, the Pope dispatched me to the Holy Land. I didn't like the order, but unlike Ibelin, I had no qualms with killing either man when I was directed to do so.

"The night I left for Sicily, Michael confronted me in Rome. Knowing he rode for Morrigan, I did not wish to hurt him. However, I couldn't have him following me. I knocked Michael out. Raphael came upon us, and I escaped into the shadows to avoid further conflict with the Horsemen. I did not see the Horsemen again until Jerusalem."

"I thought Richard never made it to Jerusalem," Grace recalled Richard being stopped in Ascon and Acre.

"He didn't. I rode into the city alone. After meeting Saladin and observing Richard, I could not kill either of them. Neither were the monsters the Pope described them to be."

"They are fortunate you regained your moral compass. I can only imagine what could have happened if you killed either man. Raphael didn't reveal who he was to you in Italy?"

"No. Our encounter in Italy was a brief, unamicable one. The next Raphael and I met was in broad daylight. The sun shined down on us. I remember thinking the afternoon was oddly calm. I stood on the Temple Mont outside the Dome of the Rock. A place held sacred by all three faiths practiced in my family. I looked down on the city around me and thought what a shame men killed one another to control some place that belonged to all humankind."

THIRTY-THREE

Jerusalem - 1191

"Haroun, the Council wishes to know if you are ready to honor your agreement with Lyal."

Rayne turned to see three men dressed in black and gold on black horses behind him. Recognizing them as the men who seemed to be ever present in his affairs the past few months, he frowned. One of them was the man he saw with Isis then again on his last day in Malta. "You three are Council messengers?"

"Not exactly." The man on the center horse dismounted and approached Rayne. "We have not formally met. I am Raphael Fiore, Morrigan's Commander of Forces and Liaison to the High Council. I come with an offer of full redemption."

Rayne noted Raphael dressed for war, not peaceful negotiations. Now that the immortal was closer, his eyes skimmed the odd armor Raphael wore; visually assessing it for weak spots should this meeting turn to conflict. He had never seen another suit of armor quite like it. Whoever crafted it designed it to be light weight, in addition to near impenetrable. Made from a mix of leather and metal, blending the popular designs of the human classical world with that of the gods, it alerted any immortal that the men who wore it held an esteemed position with the Council. The dagger off Raphael's belt and the uniquely dark-colored sword on the opposite hip warned Rayne he was not a diplomat of any kind. "In exchange for?"

"Nothing. I merely need to know if you wish to remain a knight with the order or if you would rather do something more purposeful."

"If I turn down your offer?" Rayne tested the being before him.

Raphael shrugged. "My men and I ride away. You will never see us again. Unless you do something requiring the Council's intervention. Let us hope that does not occur. It would upset me a great deal to kill a good man like yourself."

Rayne laughed at Raphael's confidence. "Many men and djinn have tried. None have succeeded."

His mouth had just shut after speaking when he found himself lying on the ground with Raphael's sword pressed into his windpipe. A booted foot rested firmly on his chest.

"I tend to achieve where others fail." Raphael grinned at the dazed expression on Rayne's face.

Never had Rayne encountered a foe that could attack without any indication or sign of warning. The man moved at a speed his mind could not comprehend even after learning things greater than he could ever have imagined existed. "What do you want me for?"

"This is not about what I want you for. You must decide what path you walk. I cannot tell you more until I know your answer. What do you want most, Haroun, redemption and freedom, or existence and servitude?" Raphael waited patiently for an honest answer as Rayne remained on the ground debating what to do.

"You may be able to redeem me, but not even Isis and Lyal could free me. What makes you think you can deliver what a goddess and her harbinger couldn't?"

A smiled spread across Raphael's face. "It was not time to free you. Their role was to prepare you for what is to come. I am the one entrusted with confirming you are worthy of becoming a balance keeper. We needed to know you were once more a man of conscience before returning your soul. You are a powerful being; destined to wield the ultimate authority and judgement of human and immortal alike.

Giving you your soul before you proved yourself was too great a risk for us to take."

"Am I to assume I've finally proven I am worthy based on your presence here, Commander?"

Raphael laughed. "Indeed, you have. You defied the Pope, sparing Richard and Saladin. That goes against the creed of the order. A djinn turned Crusader, placing himself at significant risk by ignoring such a directive demonstrates the selflessness we needed to see. I can get your soul back if that is what you want."

"Why would you do so? To indenture me to yourself?" Rayne doubted the man would offer such a precious gift without strings attached.

"You are hard of hearing, Rayne. I do not seek your servitude. We never force or trick individuals into our ranks. Doing so makes internal enemies and creates weaknesses that can be exploited. What I intend to offer requires your full commitment, freely given without conditions. If you accept, you are free to leave at any time of your choosing. Now, tell me, what say you to the crossroads you face?" Raphael removed his foot from Rayne's chest.

Still skeptical of Raphael's strange proposition, Rayne sat up. "Redemption, with a right to determine my own fate?"

Raphael offered Rayne his hand. "Only take it if you are prepared to begin the most demanding and rewarding journey you shall ever know."

Rayne weighed his choices: uncertainty, but a chance to be master of his own fate or the comfort of the known in being the silent arm of the Pope. Redemption and freedom seemed the more frightening option. Making up his mind, Rayne firmly clasped Raphael's hand.

"Haroun Ibn-Ziyad and Richard Dalglese cease to exist today. I wipe your slate clean to begin anew. Your sins are forgiven. Arise one of Morrigan's Horsemen, Rayne." Raphael hauled Rayne to his feet.

"A Horseman?"

"Yes, a Horseman. Allow me to introduce your brothers-in-arms." Raphael and Rayne walked to the two mounted soldiers. "This is Gabriel, and the man scowling at you is Michael. I believe the three of you know one another."

Rayne shook Gabriel's extended hand. "We've met."

Unlike Gabriel, Michael continued to glare down at Rayne.

Raphael chuckled at Michael and Rayne. "I see we are going to have to do a little work when it comes to camaraderie between you two. We also need to get you a mount and proper uniform."

"I already own a horse I trust, and will never don a uniform for an organization I know nothing of." Rayne studied his new peers, a bit apprehensive about what he committed himself to. "Explain to me this role of Horseman."

"Have you read the Bible, Rayne?" Michael grinned as he asked the question.

"I have."

"You are now War. As in the War from the Four Horsemen of the Apocalypse, the being who rides with a great sword after the second seal is broken on a red horse, or at least according to Christianity's twist on us."

All three men laughed at the look of horror on Rayne's face.

Gabriel understood why Rayne second-guessed his decision. "It is not as bad as it sounds."

"Seeing the terrified look on your face is payback enough for knocking me unconscious in Rome. Welcome to the Horsemen, Rayne." Michael offered his hand to his new peer.

Rayne grasped it, still unsure what to think.

Raphael set a reassuring hand on Rayne's shoulder. "You will get used to the various ways man views us. Our charge is not to end the earth. We are the protectors of humanity. We prevent evil from rising and keep the curtain in place between man and myth. Now, let us get your soul back."

"Commander Fiore, I see you recovered my wayward minion." Isra's voice sounded from behind them.

Dread shot through Rayne. The past few years had given him hope he would not encounter his old master again.

"Morrigan's new Horseman is in need of his soul, Isra." Raphael turned with a forced smile on his face.

"Morrigan does not want this man in her ranks. He is a deserter," Isra said, unimpressed by the presence of Morrigan's officers.

"I believe he is a victim of circumstance. Where should we start negotiations?"

Isra summoned Kamar and Narciso to her side. "The only thing I will settle for is his return, Commander."

Gabriel and Michael dismounted and stepped forward to stand beside their commander.

Raphael let out an annoyed sigh. "Must we travel this path, Isra? You will lose the two other mercenaries you prize."

Isra's eyes locked on Rayne. "You are welcome to fulfill Haroun's agreement."

"If you can best me, you may have me. But if I best you, you give me Haroun's soul and the contract for him." Raphael knew Isra wouldn't be able to resist the offer.

Kamar and Narciso simultaneously lunged for Raphael. The commander vanquished both before either could reach him.

Raphael calmly returned his sword to its sheath. "The agreement was if *you* could best me, Isra."

The overseer laughed then engaged Raphael.

Rayne anxiously watched the two spar. This was only the second time Rayne had seen Isra draw her blade. She preferred to have others fight her battles.

The confrontation ended quickly. Raphael disarmed Isra and held her captive.

"Take him. I do not need him with having Kamar and Narciso." Isra vanished, leaving Raphael holding the sealed contract obligating Rayne's soul to her.

Raphael broke the seal and burned the document. He smiled at the way the silver disappeared from Rayne's eyes; the man was once again whole.

"Thank you." Rayne did not know what else to say.

Raphael clapped him on the back. "It is time for you to meet Morrigan and see your new home."

Rayne mounted Fahkir then looked at the mosque and scenery around him. He was free; gifted a second chance to live a good life. He turned his face heavenward. *I will not squander what you have given me. I will strive to be better.*

Gabriel grinned, hearing the man's silent prayer. "Rayne, yallah!"

***

Córdoba - 812

Grace took Rayne's hand in hers. "You certainly fulfilled your vow."

"I try my best to every day since Jerusalem."

"With the others' acceptance of you, your transition to Horsemen must have been a smooth one."

"I wouldn't say that. The journey had plenty of challenges. Morrigan almost demoted me after Lucien and I crossed paths in France. Michael kept me from killing him. Word of the altercation reached Morrigan. If Raphael had not been present to soothe her temper, I wouldn't wear the uniform I do today."

Grace doubted Morrigan would throw Rayne out of the Horsemen once he disclosed Lucien and his prior encounters. "How bad was the fight?"

"I am not proud of that moment, Grace. I lost all control seeing him. I beat him to a bloody pulp. Michael pulled me off Lucian after I drew my dagger to finish him. Morrigan would have been justified in casting me out. I behaved as a djinn, not one of her officers. She intended to do exactly that even after hearing of Lucien's and my past. I still to this day do not know what Raphael and Gabriel shared with her that caused her to commute my sentence."

"You and Dante have never shared much about Gabriel."

"Dante never really knew Gabriel well. It was Gabriel's position that Dante took in the Horsemen after Qasim, and I assume Gaelin, killed Gabriel. We never did confirm the identity of his assailant. It was Gabriel who warned me the time was nearing for our paths to cross again."

"What do you mean he warned you?"

***

Carthage - Twenty-two years earlier

The call for help resounded around Rayne. He turned Fahkir westward. Gabriel was assigned as escort to the human and immortal forces trying to prevent local mercenaries from taking commissions from the Hasan. "Your status, Gabriel?"

"We are being overrun. What in god's name is that?" Gabriel broke contact to focus on the troops that surprised them.

It only took seconds for Rayne to reach Gabriel's location. Bodies and severed limbs lay strewn across the countryside. Whatever attacked the peacekeeping force appeared to be gone.

Taking in the grotesque scene around him, Rayne dismounted. He had seen hordes of demon and djinn kill like this, but never humans. Demon and djinn lacked the ability to kill immortals. What sort of creature could annihilate an immortal unit?

Spotting Gabriel lying several feet from the human and guide corpses, he ran over to him.

"Rayne." Gabriel winced, but smiled up at his peer.

Rayne knelt down and took his hand, hoping to heal Gabriel enough that he could hang on until one of Morrigan's healers could reach them.

"Warn Morrigan one of our own did this. I am not sure who, but the Hasan has someone assisting them from the immortal realm."

"You will tell Morrigan yourself." Rayne tried to hide the grief in his voice.

Gabriel let out a pained laugh. "How were you ever an evil enforcer with how poorly you lie? I won't see Sasainn or the goddess again. I have always known my time with the Horsemen was temporary. We were waiting on the one to be ready to join us. The one prophesized to destroy this new enemy."

"Stop these nonsensical ramblings, Gabriel."

"You know I speak the truth, Rayne. The Council keeps one last secret from you. It is time you know it. You are the cornerstone..." Gabriel sharply inhaled, his life ebbing away. "The cornerstone of the prophecy the Fates whisper behind closed doors. The foundation and the balance keeper. Remember that always. The Hasan, the Hasan are hunting for the others foretold of in the prophecy. One of them is the moon. She walks the earth, Rayne. You must find her before Rasil does. If you fail to, greater strife befalls us."

"How can I protect someone I do not even know?" Rayne hated how Gabriel's last moments would be spent as a messenger. The Fates should have let the immortal leave the world peacefully.

"You met the moon, on the Watchtower in Jersey."

Rayne grappled with comprehending what Gabriel disclosed. "Rasil hunts my future wife?"

"Her and another. The other's identity has not been revealed to me."

Michael and Raphael materialized on either side of Rayne. Raphael cursed, seeing the severity of Gabriel's wounds.

"We all face death, Raphael." Gabriel looked up at his old friend. "The Fates say it is time for your protégé to rise, Commander. They hope you taught him well."

Hearing approaching horses, the three uninjured Horsemen prepared for another attack.

Gabriel grabbed Raphael's hand to get his attention. "They are friend, not foe."

Dante and Caitlin rode around the curve of trees with a group of regular cavalry and foot soldiers following them.

"Caro Dio!" Dante muttered, taking in the carnage around him.

Gabriel's eyes focused on Dante. "The one I am the placeholder for arrives to assume his rightful place."

Rayne turned his head, following Gabriel's gaze. "Dante? He is too young."

"He is no longer a child, Captain. The Council knows his destiny just as they know yours." Gabriel coughed, beginning to gasp for air. "He is ready for the promotion, Rayne. Tell Morrigan the time has come for him to wear the black and gold."

"She will learn of the Fates' wishes. There are at least three individuals in the prophecy I have heard. If I and my supposed wife are two, who is the other?

"That I do not know. More will be revealed in time." Gabriel's gaze shifted to Caitlin standing in the distance. "So much loss and grief in such a small window of time. The realms need you more than even the Council can imagine. Protect all of them, Rayne. Come what may, swear to me you will."

"I will never forsake my oath, Gabriel. I will always do my best to protect all you and the Council ask me to."

"You are an honorable man, Rayne. May God forgive my trespa..." Gabriel's head rolled to the side mid-word. The immortal's spirit departed the realm of the living.

Admiring how Gabriel clung to his mortal faith while still serving the Council, Rayne gently closed Gabriel's eyes. "They all will forgive you. May your soul find peace in the afterlife."

"Gabriel!" Dante called the Horseman's name, now running towards them. He couldn't fathom how the Hasan killed a Horseman. He reached for the immortal, needing to see for himself that Gabriel was no longer with them. Images of Gabriel's final encounter played in Dante's mind as his fingers made contact with Gabriel. While he had experienced visions before, this one was intensely different. It placed him in the middle of the action. All of his senses engaged while he saw events through Gabriel's eyes.

The Hasan ambushed the envoy. They were overrun in mere minutes. Gabriel held off those he could. As Gabriel called for the other Horsemen, a man with no face drew closer, his sword slashed through his armor, dealing the unrecoverable gash across Gabriel's stomach.

Dante winced from a burning sensation across his own abs as the blade tore through Gabriel's. The taste of blood filled his mouth.

Rayne looked up at Raphael after hearing Dante inhale sharply and seeing his body jerk as if stuck by a blade. Only a Horseman could have such powerful visions. *Dante truly is one of us.*

Raphael nodded. *With Gabriel gone, he will need another to guide him when I am not around. Are you up to the task, Captain?*

As if I have a choice. The gods help us with Dante joining our ranks. Rayne hoped Dante would live up to the Fates' expectations.

Coming out of the vision, Dante shared what he saw. "Gabriel fought Qasim and someone else. I cannot see the other man's face. It was the faceless man who killed Gabriel."

"We will find them, Dante." Raphael set a hand on Dante's shoulder, severing the connection between Dante and Gabriel. "In the meantime, you and Caitlin keep pressure on the Hasan. Michael, Rayne, and

I need to return Gabriel's body to Sasainn. We will regroup with you in a day or two."

Sasainn -

Morrigan looked out the tower window to see four horses, but only three riders. Where was the fourth rider?

After the gates opened and the Horsemen filed into the courtyard, she noticed the body draped over the fourth horse's saddle. She shook her head, terrified the Fates' warning of dark days coming turned out to be worse than expected. She ran down the tower steps and into the main hall.

The three Horsemen turned to her after settling Gabriel's body on a nearby table. She looked like the stereotypical portrayal of an angel coming towards them in her green and gold robes; her long blonde hair floating out around her.

"Gabriel!" Lavender eyes filled with tears as Morrigan's hand rested against the dead man's face.

Raphael gently touched her shoulder. She looked over at him. Her other hand settled on his arm.

By the nod of Raphael's head, Michael and Rayne knew the two privately communicated with one another.

"What message do you have for me, Captain?" Morrigan startled Rayne.

Not anticipating she would wish to speak with him instead of Raphael, Rayne had to clear his throat before answering. "Gabriel wished you to know that it is time for Dante to take his place amongst the Horsemen."

"No." Morrigan shook her head.

Raphael didn't understand the goddess's refusal to promote Dante. "Morrigan, he is more than ready."

"He is needed in the general cavalry."

Rayne had never seen Morrigan refuse the Fates' direction before today. "I second Raphael's statement, goddess. He fights and rides as well as any of us. He knows most of our maneuvers and possesses our abilities."

"Which is precisely why he will remain with Sean and Caitlin in Carthage," Morrigan snapped before spinning on her heel and heading towards her library. She needed time, time to accept everything.

"Dante is romancing your granddaughter. Fraternization of that nature is deadly on the battlefield." Michael pricked a nerve in Morrigan.

The goddess froze in place.

Rayne wondered about Michael's sanity to disclose such a thing when Morrigan was angry and grieving. "Are you trying to get Dante banished to Tartarus?"

Morrigan looked back over her shoulder at the Horsemen Commander. "Raphael, is this true? Has their relationship gone beyond flirtation?"

Raphael's baffled expression shared Morrigan was well aware of the fact Dante and Caitlin were falling for one another. "You already know that it has, mia dea."

"Send word to Dante that he will temporarily ride with the Horsemen until he proves to me he is worthy to be one of you. Ensure Dante understands if he fails to appear when he or the Horsemen are summoned, I will strip him of his rank and toss him from my forces. Order him to stay away from my granddaughter. Caitlin needs to be focused on recapturing Qasim."

Raphael bowed, paying all proper respect to Morrigan. "As you wish, goddess."

"When you return from speaking with Dante, I request a private audience with you in my library, Commander Fiore."

"Yes, goddess." Raphael again inclined his head.

Morrigan left the men alone in the main hall.

Raphael scowled at Michael. "There was no need to bring up Dante and Caitlin's affair."

"It worked, didn't it?" Michael earned a second glare from Raphael.

Rayne didn't like Morrigan's out of character behavior. The way Raphael stared at him only worsened the dread in the pit of his stomach. "Why did Morrigan react as she did to Gabriel's last request?"

"She is struggling, as I am to accept that our failure to imprison Qasim now jeopardizes the security of our realm and the human one. Rayne, more than guiding Dante is going to fall on your shoulders."

Rayne looked away from Raphael. "Gabriel mentioned the cornerstone prophecy."

Raphael knew Rayne worried about the woman from the Watchtower. "Do you wish to search for her?"

"I do not know where to look. She always came to me in the past."

Raphael smiled. "Then let us hope she seeks you out again. Until then, we have a rogue immortal and his human ally to hunt down."

Córdoba - 812

"I always searched for your face every place we rode. I even tried to summon you several times. Hoping to find you before Rasil could." Rayne pulled Grace against him, regretting that he hadn't discovered her before the Hasan did. "I wish I could have prevented all your suffering."

"That was not your fault, Rayne." Grace hated how he added the torture Qasim meted out to her to his list of failures. Dante had once done the same. Neither of them were responsible for what Qasim did. "If you need to blame someone for it, blame Qasim and the Fates."

Raphael rapped on the door.

Grace glanced at the window. The sun had set. Fear for Rayne's well being struck her. "Don't go. Take one night off. Please. Search for Isra tomorrow."

"The faster she is captured, the faster we can return home." Rayne wondered what brought on the fearful pleading.

"Stay with me, Rayne."

A second knock on the door caused Grace and Rayne to look towards it.

"Let Raphael in. You have nothing to fear."

Grace begrudgingly opened the door and greeted Raphael.

Rayne joined Raphael on the porch. "I will see you at dawn."

"Please be careful, Rayne." Grace forced a smile, not liking his insistence on tracking Isra tonight. The overseer would be furious about Grace's earlier assault. Temporary vanquishing was painful for a demon or a djinn. She hoped Rayne did not bear the brunt of Isra's wrath for her actions.

Rayne gently held Grace's arm by the elbow. "What troubles you so much tonight?"

"She is going to retaliate. I can already feel things reeling."

"Isra will never come near you or the children again after receiving Kamar's head."

Grace looked away from him. "I wouldn't be too certain of that. You take an unnecessary risk going after her tonight."

Rayne's fingers cupped her chin as he brought her gaze back to his. "You will see me at sunrise or shortly thereafter."

Trying to shrug off the guilt tugging at her conscience, Grace nodded her head. "I love you. Onore e gloria, Commander."

"Morrigan Victoria, my love." Rayne smiled reassuringly. *Nothing foreboding looms in either of our destinies tonight.*

Grace kissed him goodbye, knowing otherwise.

THIRTY-FOUR

Elysium

Dante stood alone in his living room, intently watching Rayne and Raphael search for Isra.

"I had a feeling you might be watching," Grace said, unexpectedly joining him.

Dante grinned, briefly looking away from the portal. "I am doing what I can to help within the boundaries set by the High Council. For you to be here, Rayne didn't want you riding with him tonight."

"He wouldn't stay home as I asked either. Do you mind if I watch with you?"

"Be my guest."

Grace sat down on the couch. "Thank you."

"Nothing eventful has happened." Dante poured Grace a glass of the wine he was drinking. "I suspect Isra went underground again."

"Maybe."

Isra wasn't hiding. She was probably still recovering from the vanquishing wound and plotting all the ways she'd get her revenge. Grace ignored how Dante suspiciously eyed her. Thankfully, he didn't sit down beside her. He went back to keeping an eye on things in Spain.

Grace debated downing her entire glass of wine in one gulp after Dante glanced over at her a second time.

"What has you on edge tonight, cara?"

"Nothing. I am just worried about Rayne. We are operating in the unknown with Isra."

Dante didn't like how Grace purposefully avoided eye contact with him. He joined her on the couch. "Rayne knows Isra and Córdoba well. What makes you believe otherwise?"

"You're reading too much into my words, Dante. What I meant was Isra has never come after Rayne prior to now. This is a personal vendetta. We usually deal with conflicts of a less personal nature."

"Bugiarda." Dante set his hand on Grace's knee.

"I'm not lying."

"No? Then why are you angry about my touching you in such a harmless fashion?"

"There is nothing harmless about it," Grace snapped, grasping his forearm.

"What do you fear I will see?"

Grace forced his hand off her knee. "I am secretly in love with Ares."

Dante laughed. "Now, you are truly lying. Ares annoys you as badly as he does Rayne and me."

"I think he annoys you and Rayne much worse." Grace set her glass of wine on the table beside the couch.

"With the wound you dealt her, Isra more than likely won't be well enough to walk in the human realm until tomorrow. You should have told Rayne the full truth of how you obtained the indenture."

"He'd be furious. I don't want to add more fuel to the fire that keeps the enforcer part of him alive."

"There is no enforcer left in your husband."

"I used to believe that. I tried to tell myself the silver eyes are just those of the High Council's executioner. That Rayne is the sacred balance keeper, so War sometimes appears more scary than he truly is. But, I'm not so sure after the past few days. I hoped getting the new indenture might quiet the wolf. It didn't. He's as restless as ever tonight."

Dante slid an arm around her. "Rayne's merely tired, Grace. He is doing his best to protect you and everyone else Isra is targeting."

Instead of pulling away, Grace instinctively turned into Dante, embracing him as fear briefly took control. Her head rested against his shoulder. He held her, providing her the soothing comfort she needed.

"Djinn and demon don't defeat Horsemen. Even ones as old as Isra."

"I hope you are right."

"Gods are always right." Dante chuckled before brushing his lips across her temple. "Perhaps, you should return to Spain and rest yourself."

Shouting drew their attention back to the portal. Rayne and Isra fought one another. Isra wielded her blade as masterfully as any Council officer did. Raphael kept the other djinn in Isra's courtyard from entering the fray.

Not believing how fast Isra countered each move Rayne made then launched rapid attacks back at him, Grace came to her feet. It was as if Grace's assaulting her earlier in the day never occurred. "She recovered quickly."

Dante gently clasped Grace's hand to prevent her from teleporting to her husband. "Rayne can manage her. Your presence there will only be a hindrance."

***

Córdoba - 812

Rayne pinned Isra down. He yanked the jewel encrusted dagger from the sheath on his side.

"You die if you kill me. Is that what you want, Haroun? To abandon your new wife and children."

"What lies do you spew now?" The way Isra held his gaze made him second-guess his decision to finish her. He stopped the descent of his hand on the off chance she spoke the truth.

"It isn't a lie. You swore a blood oath. A contract soul bound. I gifted you your immortality. Permanently vanquish me, and you vanquish yourself." Isra sliced open her left palm against Rayne's blade.

Smarting across his left palm caused Rayne to look at his hand. Blood dripped from an open wound, running down his wrist like red paint down canvas. The glistening of it against his uniform sleeve in the moonlight and the dampness against his skin made Isra's revelation all the more shocking. "What in Hades?"

"Is that proof enough, Haroun? Master and servant eternally bound."

Rayne glanced over at Raphael; the dumbfounded expression on Raphael's face cautioned Isra may be telling the truth.

Rayne kept a tight hold of Isra's arm as he stood. "On your feet."

Isra brought her own blade down upon herself, severing the arm Rayne held at the shoulder. Rayne reflexively released her due to the extreme pain traveling down his own limb.

Isra vanished from sight.

"How did she do that?" Rayne massaged his upper arm, trying to stop the torturous throbbing.

Baffled by what he witnessed, Raphael shook his head. "I am not sure. While highly unlikely, maybe, you two are still bonded."

Grace walked toward Raphael and Rayne. "Why did you let her go?"

Seeing his wife only worsened Rayne's mood. "What are you doing here?"

"Never mind what am I doing here. You had her. Why didn't you kill her?"

"The matter just became a great deal more complicated."

"I would say so if the High Council balance keeper let an overseer best him." Grace's hands rested on her hips as she shot him a glare. "I've never seen you hesitate or miss a target before tonight."

"Grace." Rayne took a deep breath, fighting to keep himself calm. "It isn't that simple."

"How complicated can it be for War to kill an ifrit?"

"I can't kill her!" Rayne shouted after the pain in his arm and shoulder sent his temper over the edge. "Christ, woman! Can you never give me the benefit of the doubt at times like these?"

"What do you mean you can't kill her?"

Rayne focused his gaze on the ground and counted to ten, forcing the enraged enforcer to quiet. "There is still some sort of bond between her and me."

"No." Grace shook her head. "The Fates wouldn't allow that. You were born a Horseman, destined to be immortal."

"My blade did this when it sliced into her left palm, Grace." Rayne held up his injured hand.

Grace gently took it and inspected the wound. While it bled a lot, the tendons in his hand were fine. It would quickly heal. "This is bullshit." She dropped his hand then sent herself back to Elysium.

Elysium -

"You need to kill her, Dante."

Dante saw the desperation on her face. He hated that he would worsen it. "Grazia, I cannot."

"The hell you can't. You can and you will."

"My ban from you may be lifted, but you know the law on interceding in this. My actions are limited to investigation and support only. I cannot do as you wish."

"Rayne cannot kill her. Unlike you, he is willing to do the harder thing and live to protect his family, not copping out with some backroom deal."

"Grace, if I go after Isra as you desire, I face Council sanction or worse. Would you leave your children no safe haven after multiple attempts on their lives? That is the consequence of doing what you ask."

"If you won't kill Isra, Dante, I will."

"You will go nowhere near Isra," Rayne interrupted their argument. "You will trust me to resolve this."

"This has to end, Rayne. Your health is taking too heavy a toll." Grace stared up at her husband as he approached her.

"Have faith, Grace. We will find a way around this new development."

"I am done having faith. I want blood. The Council and the Fates can go to Hell with all these little surprises they place in our paths."

"Careful with your desires, leof. The ones you are having lead to a dark path you never want to walk." Rayne ignored the way the enforcer stirred within him. The djinn wanted to fuel Grace's rage until it blazed like a wildfire of dark flame that could only be controlled under his masterful hand.

Not liking the darkness he sensed in either of his companions, Dante set a hand on each of their backs to ground them firmly into the light of good once more. "There is a High Council meeting tomorrow afternoon. The Fates will be there. I will find out what I can about this master-servant bond between Rayne and Isra. In the meantime, both of you should go home and try to get a few hours' sleep."

CHAPTER

THIRTY-FIVE

Córdoba - 812

Rayne only managed brief interludes of sleep before horrifying images forced him back into consciousness. The nightmares blended past and present. He wished he could force Isra's meddling from his mind. He climbed out of bed and went downstairs, so he didn't disturb Grace. Rayne absentmindedly thumbed through a book, hoping it might distract him enough to quiet his mind.

"The sun god desires your wife," Isra whispered to him.

He ignored her. She wasn't going to torment him more tonight.

"You saw the way she enjoyed his attention in your very home a few days ago," Isra continued. "Anne betrayed you for a djinn's affection. Can you imagine what a woman would do for a god, especially once she has shared his bed? There are many stories of Dante's conquests. The muses and two goddesses fight for his attention with the rumors of his stamina and the attentiveness he pays to his lovers."

Rayne slammed the book closed. "My wife, while flattered like any woman is by Dante's charm, does not want the god as a lover. She is faithful in her vows to me."

"As you were so certain Anne was?"

"Grace is not Anne."

"What makes you so certain Grace does not entertain amorous thoughts of Dante? She offered herself to him in exchange for protecting you the night Umar died."

"You will not sow seeds of doubt between my wife and me."

"Perhaps you don't care as you are the one taking others to your bed. A female guardian stole a contract for you."

Rayne wore Isra down for her to shift tactics. He almost smiled to himself, picturing the annoyed expression most likely on the djinn's face. "I know nothing about whatever occurred between you and this guardian. My wife is the only one who shares my bed. Infidelity is not a nerve you may pluck within me."

Isra scoffed. "That is a lie, Haroun Ibn-Ziyad. I sense jealousy in you anytime Dante looks at your new wife."

"There is nothing for me to be jealous of. What you most likely sense is my annoyance, which you cause, and the natural tendency a man has to be possessive of his spouse. Nothing more."

"The enforcer never liked when others touched things that belonged to him, especially when he valued whatever others dared to lay fingers on. I smell hints of fear and insecurity within you."

Rayne didn't respond. Isra could rant for the next century before he'd acknowledge her presence again.

Growing angry with his silence, Isra snapped at him, "Time will tell the truth, Haroun. It always does."

Drowsiness at last set in. Rayne returned to the bedroom. As he drifted off, Isra once more taunted him. The damn demon hadn't found something else to do after all. Every time his eyes closed, Isra would pipe up again. Dawn finally brightened the room. Daybreak meant Isra would need to seek sanctuary somewhere. Hopefully that would give him a few hours of reprieve from her taunting and squawking.

Feeling the bed rock as Rayne left it, Grace woke. She frowned at how he stared out the window. "Isra not allowing you to sleep?"

"I wish I could silence her."

"You'd think the Council wouldn't allow an overseer to whisper in a balance keeper's ear." Grace got out of bed and walked over to him.

"You need to rest. A couple more hours of sleep will allow you to put a barrier up against her."

"I can't sleep."

"Rayne, Isra can't destroy Córdoba overnight."

"Córdoba is the least of my worries. I am more concerned that my wife is demanding blood. There was vengeance and wrath mixed with your anger last night. Almost as strong as mine can be."

"Isra is trying to take my husband. To forever separate me from the man I share a soul bond with. She also threatens my children. I would fight to the death for all three of you."

Rayne ran his thumb across her cheek. "Isra will never take me from you. She may infuriate us both, but she nor anyone else will ever separate us, Grace. Never let that kind of fear overrule the good within you again."

"Let's go back to Sasainn. She can't reach you there." Grace hoped he would listen to her. "I am only asking for one day, then you can have eternity to hunt down Isra. We'll figure out a way for you to sleep"

She loved the way Rayne gently brought her against him then kissed her. His fingers crumpled the bottom of her nightgown before he pushed it upward. His knee slid between her thighs to keep the material from falling and covering her lower body again. "I think you've solved your own dilemma, Commander."

His hands cupped her bottom, bringing her hips closer to his. "I am glad you are willing to try what I have in mind to wear myself out."

"Come to Sasainn with me. We'll spend the day in bed." Grace whispered in his ear.

Rayne grinned at the seductive offer, drawing her nightgown over her head. "I would rather take you right here, right now."

"Maybe Isra will sever the connection if she hears how much your wife enjoys the way you make love to her."

Rayne let out a loud laugh. "Normally, I would object to anyone else being in our bedroom when we make love, but in this instance..." He paused to kiss Grace. "I am willing to make an exception if it earns us respite from Isra."

The front door opening, then banging shut, ended any chance of early morning lovemaking.

"Haroun! Haroun! Are you here?"

Recognizing his brother-in-law's voice, Rayne uttered an annoyed groan. "Damn Hussein's timing. Whatever brings him here better be important."

"Haroun?" The voice moved around under the floor beneath them.

"Upstairs." Rayne gave Grace an apologetic look as his arms dropped away from her.

Someone clomped up the wooden steps to the second floor.

Grace pulled on her robe. "Whatever this is, it can wait."

"Hussein would not be here this early if he or my father could handle the matter." Rayne opened the bedroom door to find out what the man needed.

Hussein cast Grace a dismissive glance before addressing Rayne. "Someone abducted Yasmina late last night. I woke, and she was gone."

Grace worried about the grim expression on Rayne's face. "Who is Yasmina?"

"One of my sisters. Stay here until I return."

"No. I am coming with you." Grace knew he wouldn't be thinking clearly between the lack of sleep and a family member threatened.

Rayne grasped her elbow. "You may stay here with Sulla and Kato, or you may return to Sasainn, but you are not going anywhere near Isra."

Grace hated that he refused her help. "Rayne, I can..."

"What was not clear about my instruction, woman?"

"As you wish, emir." Grace's livid tone conveyed her unhappiness with being asked to stay behind again.

"Do not start, Grace. Isra already has one family member. I don't want to risk her taking two."

"Maybe Yasmina went for a walk, or ran away from a controlling medieval husband."

Rayne laughed at both suggestions. "You know that isn't the case. Hussein dotes on my sister. Yasmina also wouldn't take a random stroll this early." He put on his shirt then grabbed his sword from the weapons chest. Turning, he caught the scathing glare she shot him. "We can argue about this later."

"If Isra has her, you need assistance recovering her."

Pulling on his boots, Rayne proposed a compromise. "I will summon Destahn and Tamir once I determine her location. You are staying here."

After Grace could no longer see Rayne and Hussein from the window, she changed into her uniform.

"Sean." Grace hoped the general wasn't out on assignment.

Sean appeared a few feet from her. "What do you need, Grace?"

"My husband is not well. I want eyes on him this morning."

Shouting arose in the courtyard. Grace drew back the curtain to see what was going on. A small group of menacing looking riders requested entry to the property. Rayne's two guardsmen took up arms and loudly demanded the riders leave.

Grace recognized what the riders actually were. "Djinn. Isra's trying the divide-and-conquer tactic again."

Sean peered out the window beside Grace. "Small enough group. We should be able to handle them."

A man with brown eyes and graying dark hair entered the room. "Lady Ibn-Ziyad, it is no longer safe here. Narciso and his men are at the gates. We will hold them, but it is best you use the passageway to flee."

"I am not going anywhere. We can defend against a djinn and his minions if they breach the barrier protecting the house."

Grace heard the gate being rammed. The wooden panels trembled even as Rayne's men-at-arms braced them.

"Narciso is not any random djinn, Lady Ibn-Ziyad. He is Isra's current primus and enforcer. He and Kamar assumed Haroun's place as generals of Isra's legions. It is better you run than risk having to fight him."

Sean contemplated their options. "I hate to say it, but I agree, Grace. Placing Rayne in the position of worrying about two simultaneous confrontations would not be a wise thing to do when he is this worn out."

"I don't like running from a winnable fight with an enemy we should be firm in standing against. Isra couldn't breach the barrier around the house. I doubt Narciso can."

"You're right. On the off chance he makes it into the house, we can defeat him. On the other hand, I have to ask at what price? You know

Isra's ploy. Do you really want to risk Rayne's health with potentially having to choose between you and his sister this morning?"

The braces started to buckle. Daylight could now be seen through the slowly widening opening in the gate.

"You haven't seen your husband at his worst, Grace. I have. Rayne can take down entire armies in mere seconds when not in control of himself. The earth responds to his rage like it does to Caitlin's. He is the bringer of the end of days, not any other Horseman." Sean glanced between the courtyard and Grace. "The gates won't hold much longer."

Grace hated that even Sean worried Rayne might break under the pressure Isra placed on him. "I can't believe I am conceding on this. Let's go."

The guard gestured to the hall. "I will show you to the passageway."

Sean smiled over at him. "That isn't necessary. Lady Ibn-Ziyad and I have other means of escape. Where do you want to fallback to, Grace?"

"Essaouira."

The gate shattered with a loud explosion. Shards of wood and the broken metal latch landed in various places around the courtyard.

"Guide, if you are going, you need to go now." The soldier gave away that he knew what Sean was.

Sean grabbed Grace and teleported them out of there.

Narciso seized the guard as he walked out of the house. "Where is Grace Ibn-Ziyad?"

"Haroun sent her back to England early this morning. He feared it was no longer safe for her to remain here."

The man's claim confused Narciso. He looked through the open front door and didn't see signs of anyone, not even a servant in the house. "Be certain to advise Haroun that Narciso called at his home today."

"Yes, sir." The guard nodded after Narciso shoved him away.

The djinn general and his minions walked out of the gates. Isra would not be pleased that he returned without Haroun's wife.

Essaouira -

Grace hadn't been to the Moroccan seaside villa in a long time. It was close enough she could quickly get to Rayne if needed, but far enough away to allow her to disappear from Isra and Narciso's purview.

The blues and greens of the Atlantic alongside shimmering cream sand enthralled Grace as much as they had the first time she saw them. The ocean view from the living room always awed visitors when they entered Dante's old home. Being typical fourth-century Roman construction and protected by a barrier spell, Dante opted to leave the back walls of this area of the house open. The sea breeze kept the room cool. Salty air and gull cries from outside welcomed Grace home.

The house had lain silent and abandoned the past few years; a sharp contrast to the loud laughter and life that filled it when she and Dante lived there. Sheets covered the furniture to keep dust and grime from ruining delicate fabric and aged wood. Grace had closed up all the areas of the house she could seven years ago due to spending most of her time in Sasainn or Spain. Memories of Dante and early days of meeting the Horsemen flooded her mind.

Sean noted the way she slowly took in the room and hadn't said a word. "You okay?"

Grace snapped out of the past. "Fine. We should check on Rayne." She attempted to conjure a viewing portal, but couldn't. "I can't see what is happening in Spain. What is going on, Isis?"

"Isra is blocking you," Isis advised from her home in Carthage, surprised to find Isra could do so.

Grace exchanged nervous glances with Sean. "Rayne is in over his head if Isra now has the ability to block us."

Isis closed her eyes to view any enchantments not placed by the Council over Córdoba. "The other Horsemen are with him. He requested their assistance a short time ago. Give me a moment and I will find a way around whatever spell Isra is using."

Isra was more resourceful than any of them gave her credit for being. Grace's anxiety lessened as images of Destahn and Tamir swam before her and sharpened to the point she could be with them.

"I can see them now, Isis. Thank you."

"Call on me if you need anything additional. I am going to advise

Osiris of what just occurred." Isis ended the communication with Grace.

Destahn and Tamir moved silently through Malik's palace. Rayne and Raphael distracted the royal guard outside. Grace was a bit surprised that Isra had the audacity to imprison Yasmine in the palace.

"Three men on your right, Tamir." Grace saw them before the two Horsemen could.

"Shukran, Defensore," Tamir said, confirming they could hear her. He signaled Destahn, passing along the message.

"I didn't know we had visual support this morning," Destahn whispered, happy to hear Grace's voice.

"You should know by now the Council is always watching." Grace brought a grin to Destahn's face.

Tamir smiled and shook his head. He intercepted the first guard to come around the corner. It only took a few seconds for the human to pass out with the sleeper hold Tamir used. He and Destahn silently took out the other two guards before they noticed their companion was down.

By as intent as his gaze was on the portal, Grace knew Sean would rather assist the Horsemen than watch events with her. "Go help them."

"How heavy is the guard around the inner chamber we need to get to?" Destahn asked, slowly lowering one of the unconscious guards to the floor.

"Surprisingly light after you take out the four in the next room. There are only three djinn in the apartment's outer chamber. Yasmina's alone in the inner chamber."

Tamir didn't like how only three djinn guarded Rayne's sister. "That's odd."

Destahn felt something was wrong, too. "Isra and Malik had to know we'd come with Rayne. Grace, are you sure there are only three djinn?"

"There's only three. Going silent, so they don't detect you."

Keeping an eye on the activities in Spain, Grace walked to the master bedroom. This section of the house was more modern construction. The exterior of this addition mimicked that of the Romans, but the interior had the amenities of the modern world. She yanked down the sheets covering the windows and removed the bar she placed through the handles of the balcony doors to prevent them from being opened. After sticking for a moment, the large pair of French doors swung forward, allowing sunlight to flood Dante's old haven once more.

Córdoba - 812

Destahn and Tamir reached the room where Yasmina was held.

Raphael shouting a warning drew Grace's attention away from the rescue team to Rayne. Sean and the two Horsemen fought what appeared to be a small army converging on them. Human mixed with demon and djinn in the enemy. The immortals carefully differentiated those who needed to be subdued from those who needed to be killed.

"Destahn?" Grace checked on Destahn and Tamir.

"We need a few more minutes, Grace."

Grace saw a unit of soldiers coming down the hall. "You may not have a few minutes."

Tamir glanced towards the room door. "How many are there?"

"Ten. They aren't human. They will be on you in about thirty seconds."

Destahn cursed, yanking his sword from its scabbard. "This is starting to feel like a setup."

More yelling and fighting from the exterior of the palace agitated Grace. "You two are on your own. Rayne, Sean, and Raphael are being overrun in the courtyard."

Rayne cut down the djinn surrounding him. The Horsemen and Sean decimated Isra's minions, but only injured the humans enough to immobilize them. Those poor mortal souls merely followed orders from Malik and did not wage war against the Council.

Another wave of men filled the courtyard, attempting to capture Rayne. Rage overtook Rayne. He seized the human guard captain then threw him down. The man squirmed, terrified; trying to breathe as Rayne settled a knee on his upper chest.

"Back away!" Rayne snarled at the troops surrounding him, Sean, and Raphael.

A loud clap of thunder rumbled overhead, and the sky blackened.

Destahn heard the thunder. "Grace, please tell me that isn't the darker side of War waking."

"Get Yasmina and get out of there."

Destahn cursed again. The strained tone of Grace's voice provided all the motivation he needed to kill the remaining djinn in the room.

The soldiers encircling Raphael, Sean, and Rayne in the courtyard retreated a few feet.

Raphael glanced over at Rayne. "They did as asked, Rayne. Let the human go."

Rayne laughed. "Isra needs to learn what happens when my warnings aren't heeded."

Grace watched as Rayne raised the Horsemen's blade above his head. He would damn himself if he didn't stop. "Rayne!" She screamed his name, praying he heard her.

Dante restrained Rayne's wrist, preventing the execution of an innocent man.

"We have Yasmina and are clear." Destahn advised, teleporting himself and an unconscious Yasmina out of the palace.

Grace exhaled the fear she felt. Thank the gods they safely retrieved Yasmina and Dante stopped Rayne in time.

"The rescue mission is over, Commander. Return to your wife." Dante sent Rayne to Essaouira, hoping that seeing Grace would soothe Rayne's temper.

CHAPTER

THIRTY-SIX

Essaouira

Rayne drove his weapon downward as if Dante hadn't stopped him. Steel struck marble, startling him. His sword made a bone-chilling clamor when it fell against the floor. The man he planned to execute no longer lay beneath his knee. The change in surroundings confused him. "Where am I?"

"Essaouira." Grace watched him stand. "Dante sent you here."

"Dante?" Rayne seemed disoriented as he approached her. He mistrustingly perused the room. The scowl on his face deepened as his eyes traveled across the picturesque view of sand and sea through the open doors to the large four-poster bed Grace stood beside then over the other covered pieces of furniture. "Why are we here, Grace?"

"What do you mean why are we here? I just told you, Dante…"

"I know how I got here. Allow me to rephrase the question. What are you doing in Morocco, in your ex-husband's bedroom, no less, when I left you in my home this morning?"

"A unit of djinn showed up at our door. I came here to avoid a conflict with them. Sulla said the djinn leading them is Isra's new primus, Narciso."

373

"Narciso wouldn't dare such a thing." Rayne stalked towards her.

"Believe what you will, Rayne. I am telling you the truth."

"So you go running to Dante because Narciso frightened you? You are more than capable of defending against Narciso, especially with Sean there to help you." Rayne halted before her.

Grace stared up into the silver eyes of the enforcer. Something bred a festering paranoia about Dante and her within Rayne's subconscious. "Dante isn't here, and hasn't been for a long time. I chose to come to Morocco as it is far enough to get off Isra's radar, but close enough to reach you quickly if you needed help."

A malicious grin upturned the right side of Rayne's mouth. "Do you really think you disappeared from Isra's reach here?"

Now Grace sensed the other being feeding Rayne's irrational line of thought. "Isra, you have no power here. Close the damn portal and give me back my wolf."

"Your wolf?" Displeased with her choice of words, Rayne's right brow lifted. "I belong to no one."

"I am not claiming to own you. We are married, Rayne." Grace grasped his left hand, showing him the matching rings they wore.

Seeing the two sapphires side by side partially freed Rayne from Isra's influence. He forced the overseer the rest of the way out of his mind. The protection spell over the villa prevented Isra from reconnecting with him.

His continued stony stare and silence worried Grace. "Rayne, I just want my husband back. I can embrace this part of you if I need to."

Rayne pushed her back against the wall. "You can embrace the monster in me? You could barely utter that statement. I despise dishonesty, Grace. I should rip out your tongue for lying to me."

"I will find a way to love the enforcer as I do the Horseman. Remember your oath, Rayne. It prevents you from harming an innocent."

"Innocent? Not with the blood I see on your hands."

"I am not afraid of you."

"You should be."

The wind picked up, lifting Grace's hair. She looked outside at the formerly calm water. The ocean churned. White caps crested growing waves as dark clouds rolled in. Sean hadn't been joking when he said nature mirrored Rayne's emotions anytime his control slipped.

"Looking for Dante?" Rayne's inquiry brought her eyes from the beach to him. "Hoping the god might show up to save you?"

"I don't need saving. If it's a fight you want, I'll fight you with everything I have, Rayne. We are equally matched."

Amused by her claim, Rayne chuckled. "We are far from equally matched, my feisty wife. You fight well, but not well enough to take down your husband."

"Shall we find out if that is true?"

"I do not need to battle with you, leof. What I need is truth, truth you are withholding." Rayne ran his thumb across her lower lip, perusing her recent memories. "Dante has tempted you on more than one occasion." He sharply inhaled as images of her and Dante sharing a kiss played before him.

Grace saw the same memory Rayne did. "I admonished Dante for crossing boundaries that night. One kiss is not worth damning your soul."

"Brutalizing a god would hardly bring damnation on one already condemned."

"You aren't condemned, Rayne. The Council forgave you. You broke free of your past. Do not return to it." Vivid silver eyes bore into her. His fingers now gripped the sides of her face.

"You tangled with Isra. I specifically forbade you from going near her."

"You never stated I was to avoid Isra before last night."

Rayne saw Grace's complete interaction with Isra a few days before. "And you lied to me about how you obtained the new indenture."

"I may have left out a few details knowing you'd be angry if you knew everything." Grace tried to slide around him, but Rayne jerked her back in front of him.

"You dare to say I failed to forbid you from contact with Isra then acknowledge I would be angry with your actions." Rayne chidingly clucked his tongue and shook his head. "You have been most disobedient to my wishes, Grace."

"Disobedient? What am I now to you, mere chattel? You warned me

Isra could potentially injure an immortal. You stated nothing beyond that." She tried yanking free after a wind gust slammed the French doors shut.

Rayne allowed her to spin as she wanted, but didn't let her go. Instead, he drew her back against his chest and tightened his hold on her.

Mad her husband held her hostage, Grace slammed her foot into his shin while ramming her elbow into his ribs. The blow forced him away, giving her enough room to free herself. "I am not going to play the docile spouse taking whatever punishment my husband feels he can dole out. Not even the djinn part of you is stupid enough to think I wouldn't fight back, Rayne."

Enjoying her fiery display of temper, Rayne grinned. "That determined spirit is one of the many things that draws me to you, leof." He forced her backward. His hands firmly planted on either side of her, imprisoning her between himself and the wall.

Grace glared up at him. His body felt as solid as the stone and plaster he pinned her to. "Damn it, Rayne! You are lucky..."

"Hold your tongue, woman! Allow me to make my expectations clear. You will avoid Isra at all times. Am I understood?"

Silver faded to dark gray. Rayne's venting and their bodies touching started to pacify the enforcer.

"Yes." Grace could barely speak from his full body weight against her.

"I cannot hear you, sweeting."

"You're crushing me. Back up, so I can speak louder."

"You need to relearn your place."

Grace tried not to laugh. "My place?"

"You will honor your husband's wishes on this matter. No more going near Isra without me. Submit to my direction. I want complete compliance going forward."

"Submit to you? Is this some weird obedience thing demons crave?"

Rayne's hand slid up her cheek until his thumb rested lightly on the side of her face and his other fingers tucked into soft curls. His lips grazed hers then drifted to her ear. "I crave assurance of your loyalty."

"I am more loyal than I should be when you are acting like this,"

Grace muttered, relieved Rayne's anger faded. "Makes me wonder why the Fates thought I would complement a being who is part djinn, part saint so well."

"They knew your strength and passion would match mine, but your softer side could soothe the beast within me when it rages." Rayne's head jerked back, surprise flitted across his face. Their conversation provided the prompt he needed to discover a way to block Isra. He would have never considered asking Grace to do what now struck him prior to that moment, but it could work if she agreed. "You said you could embrace the enforcer. Show me you can, Grace. That you aren't merely speaking hollow words. Agree to be the enforcer's submissive."

Grace laughed at how crazy the request sounded. "Any djinn, you or otherwise, wanting my submission would need to earn it."

"After all these years, have I not earned your love, your respect, your fidelity? If I have failed to do so, there is no hope for us."

The seriousness of his tone perturbed Grace. He truly wanted her to consider what he asked. "You have all those things from me, Rayne. Why are you demanding this? What does forcing me to be submissive do for you that my love as it is doesn't?"

"The type of submission I am asking for is given, never forced, leof. It is gifting full and complete trust to the enforcer. It is placing faith in me, even with my darker side, to never harm you or exploit the precious, fragile bond between an enforcer and the one they choose to claim."

"You are asking me to go against everything I am, Rayne."

"I need you to do this, Grace. It destroys any lingering tie between Isra and me. You wanted a way to enable me to kill Isra. Binding yourself to the enforcer is how we circumvent the blood oath. The enforcer is surrendering himself and his sword to you. After an arrangement such as this is struck, the enforcer will be at your mercy as much as you are his."

"Rayne, I, I am not the submissive type. You say you are attracted to my feistiness and fighting spirit. Will you still want me if all of a sudden I am honoring your every whim, blindly doing what you ask me to do?"

"You misunderstand what I ask of you. I never want you to lose the fighting spirit within, Grace. I love your independence and your fearlessness. The passion you possess at all times. I am not asking for you to stop being anything that you are. I want you to place your full trust in me; to trust that I know well how to tame the stubborn side of you when it needs to be done. That I know when to demand you be obedient and when to let you do as you wish. There is a difference between obedience and fear."

"I really don't like that word."

"Allow me to reframe the concept in terms you like then. Periodically, I will remind you that you are a loving wife, who respects her husband's need to keep her safe. A loving wife who values not adding to her husband's woes, and will do what he requests of her in turbulent times."

Grace wondered if Rayne realized he talked out both sides of his mouth. "After you slam me into a wall twice today, you want me to believe you know how to tame my stubborn side? That you did such an assholish thing to remind me to be a loving wife?"

"I apologize for allowing the djinn to countermand my more diplomatic nature. While I upset you, I didn't hurt you, nor did I raise my hand to you. I merely subdued you."

Rayne backed away from her. The decision needed to be hers alone. It could not be influenced by intimidation or any other emotions the physical contact of him having her up against the wall might provoke. He ignored the enforcer who silently taunted him with doubts of Grace having the courage to embrace him. He had once thought of making Anne the same offer and look at how that turned out. The woman deserted him, preferring Lucien instead.

Debating what to do, Grace frowned. Place blind faith in this part of her husband she only recently learned about, or risk the fallout of rejecting him. The enforcer clearly craved dominance and control. He had no problem being a misogynistic tyrant. Then again, most male immortals didn't act much differently toward women. Rayne only did normally because of his exposure to other centuries and working for two goddesses now. Though, he still had his days when his medieval mindset would override his common sense. While she knew she wouldn't lose Rayne if she said no, it would deal a devastating blow to him. "If I do this, you must swear to me, you will never lay a hand on me in anger."

"When have I ever struck you, Grace? And the night in Sasainn when you stabbed me doesn't count. I was defending myself from a vicious assault, and even then, I did everything I could not to hurt you before we came to blows with one another."

"I was possessed by a demon parasite!" Grace snapped at him. "That whole experience is exactly why I want the enforcer to understand if I agree to this arrangement, abusive behavior will not be tolerated. So we are perfectly clear on the consequences of your darker side breaking your word, I will personally turn you over to Isra if you ever strike me."

"I give you my word as an enforcer, I will never raise my hand to you in anger. Regardless of whether or not you accept me as your master."

"My master." She shook her head. It was difficult enough to wrap her mind around the fact she was married to a former enforcer, much less agree to ever call him master like an underling.

One of the first lessons she learned from Raphael in the immortal world was one must learn to make difficult, blind leaps of faith. Only after they were made would one learn of whether or not they would be punished or rewarded. Grace doubted her wisdom in agreeing to this. For all she knew, Isra could be manipulating them both. She stepped forward, closing the distance between them to show Rayne she was willing to attempt this. "What do I need to do?"

Grace completely silenced the antagonistic voice within Rayne. His darker side's cynicism shifted to curiosity then fascination. Her willingness to ensure he remained free won the enforcer's loyalty and admiration.

"Relax, leof." Rayne's voice turned soothing: soft, deep, and inviting, as it frequently did when they made love. "Open your conscience to me as you have your heart." He slid an arm around her. "Freely comply."

She leaned into him. Everything still alarmed a small part of her. He could see the terror Qasim and Rasil instilled in the young mortal soul who naively trusted men shrouded in similar darkness. She had buried that part of herself almost as deeply as he had his past as an enforcer. Both the Horseman and the enforcer wanted to erase the mark those two left on her spirit. "I am not them, leof. I will never take what you gift me for granted. Do not fear what might happen. Your wolf will always protect you. I'll guard you zealously from anyone who wishes to do you harm, including myself should that dark day ever come."

Grace's eyes turned hazy. Her heartbeat grew louder and slower in his ears.

"You truly are a phenomenal woman." He noted the way her lips parted the closer he brought his face to hers. She involuntarily groaned when he kissed her. "I ask you again, do you understand your husband's earlier direction?"

"Yes," Grace breathed the word.

"Good."

The husky whisper in her ear almost brought her to her knees.

"You will not defy the master of your soul ever again. I will not tolerate it."

"I own my soul."

"You entrusted your soul to me when you spoke the binding spell in the courtyard, then again a few minutes ago by agreeing to this." He brushed his mouth against hers. She instinctively divided her lips, wanting to taste him once more. Rayne denied her. "Who have you entrusted your life to?"

"You, Haroun." Grace pulled Rayne's face to hers.

While Rayne's mouth rested on hers, he didn't grant her the deeper kiss she wanted. He waited until her lips started to close. His tongue flicked forward, preventing them from meeting. She surrendered completely to his ingress on her being. Now he allowed her to take everything she wanted from him. Grace greedily kissed him over and over again, unable to get enough of the new energy connecting them.

"What is this?" Grace could barely get the question out with how badly she craved Rayne.

Rayne grinned. "Lust."

"I've experienced lust before, with you, and it was nothing like this."

"You weren't bound to the enforcer. Sins are much more tempting for a djinn or demon than other beings."

"Am I a djinn now?"

"No, my beloved. You're only feeling what I do as an enforcer."

"Do you always experience all seven deadly sins with this intensity?"

"Yes. It's the curse all djinn and demon must bear." Rayne

wondered if Grace would sever the new bond between them. Shockingly, she only opened her subconscious more, strengthening her tie to the enforcer and Horseman alike.

"You shouldn't carry such a burden alone." Grace dived deeper into the abyss of the power her husband's soul held. Drowning in the darkness of wrath and lust, her knees crumpled. Rayne's firm embrace kept her from toppling over. Yearning intensified to raw hunger. She unconsciously shifted against him. The black material of the shirt and tunic on his shoulders bunched underneath her fingers. She wanted to rip off the protective body armor he wore along with his clothing; to feel his skin against hers. She'd give anything to have him inside her. "I need you, right now, Rayne."

Rayne slowly guided her hips downward against him. The feeling of him swollen and hard, pressing up into her through their clothing intensified her desire. She hated the layers of material preventing her from having exactly what she wanted.

"I will happily give you what you want. Swear there will be no more encounters with Isra."

"I can't promise you that, Rayne. I will not stand aside as she harms you or our children"

"What do you not understand about Isra being my fight, not yours?"

Wrath replaced the lust Grace felt. "The enforcer really doesn't like to be told no."

She studied her husband. The fury in his eyes warned she treaded dangerous waters. But Grace sensed something else: fear, fear of loss. Rayne hid fear under the churn of wrath. That's why she rarely saw it in him alone or in any battle they fought.

"I fear losing you more than anything, Grace. Why do you think I am asking you to never face Isra alone?"

"I will not seek Isra out again. If she and I have any further encounters, I will make certain you are at my side."

"No further encounters." Rayne picked her up and carried her to the bed.

"I can't guarantee that," Grace said, staring up at him from the bed.

Rayne took her hand in his. "Then I can't give you this." He slid her palm down his groin, rekindling the lust they both felt earlier. "It's a fair trade, leof. You relieve my worries, and I relieve that delightful, all-consuming ache growing in you."

He jerked off her boots then unbuckled her belt. Her lips meet his when he leaned forward and gripped her waist band. He yanked her pants downward, anxious to see Grace freely bend her will to his. "I can wait an eternity for your compliance if I must, Grace. How long do you think you can endure the longing for me?"

Rayne's fingers traced small circles on the insides of her thighs.

"An hour?"

Now they glanced teasingly over the soft cotton underwear she wore.

"Two hours?"

He shifted his hand, pressing upward so the length of his fingers traveled her core.

"An entire day?"

He pushed aside the material preventing contact between them, and grazed her flesh with the tip of his finger, making her moan. "It will only get worse, Grace. The ache will grow to a raging fire demanding satisfaction. Its flames will consume you until I alone extinguish them."

Rayne slowly slid one digit inside her. "You're so wet and ready for me. Why deny yourself, leof?"

He loved the way she panted then writhed from the feel of his finger slipping in and out of her. She whimpered as he added a second one, heightening the sensation rippling through her. Her hips undulated in time with their pulsing. "Wouldn't you rather my cock inside you? The length and girth of me filling that sweet body of yours, your skin against mine."

"That is exactly what I want, Rayne."

"Agree to no more encounters with Isra, and I'll take you, Grace. I'll fuck you just like you are imagining me doing right now." He joined her in the bed.

The way his chest brushed against her as he slowly stalked up her body until they looked eye to eye was a whole new form of torture she never imagined existed. She grasped his shoulder and let out a frustrated groan. "Fine. I will not seek out any fights with Isra."

"While that pleases me, we both know it isn't what I requested. No encounters is what you need to agree to."

"I won't agree to avoid her if she comes to me."

"Oh, and we were so close to an accord." Rayne pressed down into her, the bulge in his pants reminded her of the reward for her compliance. "Are we starting all over again, Grace?"

"Rayne!" Grace slammed the bottom of her closed fist against his shoulder, wriggling beneath him. No wonder demons were crazy if this was how intensely they craved sex and killing. She detested the "No hitting, leof," he murmured before kissing the tender flesh below her ear. Her fingers grasped his hair as his tongue stroked her skin. The pressure of his lips sealing themselves against her neck brought forth a loud cry of pleasure and protest. "Damn it, Rayne! You wouldn't ever be cruel enough to deny me when I mostly gave you what you want."

"Wouldn't I?" He ripped open her shirt. The small black buttons holding it shut flew in various directions around the room. "There is no negotiation with an enforcer. Give me what I want, or I will savor every second of sweet hell I put you through until you ultimately do as I ask. You only torment yourself."

A cool breeze swept over Grace's skin, contrasting with the warm hand grasping her breast. The simple strumming of Rayne's thumb against her nipple drove her insane. Her feet traveled down the smooth leather of his boots until they found the metal spurs he wore. The freezing steel coated in gold caused her toes to curl; her legs instinctively retreated upward.

"I will torture you for centuries if it ensures your safety, Grace."

Her hand scaled Rayne's side until her arm hooked around his shoulder, bringing him closer, wanting his body to erase the momentary chill. She closed her eyes, raising her head to kiss him.

"Not until you please the enforcer. Until then, you will only experience what I want you to, not what you desire."

"I can't take this anymore. I need you inside me, Rayne. Please."

Rayne gripped her outer thigh after her leg wrapped around his. "Your word you will not confront Isra in any capacity again without my knowledge or permission."

"Rayne," Grace groaned his name, not wanting to speak of Isra any longer.

"Say it, Grace."

She opened her eyes after her fingertips traveled warm skin instead of his uniform shirt. They both lay completely nude. "Did you vanquish your clothes?"

"Stop stalling, or I'll take you over my knee instead of granting you what you desire."

Grace entwined her fingers in the soft, black waves of his hair. "You promised you wouldn't raise a hand to me in anger."

"I am definitely not angry, and you'd more than likely enjoy what I plan to do once you're laying over my knee."

Her mouth pressed up against his. He once more wouldn't allow her another kiss.

"Say what I want to hear, leof."

"You once warned me never to strike a bargain with a djinn."

A deep chuckle relayed he found her excuse entertaining. "That doesn't apply when I am the djinn." He rubbed the tip of himself tantalizingly along her. "All you have to do is say there will be no more encounters with Isra of any kind, and this is yours."

"It's already mine." Grace impatiently arched up against him.

Rayne pinned her arms down on the bed and turned slightly to prevent her from taking him into her. "While that may be, I am not inclined to let you enjoy your rights to it at the moment."

"You Middle Ages, arrogant, demon ass! Stop tormenting me!" Grace couldn't resist the lust consuming her any longer. Another frustrated squeal left her lips before she looked up at him again. "You win, Rayne. I concede. Now, please, may I have the pleasure of fucking my husband?"

"State my terms, leof."

"You have my word, Rayne. No further encounters with Isra. I also concede to whatever else you desire as long as you take me right now."

"Whatever else I desire? You more than please me, beloved. I will happily grant you exactly what you wish." Rayne uttered the words in djinn.

Lost in the rhythm of their bodies moving together, Grace didn't understand what he said. He could be cursing her to hell for all she cared. She only wanted him to drive himself deeper and deeper into her.

Rayne did so until her body convulsed around him. Her fingernails sunk into his skin. The high-pitched cry she let out confirmed he brought her to climax. He stared down at her, savoring her completely exposed and vulnerable. Her soul laid bare. His to claim as he did her body. *We are in each other's blood, in the darkest depths of our being.* Rayne ran his fingers across her collarbone and down to her heart. *You are mine, and I am yours, mia luna.*

Grace's eyes fluttered open. She had heard those words before, over a decade ago in Rome. All these years, she thought a spell caused the strange amorous connection that afternoon, but feeling the same intense joining now, she realized the spell merely exposed the entirety of Rayne's being; the intoxicating combination of virtuous Horseman blended with fallen enforcer. She rested her palm against his cheek, staring up into silver eyes, no longer concerned by the color. *Fated.*

Rayne smiled. "We aren't finished yet. Turn over."

Before she had completely rolled to her belly, he tugged her hips backward, so she took him in completely once more. They groaned together.

"My wolf."

"Yes, my love. Your wolf. Yours alone." Rayne's hand found her core. His fingers moved in time with his hips. The soft moans falling from her lips beguiled the enforcer. He found his match. The perfect blend of unconquerable fighter, passionate lover, and woman not afraid of what he was or what he may demand of her. "Submit to me again, Grace. Promise me I am your only master."

"I have no master."

"You said you loved my darker side. I freely indentured that part of myself to you." Rayne's palm traveled down the curve of her hip. "I need the same from you. Finish binding our beings, so no one, no creature, may ever again come between us." He gently pinched her nipple between two fingers bringing forth another ecstasy-filled moan. "Claim all of me, luna."

"Yes, Rayne."

Rayne lightly tapped her bottom. "Yes, what?"

"Yes, master. I bind myself to the enforcer."

"You eternally submit to the djinn?" Rayne's voice deepened as the enforcer emerged to receive her vow.

"You are forever the only being I will call master, Rayne. I eternally submit to War's wishes. Now, stop demanding things of me."

"That borderlines disobedience. I am starting to think you want me to reprimand you." His palm came in contact with her skin a little harder this time.

Grace smiled over her shoulder at him. "As I said, shut up, and finish with me."

Rayne gave her a third spanking. The passionate cry she uttered in response confirmed she enjoyed the rough play. His fingers grasped her hair, giving it a tug as he took her.

"Don't stop, Rayne," Grace protested when he slowed their pace.

"I have no intentions of doing so. I merely want to ensure I am not hurting you."

"I'll let you know if you hurt me in a way I don't like. I thought you already knew I like it rough on occasion."

"I am being a bit rougher than normal. But since it pleases you." He grasped her hips tighter, yanking her back against him, driving himself into her.

"Rayne, yes, just like that." Grace's body trembled more and more. "Master!"

Rayne groaned in her ear, his hand traveling downward along her belly, seeking the tender, swollen button of her sex. "I love you calling me master, Grace."

"My master," Grace mumbled, nearly collapsing from the intimate stroking and the sensation of Rayne inside her.

Grace's hand settled on top of his. "I can't take this. It feels too good."

"Too bad, leof. I am not stopping until you climax again. Perhaps I should say, you are not stopping until you climax again for me." He changed the position of their hands and guided her finger in a circle against herself.

"Keep going," Rayne whispered in her ear, moving his hand away. By the timid movement of her fingers, he knew she wasn't sure what to think of the request. "Pretend your hand is mine, Grace. We both know you need more of a touch like this." Rayne once more guided her fingers with his. "You know exactly how to pleasure yourself with how you tell me what you like and don't like."

Rayne slowly went deeper into her. He gradually increased the speed he took her with, ensuring she remained in sync with him. Feeling the dampness growing around him, Rayne lightly spanked Grace.

"That feels so good, Rayne."

"Take your pleasure, Grace."

He brought his palm down against her backside again, letting her set the pace now. She repeatedly bucked back against him until they both could stand no more. A guttural rumble escaped Rayne, matching the intensity of the pleasure-filled shriek that came from Grace. They collapsed forward, onto the bed.

Rayne kissed the back of Grace's shoulder before resting his cheek against it. He laid on top of her, catching his breath, before rolling onto his back. Grace curled up against him. She ran her fingertip over a small scar near his heart. Had it really come from an arrow in his youth as he once told her, or had he incurred the injury as a djinn? Truthfully, it didn't matter. After today, the enforcer no longer scared her. He was simply another piece of her husband. A frightened and wounded creature who needed to be reminded he wasn't facing the world alone; his wife stood beside him in the dark, and she was as strong as he was. "You are in my blood, the darkest depths of my being."

Stunned by what she whispered, Rayne opened his eyes. "Grace, don't...."

She placed her finger against his lips. "I know what I speak. Let me finish the words. You are mine." Grace watched Rayne's eyes turn luminescent silver. "and I am forever yours. May you eternally be my wolf and my master, Haroun Ibn-Ziyad."

"My sword and soul are forever yours alone, my beloved." Rayne kissed her, cementing the ancient djinn vow. Becoming his submissive was enough to dissolve the last remanent of Isra's hold. He never expected her to swear a lover's oath to the enforcer. "You amaze me, Grace. No other has loved me as you do."

"We're both one of a kind, Rayne. This afternoon was incredible. You need to let the enforcer out more often."

"Does your husband, the Horseman, no longer satisfy you?"

"He more than satisfies me. Making love to him is my favorite thing to do. But playing with the part of him that fucks like a demon is a close second." Grace smiled at the way his brows rose before he laughed.

"Since it pleases you, I will see what I can do to accommodate your request every now and then." Rayne shook his head. "Fucks like a demon. Never imagined I'd ever hear you describe me in such a manner."

Her giggling beside him brought a grin to his face. Welcoming sleep for the first time in days, his eyes slowly closed.

Grace watched the slow rise and fall of Rayne's chest. Lifting her head, she admired the relaxed features of his face. No dreams or nightmares disturbed him. She finally had her husband back after days of him teetering between light and dark. She pulled one of the spare sheets over them and indulged in an hour-long nap herself.

The ocean called to her after she woke; she picked up Rayne's shirt since hers couldn't be closed any longer and put it on. She quietly walked out onto the back deck to enjoy the sunshine and listen to the now calm sea lap against the sand.

What was it about this place? Some of her most crazy, passionate moments had been spent here. First, with Dante, and now Rayne. Was it the sea air? Or did she connect with the men the Fates bound her to more deeply here?

"I prefer to think it's the fact you choose to let go when you feel loved more than the particular place." Rayne intruded on her thoughts, joining her. "After all, we've had intense moments in Rome and Andalusia before."

"So, it was the enforcer who whisked me away to some foreign place after I made love to you in the baths of Caracalla, and that Ares feared when I asked him for help."

Rayne guiltily smiled, displaying the two dimples she adored. "Yes, it was."

"Why didn't you tell me then?"

"I don't think you would have handled the news that I was once a djinn well. You were struggling as it was with being torn between Dante and me. Not to mention, I was mortified an enemy had figured out who I once was when the Council promised my past was erased."

"Fair enough." Grace kissed him then watched the gulls play on the breeze over white-edged, turquoise water. "You should have slept longer. How are you feeling now?"

"Surprisingly, well rested for the first time since all of this started." Rayne admired his wife before taking in the serene setting of sand and sea. "Thank you, Grace."

Genuinely confused, Grace looked up at him. "For what?"

Rayne's arm wrapped around her waist, bringing her against his side. He kissed the top of her head. "For maintaining your courage in facing Isra and ensuring only one woman ever has dominion over the enforcer going forward."

"As if I'd ever let Isra have you." The mischievous grin on her face forewarned a playful remark was forthcoming. "Men who make love and fuck like a demon are hard to come by."

Rayne rolled his eyes and swung her around, towards the house. "Inside with you, you half-dressed, foul-mouthed heathen."

"So you can have your way with me again in Dante's old bed?" Grace caught the slight raising of his brows and the interested, lopsided grin on his face as they walked toward the house.

"If that is what you desire, leof, I am more than happy to oblige."

"Aren't you supposed to say your wish is my command? That's what all evil djinn who grant wishes that are actually curses say in stories."

"You are mixing up different beliefs about djinn. My family thinks djinn and genie are separate creatures entirely. Not to mention I am an enforcer, a military commander, not a wish granter confined to a bottle."

"I'd argue you're also a wish granter." Grace stopped just inside the doorway. She loved the soft chuckle she heard and the way Rayne lovingly stared down at her.

"Only for you, my love. Only for you."

CHAPTER

THIRTY-SEVEN

Essaouira

"Are you going back after Isra?" Watching Rayne dress, Grace worried he might.

"No. I am honoring my wife's earlier wishes and going to Sasainn. I have a feeling I will get a very good night's rest tonight."

"Because of how this morning ended?"

"Partly." Looking at Grace still lying in bed with a sheet draped loosely over her, Rayne appreciatively grinned. Their lovemaking had been as intense as the preceding encounter binding the enforcer to Grace. He buttoned the last two buttons on his shirt. "But mostly because Isra can no longer provoke the enforcer. Your binding yourself to my darker side prevents anyone from manipulating my fears; for no one can ever take the thing my entire being desires most." He offered her the protective tunic he normally wore over his shirt so she had something to wear after he had ripped apart her shirt.

Grace took the tunic from him and pulled it over herself. Seeing her stand, he held out his hand to her. "Are you ready to go home?"

Grace picked up her boots and pants, then settled her hand in his. He teleported them to their home in Sasainn.

390

Sasainn -

After a bath and late lunch, Rayne took a second nap for the day. Grace worked downstairs at the dining room table, so she didn't disturb him. The more he slept the next day or so, the better.

Raphael appeared with an envelope in his hands. "Ibelin requests your presence at the Vatican."

Grace took the envelope to see what caused the summons. Inside it was a newspaper article claiming another journal detailing more information on the man referred to as the Left Hand of God had been discovered. The picture in the center of the page contained a miniature silver wolf's head medallion like the one in the drawing that disappeared the night of the earthquake. "Rayne swore the medallion couldn't be traced back to anyone."

"We cannot chance any sort of exposure in the mortal realm, Grace. As the Warwick Endowment funds Dr. Blackburn's research, you need to pull it. We need to identify who this new colleague of hers is that is helping her find these lost items."

Grace wrote a quick note to Rayne, so he wouldn't worry if she was not back by the time he woke up. "Her new colleague? Who is assisting her with digging up information she shouldn't?"

"I am not sure. The article only mentions Blackburn and her research assistant. Ibelin confirmed an unauthorized party was in the archives with her for the past several days. "

"Why didn't he investigate the other party then if he knew they were there?"

"He wasn't in Rome at the time. The security breech was reported to him upon his return. There's more. The Pope appointed a new director to oversee the archives three days ago. Needless to say, the director was livid when he learned of the situation and Blackburn's refusal to disclose the name of whoever was with her. It took Ibelin an hour to calm him down."

Hearing Dr. Blackburn wouldn't cooperate with the new director's requests puzzled Grace. "Why would Abigail not want to share the names of those on her team?"

"I hope you can learn the answer to that. Ibelin said to call him when you get there."

———

Rome - Present Day

Grace went to modern day. She tried to call Blackburn and Rossi first, hoping they might share their side of events with her. Neither answered their phones. She dialed Mirko's number. Thankfully, he picked up after the first ring. "Mirko, it's Grace Warwick. Are Dr. Blackburn or Dr. Rossi around?"

"They are attending a conference in Firenze. Dr. Nascimbeni requested I send their calls to his office while they are away for the next couple of days. Would you like me to transfer you to him?"

"Dr. Nascimbeni?" Grace didn't know the name.

"Ah, you hadn't heard. He is the new Archival Director. The Pope transferred him to the position last week."

Grace debated whether to call Ibelin or speak with Nascimbeni. Knowing that a director or higher would need to be the one to officially pull all funding for Blackburn's fellowship, Grace decided she'd call Ibelin later. "Dr. Nascimbeni can probably assist me. Please put me through to his office."

"Pronto." A deep voice came on the line halfway through the first ring.

"Dr. Nascimbeni? My name is Grace Warwick. I am one of your donors."

"What interesting timing, Signora Warwick. I was just thinking about you and the generous funding you offered our institution. Ibelin mentioned you might visit Roma soon. Would you have time to meet with me while you are in town? I like to get to know all the individuals doing research on the Church along with our more benevolent donors."

His brusque tone and the way he phrased his request didn't sit well with Grace. "I am actually in Vatican City now. Would a meeting in, say, twenty minutes, work for your schedule?"

"As Fortuna would have it, that works perfectly, Signora Warwick.

My assistant will be looking for you at the main entrance of the museum."

"Great. See you then." Grace hung up, took a deep breath, then called Ibelin. Of course, he didn't answer his phone.

Dante. Grace reached out to the god for help.

Dante walked out of the crowd in the square. "What is wrong for you to call me?"

"I'm not sure. Raphael sent me here to investigate a few things. I have a meeting with the new Vatican Archival Director. Something isn't right about this impromptu meeting."

Dante glanced up the road toward the dome of St. Peter's. "What's the Archival Director's name?"

"Dr. Nascimbeni."

"I will return in a moment." Dante turned to leave.

Grace caught his arm. "Where are you going?"

"To see if the man appears to be a threat."

"You can't just pop in and out of the Vatican with Ibelin there."

"Ibelin and I know one another. Wait here."

"Dante!" Grace let out an exasperated breath after he vanished.

Not knowing how long Dante would be, she ordered a coffee from the coffee shop behind her and sat down. As she finished her espresso, Dante appeared in the seat across from her.

"You have nothing to worry about, cara. The man's harmless. I believe the modern term for him would be a... come sei dice?... a nerd? Nascimbeni is one of those quiet, academic types; an awkward man with glasses, who most likely spends his nights alone reading some boring book on philosophy or something dull like that. But on the off chance that is a false appearance, I will keep an ear out for another summons from you."

Surprised by Dante's description, Grace suspiciously stared at him. "Since when do you use the word nerd or find philosophy boring?"

"Ibelin taught me the term. It is how he referred to Nascimbeni. Ibelin will be nearby if you need any assistance; however, after seeing the new director myself, I am certain you will know how to manage the man." Dante stood and pushed his chair in.

"Wait, where are you going?" Grace asked, watching him leave. Dante gave her a sidewise glance and grinned, but kept walking.

"Cavaliere!" He continued on until he disappeared into the throng of people outside. Why had he ignored her? Frowning, Grace took her empty cup to the counter then headed towards the Vatican Museum.

A young man, small in stature, with dark hair and glasses, waved to her as she neared the Vatican entrance. "Mrs. Warwick?"

"Yes?" Grace suspected he was Dr. Nascimbeni's assistant, but had never met him prior to today.

"I recognized you from the newsletter picture taken of you and your husband at Sant'Angelo the night of the earthquake. I am Tomasso, Dr. Nascimbeni's assistant. Please, come this way. Dr. Nascimbeni has several appointments today, but squeezed time for you in between his meetings."

Grace couldn't help smiling, thinking about Dante calling the director an academic nerd. If he looked anything like his assistant, that was a pretty accurate description. The two of them walked inside the museum then into a side hall that led to the museum staff offices.

"Please wait here while I let Dr. Nascimbeni know you arrived." The assistant directed Grace to a chair before knocking on a closed door. Not waiting for an answer, the assistant poked his head into the office and announced that Grace was there.

After being waved over, Grace walked into the director's office and extended her hand. "Dr. Nascimbeni, a pleasure to meet you."

The man who stood to greet her definitely wasn't what she would describe as a nerdy academic. The only thing close to nerdy about him were the glasses on his face. Maybe Dante mistook the assistant for the director.

Grace had to look up at the man due to his height. Piercing green eyes contrasted against light brown hair highlighted with streaks of copper and gold. He wore a custom-made brown suit that perfectly covered broad shoulders. The suit jacket hung open, revealing a starched white dress shirt, which Grace guessed was also custom tailored. The way the shirt tapered at the waist hinted at a fit body underneath.

He grasped her outstretched hand. "The pleasure is mine, Signora Warwick. May I offer you some caffè or water?"

"No, thank you." A surge of familiar energy traveled between them. Visions of the man with the cardinal at the Castel Sant'Angelo flashed in her mind.

He smiled, almost as if he could read her thoughts. "I know the last name is challenging. You may call me Michael if you would like."

"Have we met? You seem strangely familiar."

Michael laughed. "I have one of those faces. People ask me that a lot. For you to agree to a meet on such short notice, I assume you have a request of me. How exactly can I help you?"

"You're an astute man. The journal mentioned in this article. I would like to see it." Grace handed Michael the paper Ibelin sent her.

Michael skimmed the article. "I am afraid that isn't possible."

"And why is that?" A nagging suspicion swirled in Grace's stomach. Something was wrong here. Maybe she should have woken up Rayne and had him come with her.

Michael smiled and held his hands up. "We do not allow random visitors to view the Popes' private artifacts without going through the proper background checks."

"As one of your donors and a researcher myself, you should have a background check for me on file. I was last here two months ago. Baelin D'Ibelin processed my paperwork himself." Grace wasn't leaving without reviewing whatever the Pope had written in the journal.

Michael let out an aggravated breath, but picked up his phone and dialed an internal extension. "Baelin, do we have a current background check for Signora Warwick?"

Grace couldn't make out the muffled response.

"I see. Hmmm... well, thank you for checking for me." Michael hung up the phone.

"It seems we do. With that being the case, Signora Warwick, I would like to show you something far more interesting than the journal." Michael walked across the room and opened a secret door hidden in the bookcase built into the far wall of his office.

Grace noted the way he strolled across the room: long, confident, decisive strides. She summoned a dagger and carefully tucked it into the inner pocket of her jacket.

Michael's eyes briefly darted to where she concealed the weapon.

Not missing where he glanced, Grace kept a wary eye on him as she walked over to him. A dimly lit staircase spiraled downwards on the other side of the open bookcase.

"After you, Signora Warwick." Michael motioned for her to go before him.

Grace wished she was in uniform instead of a business suit. Her instincts screamed not to trust the director. Forcing herself to get a grip on her fears, Grace stepped down onto the first tread.

Michael joined her then triggered the closing mechanism for the door. The bookcase slid back into place. He didn't say a word as they descended the staircase. Reaching the bottom, she followed him down a passageway into a restricted area. A metal fire door prevented them from going any further. Michael entered an alarm code on the keypad beside it. The electronic lock clicked and the door automatically opened, revealing a frescoed room that must have been older than the Vatican itself. After they entered, the door faintly shut behind them. The soft mechanical hum of the deadbolt sliding into place put Grace even more on edge.

"You can relax, Grace. You aren't in any danger. We needed to continue our discussion away from any potential eavesdroppers." Michael opened a large safe in the room and pulled out what looked like an elongated, horizontal file cabinet drawer. "What I am about to show you doesn't exist as far as the Vatican is concerned." He lifted a black scimitar from the drawer. A red tassel hung from its engraved hilt.

Grace recognized it. "A sword from the Cordovan Caliphate? With the engraving and the red tassel, this is from one of the Emir's personal guards or a high-ranking officer in the Emirate's army."

"I am impressed, Signora Warwick. It belonged to a Cordovan general, not a member of the haras." Michael held it out to her.

"That is at least a thousand years old. I don't have gloves on to safely handle it. The last thing I would want to do is damage an artifact in such excellent condition."

"The oils from your hands won't harm it. Please, take a closer look."

Grace took the sword and pulled it from its sheath just enough that she could see an inch or two of the blade extending from the hilt. The polished steel looked as if a smith had forged and polished it only yesterday.

Michael retrieved a second sword from the drawer. It was more European in design. "I would be curious to hear your analysis of this weapon as well."

Grace carefully set the scimitar on the table beside her, then turned to take the new sword. She noticed the wolf in the weapon's guard as Michael settled the heavier weapon in her hands. The medieval sword reminded her of Rayne's blade. Both weapons were weighted in the exact same places. She didn't even need to take a practice swing to test that. Recognizing the wolf emblem after examining the guard and hilt, dread filled her. "An arming sword? Or at least that is what I am guessing. Interesting wolf design in the hilt and guard."

By the stare Michael shot her, he wasn't buying that she guessed at anything. "Fine. It's a medieval knight's weapon. More than likely a knight of the Order of Constantinople. Please tell me this isn't the sword of a papal assassin. That it is a random artifact discovered in the Vatican's vaults or on the grounds."

"You hold the Left Hand of God's blade. He returned it to the order after renouncing his position."

Michael pulled a box from the drawer and set it on the table. "There is more you should see."

Grace didn't like the way he pushed the box towards her after he removed the lid.

Noticing her troubled expression, Michael said, "You came here for answers. Today is the only day they will be available to you."

"So much for having nothing to worry about. I am going to smack Dante the next time I see him," Grace muttered, pulling the box closer. Inside it were a heavy, long, red and black cloak, a jeweled cross hanging from a gold chain, and several letters.

Michael smirked at her mumbling, but didn't say anything.

Grace opened one of the letters and read an order issued by Clement for the execution of a marquis and a bishop who allegedly committed heresy. The letter in the box immediately behind it confirmed neither man was a threat any longer. Even composed in an old mix of Latin and Italian, the strokes made by the quill were all too familiar. Certain letters matched Rayne's modern handwriting perfectly. There was no denying he authored the response, even with his signature missing. She sighed, setting down the note; wrestling with how to respond to whatever fishing expedition Michael took her on.

Michael laid the miniature silver medallion mentioned in the article on the table beside the box.

Grace picked it up and ran her thumb across the wolf's face, thinking about how much her husband endured. "Why are you showing me these things?"

"You need to know the Left Hand honestly believed he was doing God's work. His desire to atone for his prior sins briefly blinded him to the fact that the human head of the Church was fallible."

"Can a pope be fallible? That doesn't sound like something a man of the Church would say." Grace looked over at Michael. He stared back at her, not saying anything else. "So, have you found new evidence into the man's identity to make such a statement? Or are you making an educated guess about his motives, Dr. Nascimbeni?"

Michael held up the garnet, ruby, and gold cross hanging from a gold chain. "You will undoubtedly find this artifact even more intriguing than all the others. The Pope created it as a means to identify the assassin no one else could ever learn about. Each man to serve as the Left Hand of God was gifted a cross, designed to be as unique as they were. If one looks closely at this cross, they will notice the blending of Islamic and Christian art in the engravings. This belonged to the one assassin no official or historian has ever been able to identify; the last remaining unknown assassin to secretly serve the Church during the Crusades. Oddly, he is also the most enigmatic member of the Order of Constantinople. Some of the more senior order members have written the man was a repentant minion of Lucifer himself. Who knows the truth? But based on documents that survived the Crusades, we do know he's the only knight to defy papal decree and then have the audacity to appear before the Pope after doing so, simply to ensure all of these items were returned to the Vatican. I admire the man's boldness to do such a thing."

Michael offered Grace the jewel-encrusted crucifix. "Turn it to the right in the light to see what appears in the center stone."

She did as instructed. The name Haroun immediately followed by Harbinger materialized. "A name? And a type of angel?"

"We both know that does not reference an angel, Defensore."

Grace eyed the man standing next to her. "Defensore?"

"Grace, I know what you are." Michael's expression dared her to deny her immortality. "To answer your second question, the Church does not use harbinger as the High Council does. But, all the popes and cardinals at the time knew of an avenging angel identified by this cross, whose sole purpose on earth was to conduct the darker tasks of purging threats to Christendom."

"The Fates and High Council really can be petty, vindictive miscreants when they want to be." Grace hated how they let Rayne continually veer off the path of greater good.

Michael laughed. "Blame Lucifer for that. The other council members worried for the man's well-being, but they couldn't simply yank a corrupted djinn back into the light. He needed to find his own way. Unfortunately, he stumbled once or twice returning home. The whole purpose behind designating a being as a balance keeper is to ensure someone protects the existence of freewill up until the point it is destructive to the larger community we reside in. Haroun does that very well. I think it's time these returned to their original owner."

"How could they possibly be returned to a man who died centuries ago?"

"We both know he is very much alive. I'd argue he lives more now than he ever did." Michael removed his glasses and placed them on the table. "I tracked the Left Hand for six months before he received the order to kill Richard and Saladin. Bastard even knocked me out the night he lost that smaller medallion you're holding. I ripped it from his neck in that squabble. Your husband's a good man, Grace."

"Who exactly are you?"

Michael grinned. "I am surprised you haven't guessed already. Let's just say Rayne's former brethren conceal his identity. One of the Vatican staff surfaced these, along with that statue of Dante, to cause havoc. That staff member is no longer employed here."

"You fired them?" Grace wondered what a human had to gain exposing the Horsemen.

"Terminated is the better word. She had more in common with Lucifer than God."

"Don't tell me you now are going to claim demons exist?" Grace maintained the pretense of not knowing what he talked about as she tried to figure out which immortal stood before her.

"When war arose in the heavens, the angels fought against the ancient serpent, the great deceiver. I threw Lucifer and his minions down to earth; casting them out on behalf of the Council. Onore e gloria, for I once donned the black and gold."

Hearing the Horsemen's battle cry, she realized the one original Horseman that married, retired, and then disappeared into history stood before her. "Never thought a Horseman would give up the sword for the pen."

"We are all well-read men, Defensore. It really isn't that unusual a fit. Not to mention it allows the Council to keep the Church from getting too close to our world. Now, take those to Sasainn, so they can't reappear in the future."

Grace worried about the one artifact she didn't see. The one that risked exposing Rayne more than these others did. "May I have the journal?"

"There is no journal. I made that story up to entrap Dr. Blackburn and force who she worked for from her lips. Isra really went out of her way to put pressure on Rayne, so he'd return home."

"Dr. Blackburn isn't a djinn or immortal. I would have sensed that. How is she tied to Isra?"

"She was a human employee, paid a small fortune to work as Isra's eyes and ears here in Rome. She made the mistake of asking Isra for immortality about two weeks ago. I always suspected there was more to our latest fellow's interest in the Crusades. When I saw the statue of Dante, then you and Rayne at the presentation, along with the surprise addition of the Crusades lecture, I knew she most likely worked for Isra or Rodrigo. Once you showed up here digging into the Left Hand of

God, and Ibelin shared that Dr. Blackburn failed to submit your background check paperwork as required, that confirmed my suspicions. Ibelin notified Rayne of your being at the Vatican to prevent you from accidentally discovering anything Dr. Blackburn could pass on to Isra. Word of the chaos in Spain the past few weeks reached Rome, prompting Ibelin and me to cut off Isra's snooping. We figured you and Rayne didn't need a larger mess to deal with."

"You sent the note and article, not Ibelin."

Michael smiled again. "Dante warned me you would start putting things together quickly once you realized who I was."

"Well, at least he gave you an accurate warning. He told me you were a nerdy, awkward academic who seemed like they were too into reading philosophy."

Michael shook his head and loudly laughed at how Dante described him. "Perhaps, the god would learn a thing or two if he picked up a book every now and then."

"We both know he can't read anything without pictures." Grace made Michael chuckle.

"While I've enjoyed meeting you, Grace, unfortunately, I have another meeting in about fifteen minutes that I need to prepare for."

Grace picked up the box in front of her. "Thank you, Michael. Rayne owes you one."

"No, Grace. I've owed him for several centuries now." Michael grinned, setting the two swords on top of the box. "When you see Rayne, tell him destiny saves us all from bondage if we maintain a grateful heart and follow our rightful course."

THIRTY-EIGHT

Sasainn

Rayne still slept soundly when Grace returned to Sasainn. She quietly opened the safe to put the letters and jeweled cross in it. Once Rayne woke, she'd let him decide what to do with the rest of the stuff.

A pink and green amulet shimmered up at her from the bottom of the box. She hadn't noticed it while at the Vatican. The silver and stone design didn't seem to fit in with the red and black assassin's motif. Grace picked it up. Pain seared through her arm. She tried to drop the amulet to stop the burning traveling through her, but magic kept it stuck fast in her hand.

There's one last secret Rayne has that the Fates forbid him to share. It is something you should know. Michael's voice sounded in her head.

Sasainn - Twenty-Two Years Earlier

Three days after the first battle in Alexandria, Sean summoned the

Horsemen to Morrigan's library. The goddess paced the floor. Rayne and Dante exchanged worried glances.

"I know we are short a Horseman. However, I must dispatch you once more. The Hasan burned a village in Algeria this morning. The Council advised there is a mutilated human prisoner the Hasan left behind a short ways from the village. I need one of you to escort me to evaluate them. The Council wishes the prisoner to be saved, if at all possible. The other two of you are to track Rasil and Qasim. If the opportunity to apprehend either Hasan Officer presents itself, you must take it. The Council does not care if you capture the men alive or kill them."

Dante dispatched his first orders as Horsemen Commander. "Rayne, War is the best one suited to escort a High Council member into Hasan territory. Michael and I will track down Rasil and Qasim, but we will hold any capture attempts until you are with us. Once Morrigan and this human reach a safe haven, contact me, so we may regroup accordingly."

Algeria -

Rayne and Morrigan journeyed south of the Saharan village. A hooded council harbinger sat beside a body in the sand. The stench of death lingered in the air. Rayne loathed how part of him could still so easily identify that unpleasant odor. Sean stood at the top of an adjacent dune, keeping a look out for Hasan soldiers.

Morrigan approached the human. "Are they still alive?"

"Barely. I sustained her the best I could until you got here." The harbinger pulled back his hood.

Few things shocked Rayne like the face of the harbinger did. "Raphael? How is this possible?"

"The Council held one last task for me." Raphael nodded toward the human. "I will cross over once it is complete."

Rayne quietly cursed in djinn as his eyes traveled the length of the human. The woman's bloodied back and the blistered skin on her shoulder horrified him. He noted the weak trembling of her body.

Sweat, blood, and sand co-mingled in her knotted hair. The swelling and bruising of the cheek facing them prevented the woman from opening her eye completely. What had she done to suffer this kind of treatment?

"With the severity of her wounds, I am surprised you kept her alive. I will do what I can." Morrigan half wondered if she could save the human. She sat in the sand next to Raphael to get a better look at the festering gashes. "Rayne, get her to drink this while I heal her back."

Rayne moved to the front side of the woman. "What language does she speak?"

Raphael handed Rayne the vial of potion they needed her to drink. "English."

Rayne removed the cork from the bottle then knelt down beside her. By the slight shifting of her head, she tried to identify who joined her and Raphael. "Do not be frightened. I mean you no harm. I know it may be difficult, but you need to drink this. It will ease the pain."

"Let me die."

Rayne, Morrigan, and Raphael exchanged glances after hearing the barely audible words. She repeated the request once more.

Morrigan looked over at Rayne. *Disregard her wishes. She needs to live.*

Rayne carefully lifted her head and placed the vial to her cracked lips. "What a strange thing to ask of someone trying to help you."

"If anyone tells him they saw you helping me, he will come back. It is better you let me die. I can't go through this again." The woman winced.

Rayne wasn't sure if the wince was from taking in the bright sunlight when her non-swollen eye briefly opened or from his slow raising of her head. He did his best to be gentle with her.

"Whoever 'he' is will regret being stupid enough to confront me." Rayne drizzled a few drops of the healing elixir onto her tongue. Her lips didn't close nor did she show any signs of wanting to fight to survive any longer. "You allow him to win by giving up. Do not grant him an undeserved victory. Have courage, you no longer face him alone."

Once more, her good eye slightly opened and she let out a troubled sigh.

Rayne took that as a positive sign. "Please, drink for me, sweeting. "

She finally swallowed, bringing a smile to Rayne's face. "That's it. Only a few more sips to go."

She continued watching him as she obediently drank the bitter medicine.

Morrigan removed her own cloak and wrapped it around the woman after the woman's back was mostly healed. "We need to find someone who will take her in."

"Diego can shelter her," Raphael suggested, aggravating Morrigan.

"The slave trader? Has death caused you to lose your senses?"

Raphael smiled reassuringly at the goddess. "Diego will not trade her. His home is miles from here. Qasim will never suspect she survived if she takes shelter in Morocco. If we leave her in a nearby safe house, we risk drawing attention to her."

"We risk the same sending her to Morocco. The Hasan have officers and agents in Marrakesh just as they do here."

"Yes, mia dea. But there are many more Hasan here. And the people in Algeria fear Qasim and Rasil to a greater extent than those in Morocco who have rebelled against the Hasan. She is safer in Marrakesh, and hiding her in Diego's house prevents any suspicion arising about a European woman appearing in the area. People will assume she is part of a new slave lot."

"The Romans do not treat slaves well, Raphael. I watched what your kinsmen did to the tribes in Britain." Morrigan recalled how the Romans had treated her and those she watched over. "If further harm befalls her in Morocco—"

"You can send a Horseman to retrieve her." Raphael cut Morrigan off. "However, I can assure you that will not be necessary if we explain her status to Diego."

"What exactly is her status, Fiore?" Rayne interjected. It wasn't often Raphael openly argued with Morrigan, nor did the Council routinely send the Horsemen and Morrigan on rescue missions to save only one mortal.

Morrigan sternly stared at Rayne; her expression conveying the reason for saving the woman was none of his concern. The goddess shook her head before speaking again. "She most likely won't survive the ride to Morocco."

Raphael took Morrigan's hand in his. "She will survive. Dante sending Rayne as escort ensures she does. It's the least we can do for her."

Not liking how Raphael phrased things, Rayne frowned. "That almost sounds prophetic, Raphael."

"It is. The Council identified her as a potential officer candidate. She is descended from one of the immortal houses. You, being the one sent, confirms she's indeed the one they seek," Raphael disclosed the woman's destiny, angering Morrigan. "Furthermore, the human obtained insider information on the Hasan for Morrigan and me."

"That was not to be shared with anyone," Morrigan reproached the commander defying Council directives.

Raphael shrugged. "You are about to ask him to take her to Diego. He has the right to know why the Council would extend protection and aid to her."

Rayne glanced down at the human woman now peacefully sleeping. "What else is the Council hiding that they want me to deliver her to Morocco? This is normally a duty Dante as commander would carry out."

Raphael grinned. Rayne had every right to be suspicious. It was an odd request. "War is the better Horseman to deliver her to her new home. You are a more experienced and cautious fighter than Dante. You will resist any temptation to engage the Hasan should they cross your path. And if you are ambushed, Morrigan and I know you will find a way to evade your attackers. Dante is vengeful at the moment. He would want to fight them instead of ensuring the woman doesn't fall back into Hasan hands. We can't risk that. Tell Diego Marcus sends the woman to him. She is never to be enslaved and is to be nursed back to health. Remind him to remember our discussion in Gaul."

"You need to get going. A Hasan rider heads this way," Sean called down to the trio.

Rayne debated how best to pick up the human with the severity of her injuries.

"The potion should prevent any pain from your handling of her." Morrigan placed a reassuring hand on his arm. "May the gods protect you on your journey."

Morrigan laid down in the sand and transformed her appearance to that of the mortal. The Hasan rider would find a lifeless corpse once they arrived.

Rayne carefully slid his arms underneath the human. "You must be something special for the Council to fool the Hasan like this."

"Raphael," She muttered after Rayne lifted her from the ground.

"Shhh, ragazza. Rest." Rayne mimicked Raphael's voice, hoping she would drift back to sleep.

Raphael and Sean assisted Rayne with settling her in the saddle while Rayne mounted. The woman's head fell back onto Rayne's shoulder. Sean stepped away from Fahkir, giving Rayne room to leave.

Raphael looked up at Rayne. "She should sleep the entire way. Stop for nothing until you reach Diego's home."

Rayne sadly nodded; this was most likely the last time he'd see Raphael. "Take care of yourself, Fiore."

"I will greet you at the gate when it is your turn, Rayne. Let us hope that is centuries away. Onore e gloria, Captain."

"Morrigan Victoria, Commander," Rayne finished the Horsemen's battle cry, hating that he bid Raphael a final farewell and hoping nothing interfered with his delivering the woman to Morocco.

Morocco - 315

Rayne rode up to the reddish gold gates of Diego's Moroccan manor.

"State your business, sir," One of the gatemen nervously said, staring up at Rayne.

"I have an urgent message that is for Diego's ears only."

An older guard walked towards them, eyeing the cloaked figure in the Horseman's arms. "What kind of message?"

"The kind requiring a Council Harbinger to deliver it."

The man paled and directed the other guard to alert Diego of a High Council Harbinger being at his door. After giving the younger guard a minute to reach the house, the older guard waved Rayne through the gates.

Diego emerged in the doorway of his home, puzzled by the hooded man holding an unconscious woman. "What trouble do you bring to my door, rider?"

"Marcus sends me. You are to give the woman shelter for as long as she requires it."

The harbinger's request surprised the Spaniard. "After all these years, Marcus Furius asks I honor our strange agreement? Bring her this way."

Rayne followed Diego inside the house to a room tucked away off the main wing.

Diego opened the room door. "Tell Marcus she will be well cared for. You may lay her there."

Rayne settled the woman on the crisp white sheets of a freshly made bed.

"Clean her and find her some fresh clothing," Diego directed one of his house slaves. "Do you require refreshment or a room yourself, Harbinger?"

"No. Once she is settled, I will be leaving." Rayne watched one of Diego's servants remove Morrigan's cloak to bathe the woman then turned his attention to Diego. He wanted to be certain the slave trader understood he wasn't being gifted a new slave. "The Council decrees that she is not to ever be traded or sold. She is a free woman, not a slave or servant."

Diego almost laughed at the immortal's words. "Do you think me a fool? She is a Hasan escapee by the mark on the back of her shoulder."

"What mark?" Rayne hadn't seen any distinctive markings on her.

The two men walked over to the bed together. Diego pushed aside the wide neck of the fresh gown his servants pulled over her. "This one."

Disgust swept over Rayne. A brand scarred a crescent moon and star into the woman's flesh. The poor woman tangled with Rasil. He was the only Hasan officer in North Africa who did such hideous things. Rayne lightly brushed his fingers across the moon, trying to remove it with a healing spell. While it faded, he could not make it disappear. "She is not an escapee. This is the traitor's mark, given to one who betrays the Hasan and is cast out of the organization."

Diego pulled the gown up over her shoulder. "Regardless of what it means, it promises harsh punishment for anyone who aids her."

"The brand can be concealed by clothing. The scarring should make her self-conscious about undressing or bathing before anyone. Outside of us and whoever branded her, no one will know she has it." Rayne stared down at the human. What had given her the courage to challenge a monster like Rasil? Anguish tore through him as the potion finished its work and her facial features normalized. While she was younger than the woman who appeared on the Watchtower, they were one and the same. He'd kill Rasil for so severely torturing her. "Marcus trusts you to care for the woman. That is the only reason she is being left with you. Do not disappoint the Council. I need to speak with her privately, then must go."

Diego nodded and waited for Rayne by the door.

"Ragazza?" Rayne used Raphael's voice as he gently woke her.

"I tried to stop him, Raphael."

"You did well, cara. The Horsemen will take things from here. You never told me your name."

"I didn't?" His words seemed to confuse her. "Waheeda. That is what they all called me."

"What they called you? Do you not remember your birth name?"

"I am sorry. I can't remember it right now. Things are jumbled. My head hurts. Everything hurts."

"It isn't important. Rest, then focus on recovering, cara. I am leaving you in the care of a friend of mine."

She opened her mouth to say something else to him.

"Shhh, ragazza. We will speak more when our paths cross again. Go back to sleep, so your body and mind heal." Rayne passed his hand downward over her face. Her head fell to the side after Somnus claimed her once more. He brought her hand to his lips and prayed the Fates would keep her safe. *I look forward to our next meeting after you are recovered, my countess.*

The intimate gesture surprised Diego. Harbingers seldom showed any attachment to those they helped. What entanglement brought together a human, a Horseman, and a Roman veteran like Marcus?

Rayne slowly lowered the hand he held and gently settled it on her stomach. He stood, then briskly passed Diego, only pausing briefly in the doorway before exiting the room. "The Council will send further instructions to you about her care."

Continuing down the hall, Rayne reported to Dante that he was on his way to rendezvous with him and Michael.

Diego followed him to the front door. "I do not want to be caught in the middle of whatever feud exists between Morrigan and Rasil."

"You do not have a choice in the matter. Keep the woman safe at all costs." Rayne did not look back as he walked out the front door. Harbingers were required to be distant from those they engaged with. It ensured mortal compliance with Council instruction.

"If he finds her here..."

A blond-haired man dressed in twenty-first century clothing stood outside and interjected himself into the conversation. "Rasil won't know she is here. The Council sent me to ensure of that."

"How can the Council send a slave I purchased last week? And what are you wearing? Where are your proper garments?" Diego scoffed at one of his recent acquisitions.

The man rolled his eyes. "Because they knew she'd be brought here. Give the powers that be some credit."

Rayne had never met the man that claimed to be a Council servant. "You are?"

"Christian. I won't be answering any further questions, Captain. You will have to place faith in my abilities to shield her."

Rayne swung into the saddle and stared down at the two men. "I question the High Council's wisdom to entrust such a precious asset to two unworthy men like yourselves."

Christian chuckled. "I am certain we are only temporary caretakers."

"We better be," Diego muttered under his breath.

Empathetic to the Spaniard's concerns, Rayne smiled. "Rest assured, Diego, if trouble with the Hasan comes, the Council will send reinforcements to you. Pray it is not the Horsemen who appear on your doorstep. We tend to be omens of ill fate." He turned Fahkir then rode out the gates, toward the horizon and twilight desert sky.

"That is what worries me!" Diego shouted, watching Rayne ride off.

Once the Horseman disappeared from sight, he motioned for Christian to come inside.

Sasainn -

"Grace! Answer me!"

A frantic tapping of fingers against her face brought her back to consciousness. She stared up into the worried eyes of her husband. "You were in the desert with Morrigan and Raphael."

Rayne wondered how hard she hit her head when she fainted. "What?"

"Michael said to tell you destiny frees us all from bondage, if we maintain a grateful heart and follow our rightful path."

"Michael? Michael has not had contact with the Horsemen in centuries. He disappeared after retiring."

"He's at the Vatican. Michael is the strange man we saw the night of the earthquake."

She wrapped an arm around Rayne's neck.He slowly brought her upright into a sitting position. His helping her flashed a similar shared moment before Grace. "Why did you not tell me it was you who delivered me to Diego's? Why'd you let me believe Diego and some Bedouin found me and brought me to his home?"

"I never told you because I thought it didn't matter much in the grand scheme of things. The High Council was very clear in their direction to limit your knowledge of the Horsemen at the time. The Bedouin story more than explained how you ended up in Marrakesh. You've never questioned it before today." Rayne noticed the amulet a few feet away. "Prompting erased memories? No wonder you passed out. Where did you get this?"

"It was in the box with the things from the Vatican."

"What box?"

"The one on the dresser. Next to the safe."

Rayne frowned, then went to investigate whatever box "Michael" had supposedly given her.

Grace heard him curse as he discovered the two swords she brought home. The way he picked up the one with the broader blade and ornate hilt confirmed he once wielded it. He brushed his thumb across the blade's edge. Surprise softened the initial skepticism and irritation painted across his face. She could almost hear him say *it's still sharp*, even though he never uttered the phrase. She watched him carefully set the sword down then rummage through the box. A second stunned expression covered his face as he pulled out something small.

"I'll be damned. Michael truly did meet with you." Rayne grinned, still not believing Michael revealed his location after all this time. Michael had sworn he wanted nothing to do with immortal military affairs once he removed the Horsemen's laurels from his collar.

Curious, Grace looked over his arm to see what he held. A gold coin about the size of a quarter rested in the palm of his hand. "An officer's coin? Dante used to carry one. I only saw it once after a guard gave it to Tamir in Damascus."

"A Horsemen's coin. Each one minted to be distinctive to the man who owns it. They confirm the legitimacy of unexpected or questionable orders that we may dispatch to a peer." He handed the coin to Grace. "Each Horseman is issued one. I seldom use mine, but always carry it."

Grace smiled as she studied the face of the coin. An imprint of the Horsemen's laurels made up the rounded border. Four horses and riders rested in the center. She flipped the coin over. An angled sword with the tip plunging downward overlaid ancient scales. The sword's tip disappeared into a serpent along the lower circular edge. "Did Michael really toss Lucifer out of the High Council meetings?"

"A few times." Rayne chuckled, recalling a meeting or two where Michael and Raphael dragged Lucifer out of the High Council round after Lucifer denounced the Council. "They banned him from ever rejoining their ranks after he sidetracked me and used me to attack the Horsemen in Malaca."

Dante watched Rayne in the stables as Rayne tended to the horses for the night. Fahkir snorted at Dante as he approached, giving away his presence.

Rayne patted Fahkir's neck, then set down the feed bucket in his hand. "What brings you to Sasainn this evening?"

"I wanted to check on you after the events of the day."

Rayne locked Fahkir's stall door in place. "We both know you aren't here because you are worried about my well-being."

Fahkir stuck his head over the door; his ears turned forward, his dark eyes watching the two immortals.

Dante walked over to the stall and rubbed behind Fahkir's ear. The gelding tilted his head toward Dante and closed his eyes. Fahkir and Vittore always loved when anyone stroked that spot. "Isra waking the enforcer makes polite discourse with you challenging lately."

"The enforcer and the Horseman have little patience for false concern. Why are you really here?"

"You need to stop alienating Grace. All you are doing is driving her to find various ways to disregard your wish for her to stay away from Isra. You have greater odds defeating Isra and Malik if you allow Grace to assist you."

"I am protecting my wife by removing her from whatever is going on."

"Isra cannot hurt her."

"You would be surprised by the harm Isra can do when she puts her mind to it."

"Rayne, I, of all people, understand the urge to protect Grace. She was human when we fought the Hasan. Anything could have killed her back then. Every day I took her into Qasim's camp or fortress, every night we spent at risk in Rome, fear and concern plagued me, especially once she conceived Tarquin. At the same time, I knew I needed her there. Fighting beside one another was the only way to defeat Qasim and Gaelin. Just as you need her to overcome this fight with Isra and Malik."

"I do not need my wife to defeat Isra. And you conveniently forget there were several times you locked Grace up somewhere to keep her away from whatever mission we undertook or ensured she had, as I recall your words, a well-armed guard of your choosing with her."

Dante scoffed. "Who was frequently the well-armed guard I left with her?"

Rayne shot Dante an annoyed glare, but said nothing.

"There was a purpose in my entrusting her to you when I wasn't there. And that purpose was more than War being the High Council Balance Keeper."

"Your purpose, or rather yours and Raphael's, was to fulfill an agreement made with the Council that I had no knowledge of."

Dante laughed now. "You, il mio amico, may not have been privy to that particular accord, but you have known since becoming a Horseman you would one day guard the moon. The Fates never concealed the face of your countess."

"No, they didn't. They gave her to you instead."

"Because you fought destiny, Rayne, telling everyone at every opportunity you were a man of war and had no room in your life for a wife or family. You weren't willing to welcome her into your world. Suspicion filled your gaze anytime you set eyes upon her those first few months. It wasn't until the night you demanded to know about the serpent in Damascus that you truly started the journey to her." Dante briefly smiled, recalling that night. "She was so flustered by the things she saw and what she felt when you touched her. I should have known then the two of you were meant to be more to one another." He paused, thinking about how oblivious he had been as a Horseman.

"You weren't naïve, Dante. You were infatuated. The Fates could have clocked us both over the head with the truth that same night and neither of us would have welcomed their news." Rayne slowly let out the breath he inhaled. "Just as I am resisting your guidance now. She's already endured more than her fair share. I simply can't stand the idea of her possibly suffering more when it can be prevented."

"She feels the same way when it comes to you. Welcome her to stand at your side. The two of you aligned are stronger than the two of you divided. Grace has already outwitted Isra once."

"Dante, I do not doubt Grace at all. With the two of us refining her combat skills, she is a formidable opponent for any immortal or human."

"Then why do you refuse her assistance?"

Unwilling to engage in conversation any longer, Rayne walked away.

Dante now realized why Rayne most likely kept Grace at a distance. "What haven't you told her?"

By the way Rayne's step faltered, Dante knew Rayne harbored another secret he wasn't ready to share with his wife.

THIRTY-NINE

Córdoba - 812

After two weeks of quiet, fighting broke out across Córdoba. Demon, djinn, and humans ransacked the city. Malik sent Saladin to Granada the previous day on a diplomatic mission then the caliph disappeared himself. None of his viziers knew where he had gone. With the mayhem in Córdoba, Grace suspected Isra intentionally made sure the two humans who could stop it weren't present. Rayne mustered the Horsemen to halt the rioting.

Grace didn't like that he did. "Why call for the others? We can suppress this small a conflict."

"This has all the hallmarks of an ambush." Rayne sensed a threat to his family. "Have you had any visions or dreams lately?"

"None that are concerning. Why?"

"No particular reason." The trepidation Rayne felt became almost unshakable. He reminded himself that his gift was not one of foresight, but of battle. If Grace had no visions, his personal fears interfered with his instincts.

Grace grabbed the hilt of the sword he secured on his waist to get his attention. "What have you dreamt?"

"I am not a visionary as you are." Rayne brushed her hand off his weapon so he could adjust it.

"You see individuals' fates."

"I see their past and their sins, Grace."

"You see more than that. Has the ruby warned you of something?"

Destahn, Tamir, and Raphael joined them.

Rayne nodded, acknowledging their arrival before responding to Grace. "No, leof. Mayhap, I fret about nothing."

"We promised no more secrets. Tell me what you dreamt." She stepped closer to him, trying to read the thoughts he hid.

"It was only a dream. Do not worry about trifling matters."

Destahn noted Grace's knitted brow and the intent way she stared at Rayne with wide eyes. "Save yourself an argument, Rayne. Let Grace interpret whatever this dream was."

Rayne's lips compressed into a tight line, then relaxed as he exhaled, giving into Grace and Destahn's request. "Destruction, as I have not seen in centuries. Isra's wrath unleashed on Córdoba and Granada. I don't know when or how. Nor could I see if good prevails."

"Sounds like a glimpse of the future to me if you can't see the outcome. What say you, Defensore?" Destahn looked at Grace for confirmation.

Grace took Rayne's hand and viewed the violent images in Rayne's subconscious. "I am at a loss with this one, Destahn. I honestly can't tell if this is a warning or an imaginary event Rayne fears. Dark visions such as this can be completely false. To be safe, you four stop the hostilities in town. I will ride out with Xander and Ares to ensure none of Isra's minions hide within your father's ranks to cause trouble in Granada."

"If you prefer, I can go with Grace instead." Raphael offered to serve as her guard.

"The Horsemen are needed with their commander. He and Córdoba are the bigger targets." Grace declined Raphael's offer.

Lyal strolled into the room. "The Ancients watch over the Moon. Entrust your wife and children to my care. The Council sends me as harbinger, Commander. Your orders are to put down Isra and all of her supporters. No quarter should be extended to Isra. She overstepped her boundaries instigating the civil unrest this morning. You are free to exercise discretion in determining who should be spared and who should die."

Rayne hated that things escalated to the point the Horsemen confronted Isra under official orders. "So, the dream is foresight, not fear."

Lyal nodded, confirming he understood the motivation behind the Council's message.

Grace reassuringly squeezed Rayne's hand. "The Fates sent warning. We will stop Isra's plotting."

Rayne smiled down at Grace before kissing her. "Prevent the spread of the fighting, leof." He signaled the Horsemen to mount up. "More importantly, be vigilant, and come home to me."

"I will return to you as soon as I can."

Grace followed the four outside. Watching them ride through the gates then turn towards town, she reflected on the events of the past several weeks. Isra's obsession with reclaiming Rayne to do whatever she plotted ensured her downfall. The Council certainly had enough of everything to issue a death warrant for her. All that was left to do was for Grace and the Horsemen to find a way to kill Isra without harming Rayne. Hopefully, the Horsemen would capture the overseer today.

Shaking off her thoughts, Grace went to the stable. She might be fighting her own battles tonight if Isra planned to make an attempt on Saladin or Granada. Diya's head protruded over her stall door.

"Sorry, girl. You are going to have to sit this one out. Unfortunately, I need Vittore tonight." Grace offered the chestnut horse a treat from the treat bucket. Velvety lips gently whisked the homemade cookie of ground oats and molasses from Grace's palm.

Hearing someone rummaging in the treat bucket, Vittore moved to the front of his stall and whickered.

Grace looked over at the large black horse. She was glad she had the stallion brought to Cordoba a few days ago in case they needed him for any reason. "All right, you unruly beast. I suppose you can have one too, especially since I need you to get me to Granada tonight."

Vittore let out a second soft whicker as Grace got his treat. "If you're good, you might even get an apple when we get back. But that requires the evening to be hijinks free. No dumping me off in a pond or any joyrides through whatever briar patch or clump of trees you find interesting."

He tossed his head a few times after Grace put his bridle on, as if telling her to hurry up. He was ready to go, and she was taking too long. Once she was in the saddle, Dante's old mount eagerly trotted out the stable door.

Grace couldn't help smiling while thinking of old times as Vittore danced in place after she halted him in the courtyard.

"Behave for me today, big guy, and that apple is all yours." Grace patted the horse's neck.

Xander patiently waited for her by the gates. "Things must be bad if you chose this monster over Diya."

"He's faster than she is, and we have a lot of ground to cover with Saladin leaving yesterday. Where is Ares?"

"Zeus delays his departure. He will meet us later," Xander advised before turning into a wolf to follow Grace. "We should be able to intercept Saladin before he reaches Granada. then find the djinn and any human stupid enough to take the bribes Isra offered within his envoy. You have the harder task of convincing Saladin to return to Córdoba early. His presence here will help prevent any more fighting."

***

Olympus -

Zeus, Ares, Theseus, and Dante stood around a portal and watched Xander and Grace set out for Granada. As soon as the Council dispatched the Horsemen's latest orders, Ares sought out Dante and Zeus, since neither attended the meeting.

Disappointed, Dante shook his head and folded his arms. "Vittore being her mount tells me all I need to know. We shall heighten the guard around Elysium."

Zeus started at Dante's statement. "Isra is not foolish enough to attack the domain of multiple gods."

"She is stupid enough to go after Rayne in my home. The risk of her attempting to abduct the children is real. We take measured precautions to ensure that does not occur." Dante hesitated, thinking through his next words carefully, mindful of the things they could provoke. "We should perform a sweep of Hades's ranks to ensure none of them changed loyalties. Hades did side with Isra when she produced the fraudulent contract until I challenged its validity."

The accusation against Hades disconcerted Zeus. "Hades would not mix himself up in this. Xander would also be recalled if Hades aided Isra."

"Zeus, I no longer trust your brother after his recent actions against myself and the Warwicks. One of us needs to keep an eye on him."

Theseus interceded before things escalated between Dante and Zeus. "I agree with Giovanni, and will handle the review of Hades's minions."

"Grazie. If you'll excuse me, I need to tend to the defense of my home." Upon reaching Elysium, Dante headed for his bedroom to retrieve his sword. He would be damned if he was caught off guard again.

Spain - 812

Grace saw her father-in-law and his men a short distance ahead. "Saladin!"

Hearing his name, Saladin halted his ranks; allowing her to catch up with them. "Grace, what are you doing so far from Córdoba unescorted?"

"You must not go to Granada. Divert course to Lucena."

"I am to meet with the Grand Councilor of Granada, Grace. I cannot ignore such an invitation."

Grace understood the difficult position she placed the man in. "Rayne sends me to you. You must dispatch a message that you are delayed a day or so due to ill health. Assassins await your arrival in Granada. Isra plans to start a war between Córdoba and Granada. Rayne is dismantling her ranks in Córdoba. If you ride ahead, her minions will capture you, and she will ransom you to force Rayne to free the troops he has in custody."

Saladin looked in the direction of Granada. "You are certain of this?"

Ares yanked one of Saladin's soldiers off his horse and tore open the man's shirt, revealing a damned souls tattoo on the man's chest. "This emblem means this one serves an ifrit. Proof enough for you, Saladin?

"Ares!" Grace snapped at the god's brash behavior.

Ares ignored her, still holding the struggling soldier. "How much did Narciso buy you for?"

"I, I, I," The man stammered, unsure what to think of the god, "swear, Saladin, I would never betray the House of Ibn-Ziyad. This man is a djinn himself with the way he appears from nowhere."

A furious glare replaced the surprise on Saladin's face.

"He isn't a djinn," Grace said, giving Ares a reprimanding stare for pulling the traitor out of Saladin's ranks as he did. "Try to use a little discretion, Ares. These are god-fearing people."

"I can assure you this one isn't." Ares pointed out another djinn riding amongst Saladin's men. "Nor is his companion over there."

Xander ripped the other rider Ares referenced from his horse. With the demon's hands on the man, the spell hiding the djinn disappeared. The Captain of Hades's guard dragged the being closer to Grace and Saladin, so the general turned diplomat could get a good look at what rode with him.

Grace studied the soldiers left around them. "Any others?"

"No. The rest await Saladin a mile or two outside Granada." Xander kept a firm grip on the creature wriggling in his grasp. "What do you want me to do with him, Grace?"

"Djinn fall under Hades's judgment, not mine."

"In that case..." Xander vanquished the djinn, spooking Saladin's men.

Grace heard the panic in the raised human voices around them. "Xander! What did I just tell Ares?"

The soldier Ares held captive screamed and begged Saladin to show him mercy. He confessed to taking the gold Narciso offered as Isra promised not to harm any of them. He would repent of his sins if only Saladin would let him live.

"Allah will judge you. In the meantime, pray for his forgiveness.

When we return to Córdoba, you must give the gold you took to the poor to cleanse the greed from your soul," Saladin said, then addressed his men. "The prophet warned us of the evil some djinn do. None of you should be frightened by their presence. Our faith and prayers protect us."

Once the murmuring slowed in his ranks, Saladin turned back to Grace. "How long must my illness last?"

"Only a day or so. Ares and Xander will go to Granada to dispatch Isra's djinn there. I will escort you to Lucena to ensure you reach it safely." Grace hoped the man would listen to her. With the beliefs of the age, she feared he would disregard the warning. She let out a sigh of relief when Saladin asked an officer he knew well to advise the Grand Councilor that he had fallen ill and would not reach Granada for another two days.

Ares swung up onto the horse the djinn had been riding. "We will ride with him to ensure he reaches Granada safely. Are you good escorting Saladin to Lucena alone?"

Grace nodded. "I can handle the escort."

Ares, Xander, and the officer departed.

"Nightfall is approaching. If we are to make it to Lucena before dark, we need to be going." Saladin turned his horse toward a fork in the road. "Never in all my days did I dream I would be under threat from an ifrit."

Grace understandingly smiled. "Your faith cautions to always be on your guard against evil djinn. I thought there was even a teaching that every person was born with a djinn companion."

"For a nonbeliever, you know a great deal about Islam."

"While I am not Muslim, I wouldn't say I am one without faith, especially after all I have seen."

Grace and Saladin conversed the entire ride to Lucena. Thankfully, the ride was an uneventful one. Dante waited outside the city gates on a white horse. Grace had to bite her tongue to keep from snapping at him. He shouldn't be there.

Dante greeted Grace first. "Lady Ibn-Ziyad, it is a pleasure to see you again. We are humbled to have you and your father-in-law visit our small city, even if it is only for a brief stay."

"Thank you for the warm welcome," Grace curtly acknowledged him.

Dante cordially smiled over at Saladin. "Saladin, it is good to see you arrived safely. I am a friend of your son's. Housing for you and your men has been secured. If you will follow me, the fortress you are staying in is a short ride from the gates."

"I appreciate your hospitality, sir." Saladin followed Dante and Grace through the gates.

"What are you doing?" Grace whispered to Dante when she really wanted to yell the question at him.

"With Rayne and the Horsemen protecting Córdoba, I figured you could use a hand. And before you ask, my mother tends to our children and Sean is supervising the guard at my house." Dante signaled the gatemen to close the gates behind them.

Grace noted how Saladin's brows rose overhearing Dante say 'our children.' "Lower your voice."

"Calma, cara. No one knows us well here."

His casually brushing off her concerns annoyed Grace. "Thank the gods for that with you riding a pale horse. If anyone recognizes you, they will fear Armageddon arrives."

Dante laughed. "I hadn't thought about the Death rides a pale horse verse."

"Of course you didn't. I have things well in hand. Go back to Elysium."

"Not until you and Saladin are safely behind closed doors."

Saladin watched Grace argue with their escort. He didn't need to hear their conversation to understand the two fought. Their body language and the irritated expression on Grace's face broadcast the disagreement to anyone observing them. Once they reached the Castello del Moral, a large cream-colored stone fortress in the heart of the medieval city, the escort who aggravated his daughter-in-law departed.

That evening, their host, Hasdai Ibn-Nagrela, offered Saladin and his men an array of local foods for dinner. A servant sat a plate of trout cooked in an orange sauce with large chunks of fresh orange before Grace, along with a small bowl of saffron rice with carrots, figs, pomegranate, and pistachios mixed in. It always amazed her how such simple ingredients with the right spices could create the most wonderful dishes, delighting the palate in the various times and places she traveled too.

She noticed Hasdai spoke in Hebrew to one of the men on his left. "Vizier, you speak Hebrew?"

Pleasantly surprised by her recognition of the language, Hasdai smiled. "Yes, Lady Ibn-Ziyad. Many of us in Lucena do. Most that live in this city are Jewish. Lucena is home to the best Talmudic schools in all of Al-Andalus."

Fascinated by the fact that the community was primarily Jewish in contrast to Córdoba or Granada, she hoped Hasdai would share more of the town's unique culture. "Please, tell me more about Lucena."

Hasdai proudly shared the city's history and went into detail about the thriving trades practiced in the area.

Once she finished her meal and had spent enough time at the table to be considered a polite guest, Grace excused herself to double check the patrol stationed on the walls. She wanted to learn more about the men guarding the property. After speaking with several men and walking the walls herself, she returned to the main hall.

Most of Saladin's men still engaged in after-dinner activities. Grace sat down at the head table beside Saladin to enjoy some dessert. Saladin nodded hello then silently sipped his tea across from her. She requested a glass of wine from a servant who walked by.

When the servant finished filing her cup, Saladin voiced an inquiry he had wanted to ask Grace for most of the evening. "Who was the man that escorted us?"

"No one of importance." Grace wished Dante let her handle this tasking alone.

Saladin placed one of the walnut cakes from the dessert tray before them on her plate then took one for himself. "I would think a man who uses the words 'our children' is someone of significance."

Grace stared down at the cake. Saladin expected her to offer some sort of response or her normal polite thank you for giving her the dessert, but she remained silent. Whoever the stranger was agitated the woman a great deal. "Why does he refer to your children as his own?"

"He is their guardian should something happen to Rayne and me." Grace partially told the truth. Technically, Dante was their appointed guardian. How in the hell was she going to explain things to Rayne's father?

Saladin took a bite of the pastry in his hand, staring thoughtfully at her. Once he swallowed the mouthful he had, he set the pastry down and reached for his tea. "Your first husband is very much alive, isn't he?"

"How did you...?"

"Only a wife or lover quarrels with a man the way you argued with our escort. I know you and Haroun are different."

Grace's head tilted sideways, her eyes briefly looked down at her wine again then back up at Saladin before she smiled. "Different is a nice way of putting it."

"Why did the two of you lie to me about your first husband?"

"We did not lie. Dante died fighting in Alexandria. As a reward for his valor, he was made a god. Those who made him one forbid him to see me until recently. They also forbade him from interfering in matters that don't threaten the immortal community. He should have never come here today."

"He comes to Spain twice now to assist you. He is the god from the morning Umar's body was discovered and the man with Tessa the evening I came to Rayne's home."

"Yes. He tracks Isra with Rayne more than assisting me, Saladin." She downplayed Dante's appearances.

"He loves my son as a brother, but must still love you as a wife to risk the wrath of the Almighty for violating whatever laws you immortals follow."

Grace didn't like what Saladin implied. "I love your son. Rayne has my full fidelity."

Saladin empathized with the situation she faced. "Having multiple spouses is challenging. Ensuring each are treated equally even more so."

Grace choked on the mouthful of wine she had. While Saladin's intentions were good, the last thing she needed was marital advice for managing multiple spouses. She only had one. Once she managed to swallow the wine, she tried to clarify things. "Our relationship is not the same as the one between you and your wives, Saladin. There is no requirement or law when it comes to polygamy in the immortal realm. Rayne is my only husband. Dante and I's marriage ended when he died.

Normally, when an immortal dies, they go to their version of the afterlife, just as a human would. Rarely do they become gods or return from the dead."

Xander sat down next to Grace. "Nor is there any other group of immortals who form the Triad as you, Rayne, and Dante do. Maybe you should listen to what Saladin has to say."

Grace shot him a sideways glance. "Aren't you supposed to be in Granada?"

"Our business is concluded there. As my presence is not welcome here, good night, Defensore." Xander disappeared.

She shook her head at Xander's exit. Overdramatic demon.

"What is this Triad he mentions?" Saladin wanted to better understand what his son had become.

How the Fates loved testing her! They pushed her to reconcile her two marriages, but now wasn't the time to do so. "The Triad is a trio of the sun, moon, and wolf that bears the responsibility of protecting humankind from evil much greater than Isra. Rayne, as the wolf, is the cornerstone and balance keeper of the group. I serve the Ancients that oversee the House of the Moon. Dante is the Guardian for the Ancients in the House of the Sun. There are those who very much believe the three of us are in a mystical marriage of sorts."

"But you do not believe this to be true?" Saladin processed what she shared.

"No. The Triad served its intended purpose. That purpose ended in Alexandria eleven years ago. The Four Horsemen are the true protectors of humanity, and I am an officer known as the Morte Defensore who assists them with that responsibility."

"As unorthodox as the Triad arrangement is, I think you are wrong, Grace. Both men care about you. If you favor Haroun, that is one thing, but if you deny this Dante his rights as a husband while bedding my son, punishment awaits you as it would me if I favored any of my wives."

"You favor Lillian. I see it anytime you look at her."

"Ah, but I do not neglect the others' security and welfare for hers."

"Good night, Saladin." Grace pushed her chair back from the table. She realized the man struggled to comprehend Rayne's and her world. He could only view it through the lens of his own.

"Grace, my new daughter, I do not mean to offend or upset you."

She smiled at her father-in-law. "You do not offend me, Saladin. There is too much occurring right now outside of my marital affairs which requires my attention. The greater good first. I can sort out my personal life later."

Exhausted, Grace left the great hall and climbed the spiraling stone staircase to find the guest room that was hers. A maid saw her in the hall and guided her to her temporary chambers.

"Do you need help preparing for bed, Lady Ibn-Ziyad?" The maid softly asked.

"I appreciate the kind offer, but can see to myself. Thank you." Grace smiled, grateful for the hospitality extended by their host and his staff.

After closing the door, Grace removed her cloak and set it on the small table along the side wall.

"As Saladin advised, you risk damnation denying both your husbands their marital rights." Dante teased, alerting her to his presence in the room.

She shook her head before turning towards him. He stood by the door in the Horsemen's armor and uniform.

"Let us pray War does not overhear such nonsense or Dead you will be once more."

"I think you meant Death, mia stella."

Grace laughed. "No, I meant dead. I'm surprised you still don't comprehend my husband has no patience for your shenanigans. What brings you back here?"

"The Council agreed to dispatch a guide unit to reinforce the human guard. I didn't want you worried when they arrive. You'll only hear from them if there is a reason for them to reveal themselves. We are also ensuring Hades's and his minions' loyalty to the Horsemen and you. I am going to Córdoba to help Rayne for a few hours before returning to Elysium. Would you like me to relay that you and Saladin arrived safely and are secure here?"

"Please do, and give him my love."

Dante rolled his eyes and placed a hand over his heart. "Forever tormented by the woman I love, loving another. Have mercy on me, Grace."

"I wasn't the one who swore to spend eternity as a sexually frustrated monk."

Dante loudly laughed, recalling the night he said that exact thing. "I never would have spoken that damn phrase had I known it would be a self-fulfilling prophecy."

"I find it hard to believe Casanova hasn't taken a lover all these years."

"Sadly, he hasn't since leaving his wife."

Grace snorted. "I doubt that."

He walked over to her, cupped her chin in his hand, then ran his thumb across her lower lip. "No other woman can satisfy me as my wife did."

"I've heard the rumor of a goddess who can."

"You should not listen to malicious gossip, cara. Oftentimes, it is spewed by petty and jealous individuals."

"Or ones told they were only one night's pleasure," she flippantly remarked.

Dante looked down at the floor.

"At least you have the humility to look embarrassed." By the tick in his cheek, she actually tweaked a nerve.

He stared her directly in the face again. "I was drunk, lonely, and grieving not being able to see my wife and son. Those factors significantly impaired my judgement. I regret that one night more than you will ever know."

His curt tone and upset expression startled her. "You don't have to justify anything to me, cavaliere. We aren't married any longer."

"Hearing you say that, hurts more than I ever imagined it could."

Grace disbelievingly shook her head. "Don't start going down that road, Dante. Not tonight."

"You are still my wife, Grace. We never divorced, and unlike humans, we do not say until death do we part. Our vows were in this lifetime and the next."

"Good night, Dante." She ended their conversation.

"Since you do not wish to speak any longer, sogni d'oro, cara." He gave her a stiff, but polite bow, then left her room.

Dante distractedly descended the stairs to the first floor. His thoughts swirled between irritation at how Grace now disregarded their marriage as if it were nothing and ensuring all plans to ensure her and the children's safety were in place. No one but Saladin noticed him as he skimmed along the wall rimming the crowded main hall then slipped out the front entrance. He continued on to the stables to retrieve the horse Theseus loaned him.

"When the vile stench of a High Council officer wafted on the wind, I didn't expect it to be that of a god." Narciso leaned against the stable wall.

Dante halted; a bit surprised to see the djinn after Ares trounced him earlier in the evening. "Due to your and Isra's mischief making, the Council placed Saladin under my protection. I go where he goes."

"Saladin?" Narciso laughed. "From what I hear, you are more concerned with Haroun's wife than Saladin tonight."

"She is a member of Saladin's entourage. It would be impolite to ignore the lady if she wishes to converse while we travel to Granada."

Coming towards Dante, Narciso smirked. "And was it polite conversation you two engaged in for you to be seen leaving her chambers at this hour or another activity you were once famous for?"

Dante maneuvered around Narciso. His arm encircled the djinn's throat. He flexed his bicep and forearm, tightening the suffocating headlock he kept Narciso in until the djinn swayed on his feet. "Haroun's wife is under my protection as well. You would be wise to remember that."

Narciso growled and struggled to get free, but Dante held him fast. All the djinn's flailing did nothing to dislodge Dante's vice-like grip. "Council members are forbidden from killing, god."

Dante coldly laughed, listening to Narciso choke and gag. "I am not a Council member. For a djinn claiming to know all I am famous for, you must then know I have a habit of being impulsive and disregarding orders if they inhibit my mission. I was also famous for cutting out the tongues of evil doers who defamed my character. Mayhap, I should remove yours?"

"Do so, and Isra will attack Elysium."

"Isra has too much to deal with here." Dante pulled his dagger then slammed it into Narciso's chest, forcing the djinn back to Hell for the night.

Angry that Narciso freely moved about Lucena, Dante called for the head of the Council guard. The guide immediately appeared. "Station two guards outside the Defensore's chamber doors and two more outside of Saladin's. There is an agent of Isra's or Narciso's amongst us. Search the house and city for them. Do it quickly and quietly to ensure we do not distress the humans or cause alarm in Lucena's militia or Saladin's ranks. When the agent is found, kill them."

"Yes, sir. What do you wish us to do if the agent is human and not djinn?"

"They won't be. Not for Narciso to come to Lucena in such a weakened state. And on the off chance they are, my orders are no different. A corrupted soul presents too much risk to the Council's desire to keep peace between the realms and their efforts to disempower Isra."

The guard's eyes widened at Dante wanting a human killed, but he wasn't about to question the former Horseman. The god understood Council laws much more than he ever would. "Shall I alert the Defensore if we locate Isra's agent?"

"No. You are to kill them immediately, then report only to me. The Council does not wish for the Defensore to become embroiled in the war Isra instigates. The Defensore needs plausible deniability should Rodrigo demand a meeting with her while she is within his territories. I am going to Córdoba to consult with Commander Warwick on matters, but will return before sunrise. Hopefully, you will have eliminated whatever traitor lurks in Lucena long before then."

CHAPTER

FORTY

Lucena - 812

Grace woke with a start. *What time was it?* She dressed then went downstairs to the main hall. Surprisingly, it was virtually empty. Saladin and his men would usually be up already if they were back in Córdoba. They all must have stayed up later than normal for only one man sat at one of the long tables eating. She stared out the window at the disappearing moon. The lightening of the night sky announced dawn's arrival.

"Is everything all right, Grazia?" Dante's voice made her jump. He sipped a cup of coffee, standing only a few feet from her. "I apologize. I did not mean to frighten you."

Seeing him with a cup of coffee in hand caused her to think about the many times she watched him drink his espresso as the sun came up in Essaouira. "What are you doing back in Lucena?"

"I promised Rayne I would look after things here this morning while he finishes calming the skirmish in Córdoba. Did you sleep well?" Dante held a cup of Moroccan mint tea out to her.

"For the most part." She accepted the warm glass. "Grazie for the

431

tea. But you really shouldn't be conjuring beverages that don't exist yet."

Dante chuckled. "Di nulla. And no one is awake enough to notice what we drink."

Grace sat down at the table closest to them. "I assume by your smile and coffee, the Horsemen and you quickly brought things back under control last night."

"Mostly. Rayne's expert negotiating and his showing how each adviser was being manipulated by an outside entity slowed the fighting amongst the humans. He is keeping an eye on two of the advisers and one of Malik's officers, who aren't happy with the truce put in place. The threat of tangling with the Horsemen and myself deterred most of Isra's djinn and demons from causing any more trouble. Narciso being the exception."

"Hopefully Rayne finds him before he can reignite things. I will try to convince Saladin to either return to Córdoba today or at least shorten his trip to Granada. That way, all we have to worry about are Isra and Malik. I am starving. I guess I need to find the kitchen, as it doesn't appear Hasdai is awake yet. They won't serve breakfast until he is."

Dante set a plate with sliced pear, fresh cheese, and figs on the table. "These should hold you over."

"No caramel apples?" She teased him about the morning he tried to convince her caramel apples were the perfect breakfast food. The hearty, deep laugh that came after her question made her smile.

"I save those for special occasions. You always preferred these to caramel apples."

"I am surprised you remembered that after all these years." Grace picked up a slice of pear.

"I remember many breakfasts you like. These, blackberry crêpes, strawberries in oatmeal, and egg white vegetable omelets were your go to breakfasts." Dante enjoyed the way she smiled again before eating her pear.

"All of which sound wonderful right now."

Grace found herself laughing as they continued talking and sharing the small breakfast platter. Dante certainly hadn't lost any of his charm or his sense of humor.

"Thank you, Dante. I needed to laugh with everything occurring." She looked down at the empty cup in her hand. Part of her wished she could read tea leaves with how they made woven patterns against the bottom of the glass.

"All will be well, stella. These recent troubles testing you and Rayne are only temporary."

"I pray you are right." She set the cup on the table.

The way her head bowed and she clasped her hands together told him she still worried. Her body language practically screamed he was wrong with the tense forward set of her shoulders. He set his hand on top of hers, pulling her out of the whirlwind of worries circling in her mind. "The gods hear your prayers. At least one is doing all he can to end your woes."

"I am forever grateful for that. Isra and Malik shouldn't be this complicated of a foe to beat. I don't understand—"

"Stop, Grace." Dante hated to see her doubting herself. "You and Rayne will overcome all of this. Do not dwell on matters out of your control any longer."

Grace drifted on familiar tides in gold pools the longer she stared into them. The quiet moment of vulnerability lured her to take refuge in the god as she had long ago. She quickly came to her feet to escape the intimacy redeveloping between her and Dante. "I need to ensure breakfast gets delivered to the men on the perimeter walls. They will be hungry after standing watch all night."

He gently caught her wrist. "Grazia, was I that awful a husband?"

"No, Dante. Other than the whole pact with the Council thing and a few Neanderthal moments, you were a very loving husband. Losing you was one of the most difficult things I have been through. Not wanting to ever go through that again is why I worry so much about Isra."

A bit surprised by her answer, Dante released her arm. "Isra cannot kill Rayne or you."

"I know she can't. But she keeps backing Rayne into very ugly corners he has to fight his way out of. Seeing the djinn my husband once was at times is concerning. I hate to think..." Grace refused to even utter what she feared most. The universe had a funny way of making utterances reality.

"You and the children keep him tied to good, cara."

"Is there any way Isra could override that tie?" She didn't like how Dante's brow shot up after the inquiry.

"Didn't you ask Theseus a similar question?"

"He doesn't know Rayne like you do."

"The only way Isra could turn him again would be by harming you or the children, and even that would never work in Isra's favor. Any action she took against you or Tessa and Tarquin would make Rayne a vengeful free agent instead of her minion. Rayne would want retribution. He would ensure Isra's death was a very slow, anguished one. Rayne, the enforcer, with or without a soul, is not a being I would ever want to find myself crossways with."

Ares suddenly standing by the table interrupted their discussion. "Rodrigo is at the city gates, demanding to speak with Saladin."

"If Saladin appears, no one will believe he is ill." Grace debated how to respond to Rodrigo.

Dante stared at Grace's uniform. The Defensore in full military dress would agitate an already annoyed overseer. "Are there gowns you could wear in the room you stayed in?"

"Yes."

"Put one of them on. We will send you to meet with Rodrigo."

"Rayne is going to be mad about this," Grace grumbled, but got up to do exactly what Dante suggested.

Dante grinned. Undoubtedly, Rayne would be mad, but they had no other choice if they wanted to maintain the farce of Saladin being ill. "He will understand. Besides, we aren't sending you out to face the overseer alone. Ares and I will be nearby you for as long as the meeting lasts."

A short time later, Grace returned to the dining hall in a period gown. Dante buckled a sword belt around her waist. "You really think it's wise for me to carry a weapon? Won't that provoke Rodrigo?"

"It isn't unusual for a woman of your standing to wear a sidearm during formal negotiations or travel through the countryside. You are also a Cordovan general's wife, and your husband descends from Umayyad and Imazighen with fierce female fighters in their family tree.

Just don't make any threatening move towards Rodrigo unless you need to defend yourself." Dante shifted the belt a bit more, so the ornate scimitar hung properly from her side.

"You better not be leading me astray." Grace had her doubts about his answer.

"I would never do such a thing, cara. We are merely giving Rodrigo a warning to act with caution and negotiate with respect. Now, let us go meet him before he does something rash."

Hasdai stood at the city gates with several other prominent citizens. Seeing Grace walking with the man sent to get Saladin, he hurried towards Ares. "You bring a woman instead of Saladin?"

"She is the better one to negotiate with Rodrigo," Dante answered for Ares.

"This is unwise. I realize you are a respected mercenary, Giovanni, but you know nothing of Andalusian politics or Rodrigo. Lucena is already in a precarious position due to it being a Jewish city. You risk all of our lives." Hasdai thought the Venetian mercenary who showed up at his home the day prior had lost his mind.

Grace hoped to placate Hasdai's fears; though part of her wondered if the man wasn't right in his assessment of the situation. "All will be well, Hasdai. We will not bring war to your door, and if, for some reason, I am wrong, the Army of Córdoba will protect you from Granada."

"The Army of Córdoba is not here!" Hasdai snapped at Grace.

"Open the gates!" Ares called to the gatemen. "Hasdai, trust us. We know what we do."

The man-at-arms near the gate looked at Hasdai for confirmation to do as requested. Hasdai muttered under his breath. His eyes briefly looked skyward. "May God go with you, Grace Ibn-Ziyad. You risk many lives this morning." Hasdai nodded to the guard by the gatemen. "Do as they ask."

Grace took a deep breath as the massive hinges on the wooden doors screeched. The guards and gatemen opened them just enough she, Ares, and Dante could pass through the gap between them. Archers stood on the walls along with men-at-arms who kept crossbows trained on Rodrigo. She calmly moved forward to greet the overseer. Dante and Ares remained a few feet behind her, formally recognizing her as the one sent to speak on Saladin's behalf.

The Spanish overseer smiled from atop of his horse. Unlike Narciso or Isra, Rodrigo looked human enough: elegantly dressed in brown, black, and gold garments, his dark hair under a velvet and feathered cap, carefully groomed and trimmed sideburns led to a well-maintained box-styled beard that rimmed his jaw and chin. His long, rectangular face gave him an aristocratic appearance. "I ask for a man, and they send me a woman."

The equally well-dressed, armed guards surrounding him laughed.

"Saladin is ill, Señor Alcaide. I am Grace Ibn-Ziyad, his daughter-in-law. I come in his place."

"Daughter-in-law?" Rodrigo studied her much more intently now. "I was not aware Saladin had any sons other than Haroun, nor that Haroun had taken a wife before he died."

"I know you are wiser than to believe tall tales, Señor Alcaide." Grace made the overseer laugh again.

"Flatterer, are you? That will not get you very far with me, Lady Ibn-Ziyad. Am I to assume by your presence here the rumors of your husband seeking to lay siege to Granada are true?"

"No. Haroun does not seek war with Granada. Neither does Saladin. He is traveling to your city to meet with the Chancellor and Vizier about diplomatic matters. Additionally, he is checking on grain stores. We travel with a small entourage of armed men for our own protection. If you have heard the rumors of war between Granada and Córdoba, certainly you have heard Haroun once more fell out of favor with those overseeing Córdoba. Several attempts have been made on our lives. I give you my word Saladin, nor my husband seeks conflict with you. My husband remains in Córdoba. If he wanted warfare, he would ride at the front of the lines as is customary for an enforcer and primus, not cowering at the back of them or sending legions forward alone."

The way Rodrigo grinned put Grace on edge. She resisted the urge to bring her hand back to the hilt of the sword. She wouldn't give the overseer any incentive to harm Lucena.

"You give me your word? The men on the walls are prepared to fire down on me at any second and are reinforced by soldiers not from Lucena. I would say you and Saladin come well-prepared for battle."

"The men are neither Saladin's nor hers. They are under another's command and are only present to protect against Isra and her minions. They have no orders to engage you or anyone else in Granada," Dante remarked, drawing Rodrigo's attention.

Rodrigo studied the hooded man on Grace's right, then the Greek god on her left whose face was openly displayed.

"Rodrigo," Ares stepped forward to stand alongside Grace. "Xander and I executed the rabble commissioned by Isra to falsely convince you of Haroun's intent to lay siege to Granada. I would not stand alongside Grace Ibn-Ziyad if Córdoba sought conflict with you after doing so. You know I speak the truth. Xander and I presented ourselves to you for permission to enter Granada yesterday. If we wanted war, we never would have done so."

"Forgive me if I am cautious, Ares. Until I know the truth of why you and these troops are in Lucena, I leave nothing to chance."

More armed men, demons, and djinn emerged from the olive grove and citrus trees behind Rodrigo.

Grace allowed her hand to settle on the sword hilt, not caring if her doing so escalated things. He wouldn't have brought the mercenaries if he intended to investigate and leave peacefully. "Rodrigo, again I swear Córdoba does not seek conflict with Granada. But if you lay siege to Lucena, we will defend the city. The men on the walls are only at arms as they fear you and your soldiers."

"A woman's word means nothing to most men, Lady Ibn-Ziyad."

"Then allow her husband to offer his word in place of hers," Rayne called out, riding up and halting Fahkir a few feet from Grace and Rodrigo. The other three Horsemen stopped alongside him. "I have no quarrel with you or anyone else in Granada. Harm my wife, or Lucena, and I will decimate the forces you foolishly brought with you then take your head as my prize."

Rodrigo shot Grace an amused look. "I thought your husband was not here, Lady Ibn-Ziyad."

Dante lowered his hood, revealing his face. "He wasn't until I requested the Horsemen's presence in Lucena. The men on the walls are under my command. As the lady states, we do not seek war with Granada. The Council only wants to calm things and protect their own."

"The sun god of Elysium graces Lucena with his presence." Rodrigo smiled over at Dante, then looked back at Rayne. "This explains how you returned from the dead a married man, Haroun. As your wife began negotiations and you offer your word as evidence of her integrity, I will conclude my discussion with the lady."

"By all means." Rayne politely inclined his head as a sign of peace to Rodrigo, but remained where he was should he need to quash any fight that may begin.

"Lady Ibn-Ziyad, I will presume based on those around you that you share their favor within the realms."

Understanding Rodrigo recognized her as an equal and an immortal, Grace relaxed. "I do indeed share the benefits and prestige bestowed upon my husband for his service to the Council. Hence, the elite guard that protects Saladin and myself. Is my word now worthy of acceptance, Señor Alcaide?"

"The word of a Council harbinger is never one I would doubt. I welcome Saladin and yourself to Granada. No one will do either of you harm as long as you are within my territory, Lady Ibn-Ziyad, but ensure your husband remains well outside Granada's gates." Rodrigo signaled his men to fall back and return home.

"I will return to Córdoba once you and your men leave Lucena." Rayne leaned forward in the saddle and caught Grace's hand then brought it to his lips, bestowing a lingering kiss on her knuckles. "I leave Lucena in your capable hands, my beloved."

Rodrigo laughed at the gesture which both confirmed Rayne would keep his promise to leave and as a warning to remember who the lady's husband was. "Have no fear for her welfare. My legions will be well warned to treat your wife with respect as long as she is in Granada. Safe journey to you, Haroun. Good day, Lady Ibn-Ziyad." He, along with his entourage of escorting officers, rode off into the distance.

Grace smiled up at Rayne. "I love you."

"And I you." Rayne gave her chin a gentle squeeze.

Grace stepped back so he could turn Fahkir and head back up the road toward Córdoba. She watched the Four Horsemen gallop off. They would disappear from sight once over the hill and out of view of those on the city walls. "You intended to call Rayne here all along."

Standing beside her now, Dante chuckled. "Si. I had hoped he wouldn't be needed, but suspected Rodrigo might want to hear the truth from Haroun himself, so yes, I requested he come to Lucena as quickly as possible. I knew you could keep Rodrigo at bay for the brief time the Horsemen needed to arrive."

CHAPTER

FORTY-ONE

Córdoba - 812

Grace noted Rodrigo's djinn and men wherever she and Saladin went in Granada. She debated whether Rodrigo was offering them protection or keeping tabs on their activities. More than likely, the actual answer was the overseer did both. None of his minions ever engaged her or Saladin. They simply lurked nearby. Once she was certain they successfully diverted Isra's coup attempt and no threats existed against Saladin, Grace decided it was time to return to Córdoba. Rodrigo stood at the city gates. He politely offered her a gallant bow as she rode past him.

She periodically looked over her shoulder, searching for djinn until she reached Rayne's estate. Seeing her, Sulla let out a long howl. Rayne immediately stepped outside the house and came toward her. She started to dismount. He caught her about the waist before her feet touched the ground. Their lips met in an ardent, welcome home kiss. Both of them relieved to see one another unharmed after several contentious days apart.

Rayne took a hold of Vittore's reins with one hand and his other rested on her hip, his arm draped around her the entire time they walked to the stable together.

After Vittore was untacked and groomed, Grace held out an over-sized apple in her palm. "As promised, an apple for your good behavior in Lucena and Granada."

The horse snorted, then his lips slowly swept the apple from her hand. Grace shook her head at how he chomped the apple in two, letting half of it fall into his feed bucket. "Well, at least you didn't try to swallow it whole."

"I'll throw in a second for good measure. You did bring her safely home." Rayne cut a second apple into four pieces, then tossed it into Vittore's feed bucket. Vittore neighed, nuzzling him. He laughed and patted the horse's neck. "It is I who am grateful to you today."

Rayne hugged Grace to him. "Dinner should be ready in an hour. That is enough time for you to take a bath and fill me in on what happened in Granada and Lucena."

***

The next afternoon, Grace walked through one of the swaths of Rayne's land. His estate manager educated her on the variety of crops cultivated on the Cordovan property. Sulla and Kato roamed between the cultivated rows.

"This seems like a lot of grain and food for only one estate."

"Your husband is a very charitable man. After we set aside what we need for ourselves and taxes, the rest is split between the local orphanage and feeding the poor. Haroun gives away a much of his wealth."

Learning Rayne continually cared for the town's less fortunate, she smiled. "Haroun has a big heart."

"Yes, he does. It is a shame the Emir does not follow his or Saladin's example."

The manger's remark surprised Grace. "Malik is required by the tenants of his faith to pay tithe and take care of the poor. Being an emir heightens that obligation."

"Malik squanders Córdoba's riches. The Emirate lost a great deal of its wealth under his father and the past few years of Malik's leadership."

"How far in debt is the Emirate?"

"The Emirate is fine. Malik himself is in a large amount of debt."

"Have you shared this with Haroun?"

"I have not had the opportunity to speak with him as frequently as I do you, Lady Ibn-Ziyad."

Riders approaching interrupted their discussion. Not knowing if whoever approached was friend or foe, Grace called Kato and Sulla over to her.

"As-salamu Alaykum, Lalla Ibn-Ziyad." The lead rider dismounted and politely bowed to Grace.

"Wa'alaykum as-salam." Grace returned the formal greeting, still not sure who the man was until the grounds keeper bowed and addressed the visitor as Emir.

"My apologies, Emir. I did not realize who you were."

Malik offered Grace a charming smile. "No harm done. Is your husband home? I hoped to speak with Haroun."

"He is assisting a family member at the moment. He should return shortly." Grace noticed how one rider watched her as she and Malik spoke. Sulla slowly made his way towards the same man. "Sulla!"

The wolf snarled before obediently returning to sit beside her, but continued watching the man he had stalked.

"They are very loyal creatures to protect their mistress as much as they do their master," Malik remarked.

"Yes, they are. You must be a good man for neither of them to bare their teeth or growl at you." Grace tested the Emir.

Flattered, Malik laughed. "I am glad they think so."

"Is there a message I should give my husband on your behalf?"

"I wished to invite him to the palace for a dinner honoring him and his father. I hope you will attend with him."

Grace politely bowed her head to the young ruler. "I will let him know of your request, and am honored you would invite me to dine at your table."

Malik handed Grace a sealed paper to give to Rayne then bid her farewell. He and his escort passed directly in front of her as they departed. The man Sulla disliked kept his eyes on Grace.

Grace mouthed the words, 'I know what you are' to him.

The man smirked and nodded his head to her.

Rayne and Destahn rode up to the house an hour after Malik's visit.

"You received an invitation from Malik to attend a dinner being held in your and your father's honor," Grace said before kissing her husband hello.

Rayne grinned. "Malik will most likely be withdrawing that invitation after Isra lost several of her djinn and demons this morning along with us scaring off half the human mercenaries she hired."

"I wouldn't be too certain of that. Malik himself brought the invitation just an hour ago." Grace held out the sealed parchment Malik had left with her. Rayne broke the wax seal and read the handwritten note. "Sulla exposed a tall, dark-haired, and dark-eyed djinn almost your height riding with Malik's entourage. He carried a Spanish rapier on his side and wore a gold cross around his neck."

"Narciso." Rayne stopped reading. Isra's primus riding with Malik was not welcome news. "Either Narciso is learning to enjoy daylight or they expected to find a lone, helpless mortal woman to kidnap. Sulla and Kato probably kept him from acting."

"Or he had second thoughts, sensing I wasn't human with the way he watched me. I also let him know I recognized that he was a djinn. This isn't the first time he has been here."

"What? When did you see him before today?"

"I already told you about the first visit. It was the day Malik and Isra kidnapped Yasmina, and I went to Essaouira. He led the group of djinn that demanded entry to the house."

"I apologize. I forgot with everything occurring. I well warned Isra what would happen if she took any action against you or our children. Destahn, please advise Malik that I must regretfully decline his invitation, as I have been urgently summoned to assist a friend in Malaca. Also, share my father is still recovering from the illness which struck him on the way to Granada, so he has not returned to Córdoba yet. His poor health slows his travels home."

Destahn nodded then left to deliver the message.

Grace wondered about the odd response. "Your father is fine. I also have to point out a loyal subject wouldn't ignore a summons from his ruler for an imaginary friend."

"Malik doesn't know the friend in Malaca doesn't exist. I am curious to see if Narciso appears in Malaca or stays here in Córdoba."

"I take it you are headed to Malaca then."

"No, I have eyes and ears there that will alert me if Narciso is seen in Malaca. I plan to stay here, but out of sight, should Narciso remain in Córdoba. If he does, that confirms he was stupidly after you today, not looking for me."

"Maybe he's acting as Malik's personal bodyguard because the Emir has gotten himself into trouble with a nonhuman entity. Your estate manager mentioned he believes Malik is in a great deal of debt and squanders funds from Córdoba's coffers."

That bit of information got Rayne's attention. "How much debt?"

"He didn't say. I am wondering if there was more to the feud between Malik and Umar than we know, especially for Malik to so readily negotiate with Isra."

Contemplating what Grace hinted at, Rayne tapped Malik's invitation against the side of his hand. "I suppose Umar exploiting Malik's mismanagement of funds to support a usurpation attempt is certainly a possibility. But he and Abdul had to spend a great deal of money. The Treasury was overflowing when I left Córdoba."

"They lost their most successful general when you, well, I guess, became immortal. No more spoils of war to keep the wealth coming in."

"The Emirate had other sources of income. Although, it does make me wonder what exactly Abdul and Malik spent that kind of money on."

"Armies and mercenaries drained many royal purses for centuries." Grace suggested, causing Rayne's brows to raise again. "Maybe you or your father should meet with whomever oversees the treasury and caliph's coffers."

Royal Palace - Córdoba - 812

"Why did you visit Haroun's wife?" Isra fumed at Malik in his private chambers.

"You have not fulfilled your end of our agreement to ensure Haroun eliminates those threatening my rule."

"You are an idiot, Malik! Provoking Haroun after the warning he sent will not force him to do your bidding. Instead, he will seize your Emirate, slaughter you and your viziers, then destroy your palace along with anything which would preserve your memory."

"Calm yourself, Isra. He is only a djinn, not God himself."

A sinister laugh rumbled from the corner of the room.

"I warned you two not to trifle with Haroun. To find another way to remove Umar and Saladin, but you did not listen. Not only is your failure to obey one much wiser threatening our hold in Andalusia, it has brought all of us under the scrutiny of the High Council. The new sun god siding with Haroun further complicates matters after you foolishly entered his home in yet another ridiculous attempt to manipulate him." Lucifer glared at the impudent human and regional overseer. "Haroun is not merely a former djinn, Malik. He is one of the High Council's harbingers. Their lead balance keeper, to be exact. Have you ever read the Christian Book of Revelations, Emir?"

Malik paled. "I am familiar with how they believe the world will end."

"Then you should be familiar with the Four Horsemen who guide the events of the Apocalypse. Haroun is the Commander of those Horsemen. You are provoking War himself. If I and my legions cannot control or defeat him, what makes you foolishly think you can?"

Lucifer left the three to contemplate his words.

Isra resisted the urge to throttle the human. Unfortunately, she needed Malik to regain her hold over Rayne. "It is best you abandon any plots to ransom Haroun's wife. Haroun killed Kamar for attempting to take his daughter, and he and Kamar were once friends. He wouldn't hesitate to slay Narciso. We can't afford to lose another experienced fighter if we wish to remain protected against the Council forces, nor do you want Haroun breaking down your door as your enemy. Mayhap Saladin may be bribed into silence if he discovers your alliance with the Almoravids."

"Saladin cannot be bought. Father and son share the same moral code. If Saladin remains in Córdoba, he will defend the people and challenge every decree I issue." Malik stroked his beard. "Haroun must have a weakness that can be exploited. Are you certain we cannot ransom his children?"

Isra shook her head. "The sun god protects them. If we managed to distract Haroun, we would never be able to eliminate the god."

"His wife wanders freely through Córdoba. Perhaps there is a way to make it appear someone else took her hostage."

Narciso chuckled at Malik's ignorance of the immortal world. "In addition to what Isra already advised you of, Haroun's new wife is not human. Kidnapping an immortal woman would draw more than Haroun's attention. The two wolves with her today belong to the traitors pack, which means the pack watches over her."

Isra started at Narciso's mention of the traitors pack. "Which two?"

"Sulla and Kato. They always did like Haroun. Now that he feeds the pack and gives them shelter on his lands, the entire pack protects Haroun's estate. It is a pity there is not another human outside of his family that Haroun would surrender himself for in order to protect them."

The djinn's words sparked a thought in Isra's head. "While there might not be a living one, there is one from his past. She is within my reach."

FORTY-TWO

Córdoba - 812

Rayne stood in the courtyard at his father's house, staring at the fountain. The painful memories which kept him away from Córdoba seemed so distant now. A new moon hung on high, reminding him of Grace. She and his mother awaited him inside. Taking one last look at the fountain, he decided to join them.

"Haroun!" A voice he hadn't heard in centuries whispered to him on the night wind. "Haroun!"

He took a step towards the ghostly figure forming near the fountain. "Priya?"

"You must flee. Take your wife and run!" The ghost glanced over her shoulder. Her body contorted as if the assassins' blades once again drove their way through her back and throat. Her mouth hung open in a silent scream, then she crumpled to the ground.

"What are you trying to warn me about? Why are you no longer at rest?" He reached out for the phantom that laid in the grass. His fingers found only turf as Priya faded from sight.

"Mother!" Rayne drew his weapon, running inside the house

worried whatever befell Priya had harmed his wife and mother. His eyes scanned any room with an open door for signs of intruders. "Grace!"

Grace came down the hallway towards him. She didn't sense danger, but something was wrong for Rayne to act as he did. Lillian stayed close behind her. His grim expression and the sword in his hand panicked Grace. "Rayne, what is wrong?"

"I want you to go to Elysium. Take my mother with you. Check on the children."

"Why?"

Rayne looked past her, scanning for any potential enemy lying in wait for them. "Just go! Do not return until I tell you it is safe to do so."

Noticing how his hands shook, Grace grabbed his arm. The last time she saw Rayne this perturbed was immediately after the battle in Alexandria. "What happened?"

"Please do as I ask. I love you." Rayne kissed her. "Now, go."

"Your mother, she doesn't know." Grace glanced over at Lillian. "Taking her to Elysium with no warning will...."

"Do as I say, Grace." Rayne's patience slipped, and the enforcer emerged. Not willing to argue any longer, Rayne sent her and Lillian to Elysium. "Dante, protect them."

Elysium -

Dante rose from his desk chair after Grace and Lillian unexpectedly stood in the middle of his study. "What occurs in Córdoba?"

"I don't know. Rayne wouldn't tell me. He insisted we come here." Grace wished she could tell Dante more.

"Lyal is here. The two of you can keep the house secure for the short time I will be gone. If anything strange occurs, call for me."

"Where are you going?"

"Córdoba, to find out what disturbs your husband so severely that he sends you and Lillian here." Dante kissed her cheek, then went to the mortal world.

Dazed by how the man vanished from the room, Lillian looked around. "Where are we?"

"Some place safe." Grace wished Lillian learned of Rayne and hers immortality another way than being thrown into Elysium.

"The man you spoke with, he disappeared like a phantom."

Grace gently grasped Lillian by the arm. "He's not a ghost, he's a god, Lillian. Dante's also a good friend."

"One of the Roman gods protects you and Haroun?" Lillian struggled to understand everything happening.

"Not exactly. Has Saladin told you nothing unusual about Haroun and me?"

Lillian shook her head. "Saladin only shared that Haroun and you are both warriors in a foreign army."

"That is one way to put it."

"I will make you both some tea to calm her nerves with what you are about to tell her." Maria said from the doorway. Grace hadn't noticed her there.

"Thank you, Maria." Grace guided Lillian over to one of the couches.

Lillian sat across from her daughter-in-law, trying to muster her courage to hear whatever needed to be said. "What do you wish to tell me, Grace?"

"Rayne and I, well, Rayne and I aren't human like you any longer. We were gifted immortality by the gods."

Grace could sense the swelling panic in the woman. "Don't be frightened, Lillian. We are not anything evil. Saladin is right. We are soldiers for a foreign army. Rayne commands the armies of the gods that protect humanity. Your son is an amazing man to handle the great responsibility he has been given. He is charged with keeping all mortals safe from immortal warfare. Not many men in his position are allowed to have families due to what the gods expect of them. The gods made an exception to this rule as Haroun, Rayne is—"

"Unique." Lillian cut off Grace. "Saladin and I always knew Haroun had a different calling. He rose in the ranks so quickly, yet remained charitable. Haroun did not gain the harshness Umar and Abdul developed. He never liked going to war until exhausting all other diplomatic means."

Grace smiled. "He is still that way."

"Saladin and I once believed Haroun brought hope to Córdoba. By being a mix of all peoples who lived there, he and others like him would instill peace for all generations to come. Then Umar..." Disturbed by the vivid memory of Rayne's blood-covered face and him holding Priya's body when she and Saladin entered the courtyard after hearing a man screaming, Lillian lost her voice. Umar had taken her son from her. He deserved the dishonorable death given to him and worse.

The loss in Lillian's eyes shared her grief better than words ever could. Grace empathetically set her hand on Lillian's knee. "Your son survived that dark time and became a being who brings hope and peace to a great many, just as you and Saladin believed. Rayne does his best to make Córdoba and elsewhere safe for everyone."

Maria returned with a tray carrying a teapot and three cups. Lillian took the glass she offered her. Maria and Grace shared an understanding smile, seeing Lillian's hand tremor as she took her first sip of tea.

"Lillian, this is Maria. Dante's mother," Grace introduced her two mothers-in-law.

"Thank you for your kindness, goddess," Lillian politely addressed Maria after setting her teacup down again.

Maria laughed. "Prego, Lillian. But I am no goddess. I am human like yourself. I remember my shock the first time anyone spoke to me about gods and immortals. Thankfully, I was in my own home when that discussion occurred. I can only imagine how disconcerting it is to learn deities exist after being suddenly sent to Elysium."

Lillian turned ashen white as it finally set in that her son sent her and Grace to Roman heaven. "Elysium? Are we dead?"

"No. You are very much alive, Lillian." Grace reassured her no one had lost their lives. "Rayne sent us here as Isra, the ifrit causing all of the trouble in Córdoba, cannot enter a god's home. Whatever happened tonight frightened Rayne for him to expose our world to you. Normally, we would not let a human know what we are or allow them to see Elysium. He's trusting you to keep a very important secret, in addition to protecting you. Would you like to meet your grandchildren?"

"They are here?" Lillian didn't think she could be anymore shocked.

"They are. Dante and Maria watch over them to ensure they are kept safe from Isra and Malik."

Maria stood and patted Lillian's hand. "Tessa and Tarquin are playing in their room. Come, let us go introduce the three of you."

It was well past midnight when Dante returned. Grace waited up for him. Before she could ask anything, he reassuringly clasped her hands in his.

"Your husband is well. He believes he saw Priya. She told him to take his family and flee."

What Dante disclosed surprised Grace. No wonder Rayne acted as he did. "Was it really her?"

"I do not know. My father swears Priya is still in the afterlife, but Rayne's description of their encounter tonight is vivid enough that I believe she warned him of something. Or Isra is an excellent actress ripping open an old wound. Either scenario is unsettling."

Grace's concern for Rayne's welfare continued to grow. "Isra and Lucifer used her to manipulate Rayne once before. Is he in any danger?"

"Rayne is perfectly safe. We need to uncover the real reason behind Isra's scheming. There is more than removing Umar from the Emirate. For her to continually go after your husband's conscience, she needs Rayne to accomplish something larger or to take the fall for whatever she and Malik are plotting."

Frustrated, Grace let go of Dante's hands. "My visit to her a few weeks ago should have been enough to warn her away. She knows what Rayne is, and that he is under the protection of the Ancients."

"Your visit? Did you break your promise to Rayne?" Dante gave her a hard stare.

The arched dark brow and disapproval in his gaze annoyed Grace. "Stop looking at me like that. I am talking about the first visit to get the contract. You would have done the same to obtain any contract that awarded my soul to a demon."

Dante scoffed. "I am a god and a man. It is my duty to protect my wife. You, on the other hand, should have never done such a thing, especially knowing it would upset your husband."

"Fourteenth-century Neanderthal!" Grace couldn't resist teasing him. The old joke between them lightened the tension they felt.

Dante grinned. "Neanderthal I may be, but my outdated thinking has kept you safe on more than one occasion, and continues to do so. Don't make me angry or I will toss you out of my cave."

She rolled her eyes. "You wouldn't dare, as you'd earn my husband's ire for doing so. Didn't you tell me a few days ago you wouldn't ever want to end up crossways with War?"

"All jesting aside, it worries me that Isra is willing to not only challenge Rayne, but the Defensore as well after you confronted her."

"Isra doesn't know I am the Defensore. I went on my own as an anonymous guardian."

"My thief, still causing extra trouble for the men in her life."

"Should the Defensore pay an official visit to Isra?" Grace debated doing so.

"Rayne would murder me if I allowed you to do such a thing. He asked that you and Lillian remain here until he can better understand what happens in Córdoba. Please do not worry him further by disregarding his wishes."

Grace smiled again due to the way Dante eyed her. He knew she rarely did as asked. "I will stay put for a day or two, as long as things do not worsen. If anything looks like a genuine threat to Rayne or his mental health, my role as guardian obligates me to ensure he is safe."

"Allow the House of the Sun to assume that mantle, for your husband's sake." Dante respected her fighting spirit, but it frequently led her into trouble. "How is Lillian handling finding herself here and learning what you and Rayne are?"

"She's shocked, but I think she will be okay. Time with Tessa and Tarquin eased her nerves along with your mother taking her under her wing. She seemed well enough when she went to bed a couple of hours ago."

"You look tired. You should go to bed yourself, cara."

"Now that you've returned, I will. And as long as the sun is diligent in his duties, the moon will stay here."

"Your compliance with your husband's request is appreciated. It eases his concerns about you doing anything rash."

"Would that husband be you or Rayne, Dante?"

The night air drew Dante closer to Grace. Sunset and the witching hour were dangerous times for them both. Acknowledging him as a current spouse only courted the Fates to unleash more mayhem. He wished the Council hadn't removed the safety net of their edict to forever keep his distance from her. "Both of us, tesoro."

Grace felt the same odd calling with Dante only a breath's distance away. "The Fates entwine our stories once more." She looked out the window to see the full moon shining then took a step back from him. "This time, we must write the narrative, Dante, not anyone else. Sogni d'oro, cavaliere."

She left Dante alone in the living room.

***

Hating that she spoke the truth, Dante closed his eyes. They needed to kill Isra quickly. Before he found himself facing off with Rayne over Grace.

"That was your moment to reunite with your wife," Lyal remarked with an amused expression from the doorway.

"You and my father need to stay out of my affairs."

"Even as a god, you fight fate as strongly as she does." Lyal found Dante's resistance entertainingly ironic. "The three of you will come to embrace what you are destined to be."

"She is happy with Rayne. I do not want to ever take that from her." Dante worried about the strain Grace and Rayne would bear with Isra's antics if the Triad reformed as predicted. "Tell the Fates to leave Grace and me alone. They risk their safety and mine by taking action on an outdated prophecy."

"Mayhap, the matter is urgent and can no longer be delayed."

A harsh distaste filled Dante's mouth as he pondered what prompted the High Council to rush the fulfillment of the old divination. "What peril exists that requires the Triad to be reunited?"

Instead of answering his inquiry, Lyal walked outside.

Disturbed by Lyal bringing up the Triad, Dante went to his study. He opened the door to discover Osiris, Isis, and his mother standing in the middle of the room as if they waited for him. "What do you want for all three of you to be here at this hour?"

Osiris took a deep breath. "Perhaps it is best if you sit down for this discussion."

Dante eyed his father and sat in the large, leather chair behind his desk.

The conversation between the four was short-lived.

"Leave my home!" Dante shouted at Isis and Osiris after they shared the proposition the Council wanted him to consider.

A bit surprised by Dante's temper, Osiris glanced over at Isis. "Dante..."

"Grace would never forgive me for doing what you ask."

"We are not asking you to hurt her." Isis tried to soothe her stepson's indignation.

Dante scoffed. "The two of you asked me to knowingly and deceitfully seduce her this very night."

Osiris uncrossed his arms and sighed as if disappointed in his son. "You are misinterpreting what I said."

"There is no misinterpreting what the Council means when they tell me the sun and moon must reunite to align night and day. We both know there is only one way to do that."

"I thought you enjoyed copulation with the Defensore," Lyal chimed in from the rear of the office.

"Say one more word about copulation, Lyal, and I swear I will send you permanently back to the deepest pits of Tartarus. Not even the Council will be able to retrieve you from there." Dante resisted the urge to hurl the letter opener from his desk at the annoying harbinger he had imprisoned in Tartarus once before.

"This must be done, Dante." Osiris hated how Dante's glare again rested on him.

"No. Find another to execute this despicable task if it must occur."

"There is no other!" Osiris barked in a rare display of anger.

"You ask me to do this, to hurt Grace, of all beings, simply because the Council is suddenly afraid of Isra? A second-rate regional overseer for Lucifer?"

"It isn't Isra who concerns us," Osiris muttered, not wanting to disclose the entire truth.

"Not Isra?" Dante scrutinized his father and Isis. Who else would they be afraid of? Now understanding what had the Council so concerned, Dante laughed. They needed to be certain the one being who could kill them all was still on their side. That's why they needed to revive the Triad. "What sins are you hiding that would bring War to your doorstep?"

Dante noted the sudden silence in the room. He shook his head in disbelief. "I will ensure Rayne never becomes the executioner you fear on the condition the Council and Fates keep Grace and the children as far from this situation as possible. And let us hope no one ever learns of our conversation tonight. It would give Rayne more than enough incentive to pay a hostile visit to Council chambers."

"The Triad—" Isis tried to reason with him one last time.

"Is no more! I ended it, Isis! Had the Council taken Qasim and Gaelin for the threat they were early on, the Triad wouldn't have been needed. If YOU had brought Rayne into Morrigan's ranks when originally planned, Haroun the enforcer would not exist. The High Council made this mess. I will be damned if Grace or my son has to clean it up any more than they already have."

Osiris didn't want to force his son's hand but would if the predicted future did not change course. "Dante, you took an oath as a Guardian and Horseman."

"I am no longer a Horseman, Father. And nowhere in any oath I took did I swear to seduce or rape women at the Council's whim."

"Rayne will never learn of tonight since he is in Spain."

"Rayne could come into my home at any minute to check on his family. The three of you do realize Rayne's mother is now here, under my roof, my protection, in addition to Grace and the children. With her morality, Grace would be shunned if Lillian caught us together, not to mention the harm done if Lillian disclosed anything to Rayne. I will not gamble with Grace's marriage or her heart. That is the final word on the matter. I will find another way to manage whatever it is involving Rayne that has the Council in their latest state of panic. Now, leave me in peace for the night."

The deities vanished, leaving Maria alone with Dante. She watched him pour golden liquid into a crystal glass. "Please, Dante. Do not start drinking as you used to. It solves nothing."

"We all need a vice, Mama. This one is better than many others." Dante swallowed the liquor in his glass.

"I am always amazed by how some gods remain ignorant with all the knowledge they possess."

"Mama..." Dante cautioned his mother not to anger him further.

"Mio figlio..."

"Why are you still up, Mama? Normally, you are retired well before the witching hour."

"Your father asked me to be a part of tonight's discussion."

"Did he?" Dante fought for control over his temper once more. His father promised to keep his mother out of immortal affairs. "You should not honor any request to participate in Council matters. You do not understand the way the immortal community or the High Council handles their affairs."

"I may not be a Horseman or a god, but I am no fool either, Dante Enzo Giovanni. Sometimes Fate changes the best-laid plans. Only a stubborn ass does not recognize this."

"Do not denigrate me, Mama! You were foolish enough to believe Osiris would spend the entirety of your mortal years with you. Or better yet, you unwisely believed a protection spell could hide your children and yourself from destiny after Morrigan warned you and Osiris that the Hasan hunted your young demigod son. We all know how your misplaced faith played out then, don't we? Perhaps, your son is wiser than you on these matters and it best you heed his guidance."

Dante's words shocked Maria. He had never spoken to her as he did now.

"If you prefer drink to your wife, who am I to judge?" Maria stomped out of Dante's study. The door banged shut behind her.

Dante looked down at the glass in his hand and the decanter on the table behind his desk. His mother's remark paired with what the Council asked him to do made him want to murder the Fates. The women and their destructive plotting. How much did they expect him, Grace, and Rayne to endure?

He picked up the elaborate Venetian glass container then flung it into the fireplace. The sound of shattering glass and the shards melting in the flames calmed his nerves.

FORTY-THREE

Córdoba - 812

"Drowning your sorrows, Commander?" Grace whispered in Rayne's ear. Her arms settled around his chest after she found him sitting alone in the living room and staring into the fire.

Rayne chuckled, resting his hand on her arm. "You are supposed to be in Elysium."

"When do I ever listen if my husband is in distress?" Grace brought a smile to his face. "What's troubling you besides Isra?"

"I am responsible for all of this. If I had killed her when I had the chance centuries ago, she couldn't have caused additional harm."

"And you might not be here protecting those you can."

Rayne closed his eyes. "I've made so many mistakes because of fear and hubris. I didn't tell you the truth until I had to." He looked up at her before continuing. "I ignored Priya's initial warning, believing I knew better. I feared truly loving a woman again after losing Priya and Anne's deception. If I hadn't resisted the prophecy or had looked harder for you before the assignment in Luxor, I could have prevented what you endured at Qasim and Rasil's hands."

"None of those things are your fault, Rayne." Grace sat on his lap.

"Anne was a lost soul Lucien exploited. Umar was the one who ordered Priya and your deaths. And me, well, while it wasn't a pleasant experience, I don't regret going through it. All I endured led me to you."

One of Rayne's arms encircled her waist. The other remained on the side of the chair, so he could still hold his drink. 'There had to be an easier path for you to find me."

"We cannot change what is predestined. Nothing you could have possibly done would have derailed the destructive course we all had to travel to get rid of Gaelin, Qasim, and Rasil. We can't truly change the future or the past if events are inevitable. I recently learned two children I saved in a conflict died a few months later from plague. They weren't destined to see adulthood."

Rayne took a drink from his glass. He savored the alcohol for a moment before swallowing it. Grace pulled the glass from his hand and sampled whatever he drank. Her eyes watered and she grimaced as she swallowed it. Rayne chuckled at her reaction to the strong beverage.

"What in the world are you drinking?" Grace asked, her mouth still puckered from the distinctive sour and sweet taste of the liquor.

"Orujo."

"Well, as strong as that is, nothing should trouble you, wolf."

Rayne smiled and set the glass down on the floor beside his chair. "If only it was the cure for what ails me." He grew somber once more, watching Grace twirl one of the lacings of the shirt he wore around her finger. "I wish I had better foresight into this conflict with Isra and Malik."

Grace stopped playing with the lacing and stared up at Rayne. "We will prevail, with minimal loss of life, Rayne. I haven't had any visions, but I know we will stop them. You need to believe that as well. Trust me, let me help you through this."

Rayne nodded. "Allow me time to ensure things are safe for you and my mother here, then I will do exactly that. Go back to Elysium, leof. I do not want to add any more sorrow or fear to the memories I have. If the Council knows you are here, so will Lucifer and Isra."

She kissed her husband. "Your mother is safe and sleeping soundly. I promise not to add to your sorrows. Do not spend the entire night dwelling on things no one can change. I love you, Rayne."

"And I you, Grace. For eternity."

Leptis Magna, Libya - Five years after Rayne took Grace to Diego in Marrakech

The crowded tavern where Rayne sat buzzed with the raised voices of drunken men and women. Disguised as a Roman military officer, he blended in with the humans. Finding it ironic he dressed as one of the very same people who subjugated his Numidian ancestors, he took a drink of the wine in his cup then popped a fig into his mouth. No one dared question his status, even though the locals recognized him to be one of their own. The Romans continually revered Numidian cavalrymen, even as the bucellarii now rose to fame. The blood of all the fiercest peoples riding in Rome's cavalries flowed in his veins, and he carried on their centuries-old tradition of fighting on horseback. He chewed slowly, contemplating the latest piece of news they received about Rasil. The shadow the locals loved to tell tales about relieved the Hasan commander of most of his arms, along with ten horses and two chests of gold, without any in the camp sounding the alarm. Whoever the shadow was needed to be careful. The shadow's recent successes promised retribution from Qasim.

"Drowning your troubles, legatus, or is it praefectus? You Romans confuse me with all of your insignia and titles." A woman whispered in his ear while sliding her hand down his chest.

He flung her hand off him. "Tribune. My coin and my weapon are not destined to be yours tonight."

"The gladius I seek is not the one on your side."

Rayne laughed then looked up at the woman standing behind him. "A prostitute and a thief?"

"A thief? I am offended to be called such a thing. And I prefer the title lupa to prostitute."

"They are one in the same, domina."

"Not when referring to the wife of the wolf. I need to speak privately with you, lupus."

Rayne raised a suspicious brow. The dim light and the material covering her head hid the majority of her face. The bright gold and peacock blue in her thin silk clothes sent mixed messages of wealth, piety, and promiscuity. Only respectable women wore a stola and palla. A prostitute caught dressing herself in such garments guaranteed a visit from the local authorities. The law prohibited women of low standing from donning the clothing of respectable Roman women, yet this woman wore both.

A drunken Michael clapped Rayne on the back. "What the hell, Dante has disappeared with two tarts. I'll pay for one night with this one if it will pull you out of the foul mood you've been in the past couple of days."

"No need for anyone to pay. I will gladly pleasure the tribune this night for free." The woman took Rayne's hand and gave it a gentle tug. "Are your accommodations here, Tribune?"

"They are indeed, domina." Michael answered for Rayne.

Rayne let out an aggravated breath and set his cup down on the counter. Ignoring the way Michael smirked at the woman's bold behavior, he stood, then allowed the woman to lead him across the room and up a set of stairs.

Reaching the second floor, the woman turned to him. "Which one is your room, Tribune?"

He opened the door to a room on their right. She slid past him to stand in the center of the small private room. The long length of her palla slipped back as her hip brushed his, revealing a concealed knife. When she moved away from him, the silk fell back into place, hiding the weapon once more. He eyed her mistrustingly as he closed the door. "You have a message for me?"

"No. I am here to prove a point." The woman lowered the silk from her head.

Rayne's throat tightened; surprise openly displayed on his face. His countess randomly appeared in his life again. He shook his head, snapping out of his initial shock. "At least now I know you are alive after you vanished from Marrakesh. Not even Christian would reveal where you had disappeared to."

"There is a reason for that. We aren't meant to cross paths for some time yet."

Rayne leaned back against a nearby table and crossed his arms over his chest. "Then why are you here?"

"You told me this very evening you regretted not looking harder for me, that you felt responsible for certain events. I am hoping this moment will prove to you, not even War, as powerful as he is, can change the trials the Fates require us to go through. That you will let go of the guilt and place the blame where it belongs; on Isra, Lucifer, and the Hasan."

"I am not certain I like the reason you are here. Not to mention, it is against our laws to change the past. How many times are you going to tempt the Council to jail you in Purgatory with flouting their decrees?"

Grace smiled. "Don't start getting righteous on me now, djinn. I am not changing any events, nor will this visit alter the future. Just promise me you won't let unearned guilt continually guide you. You're a good man, Rayne."

"A good man married to a thief with the blatant display of pilfering I witnessed downstairs. What does that say about my character for me to choose a spouse with such a profession?"

She couldn't help laughing at the dubious look he shot her. "I use my skills for good once we marry, and truthfully, I am working for good now. Did you fail to notice who I relieved of their coin?" Grace held her hand up. A chain with the Hasan emblem dangled from her fingertips. "Each man sells his services to the Hasan. The rest of the men I leave for others to rob. You're surrounded by the enemy, Captain, but you already know that."

Rayne shook his head. "What a pair the two of us must make." He crossed the space between them to hold the Hasan pendant in his palm, then he slipped the chain from her fingers and stared down at what he held.

"We're undefeatable when we work together, wolf."

He grinned, his gaze meeting hers. "Now that, I believe. You are something else to survive what you have, to break Council laws, then ask me to make you promises I am not certain I can keep or even truly understand."

"Leaps of Faith, Horseman. They rarely go unrewarded."

"State your terms again, leof. So I may give them my full consideration."

"Promise me you won't let guilt consume you, especially for things well beyond your control."

"What is my reward if I make this promise?"

Grace winsomely smiled, staring up into eyes dissecting her every word and movement. "You'll learn what it is *if* you come to me in Elysium, on the night you find yourself in Córdoba, sitting before your fireplace, contemplating all the strange events in your life after Isra's actions require you to return home."

"Elysium?" Not expecting to hear that, Rayne's brow knitted. "Are you telling me I am married to a dead woman?"

"No. I'm very much alive thanks to you and your devotion to your loved ones. You needlessly send me to a god in Elysium for safekeeping when life gets a little rough. What you should do instead is allow me to fight beside you in Córdoba. But fear brings out your stubborn side. At times, I think you are more thickheaded than Dante."

Rayne scoffed at her comparison. "No one is more stubborn or impulsive than Dante Giovanni."

Grace raised her palla back onto her head. "Good night, Rayne."

"Wait." He grabbed her arm. "I haven't given you my word yet."

"Your heart already made the promise your lips are refusing to speak. I've been married to you long enough to know your decisions without you needing to say them aloud."

He wanted her to stay longer. Her presence always allowed a welcomed calm to settle over him. "When will I see you again?"

"When the Fates decide we should next meet."

"At least give me your real name."

"I can't. That risks altering events which are soon to come. I wouldn't want to change anything that ultimately brings us together."

Rayne sighed. "Are you always this much of an enigma?"

"I prefer to think of myself as more of a shadow in the night and an oracle of a promise to you that a better future is yet to come." Grace kissed his cheek and hugged him.

His arms tightened around her. "Don't get yourself killed stealing from Rasil and Qasim before we can meet again."

"I won't. Not with the training I received from Ares and the pair of blades War gifted me to protect myself with. Thank you for them."

"I'm afraid I know nothing of this nonsense you speak."

She laughed at his half-hearted denial. "Did you think I wouldn't discover who had the knives made for me, with them being Spanish steel and decorated the way they are? They still serve me well, wolf. Until the next time we meet."

"The next time we meet? You promised me a pleasurable evening," Rayne teased, not letting her go.

"If we make love now, it will ruin what is supposed to be our first time. And that is one of my favorite memories of you. But I suppose no harm can come from giving you something to look forward to." Grace pressed her lips to his, allowing him several long, deep kisses.

A loud moan and a woman crying, "Fuck me, Commander" in Latin interrupted their kissing.

Rayne shook his head as Grace laughed after hearing Dante's muffled voice on the other side of the wall.

"May I recommend you request another room, Captain? Otherwise, I'd wager you are in for a long night." She grasped the length of him in her hand, slowly bring her palm upward. "Especially with my not staying to help with this."

Grace left the past and returned to Elysium.

Elysium -

Rayne stood in the guest bedroom doorway waiting for her. "Point proven, leof. I come to collect my due."

"Your due?" Grace pretended not to know what he wanted, smirking at the annoyed scowl on his face.

"The pleasurable evening I was promised and then denied." Rayne shut the door. "I intend to pay you and Dante back tenfold for the restless night I endured between being left wanting by my evil temptress of a wife and the racket from Dante's conquest of two women in the room next to mine."

More than happy to honor the offer she made, Grace walked over to him. "Revenge really can be sweet."

"At times." He possessively embraced her; his mouth descended on hers, hungrily tasting the woman he desired.

Grace unbuckled his belt and undid his pants as they kissed. Her fingers encircled the circumference of his hardened, warm flesh; sliding from base to tip. She dropped to her knees before him. The way she kissed his thighs then slowly took him into her mouth brought forth an approving, low moan. Her aqua eyes stared up into his as her tongue brushed against his skin.

"By the gods, woman, just when I think I have you figured out." Rayne closed his eyes, his fingers delved into her hair, lightly massaging her scalp. His body shuddered from the steady cadence of being drawn in then pushed away before Grace exquisitely reclaimed what she had given up and then took more until she encompassed all of him. Her fingers stroking and teasing him as much as her mouth did. She remained on her knees until he grasped the sides of her head and in a hoarse whisper demanded she stop.

"What's wrong? Am I not pleasing you as promised, my wolf?"

"You are more than pleasing me." He offered her his hands to help bring her to her feet. "There is only one thing more pleasurable I can think of than your lips wrapped around my cock." His arm curled under her and he lifted her upward against him. "And that is being inside you."

He plunged himself into her welcoming body. Her legs eagerly enfolded his waist. He turned, so Grace's back rested against the door slab. A soft percussive beat followed every thrust he made. Enjoying the rhythmic reverberation of their bodies moving together against oak intermingled with the high-pitched squeals and pleasure-filled moans escaping Grace, Rayne took her slightly faster. She whispered his name as he brought her closer to climax.

"Louder, sweetheart." Rayne smiled at how her voice raised the second time she called his name. "Let all of Elysium know who takes you."

Her nails raked over his back before her fingers clutched at his shoulders as love making turned to something much more primal. Raw need to conquer set in. Grace's hips rolled to meet the full force of his, drawing him in deeper. Rayne laid waste to Grace's being until she surrendered everything to him, quivering and crying out. Taking Grace against the door in Dante's home gave him an intoxicating sense of carnal satisfaction. He relished the thought of Dante being reminded of what he would never have the chance to enjoy again.

Dante rubbed the bridge of his nose. The banging coming from down the hallway crescendoed. He didn't need this tonight on top of everything else. He drank straight from the bottle as Grace shouted Rayne's name. Hopefully, that was the end of the passionate interlude. Thank the gods his mother had left and his other guests were sound sleepers.

"You've made your point, Rayne," Dante mumbled before downing another mouthful of grappa.

After a half hour of silence, Dante heard moaning from down the hall. He shook his head then looked up at the ceiling. "Do you hear that racket? That is War claiming what is his, in my home. And you fools wanted me to seduce her tonight. We'd all be dead if I had agreed."

Grace made breakfast for Tarquin and Tessa. She looked up to see Dante stroll into the kitchen wearing one of his old Horseman's uniforms with his sword on his side. By his manner of dress, he headed to Spain to help Rayne unweave the web Isra and Malik wove between the city's elite.

"No golden armor today?"

Dante grinned, but spoke in an acerbic tone. "The Council can keep my godly vestments."

Grace knew by the bitter edge in his voice the Council had done something to upset him. "Whatever trouble the Council stirs, I hope you put a quick end to it."

"Uffa, the trouble they stir is nothing for you to fret over, cara. I ride with the Horsemen today, so should appear as they do."

Dante obviously didn't want to discuss the matter, so Grace let it drop. "Perhaps a cup of coffee before you go, cavaliere? You look exhausted."

"No, grazie, cara. I am already late in meeting Rayne."

"You're turning down coffee?"

"As I said, I am late in meeting your husband." He ignored the suspicious look Grace gave him. His stomach rumbled from the whiff of warm pancakes drifting up from the kitchen table. "Stay out of trouble, cara. Neither Rayne nor I need the added stress today."

"Be safe yourself." Grace walked back over to the stove to flip the two pancakes cooking on the griddle.

"Tarquin." Dante distracted himself from the temptation of lingering in Elysium.

The boy stopped eating. "Yes, Papa?"

"Watch over your mother and sister while I am gone."

"I will, Papa."

Tarquin's answer brought a smile to Dante's face. He tussled his son's hair then walked over to Grace.

She pulled a plate from the cabinet and set it down on the counter before facing him. "Give Rayne my love."

"Certo, mia bella stella." Dante kissed her on either cheek. "A presto, Grazia."

"Buonna giornata, Commander. Since you are a Horseman for the day."

***

Córdoba - 812

"You used to be punctual, Dante." Tamir teased the sun god, who joined them an hour later than planned.

Dante shot his companions a stern look. "I overslept. Various matters kept my awake late last night."

"Careful, Tamir. The man obviously hasn't had his morning coffee." Destahn added to the jesting.

Dante ignored the two, urging his horse forward to ride alongside Rayne. "Grace sends her love."

Thinking of his wife, Rayne smiled. "That both pleases and worries me."

"Lyal is under strict orders not to allow Grace or the children to leave my house."

"You still severely underestimate Grace's creativity in protecting her loved ones if she suspects any of us are in danger."

"After offending my mother last night, I am sure the two of them will be too busy plotting ways to torment me to worry about anything else. Hopefully, your mother's presence in Elysium will prevent them from coming up with anything too heinous."

"You offended Maria? That certainly is out of character for you."

"My father went behind my back and involved her in a Council matter. I expressed my displeasure about the situation in a harsher manner than I meant to. I tried to apologize this morning. It did not go well."

"Maria will forgive you for whatever you said. Be thankful she is a mortal soul. That prevents Grace from teaching her too many ways to get even. It's not often I see you looking so tired. You can leave the tracking to us today if you need time to mend things with your mother."

"Eh, it wasn't the argument with my mother that kept me awake. Other Council nonsense did. Certain members scheme more than you would suspect. Always stirring up chaos. There are days I wish I were still a Horseman, so I had some distance from the going-ons of the Council. How Raphael has put up with them for centuries, I will never understand. Ten years as a Council advisor is more than enough to make me want to become a recluse tending solely to matters in Elysium."

"Perhaps share your wishes with your father."

Dante scoffed. "My father is the biggest instigator of the lot. You are fortunate to have caring mortals as parents."

Rayne empathetically laughed. "Parents only want what's best for the children."

Dante shook his head in disagreement. "Are we going to the palace first or where Isra was last spotted?"

CHAPTER
FORTY-FOUR

Elysium

"I need to return to Spain for a few minutes," Grace said, putting away the last of the dishes she washed.

Hearing Grace intended to go to Spain alone, Maria panicked. "Rayne told Dante that you mustn't be in Córdoba unescorted. Dante also ordered Lyal to keep you and the children here. You should wait until Dante or Rayne returns, so one of them may accompany you."

"I will only be in Córdoba for a few minutes to pick up some clothes from the house."

"Grace, ragazza, if my son and your husband feel it is too dangerous for you to be alone in Córdoba, listen to them. I once disregarded a similar warning. It cost my daughter and me our lives. And the brutality Dante endured afterward...." Sorrow filled her brown eyes. Dante's words from the night before sounded in her head.

"That day and today are vastly different scenarios. The horrible day you mentioned was sadly fated. Unavoidable. There is nothing fore- boding written like that for me. I would know with what I do." Grace hugged Maria. "And I won't be alone. Sulla and Kato are there. Besides,

I am a High Council Officer trained by your son, Ares, and Rayne. I am not as defenseless as your son and my husband like to make it sound."

"Be careful, Grazia. Dante is already angry with me. I do not want to make matters worse."

"Angry with you? About what?" Grace had wondered why Maria hadn't been her normal, joyful self all morning.

"It's nothing important. I was upset that he is drinking again."

"Drinking?" Why would a woman who indulged in a periodic drink herself would be so concerned about her son doing so?

"He would not want you to know this, but he drank heavily when he first ascended. The loss of you and Tarquin..." Maria's voice trailed off as she had second thoughts about disclosing things to Grace. "Dante hasn't drunk himself into a stupor in a few years. Last night, I discovered him doing so in his study after you and the children went to bed."

Grace hated to hear Dante fell back into destructive dependencies. "Perhaps last night was a one-time thing. I will speak with him about it."

"No. It is something he and I should resolve." Maria shook her head and forced a smile. "Be safe in Spain. When you return, I will teach you and Lillian to cook seafood risotto. It is one of Dante's favorite meals. Rayne enjoys it as well."

"Sounds wonderful."

<hr>

Córdoba - 812

Unsure of how long she'd be in Elysium, Grace packed a few changes of clothes. She picked up the wolf's head medallion Rayne left on the dresser and sat down on the bed. She traced the outline of the wolf before standing up again. Kato nuzzled her palm and brushed his head against her side as if to ask what was wrong.

"Nothing a wolf would understand." Grace petted the wolf.

"I may understand more than you believe I will."

The wolf changed into a man. She had to stare up at him once the transformation was complete.

"You're a shapeshifter." Grace guessed at what the wolf/man was.

"Reformed djinn. Sulla and I were not as fortunate as Haroun in the dispensing of our servitude. Several of us earned our freedom, but must spend the rest of our days on all fours. They call us the traitors pack. Haroun took pity on us. We inhabit this house when he is not here."

Still processing the pack of wolves were once humans or djinn, Grace was at a loss for words. "I am sorry if we kicked you out of your bed."

Kato smiled and took her hand, leading her to the sitting room of the master suite. "I prefer the floor."

He gestured to the large chair Rayne frequently used. Grace sullenly sat down. "What troubles you, Grace, if I may call you that?"

"Of course you may, Kato. Fate upsets me this morning. Unfortunately, you can do nothing about the three of them. I also worry about Rayne. I don't understand why Isra harasses him after centuries of leaving him alone."

"There are rumors she and Malik formed an alliance against Rodrigo to lay claim to all of Iberia. They need Rayne and his men-at-arms out of the way to accomplish that."

"I am not certain she wants him out of the way. I would bet she more than likely needs Rayne to defeat Rodrigo with what I hear of him and his mercenary forces. He's one of the few overseers to amass a large army of humans, demons, and djinn loyal to him. He's figured out reward works better than punishment, unlike Isra. She seems to be losing her foothold in Spain to him." Grace studied the gray eyes of her new friend. "You were the wolf at the games in Rome."

"Yes. Sulla and I were once soldiers. I was an optio, and Sulla a centurion. Our centuria was slaughtered in a surprise attack here long ago."

Grace wondered if he and the famous enemy of Caesar were related. "Are you related to the senator who challenged Caesar?"

"We are from the same family, but I am not the man you identify." Kato glanced over his shoulder.

Grace wasn't sure what to think when he turned beast once more, circling around her chair with hackles raised.

Sulla appeared in the doorway, emanating a rumbling warning to whatever spooked the two former legionnaires.

Grace grabbed one of her daggers, then went to the front door. She glanced back at the wolves. "There's a rider at the gate."

So much for no conflict. She stepped into the courtyard as the gate opened, allowing the rider in.

Recognizing Rayne's uncle, Grace relaxed. "Mohammed, what a pleasant surprise."

"Sherifa sent a message that Lillian is missing. They have searched the house and markets for her. Is she here?"

"Rayne asked her to visit a friend in Montoro. He fears for her safety with Saladin gone and the attack on Yasmina. He took her there late last night after receiving word someone watched Lillian at the market and intended to do her harm." Grace hoped her story sounded plausible.

The tension left Mohammed's face, and the man raised his palms upward, thanking Allah that Lillian was safe before he looked down at Grace again. "Tell my nephew to inform others of his plans next time. We feared the worst with the strange happenings around the city."

"Strange happenings?"

"Nothing for a woman to concern herself with. Now that I know Lillian is unharmed, I must return to my work for the day. My fields don't plant themselves. Give your husband my well wishes and may you have a blessed day, Grace."

"Ma'a salama, Mohammed," Grace politely said goodbye, then watched Rayne's uncle ride out of the gate.

Kato stood beside her in human form once more. "You lied to Mohammed. Why?"

"I don't think he would believe me if I told him the truth. Lillian is in Elysium, where I need to return. I've already been gone for more than an hour. Lyal will alert Dante or Rayne to the fact I am in Córdoba if I linger here much longer. The two of them showing up angry in Elysium to argue with me about disobeying orders would traumatize Lillian. She has had enough to deal with the past twelve hours. The last thing she needs to witness is two angry immortals berating her daughter-in-law."

Kato chuckled. "We will stand guard over the estate and your husband. If we hear anything more of Isra or Rodrigo, we will send word to Rayne."

Grace picked up the bag she packed along with the two knives she had carried for over twenty years, then returned to Elysium.

***

Lillian and Maria sat in the living room talking while Tessa and Tarquin entertained one another. Lillian seemed to be taking everything well.

The three women and two kids prepared a small feast for the evening meal. Maria taught Grace and Lillian how to make a seafood risotto seasoned with saffron. Lillian made a chicken tagine seasoned with a mix of nutmeg, cinnamon, cumin, paprika and cardamon. She showed Grace how to fry eggplant then add honey to it along with how to make rose water syrup to pour over baklava and to flavor a fragrant tea. As the main dishes finished simmering, Grace excused herself to take a bath.

"Use the large one in Dante's bedroom. It is deeper than the one in the guest bath. He nor Rayne will return for a bit," Maria suggested, checking the artichokes steaming over the fire.

"I do not want to upset Dante by invading his personal space."

"If my son would mind you using his bath, I would not advise you to do so. Go relax, Grace. You have earned it after the past several days. I will put some towels and soap out for you if you want to grab your robe from your room."

Grace picked out a gown to wear to dinner. After laying it on the bed, she walked down the hall to Dante's bedroom. The large room definitely fit him. Colorful frescoes framed by green and white marble columns decorated the walls. A four-poster bed covered by a hunter green Venetian velvet comforter and pillows in matching green, black, and gold sat in the center of the far wall. Grace ran her hand over the comforter. The soft, plush fibers caressed her palm. Dante always enjoyed luxuries in his private spaces. So strange for a man who frequently shunned them elsewhere.

The sprawling white marble floor extended into the master bath. Dante's tub was more like a small pool than a bathtub. Grace slowly descended the steps into the warm water. The scent of jasmine floated around the room.

Grace discovered a carved-out niche that allowed one to stretch out and soak at the far end of the tub. She picked up the bar of soap and smelled it. The sweet fragrance of summer peaches actually made her mouth water. She could almost taste the delicate orange and red flesh of the fruit on her tongue.

"I need to remember to ask Maria where she got this," Grace said to herself as she lathered up her arms.

After washing, she closed her eyes, enjoying the quiet and warm water. Every once in a while, she could hear Tessa laughing or the muffled sound of Lillian and Maria talking. If only their days routinely returned to such a calm existence. Feeling as if someone watched her, Grace opened her eyes. She slowly scanned the room, but didn't see anyone. Not caring for having company while she bathed, Grace climbed out of the tub, dried off, and put on her robe. She walked into the bedroom and pulled out the dagger Dante kept in the chest of drawers near his bed.

"Is everything all right, cara?" Dante asked from behind her.

Grace spun around. "Dante? How long have you been home?"

"I just returned from Spain." Dante's left brow lifted a bit higher than his right one, his head cocked to the side before his eyes swept down her body then back to her face. "I am a bit surprised to find you in my bedroom, wearing only a robe, and holding a knife, no less."

Feeling stupid, Grace set his blade on the bed. Her imagination must have been playing tricks on her if Dante didn't sense anything out of place. "Maria said I could use your bathtub. Toward the end of my bath, I felt like someone watched me."

"Someone watched you?" Dante picked up the weapon she had put down. "Stay here."

"What are you…" Grace didn't finish her sentence after Dante held up his hand then placed his finger in front of his lips, cautioning her to be quiet.

Dante searched the bedroom and bathroom. Nothing appeared to be out of place. The only things he didn't recognize in the room were the bath oil and bar of soap Grace smelled like. The large window on the back wall remained locked. Coming out of the bathroom, he went out onto the balcony since he regularly left his room doors open. Nothing was amiss out there or in the rear yard of his home. He returned to Grace and laid the dagger down on a table near the bed. "It must have been your imagination, cara. No one is here but us."

"Maybe."

Dante placed an understanding hand on her arm. "We are all on edge. Rayne and the others returned with me. He is speaking to Lillian right now. So nothing is misconstrued about you being in your robe and with me in my bedroom, mayhap it is best you make your way to your room."

Grace took a deep breath and nodded. "Thank you for checking things out."

"My pleasure, cara."

As soon as Grace departed, Dante quietly closed his bedroom door. One of his curtains moved, but there was no breeze. "I well warned you to leave Grace alone."

A curvaceous, tall, mahogany-haired woman in a white gown appeared in the doorway. "I came to see you. Instead, I find your ex-wife in your bath."

"Allow me to reiterate my earlier warning, Volupta. *My wife* is to be left alone. You will not like what happens if I discover she is the unwitting victim of any scheming by yourself or anyone else acting on your behalf."

"From what I hear, she no longer considers herself your spouse. It's most entertaining watching you play house, taking care of her two children, and at times, her."

"Must I remind you, you are no longer welcome in my home."

"I am surprised Rayne did not strangle you when Grace confessed to offering herself to you. It's a shame Hades never got to tell the court how the two of you pawed at one another in your bed while lip locked. Or how her robe was undone, and you rested yourself between her bare thighs. You may fool the Council at times, but I know what you are. I saw you and her with my own eyes that night."

Dante let out a mocking laugh. "You spend one night in my bed and claim to know everything about me? You are no more an expert on me than you are an expert in Council matters. Unleash your worst on me, goddess. My pathetic, drunken self has earned your wrath, but leave

Grace out of the dispute between us. My wife has committed no wrong against you."

Volupta huffed at the god who declined her recent advances. "Your wife. She is not worthy of a god. She is plain, and boring, other than her hair, Dante. Her hair is quite lovely. With all the beautiful human women in the world, you took such an average example of one as your wife."

"Jealousy does not become a woman such as yourself, goddess."

Volupta shot him a murderous stare. "I am not jealous of that former human. You have goddesses willing to ease your loneliness, yet you turn us away for such a plain, former human enraptured with War."

"I enjoy my solitude. As for the plain, boring, former human, Grace possesses a greater beauty than any goddess offers. It's interwoven with every fiber of her being. If Grace ever seeks my bed again, she will obtain the exact thing you desire."

Volupta slapped him. "You insolent half-breed. To think I once thought you worthy to be my lover."

Dante grasped her wrist. "Strike me or come near my wife ever again, and this half-breed, will end you, Volupta. Leave. Now. Before I teach you the manners that Cupid and Psyche failed to."

Grace helped Maria and Lillian set the table. As she set a platter of risotto down, Dante walked into the dining room with a disgruntled expression on his face. His hair still slightly damp from bathing before dinner. "What's wrong, cavaliere?"

Maria looked up from placing silverware next to each plate. Something definitely troubled her son.

"Niente, Grazia. I am only tired."

Lillian passed in front of him, carrying the tagine she had made.

Dante reached for the heavy serving dish. "Allow me to take it for you."

"Thank you, Dante." Lillian gladly turned over the tagine then disappeared into the kitchen to fetch another of the remaining plates and bowls filled with food.

Rayne joined the growing group in the dining room now that he had cleaned up and changed. Seeing his mother, Maria, and Grace flitting about the room, setting food on the table, he nodded to Lillian. "Mother."

Lillian gave his arm a gentle squeeze as she passed him, then disappeared into the kitchen.

"You ladies prepared a feast worthy of a king," Rayne complimented the three women as he stared down at the growing amount of food being placed on the table. "What can I help put out?"

"You can open the wine and bring it out," Grace advised, stopping briefly to kiss him.

"Grace, your gown is quite lovely." Maria smiled from across the room.

Uncertain as to what caused Maria to remark on the simple dress, Grace looked down at what she wore. Rayne and Dante both took in the woman's appearance. Her long golden hair hung freely around her shoulders, a simple short-sleeved white chemise with a low neckline was covered by a square necked gold-colored kirtle that laced up the front.

"Yes, it is." Rayne stepped forward and brought Grace's hand to his lips. "But not near as lovely as the woman wearing it. I am a blessed man to have the honor of calling her wife."

Grace appreciatively smiled up at Rayne before kissing him.

Dante chuckled at how his mother's attempt to get him to flatter Grace failed due to Rayne taking advantage of the opportunity presented. So she hadn't abandoned the course his father set as he hoped she would. "Mama, may I speak with you for a moment?"

"Certo, mio figlio." Maria strode past him into the kitchen, ignoring the raised brow and chiding expression he gave her.

A few minutes later, Maria almost shouted at Dante.

"Abassa la voce, Mama." Dante wished his mother would lower her voice.

"What is that all about?" Grace started for the kitchen.

Rayne caught Grace's hand, stopping her from leaving the dining room. "They had some sort of disagreement last night. I'd wager they are working things out. Let's give them another moment before going into the kitchen."

Maria's voice raised a second time. The only word Grace recognized in the rapid-fire Venetian dialect was Volupta. She could see the two of them through the open archway. Maria lightly popped Dante's shoulder with the wooden spoon she held. Dante glared at Maria, but continued to speak calmly. Grace choked back a laugh. It was so strange to see someone scolding Dante the way Maria was.

"Mother." Rayne intercepted Lillian as she headed for the kitchen again. "Tell me about the tagine you made. It smells delicious."

Rayne periodically looked over Lillian's head to see if Dante and Maria had finished their discussion. Thankfully, they seemed to work through whatever matter they discussed fairly quickly. Once Maria came out carrying the plate of steamed artichokes, he went into the kitchen to open the wine.

"Everything resolved?" Rayne asked, screwing the wine key down then pulling out the cork from the bottle Dante handed him.

"Si. Thank you for giving us a few minutes alone."

Rayne smiled and nodded, then opened another bottle of wine. Even with all the Horsemen, Grace, Dante, Lillian, Maria, and the children eating together tonight, Rayne doubted they'd finish the extravagant meal.

Once everyone was seated, Lillian went back into the kitchen for the round tray filled with fried eggplant drizzled with honey and sea salt. The smell of fried eggplant wafting up from the table towards Rayne conjured memories of eating at the banquet table in his parents' home as a child. Biting into the warm slice of eggplant he held, Rayne's eyes closed. The sweet honey and crunching of sea salt coalescing with thyme brought a smile to his face as he savored the simple dish he had not eaten in years.

Grace had never seen Rayne enjoy a meal so much. She giggled at how pronounced the dimples in his cheeks were even with his mouth closed and the barely audible "mmmm" that sounded from his lips. Good memories always made flavorful food taste better. She cut a piece of the eggplant on her plate to try it. Her reaction to the fusion of flavors was similar to Rayne's. He chuckled knowingly beside her.

"How have I not eaten these before? They are heavenly."

Lillian beamed at her son and daughter-in-law, delighted they both liked the eggplant so much. "Fried eggplant with honey and salt was one of Haroun's favorite foods when he was a child. Now that you know how to make them, I am sure he will request them often."

"You taught Grace how to make these?" Rayne asked, surprised she had.

"I did. She made most of the slices on the plate. Maria and I taught her our tricks to preparing each dish you see. She is an excellent student, so is little Tessa."

"Tarquin and I made dessert," Tessa announced from across the table.

Rayne smiled at his daughter happily sitting in between Lillian and Dante, eating eggplant and a small artichoke made special for her. "I look forward to trying the dessert you two made."

Laughter resounded through Dante's house as dinner went on. For a couple of hours, the group forgot about Isra and Malik. They told stories and joked as they once used to in Essaouira or in the dining hall of Morrigan's castle in Sasainn. Rarely did the Horsemen all gather as a group around the table anymore. Maria and Lillian added to the merriment, sharing entertaining tales about mischief Dante and Rayne caused in their youth.

Rayne's arm rested around Grace while she finished her wine. It was nice to have a brief sense of normalcy in tumultuous times.

"It's getting late. I am going to get the children ready for bed," Grace said before kissing Rayne then standing up.

"Mama!" Tarquin protested, annoyed at how he was being made to leave the table while the Horsemen still drank and conversed.

"Tarquin." Dante raised a brow, giving his son a scolding look. "The day will come when you stay at the table with all of us until the witching hour. But that day is not here yet. Go with your mother and sister."

After the table was cleared, Rayne strolled with Lillian around Dante's gardens.

"You and Grace seem enamored with each other." Lillian broke the silence they walked in.

By the tone she used, his mother laid the groundwork for a more intrusive question. Rayne quietly took in a deep breath before responding to the remark. "We love one another a great deal."

"And you trust this god, Dante, to leave your wife and children in his care?"

"I do."

"Even with his being Grace's former husband and lover?"

Rayne halted and stared down at his mother. "Yes. Is there a reason you ask inquiries of this nature?"

"No. Yes. I am trying to understand your new world, what you have become. Most men I know, including your father, would not want their wives staying with a former lover or husband for fear of..."

"Dante would never assault or ransom my wife, nor would Grace and he engage in any sort of questionable relations, if that is what you are concerned about."

"The way he looks at her at times. He is still in love with your wife."

"I am well aware of Dante's feelings for Grace. Mother, I trust my wife. The reason I believe Elysium is the safest place for Grace and the children, along with you at the moment, is because Dante would surrender his existence if needed to keep all of you alive. He and I are old friends. He won't do anything to compromise my marriage or our friendship."

"If that is true, why the possessive display throughout dinner?"

Bewildered, Rayne wondered what he had done for his mother to say such a thing. "Possessive display?"

"Your arm remained around Grace's waist or rested on her shoulders. You also kissed her more than once at the table."

Rayne grinned. "Mother, that was not being possessive. In our world, and the time Grace is from, showing affection to your spouse in public is expected and a normal occurrence. You will find the immortal community has a different interpretation of what is and is not acceptable when it comes to demonstrations of friendship and love than we do in Córdoba. I rather enjoy being able to be reasonably affectionate with those I care about. It was a change for me to embrace, but one I find most welcome."

Lillian worried she may have offended Dante or Grace by not engaging in the same actions she observed tonight. "Am I behaving in a manner that is acceptable to our host and your friends? I do not wish to offend anyone."

"You have not offended anyone. None of us expect you to act as we do. We all are very sensitive to the fact that different people have different standards of conduct and social expectations of men and women."

Lillian offered her son a timorous smile. Everything about her new surroundings still dumbfounded her. "When may I return to Córdoba? Your father will be concerned if I am not at home when he returns."

"Hopefully late tomorrow or the next day. There are still one or two things I wish to investigate before taking you back, especially with Baba gone." Rayne understood why his mother would be anxious to return home and how disconcerting everything must be for her.

"Speaking of your father, he told me about Grace protecting him and his men in Lucena, along with her handling a local warlord when he appeared at Lucena's gates. Maria claims Grace is as much a soldier as you and Dante are."

"She is indeed." Rayne proudly smiled, thinking of how far Grace had come over the years.

"Then she should be honored as such." Lillian gently tapped the jeweled dagger hanging from his side.

Rayne contemplated the suggestion. "A familial dagger is only given to the men of the Ibn-Ziyad family who serve in the armies. Giving one to a woman would break the old traditions you vehemently uphold."

"I am slowly coming to like the idea of beginning new traditions, especially after learning how women in the immortal world stand on more equal footing with men. Perhaps it is time to change some of our old ways."

Rayne loudly laughed, hugging his mother. "You always were the wisest of my teachers. I will do as you suggest. Though be careful what you take back to the human realm. I wouldn't want to learn my mother was imprisoned or burned at the stake for challenging the patriarchal ways of the medieval world."

Elysium

Grace went to Dante's study to wish him goodnight. She peered inside the open door, but there was no sign of him. A shard of broken glass with gold leaf on it near the fireplace caught her eye. She entered the room and bent down to pick up the piece. When she did so, she spotted several other matching fragments scattered on the tile and near the stone hearth. She recognized the remnants of the Venetian decanter. Glancing back at the office bar, only the crystal decanter and a few bottles of liquor remained. Why did Dante destroy the one his father had given them as a wedding gift? Between this and Maria sharing he was heavily drinking again, Grace worried about him. She walked to his bedroom. Like the study, it too was empty. Where had he gone?

"Nowhere." Dante's voice answered her unasked question. His body briefly brushed against hers, warning he stood directly behind her. "I was putting the leftover wine away."

The smell of fresh peaches wafted up from her skin and hair. Dante's eyes closed; he inhaled the alluring scent again. His mind raced back to their wedding night and the night they developed their plan to ensnare Qasim. She had bathed in the same oil and soap then. His hands settled on her waist. He originally intended to remove her from his bedroom doorway, but memories of her naked and laughing caused him to step closer to her instead. He nuzzled the side of her head.

Electric, frenetic desire shot from the skin his nose touched, down Grace's torso all the way to her toes. His grip tightened covetously on her hips while his lips glided over the soft skin of her neck. She reflexively grasped the muscular thigh pressed up against her. Her head turned, welcoming his seeking lips. The passion building treacherously between them with each touch of their tongues. Images of them entwined in his sheets played in her head.

"Grace," Dante murmured her name, his fingers undoing the front lacings of her kirtle. "You torture me to no end, stella. One minute cold and distant, the next imaging me taking you in my bed."

Yanking her soft chemise open and down once the laces gave way, Dante cupped and caressed her exposed breasts. She whimpered, reclining against him, her arm curling around his neck, and her head falling back onto his shoulder. Dante admired the woman slowly surrendering to him. Not even a master artisan like Michelangelo could capture the intricate details of her lost in uninhibited rapture: her eyes closed and lips parted, golden curled tendrils falling over her shoulder and his, the creamy swell of her breasts contrasting against the darker hue of his palms cradling them while his fingers painted their pink-colored peaks in light, circular strokes, transforming their hue to a flushed rose.

"Ease this endless ache you cause me, mia stella." Dante swept the side of her skirt upward; his fingers whisked the inside of her thighs, slowly rising higher, seeking her core. After lightly skimming the conjunction of where her thighs met, his hand slipped down her belly, under soft cotton, until he found the prize he sought. A breathy ahhh fell from her lips as the tip of his finger grazed the swollen jewel of her sex.

Grace's body hummed and her nerves sang from his masterful strumming of sensitive flesh. Every inch of her tingled. She clutched the doorframe for balance. "Rayne could..."

"He won't, amore. Do not fear for your marriage. I will conceal everything between us."

The dampness against Dante's fingertips grew, allowing them to more easily glide in the variety of patterns he traced against the tender nub. He groaned, enjoying her heightened arousal. Feeling her body quake, his fingers delved into the exact place he longed to bury himself.

"Dante."

He edged her closer to the brink. "Si, cara?"

She didn't answer, but instead, turned to face him, her hands frantically clasping at the back of his shirt. The way she vigorously kissed him urged him to forge her into the living masterpiece he envisioned. Dante loosened his pants then pressed their bodies tightly together; his erection slipped between her thighs. He ever-so-slowly rocked his hips; tormenting them both with the intimate friction of skin against skin without him entering her. He continued doing so, backing her into the room and towards his bed.

The velvet comforter tickled the back of Grace's knees once they reached it. She instinctively laid down, bringing Dante onto the bed with her. His teeth grazed one of her nipples before his tongue flicked around it, easing the sting the light bite caused. He alternated suckling each breast until Grace arched up underneath him and her fist seized the hair on the back of his head, a loud cry escaping her lips.

"Cavaliere! I want..." Grace couldn't finish the sentence with how he lightly nipped the pink tip in his mouth.

Dante rolled, so she sat astride his waist. "Take what you desire, Grazia."

Grace panted, staring down into golden eyes. "You normally do the taking."

Dante laughed. "Si, ma stasera, you must claim me. I do not want you later regretting embracing the Triad, mia stella."

The mention of the Cornerstone Prophecy dampened her desire. Still, all she had to do was shift her body to slide down the length of hard flesh displaying Dante's ardor for her. Her body and heart traitorously demanded gratification; her mind screamed, you compromise everything. The way Dante patiently waited for her to make her choice only made the decision harder. She leaned forward and kissed him.

Her hips tilted, entrapping the tip of him in the folds of her opening. Tempted to thrust upward into the body he hungered for, Dante seized her hips, forcing her lower body to remain still.

When the kiss ended, Grace gazed down at him again. "I can't do this. I want to, Dante. By the gods do I want to, but I can't." Her heart pounding and still breathing heavily, Grace forced herself off him. "Not right now, not while my marriage is in turmoil. Rayne would never forgive me."

"When you are ready then." Dante sat up, took her hands in his, and laid his forehead against hers. "One day, Rayne, you, and I will embrace what is to be. You needn't fear losing either of us."

Both of them sat quietly together, tormented by insatiable yearning and obligation to vows they freely gave others. Neither able to convey their feelings in words, their lips met, sharing one last kiss.

Grace slowly slid off the bed, relaced the bodice of her kirtle then smoothed her skirts and hair. "I am sorry, Dante. We need to stay away from one another. This can't happen again." She fled the room before something could tempt her back into his arms.

Frustrated, Dante laid back on his bed. He should have never given into temptation. The lavish meal, the peach soap and bath oil, Rayne walking outside in the gardens with his mother, Grace in his bedroom doorway; all warned of the Fates' meddling. He hoped he hadn't destroyed what precious trust he had earned back from Grace with the one moment of lecherous weakness.

The liquor down the hall whispered his name, promising numbing relief from the now agonizing craving for Grace. Resisting its call, Dante got up and slammed his bedroom door shut. Vice and impulsivity placed him in a precarious enough position tonight, he wouldn't add to it. No more drinking anytime Grace was present in his home. It removed too much of his inhibition that kept his desires in check. He needed to be on his guard, especially with his own mother and father scheming with the Fates against him.

Grace's perturbed expression and the quick, forceful strokes of the brush through her hair held Rayne's attention as he watched her ready for bed. "You seem flustered, leof. What's troubling you?"

"I am annoyed by Isra's most recent ploy." Grace drew the covers down, hoping Rayne believed the bogus excuse.

Rayne frowned, but didn't inquire further. Concerned about whatever troubled her, he walked to the bed and stood behind her. She jumped when his fingers ran down her arms in what would normally be a welcome caress. "Do not let Isra trouble you, especially after such a wonderful evening." He kissed her temple, trying to soothe her angst. "Thank you for taking care of my mother and the brief respite from the difficulties in Spain."

"You're welcome." Grace forced a smile and glanced over her shoulder at him. "Your mother and Maria planned the dinner. I only helped prepare things. We should get to bed. It's late. I know you and the others will want to be out tracking Isra at sunrise."

Rayne watched Grace lay down then joined her in the bed. He wrapped an arm around her and gave her a goodnight kiss. "I love you, Grace."

Grace stared across her pillow into calming ocean-colored eyes. "I love you too."

Rayne caressed her cheek with his thumb. "I will gladly listen to whatever troubles you when you are ready to share it." Her gaze drifted downward. "Leof, I know it isn't Isra who bothers you. I sense the same turmoil I used to in Rome and Sasainn when we first courted."

"Rayne." Grace searched for the words to tell him the truth after he referenced the days she found herself caught between him and Dante. She finally brought her eyes back up to his.

Rayne's hand traveled down her side to rest on her hip. "The Fates rekindle feelings between you and Dante the longer you are in Elysium. I see it, along with everyone else."

"You stood by me when Dante chose to walk away."

"I will always stand by you, Grace. Regardless of what trouble the Fates stir." Rayne drew her against him, reassuringly holding her. "I will bring you back to Córdoba with me tomorrow, so you no longer find yourself under duress."

Grace doubted he'd be so forgiving if he ever learned how far things had gone between her and Dante. "You have to be the most understanding being in the realms to so casually deal with another man tempting your wife."

"I am empathetic to where fallibility can lead us. Moreover, I am soul bound to my wife. No one, djinn or god, can ever take her from me, no matter how hard they may try. We will survive these distressing times and whatever the Fates send our way."

CHAPTER

FORTY-SIX

Córdoba - 812 - Two weeks later.

After no more concerning issues with Isra, Rayne returned Lillian to Córdoba. Unfortunately, the political intrigue in Malik's court continued to escalate. Rayne, Saladin, and Grace met with various advisors and their wives trying to better understand the financial state of the Emirate. Every lead they uncovered turned into a dead end or a dead body, frustrating the three of them. Priya hadn't made any more appearances. Grace and Rayne assumed whatever disturbed her had passed. Isra vanished from the Andalusian city as well.

Grace rummaged through Rayne's desk looking for the note he asked her to retrieve. Where was it? And why was his normally organized desk suddenly such a mess?

A shuffling sound followed by a loud crash, as if something suddenly fell, came from outside.

Grace, Sulla, and Kato looked toward the window, but didn't see anything out of place.

Grace glanced back at the scattered papers on Rayne's desk. "Something is definitely out there, and considering Rayne is meticulous in how he keeps everything, I'd wager whatever it is has been in the house."

488

She walked into the great room to look out of the front windows.

Kato pushed her back into the side wall. "It's a djinn. Don't let him see you."

Grace pulled one of the scimitars hung on the wall from its scabbard. Footsteps traveled the front porch, moving toward the door. "How did they enter the house?"

Kato leaned sideways to steal another look out of the window. "I am not certain he did."

"Then who else went through Rayne's desk?" Grace slid along the wall and moved closer to the front door. The djinn didn't know they were there. Hopefully, it would leave without a confrontation. "Our visitor seems to be confused or unsure of himself."

"The djinn can't enter. The protection spell keeps him out." Sulla took arms himself. "Strange. He doesn't seem to be searching for you or us."

"Who is he looking for?"

"I am not certain. But whoever it is, I suspect they have taken refuge here."

Something charged into Grace. Other than knocking her down, no harm was done. She wasn't sure what her assailant was.

"Please. You have to save him!"

Scarred gray skinned hands gripped Grace's shoulders. Round, light brown eyes with golden flecks stared at her. There was something pleading in the creature's eyes when Grace looked into their depths. Dull, scraggly black hair framed a marred, gaunt face.

"Do not strike me. I come to warn you." It could barely get the words out with being wounded from a prior entanglement with what Grace assumed was the djinn outside the door. "Your husband... Isra intends to kill him, since he will not surrender himself."

Grace slowly lowered the scimitar she held. What was this new being? It seemed harmless enough for a djinn to hunt it and for it to ask for help.

Kato snarled, lunging at their visitor. Grace pushed the wolf away. "Stop, Kato! I want to hear whatever it has to say."

Kato sat, but continued growling. The injured creature mumbled a thank you to Grace.

"Why do you warn me?" Grace doubted one of Isra's djinn would suddenly seek to aid Rayne.

"I loved him once." Priya's human face flickered before Grace.

Grace recognized the woman from Rayne's past. "Priya?"

The creature nodded. "Yes. She is conjuring Haroun's past to ensnare him. I refused to do as she asked. Isra caused my wounds and turned me into what you see. She showed me you and your daughter hoping to tempt me into a jealous rage. When her attempt failed, she tortured me, and issued orders to hunt you and Haroun down. I escaped to warn Haroun, but no one was here."

"You went through Rayne's desk." Grace said, now understanding why the normally immaculate desk was in such a chaotic state.

"I hoped his correspondence would reveal where he might be since he wasn't here. I hid when you and the wolves arrived. Haroun needs no further grief added to that he already carries. Grief corrupts him. He is powerful, Grace. He always has been. Warn him not to trust anyone here, not even those closest to him."

"I promise I will tell him everything. Allow me to help you, Priya. Haroun would never want you to suffer like this. I can take you to someone who can heal your injuries and see you safely back into the afterlife."

"It is too late for that." Having survived long enough to protect her former fiancé, Priya's eyes closed.

"Osiris!" Grace hoped the god heard her.

Lyal materialized before Grace. "He cannot help her."

"I can't let her soul be lost. Priya is innocent in all of this. She only suffers because she loved Rayne long ago."

"I will take Priya to Anubis, so your husband never discovers her fate."

"Can Anubis heal her?"

"If he cannot, he can ensure her soul passes the test of the scales then usher her back into the afterlife, so she isn't trapped here on earth." Lyal held out Rayne's familial dagger. "You must end the standoff between Rayne and Isra before it escalates again."

Grace yanked the dagger from her hand. "How could you take this from Rayne when he hunts Isra?"

"He will not kill her until he has no other options. You, unlike your husband, have no issue terminating Isra."

"Lyal, Rayne cannot kill her."

"She deceives him with a spell."

Grace let out an irritated sigh. "Then go tell him that and how to override it."

"The moon must dispatch Isra, not the wolf."

"I gave him my word never to confront Isra alone again. I cannot go back on that."

"Lillian is her next target. An invitation from Malik was secretly sent to Lillian requesting an urgent meeting this afternoon regarding Haroun. Who do you think truly sends the invite?"

"Why are you telling me instead of Rayne?" Grace knew there was more. Lyal whispered the reason in her ear. "He wouldn't. Rayne has mastered controlling his darker side."

"How well do you think he will control it, seeing his mother sliced into pieces by Malik and Narciso? There will be no bringing him back. End this."

"Rayne would never go down that road."

Lyal eyed Grace. "Why wouldn't he?"

"I know my husband. He won't turn."

"You've seen Rayne's wrath yourself. You do not honestly believe he would be consolable if someone killed his mother."

"At first, no. Rayne would be angry, and would most likely go after Isra and Narciso, possibly Malik, but nothing more than that. Rationality would start to set in for him once he caught up to those three."

"What makes you so certain?"

"The enforcer swore a new oath to another."

"The only oath that could eternally bind an enforcer is a mutual one taken with a soul mate of the opposite nature. Considering Rayne's dominant personality, he would have to take a submissive."

"He has one. She just isn't what most folks think a submissive should be."

Repulsed by what Grace has done, Lyal's upper lip rose in a disgusted sneer. "Did I not teach you never to lower yourself to such things?"

"Lower myself?! After all the things you've done, you dare to judge me?"

"You are the descendant of a goddess. He is a djinn. If anything, War should be the one serving you."

"Rayne and I are equals, Lyal. It's a mutual exchange. Neither he nor I buy into this stupid hierarchy the rest of you follow. It also ensures his loyalty to good. He'll obey any order I give if, on the off chance, he turns into the monster you claim he will." Grace threw her hands up in the air. "Why am I justifying this to you? He's my husband. I'd do anything for him. End of discussion. Get Priya to Anubis."

"Isra kills you. There will be no barriers to prevent Rayne from falling under Isra's control."

Grace doubted Isra could do anything more than annoy her. "She can't kill an immortal, Lyal."

"She steals Lucifer's harbinger blade. Rayne refuses to listen as you are. In a week, you will be dead, and your husband an enforcer once more."

"I would foresee that."

"The Fates showed Rayne instead. He doubts the dreams."

Grace needed proof of Lyal's claim. "I won't break my promise to Rayne. What is the vision the Fates gave Rayne, so I can convince him to take action on it?"

"See for yourself." Lyal shoved Grace, sending her stumbling through time.

FORTY-SEVEN

Granada - 812 - Three weeks into the future.

Grace hated the scene she found herself in. Men, women, and children lay massacred around her. Building roofs and facades were charred. Billows of black smoke hung in the sky. Chunks of stone created scattered patterns between corpses on the interior streets that ran the length of damaged wall; telltale signs of projectiles launched from mangonels. Someone intentionally raised Granada. Blackened fields spanned the horizon outside the shattered city gates. The battering ram used to open them lay abandoned a few feet away. This wasn't a siege to take a city; whoever attacked intended to destroy it, so it wouldn't be habitable ever again.

Terror swept across Grace's features. Lyal loathed the idea of Rayne turning as much as Grace did, but did not carry the sense of denial that it could happen. "Your husband's darker side unleashed."

"Rayne did this?" Grace couldn't believe he would slaughter an entire innocent population. "Why?"

"One brief slip of subduing the enforcer gave Isra the opening she needed."

Praying Rayne could be brought back to the Horsemen if she found him, Grace transformed her clothes to her uniform. "Take Priya to Anubis and stop Lillian from accepting that invitation. If you can't do both, have Xander and his men intercept Lillian. Isra can't suspect we are on to her plans. I will find and put down Isra. And if need be, Rayne."

Fighting War himself may very well end her. Having to imprison or kill the other half of her soul would destroy her.

"The Fates say there is more you must learn. Find your husband. Only after you speak with War, may you return to the present to stop this from occurring." Lyal abandoned Grace in the future after delivering the Fates' message.

"How in the hell am I going to outwit Rayne without help? War is no fool," Grace muttered, looking skyward. Of course the Fates offered no assistance. They rarely ever did. One life! Grace reminded herself of the question asked of all harbingers and guardians. Is one life worth all of humanity?

Focusing on the task at hand, she looked at the footprints left by ash-covered boots and how the sand and dust layer over the cobblestone shifted, leaving multiple outlines of hoofprints and more booted feet. The attacking party moved northward through the town. Grace followed the tracks to the large square in the center of the medieval city. The worst of the fighting appeared to have occurred here and not at the walls as she first believed. Rayne and Isra caught the town by surprise. Grace could almost envision the panicked people fleeing to the center of town; vainly hoping to find some protection by congregating in larger numbers. Their attempt to find refuge sadly turned into a mass execution.

She carefully stepped over corpses starting to bloat in the afternoon heat. Thankfully, the stench of decay didn't mingle with that of blood in the air yet. The gurgling of the fountain in the center hauntingly reverberated off the building walls surrounding it. Death had a way of silencing even the sparrows and doves one would normally hear in a city center. Her own boots left red prints behind her while she made her way over cobblestone, now dyed dark red from the blood flowing over them. Nothing living seemed to remain in Granada.

A moan sounded from behind an overturned cart. Someone was still alive. Grace carefully made her way around the strewn contents of the cart and found who she assumed was the driver beside it. She knelt down to inspect his injuries.

He winced as she touched a cut on the side of his face. "Will I live?"

"If we can get you help, you should." Grace tried to heal the large gash across his chest enough to stabilize the man without drawing attention to herself.

"Are you a healer?" The man was confused as to whether a soldier or healer tended to him.

"No, I am not a healer, but I am familiar enough with tending injuries like yours. What happened here?"

"A woman demanded we turn over the town treasury and food stores. When we refused, she unleashed her army upon us."

Grace tore his tunic the rest of the way to get better access to his wound. "Did you see who led this army?"

"The Devil of Andalus himself, Haroun Ibn-Ziyad. All these years I thought him a mere myth."

"You are certain it was Ibn- Ziyad? That some entity isn't trying to frighten people with an old tale?" Grace still couldn't believe after being a Horseman Rayne could kill like this.

"One man called him by name. The general rode in black with the blood red scimitar on his side as he is often described. His two wolves accompanied him. There is no mistaking the monster I saw."

Footsteps approached from an alleyway behind her.

"They return," the man she helped whispered.

"Ensure there are no survivors." A broad-shouldered sentry ordered the soldiers with him. The four began checking the bodies scattered around the square.

"Stay quiet; no matter what they do," Grace cautioned her compatriot before looking around for a better place to hide. The four hadn't noticed her yet.

Not seeing a nearby spot she could conceal herself in, she laid down beside the driver and kept a watchful eye on the soldiers. Maybe she could follow them back to wherever they camped and find Rayne.

The smallest of the bunch came around the back side of the wagon. Grace held her breath, hoping he would think she was dead. He tilted her body with his foot. She forced herself to remain limp. He only briefly glanced at the man next to her before moving on to the next group of corpses.

She shifted, accidentally bumping the wounded man in the side. He let out a pain-filled groan. The muted sound was enough to catch the djinn's attention. The djinn retraced his steps back to them. Grace once more held her breath and focused on staying still.

The gold of one of her collar devices was now visible from under her cloak. He leaned closer to her to inspect it. His breath smelled of rotting fish. A clawed finger shifted the gold device in the sunlight. It was fair spoils for his work that day. When he tugged on the laurels, his foot slid forward, sending dust into Grace's face. Knowing she couldn't stop the sneeze tickling her nose, Grace slowly pulled the dagger on her hip then swung up, aiming straight for the djinn's chest. The blade sliced through his uniform and into his skin as she sneezed. The loud achoo bouncing off stone walls alerted the unit roving the empty streets that someone survived their wrath.

The djinn howled in pain, but her blade had missed its mark. Grace cursed. She swung behind him and slit his throat. Shouting came from all around her, along with the sound of hoofbeats.

A mounted djinn officer rode into the square with the fresh troops.

"Narciso," Grace whispered the enforcer's name. His presence confirmed Rayne and Isra must be nearby.

Dark eyes locked on her. "Take her alive! I want to know who she is and why she is here."

Grace managed to fight off several of the horde swarming her before something collided with the back of her skull.

A deluge of frigid water pouring over Grace brought her back to life. Sputtering, she opened her eyes to find herself on a stone floor in an expanding puddle of water. A length of chain ran from the wall to her wrists. Her weapons lay on a table several feet away. Two lower-ranking djinn stood on either side of her.

"Your name!" A demon demanded. By his formal attire and the

ornate insignia on his clothing, she assumed he was an officer of some sort.

Grace glared at the demon the best she could despite the splitting headache she had.

The demon backhanded her. "Insolent woman, you will tell me your name."

"The only one I will give my name to is Haroun Ibn-Ziyad."

The demon laughed. "The Primus has more important matters to deal with than some woman who has forgotten her name."

One of the guards kicked her in the side, causing her to wince. "Your name."

Grace slowly climbed to her feet, but said nothing.

"We will make you speak yet, woman." The demon forced her into the wall, raising a glowing, red fireplace poker near her face.

"My name is Death. I come to avenge the humans." Grace yanked the man's weapon from his side, tilted the long blade sideways, then ran it through his rib cage.

The demon stood with mouth open as she speared him with the poker he had initially held before turning to dust. She vanquished the closest guard to her before turning to face the one guarding the dungeon entrance.

Damn it! The last guard was human. "Stand aside, and tell me where Haroun Ibn-Ziyad is, in exchange, I will spare you."

The human screamed for assistance to subdue a prisoner.

Kato and four other guards sprinted into the room. Grace killed the four djinn, but hesitated when the human who called for help swung at her.

Kato noted her hesitation in attacking the human mercenary. "Send the humans to secure her."

Hoping to correct her error, Grace quickly knocked the man to the ground.

Six human officers and their soldiers flooded the cell. She poorly defended herself to mislead Kato and the mercenaries. The humans would let their guard down if they believed she was some random, angry, incompetent female swordsman. She surrendered after a brief encounter. The closest two mercenaries seized her chains.

She held her head high and stared directly at Kato. "I demand to speak to whomever the highest-ranking individual is here."

"Prisoners, especially women, don't make demands." The guard on her left snarled.

Grace brought the length of chain securing her wrists over the man's head and choked him. "I am not just any prisoner. Now, who in this room is your commanding officer?"

"He reports to me." Kato slowly approached Grace. "Do you honestly think you can fight us all?"

"I am willing to die finding out how many of you I can take into Hell with me. I am not that much different a soldier than you." By the slight widening of Kato's eyes, he understood she implied she was immortal.

"The man will die if you keep the chain that tight."

"I have no qualms killing a worthless mercenary, especially after what was done to Granada today. If you do not value life, why should I?"

Unsure whether the woman bluffed or would kill the man she held prisoner, Kato frowned. "I may value life more than you believe I do. State your terms, woman."

The man she choked swayed on his feet, warning he was close to passing out. Grace didn't loosen her hold. If she did, she would lose the bit of leverage Kato gave her. "Take me to Haroun Ibn-Ziyad, or I will decimate every man in here, including you."

Kato closed the distance between them. "Do you know who you challenge, woman?"

"Have you earned your right to walk again or did you swear a new oath to Isra to stay in human form this long, wolf?" Grace tested the creature once her friend.

The inquiry halted him a foot from her. Gray eyes more closely studied her face.

"If you truly value the men's lives in this room, take me to Haroun, Kato. Now."

The guard's knees buckled as the man blacked out. Grace released her hold on him, letting his body collapse to the floor then removed the wedding ring from her hand. She tossed it to Kato.

Surprise flickered on his face as he looked at the ring. Kato knew the stones and design. "You can't be..."

"Onore e Gloria, lupus."

Kato moved closer to get a better look at her. Recognizing her now, he shook his head in disbelief. "The Primus will not be pleased with a prisoner demanding a meeting at this hour."

"I am not afraid of displeasing him. I suspect the enforcer will be angrier to learn of your failure to inform him I am here."

Kato laughed. "We shall see, woman. Who shall I say requests an audience with General Ibn-Ziyad?"

"You can advise him the moon seeks private discourse."

One of the mercenaries roughly grabbed Grace's arm. "Give Kato your real name."

Grace punched the guard in the face. "That is my real name."

She knocked the other man now holding her sideways and onto the floor. "Kato, we both know I could kill everyone in this room if needed. Save me the trouble and take me to the one I seek."

The corner of Kato's lips curved into an amused grin. "Guards, pull up her cloak hood. It and the dark will prevent her from learning to navigate the halls."

After the guards settled the hood in place, they led her forward.

Kato politely bowed and gestured to his right. "This way, my Lady Moon."

Flanked by human guards, Grace walked behind Kato through the dismal, dank bowels of the palace Isra claimed. Her eyes adjusted to the dark. An occasional torch provided minimal light for any human to navigate the twist and turns of the labyrinth of murky halls. After turning one corner, the dark gave way to a brighter orange glow of fire pits set outside an enormous, arched wooden door. Two hulking demon sentries with large tusks reminding Grace of boars stood on either side of it. She guessed by their stopping they had reached Rayne's quarters. She wondered if the demons protected Rayne or imprisoned him.

Kato knocked on the door slab with the side of his fist. A muffled response of "enter" confirmed Rayne occupied the chamber. Kato turned the knob, then gave the heavy door a hard shove, forcing it open.

Grace tripped on the small step up into the large room. One of the mercenaries jerked her upward, but kept her from crossing the threshold. She noticed the scimitar along with the Horseman's blade resting on a table in the center of the room and a djinn general's jacket draped over the chair behind it. A half-drunk glass of what looked like whiskey sat on the far corner of the wooden top opposite the two weapons. A dark wood bed rested diagonally in the corner farthest from the door.

Her eyes shifted to the right, searching for her husband. He stood shirtless, staring out the lone window in the stone wall. Other than the dim moonlight shining through the open window and the wavering orange glow the fireplace cast, the room was pitch black. The four scars on Rayne's back held Grace's attention. Reminders to her of what the man who bore them had lived through.

"Why am I being disturbed at this hour?"

"The men captured a survivor," Kato explained the intrusion.

"There were to be no survivors."

"I am as surprised as you to learn Narciso took a hostage. Particularly, one who refuses to speak with anyone other than yourself."

Rayne turned to learn what prisoner had the courage to demand his attention. Due to the cloak the prisoner wore, he could not identify the detainee from where he stood.

Grace resisted the urge to call out to him. Silver eyes, longer hair, and a short beard forewarned Rayne may no longer be himself.

"She came upon Narciso and his guards after the attack."

"She?" The lifting of a dark brow broadcasted Rayne's automatic distrust of whomever Narciso imprisoned.

Kato motioned for Grace and the two guards to enter Rayne's quarters. One of the soldiers shoved Grace through the door. Playing the part of a weaker foe, she tumbled forward onto stone. None of the demons or humans made a move to assist her in getting back to her feet.

"She killed Narciso's interrogator and the djinn detaining her. Hearing the ruckus from the dungeons on my way to my own quarters, I intervened in the brawl. When I asked for her name, she advised it was Moon."

Grace could feel Rayne's gaze searing into her. She forced herself to keep staring at the gray stone mere millimeters from her nose.

"Moon?" Rayne picked up the glass from the table, took a long swig then loudly swallowed the mouthful of liquor before setting the glass down again. The prisoner hadn't moved from the spot where she fell. "What is it you wish to tell me, woman?"

I cannot speak with you in mixed company, wolf.

The loud humph that escaped Rayne's lips confirmed he heard her words. He studied the being laying subserviently on the floor. Her hands tucked under her chest to prevent any injury to her face when she had fallen. Something did not sit well about her presence. Rayne heeded his instincts and offered no response to her remark.

"Kato, can none of you properly manage the interrogation of a woman?"

"She carried these." Kato handed Rayne her weapons and ring.

Rayne dropped the daggers on the desk beside him, but stared grimly at the ring. "Leave the prisoner with me."

"General, I think it is unwise—" One mercenary started to challenge their new leader.

"I said leave us!" Rayne shouted, sending the guard scampering for the door. "Kato, ensure none of your men ever act insubordinately with their general going forward, or I will instill the discipline in your ranks that you have failed to."

"My men will never disrespect you again, Primus." Kato bowed and directed the guards to follow him.

Neither Rayne nor Grace changed positions. The loud grating of a key in the old iron lock broke the silence in the room. The screech of the locking bar settling into its resting place sent a shiver through Grace. She hoped the ominous sound was not an omen of ill fate.

Rayne turned his back to the woman. It was a simple, but telling test of a foe's intent. He heard her slowly climb to her feet. She did not make any threatening movement toward him. Seeing Grace's wedding ring unnerved him. Lost in thought, he ran his thumb over the vibrant blue sapphire. "Where did you obtain this ring?"

"My husband gave it to me the night we married."

Rayne's fingers closed around the jewel. "May I ask his name?"

"Which one would you like? He has three." Grace lowered the hood that covered her head. She took a hesitant step forward.

His eyes rested on her once more. "How?" He breathed the word. Was she a ghost sent to haunt him?

"Rayne."

The scraping of her chains against the floor added to Rayne's belief a dead woman walked towards him.

You should be at peace, not in chains wandering the earth.

Grace ignored the unspoken remark. "Rayne was the name I loved most. Followed by his human one, Haroun Ibn-Ziyad."

Needing proof that she was not a specter, Rayne took her face in his hands. "How are you alive?"

"I never died, Rayne. I was warned of what would occur."

"Isra and Narciso..." Rayne couldn't finish the sentence. His hands trembled. The woman was no ghost. She lived more than he currently did.

"Neither has the ability to kill an immortal. You know this. I kept my word to never again go near Isra alone."

"No! You did not." Rayne blinked back the tears forming in his eyes. Tonight was some sort of trick. Needing distance, he retreated from the woman. *What cruel hoax is Isra playing now?*

"This isn't a hoax, Rayne."

"You're dead." He shook his head. "After Priya warned you, you went after Isra without me or anyone else. You humiliated her in front of her field commanders, but foolishly left her alive. We thought the defeat finished things, and we returned home. But our assumption was wrong. Isra carefully planned her retaliation against you and me. She waited until the Council dispatched me on assignment, leaving you and the children alone. Isra stole Lucifer's harbinger blade. Narciso and she... you had no chance with the way they surprised you. The wounds you sustained... I arrived home too late. You were barely conscious when I lifted you from the floor. You died in my arms, Grace. My arms!" Rayne paused, reliving those horrific moments. "Isis nor anyone else could revive you. While I was with Isis, Narciso took Tarquin and Tessa. He and Damien colluded with Sanjur to keep Dante out of the way. Your death and the disappearance of our children drove Dante to darkness, as I have never seen. We tried everything we could to bring him back into the light, but nothing worked. I had no other choice than to sentence him to damnation in Tartarus. I... I could not save any of you. Our children...." Rayne's voice broke, recalling how Tessa and Tarquin had cried out for him the last he saw them.

He had arrived in Elysium before Dante, but Narciso and Sanjur already held Tessa and Tarquin hostage. Tessa had wailed, terrified, with her arms extended toward him as Narciso carried her away. Tarquin's voice wavered once the boy spotted him and shouted, 'Daddy, help us!' then futilely yelled for Dante. Rayne shut his eyes, trying to forget their pleading. By the time Dante arrived, Narciso and Sanjur were gone. "Do you have any idea of what it is like to fail your family so?"

Wanting to console him, Grace took a step forward. The blade of his scimitar against her throat halted her.

"What hell it is to hold your wife as she struggles to take those precious last breaths? Then to have her go limp against you as her soul departs? To helplessly watch your children be abducted from the one place they should have been safe?"

His wrath and pain made the air crackle around them. The edge of the razor-sharp blade skimmed the side of her neck as he closed the distance between them. His practiced hand was the only thing that prevented steel from slipping into flesh and muscle, relieving her of her life.

"I do not know who or what you are, but I can assure you, I am not naïve enough to fall for whatever ploy Isra concocted. My wife is dead. You are not her."

Unable to read Rayne's thoughts any longer, Grace took a deep breath. He intentionally shut her out. The hatred and anger in his gaze suffocated her. She may as well have been standing in the pits of Hell, engulfed by eternal fires of dark flame. This incarnation of the enforcer scared her more than anything ever had. With witnessing her murder, losing his children, then issuing an immortal death sentence to Dante, she understood why Rayne became what he was. Forcing aside the fear screaming for her to run, Grace mustered the courage to try and reach any remainder of the man Rayne once was that might exist in the dark soul staring her down.

"I am not sure what artifice you are under, my wolf, but none of those things ever happened. When Priya warned me, I came only to you. That is why I am here now." Grace slowly pushed the blade aside; betting the man she loved still survived somewhere within the enforcer. That in a moment of blind rage, he wouldn't end her existence.

The firelight deepened the dark circles under former loving blue eyes. Mistrust and suspicion took up permanent residence in silver orbs. Dark bruises covered Rayne's torso along with several deep, jagged gashes. He flinched when her fingertips ever-so-lightly grazed one of the cuts. Were they wounds from battle? Or did Isra torture him to keep him under her control?

"How do I know Isra does not test me further?" Rayne's inquiry brought her eyes up from his chest to his face. He desperately wanted to believe the aqua eyes searching his belonged to his wife. He would give anything to see her alive again.

"I am no more a test of Isra's than you were Osvaldo's bounty hunter. I make the same offer as you did in Santa Maria Maggiore. I will help you run, if you so choose," Grace shared something only they would have knowledge of to confirm she lived.

His weapon fell to the floor. The Horseman reawakened within the enforcer. "Grace?"

She rested her hands against his chest. "My ring for your heart, Lothario."

Rayne's hands covered hers before he kissed her. The immortal bond they shared resonated through him. He smiled for the first time in days. Grace truly found her way back to him. He slid her wedding ring onto her finger. "How can I give you something you already own, my Lady Warwick?"

"Entrust me with it again anyway, wolf."

"I commend myself into your care, guardian. Heart, body, and soul." His lips covered hers once more.

Grace stared up at him when the kiss ended. "We need to return to Córdoba."

"I cannot leave Isra's ranks."

"What keeps you from doing so?"

A loud knock on the door interrupted their reunion.

Not waiting for his permission to enter, Isra stormed into the room. "Where is the prisoner from Granada?"

Rayne pushed Grace behind him. "What prisoner?"

"Narciso said a woman killed three of your men before being taken prisoner."

"The female djinn killed one of his who was careless. Narciso exaggerates the situation as usual."

"He also reported a woman was brought to the palace in chains, then to your chambers only a short time ago." Isra half expected Rayne to deny the presence of the woman she knew stood behind him.

Instead, Rayne turned sideways, revealing Grace. "A human. She is not the djinn who engaged Narciso's men. She is a servant from Rodrigo's palace. I spared her life so that I may have entertainment while we are here. You have never forbidden me from taking spoils of war. Kato executed the djinn Narciso rants about."

"A human? I thought your conscience couldn't bear harming the innocent any longer." Isra remained suspicious. "Why have you chosen to take this one as a pet?"

"She is far from innocent. This mortal is an intoxicating mix of vulnerability and sin. The kind of sin which warrants nurturing, not a death sentence." Rayne pulled Grace's cloak from her shoulders and tilted her face up towards his. "I am going to take great pleasure in exploring your darker side, woman."

"Please don't hurt me," Grace pleaded in a hushed frightened tone.

"I have no intention of hurting you. At least not in a fashion you will not enjoy. Is there anything additional you need of me, Isra, or may I be left in peace the rest of my evening?"

Isra watched the way Rayne grinned at his prisoner. "Besides this woman you left alive, are Rodrigo and his minions eliminated?"

"They are no more. Rodrigo's gutted remains and head are hung from his castle walls to remind those of who now rules here." Rayne kissed down Grace's neck then groped her breast. Grace tried to jerk away.

"You'll soon welcome my touch, corazón." Rayne brought Grace's body back against his.

"You disgrace me with your words and actions, djinn."

Rayne laughed. "There is no disgrace in what we do. Part of you secretly begs for more even though you protest. I will stoke those carnal desires until they consume you. But first, you will learn to please your new master. We shall start slowly, with simple orders. Kneel."

"General." Grace hesitated to do as asked.

He placed a finger against her lips and softly repeated the order. His eyes locked with hers. Grace slowly sank to her knees. "Address me as master, as you did Rodrigo."

"Rodrigo promised me to the captain of his guard. You cannot take what is promised to another djinn."

"Rodrigo is dead by my hand. You are now the servant of Haroun Ibn-Ziyad. I shall have what Rodrigo promised to Inigo."

"I will not forsake my oath to Inigo."

"Inigo is dead as well, corazón. You forsake nothing accepting a new master. Do we understand one another?" Rayne ran his thumb across her lower lip.

She nodded, hoping they fooled Isra. "Yes, master."

"Disrobe, then await me in my bed."

Grace shook her head. "I will not reveal myself to anyone but you."

"Isra cares not about your state of dress!" Rayne yanked Grace to her feet, tore open the top of her shirt, then shoved her towards the bed. "Do not disobey me again. When my mistress departs, I expect to enjoy all my spoils offer without delay."

Grace climbed into Rayne's bed. She acted as if she was crying and loosening her shirt with her back to him and Isra.

Isra laughed in a manner that made Grace's skin crawl. "My primus finally returns."

Rayne slammed Isra into the wall. "I am much worse than my prior incarnation, Isra. He did not know what power he held. The old Haroun retained a sliver of his humanity. I have none. You took it from me when you killed my wife. One of these days, the fiend you created will slay you."

"Without the dagger, you can't." Isra slapped Rayne hard enough his head snapped back. "Release me, Haroun, or I will take your new pet away."

Rayne reluctantly set Isra free.

Isra looked at the woman sitting on Rayne's bed. "Girl, you are the whore of a disgraced djinn. Be thankful you share similarities with his dead wife or you would have met your end as Inigo did."

"She is nothing like my wife." Rayne struck out at Isra again.

Isra caught his fist. "Test me again, and sweet, innocent Tessa shall become Narciso's reward for today. You know how he enjoys little girls."

A portal opened, revealing Tessa hugging a doll, alone and frightened in a cell. Grace quietly gasped.

"Daddy!" Tessa called out, almost as if she could see Rayne.

As the portal closed, Grace heard Tarquin tell his sister not to be afraid. The children were together wherever they were.

Rayne muttered a threat in Kabyle, earning a sharp retort in the same language from Isra.

Isra laughed. "Enjoy the rest of your evening, Primus."

Rayne waited a few minutes to ensure Isra had left before approaching Grace. He needed to repress the darkness raging through him. The last thing he wanted was to accidentally injure Grace with the enforcer in full control.

Grace watched him from the bed. "Where is the dagger?"

"Destroyed. I am trying to keep what remains of my family alive while I figure out an alternate way to finish Isra."

"By slaughtering innocent people and raping women?" Grace couldn't believe Rayne placed their family before the souls taken earlier that day.

"Rodrigo was a rival djinn. You know that. The only woman I have inappropriately touched since being blackmailed into Isra's ranks again is my wife. I apologize for doing so."

"Rayne, your minions annihilated an entire medieval city today. They didn't just kill Rodrigo and his underlings."

"That was not the order I gave. When I left, only Rodrigo and the soldiers loyal to him were dead."

"Then your ranks disobeyed their general. Only one soul was alive upon my arrival in the main square. Not a man, child, or woman was left breathing."

Rayne sat on the bed beside Grace. "I should have never left Narciso unsupervised."

"I am relieved my husband wasn't the executioner this afternoon."

"Going forward, I will be the last one to leave the field," Rayne promised, mortified by what Grace shared. "Kato will escort you back to the dungeons once Isra retires. He will ensure you safely escape. We must be careful. If Isra or Narciso discover who you are or figure out Kato intentionally aided your departure, the children or my parents may suffer the consequences. I will have a few of Narciso's officers escort you with Kato to limit suspicion. They are gullible enough to fall for any trick you may use to evade them."

"Rayne, I am not going anywhere. Why are you allowing Isra this much control over you? Why are you so frightened of her?"

"I do not fear her. I fear the death of my children." Rayne upturned his wrists then held them out to Grace. "War can no longer strike as he once could."

Grace ran her finger over the cold metal bands surrounding his wrists. She hadn't noticed them before. "What are these?"

"Lucifer's devious inventions. I cannot kill Isra as long as I wear them. One is linked to Tessa, the other to Tarquin. If anyone other than Isra removes either of band, the child tied to the restraint dies. If I disobey her, our children die. If anyone besides Isra tries to remove the devices on the children, they die. I will not sacrifice our children."

"I didn't see similar bands on Tessa's wrist. What creates the tie between these and the children?"

"Narciso placed thin titanium collars around Tarquin and Tessa's necks. They are concealed beneath the children's clothing. The collars are filled with explosive material that is deadly to human and immortal alike. They detonate if tampered with or if someone without Isra's energy signature removes the ones on my wrists."

Grace frantically thought through how to free her children. "Dante could shield them from the blast."

"Theoretically, he could, but he is not in a position to help. The corruption of his soul with the loss of you and the children turned him into a being you wouldn't recognize. He handled matters much worse than I did."

"If I could reach Dante, bring him back to the light, and if you had the dagger, we could end all of this with no harm to your parents and the kids. Do you know where Isra detains Tessa and Tarquin?"

Rayne shook his head. "No. She moves them each morning."

Kato's raised voice arguing with Narciso warned them of the djinn's approach. "Haroun gave orders not to be disturbed."

"I do not give a damn what Haroun orders. His concubine killed several of my most valuable men. He owes me recompense for that."

"Take up the issue with him in the morning."

"Fetch your general, Kato!"

Kato growled at the only other of Isra's djinn equal to Rayne. "He is training the new concubine to service him. I know better than to intrude on that session."

Hearing the reason Narciso couldn't disturb Rayne, Grace sighed. "Training a new concubine? Nice to see you mourn your wife."

"I mourn my wife with every breath I take." Rayne hated the repeated interruptions that risked Grace's life. "I am sorry for tonight."

Rayne shoved her from the bed. The surprise at finding herself on the floor displayed on her face as he hoped it would. Narciso forced open the door as Rayne stood over her.

"I will not tolerate any more insolence, human! Now, let us begin again. Kneel before your master."

"What?" Grace wondered what had come over her husband.

"I said kneel, woman."

Rayne jerked her upright. As he pulled her forward, she noticed Narciso's hulking frame moving towards them.

"Eyes on me, jamila." Rayne calmly directed, giving the appearance of preventing the woman from looking at the door.

"Yes, master."

Narciso intended to challenge Rayne's position as lead general for his keeping Grace alive.

How many are there? Rayne asked Grace.

Only Narciso. Kato is alone in the hall.

Rayne kept his eyes on Grace. "Your business with me will wait until morning, Narciso."

"The bitch you bed killed my personal guard. Give me her life for theirs." Narciso took a step forward.

The wrath within Rayne swelled to a murderous bursting point. His eyes turned the color of mercury. The promise of death in retribution for Narciso's audacity to demand Grace etched itself across Rayne's face.

"Master!" Grace seized Rayne by the waist with both hands, hoping she could shift the direction his emotions dangerously veered in. *Do not let him provoke you. We will be separated once more if you allow fear and anger to rule your actions.*

Rayne ran his fingers through Grace's hair. Her words brought back some sense of self-control. "Then you failed to train your soldiers properly."

"Please, Haroun." Grace clutched his right leg. "Allow me to stay with you. I will do anything you ask."

"Serve me well and you shall remain at my side, mortal." Rayne continued stroking her hair. Grace subserviently laid her head against him. He glanced over his shoulder at Narciso. "The woman is easily tamed, as you can see. So wanting of my approval and attention. She gives herself completely if another threatens to take it away. She is the epitome of how I expect my subordinates to behave. Learn from her example, Narciso."

Narciso brushed aside the comparison of himself with the human. He was far from Haroun's servant. "I expect compensation ...."

"Narciso, if you disrupt my evening any longer, I will tell Isra of your disobedience today. You know the penalty for failing to follow the orders of a superior."

Grace's cheek resting against Rayne's hip only further aroused the enforcer. He struggled to suppress the beast within demanding the primal pleasure of making Grace submit to his every whim after he spilled Narciso's blood for disregarding his direction.

Narciso growled from the doorway. "I followed your orders."

"My orders were to clean up the bodies after ensuring the demon and djinn loyal to Rodrigo were dead, not to slaughter the entire town."

"The hordes let off a little steam. What are a few dead humans?"

"The humans mean nothing. Your defiance of my instruction is what troubles me."

"If a fellow general making a decision when you are not present bothers you so, perhaps you shouldn't be primus, Haroun."

Rayne teleported to Narciso then struck him hard across the face. "You will never..." Rayne hit him a second time on the opposite side. "flout an order..." A third blow caused Narciso to cower. "I give again. Nor will your men. You've lost your position as Isra's primus. I alone command the legions. Never again will you dictate any order without my approval. Remember well which one of us is now the primus from this day forth."

"You have my fealty, Haroun. I and my men will obey your direction." Narciso backed down. "The woman killed some of my best men. May I not have recompense for her actions?"

Rayne laughed then pointed at Grace. "This woman killed some of your best men? She fears what we are. I do not believe this petrified being is capable of killing a djinn, much less your best men."

"I saw her—"

"You saw her?" Rayne cut him off. "Let us test your murderess, shall we? Woman, come here."

Grace started to stand.

"Crawl." Rayne halted her rising.

Grace bit back the retort forming on her lips and slowly crawled to Rayne. She kept her gaze on his feet, so she didn't tell Rayne off like she wanted to. When she reached him, Rayne jerked her face upwards so abruptly she gasped.

Rayne smirked, then looked over at Narciso. "Do you still expect me to believe this submissive creature killed your men when she cowers and crawls to me?"

Narciso snarled at the way Rayne mocked him. "She is playing you for the fool, Haroun. Armed, threatened, and degraded, she would behave differently, especially if she believed she could escape from here."

"Even threatened or degraded, she will not strike out." Rayne picked up one of her daggers from the table and forced it into Grace's hand. Grace winced when he pulled her hair, but did not counter his actions. "I see no killer, Narciso. Shall we try degradation?"

"Open your mouth, woman," Rayne gruffly ordered, turning away from Narciso. He pulled Grace's face into his groin and slid two fingers between her lips.

Grace gagged and slapped Rayne's thigh. Afraid she'd stab him as Narciso expected, she dropped her dagger. The pressure of his other hand on the back of her head prevented her from pulling away. Rayne moved his fingers back enough she no longer choked, but that was the only reprieve he allowed her. She nipped his fingers, cautioning him he took things too far.

Noting the way Rayne's jaw clenched, Narciso let out a loud laugh. "It appears she isn't as obedient as you claim."

"She will learn as you did a few moments ago." Rayne fisted a handful of Grace's hair, applying enough downward pressure that her eyes met his again. "Human, if you wish to stay alive, you will refrain from using those teeth in a manner which displeases me."

Grace shot him an angry glare, but slowly moved her head, sucking his fingers. She'd definitely be paying him back later for this.

"One brief moment of resistance. She is hardly a fighter, much less a killer." Rayne looked over his shoulder at Narciso. "Disregard my direction again, and I will demand your sentence be much worse than life on all fours. Now, get out. So I may finish with one who knows how to please her master."

"Careful she doesn't bite your cock off, Primus. She's a wolf in sheep's clothing." Narciso slammed the door behind him as he exited.

Thankful the ploy worked, Rayne withdrew his fingers from Grace's mouth.

"I should stab you for what you just did!" Grace hissed at Rayne as he hoisted her to her feet. She punched him in the chest after she yanked free of his grip.

"That crass display spared your life. Stop berating me and send yourself back to wherever you came from."

"The second I use my powers, Isra will sense me."

"She already senses something off about you. Why do you think Narciso was stupid enough to barge in here?"

"He wanted to challenge you."

"No, leof." Rayne brought her against him again. "Isra fueled his resentment. She couldn't care less if I killed him. She wants to know why I dared to put hands on her since I have not done so since she assassinated you and took the children."

He ran his hands down her back, then slowly kissed her, sensually reminding her and himself that their union was timeless. His beard tickled her cheeks as Grace's fingers lightly gripped the nape of his neck, her mouth more firmly moving against his. Rayne groaned, the darker side of him taking over. He pressed her into the wall; the probing of his tongue grew invasive, warming embers of passion, kindling them into lustful flame. "You provoke the enforcer as much as Isra does tonight."

Not believing how much the events of the evening aroused the enforcer, Grace laughed. "When was the last time you were with a woman, Primus?"

"Weeks ago. When I last made love to my wife."

"We will have to remedy that, master." Grace ran her hand up his chest, testing Rayne's ability to control the baser part of his being.

"You vile, evil woman. You tempt the devil well beyond sin. When you should be fleeing for both our sakes." Rayne gave her a wicked grin before kissing her again. "As much as I want to take you to my bed, you need to go. We only have seconds before Narciso reports the woman from town wasn't executed as I claimed. You must leave."

Grace wrapped a leg around his and entangled her left hand in his hair. "We leave together, or I don't leave at all."

"Grace, we don't have time to argue about this."

"You swore an oath to me, Primus. You leave with me or you lose my submission."

"By the gods! Do you not understand I have no choice with the children and my parents held hostage?"

"I am giving you a choice. Right now. Finish Isra and leave with me, or I die in your arms tonight."

Rayne could hear a messenger reporting to Isra that they came under attack. The Horsemen and High Council officers seized the fortress and the city. "You executed a siege on Granada? Are you insane? Why would you do such a thing without line of sight to the consequences?"

Isra's fury coursed through him. She now knew who the woman was in Rayne's quarters.

"It's a chance I had to take. Isra cannot have you or be allowed to conquer anywhere else."

"Our children, Grace!"

"Dante is with them. All he needed to hear was Tarquin's voice to find them, which he did through the two other members of the Triad."

"The Triad ..." Rayne started to disagree, but something cold against his belly halted his words.

"Is intact, Rayne. Dante has not fallen. I sent Lyal into the past to warn him while you argued with Isra. I will not allow Isra to blackmail you any longer. Make your choice. Trust your wife or serve Isra."

Rayne glanced down to see the sapphire hilt of his dagger. Grace brought him salvation. The door colliding against stone announced Isra's arrival. Rayne's fingers closed around his weapon's hilt.

Grace held the sheath tightly. Rayne would need to flawlessly pull off his assault. "I love you. In this lifetime and the next," she whispered, knowing it may be their last seconds together.

His eyes remained focused on her. Silver faded to ocean blue. War rebelled against his new bonds.

Thirty paces. Grace counted Isra's steps.

Twenty. Her hand fell from his hair.

Ten. She moved her leg, so Rayne would have all the room he needed.

Rayne drew the blade, but kept it hidden between him and Grace. Once Isra was close enough, he twisted and plunged the weapon into Isra's chest. "Down, Grace."

She dropped to the floor. Rayne's sword barely missed striking her.

Isra burst into a cloud of black ash as Rayne's scimitar severed her head.

Rayne let out the breath he had been holding. He was free.

Narciso stood in the hall and screamed for guards to aid him as Haroun murdered their mistress.

Rayne teleported to the open doorway and killed Narciso, but he wasn't fast enough to stop the alarm. He barred the door then pushed the heavy table against it. After whispering an incantation, he threw the bottle of whiskey at the threshold.

"The spell won't keep them out long." He grabbed the Horsemen's blade from the top of the table and handed Grace her daggers.

Kato and Sulla joined Grace and Rayne. They could hear the hallway filling with guards. Loud pounding came along with screeches as demons and djinn tried to force their way into Rayne's chambers.

"Your parents are jailed in the old castle. We will never reach them in time," Sulla shared what he learned.

"Raphael and Destahn are there. They held their strike until we could confirm Dante found the children. We hadn't anticipated the restraints Isra created for the three of you." Grace astonished Rayne.

Rayne needed to know she spoke the truth. *Fiore?*

Your parents are safely in Sasainn. Dante retrieved the children and has them in Elysium. Get yourself out of harm's way, Warwick. Raphael confirmed the other Horsemen had completed their end of the mission.

The room door exploded into splinters. Rayne hurled dark flame at the whiskey on the floor, igniting the threshold and momentarily spooking the djinn and demons in the hall. Bolder than the rest, Isra's most recently promoted officer charged through the black flames. Rayne grabbed a hold of him. Grace, Sulla, and Kato cut down the ones who streamed in after seeing the officer survived.

"Stop!" Rayne shouted at the horde in the hall with the younger djinn trapped in a headlock. "Swear allegiance to me, and you live. Fight me, and death awaits you. You all know well who I am."

Panic gripped Grace. "What are you doing, Rayne?"

The djinn Rayne held snarled. "One of us will end you, Horseman or not. Isra's murder cannot go unavenged."

Rayne killed him, halting those who moved towards them. "Do not foolishly test me as Juan did."

Black flame climbed stone walls as if they were wood kindling. The building tremored. A jagged crack traveled the length of the hall floor, threatening to divide it. Silver returned to Rayne's eyes. Witnessing a hint of what War could do, human, demon, and djinn quickly dropped their arms and went down on bended knee.

"Get out of here," Rayne whispered, staring at Grace.

Grace didn't understand. Isra was dead and Rayne free. "What?"

"Leave, Grace."

"What are you doing?" Grace took a step towards her husband. Mastering djinn legions would trap him permanently in no-man's-land between good and evil.

"Atoning for my sins. Isra's legions will never be a threat again." Rayne walked amongst those kneeling. Stopping at each djinn and demon, he placed a hand on their shoulder to determine if they were too far gone to save. Any with a clouded future or that provoked images of betrayal he executed. While the legion members remained silent, fear surfaced on multiple faces.

"No, Rayne, not with what we risked to save you."

He offered her a sad smile. *I will find my way home to you, leof.*

Rayne summoned the one being he could always entrust his family to. "Dante!"

Grace shoved Dante away from her. "I am not leaving, Rayne!"

Dante saw the torment on Grace's face. She wasn't going to come willingly.

An overly confident demon charged Rayne.

"Take her!" Rayne yelled, the blade in his hand slicing through the demon's belly.

Dante's arm encircled Grace's waist. Rayne looked back at her.

"Rayne!" She screamed, reaching for him. Her tone pleading he come with her. He rapidly drifted from her outstretched hand.

FORTY-EIGHT

Córdoba - 812

Grace's tortured scream echoed throughout the house.

Sulla and Kato paced nervously. Kato whimpered, approaching her after she collapsed to her knees.

Lyal pushed the wolf back. "Allow her space." The harbinger gripped Grace by the shoulders. "You can stop this."

Relieved to find herself in Rayne's Cordovan home across from Lyal, Grace calmed herself. If Rayne ignored such vivid premonitions, she would do what she must. "How much time do I have to prevent what I just saw?"

Lyal pulled back the window curtain, so Grace could see twilight skies. "Not much. Nightfall has come. "

Forgive me, Rayne. Grace didn't know if Rayne could hear the apology. Something blocked the connection between them.

"Sulla, warn Rayne Isra's strike will be soon and more brutal than expected. He mustn't ever lose hope if she wins this round."

"I will send one of the pack members to warn him. Kato and I promised we would stay with you."

"I don't need protection. Go warn my husband."

"Isra and her minions are not an enemy an immortal woman can face alone. She and her legions are on the move during daylight. They hunt for you and your children," Sulla challenged the order she gave.

"I am well aware of what she is and what she is doing." Grace retrieved her sabre and daggers from the weapons trunk at the foot of Rayne's bed. "Arturo."

Raphael's aide materialized beside her. "Defensore."

"We need to ensure my children disappear from any location Isra knows about. Take Tessa and Tarquin to Gage and Caitlin at D'Orme in the twenty-first century. I will retrieve them once it is safe to do so. Tell Gage to release the children to no one other than myself or Dante."

"Yes, Defensore."

The woman issuing orders and arming herself confused Kato. "Where are you going?"

"To prepare for war. Is Rodrigo still in Granada?"

"Granada is his power base. He does not wander far from it."

"Kato, I do not have time to explain everything. I need you..." Grace paused, looking down at Rayne's dagger in her hands. Did she risk sending him the dagger, or did she keep it?

"You need me to do what?"

"Take this to Rayne. Do not stop for anything until you reach him. Narciso is looking for the blade. Isra plans to destroy it. Be certain Rayne knows that. Make him swear to never let it leave his person, and most importantly, he needs to keep it concealed at all times."

Kato took the dagger, but remained staring at Grace with a worried expression.

Grace opened the door for the wolves. "He will need both of you in what is coming."

Sulla nodded and transformed into a wolf. Kato hesitated, but did the same, then followed Sulla out the front door. The two stopped in the archway of the gate. Kato looked back at her.

"Do not fret, Kato. I go to Elysium. Isra will have to fight a god if she wants me." Grace took a deep breath. She had no other options left with as quickly as darkness descended on Córdoba. She had to warn Rayne and buy them all time.

Hell -

"Get out!" Grace ordered the demons standing around Lucifer to leave.

"Defensore?" Lucifer smiled at the woman wearing a black and gold uniform striding towards him. The way she dismissed his minions entertained him. "It's been centuries since I've received a visit from a Council Harbinger."

"I am not here on behalf of the Council."

Lucifer's smile broadened and his eyebrows lifted before he laughed. "Come to make a personal deal with the Devil then, Mrs. Warwick?"

"I'm not that stupid, Lucifer. But I do need to speak with you." While the demon guard stepped back, they didn't leave as requested. "Privately."

Lucifer nodded to his two bodyguards. The demons vanished from sight. "My attention and time are yours, Defensore. If you aren't here on behalf of the Council, how did you enter Hell? My home isn't exactly open to the immortal community."

"The High Council is not the only organization I protect."

Lucifer poured himself a drink. "I heard rumors of ancient blood flowing through your veins. So, Rayne finally embraced ownership of the moon after denying the prophecy for so long. If you aren't here as harbinger or to barter for a favor, what are you here for?"

"Information."

"What type of information?"

"I need to understand why Isra is suddenly so interested in having my husband back under her thumb, since you claim to have nothing to do with recent events. Is it possible for the Devil to have a rogue agent on the loose?"

Lucifer sat down on a black leather sofa. His eyes rested on the wife of the one immortal he hesitated to provoke. He sipped the dark liquid that swirled around in his glass as he brought it to his lips. "I would be more interested in hearing your theories on what Isra is up to."

"Isra isn't smart enough to come up with a plan like this on her own, nor do I believe you lost control of one of your regional overseers.

There are plenty of reasons for you to mastermind a coup. Not to mention your past behavior of pulling crap like this. My husband's escaping you worsened the blight on your already despicable reputation. You once wanted the power he holds as universal balance keeper. Throw in the Council casting you out of their ranks after learning you detained and concealed the man they searched for to complete the Horsemen, and I see a prime motive for a vengeful act."

"You are clever, Grace. But not as clever as you believe yourself to be. I exploit windows of opportunity more than masterminding the type of plot you envision. I have zero desire to return to my position on the High Council; being limited by all kinds of boring rules and stupid ethics I don't agree with, and lastly, your husband escaped Isra, not me. Once I realized that Haroun's fate was predestined, I had no use for him. Isra foolishly thought she could control him. I warned her then, as I do now, that she is wrong. Demons and djinn are like greedy, spoiled children, Defensore. Sometimes they must learn the hard way. Just like when you tell a child a flame can burn them and then they stick their hand in the fire anyway."

"So be a good parent and punish your evil spawn for disobeying."

"What makes you think I am not doing so by allowing her to act as she is?" Lucifer took another drink from his glass.

Grace bit back her initial retort to the question and rethought her approach. What would motivate Lucifer to aid her and Rayne without her having to trade something in return for his help? Did she appeal to his narcissistic nature and vanity? She loathed the idea of playing the bootlicker. Lucifer would see right through that. Worse yet, he would have no respect for anyone who resorted to those tactics. Lucifer loved attention, power, and being the one in charge.

Realizing what card she held that might provoke Lucifer enough to assist her, Grace mustered the most serious expression she could. "I've foreseen her rise to power in Spain. My husband, forced into her service once more, secures more than Spain for her. With Rayne doing her bidding, she grows more powerful than you. You are oddly absent in that future."

A brooding scowl erased the snide grin from Lucifer's face.

"You said you weren't here as harbinger, Grace." The Devil stalked towards her; his face turning a mix of red and black, the horns on his head visibly growing, and raven-colored feathered wings spread out from his shoulders.

"I'm not. I want to prevent the vision from becoming reality. I lose more than my husband if I don't. Not even you want a corrupted, soulless War walking the earth, Lucifer."

"Then you are here to make a deal after all, Grace. What is a guardian willing to trade for her husband's soul?"

"Your life, Lucifer. If we can't stop the future I foresaw, you should know Rayne seizes command of the European legions and your regional overseers. They all swear allegiance to War then conquer the human realm. Where do you think those thousands of lost souls, demons, djinn, and Rayne turn to next for plunder? They'd need more strength to battle the Council or to defile the grounds of the Ancients. The only logical place left after human earth is Hell. War and his legions will storm your gates. You can't possibly defend against such a horde. We both know what the outcome of them taking over Hell is, especially if Rayne is trapped here with the legions. He has little patience for you. And let's not forget the fact he holds you directly accountable for his subjugation to Isra. Toss in my death and that of his children on top of everything else. He'll end your miserable existence before you even know he has entered your personal chambers."

Lucifer's eyes flashed red. "You're lying."

"Is it in a guardian's nature to lie, especially to a fellow immortal?" Grace kept her gaze locked with Lucifer's.

Overwrought stillness befell the room. Both beings scrutinized one another. Black wings slowly folded into Lucifer's back.

"On the off chance you are telling the truth, what do you require of me, Defensore?"

"Isra uses a set of silver bands to control Rayne. I suspect she gets them from you when she steals your harbinger's blade."

"That's preposterous. She would never get away with taking my harbinger's blade."

Annoyed by Lucifer's denial that Isra could steal from him, Grace glared at him. "Tomorrow morning, you will find your safe open and the blade gone."

"Even if she took my blade, which she can't, she couldn't possibly obtain these bands you speak of."

"So you know what the bands are?"

"Of course I do. The reason I know she can't obtain the bands is the High Council had them destroyed after..." Lucifer drifted off into his thoughts, now pondering Grace's words.

"After what?"

"After they learned I plotted The Battle of Carcassonne."

"The Battle of Carcassonne?" Grace wasn't familiar with the conflict.

"A little skirmish where a few humans died." Lucifer rolled his eyes. "Honestly, Rayne killed more djinn that day than Lucien's forces did humans, but the Council still added it to the list of reasons to bar me from their ranks."

"What?"

"Your husband, ever the damn good deed doer, turned on Lucien, massacred a sizable portion of Lucien's ranks, then tried to disappear into the countryside of France. Of course, that couldn't go unpunished. Rayne was so unmanageable back then. I've never seen such a disobedient djinn like your husband. We caught him and dragged him back to Lucien's dungeons." Needing to wet his now dry mouth, Lucifer sipped from his glass. "We had to devise a way of controlling Haroun before he could serve any useful purpose."

"So you made the bands. How did you possibly get them on him? He would have fought you to the death before allowing such a device to be placed on his wrists."

Thinking back to that day, Lucifer fiendishly smiled. "A great deal of sedative. Enough to take out an elephant. Lucien and I had to force a tube down his throat to get him to drink it all. He killed the other two djinn we sent to do it. It took a few hours to kick in, but he eventually passed out. While he was unconscious, we placed the bands on his wrists, and sent the collars to his mother, one of his sisters, and his cousin, Nezha. All three women, flattered by the gifts, tried them on, then learned they couldn't be removed. When Rayne woke, we warned him not to take off the bands or one of the three women would die."

A cruel laugh departed from Lucifer's lips, warning Grace the story got worse.

"We then cautioned him that any attempt to remove the collars from the women would result in them dying. As angry and desperate as he was to get free, I knew he'd act foolishly. He yanked the band from his right wrist. A scream rang out around all of us, followed by the thunderous rumble of an explosion. Poof! Nezha vanished from the three portals before him. Well, actually, it was more her tiny bits and pieces scattering into time and space than her vanishing." Lucifer took pleasure in a sickening dramatic pause.

The way Lucifer's lips twisted in a sinister grin tormented Grace. "Rayne must have been devastated."

"He was more than devastated. Lucien and I took him to Córdoba, so he could see for himself what occurred after he accused me of deceiving him. That the noise and Nezha's disappearing were only a trick of some sort. I will never forget the mortified expression on your husband's face as he looked at Nezha's limbs scattered around her room. Her blood and flesh randomly dotting the walls. Not even Priya's suffering broke him as this did. Rayne fell to his knees, clutching what was left of her clothing; cursing me and himself. When he finally looked up from the garment, his eyes forever changed to silver. In that solitary moment, darkness claimed a soul born of light. Rayne freely placed the band back on his wrist and then agreed never to return home. Isra's servant fully submitted to his indenture."

Now seeing the past through the Devil's eyes, Grace hated Lucifer almost as much as Rayne did. "You stole my husband's humanity by leveraging his family. No wonder part of him is so afraid the same will occur again."

Lucifer laughed, conjuring a box. He flicked open the lid then picked up one of the collars resting in the case. "I stole nothing. That's the beauty of it. Rayne imprisoned himself. The dark irony of freewill."

"You left him no other choice, Lucifer. He couldn't die to escape you. He also couldn't hang onto what helped him stay in touch with his humanity."

"And now you are faced with doing the same, if you want to save your children and end Isra."

Grace watched him slowly approach her. "I thought these were destroyed."

"The ones I used on your husband were, but not the entire set. The Council didn't know there were more."

Lucifer settled the collar around Grace's neck, but did not secure the restraint in place. He placed one of the wrist bands in her hand. "I am curious, Defensore. In your vision, did you wear a collar or a band like your husband?"

"I wore neither." Grace carefully removed each piece from her body. She stared down at the case Lucifer extended to her.

"Take them, Grace."

"You should destroy them."

"I've had a vision this afternoon as well. You need these as much as Isra does to put the fear of God in your husband. Is your charge not to protect *all* beings from wrongful death? Do you have the courage to save us all, good and evil alike, Defensore?"

Grace hated how the smile on Lucifer's face widened after she grasped the box. "Let me be clear in what is being exchanged for these, Lucifer. Your life for aiding in eliminating Isra. Nothing more. With what you just disclosed, I would be more than justified in executing you. The Council wouldn't even give me a slap on the wrist for doing so without authorization."

Lucifer chuckled, then returned to his spot on his couch. "Consider these a gift. You take care of a mutual problem which troubles us both. Now that I've given you the tools to carry out your misdeed, how do you intend to incite your husband enough that the enforcer surfaces to draw Isra out of hiding? You can't fight here. Council law prevents it."

"Why would I need to surface the enforcer?"

"Isra won't come out of safe haven to tempt Rayne. You will have to give her a powerful incentive to return to Córdoba. With the threats your husband sent, how many times all of you have defeated her, and each of you actively hunting her, the only thing that will draw her out is Haroun Ibn-Ziyad: broken, desperate, betrayed, and djinn once more."

Grace's confidence faltered. Using the collar and wristbands was one thing, to demoralize her husband was another. "Bringing the enforcer back risks exactly what I am trying to prevent."

Lucifer shook his head. "Such a shame you wasted both our time today. It always comes down to that one simple question for you guardians. What is one life worth?"

Grace studied the leather box in her hands. "There has to be another way."

"No, Grace. Sadly, there isn't." Lucifer set his glass down on the end table beside the sofa and walked over to her. "Allow me to rephrase the question in a way that might help you with your decision. What exactly is Rayne Warwick's life worth to you? Would you really trade your happiness and freedom for his, or was that merely hollow moral bluster for yourself and the Council?"

"I will lure Isra out, without the enforcer, Lucifer."

Lucifer laughed. "Stubborn, just as your husband is. I am feeling generous today. I'll do one other thing to help you. Do not squander this opportunity. Isra is cast out. Hell offers her no sanctuary."

"Why so readily do that?"

"This isn't the first time Isra has tried to take over. She clearly didn't learn the lesson she should have when she lost Haroun in France."

Grace couldn't hide the surprise on her face. "It was you that gave Rayne back his conscience."

"Confusing, isn't it? I am no fool, Grace. I knew what Isra intended to use your husband for then, just as I do now. It took a few weeks for his conscience to fully root again. And once he regained a touch of humanity, it drew Lyal right to him. The only thing that gave me greater pleasure than observing Isra as Narciso reported Haroun vanished with no trace from the field was the beating I dealt her for sedition against her master." Lucifer picked up his glass and swirled the liquor in it, focusing on the miniature whirlpool that formed in its center. "Self-preservation, or survival instinct if you prefer a more politically correct term, it's the one motivation within all beings that we can never ignore."

Córdoba - 812

"You said you were going to Elysium," Lyal snapped, following Grace through the front door of Rayne's Cordovan home.

"I had to do something first." Grace continued on to the bedroom and unlocked Rayne's weapon chest. She pulled out the bejeweled dagger Rayne gifted her a few days ago and held it out to Lyal. "Is this close enough to Rayne's dagger that you would believe it is his?"

Lyal shook her head no. "This is a woman's weapon."

"If you didn't know it was made for me, could it pass as the dagger Saladin gave Rayne?"

"No. The blade and hilt are narrower in design. Isra would never believe this was a Rayne's familial dagger if that is who you are seeking to fool."

"Isis." Grace summoned the goddess.

Isis answered the question Grace had for her before Grace could voice it. "I can't transform the weapon, Grace, and you cannot take Rayne's from him with what is at stake."

A loud rumble of thunder and a flash of lightning distracted the three immortals.

The storm transfixed Grace in place. It wasn't nature putting on a display. It was time unraveling. "Is Lucifer right? Do we need the enforcer to determine the outcome either way?"

Isis took in a troubled breath before answering. "We need the Triad to end this."

"I can't reunite the Triad. Not now."

"Then you need the enforcer. Either path requires you to deceive Rayne."

Grace watched the storm outside. "There are days I really hate you and the Council."

"I know you do not understand our ways, Grace. But remember this. There are degrees of deception. Follow your instincts." Unable to guide her anymore, Isis left.

Grace crossed her arms; hugging herself as another bolt of lightning streaked a purple, red, and white jagged path through the clouds.

Lyal watched Grace struggle with deciding what to do. "You saw a sample of the destruction Isra will bring to Spain. Warfare will spread well beyond Spain's borders after her conquest here. Rayne will be the weapon wielded either way. It is better you are the one wielding him."

"The cost will be devastating if I do so. I can't do that to him."

"You preserve his soul and your existence, even with the price paid. You save humanity and keep your children from harm. Uphold your oath to the Ancients and the Council."

Kato and Sulla ran into the winds. The rumble of thunder and lightning periodically illuminating the ever-darkening sky spooked them. But they would not fail the immortal who aided the traitors pack. Kato spotted Rayne walking with Destahn and Raphael outside the palace gates.

"Haroun!" Kato shouted, shifting to human form mid-stride.

"Kato?" Rayne wondered what had Kato and Sulla running towards him.

"Your wife, your wife says there is danger. Sulla and I come to warn you."

"What kind of danger?"

"Something involving Isra. Grace had a vision of what is to come. It is the same as the dream you've been having."

"No. I would never turn." Rayne momentarily panicked. Grace had to have misunderstood her vision. "Where is she now?"

"Elysium. She is going to the god to defend against Isra."

Grace seeking sanctuary in Elysium eased Rayne's fears. "Grace is safe there. Isra can't enter Dante's home."

"There is something else." Kato handed Rayne his familial dagger. "Do the other Horsemen speak djinn?"

"No." Rayne took the dagger, guessing Grace sent it to him so he could kill Isra if he could find the damn overseer.

"Good. She said to ensure only you heard the rest of what she had to say."

What Kato told him next, confounded Rayne. "Did she explain why?"

"What's going on?" Destahn called, not liking the perplexed look on Rayne's face.

Rayne held his hand up, signaling Destahn and Raphael to keep their distance. "I will fill you in momentarily."

"Grace said she had no time to explain anything more. She also insists Sulla and I stay with you."

"Come with us then. She would not ask you to do such a thing without purpose."

"Everything okay?" Raphael asked as Kato shifted back to a wolf and the wolves followed Rayne over to the other two Horsemen.

"No. Grace sent Kato and Sulla with a warning of full warfare between Isra and the Council. Isra's first strike will be soon."

"Explains the change in weather." Destahn thought it odd Grace sent the wolves. "Why didn't she come tell us herself?"

"She went to Elysium to warn Dante of something."

"We better find Isra, then. Maybe we can preempt whatever hell is about to break loose." Raphael hoped they could slow things down and move as many mortals out of the way as possible.

"I think we need to find your wife first," Sulla interjected as the Horsemen started back for the palace.

"She's safe in Elysium, Sulla."

"I do not think she is there. The black-eyed woman with strange hair returned to the house looking for her after she couldn't find her in Elysium."

Rayne halted. "Lyal said she wasn't in Elysium?"

"Grace was asking about Rodrigo, Haroun. I suspect she rode for Granada instead of going to your friend, the sun god."

Destahn looked over at Rayne. "Rodrigo is more of a threat than Isra with his men and arms if Grace accidentally provokes him."

"Grace! Where are you?" Rayne reached out to his wife. After a minute passed with no answer, he called for her again. "I swear I will take her over my knee if she is courting trouble with Rodrigo. We can't fight a three-fronted war without putting too many humans at risk."

Raphael hoped for all their sakes Grace wasn't in Granada with how agitated Rayne became. "Give her a chance to answer. She may be speaking with Dante. You know how hotheaded he is. She might be having to calm him down."

"Only one way to find out." Rayne prayed Dante would answer, since Grace didn't. "Dante, is Grace with you?"

Rayne's inquiry startled Dante. Why would Rayne think Grace was in Elysium? "No. Is she not in Córdoba?"

"Keep an eye out for her. She told Kato she is coming to you."

"I will let you know when she arrives."

The enforcer stirred within Rayne. Trepidation plagued Horseman and enforcer alike. "She isn't with Dante. Excuse me for a minute."

Rayne moved several feet away. He hated to resort to this, but Grace left him no other choice.

"Grace Ibn-Ziyad, come to your master." Rayne summoned her in djinn. She immediately appeared, head bowed and bended down on one knee before him. He quickly yanked her to her feet. "Get up before anyone sees you."

"If you don't want others to see you've taken a submissive, then you shouldn't have summoned me like you did," Grace snapped, furious he did such a thing.

"Don't send mysterious messages and ignore my inquiries or lie about where you are going, and I won't ever need to do this again. Now what is going on?"

Destahn watched Rayne and Grace arguing. "Since when does Grace understand djinn dialects?"

"I don't know, but she certainly understands whatever Rayne is saying to her." Raphael kept a close eye on the two, thinking the events of the day were odd indeed. "Rayne doesn't want anyone eavesdropping on their conversation to use djinn to converse with her."

"At least we can understand half of it." Destahn frowned as Grace raised her voice and demanded Rayne listen to her.

***

"Enough, Grace!" Rayne snarled, losing his temper. "Were you in Granada? Answer me with the truth, woman!"

"No. I was someplace else you wouldn't be happy about. Though I do need to go to Granada to warn Rodrigo. If I can convince him to take me seriously, the humans in the area may be sparred Narciso's wrath if things go south and you do attack Granada for Isra."

"Do you hear yourself, Grace? You cannot walk into Rodrigo's domain and warn him of warfare, especially not of a battle with me leading the strike. He will attack Córdoba. The second the name Haroun Ibn-Ziyad leaves your lips, you condemn every innocent soul here. There isn't a djinn Rodrigo fears except for me. He won't want to take any chances of Isra making the first strike in an attempt to usurp his territory. We will find another way to stop this vision of yours."

"We cannot leave things to chance. I saw the bodies myself, Rayne. Women, children, men - everyone of all ages slaughtered in one afternoon. The only people alive within Granada's boundaries are you, Isra's legions, and the human mercenaries that work for them."

"I won't turn, Grace. Even if I did, the enforcer is sworn to you. He only serves you. That is the whole point of the full soul binding between us. I asked you to do such a thing for the sole purpose of preventing Isra from ever commanding that part of me. As long as you are alive...." The gravity of what he said sent a shudder through him.

"No." Rayne shook his head after Grace looked away. "Look me in the eye and tell me you are alive in this vision you've had."

Grace hated the way he stared at her.

"I will tear apart all of Spain stone by stone to find Isra and Narciso before that happens." Rayne backed away from her.

"Stop, Rayne."

"She dies. She dies now, Grace." Rayne drew his sword.

"Rayne, you damn yourself if you do this."

"So be it." He started for the palace.

"It's your wrath that brings about your downfall. Just as it did when Priya died. Don't let the past repeat!" Grace called after him, but he kept walking. The Fates would punish her for disclosing too much of the vision. "I live, Rayne. I live because Lyal disobeys Council laws and warns me in hopes I can keep you on the side of good. But you don't know that until it's too late. Isra plays off you not knowing the change in my fate. She uses your pain and anger against you. Don't give Isra an advantage by acting like this."

"I will not risk your life, Grace," Rayne growled over his shoulder; his eyes locked on the palace a short distance away.

"Then she's already won."

After Rayne no longer acknowledged her, Grace did the only thing she could to stop him. "Your blade is in my service, Enforcer. I order you to stand down. You are my primus, not hers any longer. I will beg you if I must. Hear me out."

To prevent himself from strangling Grace for wielding their bond, Rayne halted where he was. Furious, he closed his eyes and sheathed his weapon. "What do you wish me to do, Grace?"

"I want you to fight when it is time, but as War, the Balance Keeper, Commander of the Four Horsemen, High Council Harbinger, Haroun the level-headed Human General – Defender of the Cordovan Emirate, The Black Wolf of Córdoba, not Haroun The Soulless Enforcer." Grace walked to him. The internal battle waged between the Horseman and Enforcer showed in the torment on his face.

Rayne swallowed hard, staring down at the woman asking him to stand down, to place her life and that of his children on the line. "I will fight as whoever I must be. I cannot watch you die, Grace. The brief time life slipped from you in Alexandria, those seconds, those seconds were the most terrifying of my existence; even with knowing I could call you back, that you would survive. Then being restrained and only able to watch as the temple collapsed with you trapped inside. I was certain... I cannot endure that again."

Grace saw the tears he held back. She felt his heartbreak and fear along with the rage simmering throughout him. She took his face in her hands. "I am not asking you to. Wage war if you must, Rayne, but do it as a Horseman. Just as you are not willing to let me go, I am not willing to surrender you to darkness. Please, Rayne. Do not force me to watch my husband be enslaved within Isra's legions. Losing you would be the most painful thing I could imagine, but knowing you were trapped as an enforcer for eternity would destroy me."

Rayne clutched her to him and kissed her as if he would never do so again.

"War it is," Raphael muttered, watching the long kiss Rayne and Grace shared. "Come on, Destahn. I already know what order Rayne is about to give."

Destahn laughed and pulled his hood up. "Is it too much to hope they may be making up after the disagreement they had?"

Grace comfortingly stroked her husband's hair. "This isn't goodbye. I refuse to let it be that. I have hope we overcome whatever plays out. And if the worst happens, Tessa and Tarquin will need you. If I can't keep you in the light, may your love for them be enough to pull you through your grief. Contemplate the next commands you give carefully, wolf."

Searching for courage to face the coming storm, Rayne sadly smiled. "I place my faith in you, mia luna. Sulla!"

The wolf obediently approached Rayne. "Yes, Haroun?"

"Spread a rumor that Narciso plans a coup in Granada. Pick whichever of Rodrigo's lieutenants you believe holds the largest grudge against their master and say he is Narciso's co-conspirator. Be certain word travels quickly. Ensure whatever tale you tell is believable. The more the djinn legions deteriorate into anarchy, the better. It expedites what the Horsemen must now do."

CHAPTER

FORTY-NINE

Elysium - The Same day

Dante stood on his balcony watching the day draw to a close. He contemplated the latest news of Isra and Malik gathering a small army. Rayne and Grace remained in Spain the past week, trying to disassemble the growing force. He wished he could join them, but the mounting threat to the children required he stay in Elysium. Perhaps it was best he couldn't go to Spain. Since the night of the dinner, Grace understandably kept her distance. He had acted on impulse when he shouldn't have. She wasn't ready to embrace the Triad, and truthfully, he wasn't certain he was either.

The fading sun set fire to the formerly blue sky, reminding Dante he could do no more. Twilight ended any power the sun held over the earth. Nightfall fell under the moon and wolf's jurisdiction. Feeling a hand settle on his arm, he started. Turning, he discovered Grace beside him, wearing a wine-colored gown he had given her. The same gown she had worn the night they watched the sunset over the Roman ruins in Sasainn. After which, they made love amongst the crumbled walls of the roofless temple, under the stars and the Hunter's moon.

"May I watch the day end with you?"

"Sicuramente." Dante had to force the word from his suddenly dry mouth. The Fates brought him and Grace to one another now as they had that night in the ruins.

Noting the lack of darkness on the horizon, Grace took a relieved breath. So far, only things in Spain unraveled. She wondered how long it would be before the storm clouds found their way to cover the skies illuminating Elysium. "Dante, join me for dinner. I could use your charm and humor tonight."

"I know why you are here, and it isn't to ask me to dinner or to watch sunsets."

"Then make this easier for me."

Dante stared out at the golden sky before them. "You know I cannot do that either."

"It's never fair when fate places us in these positions. You gave your life once for me and Tarquin."

Dante detested how the Council repeatedly forced them to make a horrendous choice to protect one another.

"This is about more than Rayne." Grace hoped he'd look at her. "Do you wish to martyr our children?"

"Grace, you still have reservations churning about your heart. I can save the children. You give me the warning needed to prevent what played out in your vision. Isra will never reach Tarquin and Tessa now that I know, nor will I allow her near you."

"And Rayne?"

"Rayne... Rayne will choose his own fate." Dante refused to wear the mantle of harbinger tonight. The Council could find another messenger to torment Grace with news that would destroy her. "He promised to find his way back to you. That should serve as a gift of hope."

Grace shook her head. "Now, you sound like a member of the Council, Dante. You truly are no better than your father."

"What do you want from me, Grace? I already live with your loathing for tossing freewill to the wind since the bargain I made a decade ago. You want me to add to the guilt I feel for that? To make promises I cannot keep? I cannot save Rayne from a fate he voluntarily accepts. Do you truly want me to lie to you? So you find false comfort in a bargain which will slowly eat away at your soul each sunset you watch for eternity.

"There is always a price, Grace. Take it from one who is paying with every breath he takes, the hell you will internally suffer for saving him, humanity, your children, yourself; it will be more than you ever imagine it could. Go back to Spain, fight alongside Rayne, and hope he is wise enough to listen to the warning you gave him. Stop Isra's playing on his fears. That is how you save him, not through conspiring against him in back channels. I will protect Tarquin and Tessa, and if needed, you, but can do no more. Not this time." Dante started toward the house.

Grace grabbed his hand, halting him. "I am sorry, Dante. I am sincerely sorry for not comprehending the sacrifice you made until now. For placing you in the position of lying as you do."

"Please, cara, I beg of you, do not ask me to destroy you and Rayne, not when I know how much you love him." Dante closed his eyes, wishing her away. Even as a god, he was not strong enough to say no when she so desperately needed his help.

"At least hold one last sunset for me. Give me that simple pleasure. It has been too long since I was lost in a sky on fire."

Dante extended his free hand, freezing the sun in place. Her fingers lingering on his tormented him in unimaginable ways. "Grazia, this may cost you everything."

"I am willing to risk that."

He took in every detail of her. The flame-colored sky gave her hair a translucent glow. The intensity with which she returned his gaze. Her name caught in his throat as the peak of the twilight hour set in. The sun and moon freely intertwined with one another. Grace leaned into him. His arms disobediently embraced her. He already tasted her on his tongue as his face drifted towards hers.

Grace's eyes slowly closed. "Play the villain, Dante. The world needs you to. I need you to."

Dante surrendered to the desire that overwhelmed him anytime Grace was so close. His lips seared hers, sealing the unspoken pact between them. "Managgia! Tell me what I must do."

He released his hold over the sun, allowing the moon to begin her ascent. His lips found Grace's again. The lack of doubt in her alarmed him. She freely wanted him after denying him. "Demand I stop as you did before."

"I am going to burn for saying this, but I don't want you to."

"Caro dio in cielo! Lie to me then." Dante needed her to resist, or he would end up taking her right there, shattering her marriage and earning her wrath all over again. Her hands skimming his shirt drove him dangerously closer to the line they weren't ready to cross. He pinned her to the column behind them.

"I've never been able to lie to you, Dante. Voglio fare l'amore con te."

"You will be the death of all three of us, Grazia." Dante hiked up her skirt. The flat of his palms traveled the soft skin of her thighs before he grasped the rounded curves of her rear, gently kneading the two globes so her hips teasingly moved against his; heightening the desire they felt. Trying to resist the all-consuming urge to undo his breeches and entomb himself inside her, Dante broke off the current kiss they shared. "Why tonight, cara? When the world is on the brink of war?"

"The world be damned, Dante. Can I not have Rayne and you both as once predicted?" Grace couldn't believe the words she uttered. They shocked her as much as they did Dante.

"And there it is! The Defensore's greatest weakness is lust for a god and a djinn," Lucifer interrupted the intimate moment. "Sorry to end this entertaining interlude without a happy ending, Giovanni. But with the prophecy floating around about the Triad, you'll be enjoying your wife again soon enough."

Dante dropped the skirt he had so zealously pulled up. Now the intensity of their emotions made sense, Lucifer manipulated them. "You better have a damn good explanation for what you instigated."

"I needed to know what sin tempted Grace most if I am to help you two head off things with Isra and Rayne. I must say, I am astonished, Grace. On the balcony, in the open, where anyone could come upon you? No wonder you and Rayne work so well. Djinn are always drawn to unbridled passion. I wrongly thought you such a conservative soul." Lucifer laughed, walking out onto the balcony. "And you, Dante, even with your old reputation, I figured a god like you would have better control of his baser instincts. Especially after hearing you've been turning down so many offers. I guess they aren't coming from the right party."

Dante moved, so he stood between Lucifer and Grace. "I do not recall asking for your assistance, Lucifer."

"You didn't. The lady did."

Not believing Grace would go to Lucifer for help, Dante turned back to her. Disbelief darkened his normally welcoming gaze. "You brought Lucifer into my home?"

Grace hated the way Dante glared at her. "I didn't think he would do anything like he just did."

"Che cosa? You didn't think, Lucifer, the one being tossed off the High Council and called the tempter of man, would cause trouble while soliciting him for assistance! That thought never crossed your mind, Grazia?"

Grace wished Lucifer had let her handle things instead of aggravating Dante. The god would most likely refuse any request they made of him now. "Dante, we don't have a choice. Unfortunately, we need his help. And as long as no further harm is done."

Enjoying the argument brewing, Lucifer chuckled. "Now that I know all I need to, there'll be no additional trouble. On my honor, Sun God, Defensore." Lucifer gave them a gallant bow.

"You have no honor," Dante growled at Lucifer. "I need a strong drink to deal with this."

Lucifer smiled and rubbed his hands together. "Pour me one while you're at it, Giovanni."

Dante grabbed Grace's arm. "You are staying right next to me until he leaves. I could throttle you for doing something as foolish as you have."

"I know it's shocking, stupid, whatever you want to call it. Just hear us out. It's either this or full out warfare. Eternal nightfall will cover the mortal realm and make its way into ours if we don't stop Isra." Grace said as Dante led her inside and to his bedroom door.

Lucifer remained on the balcony, watching the two of them.

"This is undoubtedly the most irresponsible thing—" Furious, Dante clenched his jaw to keep from saying anything more. Grace had done some ludicrous things in the past, but this, this was absurd. Of all beings to ask for help! Rayne would lose his mind if he knew Grace conspired with Lucifer. The way she apologetically stared at him only irked Dante more. He held his hand up, silencing her when her mouth opened to plead her case. "Do not say another word! Nothing justifies this, Grazia!"

Grace waited for the usual tirade in Italian and Venetian Dante normally erupted into when something made him this livid. Surprisingly, he said nothing more, his eyes shifting between Lucifer and her.

While it went against his better judgment, Dante reluctantly conceded. "Beelzebub, to my office. Now, or I throw you off the balcony and banish you back to Hell."

"You know I hate that name." Lucifer eyes flashed red.

Dante grinned. "If you don't want me using it regularly, start complying with my instructions."

The three passed Maria in the hall. Recognizing Lucifer, Maria crossed herself and gave Dante a mortified look.

Dante held up his hand to stop his mother from making any inquiries. "Keep the children in their rooms and away from my office. Lucifer will be departing as soon as our meeting concludes."

Maria nodded, then hurried off toward the playroom.

Grace remained standing once they reached Dante's office. Lucifer made himself at home in one of the large chairs opposite Dante's desk. The two watched Dante pour himself a drink.

Lucifer held a finger up in the air, trying to get Dante's attention. "I'll have the brandy."

"You will have nothing, as you are not staying long enough to consume anything." Dante pushed the ornate cork back into the crystal decanter. His eyes never left Lucifer while he made his way to the chair behind his desk. Once seated, Dante took a deep breath, composing himself, only so he wouldn't lash out at Grace again. She wouldn't seek out Lucifer's assistance unless she believed she had no other option. "Now, Grazia, explain to me what il diavolo is doing in my home."

CHAPTER

FIFTY

Córdoba - 812

Kamar's old legion was destroyed along with half of Narciso's. The rumor of a coup was spreading through Córdoba and Granada, aiding the Horsemen in expediting the weakening of Isra's ranks. Rodrigo culled any djinn, human, or demon he mistrusted from his legions. Malik's viziers were in a panic. Malik allegedly had gone to meet with the Almoravids to solicit more support after he learned the djinn division protecting the palace was massacred by four men in black.

Rayne left the djinns' heads on pikes outside the palace gates to send a declaration of war to Malik and Isra. He made certain humans saw the Horsemen raising the pikes, so whispers of the Four Horsemen appearing on earth to slaughter rogue djinn traveled through the region.

Immortals wanting nothing to do with either side fled the area. They recognized warfare as the region had not seen may soon begin. Christians feared the end of days had come with the storms raging and the sightings of the heavenly messengers from Revelations. Members of other religions prayed for deliverance from Mother Nature and the conflict brewing in the city streets.

The Horsemen split into pairs to eliminate the remaining djinn and

539

to encourage the locals to either leave or barricade themselves inside their homes. Sean's guide teams helped spread the word for anyone staying in Córdoba to gather supplies and hunker down.

Rayne watched several families leave the city to head for their country estates. He and Destahn ensured the road remained clear after receiving reports of Isra's djinn attacking anyone who tried to flee. He hoped the original premonition of what was to come had been disrupted enough the scales now tilted in his favor. Because of the unexpected chaos, Isra delayed the predicted strike on Córdoba. It took some arguing, but he convinced Grace to return to Elysium. Dante requested a formal guard be placed around his home to ensure Grace's and the children's safety. Rayne hoped Dante and the Council guard could provide his family the protection he couldn't with having to manage things in Córdoba.

"Rayne!" Grace riding towards him pulled him out of his thoughts.

"Grace? What are you doing here?"

"I have the letter you wanted. Sulla found it for me." She handed him the document.

"You should have sent Sulla or Arturo instead of bringing it yourself."

"I wanted to see my husband since I haven't for the past three days. To make sure he is well and not overextending himself as he tends to do." Grace watched Rayne open the letter and read it.

"Your husband is fine, and trying his damnedest to ensure you don't fall victim to Isra. You can't keep testing the Fates, leof."

"Then don't ask me to look for things you misplaced." Grace teased, surfacing an amused smile on Rayne's face as his eyes finished skimming the letter. It sharply contrasted against the ominous black hood concealing his identity unless one stood only a few inches from him. "We both know you miss me, Commander."

"I do indeed. Every night I ask the Fates to quickly resolve things here so I may be with my wife and children again. I also ask them to grant my hardheaded wife patience and the wisdom to keep herself safe. They must no longer hear my prayers."

"Or they know you need help." Grace earned another sideways glance. "Why did you want the letter?"

"It proves Malik is sending funds to the Almoravids." Rayne carefully folded the letter shut, casting a glance to his right after noticing another wagon and family coming through the city gates.

"I still don't understand why he is in league with the Almoravids. They're more conservative in their religious viewpoints and are surely a threat to his rule."

He tucked the letter into his jacket. "He needed an ally to take on Umar, especially after my refusal to kill him. Abu Bakr is expecting Malik to maintain their alliance. We scared Malik into agreement with Abu Bakr's demands. Malik rode out to meet him this morning. If Narciso wasn't robbing and killing those fleeing the city, I would have followed Malik to gather evidence to turn over to the Cordovan Court."

"Córdoba is fortunate to have its wolf back."

"I am blessed that my wife only sees my finer qualities."

Rayne leaned towards her. Grace savored the kiss he gave her. She hated how recent events separated them.

"This fight tries us both, leof. As you regularly remind me, stay the course. It will be over soon."

Lyal materialized beside Rayne. "Commander, Isra and Narciso have your mother."

He muttered a djinn profanity before addressing Lyal. "Raphael is not far from my father's. You and Raphael intercept Isra. I will join you momentarily."

Lyal nodded then departed.

"Now that Isra shows herself, I want you to go back to Elysium, Grace."

"If war is upon us, you need all the help you can get, Rayne. I am staying here."

"The hell you are. I need to know you and the children are safe."

"We have always fought side by side since marrying. Your fight is mine, Rayne. Dante can keep Tessa and Tarquin safe. Now, let's go rescue your mother." Grace started to turn Diya, so they could ride toward Saladin's.

Rayne seized a hold of Diya's bridle, keeping the mare in place beside Fahkir. "Forgive me, Grace."

"Forgive you? For what?"

"As the High Council Balance Keeper, I exile you, Grace Warwick, to Elysium. You may not leave the boundaries of Dante's home until I end your banishment."

"Don't do this, Rayne." Grace panicked; she hadn't anticipated him doing such a thing.

"I am sorry, Grace. You will not fight this round with me."

Elysium -

Grace found herself in Dante's office.

Startled to see Grace back so soon, Dante crossed the short distance between them. "What's wrong? Why do you look so rattled?"

"He exiled me here." Grace still couldn't believe Rayne banished her from the mortal realm.

Her answer confused Dante, very few beings could issue such a decree against a High Council officer. "Who exiled you here?"

"Rayne. He decreed it as the Balance Keeper."

Dante placed a reassuring hand on Grace's shoulder. "This may play in our favor."

"I am not certain it does."

Hearing the tremor in her voice, Dante embraced her. "All will be well, Grace. Rayne is doing what he feels he must. Isra can't reach you here, and with the contingencies in place for the children, she nor Narciso will ever be able to blackmail Rayne."

"Forgive me for intruding on such a touching moment, but it's time, Defensore." Lucifer now sat in one of the chairs across from Dante's desk.

Grace hoped Lucifer was wrong. "It can't be."

"The ruckus your husband and his men cause in Spain forced Isra out of Hell. With the losses Narciso is incurring, she can't afford any more if she hopes to defeat Rodrigo. She's making her last stand. It is time to play your hand, Grace."

"We can't. I still need the dagger, and it's back in Spain."

Dante wondered why she needed a particular dagger. "What dagger?"

Annoyed, Lucifer sighed. "We've got one shot at this, Grace. Don't tell me you came all the way to Hell and courted the Devil for nothing?"

"Stop it, Lucifer." Dante loathed how Lucifer antagonized her. "Grace, tell me what dagger. I will retrieve it."

"You can't. I have to be the one who carries it." Grace wished Dante could go get it. It was certainly less risky if he returned to Córdoba instead of her. "Is there any way around Rayne's edict?"

Lucifer helped himself to the decanter of brandy on the bar. "A rogue harbinger can circumvent him. The Council forgot to strip her of that power, and you know Lyal, she isn't about to point out their oversight." Lucifer inhaled the aromatic scent of caramel, citrus, and vanilla before sampling the golden liquid in the glass. "I must say, Giovanni, you have excellent taste in liquor. You should come to Hell and join me in a drink or two one night."

Dante was tempted to swipe the glass out of Lucifer's hand. "I'll pass on that offer. As soon as this business with Isra is over, I revoke any permissions granted for you to enter my home."

Grace hoped Lyal could still hear her. "Lyal, I need to get into Saladin's house."

"Cara, no. We need to discuss this plan of yours..."

Lyal materialized in the room long enough to grab Grace then disappeared once more.

"... first." Dante finished the sentence with a groan. "Che cazza!"

"Pour yourself a round while you still can, Dante. It's going to be a long night." Lucifer chuckled. While Dante agreed to everything, he still didn't like it. "Almost as long as the one a few days ago when you got a sample of the wife you are missing, or better yet, the following two nights when Rayne and her were rather amorous with one another once they thought everyone was asleep."

Dante slapped the glass out of Lucifer's hand, spilling the drink down Lucifer's suit. "Next time, ask, instead of helping yourself."

"Tsk Tsk, Giovanni. You're as ill-mannered as Rayne was as a djinn."

"Ill-mannered!" Dante pinned the Devil against the wall with one arm in Lucifer's throat, then pressed the freshly sharpened steel point of his sword into the Devil's chest. "Continue to disparage Grace, I, or any other member of my family, and I'll end your existence. If you ever again exploit my desires or hers in a manner that harms her reputation or her marriage, another demon will be on your throne in Hell. Do we understand one another?"

Lucifer's black wings unfurled. "Careful, Dante. Or you'll be the one explaining to poor Grace why I have withdrawn my assistance. It will be a thousand times harder to save her and Rayne without me. Your willingness to be the noble hero for your ex-wife so astounds me. It's only to your benefit if she dies. Osiris would send her to you. The two of you would spend eternity together here in Elysium."

"Rayne makes her happy and is an outstanding father to my son. That matters more than any selfish desire I harbor, Lucifer. But I don't expect you to understand that. Love and selflessness are well beyond your grasp."

<hr>

Córdoba - 812

"Isra's minions are here," Lyal whispered as she and Grace stood in the hallway of Saladin's home.

"Which means Rayne will be here any second now. We need to work fast." Grace opened Saladin's bedroom door, startling a demon ransacking the room.

Not wanting the lone demon to sound the alarm, Grace grabbed a large candlestick from beside the door and struck it upside the head, knocking it unconscious. Lyal tossed her a knife. Grace sliced open the demon's throat, vanquishing it. "What are they looking for?"

"Isra thinks the dagger is here, since it wasn't found in Rayne's home." Lyal kept an eye on the demons in the courtyard from the doorway.

"How did Isra get into our house?"

"Narciso bribed the estate manager's child to search the house."

"He bribed a ten-year-old boy? How low will he stoop?" A second demon appeared in the center of the room. "Stupid question. No need to answer that."

Grace stabbed the demon before it noticed her. She needed the keys to Saladin's weapons chest. She should have asked Lillian where they were when she had the chance a week ago. "Where do you hide your spare keys, Saladin?" She muttered to herself, tucking the knife into her belt and scanning the room for where they could be hidden. The mess made it harder for her to guess. The massive wardrobe holding Saladin's arms looked similar to the one in Rayne's home. When Rayne went to bed or was working around the Cordovan house, he kept the keys to his weapons chest in a secret compartment built into the wardrobe.

Grace carefully navigated her way through the overturned furniture and items scattered across the floor to the wardrobe. She found a well-concealed lever in the decorative side column and gently pressed down on it. A small compartment popped open, revealing the keys she looked for.

"Like father, like son." Grace smiled, picking up the keys, then unlocked the large cabinet storing Saladin's weapons and armor.

"Please be here." Grace's eyes skimmed Saladin's collection of armaments. Towards the bottom of the cabinet, the dagger she searched for lay on a black velvet pillow.

The bedroom door opened unexpectedly as she reached for it.

Destahn stuck his head inside the room after noticing the broken lock on the door. He wasn't sure if he or Grace was more surprised as they recognized one another. "Grace? What are you doing here?"

"Sorry, Destahn." Grace nodded to Lyal, who stood behind him.

The harbinger knocked out the Horseman Captain. Rayne and Tamir's voices drifted upstairs from the first floor. By the way they grew louder, the two headed for the staircase.

Grace quickly grabbed the dagger. "Lyal, time to go."

Rayne found Destahn lying half in the hall and half in his father's room.

"Destahn?" Rayne turned his fellow Horseman over, then gently tapped his face.

Destahn came to confused. "How did I end up on the floor?"

"That's a good question." Rayne noticed the open doors of the weapons cabinet and his parents' belongings flung all over the place.

Whoever had been there was gone now. "What happened before you blacked out?"

Destahn shook his head, still a bit dazed. "I am not sure. If I didn't know better, I would say Grace was here."

Destahn's answer troubled Rayne. He crossed the room to the wardrobe. Nothing appeared to be missing other than the arms his father carried today. He started to close the cabinet doors when he noticed the empty depression in a small black pillow resting on the bottom shelf. Opening them all the way again, he realized his father's sapphire-hilted dagger was missing. Why had someone taken his father's ancestral dagger?

Destahn rubbed the sore spot on the back of his head. "Anything missing?"

"Yes. You said you thought you saw Grace?" Rayne doubted Grace was the assailant or thief with his banishment of her. She couldn't leave Elysium.

"I am almost positive it was her. She apologized before whoever was with her knocked me out."

Rayne placed a hand on Destahn's shoulder to see what Destahn had. Shockingly, Grace stood in the same spot Rayne did, holding his father's dagger.

Raphael ran into the room. "Something odd is occurring. The demons that have your mother. They're Xander and Lucifer's minions, not Isra's."

Rayne shut the cabinet doors and locked them. "Then they should have no problem releasing her to you and me."

FIFTY-ONE

Córdoba - 812

*R**ayne!* Grace sounded distressed with the way she called his name. *Rayne, please! Answer me. We need your help. We can't hold them alone.*

Rayne frowned. Dante should be in Elysium. He was nearly undefeatable as a Horseman. His promotion to god should have strengthened the man's ability to fight. Why was his wife suddenly begging for help? *Dante, what is happening in Elysium?*

He continued riding in the direction the demons had gone with his mother. After Dante didn't respond, he halted Fahkir. Could Dante not hear him? *Grace, is Dante not there?*

The clamor of sword play filled his head now that he acknowledged her.

He's here. We are being overrun. Come get Tessa and Tarquin, since I can't leave with them.

Images of Grace and Dante fighting off several demons flashed before him. A continuing flow of demon hordes invading Dante's home threatened to overpower Grace, Dante, and the guide soldiers trying to maintain control of Elysium.

The other three Horsemen stopped their horses with Rayne dropping back. Destahn turned his mount around to find out what distracted Rayne.

"What's wrong?" Destahn asked, not liking the grim expression on Rayne's face.

"There's trouble in Elysium. Retrieve my mother while I assist Dante and Grace."

<hr>

Elysium -

Two demons jumped on Rayne as the Horseman entered the fray. The three immortals tried to defeat the endless mass of monsters that kept appearing. Each seemed to target Dante and Rayne's wrists, confusing Rayne.

Rayne severed the head of a demon that leapt at him. "Where are Tessa and Tarquin?"

"We told them to hide in their room and lock the door," Grace yelled back, stabbing the demon in front of her.

Lucifer seized Grace. Rayne took a step toward them. "Stay right where you are, Commander."

Grace stared at Rayne. Her arms bent upward; her fingers grasped at something near her throat. Rayne debated whether to free her or to go for the children.

Get Tessa and Tarquin out of here. Don't worry about me.

Rayne spun his blade and grounded his stance should he need to fend off more of Lucifer's guard. "Lucifer, allow me to pass. The children are innocent. Let me take them from here, then I will return to settle whatever this is about."

"None of you are in a position to negotiate, Commander. I rather relish the idea of wielding the Triad. Enslaving their children ensures their compliance with my commands."

Grace struggled against Lucifer. "We aren't yours to wield."

Dante noticed a strange band on his wrist and tugged at it. "What are these?"

Rayne immediately looked down to discover bright silver bands around his own wrists. A shimmering silver band around Grace's wrist now stood out against the black uniform shirt she wore. *No. The Council promised those were destroyed.*

Dante glanced over at Rayne. *What were destroyed?*

Realizing Dante had halfway removed the band, terror gripped Rayne. "Stop, Dante! You mustn't remove it. Push the restraint back in place."

Dante gave Rayne a perplexed look, but did as he wished.

Lucifer sardonically smiled. "The past does have a tendency to repeat itself. Doesn't it, Rayne?"

"Who wears the collars, Lucifer?" Rayne could already guess at the recipients.

"Lower your hands, Grace, so Rayne can see your pretty new necklace. I wasn't trying to strangle you, not with needing your husband to behave."

Grace loosened her grip on the metallic band Lucifer placed around her throat, revealing it to everyone in the room.

Rayne slowly lowered his sword. If Lucifer had the courage to collar Grace, Lucifer already had Tessa and Tarquin, and had done the same to them. "I'll do whatever you ask, Lucifer, as long as no harm comes to my wife and children."

Lucifer snickered at how quickly Rayne surrendered. "See how much he loves you, Grace. If anyone else wore the collars, your husband would fight to the death. But Rayne would never let you, Tessa, or Tarquin perish."

Dante's gaze locked on Lucifer. "What are these for you to put your weapon down, Rayne?"

"Excellent question, Dante. Rayne, educate the god on your new bonds."

Rayne cursed before looking over at Dante. "The restraints are tied to a collar around a victim's neck. If someone, not the owner, removes either the bands from us or the collar from whomever Lucifer placed it on, they will die. If we remove the bands, whomever wears the coordinating device dies. If we disobey a command we are given..."

"One of the collared individuals dies," Dante finished for him. "You do not even know where the children are, Lucifer. I had one of the guards take them from Elysium."

Lucifer smiled, waving his hand in the air to open a portal. "Is this not Tarquin and sweet, little Tessa?"

Dante, Grace, and Rayne could clearly see their children and the collars around their necks.

"No!" Grace gasped. "They're only children, Lucifer. They are no threat to you."

"Young, old, makes no difference to me, Defensore. All die at some point and time. As for their escort..." Lucifer held up a severed head. "He didn't get out of the garden. Now, put your weapon down, Giovanni."

Dante dropped his sword and kicked it towards Lucifer. "You die once Grace and the children are free."

Lucifer jerked Grace back against him. "Remarks like that are why your dear children wear the collars, Grace. Dante and Rayne are very much a threat to my plans. The only way I have to ensure they stay out of my affairs is to hold you and the children hostage."

Grace glared over her shoulder at Lucifer. "Have you not heard of the Cornerstone Prophecy? Uniting the three of us in any manner guarantees your end."

Lucifer laughed. "I am familiar with the prophecy. If what you say is true, the Triad returns, but this time, united by darkness and fear. Subservient to me, not the Council."

Rayne shook his head. He should have foreseen something like this would occur. "None of us fear you, Lucifer."

"But you do fear harming your children. Hence your compliance. And you detest the idea of injuring your beloved Grace. It will be interesting to learn which of you three ends up murdering Tessa and Tarquin."

"We won't give you the satisfaction of finding out." Grace drew Lucifer's gaze. "We will end you and Isra instead."

"Pride is a sin, Grace. One that blinded your husband twice now." Lucifer let her go then stepped in front of her. "Shall we see if you suffer from the same weakness? Summon the other Horsemen."

"Why?"

Lucifer chuckled. "Perhaps Isra's ambitions have become my own. The Horsemen and yourself removing her ensures no one suspects I am the one behind her and Rodrigo's fall."

"We aren't your pawns. You want the other Horsemen, bring them here yourself."

"Aren't you and Rayne the perfect hardheaded pair? You'll learn, Grace, just like he did. I will be kind at the moment and pretend you did not refuse me. You have an hour to reconsider your words." Lucifer shoved Grace hard enough she fell. His demons followed him out of the room.

Gates appeared in the hall, kitchen, and foyer archways, trapping Grace, Dante, and Rayne in the living room.

"Call the others." Rayne helped Grace to her feet.

She shook her head. "No."

Reminding himself that Grace hadn't previously tangled with Lucifer, Rayne bit back the scathing reprimand forming on his lips. "Tessa and Tarquin will die if you don't. You do not want their deaths on your conscience."

"One life, Rayne."

"Do not deride me, Grace. I know more than you ever will what one life may be worth. You gamble with our son's and daughter's lives."

Grace folded her arms over her chest. "Lucifer may be lying about the collars around their necks. They look different from mine."

"Lucifer doesn't lie about matters like this!" Rayne wished she would listen to him. Why did her obstinate nature always kick in when it could do the most harm?

"Would the two of you stop bickering?" Dante snapped at them. His raised voice caused one of the demons guarding them to turn in their direction.

Grace dropped her arms to her side. "What do you mean Lucifer doesn't lie? He's the Devil. That's what he does, Rayne."

"Lucifer manipulates through degrees of truth, as difficult as that may be to believe. He thrives on others tormenting themselves."

Dante rotated his wrist. The silver band shimmered in response to the movement. He frowned at the light play that confirmed Lucifer didn't lie about the link between the restraints and the collars. "How do you know about these, Rayne? I've never seen such devices before today."

"This is not the first time Lucifer's used them. I killed my cousin Nezha by removing a band from my wrist after I doubted Lucifer's warning of what would happen if I did so."

Grace shook her head, her lips pursed as she gave Rayne an irritated stare. "And you didn't bother to report the bands to the Council, allowing Lucifer to use them against Council Officers a second time!"

Stunned by Grace's accusation, Rayne's voice defensively raised. He leaned toward her as he spoke. "I did report them. The Council swore they destroyed them and that no more existed."

Rarely did Rayne lose his temper as he started to now. Concerned by his out of character behavior, Dante moved closer to them. "Call the Horsemen to arms, Grace."

"I am not giving Lucifer the Four Horsemen."

"Mia stella, we do not have a choice."

The term of endearment and tone Dante used provoked the already enraged enforcer in Rayne. "She is not your anything any longer, Giovanni."

"Rayne." Grace set her hand against Rayne's chest. "Please don't. Lucifer wants us fighting one another. You know how this works. He divides us, making it harder to stop whatever he is up to."

Lucifer reappeared in the hallway, holding Tessa. "She really is an angelic little thing, considering the character of her father and mother."

Grace walked up to the gate keeping her separated from Lucifer. "If you hurt my daughter..."

"Oh, I won't harm her. Tessa and Uncle Luci have actually been having quite the fun evening together. It will be you failing to follow orders that harms her, Grace. She's got about ten minutes until... well, you know. Tell your mother goodbye, Tessa"

The little girl trustingly laid her head against Lucifer's shoulder. "See you later, Mommy."

"Your mother is sad. Maybe she needs a kiss, Tessa?" Lucifer noticed Rayne's scowl deepening and the brief flash of silver in Rayne's eyes.

"Don't be sad, Mommy. Love you." Tessa brought her hand to her mouth then blew Grace a kiss.

Lucifer lifted the collar around Tessa's neck with a finger. "Tick Tock, Defensore."

His laughter lingered in the air after he vanished.

The anguish on Grace's face made it near impossible for Rayne to quiet the enforcer. He wanted Lucifer's head with what the Devil dared tonight. "Summon the others, Grace."

Tears slipped down Grace's cheeks. "I love Tessa more than anything, but how can I honestly choose between her and sacrificing two entire realms with thousands of living beings?"

Grace grieving the potential loss of their daughter tormented Rayne. Fighting to control the rage building within him, Rayne clenched his fists. "She will not die, Grace. You are going to do exactly as Lucifer asks. The Horsemen don't take orders from him. Even when he holds their commander hostage."

Lucifer returned without Tessa. He boldly stood in the living room across from the three immortals. "Why all the waterworks, Defensore? Listen to your two husbands. Doing so will help you avoid making a decision you'll only live to regret."

Dante punched Lucifer.

The Devil staggered back, massaging his jaw. "Must I remind you of who your new master is?"

Dante scoffed. "I do not call anyone master."

"Lucifer, spare Tessa, and I will muster the Horsemen." Rayne took on the burden Grace didn't want to carry.

"Gallant of you, but Grace has to issue the order if Tessa wants to see another day. I am not unsympathetic, Rayne. Women always take the transition to damned servant much harder than men. Grace has an extra two minutes to change her mind." Lucifer disappeared again.

"So generous of him." Grace embraced Rayne.

Rayne held her tightly. *Give our daughter another day. Bring the Horsemen here. All Lucifer can do is keep us locked up. Trust me. He will pay for tonight. Once we get free, there's no place Lucifer can hide from us.*

Grace looked up at him. He nodded, confirming the decision was the right one. The fact that blue eyes continued to observe everything helped calm her anxiety.

"Horsemen..." Grace second guessed Rayne and herself.

"Finish the order, Grace." *Don't let fear rule you. The Horsemen and Defensore have never lost a battle when they fight together. We will not incur a loss now. Lucifer will regret the request he's made.*

"With the Defensore!"

Rayne smiled. "There's my brave wife."

Tamir, Raphael, and Destahn answered her call.

Destahn glanced around, surprised to see the iron gates trapping them in Dante's living room. Dante wore his Horsemen's uniform and was armed. Rayne looked angry, and Grace's face was tear-streaked. "What occurs here?"

"Lucifer has Tessa and Tarquin." Dante filled in the other Horsemen.

Destahn couldn't comprehend how Lucifer managed to kidnap Tessa and Tarquin then imprison Dante, Grace, and Rayne. "Why are you three letting Lucifer cage you, instead of rescuing your children?"

Rayne held up his hands, displaying the restraints he, Dante, and Grace wore. "Our options are limited at the moment."

Lucifer loudly clapped from the hallway. "Well done, Defensore. Tessa lives another day. You learn faster than your husband did. With you six out of the way, I can finally accomplish a few things. I think you've earned a special reward, Grace. Moloch, kindly escort the lady to her new quarters."

The demon chuckled and headed for Grace. She tried to evade him. Moloch grabbed Grace about the waist.

"Get your hands off me!" Grace clutched Rayne's arm, using him as an anchor to resist the demon yanking her backward.

Not liking how Lucifer wanted to separate the Horsemen and Grace, Rayne took a firm hold of his wife and freed her from Moloch's grasp.

"Do you never learn, Haroun? She spared your daughter, and now you jeopardize Tessa, her brother, or Grace with this nonsense," Lucifer chided. "Let Grace go."

"Where is Moloch taking her?"

"No need to worry." Lucifer smirked. "She'll be down the hall in Dante's room for the night. His bed will be more comfortable than the floor the five of you will enjoy. It also ensures you and Dante don't try anything stupid. Now, stand aside. So we are clear, that is a command, Haroun."

Rayne reluctantly let go of Grace.

Lucifer motioned for Moloch to bring Grace forward. "If the five of you are good, you'll see Grace for a bit in the morning."

This time Grace compliantly went with Moloch into the hall. They waited for Lucifer on the other side of the gate.

Destahn strode toward Rayne and Lucifer. His hand on his sword. "Define good, Lucifer."

"Hand off the blade, Captain," Lucifer cautioned. Two more demons appeared between the Horsemen and Lucifer.

"Stand down, Destahn. He's merely testing us." Rayne's eyes searched the hall for signs of other demons. "Lucifer knows better than to actually harm Grace. He's already condemned himself taking the children hostage."

Lucifer sardonically laughed. "This all feels oddly familiar, Rayne. I have the thing you value most. You're behind bars you can't escape. This time, the Council harbingers are imprisoned with you. No one is coming to your aid."

"Grace and I are stronger than the two souls you tortured back then. Make no mistake, Lucifer, any harm comes to my family, and these bars won't contain my wrath."

"Since it appears you and your men need clarification on what I expect from you, there are to be no escape attempts. As long as the five of you stay put, I could not care less what you do to entertain yourselves."

Lucifer teleported into the hallway. "Secure her then make sure they all remain caged for the night."

Moloch nodded, giving Grace's arm a tug. Dante and the Horsemen watched Moloch take Grace to the master bedroom. Moloch shoved her inside it. The sound of iron clanging shut followed by Grace's hands wrapping around newly installed bars confirmed Grace wasn't harmed.

Rayne reached through the gate in front of him and yanked Lucifer forward by the shirt. "In the future, keep Moloch away from my wife and daughter."

"Or you will what? Make all the threats you like. You can't act on them as long as you wear the bands."

Raphael wondered what Rayne might actually do to Lucifer. "Let him go, Rayne. You'll have your chance for retribution."

Rayne released Lucifer.

"Moloch, stand guard outside the Defensore's cell for the night. She attempts to escape or these five do anything rash, I trust you know how to handle the situation." Lucifer grinned at Rayne then vanished.

Rayne cursed. Why couldn't Lucifer have chosen another demon guard?

None of the immortals said anything more now that Lucifer was gone. The five sat spaced out around the room, each contemplating what to do.

"We aren't really going to stay here while Lucifer is doing the gods know what?" Destahn spoke up, not believing Rayne hadn't issued some sort of directive yet.

Rayne remained focused on the hallway, watching Moloch standing by Dante's room door. "For the moment we are."

Raphael didn't like that Lucifer selected the demon of child sacrifice to guard Grace. Moloch had quite the reputation for rape. At three thousand years old, the demon would be a challenging adversary to take down. "Moloch is an interesting choice of guard."

Rayne glanced over at Raphael. "At least he isn't the one keeping Tessa and Tarquin captive. Grace stands a chance against him if it comes to that. I hope, for all our sakes, it won't."

Dante stewed in an oversized chair in the corner. He stared pensively at the floor. Tamir and Destahn sat across from one another, unsure what to think. While it wasn't unusual in troubling times for Rayne to be calm and quiet as he worked through strategy, it was highly out of character for Dante to be stoic and silent. The former Horseman rose to glory based on his brashness and quick maneuvering to overtake an enemy. Dante was impulsive to a fault.

After another half hour of nothing happening, Destahn let out an exasperate breath. "I can't take this. What are you so fascinated with in that damn hallway, Rayne?"

"Those in it." Noticing a newcomer walking out of the shadows,

Rayne stepped away from the wall he leaned against. He moved closer to the iron gate keeping him prisoner to get a better view of whoever it was. Recognizing Lyal, Rayne resisted the urge to grin. Moloch hadn't noticed her. The harbinger brought her finger to her lips, signaling Rayne to remain quiet.

Do nothing that will endanger my wife and children, Rayne warned, half relieved to see Lyal and half worried she'd do something brash getting them all killed.

Lyal smiled, slipping between the bars covering Dante's bedroom door.

That particular smile brought trouble with it. *I swear I will hold you accountable for any harm that happens, harbinger. You'll find yourself back in Tartarus.*

Stop threatening me and worry more about your own predicament, Commander, Lyal snarkily responded.

"And since when are you so quiet?" Destahn directed the inquiry at Dante.

"Mayhap time as a god has changed my reaction to things, Destahn." Dante shot his former peer a glare then went back to examining the swirling pattern in the marble tile beneath his feet.

Destahn guffawed at Dante's comment.

Raphael noticed the perturbed expression on Rayne's face. "What is it, Rayne?"

"Lyal's here. She slipped past Moloch unnoticed."

Raphael knew that wasn't possible. "No one gets past Moloch without being noticed, not even a harbinger."

"Something's wrong about all of this," Rayne whispered back.

Tamir voiced another perplexing thing. "Does it not seem odd to anyone that Lucifer did not confiscate our weapons?"

"Yes, it does." Rayne headed straight for Dante. "It is also strange Lucifer and his minions breached a god's home as they did."

Not intimidated by the scowl on Rayne's face, Dante rose. "What are you accusing me of, Warwick?"

"Nothing, yet. But I do wonder how exactly Lucifer and the demon horde broke through a barrier that effectively kept them out until today."

"Commander," Moloch said, causing Rayne and Dante to look towards the gate. Realizing there were technically three commanders imprisoned in the living room, Moloch clarified which one he referenced. "The sun god. Lucifer wants a word with Giovanni."

Rayne shook his head, letting out a loud huff. "Why would Lucifer want to speak to you?"

"Non lo so." Dante's shoulder slammed into Rayne's as the god pushed past Rayne to see what Lucifer wanted.

Rayne resisted the urge to clock Dante for the challenge.

The iron gate opened then slammed shut behind Dante. Dante glanced back to see the scowl on Rayne's face deepen. The unspoken accusation of Dante betraying the Horsemen and Grace tolled like a death knell.

"I've never forsaken any of you," Dante grumbled, following Moloch down the hall.

Reaching the master bedroom, the gated door swung open, and Dante stepped inside. A forlorn Grace sat on the bed. Lucifer leaned back against Dante's dresser across from her with his arms crossed in front of him.

"Are you unharmed, Grace?"

Grace's spirits lifted slightly seeing him. "I am fine."

"Now that we've established she is perfectly safe, Dante, I need your assistance with getting the Defensore to understand a matter. As you're more open-minded than her husband, I hoped you might help me persuade her to see things from a different point of view."

Destahn laughed after hearing why Lucifer sent for Dante. "He chose the wrong one of us for that task. Lucifer obviously isn't familiar with how often Grace and Dante used to butt heads over everything. I give it five minutes before Lucifer and Dante are fleeing the room with everything not nailed down being hurled at them."

The door to Dante's bedroom shut, muffling any further discussion.

"Be at the ready should we need to intervene in this discussion."

Rayne removed the loops keeping his dagger in its sheath. "You three can do more than I can to protect her at the moment."

Tamir mirrored Rayne in prepping his weapons for a fight and re-tightening the straps of his cuirass that he had loosened. "We'll need to get past the gate to reach her."

"I'll take care of the gate and Moloch. You three focus on Grace."

Destahn wondered why Rayne hadn't already ripped the door from its hinges, since it sounded like he could. "If you can take down that gate, do it, and let's kill a demon or two."

"Patience, Destahn. I've been through situations like this with Lucifer and Isra many times before. They always end up doing something rash when things don't go as they wish. I have a feeling we'll have our opportunity here shortly. Whatever Lucifer wants, Grace needs to agree to it willingly."

FIFTY-TWO

Elysium

"I won't do it." Grace's raised voice warned things escalated.

"Grazia, per favore, ascolatami." Dante sounded exasperated.

"Vai all'inferno con Lucifero, Dante!"

Rayne and Raphael smiled at how Grace told Dante and Lucifer to go to hell.

The door opened, and Lucifer stepped out of the bedroom. "Moloch!"

Rayne gripped the bars, prepared to tear down the gate should Grace need assistance.

Dante blocked the open doorway, preventing Lucifer from re-entering the bedroom. "Give me more time. You know as well as I do the second you sic Moloch on her, she will never agree, and Rayne will demolish every wall in my home to get to her."

"How do you intend to get her to cooperate? She refused you three times."

"I was married to Grace, Lucifer. I know how to win her over. We either allow her time to rationalize things or we give her what she wants."

"I am not about to release War simply because she desires I do so."

"Lucifer, if she wants her husband in return for what you ask, you can give her exactly what she wants without releasing Rayne."

"Dante, don't," Rayne warned from the gate.

Lucifer looked down the hall at Rayne. "Now I am curious to learn what you have in mind, Giovanni."

Dante pulled his hood up and spoke in Rayne's voice. "All the Horsemen can present as someone else when needed. In the dark and at a distance, she won't know the difference between War and Death."

Lucifer chuckled. "I had no idea the four of you could do that. Let us try again, Giovanni."

Rayne hated how slowly time passed as he stared at the closed bedroom door. Periodically, he could hear Dante or Lucifer talking, but couldn't make out what they said.

"Dante is stalling Lucifer to give Sean time to locate the children. You know Grace can tell the two of you apart, even if Dante stays at a distance and uses your voice to speak." Raphael tried to ease Rayne's angst.

"Lucifer shouldn't be learning what the Horsemen are capable of. The more he knows, the more he will exploit our skills and vulnerabilities."

Destahn joined them. "That skill isn't going to serve him well. We can cause more chaos for Lucifer than he can for us. Allow me to prove my point. Moloch!"

Hearing Lucifer say his name, the demon looked towards the master bedroom. When no additional orders came, Moloch went back to facing forward.

"Moloch, you worthless bastard, fetch me a brandy. I am parched after dealing with Haroun's stubborn-ass wife. Oh, and schedule Giovanni for an hour on the rack since he failed to win her over."

Now realizing where the voice originated from, Moloch growled at the three Horsemen near the living room gate.

"Moloch!" Lucifer opened the bedroom door and yelled at the startled demon. "When your master calls, he expects you to answer."

Watching Moloch follow Lucifer into the bedroom, Destahn laughed. "I couldn't have timed that better."

Rayne actually chuckled to himself. Normally, he wouldn't find that kind of antic amusing, but after the day it had been, the levity of the situation struck him harder than usual. He nodded to Tamir after he walked over to the group.

"You promoted a child to Horsemen Captain." Raphael grinned as he spoke.

"It appears so." Rayne sobered again, trying to figure out what Lucifer wanted of Grace.

Tamir clapped Rayne on the back. "Keep the faith. We've all made it this far, Rayne."

Another quiet half hour passed. Raphael and Tamir fell asleep on the couch. Rayne allowed himself to doze as he leaned against the wall. This wasn't the first night he had to sleep as he could standing up.

"No!" Grace yelling woke the sleeping Horsemen. The word rang through the house again. Rayne cast a nervous glance at the bedroom door.

Lucifer appeared in the doorway, pointing at Rayne. "You! Do you honestly think you've outwitted Isra and me with what you've done?" Lucifer noted the smirk that vanished as quickly as it tweaked the Horseman's lips. "Oh, Haroun, your gloating won't last long. You are about to learn your little trick doesn't stop a damn thing!"

Destahn hadn't seen Lucifer mad like he was now. "What is he ranting about?"

Rayne shrugged. "I honestly do not know."

"Lying is a sin, Commander!" Lucifer scoffed at Rayne pretending not to know what he referenced. "No matter. There are other methods..." Lucifer re-entered the room, slamming the door behind him.

"Lucifer, you worthless, son of a bitch!" Grace screamed.

Rayne didn't like that he couldn't see what was happening. Lucifer must have severed the tie between him and Grace. Dante cursed then called Grace's name. A crash sounded within the bedroom followed by Lucifer's laughter. Worried Grace might be in danger, Rayne ignored how metal singed his hands as he yanked the gate backward. The loud cracking of hinges brought Moloch into the hallway. The other Horsemen stood behind Rayne with weapons in hand. Moloch drew his blade.

"Lucifer!" Moloch called for his master.

Lucifer dragged Grace into the hallway. "Since she won't comply, Giovanni, she leaves me no other choice."

Dante followed them. "Do nothing that harms her, Lucifer."

"She won't be the one harmed. Now, Grace, I am giving you one last chance to tell me where the Heart of Osiris is since it isn't in Petra."

Grace jerked free of Lucifer. "I don't know where it is."

"I command you tell me the location of the relic, Defensore."

Tessa appeared in Lucifer's arms.

"Please, Lucifer." Grace paled. "I don't know."

"My patience runs out, Grace."

"I can't give you the relic. I don't know where they moved it to."

"Moloch, relieve the Defensore of the bracelet on her right wrist. Tell your daughter goodbye."

Grace tried to free herself from Moloch's grip. "Take my life instead of hers."

"Do you think me an idiot, Grace? You are soul bound to a god and a Horseman. Not to mention some djinn lays claim to your soul."

"I didn't offer my soul. I offered my life. Keep me as a hostage. Sell me off to the highest bidder. I don't care what you do. Just grant my children and Rayne their freedom."

"I have no use for a hostage. Moloch, finish your task."

Rayne teleported beside Grace, grasped Moloch's wrist, and stopped the demon from removing the restraint.

Dante ripped Tessa from Lucifer's arms. He hugged the little girl to his chest. Tessa cried and called for Grace.

Rayne freed Moloch's fingers from the band and shoved the demon away. "Dante has Tessa, leof." He pushed the band back in place on Grace's wrist then held his wife. She clung to him, sobbing now that the threat to their daughter passed. "She's safe, Grace. Tessa's safe."

"I've changed my mind, Defensore." Lucifer stared thoughtfully at Grace. "I'll accept your offer. Your life in exchange for the children and

Rayne's freedom. Rayne is free to go at dawn. As a good faith payment, I will release the children to whomever you wish and allow you to remain with Rayne until sunrise. After that, you go on the market to the highest bidder. Such a pity Horsemen are forbidden from engaging in soul trafficking, your husband won't be able to buy your freedom. It will be interesting to see where you end up."

Rayne's hold tightened on Grace. Lucifer wasn't selling her to anyone. "You cannot auction off a soul you cannot lay claim to."

Lucifer laughed. "There is nothing you can do to stop me, Rayne. She freely made the bargain."

"Under coercion."

"A deal is a deal, Rayne. The only one who can prevent the sale is the djinn she bartered with, and I know he won't come to her aid. He has too much pride to publicly expose the fact the Defensore has a master other than the Council. He knows the humiliation she will suffer if anyone learns of their arrangement."

Rayne took a threatening step toward Lucifer.

"Careful, Haroun. Others might read into your actions and discover the truth about your wife and this mysterious master of hers. What is the penalty for treason against the Council again? I've forgotten after so many years," Lucifer taunted Rayne in djinn before looking over at Moloch. "Moloch, fetch me a servant's collar, and be quick about it. In the meantime, who do you wish your children be sent to Grace?"

"To the Arsceneauxs as temporary caretakers until you leave my home then they come to me," Dante interjected, gently rubbing Tessa's back and doing his best to stop her crying. "I am their legal guardian if they cannot be with their parents. I will watch over them until their father is ready to bring them home again."

"The decision is Grace's, not yours, Giovanni." Lucifer took the jeweled collar Moloch offered him. "Interesting selection of collar, Moloch. Much nicer than I would have given her."

Grace closed her eyes as Lucifer traded the servant's collar for the titanium ring encircling her throat. Lucifer looked at the Horsemen standing nearby with swords still drawn.

"All of you, put your weapons away." Lucifer turned back to face Rayne and Grace. "Now, Defensore, where do your children go?"

"Do as Dante asks. That was the initial plan for them. The Arceneauxs are expecting them."

A new demon appeared in the hall next to Lucifer. "Deliver Tessa and her brother to Caitlin and Gage Arceneaux."

Grace watched Lucifer take Tessa from Dante. He didn't remove Tessa's collar. "Wait! Lucifer, remove the band from her neck. You have Rayne's and my compliance."

"I am sorry, Grace. As I need assurance her father will remain cooperative until sunset tomorrow, she and Tarquin will have to wear the collars a bit longer. But at least you know they are somewhere safe, as long as their fathers don't do anything stupid. And as I promised, I leave you with Rayne for the remainder of the night. Now, the lot of you, back into the living room."

Rayne stopped alongside Lucifer. "I will come for you the moment my children are safe."

Lucifer tsked and shook his head. "Look at what you did to my gate and Dante's wall! Such an impolite house guest, Rayne. I'm not sure if you or your wife is more troublesome tonight."

"Lucifer, I would like a private word with you." Dante looked troubled as he uttered the remark, staring directly at Grace.

"I had a feeling you might. Remain here then, Giovanni." Once the Horsemen and Grace stood in the living room, Lucifer snapped his fingers, returning the gate and wall to their original condition. "Treasure your time while you have it, Grace. I will collect what I am owed."

Lucifer and Dante walked into Dante's bedroom again. After the door closed, Rayne's eyes traveled Grace's body, looking for signs of injury with how she had struggled against Moloch. "Are you hurt?"

Grace wouldn't look up at him. Rayne lifted her chin, forcing her to make eye contact. "Why did you offer yourself to Lucifer?"

"One life, Rayne."

"One life be damned."

"Rayne, the world needs you. It can go on without me, but not without the Horsemen."

"I nor the realms are worth your enslavement."

"Your and the children's freedom are well worth the trade."

Wishing he could undo the agreement she made, Rayne embraced her. "Once Tessa and Tarquin are safely hidden away, Hell will be the first place I head."

"Kill Isra, then come for me." Grace pressed her cheek against his and closed her eyes, allowing his strength to seep into her being and reinforce her own weakening resolve.

"You are one of the strongest women I know, Grace. Never doubt yourself or your ability to endure," Rayne whispered before kissing her temple.

Appreciating his words, Grace sadly smiled up at him. "At least the agreement ensures Isra can never command the enforcer. I am too prized a servant to ever be killed. I doubt Lucifer will find a buyer. Most in the immortal realm know who I am and who my husband is."

"I'd gladly serve Isra for eternity if it meant you were free."

"Never say that again, Rayne Warwick. If she gets you, what I just did was for nothing. End Isra, and protect our children. Continue being the great commander you were destined to be. I will be okay."

Moloch didn't like the hushed interaction between the Warwicks. "What are the two of you murmuring about?"

"Can I not comfort my wife?" The expression on Rayne's face dared the demon to open his mouth again.

Moloch snorted, but went back to ignoring them.

Grace softly laughed. "My handsome, steadfast saint."

"I am far from being a saint." Rayne kissed her. "I'll find a way to free you."

"I need to borrow your wife, Commander. I'll return her in a bit," Lucifer said from the gate.

Before Grace could protest, she found herself in the hallway with Lucifer. "How..."

Lucifer chuckled. "Forget our bargain so quickly, Grace? I can bring all I own to me that swiftly. Pity someone else has the pleasure of you calling them master. That really should be how you address me going forward, at least until we find you a new one. Now, come along."

Grace followed Lucifer to Dante's bedroom.

Rayne once more waited at the gate. Why had Lucifer brought her back to Dante? He heard more arguing from down the hall. Whatever Lucifer wanted, neither Grace, nor Dante were happy.

Grace stormed into the hallway. Dante grabbed her arm. She spun and slapped him. "Return me to my husband. I was promised the night with him."

Lucifer laughed, stepping into the hall. "Indeed, you were. You are quite the hellion, Grace. Slapping a god like that. Maybe I will keep you."

"Wait until you see what I do to you when I have a blade in my hand," Grace remarked, heading toward Rayne.

"Oh, now that, I can't let go unpunished, pet." Lucifer reached for Grace. She vanished as his fingertips brushed her arm then reappeared beside Rayne.

Rayne grinned, wrapping an arm around Grace. "A deal is a deal, Lucifer. She spends the rest of the night in my company. Unless, you are releasing her from the agreement."

Noting the silver eyes locked on him, Lucifer walked the rest of the way to the gate. "I guess I can let the one offense slide."

Rayne leaned forward and spoke in djinn so no one else heard what he said. "You'll let all her offenses slide. Harm her, and I will pay each injury back tenfold, starting with the plucking of every black feather from those wings you treasure above all else."

"Are you threatening a deity, Commander? We wouldn't want the Council thinking you've gone rogue. Not even you could outfight and outrun those they'd dispatch to eliminate a corrupted Horseman. And what use would those thoughtlessly uttered threats be to poor Grace if you're locked away in Tartarus?"

"Lucifer!" Dante called, distracting the Devil. "Our negotiations are not finished, or have you lost interest in the location of the Heart?"

Lucifer disappeared. Grace assumed he went back to the bedroom. "Rayne, we need to warn Rodrigo about Lucifer's plans."

"Unfortunately, leof, until the restraints are off my wrists, I can't go anywhere or warn anyone."

"Send Destahn or Tamir." Grace glanced over at the other Horsemen.

Rayne stared at the collar around Grace's neck. "I won't risk your life or the children's to interfere in a djinn conflict, nor will I give Lucifer incentive to separate us again before sunrise."

"We both know this is more than a djinn conflict. Lucifer won't hurt me. He will already be dealing with the ire of the Council for accepting my offer, in addition to your anger. Help the mortals in Spain."

Rayne ran his finger along the edge of her collar. At least it was padded and soft, so it wouldn't cut or bruise her neck as many servants' collars did to those who wore them. "You overestimate how much Lucifer fears the Council and repercussions for his wrongdoing. You should have never made the offer you did."

"Then I hold onto hope that you will free me."

The gate over the master bedroom door fell with a loud clang. It tremored on the floor as if someone had dropped a coin. All four of the Horsemen and Grace turned to see what happened. Dante and Lyal walked out of the room together. The livid expression on Dante's face broadcast the god's displeasure about something. The two immortals headed for the living room. Halfway down the hall, Dante seized a hold of Lyal and forced her into the wall. His dagger sliced open her throat. He flipped the blade then drove it downward into the harbinger's chest. Lyal's blue and black hair changed to a burgundy and violet hue before her body vanished.

"Isra!" Rayne mumbled the overseer's name. Isra had hidden herself in Dante's home disguised as Lyal.

"Rayne, take care of Moloch," Dante shouted, killing another djinn a few feet from where he had vanquished Isra.

Moloch glanced between Dante and Rayne.

Rayne again ripped the gate from its hinges, then charged forward, smashing into Moloch with it. Moloch collided with the wall, shattering plaster and leaving a crater-sized outline of himself in it. Tossing the gate aside, Rayne drew his sword.

"Moloch!" Dante called the demon in Lucifer's voice.

The demon only slightly twisted toward Dante, but that split second allowed Rayne to plunge the length of his sword between the demon's shoulder blades. Moloch and the bars imprisoning them all dissolved.

Rayne wanted Lucifer's head for enslaving Grace. "Where is Lucifer?"

"Distracted. I lied to him about the location of the Heart. We only have a few minutes before he returns. Grace, I am not certain of the consequences if you fight against Lucifer." Dante offered her the two blades Moloch had taken from her.

Grace strapped them in place on her sides. "I intend to see everything through, Dante. I have my reasons for making the agreement I did."

Dante nodded. "Do what you must then."

Ena entered the room after receiving the all clear from Dante. "Commander Warwick, your mother is in custody, as ordered."

"I gave no such order." Rayne glared accusingly at Dante.

"I sent the order under your seal along with Xander's men to keep Lillian safe until Sean or Ena were available to go to Spain," Grace explained things to calm Rayne's temper. "Lyal warned me that Lucifer and Isra targeted her. I hoped Xander might reach her before they did. From the sounds of it, that may not have happened."

"Xander's men reached her at the same time Lucifer's did." Raphael now understood the odd assembly of demons he spotted with Lillian.

Dante frowned at how Rayne continued to stare at him. "You can trust me, amico. No one's betrayed you. Grace and I were preparing for battle here as much as you have been in Spain. Her foresight saved your mother's life. I wish the Fates had warned of Isra pretending to be Lyal. Lucifer and his minions would have never made their way into my home if I had known who would let them in."

"Defensore, my team is with Lillian now. Xander's guard frightened her after Lucifer's minions attacked. We thought the switch would make her feel safer. Do you have any concerns with that?" Ena hoped the change in guard didn't earn her a formal reprimand with as agitated as Rayne appeared to be.

"None, Ena." Grace appreciated Ena's thoughtfulness. "Please tell the guides to release Lillian into Saladin's custody within the next hour. The presence of he and his men will keep the djinn away from her."

Rayne wasn't sure he could handle any more disturbing surprises. "I cannot believe you had my mother arrested. What other preparations have you and Dante made that I should know about?"

"Forgive me, Commander, this will only take a second," Arturo interrupted their discussion. "Defensore, Dante's Horseman's Blade as requested."

Grace took the sword from the guide. "Saddle Vittore and Fahkir. Bring them here along with the mounts of the other Horsemen. Be quick about it."

Arturo thought he misheard her. "Vittore?"

"Yes, Vittore." Grace tossed Dante his weapon. "Death leads the Horsemen today."

Destahn thought Grace lost her mind. "We have a commander. The god does not need to assume his former position."

"D'Accordo. Rayne is perfectly fit for command," Dante agreed with Destahn, settling his old weapon in place on his hip anyway.

"I need all Four Horsemen, Dante. If this fails, Tessa and Tarquin need Death to shield them. We know Raphael can't do it. He doesn't have your lineage."

Rayne took Grace's hand. "Why do Tessa and Tarquin need Dante to shield them?"

"He serves as a failsafe. Dante is the only one of us who can protect the children based on the vision I had. That is why I agreed to his earlier request of the children being brought here once Lucifer leaves. You know how difficult that is for me to agree to, I would much rather they stay with Caitlin and Gage."

"What have you not shared, leof?"

Grace swallowed; her answer would only further upset him. "I can't tell you."

"You can't tell me?" Rayne wrestled with rage once more. "You asked me to fight, to save us all. I cannot do that if you won't disclose everything. Will you truly leave me blind on the field?"

Grace gave Rayne a pleading look then whispered. "I am under order."

Whose orders? When Grace didn't respond, Rayne grasped her by the arms. *This secrecy, all this deception, isn't in your nature, Grace. Tell me what you have not.*

Please, Rayne. This tasking is difficult enough.

Tasking?

Rayne, he will kill Tessa and Tarquin if I say more.

I will not allow that to happen.

My silence protects you and them.

Protects me? Rayne's brows shot upward. Anger triumphed over rationality. What did Lucifer plan to frighten Grace to this extent? *Must the enforcer ask you to learn the truth?*

Stop asking questions I can't answer. He can hear us. Needing to compose herself, she turned away from Rayne.

Rayne started at the warning she gave. His eyes immediately shot to Dante. The god closely watched them. Dante was the only one present besides himself who spoke djinn. Rayne slid an arm around Grace and drew her backward until she rested against his chest. His finger traced the lower edge of the collar she wore. He could hear her heart beat quicken. Succumbing to the enforcer, the walls she built to keep him out of her mind lowered. He whispered to her in the djinn's ancient tongue. "No agreement you may broker destroys our bond. We remain forever tied, in our souls, in our hearts, and in our blood. Now, tell your master what fool tries to take that which is rightfully mine."

He still listens, Rayne. Trust me as I do you. My fidelity is only to you, even wearing his collar.

"I will gift you what you ask, my love. Proceed as you must. I will play along." Rayne kissed the side of her head, releasing her from the enforcer's influence. He hoped his instincts screaming Dante betrayed them were wrong, and it was indeed Lucifer who owned the collar, not the god. "For now."

"Any particular reason you speak in djinn lately?" Destahn asked, confused by what exactly he had just witnessed.

"It ensures certain conversations remain between my wife and me."

Dante grinned at how Rayne tested him. "Grazia, time is short, and we have multiple masters to please."

"Xander." Grace mustered Hades's Captain.

Xander arrived armed with two of his strongest demons. "You know I must object to what you are about to ask, Grace. This has to be the most ridiculous thing I've been tasked to do."

"And, yet, you're here anyway." Grace turned to Rayne. "Please give me the Commander's ruby."

Rayne stared down at the ring granting him authority over the High Council forces. It was only supposed to leave a Horsemen Commander's right hand upon his death or retirement. He slowly slid the ring off his finger then set it in Grace's palm. He closed her fingers around it. *I freely place our fate in your hands, leof.*

Did Kato not give you the dagger? Grace didn't see the weapon on his belt.

Rayne pushed back the side of his jacket, revealing the blade beneath it. Grace allowed herself a brief glance downward. The knife was barely visible tucked into the protective gear he wore. *Concealed, and on me at all times, as you requested.*

Hoping no one else noticed what he showed her, Grace rested her hand on the hilt of his Horsemen's dagger. "I need you to surrender your sword and dagger."

"Both my weapons? Is there a reason you're disarming me?"

Grace unhooked the Horsemen's dagger from his belt and handed it to Xander. "I think you already know."

Rayne shook his head, letting the side of his jacket fall back into place, then unbuckled his sword belt. He stared Grace in the eye as he pulled the belt off. He broke their eye contact to carefully wrap the leather strap around the sword and sheath before offering it to her.

"Thank you for your cooperation, Commander." Grace took the sword. Her hands trembled, clutching it as if having second thoughts.

"Gracie, you must surrender his harbinger's blade," Xander said, gently pulling the sword free of the death grip she held it in. He handed the sword to Ena. "Take this to Isis."

Taking the sword, Ena cast Grace and Rayne a worried glance, not understanding why the Council suddenly turned on the man they had deemed worthy of being their balance keeper.

Xander cleared his throat, prompting the guide to leave.

Lucifer returned with several new minions. "Rayne has not surrendered all of his weapons."

"What weapon do you accuse me of retaining?"

Lucifer gave her a chiding stare. "Grace, give me the knife Rayne revealed to you."

Grace reached under Rayne's jacket. Her hand brushed his side, but the weight of the hidden weapon did not shift. The sensation of something sliding along his ribs as if she pulled an object free from the leather and metal plate that protected his back startled him.

Rayne, honor your oath. No matter what may come.

Dreading whatever unfolded, Rayne nodded, acknowledging he heard her words and would do as asked.

Grace held out Saladin's dagger to Lucifer. Its similar design was enough to fool anyone not intimately familiar with the one Rayne carried. "Here is the weapon you seek."

Now Rayne understood why she stole his father's dagger. Grace secretly tried to sabotage whatever Lucifer had planned. As he stared down at her, he noticed the gems in the center of the collar formed an ancient sun. He grasped Grace's wrist as if trying to stop her from giving Lucifer the dagger. *Share one thing with me, leof. Do you know who benefits from the servant's collar on your neck?*

Her eyes shifted to Dante before settling on Lucifer. Rayne noted where they briefly rested. A lethal rage stirred in Rayne's chest. His supposed friend and ally entrapped his wife. The Council executed corrupted gods as quickly as they did any other corrupted immortal. What did Dante gain by aiding Lucifer that was worth his life?

Lucifer laughed and lifted the band in place around Rayne's wrist. "Careful where your thoughts stray, Commander. You wouldn't want to be responsible for inflicting harm on little Tessa or Tarquin."

Grace tapped Lucifer's hand with the hilt of Saladin's dagger, drawing his attention away from Rayne. "You wanted this."

"I did. Isra will be pleased to receive it." Lucifer grasped the weapon. "Carry on, Defensore."

Dante extended his hand for the Commander's ruby. "Give me the ring, cara."

Grace set the ruby in Dante's palm.

"Wrap things up, you two," Lucifer sneered at Grace and Dante.

Grace placed a hand in front of Dante as he stepped forward. "I alone will see to this. Xander, I commend Haroun Ibn-Ziyad into your custody. Rayne Warwick is stripped of the rank of commander and recused from the Horsemen. Arrest my husband for treason and murder."

Destahn blocked one of the demons. "There are no grounds for those charges."

"Captain, stand aside before you face obstruction charges." Grace maintained an even tone addressing the Persian protecting Rayne.

Destahn drew his weapon, turning on Grace. She didn't resist when he took her hostage. "Recant your order, Defensore."

Dante grasped Destahn's weapon hand to keep the Captain from accidentally injuring Grace. "Destahn, let her go."

Tamir could not support the arrest of an innocent man. "I second she releases Rayne. The charges are not justified."

"I like this no more than you or Tamir, Destahn." Grace appreciated how Dante wedged himself between her and Destahn. She kept an eye on the sharpened steel a few inches from her. If Destahn attempted anything stupid, Dante could move her out of harm's way.

Destahn looked at Rayne for guidance.

Rayne offered his hands to Xander's men. "This misunderstanding will be sorted out, Destahn. Release Grace. She only does as she is directed."

Begrudgingly, Destahn let go of Grace.

Lucifer smiled at Rayne's yielding. "Your peaceful compliance with this matter assists more than the Council and Grace. Your children are most appreciative."

"Threaten my children once more, Lucifer, and when I am free of these restraints, you will suffer in ways not even you can imagine."

Lucifer smirked. "You never did know when you were beaten."

Dante pulled Grace back, so she was out of the way.

Grace watched the guards securing unbreakable shackles to Rayne's wrists then do a quick search for any hidden arms. Miraculously, they overlooked the dagger carefully tucked between the protective tunic and body armor he wore. Her courage faded seeing her wolf in chains. *He doesn't deserve this, Dante.*

There is no other way, tesoro.

Rayne heard the exchange and looked over at them. Dante brushed his lips against the side of Grace's face.

"Rayne." Grace tried to take a step toward him.

Dante prevented her from moving. "You must see this through, cara."

"See what through?" Rayne demanded. *Let her come to me, Dante.*

It is safer if she stays with me.

For some reason, I doubt that. Rayne ripped the chains from the guards' hands and walked over to Grace. "Swear to me no one has harmed you."

Grace placed her hand over Rayne's heart. "No one has harmed me." She forced a smile as he took her face in his hands.

"What am I to believe with your actions, leof?"

"Believe I do what is best for all of us." Grace pulled away then glanced over at Xander and his two men. "Xander, bring the enforcer forth."

Xander hesitated to do as asked. "Grace, this isn't wise."

"If I or Dante must do it, his suffering will be worse. Spare him that indignity."

Xander seized Rayne.

Rayne's eyes locked with hers. *Don't betray the trust I place in you.* Xander's teeth sunk into his neck. Black flame consumed the two. When the fire extinguished itself, eyes of molten silver stared reprovingly at Grace. Isra's most powerful primus stood before them. Not even her vision had prepared Grace for the strength the enforcer projected in the flesh. She could see why so many feared and respected him, why Isra wanted him at the head of her legions. The lethal allure of the enforcer mesmerized Grace.

Xander let Rayne go. Rayne straightened, standing taller. A disdainful sneer emanated from him as his gaze swept around the room, taking in the soldiers, Horsemen, and demons before settling on Grace.

Grace shivered; torn between wanting to run from him and kneel before him. A magnetic attraction always existed between her and Rayne, but what she experienced now was visceral, carnal; Horseman, human, and enforcer merged into one being that owned her heart and soul. Dante had to tighten his hold on her to steady her on her feet.

Noting the effect he had on her, Rayne briefly grinned before the stern countenance of a confident djinn commander returned.

"Careful with him, Grace. Haroun, the Enforcer, always made me nervous. Now I have to worry about his abilities merged with those of a Horseman," Xander cautioned after unleashing one of the most unpredictable djinn enforcers in history.

"She is the one being in this room who has nothing to fear from me. Enlighten me as to how I may be of service to you, Defensore."

Grace needed to know which part of her husband remained in control now that his three selves were exposed. "General Ibn-Ziyad?"

"The general you seek died centuries ago. Only Rayne Warwick stands before you now." Rayne switched languages to djinn. "I am at your disposal for whatever you require, my beloved."

Grace smiled at the defiance in his eyes before Rayne politely inclined his head to her. War was incorruptible.

Xander guffawed beside Rayne. "Now I've seen and heard everything with an enforcer like Haroun Ibn-Ziyad flattering the Defensore at a time like this. Deadly and courtly in one big, ugly package. Shall we take this show on the road, Grace?"

"Absolutely." Relieved that Rayne truly mastered the enforcer's darker nature, Grace turned to Dante. "Commander Giovanni, are the Horsemen ready to ride?"

"At your order, Defensore."

Rayne seized Grace's arm and spun her to face him. "Disclose what you have not shared."

"I... I serve another, Rayne. I can no longer speak freely."

Rayne shot Dante a glare. "Has your new master shared a weapon from Lucifer's armory is missing? One that is used to kill immortals. Do not travel this course, Grace."

"You know I cannot abandon it."

Furious with everything and questioning the Fates, Rayne hung his head. Perhaps the enforcer was better suited to handle Isra, Lucifer, and Dante, since the Horseman was not worthy of favor any longer.

Grace shouldn't disclose much more, but the doubt in Rayne scared her. She'd be damned if she gambled everything for nothing. She placed her hands on his chest to get his attention. "Don't surrender to wrath. The heart of the wolf with the courage of a Horseman makes you more than mere djinn. You seize command of the legions. All of them, good and evil. Neither side will be able to wage war or make a change without engaging you. You hold both realms hostage. Hell is what she's after. Lucifer wants the rest. Don't give it to them. No matter the cost. Stand fast, Rayne."

I will not waiver, leof.

How do I kill Isra?

Rayne let out an exasperated breath. "Watch carefully for the opportune moment. You want her alone, without Narciso or any of her guards. Go directly for her heart. The dagger must be fully submerged. Your fingers buried in her chest with the blade. You should feel bone against your skin; otherwise, the blade is not deep enough. Then immediately take her head. You must not hesitate. If you miss your mark, at that proximity, she will do her best to end you."

"I won't miss."

"Defensore, do not test those over you," Lucifer interrupted the hushed conversation.

Grace handed the free end of the chain to one of the demon guards. "Keep a good hold of this in the future. He frees himself and Isra will become the least of our worries."

Rayne knew Grace was trying to share more with the remarks about what was to come without disobeying Lucifer. *Hope is eternal, Grace.*

She briefly smiled. The simple phrase promised he wouldn't back down from the fight ahead.

Dante raised a skeptical brow, but did not say anything.

Grace motioned for the Horsemen to move out and walked to the door.

Rayne stopped beside Dante as the guards led him forward. Dante settled a hand on Rayne's back. Grace wondered what the two silently discussed. Dante shrugged before following her.

She halted Dante once he reached the doorway. "What did you say to Rayne?"

"I never said a word."

"I know otherwise."

Dante hooked a finger under her chin. "You know nothing, tesoro. Silence serves you better in moments like these going forward."

"My husband watches."

"He won't be your husband much longer." Dante spoke loud enough for Rayne to hear.

"Traitor." Grace hissed the word in djinn.

Dante laughed and responded in the same tongue. "You forget your place, my lovely new servant. I shall remind you of it later."

Noticing Rayne glaring at them, Dante left a lingering kiss on Grace's cheek, trailed his hand down her back, then motioned for her to lead the way.

Grace glanced back at Rayne. He raised a brow and looked away; subtly signaling he heard everything. Without saying anything more, Grace obediently led them all outside.

CHAPTER

FIFTY-THREE

Elysium

Vittore's ears pricked forward. He neighed as Dante approached him.

"Missed me, Vittore?" Dante patted the stallion's neck and swung into the saddle.

Grace shocked the groom holding Fahkir's reins when she mounted instead of Rayne.

"Follow us with the prisoner," Grace directed the demon guard before wheeling Fahkir towards the gate.

Destahn glanced over his shoulder at Rayne. "This isn't right, Grace. Why is Rayne in chains while you are on his horse?"

"There is a reason for it."

Not liking the chaos occurring, Dante wished he never agreed to any of this. The Fates be damned for making him and Grace the main conspirators in this destructive betrayal. He maneuvered Vittore, so the horse blocked the main gates, preventing Grace from riding through. "Aspetta, cara!"

His actions confused her. "Why do you...?"

Dante almost pulled her out of the saddle, giving her a heart-stop-

579

ping kiss as he used to do before he left on an assignment. "It is bad luck to break old traditions when one rides to war. Now, the Fates have no excuse not to grant me victory."

Legitimately surprised by the kiss, Grace's hands rested on Dante's shoulders. The delay in her pulling back from him confirmed the two had reunited for everyone watching.

"I am looking forward to when all of this is done, amore. After last night, I am most eager to have you in my bed again." Dante let the passionate moment of him and her on the balcony surface in his mind so Rayne would see it.

"What in the hell are you doing, Dante?" Grace whispered, fighting the urge to smack him.

"You need an angry enforcer, do you not?"

"Rayne is mad enough."

"He wasn't until a few moments ago, cara. Rayne the enforcer's anger simmered continuously. It needs to do so again if you want Isra to believe her enforcer is back."

Grace snuck another glance back at her husband. If looks could kill, Dante and she would be shredded into tiny pieces, stomped on, and then scattered across the ground.

"Prego, Grazia."

"I didn't thank you," Grace snapped, this time swinging for Dante.

Dante caught her hand and yanked her into him again. "I have missed this fiery nature of yours, cara. We both know where heated moments lead us."

Grace turned her face away from his when he attempted to kiss her again. "Sei un grandissimo stranzo, Dante!"

Dante laughed, letting her go. He gathered his reins in his hand. "Horsemen, fall in behind the Defensore and me. We go to Córdoba."

Córdoba - 812

They rode for about a half hour through the Spanish countryside, keeping to the outskirts of Córdoba. Grace halted the group and scanned the horizon for something.

"Care to share your thoughts, cara?"

"Not particularly after you impulsively cost me my marriage."

"My actions did not cost you anything more than yours already had. I am ensuring you deliver the enforcer as requested."

"Why do you always think you know better than everyone else?"

"Mayhap in this instance, I do."

Grace let out a frustrated breath. "Stick to what we agreed upon going forward."

Tamir rode over to her and Dante. "Why are we stopped, Grace?"

Grace pointed in the direction of some approaching riders. "Who we wait for arrives. I hope my lion has not lost his fierceness since becoming a god with the additional trouble he stirs up and no chance of turning back now."

The chuckle from under the hood assured her Dante maintained his skills. "I wouldn't dream of retreating from this fight, amore."

Dante shifted the reins to one hand, leaving his weapon hand free to draw his blade if needed. His doing so cued the other Horsemen to be ready. Xander grumbled behind them all, pulling his blade. Rayne straightened, preparing for a potential fight.

Vittore pawed the ground and snorted. In contrast to Vittore, Fahkir's head came up higher and his ears turned forward, but the gelding remained still as stone, waiting for whatever command his rider would give him. All Grace had to do was lightly tap his sides, and he'd charge forward: bravely, reliably, without spooking or flinching, just like Rayne in combat.

"Calma, Vittore." Dante stroked Vittore's neck.

Grace nodded to Dante. "Let's go."

The two of them rode out to meet the oncoming riders.

Destahn shifted nervously in the saddle and looked back at Rayne. Rayne was surprisingly calm. Besides the chains, the only out of character things about War were the dust covering his normally spotless uniform and luminescent silver eyes. Rayne intently monitoring everything without the slightest hint of concern disturbed Destahn as badly as the charges Grace used to arrest Rayne.

Knowing Destahn once again debated mutinying, Rayne eyed his disgruntled captain. *Destahn, obey the Defensore's orders.*

Are you insane? The woman wrongly strips you of command and puts you in restraints.

We stand by Grace. Do whatever she asks, Captain.

Destahn shook his head. *You are a fool to order such a thing.*

Tamir nodded in acknowledgment of Rayne's order.

Raphael frowned. *I am inclined to agree with Destahn's thoughts on today, but will do as directed. As far as I am concerned, War still commands the Horsemen.*

The four watched a rider with armed escort approach Grace and Dante.

"Hello, Malik." Grace greeted them.

The caliph halted his envoy, wondering who spoke to him. Malik couldn't see the woman's face. "Do I know you?"

"We haven't formally met, but we share a mutual interest."

Malik eyed the soldiers behind her. "Which is?"

"Haroun Ibn-Ziyad."

"The coward fled after his wife killed a loyal general of my father's."

"What if I shared that I had Haroun and his wife in my custody? What would they be worth to you?"

"His wife-nothing. But Haroun, Haroun would make you and your friends very wealthy."

Grace leaned forward in the saddle. "How wealthy, Emir?"

"More than a woman could imagine."

"Tell Isra, I can imagine a great deal more than a twenty-nine-year-old caliph."

Malik's assurance vanished. The woman knew he had struck a bargain with the djinn. "We are returning to the palace. Perchance would you care to join me there to continue this discussion in a more private setting."

Grace almost laughed at the worried expression on Malik's face. "It would be a pleasure to, Malik."

Malik recovered his composure then smiled. "You and your men are welcome to ride back with us."

Grace nodded to Dante, who relayed the message the Horsemen were to follow Malik to the palace.

Rayne shook his head, but remained silent; his expression grimmer after his gaze met Dante's. When prodded by the guard to move forward, Rayne complied.

The group stopped again for a short break not far from the palace. The tall towers and walls could be seen in the distance. Grace turned Fahkir and made her way to where the Horsemen remained next to their imprisoned commander. The display of solidarity reminded Grace their loyalty lie with Rayne more than her or the Council.

"Tamir, inform Saladin his son has been arrested and is sentenced to be executed. An envoy brings Haroun to the palace as Malik wishes to witness the man's death himself. Stress to Saladin, if he rides to the palace immediately, he can stop the execution. But he must come now."

Tamir thought she lost her mind to ask him to do such a thing. "You start a mortal war with a message like that."

"I am well aware of what it will do, Tamir."

"You've lost your way, Grace. You are the one who should be relieved of command."

"Do as she asks, Tamir," Rayne backed Grace's strange orders.

Tamir scoffed before addressing Grace again. "I only do this out of respect for my commander."

Watching Tamir ride off towards the city, Xander wondered if Isra corrupting Grace was a greater risk than Rayne changing sides, as he had been told. "Do you plan to make a martyr of a second husband, blondie?"

"Can a djinn be a martyr? Or do they merely disappear into darkness?" Grace shuddered at the cold stare Rayne gave her. "I divorce you, Rayne Warwick."

Rayne blanched. How could she utter those words today of all days? After all he was willing to do for her?

Lucifer appeared beside Grace. The grin on the Devil's face further rattled Rayne. "Finish the words, Grace. Dante has always been your destiny."

Rayne dragged the guards holding his restraints towards them. "Do not listen to him, Grace. Anything Lucifer tempts you with is a lie!"

"You told me Lucifer never lies. I divorce you, Richard Dalglese."

Rayne's worst nightmares came to fruition. He lost everything: the woman he loved, his children, the new life he had known. "In your darkest moments, I have never forsaken you, Grace! Why do you desert me?"

Lucifer smiled then whispered something in Grace's ear.

After Grace said nothing more, Rayne feared his fate was sealed. "If you so wish to have my blood on your hands, may it flow freely. May you bathe in it, since my life suddenly means so little to you. It will stain your conscience and your heart. I will stare back at you every time you look upon our daughter, Grace. Tell Tessa her father's last wish was that she know nothing, but happiness, and that I love her."

The pang of guilt from the duplicity of her actions was almost too much with Rayne asking her to convey such a message to Tessa. Grace raised her hood, hiding her face since it displayed her emotions. She couldn't keep her defenses up. Rayne would sense her lies if she remained so close. She cantered over to Dante and Malik.

Dante offered her his hand. "Allow me to do this. Hurting him is too much for you."

"I can bear it, Dante." Grace clasped his extended hand.

"Bugiarda. I will finish the task, then take the fall." Dante looked over at Malik. "Emir, ride ahead. We shall catch up with you shortly. There is an important matter I wish to discuss with my lady employer before negotiations begin for Haroun."

Malik nodded then he and his guard rode out.

Dante signaled Xander and the other Horsemen to come over. As they drew closer, he called for Lucifer.

"What is it you need, Giovanni?" Lucifer hadn't expected to be called to Spain again.

Dante handed Lucifer a black pouch. "As agreed, here is what you asked for in exchange for giving me back my wife."

Lucifer shook the pouch and grinned. "We should do business together more often. She's all yours, Commander."

Dante looked over at Rayne. *I told you I would use other means to reclaim Grace.* He removed the bands from his wrist and then held one up, ensuring Rayne saw it. *Lucifer didn't lie when he shared these were the one thing which could scare you enough that you wouldn't fight back.*

Rayne ripped him from the saddle. "Never would I have believed you capable of conspiring with Lucifer."

Dante laughed, climbing up from the ground before striking Rayne hard enough the blow sent the weakened Horseman to his knees. "Careful, Rayne. Do not forget who else is bound by the bands you wear. Respect the gods who rule over you should you ever want to see Tessa again."

"You conniving whoreson! You collared my wife and placed an explosive device on my daughter." Rayne launched himself at Dante.

Xander and his men restrained Rayne, but not before Rayne landed a punch, sending Dante into Lucifer and Vittore. Vittore stumbled sideways then reared, trying to get out of the path of the brawling Horsemen.

Xander hooked his arms under Rayne's and locked his hands together against Rayne's chest, straining to keep Rayne away from Dante. "You must calm yourself, Rayne! You do not want the Council turning on you for striking down a deity, nor do you want to harm your daughter. Acting on your current emotions condemns you and Tessa, not Dante."

"Rayne!" Grace worried Dante pushed Rayne too far. She jumped to the ground.

Dante yanked her backward after she reached for Rayne. "The djinn is not worthy of your compassion, Grace."

"Enough, Dante! You already torture him having me and the children. There is no need for additional cruelty."

Rayne shrugged off Xander's hold after it loosened. "A rogue god will not exist as long as I draw breath, Giovanni."

"Do you hear the veiled threats he makes, tesoro? Remember what I showed you last night? That enforcer is not your husband, nor the man I once called friend."

Grace hated the way Rayne stared them both down.

Dante spun her, so she faced him. "Mia Grazia, please do not fret over his fate. It is well earned by his past transgressions. I will heal the heartbreak you now suffer. I swear, with the life I will give you and how I will make love to you, he will quickly become nothing but a distant memory. Rayne Warwick issued his own death sentence when he led the massacre in Granada yesterday. Have you forgotten what Lucifer and I showed you, Grace? All those children cut down by his hand."

"I committed no such offense!" Rayne couldn't stop the declaration from slipping out. Tears and condemnation filled Grace's eyes when she looked up at him again. "Grace, you saw me yourself in Córdoba. I never went near Granada. I would never...."

"Dante took me to Granada. I saw the bodies, Rayne. The only survivor recognized you and heard Kato address you by name!" Grace shoved something against Rayne's chest. "This lay amongst the corpses."

Rayne looked down to see she held the wolf's head pendant. His father's ring also hung from the chain. The clasp on the chain was broken. Did Isra frame him as she had Grace?

"The crest may be reproducible, but your father's ring isn't. And you certainly aren't wearing it. I saw you place the ring on the chain a few days ago, then put it in the safe, a safe only you and I can open."

"I have no idea how the ring and crest ended up in Granada, but I swear on my life, I was not there. Grace, you cannot honestly believe I would annihilate an innocent population. You saw my servitude to Isra. I resisted such orders other than one time when Lyal directed me to issue the decimation directive. While I am guilty of slaughtering men of war, demons, and other djinn, along with pillaging and destroying property, I avoided killing women, the helpless, and children."

"I'm sorry, Rayne. You lied to me about your prior sins. What makes you think I believe a word you say any more?"

The way Grace leveled the last question at Rayne even took Dante aback. Horseman and god watched her walk away.

"You dug your own grave, Rayne. Even so, she falsely holds out hope you'll save your family," Dante said as he and Rayne saw how Grace laid her forehead against Fahkir's neck. Her fingers lightly traveling the smooth, glistening black coat. The gelding nuzzling her cheek gave away the moment of weakness Grace allowed herself to openly have before climbing into the saddle.

Grace's grief sobered Rayne. No one should ever make his wife falter. While she said one thing, her actions contradicted every word she uttered. Grace continued to sacrifice herself in hopes of keeping him alive. She rode his mount. She traded her freedom for his. She came to his side when Dante worsened his suffering. What had she foreseen to do all of this? For her sake, he would wait until the right moment to strike out at Dante. "Lucifer and you will pay dearly for everything you've taken from me."

"Prophecy is not one of War's gifts." Dante shot back before remounting Vittore. "And with what is planned for you, Rayne, you will not have the opportunity to make that prediction reality."

Resisting the urge to respond, Rayne ground his teeth together. He tucked the medallion into his jacket pocket. Feeling someone watching him, he looked up to find Grace staring at him. Lucifer stood near her now. The fear he continually felt in her wrenched his heart as badly as her divorcing him did. She emotionally crumbled before him. The sadness in her eyes. Her distress barely masked on her face. The dogged spirit which drove her forward in times of strife was now nonexistent. Her hands trembled as she picked up the reins when Dante rode up alongside her and Lucifer. Rayne placed his father's ring on his right ring finger since Dante currently wore the Commander's ruby. He'd reclaim it when he took his wife and children back from the deceitful bastard he once called friend.

"Now that the theatrics are over, I will leave things in your and Grace's capable hands, Giovanni," Lucifer addressed Dante then returned to Hell.

The heavily armed Clan of Ibn-Ziyad blocked the entrance of the palace. Tamir and Saladin occupied the customary center spot denoting their leadership over the group. The horse Saladin rode snorted and tossed his head as the entourage traveling with Malik drew closer.

Viewing the small army accompanying his father, Rayne cursed. *Worsening the conflict throughout the city is the last thing you should be instigating, Grace. What are you thinking bringing Malik and my father face to face like this?*

If Grace heard him, she ignored the inquiry.

Destahn positioned himself alongside Rayne. *I do not mean to challenge your earlier orders...*

I was not aware of the depth of Lucifer's interference. I thought something different may be in play. Hold at the ready until I order otherwise.

Dante overheard their discussion. "Destahn!" He motioned for the captain to fall back into formation with the other Horsemen.

Destahn flashed the hand signal for at the ready prior to riding back to his place in line.

"Do not make me relieve you of your position, Captain," Dante reprimanded Destahn for his insubordination.

"My loyalty is to you and the Council, Commander." Destahn choked down bile as he replied, but said nothing further.

Dante looked at Rayne. *Must I add instigating mutiny to your list of charges, Warwick?*

Rayne laughed. *It will complement the one of conspiracy to corrupt a guardian that I intend to execute you under.*

Grace freely came to my bed. Mayhap, you shouldn't make a habit of neglecting your wives and they wouldn't so readily seek the company of others.

"Commander, I need an escort," Grace called to Dante, unaware of the exchange between him and Rayne.

Dante grinned before answering Grace. "On my way, mia stella."

Grace and Dante rode forward with Malik and his bodyguard to greet Saladin. Tamir nodded to them once they reached him and Saladin.

Recognizing Fahkir, Saladin frowned. The strange rider on the horse confirmed Malik or the riders with him had Rayne in custody. Rayne wouldn't freely part with the gelding.

Malik worried about the way Saladin positioned his men between the palace and them. "Saladin? What brings you to my door?"

"Malik." Saladin appeared calm, but had the same tells Rayne displayed giving away the man's preparation for war. "I am told my son is to be executed. I believe there is a grievous misunderstanding for the execution order to be issued."

Grace spoke up before Malik could. "There is no misunderstanding. Haroun plotted with his wife to kill Umar. She succeeded in the tasking. Malik simply ensures justice is done."

Saladin had hoped to resolve this situation diplomatically. "From what I hear, you have no evidence of their guilt. How can you condemn them?"

"The same way he condemned Abdul and removed the threat Umar presented."

Malik stared at the woman, wondering how she knew what she did.

Saladin's patience slipped. "Why am I speaking to a woman instead of the man I make inquiries of?"

"Because your dispute is with a woman, not her pawn."

Teleporting to sit behind Malik on his horse, Dante placed his sword across Malik's throat, taking him hostage.

Tamir and Raphael disarmed Malik's personal guard and forced each man to kneel on the ground. Destahn drew his weapon, but remained back with Rayne, disobeying Dante's direction to disarm the remaining members of the haras.

Malik reached for his dagger.

Dante pressed his blade closer to Malik's neck. "Do not be foolish, Emir."

Malik's hand fell complacently back to his side.

Seeing the Horsemen eliminated any threat from Malik, Grace shouted up at the group watching them from the walkway above the palace gates. "Isra! I have two things that belong to you. Come out, and you can have them back."

Saladin's hand moved to his scimitar. He hesitated in pulling it with not knowing if he faced a human or djinn. "What are you, woman?"

"A broker of life and death, Saladin. Stay your hand. My quarrel is not with you or your men."

Isra didn't emerge from the palace. Grace looked over at Dante. "The ifrit does not value the mortal. Perhaps she will value Haroun more. Kill Malik. He is of no use to us."

Malik cried out, begging for his life after Dante yanked his head backwards for a clean target area.

"Do not be hasty in our dealings." Isra appeared in front of everyone. "What do you offer me, woman?"

Grace glanced back at Rayne. "A runaway soldier."

"In exchange for?"

"Retribution."

Intrigued by the woman's audacity, Isra cackled. "What sort of retribution?"

"The type that requires a large payment. Xander, bring the enforcer."

Xander led Rayne forward. Pleased with the payment offered for whatever this rogue guardian sought, Isra smiled.

Tired, hot, and angry, Rayne glared at Isra and Grace. So this was his fate, to be traded back to Isra. What had Lucifer and Dante said to Grace to convince her he deserved this?

"He is yours, if you wipe the slate clean, destroying any accusation about me killing Umar." Grace pulled down her hood, so Isra could see her face. "I do not appreciate being framed. As the Defensore, I cannot have a tarnished record."

"You did not tell me Haroun's wife was the Morte Defensore!" Isra blamed Malik for the misunderstanding.

Malik didn't know what to say. He didn't even know what a Morte Defensore was.

Rayne shook his head in disbelief. Why did Grace ask for such a thing? Her name was already cleared.

Xander set a hand on Rayne's shoulder, getting his attention. *Bite your tongue, Commander.*

Isra reached for the chains Xander held. "Your reputation and innocence will be reclaimed by nightfall, Defensore."

Grace nudged Fahkir's sides with her heels so he moved forward. Positioning the horse between Rayne and Isra, she forced Isra to back away from Rayne. "As you said, Isra, do not be so hasty in our dealings. I prefer to conduct negotiations of this nature in writing." Grace extended a contract to Isra. "Sign the indenture of our terms, and Haroun is yours."

Skeptical of Grace's motives, Isra hesitated to accept the document. "I understand you are relatively new to the immortal realm. Allow me to assure you that bargains with an overseer are rarely documented. We always deliver exactly what one requests. Do you not trust me to do as I say?"

"I learn well from other's mistakes. The contract provides me a bit of assurance that there are no delays, misunderstandings, or accidents with restoring my reputation as occurred when Haroun bargained with you. No signature, no enforcer, Isra."

Isra looked from the one servant who escaped her to his wife. "Tell me, Defensore, why barter your husband?"

"If the enforcer is not a satisfactory payment, what else is it you seek?"

"I find it odd a woman would trade the man she loves to clear her own name."

"You overestimate my feelings for Haroun. A contract with the Fates and Council is what binds he and I, not love. My heart belongs to the sun. The fact you are ignorant of the whole arrangement makes me think Rodrigo may be the better overseer to bargain with. I rescind my earlier offer." Grace pulled the contract back, turned Fahkir, and gestured for Xander to follow her.

Dante released Malik then settled himself back into the saddle on Vittore.

"Wait!" Isra stepped in front of Fahkir. "Forgive my lack of knowledge about the contract, Defensore. I can assure you I am as powerful as Rodrigo, if not more so. You chose the correct overseer to negotiate with."

Grace laughed.

Insulted by Grace's laughter, Isra hissed. "I could annihilate you in one blow, Defensore. You've only been immortal for a decade, which makes you weak."

Grace leaned forward in the saddle, trying to be as intimidating as she could. "Do I behave like one that is weak? Do you mistakenly believe me to be some simple, former human servant of the Council, Isra?" She dangled the medallion identifying her as a Guardian of the Ancients.

Recognizing Isis's emblem, along with the wolf and lion, Isra swallowed hard. "Which god do you serve?"

Dante cleared his throat, drawing Isra's attention. "Can you not see my mark upon her?" He lifted his head slightly higher, giving Isra a clear view of his face.

Isra unconsciously took a step backward. The sun god himself rode in the Horsemen ranks with a descendant of Isis. "I did not recognize you in the commander's uniform, Giovanni."

"Tread carefully now that you have, Isra."

"We each have our appointed executioners, Commander. Even you." Isra grudgingly held her hand out for the contract. "May I see the contract, Defensore?"

Grace gave Isra the agreement. Isra only read the first couple lines. Finding nothing worrisome, she placed her seal on the bottom of the parchment before returning it to Grace. Rolling up the signed scroll, Grace looked over at Rayne. He stared up into sea-colored eyes, terrified Grace sold him back into servitude.

Movement in Saladin's ranks distracted Grace. Saladin's men began to shift and whisper. Someone frantically pushed their way through them.

Annoyed that Grace failed to immediately hand over Rayne, Isra tapped her foot. "You have your signature, Defensore."

"So, I do. Turn him over, Xander."

The way Rayne whispered her name tore at Grace's insides. The defeat and hurt in his expression made it hard for her to breathe. His face screamed how could you?

Xander and his two men escorted Rayne to Isra.

"No!" A woman's voice cried out. "My son committed no wrong. I killed Umar. I should be the one sold to the ifrit."

Lillian threw herself into Rayne's chest.

Rayne held his sobbing mother. The past twelve hours left him in a state of disbelief. He never imagined Dante would betray him, Grace would give him to Isra, or that his mother was capable of hurting anyone. She hated to kill insects that invaded her home. How could she have the fortitude to take a human life?

"I stole the dagger, thinking it was Haroun's. I did not know it belonged to Grace. Forgive me, Rayne. I only wanted you to be free to return home and to avenge what Umar had done to you and Priya. I never meant to condemn you or your wife. I did not know what you have become or the laws you now live under. Isra, take me in my son's place."

Pleased with the shift in events, Isra greedily grinned. "Two souls in one morning."

"Isra, the contract is only for me. Do not think of claiming my mother."

"No need to bargain with her, Rayne." Grace dismounted, preventing any negotiations between Rayne and Isra. "Lillian remains free. Attempt to conscript her, Isra, and you risk your existence once more."

Grace pulled the gold collar devices from her uniform then laid both of her blades against Isra's neck, revealing she was the one who took the forged contract for Rayne.

Narciso and two other djinn materialized with Isra threatened. The three came towards Grace.

The jingling of chains behind Grace cautioned that Rayne prepared to come to her defense. Destahn now stood alongside her. Raphael dismounted, making his way toward them. Dante pushed aside his cloak and grasped the hilt of his sword.

Isra held her hand up, preventing Narciso and the other djinn from coming any closer. "I have lost interest in Lillian, and do not desire conflict with you, Defensore. I only want what I am owed... Haroun."

Grace lowered her daggers, but kept a watchful eye on Narciso and Isra. "Tamir, escort Lillian to Saladin."

Tamir offered Lillian his hand. "All will be well, Lillian. Let us return you to your husband."

Lillian took it, but looked back at Rayne.

Rayne nodded reassuringly to his mother. "Go."

Lillian turned to Grace. "Please don't give her my son."

"I am bound to the terms of the contract, Lillian. Now, please, go to Saladin. You aren't safe amongst us and the djinn."

Tamir gently led Lillian away.

"You swore an oath to protect the innocent. My son has committed no wrong! You violate your oath giving him to Isra! Do you truly not love him? How can you not protect him?" Lillian pleaded with her daughter-in-law. "He is a being of hope, not darkness, Grace! As is his daughter. Both are worthy of being safeguarded by guardians like yourself!"

"Silence woman!" Narciso snarled, taking a step towards Lillian and Tamir.

Not willing to take any chances of things escalating to the point she could not control them, Grace engaged him. Their blades met, beginning a dance of deadly swordplay.

Raphael drew his weapon and looked for an opening to exploit.

"Stand down, Raphael. She has him," Dante ordered, confident by the way Grace attacked and deflected Narciso's blade she would be the victor. If Raphael joined in before needed, Grace would appear weak to the other djinn and demons, risking an unnecessary battle with humans in the way.

A few seconds later, the altercation ended with Narciso vanquished.

Grace sheathed her sabre and turned to Isra. "Do all your djinn disobey your orders, Isra?"

"He acted on mine. Drop your weapons and give Isra Haroun. You and your men are outnumbered," An overconfident Malik directed, signaling his archers.

"Take cover!" Destahn shouted to Saladin as Malik's archers took aim at them all.

A barrage of arrows fell from the palace walls. Two struck Grace. Dante leapt off Vittore to help Tamir shield Lillian, since she was caught in the line of fire.

Rayne ripped free of his chains and picked up Narciso's rapier.

Isra grinned, thinking her enforcer reacted from blood lust. "Kill them, Haroun!" She relished a triumph over the Council officers toying with her. "Show no mercy to any of them."

Instead of attacking the officers he stood amongst, Rayne scaled the palace wall. In mere seconds, he slaughtered the unit of archers firing on the Horsemen and Grace; shocking everyone, including Isra.

The other Horsemen took down Malik's soldiers who flooded out of the palace gates to weaken any further opposition.

When the barrage of arrows stopped, Dante knocked Malik to the ground. "I will dispatch you if you do not give the order to halt the attack."

Malik shouted for his men along with Isra's demons and djinn to stand down.

Still aghast that Rayne scaled a two and a half story wall then took out the archers so easily, Grace pulled the arrows from her arm and chest. Rayne's eyes met hers when she looked up at her husband again. She dropped the arrows in her hand.

Destahn noticed Rodrigo and his legions forming up at their rear. "Grace, we have a bigger problem than Isra."

She turned and saw what Destahn did. Rodrigo couldn't have worse timing. "Xander, Lyal, I need troops between us and Rodrigo. Ensure Rodrigo does not come any closer."

Xander's demon ranks, along with Lyal, formed a barrier to keep Rodrigo at bay.

"Must we begin again with relearning your place is subservient to your mistress, Haroun?" Isra launched into an angry tirade, staring up at Rayne. "You will do as you are commanded."

Preoccupied with Rodrigo's lines, Rayne ignored Isra and her ranting. All Rodrigo had to do was sweep forward to wipe out his mother, his father, and his father's men. Grace and the Horsemen would be caught in the center having to fight on two fronts.

Sean, we may need your assistance. Rayne hoped the guide could still hear him.

Dante put me on standby earlier. I have a unit ready to dispatch and have been watching the entire time, Rayne. Focus on whatever you need to do to quell things there.

"Who is in command here?" Rodrigo shouted, taking in the assortment of beings before him.

"I am. We have no fight with you, Rodrigo. My business is strictly with Isra," Grace yelled back, pulling her sabre again, and doing her best to keep an eye on each overseer.

"Then move out of the way, woman. I have quarrel with Isra if it is true she has regained Haroun."

"Allow me to finish my dealings with Isra. Once they are concluded, I will gladly relinquish the field to you. I believe we share a similar objective," Grace countered, praying the Fates would back her up.

"She speaks the truth, Rodrigo. The woman is a Council Harbinger sent to ensure justice is served," Xander said. His supporting Grace lent credence to her words.

Rodrigo watched Rayne on the walkway above. "As long as Haroun does not advance on our ranks, we shall grant what you request. If he or Isra cross your lines, I give the order to decimate Córdoba."

"We accept your terms, Rodrigo," Rayne answered for Grace. "I will not advance Isra's legions in exchange for the human and Council forces being allowed safe passage from between our ranks."

"I did not grant you authority to negotiate terms, Haroun!" Isra growled up at Rayne.

"Do not be foolish, Isra. As weak as your legions are, we cannot fight Rodrigo and the High Council, even with me as Primus. The Defensore killed Narciso. Your next commander has half the experience he did and not even a third of mine. We allow the humans to go free. By doing so, the Council will have no reason to interfere in our conflict with Rodrigo. Finish your negotiations with the Defensore then send her on her way."

"You forget who you now serve!" Isra didn't like his usurping her authority before Rodrigo. "Now, kill the Council officers as directed."

Rayne dropped Narciso's sword. Everyone watched as the rapier hurdled downward. The blade slid into the earth between Isra's boots. Defiance etched itself across War's face when Isra's gaze met his.

Isra pulled the weapon on her side. "Today you will pay dearly for your disobedience, Haroun! I no longer have the patience for it as I once did."

Rayne started to warn Grace, but his words came too late. He teleported to her, hoping to bear the brunt of Isra's strike. Even though it took only took a millisecond to reach Grace, he wasn't fast enough to spare his wife.

Destiny played out before him. A flash of red and black confirmed Isra had Lucifer's old harbinger blade. Grace collapsed after steel found her side. Rayne caught her as she crumpled. Her sabre fell from her hand, rolling across the ground.

"No!" The word Rayne shouted reverberated through the landscape. "Grace." He shifted her limp body in his arms. Blood dampened the sleeves of his uniform, causing them to stick to his skin. He could hear a faint heartbeat, even though she didn't breathe. "Grace, don't cross over. Stay with the living."

Time froze as Rayne laid her on the ground, pinched Grace's nose shut, and then gently opened her mouth. His mouth settled over hers. He filled her lungs with air from his own.

Isra took a step toward the immortal trying to resuscitate his wife. The way he tilted his head to listen for any sign of life made her laugh. "How many must die for you to learn to obey? First Priya, now your beloved Grace. Shall your father or mother be next?"

"Move even a millimeter in my mother's or father's direction, and I will end you."

"You forget, you are mine once more. If you will not fight as commanded then we abandon the field until you will do so."

Grace took a shallow breath, giving Rayne hope she might survive. "I am not going anywhere until my wife is conscious again."

"She is dead, Haroun."

Rayne rested his hand over the wound in Grace's side, willing it to close. "No, Isra. She hasn't crossed over yet."

Isra reached for him. Rayne called forth dark flame for the first time in several centuries. The ground trembled before it broke through the earth's surface, forming a circle around him and Grace. Isra jerked her hand back to keep from being burned. The barrier of hell fire would keep Isra at bay, hopefully allowing Rayne the time he needed to stop Grace's death.

Djinn, demons, and humans whispered, starting to panic. Isra and Rodrigo ordered the demons and djinn to stand their ground.

"Find courage, men," Saladin shouted over the wind and raised voices. "Haroun returned to Córdoba to protect us from Isra. It was her dark magic that corrupted my son. Allah shattered her hold over him, so he could save Córdoba from ruin. You see for yourselves the evil around us. The djinn and darkness Malik brought into our midst just as Umar did to gain favor over my son. Will you risk your souls and families by deserting the Emirate, or will you fight for them with the general you once revered?"

Rayne glanced up at his father and mouthed the word 'shukran' for his willingness to battle beside him in the chaos unfolding. Surprisingly, none of his father's men fled as some of Malik's royal guard had.

Once her legions quieted, Isra returned her attention to Rayne. "So you've chosen the traitors pack over servitude. You always were foolish, Haroun."

"I would rather spend eternity on all fours than serve you or Lucifer."

Sulla and Kato slowly crept through the soldiers. The wolves positioned themselves outside the ring of fire, growling at the Isra with hackles raised.

"Grace." Rayne focused on his wife again. Her skin warmed some. Her pulse beat stronger against his fingertips. "Stay with me, leof."

Dante noticed Isis concealed in a cloak, standing a short distance from Rayne and Grace. The goddess would only risk discovery as she did if the Fates contemplated severing the thread of Grace's life. *Isis, do not let them cut her thread. Offer my soul in place of hers. Elysium does not need me.*

Isis remained still, watching Rayne and Grace.

Isis! Dante's voice hissed in the goddess's head. She held her hand up, silently warning him to be quiet.

Rayne looked over at Dante. *Dante, heal her the rest of the way, since*

I cannot. He extinguished the ring of dark flame, so Dante could safely come to them.

I cannot. She isn't at Elysium's gates. Dante hoped he spoke the truth with Isis being present. *This wasn't supposed to happen, Rayne. It wasn't part of the—*

Rayne glared up at the god. "After everything the Fates shared, how could you not entertain the possibility the worst could play out with your scheming? That she would ultimately pay the price for it!"

"Rayne, I—" Dante started to apologize.

"Nothing you say can remedy this, Giovanni. Heal her or summon someone who can." Rayne had no patience left. Grace needed a divinity to heal her or she'd die. He frantically debated where to take her if Dante wouldn't help her.

"You damn yourself for a woman who cares little for you. She deserted you for the sun god, Haroun." Isra tried once more to assert her claim over Rayne.

Isra's words brought every ounce of wrath Rayne ever felt out in his being. Her face paled after correctly interpreting the death sentence in his stare.

The winds shifted direction then churned around the palace. A loud crash of thunder rumbled as the last bits of light disappeared from the midday sky.

"If she dies, Isra, I will destroy everything you value: your men, your djinn, your properties. I will leave you alive to watch it all burn and then I will come for you. You will not receive a merciful death. I will take great pleasure in making it arduous. I will peel your flesh from your body, sever every tendon, ligament, and muscle; break your every bone before plucking a different organ from you over a month's time. Leaving you to slowly rot chained to the gate of your new home, so the vultures pick your eyes out and vermin gnaw at your remains. Not even Lucifer and all the armies of Hell will be able to save you."

"Isra better thank the Fates I live with the death you have planned for her," Grace whispered, gently grasping Rayne's upper arm.

"Grace?" Rayne was almost afraid to believe she stared up at him.

"Yes, my very vengeful saint?" She smiled as she spoke.

Her smile puzzled Rayne. "You, you aren't hurt any longer?"

"No. Isra only knocked the wind out of me."

"She did more than knock the wind out of you."

Grace moved her arm, showing Rayne where the blade had pierced her side. There wasn't so much as a scratch on her cuirass or a tear in her protective tunic or shirt.

"You were at death's door." Rayne couldn't comprehend how she was suddenly healed. The blood soaking his shirt sleeves disappeared as well.

"Deception comes in degrees, or that's what I've recently been told."

"Deception?" Rayne muttered, confused.

"You remain steadfast in your oath to me, Rayne. Leaps of faith seldom go unrewarded."

Rayne was afraid to hope Grace hinted everything they went through the past twenty-four hours was for a planned purpose. "I am a damned fool to listen to a woman who traded me to an ifrit."

"Who can do nothing with you as long as I draw breath."

He helped her to her feet. She extended a hand to wipe away some sweat and dirt by his eye. The broken pieces of chain still on his wrists clattered with the rapid step back he took. He removed the grime that threatened to drift forward and cloud his vision himself.

Dante glanced over at Isis. The goddess knowingly smiled over at him. Isis, not the Fates, weakened then healed Grace. Fooling everyone present. Relieved, Dante shook his head. Who all's assistance had Grace enlisted to save Rayne?

Isra didn't understand how the woman lived. She glanced at the weapon in her hand. "How did you survive a blow from Lucifer's blade?"

"Thank the gods she did, Isra." Rayne eyed Dante, Grace, and Isra with distrust. He took Grace by the arm. "My mother is not part of whatever occurs here."

The edge to Rayne's voice warned Grace they had pushed him to his breaking point. The slight tremble of his hand betrayed his struggle to control the wrath circling within him. "Rayne, I would never—"

"Do not utter what words you are about to after what has transpired."

"Careful how you speak to her, djinn." Dante maintained the role of Grace's new lover.

Rayne shot him a contemptuous glare before focusing on Grace again. *I am not certain what lies Lucifer and Dante crafted for you to surrender me, but swear to me you will never trade Tessa in retaliation for whatever sin you believe I committed.*

Grace laid her hand on his chest, re-strengthening the connection between them that Isis had weakened. "Calm yourself, my wolf."

Isra didn't like how coolly Grace stood before an enraged Rayne. "Your wolf? According to the agreement, he has a new master."

"You are right, Isra. He does." Grace extended the rolled parchment to Rayne.

He cautiously took the agreement from her. "Why do you give this to me?"

"It's yours. You see, the agreement giving you to Isra is null and void because Isra didn't clear me of the bogus charges. Your mother did." Grace unlocked the cuffs around his wrists. She let each of them fall to the ground, driving home he was free. "Additionally, Lillian's confession triggered a penalty clause. The role of master and servant are now reversed."

"What?" Isra ripped the scroll from Rayne's hand, frantically opening it.

"Didn't anyone ever tell you to read what you sign, especially the fine print?" Grace watched Isra read the clause referenced. "Consider this your eleventh anniversary present, Haroun Ibn-Ziyad."

The realization of what Grace had done set in. Rayne grinned down at her. "You divorced me."

"No, I divorced Richard Dalglese and Rayne Warwick, neither of which is your given name. I only said the phrase twice, and never turned my back to you, which means we are still married. Or do I misunderstand your customs?"

Rayne laughed, embracing his wife. Thank the gods she never truly abandoned him! "You understand them too well. Regretfully, the gift I had in mind for you would never come close to equaling what you give me."

"What you give me each day is much more valuable than a djinn." Grace kissed him, changing his eyes back to the blue she loved. Xander's illusion paired with Rayne's fear and anger worked perfectly to deceive those it needed to. "I love you, Rayne. I am so sorry for today. Isra needed to see the enforcer. Without him, she never would have bargained with me."

"This wrong is easily forgiven." Rayne lowered his lips to Grace's.

Saladin thought his son mad to act as he did after Grace traded him to Isra. "I fail to see the humor you do, Haroun. Did your wife not offer you to an ifrit?"

"She did. And by doing so, she gifted your son a life with no fear. Forgive your new daughter. We have much to celebrate this afternoon."

Dante shoved Malik towards Saladin. "We leave this one's judgement to you, Saladin. His younger brother is old enough to rule and is a much wiser man."

"Not to mention loyal to Córdoba instead of the Almoravids," Rayne disclosed Malik's betrayal of the Emirate.

The three immortals watched Saladin lead Malik to the Master-at-Arms for formal charges of corruption.

Dante grinned over at Rayne. "What do you intend to do with such a special anniversary present?"

Rayne pretended to study Isra. "I haven't decided yet."

"Be merciful, Haroun. I treated you like a god when you were in my favor," Isra groveled with her new master.

"Merciful?" Rayne drew his jacket back and locked eyes with Grace. "Torturing me and framing my wife is far from showering me with reward."

"Lucifer, I served you loyally. How can you give me over to Haroun?" Isra alerted the group to the Devil's presence.

Lucifer scowled at his former minion. "I warned you that you too greatly risked our ranks luring Haroun here. Did you honestly think you could use him to overtake Hell, Isra?"

"I had no intentions of..."

"Do not even try to lie to me!"

Rayne shifted position and lightly tapped his fingertip against the weapon he concealed while Lucifer and Isra argued. Catching the subtle cue, Grace smiled.

Getting nowhere with Lucifer, Isra drew Rayne's attention again. "Haroun, if I knew you actually loved the woman...."

One of Rayne's brows raised, as an incredulous expression covered his face. "You wouldn't have behaved any differently, Isra."

Isra huffed. She held her head higher and stepped closer to Rayne and Grace. "You cannot kill me, Haroun. I made you what you are."

"You didn't make him into anything he wasn't already, Isra. You merely corrupted his purpose." Grace wasn't going to allow Isra to keep manipulating Rayne with that lie.

"Do not listen to your wife, Haroun. You die if you eliminate me."

Unfazed by Isra's remark, Rayne shrugged. "I have no intention of killing you."

Pain exploded from something piercing Isra's chest, preventing the overseer from voicing any sort of retort.

"He isn't the one the High Council issued your execution order to." Grace watched the agony on the overseer's face that tormented so many others. She drove the dagger deeper until her fingers found bone. Her fist disappeared completely into tawny skin. The only part of the hilt which could still be seen outside Isra's chest was the sapphire. Grace twisted the dagger sideways to ensure it lodged into Isra's heart. "But I will give him the pleasure of finishing what I began."

Isis tossed Rayne his Horseman's Blade. Hearing Rayne's sword scrape against its scabbard, Grace ducked out of the way. The enchanted steel sliced effortlessly through Isra's neck. She exploded into a fine black dust. This time, she wouldn't heal and return to bother anyone.

Grace stood back up. "It really is amazing what we accomplish when we choose to trust one another, even under difficult circumstances."

Rayne smiled at the way she reminded him they were stronger together. "Speaking of trust in difficult circumstances, I am going to have to ask you to trust me now."

"What else remains to be dealt with besides Malik?"

His thumb brushed her cheek. "I love you, Grace, but there is one more thing that must be done."

Grace watched Rayne walk toward Rodrigo's lines. He stopped in the open space between the palace and the waiting rival army.

"I am Haroun Ibn-Ziyad, Horsemen Commander, and the lone surviving Primus of Isra's legions. The High Council's chosen balance keeper. Raise your weapon against me, you perish beneath my blade. Do as I ask, and you may see the sunrise tomorrow."

Grace grasped what Rayne intended to do. "Rayne, no! There is no need for you to do this."

He kept his eyes on Rodrigo's forces and Isra's now leaderless ranks. Thankfully, confusion kept them from erupting into chaos. "Don't be afraid, Grace. I will find my way home to you."

Rayne turned, surveying the human, demon, and djinn soldiers on the walls that Isra loaned to Malik. "I demand all of Isra's legions and commanders swear fealty to me, or face the judgement of the Horsemen. We will not be merciful to anyone who does not give me their oath."

Grace dropped the dagger she held and started towards Rayne. She'd be damned if he trapped himself between good and evil, as he had in her premonition.

Dante's arms seized around her waist. "Allow him to do this. It ensures peace between the realms, Grazia."

"We changed fate."

"Rayne asked you to trust him. Honor his request."

"I gambled everything to stop this. To keep my family intact." Struggling to understand what went wrong, Grace stared up at Dante, hoping he could provide her the answers she desperately needed.

"Nothing went wrong. Your family is safe. Rayne is ensuring humanity and Córdoba are as well. The Horsemen and Defensore must be unified in front of Rodrigo. Otherwise, the Council Forces appear fractured. Even as reserved as Rodrigo is, that is too tempting a scenario for a demon not to exploit."

Grace stayed with Dante. Isra's commanders and those they led slowly knelt before Rayne. Each officer and senior enlisted member presented themselves, swearing loyalty to him. The lower-ranking djinn and demons, in unison, shouted their oath of servitude. As he had in the vision, Rayne executed those he could not trust to remain loyal.

After Rayne severed the first djinn's head, Rodrigo's men readied for war. The movement of arms and soldiers along his lines troubled Grace. "Rodrigo prepares for conflict, Dante. Rayne may not bring about the peace you think he will."

"Rodrigo is being cautious. He is confused by Rayne's actions. Nothing more."

"I don't like this. We need to be prepared if all hell breaks loose." Grace wasn't leaving anything to chance. "Horsemen! At the ready."

Rayne smiled at how Grace rallied the other Horsemen, but stayed back. She provided the display of uniformity he needed to keep control of the field.

The three remaining Horsemen remounted their horses then spread out in a defensive line with Grace at their center. Xander's men had relaxed with things seeming calm.

"Xander, strengthen that front line."

"We stand ready, Defensore," Xander acknowledged the order and signaled his men to close the gaps in their ranks.

Saladin shouted orders to his men, preparing to assist in any way he could.

"This is not your fight, Saladin. Protect Córdoba if our lines are breeched. Otherwise, stand down," Grace directed, not wanting any more humans than necessary in harm's way.

Saladin nodded then had his lines fall back into defensive positions around the palace and city gates.

Rodrigo rode to the front of his troops. "Harbinger, if your assignment is to ensure justice is served, explain to me how that is done by giving Haroun Isra's legions."

"I prefer not to shout across the distance, Rodrigo. May I approach your lines without fear of assault?" Grace replied, climbing back into the saddle.

"You may." Rodrigo extended Grace the courtesy of safe parlay.

Grace looked at Dante. "Come with me."

Dante whistled for Vittore. The horse loped over to him. He swung onto Vittore's back, then he and Grace rode to the overseer of Granada.

Rodrigo recognized the woman from Lucena. "Lady Ibn-Ziyad?"

"Morte Defensore Ibn-Ziyad," Dante corrected him.

Rodrigo grinned at how Dante rode with her again. "Commander Giovanni, always a pleasure to see you in Spain. Now, Defensore Ibn-Ziyad, please, answer my earlier question."

"You have nothing to fear with Haroun taking command of Isra's legions. He does not seek war or to take over your region. My husband merely wishes to safeguard Córdoba and his mortal family. By controlling Isra's army and using them defensively, if needed, he ensures that."

"Haroun Ibn-Ziyad once laid siege to Spain and France, Defensore. My legions along with human soldiers suffered under his attacks. What is to stop the same from occurring again?"

"Haroun only waged war, as he was under Isra's control. He no longer is. Haroun rides on behalf of the High Council. The Horsemen's oath prevents him from taking life without sanction. That should give you all the reassurance you need." Grace hoped her answer appeased Rodrigo.

Rodrigo's features turned thoughtful. "Even immortals fall victim to lust for power. Your husband is part enforcer. We crave bloodshed, influence, and wealth. What makes you think Haroun may not one day fall victim to them again?"

"I think there are greater odds of hell freezing over, Rodrigo." Grace laughed, doubting Rodrigo understood the modern-day phrase. By the puzzled expression the overseer gave her, he didn't. "Rayne has more wealth than he knows what to do with. In fact, he gives a great deal of it away. As to bloodshed, he never really succumbed to bloodlust as the rest of you did. In his duties for the Council, he does everything he can to prevent conflict. Lastly, there is not any more powerful a position than universal balance keeper for the High Council. He can kill god, demon, and djinn alike. Would an enforcer want to risk losing that rare ability?"

"My wife fails to mention I am no longer a djinn. She and Xander used magic to create an illusion that I remained one to entrap Isra today," Rayne interrupted their discussion as he walked over to where Dante and Grace met with Rodrigo. "The Council gave me back my soul centuries ago."

Rodrigo gave Rayne a skeptical look. "Soul or not, I sense the enforcer still in you, Haroun. I also watched you summon dark flame."

"What you sense is a soul destined to be War and the Protector of the House of the Moon. As to the flame." Rayne held out his hand. A swirl of white and blue fire danced in his palm. The colors shifted to purple, red, then green. "I can summon any kind of flame imaginable when engaging immortals. Normally, I prefer not to, as rarely is it necessary. The one power I held as an enforcer that frightened Isra was my ability to control dark flame, which is why I deployed it today." Rayne closed his hand, extinguishing the magical fire.

"I need more than this display as reassurance you will not attack Granada, Haroun."

"The only other reassurance I can offer you is the sliver of enforcer remaining in me has sworn an oath to one who would never condone conquest or an unprovoked attack against Granada."

Rodrigo noted the way Rayne looked over at Grace when he mentioned swearing an oath to another. "The Defensore is honorable. Men like you and I are not, Haroun. If the Defensore wields the wolf's sword, there is no reason for me to fear Córdoba."

Rodrigo signaled his legions to return to Granada. "Lady Ibn-Ziyad, give me no reason to regret my decision today."

"I promise. You will have none." Grace doubted Rodrigo would leave Córdoba.

"May I ask you to do one more thing on my behalf, Defensore?"

Leery of making any sort of an agreement with a djinn, Grace cautiously answered. "It depends on what you want me to do."

"Give my regards to Lyal."

Rayne laughed and placed his hand on Grace's thigh. "That, she most certainly can do."

"May we meet again under more friendly conditions, Defensore. Haroun, Córdoba and Granada are at peace once more." Rodrigo and his personal guard rode off in the direction of Granada.

Rayne moved his hand to Fahkir's neck. "Scoot up, leof."

"Why did he ask me to give Lyal his regards?" Grace inquired as Rayne settled himself behind her. He turned Fahkir back towards the palace.

"They are acquainted with one another."

The response Grace started to say died on her lips as the legions they rode past bowed; paying respect to their general and his wife. "You didn't disband them?"

"No. I have other uses for them. They will limit any of Rodrigo's ambitions should he ever decide to attack Córdoba. With Sulla and Kato overseeing them, they are no threat to anyone left intact. I will also make periodic appearances to ensure they do not forget they now serve War and the Council."

Rayne halted Fahkir in front of Destahn, Raphael, and his father. Grace watched him dismount. After a few minutes, Grace slid out of the saddle herself. While Rayne, Saladin, and the other Horsemen talked, Grace walked over to where she had dropped Rayne's dagger. She brushed the dust off the sheath and rubbed the sapphire stone against her sleeve to remove the grit from it. Relief flooded through her now that Isra was gone and Rayne eliminated any future threats of retaliation by taking command of her ranks. She clutched the weapon to her chest and thanked all those who watched over them for granting them a favorable outcome.

"I am afraid to inquire what you are thinking about with how tightly you are holding my dagger." Rayne's voice caused her closed eyes to open.

Grace smiled up at the man standing beside her. "I am wondering if there are any more secrets from your past I should know about?"

Rayne offered Grace a pensive look. "Not that I can think of at the moment."

"You are not funny, Rayne. If I learn of anything else troubling, I will vanquish you as I did Isra."

"Do not threaten me, woman. My patience runs short today." Rayne playfully jerked the dagger out of her hands.

Grace pulled Rayne's face down to hers and kissed him. His arms encircled her; his lips yielding to hers. The past could no longer torment either of them.

After the kiss finished, Grace thumped her fist against his chest. "Never put me in a situation where I must gamble with your life again, Haroun Ibn-Ziyad."

"You know I can't make that promise with what we do."

Kato and Sulla growled from nearby. The sound grew louder when Osiris and Dante neared Rayne and Grace. Osiris shushed both beasts. Sulla sat, but Kato continued to snarl. Kato sensed Grace's apprehension about Osiris's presence.

Rayne shot the wolf a scolding glance. "Kato, Osiris will not harm her."

"As your husband is safe, your authority is revoked, najmati." Osiris struggled with what more he had to say. "In all my days, I have never sought to hurt you, Grace. I am sorry for all that you suffered. I did try to prevent..." Osiris stopped. He could not disclose the various events he argued against. To do so would reveal aspects of fate, not even immortals beyond those on the High Council should know.

Rayne offered Osiris an understanding smile. He and the god had previously discussed Osiris's regret stemming from past events.

Osiris's apology genuinely shocked Grace and Dante. It was not often a god issued one. Dante had never heard his father sincerely apologize for anything prior to today.

Grace offered Osiris her hand. "Today erases the past. Thank you."

Osiris took it then kissed each of Grace's cheeks, happy to have peace with her once more.

"None of my demons or djinn will bother you again, Rayne. Well, at least not over an extinguished contract." Lucifer startled all of them. No one had noticed he stood amongst them.

"Why would you..." Rayne decided it best not finish his inquiry.

"Isra stupidly intended to use you to come after me. I have no desire to face War. Especially when I can profit from the misery you met out. I mean the justice you deliver on behalf of the Council. Unfortunately, all of our paths will cross again; as foes, as we should be."

Grace frowned after Lucifer vanished. "Maybe we should have vanquished him, too."

Dante handed Rayne the Commander's ruby. "Not a wise thing to attempt, Grazia. Lucifer mostly knows his limits, and we carefully keep him in check."

"That's debatable." Grace thought otherwise.

Rayne and Dante stared at one another, uncertain of what to say after everything.

Recalling what Rayne alleged earlier, Dante's eyes narrowed. "Conspiracy to corrupt a guardian? As if I would do such a thing." The emerging grin on Dante's face gave away the lack of malice in his disgusted stare. "I had forgotten that charge even existed."

Rayne laughed and shook his head. "You lobbed instigating mutiny at me. What else was I to think seeing you paying off Lucifer after kissing my wife?"

"Our wife." Dante winked at Rayne before reaching for the band on the Horseman's wrist.

Rayne grasped his hand, preventing him from removing the band. "Where are the collars?"

"In the High Council vault, where they belong, until I destroy them this evening. Tessa is safe, Rayne. I could never harm her. You should know that." Dante pulled the restraint from Rayne's arm.

"One can never be too careful." Rayne handed Dante the second one from his other wrist.

Dante smiled. "Take good care of my son and his mother."

The god turned then walked west, toward the sun.

Grace couldn't believe Dante chose to disappear from her and Tarquin's lives. "Where are you going, Dante?"

Dante turned to find Grace following him. "You no longer need my assistance. A god may not remain in the mortal realm indefinitely, cara. You know this."

Grace hated saying goodbye after finally making peace with him. It didn't seem right for them to be separated all over again. "Cavaliere, you never falter when it is important."

Flattered by the compliment, Dante grinned. "I love you from afar until the time comes to do otherwise, Grace."

"I love you too, Dante."

"You saying that makes playing the villain more than worthwhile, cara. As you told Rayne the other night, stop feeling guilty about everything. You did what you must. The three of us will come to terms with everything."

"I pray you are right, Dante. I worry Rayne won't see things the same way."

"Omnipotent being with the power to rewrite fate." Dante winked. He smiled at how her eyes lit up when she laughed.

"And what have you written?"

"Not a thing beyond saving Rayne, my muse. We are all where we are supposed to be."

Grace embraced Dante, holding him as she did when they were once lovers.

He noticed Rayne watching them. "Rayne wonders what we are discussing. You should return to him."

"I will watch for you in the sunset each night," Grace whispered before letting him go.

"You will find me there, looking down and admiring you, cara." Dante gently pulled the servant's collar from Grace's neck. He brushed his knuckles across her cheek, reminding her of the last time they saw one another in Greece.

"Don't go." Grace couldn't stop herself from uttering the words, trapped in the memory of losing Dante all over again.

"Grazia, mia stella. Do not fear my leaving. I will be there when you need me. This time, you will see me in those troublesome hours." Dante stole one last kiss from her before stepping back and giving her a gentle push in Rayne's direction.

Ignoring the fleeting surge of jealousy after observing the tender moment between Dante and Grace, Rayne secured his familial dagger back in place under his jacket. He glanced over at Dante thankful for the god's friendship as Grace walked towards him. Dante saluted him before disappearing into the horizon.

"You promised to take me home once this was all over, Commander."

Rayne's arm encircled Grace's waist. "Yes, I believe I did."

FIFTY-FOUR

England - Modern Day

Rayne dried himself off after a bath. He wrapped a towel around his waist and entered the bedroom to get fresh clothing. Grace stood out on the balcony with Lyal and Khonsu. He watched the three through the window as he dressed. Whatever this meeting was about, it was a short one. Grace bowed respectfully to Khonsu then Lyal. Both the harbinger and moon god vanished.

Grace turned toward the house. She saw Rayne standing in the doorway.

"Everything all right, leof?"

Grace embraced him and held onto him as if he would vanish. "Now it is."

Rayne took a deep breath and lightly soothed her back. "You demand I keep no more secrets. Must I make a similar request of you?"

"No. I thanked them for the warning. This afternoon would have ended very differently without Lyal looking out for you and me."

"Whatever that ending looked like, I am glad you thwarted it."

"You aren't going to ask any questions?" Grace honestly was surprised by the fact he didn't push the issue further.

"There is no need to. You would not have gone to the lengths you did to ensure my freedom and Isra's end if the day ended happily."

"I love you, Rayne. Thank you for somewhat trusting me today."

"For a while there, I was certain you made a fool of me."

"You should know I would never divorce you or trade you to a demon." Grace rested her hand on his chest, staring up at him.

"Old fears, Grace. The rational man in your husband knows that well. But the enforcer terrified of the past repeating didn't learn that until today. The collar you wore and Lucifer taking the pouch from Dante almost ended me."

Grace smiled up at him. "The servants collar was nothing more than costume jewelry, unlike the bands Lucifer placed on your wrists. The old devices were a very convincing touch to the plan. Lucifer definitely did not want a corrupted War around. Isra pissed him off, interfering in whatever plans Lucifer had for Malik. His swapping the real harbinger's blade with the fake one knowing Isra would steal it, then his appearing in Elysium was sheer genius. Who would have thought the Morning Star would help someone with no strings attached?"

"Lucifer helped himself today. If I were not a legitimate threat, he wouldn't have played along. Either way, I never imagined I'd see the day I would have any sense of gratitude for something Lucifer did." Rayne looked up at the sky then brought his gaze back to Grace's before smiling at her again. "Has Lucifer recently developed the gift of foresight to know so much before it happens? I don't recall that being one of his abilities."

"Someone may have tipped him off."

Aware of who that someone was, Rayne smiled. "I am grateful they did."

Grace drifted to the balcony's edge with a sullen expression dulling the light in her eyes.

Guilt? He knew the weight pressing down on her well. With the way her fingers gripped the ledge and her shoulders tensed, she struggled to confess something. He sensed the spiraling hurt within her heart.

"Grace." His fingers slipped under the soft skin of her chin, lifting her face. She closed her eyes, trying to hide whatever sin she committed. "Sweeting, look at me."

She honored his request, but words still would not come.

Tears? Rayne invaded her thoughts. Flashes of multiple discussions between her, Lyal, Isis, and Lucifer, their children collared, him enslaved, Dante imprisoned, and finally, the root of her strife, she and Dante together. Grace freely risked losing everything she held sacred to ensure he, Tarquin, and Tessa remained free.

"Let the past go. You did what was necessary." Rayne held her tightly again. "Since you need to hear it, I forgive you. For everything."

"How can you? We lied to you in the worst way. I couldn't tell you anything for the plan to work. I was so scared you'd see through me. That we'd lose everything, that I would lose you and the kids. I should probably feel more sorry for deceiving you than I do."

Calm, strength, and compassion flooded into her. Rayne's arms provided her an impenetrable safe haven anytime she needed one.

"None of that matters anymore. I understand what you did and why you did it." His lips brushed her temple. "I love you, Grace. Even if you had gone to his bed, I would forgive you. I long ago accepted the possibility one day I may begrudgingly have to share you with Dante. No one has ever hidden that part of the prophecy from any of us. I am grateful the Fates have held that portion back as long as they have. We will survive all of this. Trust in your wolf. He's eager to heal and put the events of the past several weeks behind us."

A wolf howled in the distance, bringing a smile to Grace's face. A second one answered the first. "Kato and Sulla wander to our twenty-first century home?"

"No, leof. That is a modern mated pair declaring their love for one another. The male promising to love and protect the female as long as they both shall live."

"Are you making that up?"

"What benefit is there for me to make up such a tale?"

"Maybe you are trying to romance your wife in a very strange, awkward way."

"I would deploy much more useful tactics to romance my wife. But since you find the wolves courting romantic, your wolf is more than happy to declare his love for you to the night." He threw his head back, emitting a loud howl towards the moon.

Grace laughed. She would never understand the craziness her immortal existence brought with it. "Instead of you standing out here howling, how about making me call you master?"

Rayne devilishly grinned, speaking in djinn. "If that is what you desire, my beloved."

"What I desire is to have and love my amazing husband for eternity."

"May our love last beyond that." Rayne kissed her, untying her robe and slowly backing her toward the outdoor couch.

"Out here?" Grace's robe fell away from her body.

"Yes, out here." Rayne removed his shirt. "Under the moon, so you are completely at my mercy. I want any passionate memories you have of lovemaking on a balcony to be with me, not Dante."

"No need to be jealous, Rayne. Things didn't go that far."

"Oh, I am not jealous, leof." Rayne's hands traveled down her spine; his palms followed the curves of her bottom, sending a jolt of anticipation through her. "A bit possessive maybe, but not jealous in the slightest. By the time I finish taking you on the couch, then against the wall of the house, and after that, wherever else I so choose to enjoy my wife, the memory of my hands and lips will be all you feel on this beautiful body of yours. You'll ache and long for me alone to repeat the experience with you. The next time we are in Elysium, I fully plan to take you against the same pillar Dante pinned you to, so even in his bedroom, I'll be the one you feel pleasuring you. Now, lay back, Grace. I want to give you incentive to keep gifting me alone your love."

CHAPTER
FIFTY-FIVE

Sasainn

Things returned to a relative calm with Isra vanquished. The Horsemen and Grace spent more time tending to administrative affairs than on the battlefield. Rayne hated admin work but welcomed calmer days. Conflict requiring the Horsemen to take arms would arise again soon enough. Without fail, it always did in one realm or another.

Staring at the stack of paperwork on his desk, Rayne debated whether to throw it in the fireplace or force himself to read another ridiculously long supply chit or request someone submitted for approval. Whatever immortal suggested implementing human practices and processes into their ranks recently needed to be given a month on the rack. He had enough papers and accounts to review, managing his personal properties and estates. The last thing he wanted was to be sitting in his office at headquarters, signing things that should be common sense purchases all day. Thankfully, Arturo would be back in a week, along with Sean, and they could take over the new duties temporarily assigned to him.

Destahn looked in Rayne's open office door. "I believe the mortals would say it's quitting time, Commander. You'd know better than me with buying a new home in the twenty-first century. What are you aiming to become, Rayne, a slum lord with properties across time?"

Rayne grinned over at Destahn. "We always have to rent a property when Grace and I go into twenty-first century England or her family wants to see Tessa and Tarquin. It made sense to purchase a home over constantly going through the headache of finding the same short-term rental again and again. And after the ordeal of Isra appearing at my other homes, this one gives all of us a trauma free space to reconnect."

"Children are more sensitive to things than most realize. I always hear folks say they are resilient, but I am not certain that is true of all youth," Destahn said, sitting down in an empty chair.

"Being a parent now, I must admit there is some truth to your line of thought. I think age plays into resiliency. Tessa is young enough the Council agreed to wipe the moments with Lucifer from her mind, and besides the periodic bad dream, memories of Isra, or the day Kamar attacked her don't seem to regularly bother her. Though she does give the pond a wide berth. Tarquin, on the other hand, remains withdrawn and on edge anywhere but England."

"I am sorry to hear Tarquin is still not handling things well. From what I understand, Dante went through something similar after his mother and sister died. What helped him?"

"Time. I am hoping the same holds true for Tarquin. He is doing better. We can go a few days now without him acting out or becoming Grace's or my shadow. The new school and environment seem to be helping. He's also discovered video games and girls. He's doing his best to capture the attention of Arsceneaux's daughter."

Hearing Aria enthralled Tarquin, Destahn chuckled. "Poor boy. Literally taking after his father. You better warn him off of Aria before Gage does. Red hair and pretty eyes just do something to Giovanni men. Dante never could say no to a redhead back in the day."

Thinking back to Dante's women-chasing days, Rayne shook his head. The gods help him if Tarquin took a similar path. The boy's looks alone would draw the girls in. If he developed Dante's charm and wit, those the boy set his sights on would be thoroughly beguiled. He could already imagine the number of angry fathers on his doorstep berating him about Tarquin's conduct with their daughters. "Thankfully,

Tarquin is much more bashful and gentlemanly than his father when it comes to the fairer sex. Come to think of it, Dante was quite bashful and courtly when he was younger and the entire time he was with Caitlin. It wasn't until after Morrigan forced the two apart that Casanova emerged."

Destahn chuckled and smirked, slapping his hand against the arm of his chair. "Speaking of Casanova, you and Grace seem to have mended things between the two of you pretty well."

"We've been working on fixing our weaker spots. I know the concept is foreign to you, but I truly do love my wife. The happier she is, the happier I am."

"The two of you were definitely working on something in here the other day. When Dante had this office, I fully expected to hear him with some tart in here every now and then. But I am not going to lie, to hear you and Grace was quite surprising. You're going to need to sound proof these walls if that is going to be a regular habit, Commander."

Rayne shook his head. "Good night, Destahn."

"Oh, come on, Rayne. You can't honestly be mad over that remark."

Rayne stood and pulled his jacket on. "Not mad at all. Just eager to get home to my wife with the reminder of that afternoon."

Destahn made a disgusted face then walked out of the office.

When Rayne got home, the house was unusually quiet. Grace was in the kitchen putting the last of the groceries she purchased away. Rayne wrapped his arms around her waist and kissed her cheek as she set a box of cereal on the panty shelf. "Where are Tessa and Tarquin?"

Grace glanced over her shoulder at him. "Gage and Caitlin took them out with their kids for hot cider and cookies down in the village square. They'll most likely be back in a couple of hours. Why?"

"Well, if they are going to be returned loud and hyperactive due to ingesting a bunch of sugar and playing with the Arsceneauxs, I am thinking I should take advantage of the opportunity to enjoy some quiet time with my wife while we have it."

"What did you have in mind?"

"Candle light. Dinner for two. Maybe some dancing."

Grace laughed. "I like the way you think, wolf, but we only have a couple of hours, not an entire night."

"That's all we need."

"Really?" Grace doubted that.

"So cynical, Defensore. Still haven't learned to fully trust in your husband again?" Rayne's arms slipped from around her waist.

"I trust you. But by the time we change, get out the door, and to a restaurant..." Grace turned toward him.

"Who said anything about going out? We've got everything we need for a romantic evening here." Rayne held up the meal he picked up on his way home. "Dinner."

He pulled a bottle of wine from the wine fridge. "Vino."

Grace shook her head, watching him take out two candles from the hutch and set them on the counter. He snapped his fingers, so flame appeared then lit one candle. "How do you do that?"

"Do what?" Rayne pretended not to know what she inquired about.

"Summon flame. I've never seen anyone, but you do such a thing."

Rayne chuckled. "All of us most likely can. Others just haven't tried. Give me your hand."

Grace extended her hand to him. Rayne rested it in his with her open palm facing upward.

"Now, close your eyes and picture holding a flame." Rayne paused for a second, running his forefinger across the center of her palm. "It begins as a small spark, but grows brighter in your hand. Imagine its heat, but without the ability to burn. See it swirling like a spinning dancer, twirling before you. Their arms lifted and reaching heavenward." His hand fell away from hers. "Very good. Don't lose your focus, but open your eyes, Grace."

Grace discovered a small green and white swirl of fire rising from her palm. "Did you conjure this?"

"No, my love, you did. I merely showed you how to ask the flame to appear. Light the remaining candle for me while I take care of our lack of music." Rayne turned on a wireless speaker then unlocked his phone searching for the music player app. He scrolled through the list of titles until he found one of the first modern-day songs he and Grace danced to long ago. After the first few notes of the slow love song escaped the speaker, Grace looked away from the flame holding her attention and smiled up at Rayne.

"Candle light and music. Now, the evening is perfect." Rayne took her hand and lightly blew across it, extinguishing the magical flame. "Dance with me?"

"How can I say no, especially in such a fine establishment as this one?" Grace settled her arm around his shoulders as he brought the hand he held to his heart.

Rayne chuckled, pulling her close and enjoying the moment. "People seriously underestimate the romance a large kitchen can inspire."

"You normally come home grumpy on paperwork days. What brings out the romantic side of my husband today?"

"Someone reminded me of how lucky I am to have such a beautiful, loving wife."

"I am afraid to ask who that someone was."

"Surprisingly, the someone was Destahn."

Grace gave him a skeptical look. "Destahn? I suppose the Captain has his charming side when he wants to. And he has been a good friend to us over the years, even with his man-child tendencies. Now, that I know the someone, I am curious, what was the reminder? Some wise words which manage to come out of his month once a millennium?"

"No. But what he said reminded me I was curious to learn what it's like to take my wife on a granite-covered, kitchen island. It's something I haven't done before, and you've encouraged me to try new modern things. I figured a little romance would help me achieve my objective."

Grace laughed. "I don't want to know what was said any longer." She stopped their swaying and leaned closer into Rayne. "Is dinner reheatable?"

"I don't see any reason it wouldn't be."

"In that case, on to new experiences, wolf."

Rayne and Grace had just finished eating when the clamor of footsteps and voices sounded outside. A few seconds later, the front door was flung open. A boisterous Tessa led everyone inside.

"Wine, candles, and Italian food? Looks like you two had a pleasant dinner," Caitlin said, taking off her coat.

"Have to take advantage of opportunities when they present themselves," Rayne remarked with a grin, standing up and taking Caitlin's jacket. He smiled over at Grace as Tessa filled her in on all the fun things they did. Tessa bounced up and down on her feet, describing the cookies, cider, and games at the fall festival.

Caitlin noticed the way Rayne continued to watch his wife and daughter. "I know that look. That's the look of a man in love and extremely content with life. A rare thing for a Horseman."

"I would say quiet is a rarer thing around here, at least lately. It was nice to have a few hours of peace alone with my wife. Thank you for that gift, Caitlin." Rayne hung Caitlin's jacket up in the living room closet.

"Dad," Tarquin stopped chatting with Alessandro, Caitlin and Gage's son, and walked over to Rayne.

Part of Grace hated how Tarquin shifted from calling Rayne daddy to dad more and more. The ordeal with Isra made her son grow up faster than he should have. She noticed how Tarquin sheepishly approached Rayne as if embarrassed about something. By the way Rayne's brow lifted a slight bit and the smile left his face, Rayne was concerned about Tarquin's behavior as well.

"Yes, Tarquin?"

"I know it's a bit childish and all, but," Tarquin pulled a bag from his jacket. "I got you a cookie tonight, too."

Watching Rayne take the large cookie from him, Grace choked up. All she could see now was a small, five-year-old boy sneaking cookies out of the kitchen just before dinner, so he and Rayne could sit down outside together in a father-son-only, secret evening snack session. And if Tarquin didn't successfully get the cookies, Rayne always made sure he had two on hand for them to enjoy.

Rayne pulled the cookie from its bag and broke it in half. "It is never childish, nor is one ever too old to share a cookie with their father." He offered Tarquin the other half. "Just don't tell your mother about the cookies before dinner."

Instead of taking the cookie half, Tarquin hugged Rayne. "I love you, Dad. I am so glad Isra's gone, and we can eat cookies together again."

Rayne put an arm around Tarquin and gently squeezed the boy. "Me, too, Tarquin. Me, too."

Once Tarquin loosened his grip, Rayne re-offered the half a cookie to him. This time, Tarquin happily took it.

"And, Dad, I promise, I won't tell Mama." Tarquin gave the same response he had given Rayne for almost six years before taking a bite of the cookie. "Though she's looking at us, so she knows about tonight."

Rayne chuckled. "I have a feeling your mother knows about all of our cookie eating sessions. She just pretends not to notice what we're doing. As we have company, I will finish eating this later. Why don't you show Alessandro whatever new game you've been playing this week?"

Seeing the boys pull out various video games from the TV stand, Rayne headed to the kitchen. "Gage, since it looks like you're here for a bit, what can I get you? Beer, Bourbon, Rum?"

"I'm the designated driver tonight. Caitlin's already enjoyed an adult spiced cider. Have any nonalcoholic options?"

Rayne opened the fridge. "Kid safe beverages it is. Looks like we have root beer, orange cream soda, and a variety of fruit juice boxes. There's also always water."

"I'll take a root beer."

As Rayne opened the root beer then handed it to Gage, Alessandro shouted, "Oh, cool! You have Eternal Watch? Let's play that one."

Grace laughed at the annoyed breath Rayne let out. "It's not that bad, Rayne."

Rayne shook his head and watched as the "Four Horsemen" showed up on the TV screen along with an opening cut scene telling some ludicrous backstory of each one. "You're not the one who has been totally misrepresented in that. None of us look like those guys or have done half the things this game claims we did."

"Pop culture loves you all as the scary medieval-looking creatures that do bad things in the Apocalypse. At least this game gave you guys creative back stories. I like how Death is on a mission to redeem himself after his wife is killed, and War's wanting vengeance against the gods for his family being murdered is an intriguing storyline that hits a little too close to home. You must admit, it is accurate in the four of you are powerful immortal warriors battling it out with a variety of forces." Grace tried to soothe her husband's ire with the game.

"How you conveniently leave out it also alleges the Horsemen are at war with one another, in addition to everyone else. The major conflict in the game is Death and War trying to take out each other, not to mention smaller battles against Pestilence and Famine. To add insult to injury, Pestilence, of all four, almost beating War so badly, that War has to make an alliance with Death to defeat Pestilence? That is not even in the realm of possibility. And our son, the child of Death, being raised by War himself, loves playing that damn game, which we agreed you wouldn't buy, then your bloody parents give it to him."

Gage smirked after taking a drink of the cold root beer in his hand. "It sounds like your larger issue with the game is that the writers and developers let Destahn get the better of you."

"I don't want to hear it from you after your tirade about someone portraying vampires as sparkly in the sun," Rayne shot back at the half-guide, half-vampire sipping root beer across from him.

Recalling his rant a few years back, Gage laughed. "Maybe Dante's right in avoiding modern day. He doesn't have to be annoyed with any of this."

"Rayne will eventually get over the game, Gage. Just like he's accepted that cookies are cookies, not biscuits, after ten years of fighting with me over that." Grace smiled at the snort Rayne let out.

"I haven't accepted anything. I simply no longer see any point in trying to teach you proper English. You Yanks so pride yourself on butchering it all the time."

"How could someone, who isn't even bloody English, claim to be teaching an American what is and isn't proper English? Last I checked, you are an Andalusian pretending to be a Brit." Grace intentionally riled up her husband.

"My mother is a Brit. I've also lived in England for nine centuries now. I think that more than entitles me to claim I am a Brit and qualifies me as an expert to teach you the English language."

"Take it from a Frenchman, Grace, he's definitely English with the sense of entitlement and superiority he just displayed." Gage winked at Grace. "Let him have this one. He isn't having a good night between using the word cookie and being portrayed as whatever that thing is on screen. What in the hell is that, anyway? A jacked skeleton mixed with a goat on steroids in a hoodie and a bathrobe over its armor?"

EPILOGUE

"Why are you in uniform?" Grace watched Rayne pull his woolen winter cloak onto his shoulders. "You are on leave with your parents visiting us for the first time in Sasainn."

Rayne secured the clasp of the cloak. "I am sorry, leof. I know I promised to be here all day, but my presence has been requested at the castle."

"It's Christmas week. Your presence is needed here."

"Raphael swears he'll have me back home within two hours."

Grace picked up his gloves. He'd want them as soon as he was satisfied the cloak rested where it should. The leather was now soft from being broken in over the years and slightly worn where the reins routinely rested in his hands. At least he didn't carry any weapons on him. Raphael might actually keep the meeting brief. "How am I supposed to entertain the kids and your parents in medieval England by myself?"

Rayne looked in their mirror, double checking everything was in its proper place. "When they wake, have Lavinia feed them all a big breakfast. Get my father telling stories about his youth or days servings as an ambassador for Córdoba. Or if you prefer, ask he and my mother to tell you embarrassing stories about me as a boy. That should work for my parents until I get back. You know how to manage the children better than I do anywhere we are."

Grace handed Rayne his gloves. "Be careful with all the snow out there. We don't need you hurt or Fahkir lame."

After he pulled the gloves on, he grasped her shoulders and kissed her goodbye. "No need to worry, leof. Fahkir is as sure-footed as they come. He'll avoid any problem areas. I promise to be back soon."

"I've heard that before," Grace muttered as he shut their bedroom door. She shook her head, listening to him quickly descend the stairs then cross the house to the front door. She walked to the window and watched him walk through the snow to the barn. A few minutes later, horse and rider emerged from the structure. Fahkir's black coat and Rayne dressed in the same color contrasted against the white, glistening landscape. Snow flew from under Fahkir's hooves only a foot from the front gate. The farther away they got, the more they reminded Grace of shadowy specters than living beings. Sure-footed or not, galloping over snow-covered fields could lead to trouble.

"Fahkir's ability to navigate treacherous landscape is as much a marvel as Haroun was to Córdoba," Saladin said from the doorway. "I will never forget a winter battle in Aquitaine. It was the worst of conditions. Normally, we would not fight during the winter, or at least not the heart of it. But we could not ignore the recent attacks on the communities we promised to protect. The snow was knee-deep and ice covered the rivers. We could see the Frankish army riding through the countryside after burning and raiding another village. Many of my men feared confronting the knights in such perilous conditions. Knowing this was the moment to capture the enemy, Rayne unsheathed his blade and spurred Fahkir forward when seasoned commanders hesitated to attack. We all watched the black horse tear through the snow toward the long line of knights. Powder flying up everywhere his hooves landed. Two of the Franks turned to stop Rayne from reaching their lines. Their horses slipped and fell on icy ground, but not Fahkir. He plowed through drifts and flew over ice as if running on spring turf.

After Rayne killed one man, then unhorsed the commander, all of us charged forward to assist in subduing the enemy. Abdul designated Rayne a field commander for his courage that afternoon. I knew it was only a matter of time before my son would be the one leading the Emirate's army instead of myself. While I could rally the men to fight, Haroun could inspire them to do the impossible, even when fear ruled them.

"You once asked me how I knew my son still lived after the announcement of his execution. I only told you half the truth. Four years after that dreadful night, Fahkir disappeared from my stables, along with all of his tack. I found this in the straw." Saladin handed Grace a coin with a wolf on one side.

Grace smiled, staring down at the wolf. "Rayne wanted you to know he was safe and well."

"Yes. He knew Lillian and I worried about him. He did not want us to do so any longer. Just as he would not want you to spend your day worrying, or, for that matter, any day fretting over the future. Live in the moment, Grace, so you may enjoy glad tidings as they draw us through times of misfortune."

Grace gave the coin back to Saladin. "If I didn't know better, I'd say you sound like one of the Council. Perhaps you and Osiris are spending too much time together."

Saladin laughed. "One does not need to be a god to be wise, especially if Ibn-Ziyad is a name they or their ancestors bear, for wisdom comes with age."

"Or legacy." Grace watched Saladin's reaction to her words. By the grin on his face, he understood she had pieced things together his son had not. "The kind that comes from ancient bloodlines. Was Tariq or Zairah the djinn?"

"Neither. The affair between the djinn and human that gifts Ibn-Ziyad men good fortune is much more ancient, and the djinn magic skips generations. There were many tales of miraculous doings of my forbearers. I believed most to be myth until I saw my own small son perform similar tasks. His nightmares only confirmed my suspicions. I had Haroun privately tutored and trained him myself to hide his abilities from those who would recognize them for as long as I could, to keep him safe, and to ensure he developed a strong moral compass to guide him."

"Saladin, you need to tell Rayne the truth one of these days. While he embraces the enforcer, he still fears that part of himself, thinking it borne from darkness, instead of understanding the enforcer has always been a part of him, and grief corrupted a being borne of light."

"I am surprised he does not know, especially with the immortal he has become." Saladin figured Rayne would have learned of his heritage.

"The Council and Fates keep secrets just as humans do. I think he has his suspicions, but doubts them, as his father nor mother have ever relayed his full family history to him. Not to mention, so many have told him he was destined to be a Horseman, but no one has ever shared why the Fates chose him over others."

Saladin took Grace's hand in his, then patted it. "I swear to speak with Haroun and tell him of his true heritage before the next full moon. I do not wish to add more to his plate today with the Council summoning him so early. While we await his return, shall we enjoy the new morning drink you introduced to Lillian and me? Qahwa, I believe Rayne called it."

Grace laughed. "Yes. Coffee. You may want to limit how often you drink it, Saladin. It isn't available in Córdoba, and won't be for several centuries. Caffeine headaches are the worst when suffering from caffeine withdrawal."

True to his word, Rayne returned two hours later. He found Grace and his parents eating breakfast. Tessa and Tarquin missing from the table meant the children were surprisingly still asleep. Lillian and Saladin smiled seeing him enter the room.

Rayne kissed his mother's cheek. "Good Morning, Mother." He hugged his father next. "Sabah al-khayr, Baba."

"Sabah al noor, Haroun," Saladin returned the greeting.

Grace knew by the way Rayne briefly chatted with his parents, but didn't sit down the Council recalled him to duty for the day. Sure enough, he turned to face her and offered her his hand.

"Grace, may I speak to you privately for a moment?"

"Of course." Grace took his hand, forcing a smile, and allowing him to lead her away from the table. "Isis better not be sending the Horsemen anywhere."

"She isn't, but unfortunately, I need to take care of a few things for the Council." Seeing the way her lips tightened into a straight line and her jaw set, Rayne gave her hands a squeeze. "Before you get mad, the good news is I can handle what is needed from here. In between meetings, I will spend time with the family. It's only one day, Grace. The Council has promised to leave us alone until after the New Year, as long as no one tries to take over either realm. I will take everyone to the Yuletide Market tomorrow to make up for today."

"I am holding you to that, Commander. Did Raphael at least feed you with calling you in early on a day off, or do I need to get Lavinia to make you something?"

"I've eaten, leof. Let me get to work on things." Rayne kissed her before disappearing into his office for the rest of the morning and early afternoon.

His last meeting for the day now over, Rayne stepped out the front door to investigate all the shouting and laughter originating from his front yard. Taking in the cheerful scene of Tessa and Tarquin along with two of their grandfathers playing in the freshly fallen snow, he smiled. Grace stood a few feet from him, observing the outdoor hijinks. Pink tinged her cheeks. She laughed at Tessa trying to convince Osiris to lie down so they could make snow angels. The god stared at the little girl as if she had three heads.

Tessa plopped backwards into the white powder covering the ground. She flailed her arms and legs, making the outline of the Christian interpretation of an angel. "This is how you make an angel, Nonno."

Osiris snorted. One of his dark brows arched as he stared disdainfully down at the little girl swinging her arms and legs all about in the snow. "I do not think your parents have properly educated you on angels."

The little girl popped back up onto her feet and admired her work for a brief second before grabbing Osiris's hand. "Now, you try, Nonno."

Tessa tugged to no avail. Osiris wasn't about to do as she asked.

Saladin snorted at Osiris's reaction to Tessa's pleading. "Since a god fears the snow, her mortal grandfather will accommodate the child."

Saladin fell into the snow. Tessa flopped down beside him.

Grace and Rayne chuckled at how Osiris rolled his eyes.

Deciding not to be outdone by a human, Osiris slowly knelt down then laid back, mimicking Tessa and Saladin. Grace's chest shook as she tried to muffle her laughter at a famous human general, her young daughter, and Osiris sprawled out in the front yard making angels together. Quite the colorful sight against the white backdrop with Saladin's dark hair, tanned skin, and black clothing; Tessa's gold curls, white jacket, beige pants, and porcelain-colored skin just a bit warmer than the snow she laid in, and then there was Osiris – dark haired under the golden headdress he wore, with a dark beard, green-skinned, and garbed in a golden and white coat.

"Perhaps Dante was right when he said Tessa will cause more trouble than her mother with the way she manipulates mortal men and gods." Rayne took Grace's hands in his. "Your hands are like ice, Countess."

Rayne rubbed Grace's fingers between his palms to warm them up. He cupped his own hands around them, lifting the sheltered cold digits to his lips. His eyes remained locked with hers while he breathed warmth into the cylinder his rounded palms made. "I insist you come inside at once, madam. I will not have my wife catch her death due to not properly bundling up in these temperatures."

Rayne whisked her through the door, not stopping until they stood before the fireplace in the great hall. A large Christmas tree stood near one window. Its ornaments shimmered from sunbeams striking against them.

"Wanted me to yourself, Horseman?"

"Indeed, I do." Rayne drew her closer. "We haven't had much time alone the past few weeks with work and our families visiting. I wanted a few quiet minutes to tell you I love you."

Grace kissed Rayne. "I love you too."

They looked out the window. Tessa, Tarquin, Saladin, and Osiris stood and analyzed each of the angels they made.

Rayne's arm rested loosely around Grace's waist. "Never would I have imagined my father lying in the snow to make an angel."

"There is always a first time for everything."

"Very true, leof." Rayne placed a kiss on her temple. "I have an early Christmas gift for you."

"An early Christmas gift?" Grace wondered what Rayne planned with the devilish smirk on his face. That particular grin always promised her an irresistible combination of trouble and delight whenever it appeared.

"Come with me."

Grace followed him, giggling like a giddy child. She barely kept up with Rayne, traveling down the hallway as he led her through the downstairs of their home. "Why are we at your office?"

Rayne didn't answer her question. He pushed opened his office door. His hand settled on the small of her back, gently guiding her into the room before entering himself.

Confusion replaced the mirth on Grace's face. A uniformed official stood with his back to them, staring out the window. A black cloak trimmed in gold hung from his shoulders, stopping just below the man's calves. Golden spurs stood out against freshly cleaned and polished black leather boots. She glanced back at Rayne, wondering how a visit from a High Council Harbinger attired so formally could be a pleasant surprise.

After closing the door, Rayne gestured toward their guest. "Grace, I would like to introduce you to Isis's newest officer. The General will be assuming Raphael's duties on New Year's Day."

The tall figure turned to face them. "Defensore, Commander."

"Dante?" Grace immediately recognized the man in a modified Horsemen's uniform.

Dante welcomed the warm embrace she gave him. This greeting was certainly better than the last one in the hills of Spain.

Grace still couldn't quite believe Dante stood before her as she pulled back from him. During his last visit, over a month ago now, he shared he was considering the Council's offer to join their ranks. "I thought you accepted the seat on the Council."

"This position is much better suited to my talents. Raphael wished to return to retirement and couldn't do so until another could take his place. Tarquin has years to go before he is even old enough to begin training for any sort of leadership role, so I volunteered to fill the vacancy."

"Are you one of us again?"

Dante shook his head no. "Low ranking god is how I will spend eternity. Would you be willing to return Vittore to me since I am in need of a mount?"

"Of course." Grace could easily give the man his horse.

Rayne softly chuckled beside them. "I am relieved to finally be rid of the beast. No more having to pen him up and almost having my arm ripped off when taking him out to pasture every time Diya comes into season. That stud is more obnoxious than you were after a few drinks back in your womanizing days."

"Can you blame him for misbehaving when he only wants to impress Diya?" Dante grinned, knowing well how unruly Vittore could be around a mare in season.

Rayne scoffed. "Diya wants little to do with him in those moments."

Grace sat down in one of the nearby chairs. "You are more than welcome to the house in Essaouira if you need a home in the mortal realm."

Rayne moved behind the chair and settled his hands on Grace's shoulders. "We need to speak about that offer, leof."

Grace looked up at him and frowned. "The villa is more his home than ours. We are hardly ever there."

"It is your property, Grace. You may give it to whomever you wish. Even so, I would like to make an alternate proposal."

Grace folded her arms over her chest, suspicious of what the two apparently schemed up together. "Which is?"

"In addition to returning the villa to Dante, he receives an open invitation to stay anywhere we do, so he may see Tarquin as he wishes.

We have an extra bedroom in each house that he could use when needed."

Dante nervously awaited Grace's response. Would she deny him that type of access? Part of him believed she would after Rayne suggested it the day prior.

Grace noticed the apprehensive look on Dante's face. After the past several months, did he believe her to still be angry with him? "Our home is always open to Dante or any of the Horsemen anytime they wish to visit."

Dante politely inclined his head. "Grazie mille, Lady Warwick. Your willingness to welcome me into your home earns my deepest gratitude."

"I expect you to be on your best behavior, cavaliere. No bloodshed."

Dante laughed. "I swear not to seriously wound or kill the Horsemen Commander. I make no such promise of zero injury during drilling or bouting. Accidents do happen."

Rayne scoffed at the hollow threat. "I can best the General anytime he wishes to test me."

Grace rolled her eyes. "I am not sure I want whatever present you have, Rayne Warwick, if it involves Dante as your co-conspirator."

Rayne walked over to his desk and reached underneath it. "Dante has nothing to do with your gift. The Council just has incredibly poor timing with their appointment considering you and I must immediately be introduced to any new Liaison since we report to him or her. I am fairly certain you will want what your husband has selected this year as a present for his family."

He straightened, holding a yawning, small, red wheaten puppy cradled in his arm. The fury wrinkles rippling its skin and a small white star on the puppy's chest added to its cuteness. Its paws were awkwardly humungous compared to the rest of its body. Grace softly cooed in reaction to seeing it. He lightly stroked the velvety head of the Rhodesian Ridgeback he held. "What say you now, leof? Shall we keep the pup or do I need to return her to her prior home?"

"We are most certainly keeping her!" Grace took the puppy Rayne offered her. The puppy licked Grace's face. Grace laughed at how the tiny rough tongue tickled her cheek and nose. "She's beautiful. How have you managed to hide her in here without me or the kids seeing her?"

"I picked her up on my way home today. Surprisingly, she's slept quietly under my desk through most of my meetings. She did have a burst of energy and attacked my feet a few times about an hour ago, but you and the kids were outside so didn't hear her barking. After a few laps around the office and some play time with Dante and I, she went back to sleep." Rayne gently rubbed the puppy's ear. "She needs a name."

"We will figure one out." Grace still could not believe he brought a dog home after objecting to her suggestion only a week ago.

"This is the breed you mentioned?"

"Yes. She's perfect." Grace kissed Rayne, assuring him he did well in selecting their new companion.

Throwing open the office door and spotting Dante, Tessa let out a loud, "Zio!" She sprinted over to him and wrapped her arms around his waist.

Returning the hug, Dante's smile widened.

Tarquin had heard Tessa's exclamation. "Papa is here?"

"I am here, mio figlio."

Tarquin raced down the hall after Dante answered him. Tarquin bear hugged his father after having not seen him for almost a month. "I've missed you, Papa. You were gone a long time again."

"It wasn't by choice, Tarquin. I would spend every day with you if I could."

Tarquin noticed the dog in Grace's lap. "A puppy!"

"So much for you having a few minutes alone with the pup." Rayne chuckled, watching Tarquin pick up their new addition.

Tessa squealed in delight now seeing the dog.

Grace wasn't sure if the children wrapping their arms around Dante or their excitement at discovering the puppy warmed her heart more. "Thank Daddy for her. She's our Christmas present."

"Let me see her!" Tessa danced around her brother, tugging on his arm. Tarquin held the puppy lower, so Tessa didn't pull her out of his grasp. "Oh, she has eyes like Tarquin and Zio's. Can we name her Oro?"

"What do you think of Oro, Tarquin?" Grace asked, petting the pup's head.

"I like it. She does have Papa's and my eyes."

"Oro it is. Why don't you take her to the hall to play for a bit? There isn't much she can get into there."

Tarquin set the dog on the floor and called her by her new name. The puppy slipped on the wood floors, trying to run after Tessa and Tarquin. She regained her feet and playfully caught up with them.

"You will be replacing your rugs within a week's time, along with several pairs of boots, Rayne." Dante grinned, taken in by the family moment. "You can finish briefing me after the holidays. Enjoy your evening."

"If you don't have any other plans for tonight, you are welcome to join us for dinner." Grace startled Dante and Rayne with the dinner invite. "The children have missed you."

Dante exchanged glances with Rayne. "If Rayne has no objections. I do not want to impose."

Rayne smiled. "You are not imposing at all. You are more than welcome at my table, Dante."

"Papa, come see the new bow Destahn gave me for Christmas." Tarquin called from the hallway.

"No shooting it in the house!" Grace yelled, not wanting another vase broken.

"Yes, Mama," Tarquin answered in an annoyed tone.

Dante chuckled then walked out of the office and down the hall toward his son.

"Do the other Horsemen know Dante is taking Raphael's place?" Grace asked as she and Rayne followed Dante down the hall.

"No. They'll find out on New Year's Day." Rayne pulled her closer to his side.

"Well, it looks like the old group is all back together again for more crazy adventures." Grace couldn't help thinking it really was amazing how the more things changed, the more they stayed the same.

Rayne grinned. "The gods help us with Dante serving as our liaison."

"We have you as the lead field commander to keep things from going too far awry."

"I think you overestimate my abilities in influencing Dante, leof."

Grace stopped in the entryway to the grand hall. "I don't overestimate anything, wolf. You have had more success in swaying Dante over the years than Raphael ever has. And if he doesn't listen to you, you can always send him to Tartarus or Purgatory. You are the balance keeper, after all."

Rayne's dimples appeared as he let out a loud laugh. "Let us hope it never comes to that."

"Kiss me to be certain our good fortune continues." Grace pointed up at the mistletoe above them.

Rayne lowered his face to hers, indulging her in a long kiss.

The all too familiar hiss of an arrow passing close to their heads, then the mistletoe and garland falling down on them ended the kiss.

"Tarquin." Grace continued to stare up at Rayne while she started to scold her son.

"It wasn't me, Mama!" Tarquin's voice vacillated when he answered.

Grace looked in the direction where Dante and the two children stood. Dante held the bow in his hand with a diabolical smile on his face.

"My apologies, cara. The string slipped my fingers while I was showing Tarquin how to properly draw it back."

Rayne shook his head. "Am I going to have to forbid you from having weapons in the house?"

Grace folded her arms across her chest. "Bugiardo."

Indignation replaced the smirk on Dante's face. His hands came up in the classic Italian what gesture before they came together as if in prayer. "Tesoro, truly, do you not believe me?"

Grace rolled her eyes. "Behave like a child, get treated like one. No dessert for you tonight, Pinocchio."

Tessa hit Dante in the leg. "You got us in trouble, Zio. Santa better not put us on the bad list because of you. Christmas is in two days."

"I'll clear matters up with Saint Nicholas, Tessa. So he knows neither you nor Tarquin fired the arrow." Rayne winked at his daughter. He reached up and yanked the arrow out of the threshold above his head. He twirled it in his hands, eyeing Dante. "Fix the hole this made and try to resist your more juvenile impulses. Otherwise, I will be asking you to seek accommodations elsewhere."

Dante laughed, taking the arrow Rayne held out to him. "Yes, Commander."

Thinking the Fates drafted an interesting new chapter in their lives, Rayne smiled. Undoubtedly, the future held promise of better things to come, along with new, challenging endeavors for them all.

About the Author

Caterina is passionate about history, music, romance, old languages, and travel. She regularly intertwines these subjects in her writing.

When not traveling or working, Caterina finds time to sing classical music, make soutache jewelry, write, paint, shoot archery, and fence. She is always up for trying something new so the list of hobbies is ever expanding.

If you would like to contact her or learn more about her and future works, you can find her on Twitter, Facebook, Instagram, and at her website, https://caterinanovelliere.com.

You can also sign up for her Random Musings Newsletter or catch her podcast, Cat-astrophic Ramblings on your favorite podcast app.

Scan the QR code below for Cat's linktr.ee profile and to easily follow her on multiple platforms.

facebook.com/CaterinaNovelliere

twitter.com/chantueserouge

instagram.com/chantueserouge

amazon.com/author/caterinanovelliere

bookbub.com/authors/caterina-novelliere

youtube.com/@catnovelliere